KT-467-374

BIRDS WITHOUT WINGS

ALSO BY LOUIS DE BERNIÈRES

The War of Don Emmanuel's Nether Parts

Señor Vivo and the Coca Lord

The Troublesome Offspring of Cardinal Guzman

Captain Corelli's Mandolin

Sunday Morning at the Centre of the World

Red Dog

BIRDS
WITHOUT
WINGS

Louis de Bernières

GALWAY COUNTY LIBRARIES

SECKER & WARBURG
LONDON

Published by Secker & Warburg 2004

2 4 6 8 10 9 7 5 3 1

Copyright © Louis de Bernières 2004

Louis de Bernières has asserted his right under the Copyright, Designs and
Patents Act 1988 to be identified as the author of this work

This book is sold subject to the condition that it shall not, by way of trade or
otherwise, be lent, resold, hired out, or otherwise circulated without the publisher's
prior consent in any form of binding or cover other than that in which it is
published and without a similar condition including this condition being
imposed on the subsequent purchaser

First published in Great Britain in 2004 by
Secker & Warburg
Random House, 20 Vauxhall Bridge Road,
London SW1V 2SA

Random House Australia (Pty) Limited
20 Alfred Street, Milsons Point, Sydney,
New South Wales 2061, Australia

Random House New Zealand Limited
18 Poland Road, Glenfield,
Auckland 10, New Zealand

Random House (Pty) Limited
Endulini, 5A Jubilee Road, Parktown 2193, South Africa

The Random House Group Limited Reg. No. 954009
www.randomhouse.co.uk

A CIP catalogue record for this book
is available from the British Library

ISBN 04362 05491 (hardback)
04362 05513 (trade paperback)
04362 05572 (slipcased edition)

Papers used by Random House are natural, recyclable products made from
wood grown in sustainable forests; the manufacturing processes conform to
the environmental regulations of the country of origin

Typeset in Bembo by
Palimpsest Book Production Limited, Polmont, Stirlingshire
Designed by Peter Ward
Printed and bound in Great Britain by
Clays Ltd, St Ives plc

F124,758
€ 22.00

Contents

Epilogue

Postscript

In the grand scheme of things, this book is necessarily
dedicated to the unhappy memory of the millions of civilians
on all sides during the times portrayed, who became victims
of the numerous death marches, movements of refugees,
campaigns of persecution and extermination,
and exchanges of population.

More personally, it is also dedicated to the memory
of my maternal grandfather, Arthur Kenneth Smithells, of
Nelson Battalion, the Royal Naval Division, who was
severely wounded at Gallipoli, and in whose steps
I trod while researching part of this novel.

Manet in pectus domesticum.

THE CAT

She was licking
the opened tin
for hours and hours
without realising
that she was drinking
her own blood.

Spyros Kyriazopoulos

I

The Prologue of Iskander the Potter

The people who remained in this place have often asked themselves why it was that Ibrahim went mad. I am the only one who knows, but I have always been committed to silence, because he begged me to respect his grief, or, as he also put it, to take pity upon his guilt. Now that he is mad, and the sun has long since dried the rain that washed away the blood upon the rocks, and there is almost no one left who recalls the lovely Philothei, it seems to me that no one would be betrayed if finally the truth of it were known. With us there has been so much blood that in restrospect none of it seems believable, and it cannot matter much if finally I tell of the last misfortune that fell upon Philothei, sweet-natured, Christian, vain and beautiful.

There comes a point in life where each one of us who survives begins to feel like a ghost that has forgotten to die at the right time, and certainly most of us were more amusing when we were young. It seems that age folds the heart in on itself. Some of us walk detached, dreaming on the past, and some of us realise that we have lost the trick of standing in the sun. For many of us the thought of the future is a cause for irritation rather than optimism, as if we have had enough of new things, and wish only for the long sleep that rounds the edges of our lives. I feel this weariness myself.

We are in any case a serious people here. Life was merrier when the Christians were still among us, not least because almost every one of their days was the feast of some saint. Little work was done, it seemed, but at least their revelry was infectious. Our religion makes us grave and thoughtful, dignified and melancholy, whereas theirs did not exact much discipline. Perhaps it was something to do with the wine. For them it was a precious and sacred thing, because they thought it was something like the blood of God, whereas for us the pleasure of it has always been soured

since the Prophet of God forbad it. Peace be upon him, but I
have often wished that he had decided otherwise. We drink, but
we dislike ourselves in drinking. Sometimes we did drink with
our Christians, and caught their high spirits in the same way that
one catches malaria from the chill night air, but, left on our own
now, there is a sadness seeping out of the stones of this half-
deserted town.

Ibrahim the Mad was one of our most entertaining when he
was young. It was said that there was a smile at the corners of
his lips from the moment of his birth, and from early boyhood
he was a specialist in inappropriate interjections. To be precise,
he perfected a repertoire of bleats that exactly mimicked the
stupid comments of a goat in all its various states of mind; a goat
that is surprised, a goat that is looking for its kid, a goat that is
protesting, a goat that is hungry, a goat that is perplexed, a goat
that is in rut. His most popular bleat, however, was that of a goat
that has nothing to say. This bleat was the perfect parody of un-
intelligence, empty-headedness, inanity and harmlessness. If you
want to know what it sounded like, just go up past the ancient
tombs to where the limepit is. It is in the wild ground near there
that Ibrahim the Mad still watches the goats, even though he is
no longer sane. You should beware of his great dog. It is a very
fine animal that takes each goat back to its owner every evening,
without Ibrahim the Mad having to do anything at all, but it is
a somewhat ready-fanged dog that recognises a stranger straight
away by the smell. If you cannot find Ibrahim there, then listen
for the sound of the kaval, and follow it. He blows it so sadly
that it makes you stand still and go into mourning. He does not
bleat himself any more, but listens to the goats as they wander
from shrub to shrub, and you will soon recognise the bleat of a
goat with nothing to say.

Ibrahim used to do it quite suddenly in the middle of a conversation, or at a solemn moment in a ceremony, and when he was
a small boy his father used to beat him for it. One day he even
interrupted the imam, Abdulhamid Hodja, who was making some
interminable point about the law, which was one of his habits,
may he rest in paradise. This was under the plane trees where
the old men sit in the meydan. Anyway, Ibrahim crept up behind

2

a tree – he was about eight years old – and bleated quite suddenly when everyone else was listening quietly and respectfully. There was a shocked silence, and then Ibrahim giggled and ran away. The men looked at each other, and Ibrahim's father leapt to his feet, his face flushed with anger and shame. But Abdulhamid was a good-natured man who was naturally dignified enough not to have to be concerned about offences against his dignity, and he put his hand on the other's sleeve. 'Don't strike him,' he said. 'I was bleating myself, and now someone else should have the chance to speak.' Ibrahim's father was called Ali the Broken-Nosed.

The men were puzzled by the imam's tolerance of such disrespect, but the word spread that the imam considered that there was something providential in the irreverence of the boy, so from then onwards his mischief was accepted as one of the normal hazards of life. Back in those days Ibrahim was a friend of my son, Karatavuk, and I can truly say that he was not mad at all, he was merely framed by God in a comical way. If you want to see him as he is now, you don't have to go up to the tombs, now that I come to think of it. Just wait until he returns with the goats, and the great dog delivers them home for the night. Ibrahim the Mad knows the name of each goat, but apart from that his head is empty enough to rent.

They say that, for a madman, every day is a holiday, but they also say that insanity has seventy gates. It is true that many of the mad are happy, as you can see by the idiots of this town who sit on the walls and grin and piss themselves, but I know that the gate through which Ibrahim travelled was the gate of unconquerable sorrow, and that his mind remains a cataract of grief. I think that back in those days many of us were maddened by hatred because of the war with the Greeks, and in all honesty I include myself, but Ibrahim was the one among us whose mind was disengaged by love.

Ibrahim blamed himself, and if I had been one of her brothers or one of her other relatives, I would have come back from exile and killed him. The peculiar thing is, however, that nothing would have happened to Philothei at all, if other things had not been happening in the great world. So it is my opinion that the blame

3

belongs more widely, not only to Ibrahim but to all of us who lived in this place, as well as to those in other parts who were bloodthirsty and ambitious.

In those days we came to hear of many other countries that had never figured in our lives before. It was a rapid education, and many of us are still confused. We knew that our Christians were sometimes called 'Greeks', although we often called them 'dogs' or 'infidels', but in a manner that was a formality, or said with a smile, just as were their deprecatory terms for us. They would call us 'Turks' in order to insult us, at the time when we called ourselves 'Ottomans' or 'Osmanlis'. Later on it turned out that we really are 'Turks', and we became proud of it, as one does of new boots that are uncomfortable at first, but then settle into the feet and look exceedingly smart. Be that as it may, one day we discovered that there actually existed a country called 'Greece' that wanted to own this place, and do away with us, and take away our land. We knew of Russians before, because of other wars, but who were these Italians? Who were these other Frankish people? Suddenly we heard of people called 'Germans', and people called 'French', and of a place called Britain that had governed half the world without us knowing of it, but it was never explained to us why they had chosen to come and bring us hardship, starvation, bloodshed and lamentation, why they played with us and martyred our tranquillity.

I blame these Frankish peoples, and I blame potentates and pashas whose names I will probably never know, and I blame men of God of both faiths, and I blame all those who gave their soldiers permission to behave like wolves and told them that it was necessary and noble. Because of what I accidentally did to my son Karatavuk, I was in my own small way one of these wolves, and I am now burned up by shame. In the long years of those wars here were too many who learned how to make their hearts boil with hatred, how to betray their neighbours, how to violate women, how to steal and dispossess, how to call upon God when they did the Devil's work, how to enrage and embitter themselves, and how to commit outrages even against children. Much of what was done was simply in revenge for identical atrocities, but I tell you now that even if guilt were a coat of sable,

4

and the ground were deep in snow, I would rather freeze than wear it.

But I do not blame merely myself, or the powerful, or my fellow Anatolians, or the savage Greeks. I also blame mischance. Destiny caresses the few, but molests the many, and finally every sheep will hang by its own foot on the butcher's hook, just as every grain of wheat arrives at the millstone, no matter where it grew.

It is strange indeed that if you should wish me to tell you how one young Christian woman died by accident in this unremarkable place, you must also be told of great men like Mustafa Kemal, and little men like me, and you must also be told the story of upheavals and wars. There is, it seems, a natural perversity in the nature of fate, just as there is a natural perversity in ourselves.

I wonder sometimes whether there are times when God sleeps or averts His eyes, or if there is a divine perversity. Who knows why one day a man drowns because a deep hole has been carved in the fording place of a river, where men have passed safely for centuries, and there was no hole before?

To speak selfishly, let me say that what remains with me, and hurts me, after the memory of the cruelty and unreason has been laid aside, is the pain of having maimed my favourite son, Karatavuk. I will always be pained by the manner of his wounding, because I brought it on him by my own hastiness, and this after he had managed to survive eight years of war unscathed! It is astounding that I did not fall mad like Ibrahim. I think of my son constantly, with his upright nature, his great loyalty and his excellent humour, and I am proud that he has been able to find an honourable way to earn his living, now that he cannot follow in my footsteps as a potter.

There are many here who say we are better off without the Christians who used to live here, but as for me, I miss the old life of my town, and I miss the Christians. Without them our life has less variety, and we are forgetting how to look at others and see ourselves. Also, since they took their icon of Mary Mother of Jesus with them, there are some who think that we have had less good luck than we did before.

I am a potter, but I am also renowned as a maker of proverbs.

I have noticed that when the Christians were here I invented light-hearted proverbs, but now that they have gone, I invent serious ones.

Since those times of whirlwind the world has learned over and over again that the wounds of the ancestors make the children bleed. I do not know if anyone will ever be forgiven, or if the harm that was done will ever be undone. Enough of this, however. The story begins, and he who slaps his own face should not cry out.

2

Iskander the Potter Remembers the Birth of Philothei

The imam visited Philothei on the day of her birth, which occurred in the early summer of the thirteen hundred and eighteenth year after the Prophet's removal to Medina, which by the Christian calendar would be, if I calculate correctly, in the year 1900.

Philothei was the great beauty of the town, and in her short lifetime this caused her more difficulties than it brought compensations. It has sometimes occurred to me that God only bestows extreme beauty upon those to whom He wishes to bring misfortune.

The birth was, I suppose, unexceptional. The mother had drunk from a bowl engraved with verses from the Koran, and in which further verses had been dipped for extra assurance, and had slept with a cross on her belly for at least a week. In addition, a woman had gone for Mihrimah Efendim in good time. Mihrimah Efendim was our midwife in those days, and no one was more deeply versed in the arts of birth. She was, as they say, of a certain age, and was tall and fat, with hair on her lip, and her mother and grandmothers had been our midwives since the first counting of time. All of us had arrived safely thanks to them.

We always knew that a birth was close when Mihrimah Efendim processed through the town with her staff of office and her two attendants bearing the birthing chair. I myself was born through this chair, and so were my own children, and I daresay that others will be born through it for a thousand years more, if God wills. It was made of propitious walnut, and the rim was solid, although polished by so many women's thighs. Many men made crude jokes about what that rim had seen. The chair had strong arms, for a woman is as strong as a man when she suffers the pains of birth, and she proves a surprising knowledge of obscenities.

Philothei came into this world when the southern wind was bringing lewd thoughts and insomnia from Arabia. I remember this because I myself was unable to sleep, partly because of the restlessness of my wife and children upon the floors and divans, and partly because of the dogs outside that had set up a howling in unison with the shrieks of the mother of Philothei. Even out in the courtyard, wrapped in my cloak, I lay sleepless, looking at the stars, and so, finally, I decided to walk about the houses.

It was a night when there seemed to be commotion even in corners where nothing was amiss. I felt malice in the air, as if there was a spirit, risen from Gehenna, that was also walking in the town. In this place there are many who die without fulfilling their obligations; they are like shadows who drift ineffectually.

I was unable to resist walking towards the sounds of the parturition, and I passed the window of the Christian schoolmaster, Leonidas Efendi, who was writing furiously by the stinking light of a wick floating in a bowl of olive oil. This teacher was a bad character, stirring up trouble. In those days all of us spoke Turkish, but those who could write did so in the Greek script. This Leonidas, however, was one of the ones who was fussing and campaigning, saying that the Christians should speak Greek and not Turkish. He forced the children to learn the Greek tongue that to them was like chewing stones, and he stirred up resentment in them with stories about how we Osmanlis had taken the land from the Greeks, and that the land was rightly theirs. I have heard it said that this place belonged once to a people called Lycians, and that the Greeks took it from them, so why did this teacher not tell the children that all land is originally stolen? Why did he not say 'Let us find the Lycians, and give it back'? That schoolmaster was like too many in that time, the kind who toss water into a pan of smoking fat, so that others, as well as themselves, are burned. I am reminded of the tale of Nasreddin Hodja, who owned a buffalo with enormous horns. He had always wanted to sit between those horns, thinking that it would be like a throne, but always he had refrained. Then one day, when the beast was resting in the grass, he could resist the temptation no more, and he persuaded his wife to help him mount the horns. The buffalo stood up and tossed him into the air, and he came down hard, landing on his unfortunate wife, so that both of them were hurt. Nasreddin said to her, 'Sometimes, wife, we must both suffer for my desires.'

Besides being a troublemaker, that schoolmaster was scrawny, he came from Smyrna and so was not one of us, he wore spectacles, he put on airs and he never took a wife.

But I should return to the matter of Philothei. It so happened that I was outside her parents' house with many others of the curious when the screaming stopped and the delivery was completed. We heard the triumph and relief in the voice of Mihrimah Efendim as she cut the umbilical cord and cried out deeply, 'God is great, God is great, God is great.' It was our custom to name every female child firstly with the original name of the first woman who was with Adam in Paradise, and so when she called out that she named the child 'Havva' we all knew that the baby was a girl, 'an extra hand at the hoeing' as some people said.

The moment after Mihrimah Efendim cried out, I swear that the whole night was changed. The dogs ceased to howl, the moon broke out from behind the clouds, there was a scent of saffron and olibanum in the air, and a bulbul began to sing in the plane tree down in the centre of the meydan, where the old men sit in the day. I was contented that this new life had begun so well, but at the same time I confess that I could not help reflecting that everything that is born, is born to die. I was standing there wondering how long this person would live, and how it would die, when the father, whose name was Charitos, came out of the house to breathe the air of relief. I approached him and tapped him on the shoulder, giving him a cigarette that I had in truth just rolled in order to smoke it myself. 'Salaam aleikum,' I said, handing him my tinderbox.

'And upon you be peace,' he replied, and then added, almost as if he were worried by it, 'It's the prettiest child I've ever seen.'

'That'll be trouble,' I said.

'The women are hanging Bibles and Korans and blue beads and cloves of garlic all over the place,' said Charitos with a wry smile, 'but I expect it'll be trouble nonetheless. Nazar deymesin.'

'God preserve us from the evil eye,' I said.

Later, after the muezzin had intoned the azan at daybreak, and

9

everyone had done their prayers, a rumour began to spread out from her parents' house, like the ripple of a stone cast into a pond, and soon there was another crowd of the curious who had gathered there to see her, to bring gifts and wish the mother a happy freedom, but also with the intention of marvelling at the reported prettiness of the child. It was one of those towns where everybody is into everyone else's business, with the women swapping gossip at the wells and in the kitchens of each other's houses, and the men doing the same thing in the coffeehouses.

Philothei's family was a Christian one, but at that time we were very much mixed up and, apart from the rantings of a few hotheads whose bellies were filled with raki and the Devil, we lived together in sufficient harmony. Therefore it was not altogether to be wondered at that people of all sorts called at the door of that house bringing small presents of coffee, lokum, allspice and tobacco, in the hope of catching a glimpse of this child who was becoming a legend before she had even uncrossed her eyes.

It had not been a particularly easy birth, as we had all known on account of the mother's wails, but even so a rich bed had already been set up in the selamlık, and the mother, Polyxeni, was propped up against cushions, smiling as she held her little finger in the baby's mouth, in order to console it for the temporary want of a breast.

I had dressed in my best clothes, I brought a gold coin, and I brought some tea flavoured with bergamot that my wife had grated herself. I duly inspected the child, drank my sherbet, and exchanged further pleasantries with Charitos, the father of the child, who was by now thoroughly tired after such a vile night of anxiety. 'God bless the mother's milk,' I said, wondering all over again how a woman can go through such hell, and then be pleased about it afterwards.

'We are going to call the child "Philothei",' said Charitos.

'Meaning?'

'It is Greek,' replied Charitos, 'and I believe that it means "Beloved by God" or "Lover of God" or something like that. Anyway, it is a very pretty name, and I am using it to remember my own mother, who also bore it.'

'You will have to ask Leonidas Efendi, the teacher who is such a keen speaker of Greek,' I said. 'He will tell you what the name means.'

'No, I will ask the priest,' declared Charitos, who, like me, had no time for stoop-shouldered opinionated bookworms who did not even know how to harvest an apple. Charitos turned his weary eyes on me, and asked, very seriously, 'Iskander Efendi, will you do me a favour? Will you take a rag and tie it on the red pine for me?'

'You want me to make a wish for you?'

'Yes. This child of mine . . .' and he nodded towards the baby, 'you said a bad thing when you said that such a pretty child will be trouble. I hope that Satan did not hear you and get any ideas, although, to tell the truth, I had misgivings of my own. Please set my mind at rest; go and tie a rag on the red pine, and wish my child an easy life.'

'Charitos Efendi, of course I will. I will tie two rags, and wish the same wish twice. But first I must see the child a little better.'

Polyxeni moved aside her headscarf, revealing the infant Philothei, and I said, 'Indeed, very beautiful.'

I have to say, though, that in my opinion this business about babies being ugly or pretty, or just like their father or their aunt, is a very tiresome fabrication of the deluded. All babies look the same, and to me this particular one appeared to be a very baby-like baby. I have had children of my own, and I cannot remember what any of them looked like when they first emerged into the light, except that they all looked like babies, and like nothing else and nobody else at all.

It was at this moment, when I was trying to be sincere about the beauty of this baby who looked exactly like a baby, that the imam entered the house.

Our imam at that time was in the very glory of his life. He was about forty-five years old, very quick and energetic, his beard was long, grizzled and finely combed, and he combined the sharp black eyes of a bird with the hooked nose of an Arab. He still had most of his teeth, and his lips were thin, the lower one protruding further than the upper. He had made the haj twice, and was therefore a hodja twice over, and he had been a softa in the school at Stamboul, where he had qualified in his knowledge of the Sunna tradition. He was able to recite the entire Koran, and was therefore not only a hodja but a hafiz. Furthermore, as if all this were not enough, he had attained the initiation of no less than four Sufi brotherhoods, so that he was one who was amply enabled to return to God and be united with Him. All in all he was a mightily learned man, who knew more Arabic and Persian words than all the Arabs and the Persians put together. Sometimes one was resigned to understanding little of what he said, and sometimes he could speak for five minutes, filling his sentences with 'nonethelesses', 'howevers', 'notwithstandings' and 'on the other hands', and you would not know what he was aiming at until he clinched the speech with the final word. Such is the advantage of education.

Why the imam had chosen merely to be an imam when he could have been a qadi in the courts, or a mullah, or an âlim, none of us ever knew. It was suspected that he might have picked up ideas that did not suit the hard old men of the schools, but in my opinion he chose to be simply the leader of our prayers because he wanted to spend the most part of his time with his hands in the earth. He was an ardent grower of vegetables.

His name was Abdulhamid Hodja, and the two great joys of his life were his wife and his horse, although it would be hard to say which he esteemed the more. With regard to his wife, he liked to quote the story of Nasreddin Hodja, who was asked when the end of the world would be, and replied, 'The world will end twice; once when my wife dies, and once when I die myself.' I cannot say that I knew his wife, since she came from another place. In those days it was forbidden by custom even to enquire after the health of another man's wife, or that of his female relatives, and consequently one knew nothing about them unless one was told. Everything has changed now, and not all of it for the better. Nowadays, now that no woman wears the çarşaf over her face, it is impossible for a man with an ugly wife to boast of her beauty in the coffeehouses. Of course, the Christian women always had their faces unconcealed, and so their husbands never did have the opportunity to bluster, and many a Christian girl never became a bride.

The imam's horse, however, was a wondrously lovely, silvery

creature that he named 'Nilufer', and upon which he lavished great devotion. He gave it a small breastplate in brass, which he polished, and which was engraved with verses from the Koran. He braided the filly's mane, tying it with green ribbons upon the ends of which were tiny brass bells, and he had a high, rich saddle that he had bought from some Yörük nomads who were on a journey through the Bey Mountains. He washed and brushed the animal, anointed it with perfumes to repel the attentions of insects, and was often to be seen embracing it, whispering endearments to it with his arm about its neck and one hand stroking the velvet of its nose. The consequence was that the horse behaved with all the capriciousness and lack of humility of a Circassian mistress, but it always gave a lift to the heart to see him cantering upon it, with his white turban wrapped around his fez, and his green cloak billowing in his wake. He was a horseman worthy of our ancestors who came out of the East. They say that a man is most a man either when he is mounted upon his wife or his horse.

As I was saying, the imam appeared suddenly at the door, left his shoes with everyone else's, and entered the room in his habitually vigorous and lordly fashion. 'Salaam aleikum,' he said to all of us, and we chorused back 'Aleikum salaam' without pausing to think about it.

Naturally, he had come for the same reason as the rest of us, which was because he was bringing a gift, and was curious to see the beautiful child. He bent down and took the infant, holding it high in the air, and scrutinising its features as if he were divining something from them. At last he sighed happily, and recited the first lines of the Koran, which I recognised because I had once learned them myself, despite my ignorance of the Arab tongue. Then he put Philothei down, and bent over, and raised her hand to his lips, and kissed it. Later, her mother found a small crimson blemish on the child's right hand, which she believed to be the exact place where the imam had placed his lips. Even the Christians, you see, believed that the imam was a saint. Certainly he had the forbearance of one, since he never took action against those vulgar and thoughtless Christians who had neither sense nor courtesy, who would throw lemon peel at him as a gesture of contempt, and hide themselves before he could recognise them. He could have caused them to be hanged, but instead he punished them by ignoring them. In his wisdom he had recognised that the worst punishment is to be beneath noticeability.

Before he left Charitos's house, he said, 'I wish you happiness with this child,' and then he went out, mounted his silvery horse, and rode away with the bright ribbons fluttering from the saddle and the brass bells tinkling at the reins.

'I wonder what he saw,' said Charitos, and I shrugged. I thought perhaps that he had had the same reaction as myself, namely that every birth entails a death.

The room was now very crowded, and people were beginning to blow thick clouds of smoke from their narghiles, and make a terrible racket in order to keep the evil spirits away. I have always hated this din and smoke, and so I made my excuses to Charitos, having to shout into his ear: 'I have work to do, a lot of clay to mix, I had better go. I will make you a water jug as a gift.' And then I remembered. 'But first I will tie two rags to the red pine.'

By now the town had burst into life, and I had to make my way uphill through those cobbled ways that were barely wide enough for a donkey. It was as if the place were conceived before the invention of carts. Who knows when that was? At any rate, I had to jostle my way past women carrying water in jars upon their heads, past dogs insolently asleep amid all the hubbub, past pedlars, tradesmen, mendicants and craftsmen, and over the legs of the beggars whose sole function in this life was to shine the souls of those of us who kept them alive by giving them the alms that would perpetuate their idleness. They kept their eyes lowered as they outstretched their palms, since it is better for all of us if such gifts are anonymous. I went to my pottery, and took one of the rags that I had been using to wash off my wheel at the end of each working day.

The red pines stood in a group of five, halfway up the slope to the top of the cliff, very near the place where lime was dug out for the manufacture of mortar. They were lovely trees, with a rich bark, and branches that fanned out as if longing to spread their shade for we who were below. I like sometimes to invent proverbs, and one that occurred to me on that day, as I looked up at the boughs, was 'The man who seeks the shade of the red pine will be shat upon by doves'. There were always a dozen or so of those small grey doves with the black ring about the neck, very pretty, but also very generous with their bodily refuse. The good things in life are always accompanied by a detriment.

The lower branches were copiously hung with rags that represented the wishes of an entire town over many years, and it was always a challenge to find a new place where a rag could be tied. Sometimes, when a wish had come true, the wisher would return and fetch their rag, so that they could use it again for another wish. In my opinion this displayed a certain paltriness of spirit, since a new rag is not difficult to obtain.

In those days I was still young enough to climb with agility, and I ascended to the very top of the tallest pine, where I tied my rag so that it would flutter like the pennant of a ship. The sun was already strong and bright, teasing out the scent of resin in the bark of the tree. The palms of my hands were covered with that tenacious, sticky, dusty black film that is caused by gripping such a tree when it is climbed. This irritated me, but then I reflected that it would be abraded away soon enough when I set down to my potting. A breeze stirred, and I forced my turban down a little harder on to the crown of my head. I could see some children playing in the waters of the ruined temple. No doubt they were tormenting the frogs.

I stayed up there for a while, making wishes on behalf of Philothei in between marvelling at the view of the town. To see such a place from above, particularly if it has a fine mosque and a church, is to be reminded that there is something miraculous in the falling out of things. In the early evenings I used to go sometimes to the top of the cliff where the land ends and the sea begins, because the golden dome of the mosque would sparkle in the scarlet light, and the smoke of all the cooking fires would carry up the delicious smell of roasting meat.

On the way down, hoping that they would be newly laid, I took four dove's eggs to bring to my wife, one for each of my sons.

What strikes me as remarkable, in thinking back, is that the birth of Philothei was the first and only time that I remember there being such a monumental fuss over the advent of a female child.

3

Mustafa Kemal (1)

Far away from Eskibahçe, past the Dodekanissos and across the Aegean Sea, one of Destiny's men is born. It is nineteen years before the birth of Philothei, the year being 1881 by the Gregorian calendar, a year during which (and thereby perpetrating one of the most entertaining ironies of European history) Macedonia gives to the world its greatest Turk, just as once it gave to the world its most-conquering Greek.

In 1881 Macedonia is the home of Vlachs, Greeks, Bulgarians, Turks, Serbs, Slavs and Albanians. In Salonika, where the child is born, there are also 'Franks' of many European origins, and a huge colony of Jews whose ancestors fled the persecutions in Spain. Half of these Jews are Muslim by religion, since their ancestors fell into disillusionment after the failures of a local seventeenth-century messiah. By the end of the Second World War, however, extinguished by the Nazis, there will be no more Jews in Salonika, and their curious antique Spanish will have all but vanished with them.

The child is born into a world where the seeds of Nazism have been long sewn, and are waiting only for the dark rain. Stirred up by Austria–Hungary and by Russia, the various peoples of the Balkans and the Near East are abrogating their long coexistence and codependence. Their hotheads and ideologues are propounding doctrines of separateness and superiority. The slogans are 'Serbia for the Serbs, Bulgaria for the Bulgarians, Greece for the Greeks, Turks and Jews out!' There has been interbreeding for centuries, but no one stops to ask what exactly a Serb or a Macedonian or a Bulgarian or a Greek actually is. It is enough that there are sufficient opportunists calling themselves freedom fighters and liberators, who will exploit these ideas in order to become bandits and local heroes in the war of all against all. Mustafa is born into a world where law and order are fast collapsing, where looting has become more profitable than working, where the arts of peace are becoming more and more unpracticable, and personal tolerance makes less and less difference.

The courtyarded house of his nativity is surrounded by high walls, and is divided classically into selamlık and haremlık. Iron bars protect the windows on the ground floor, and lattices screen those on the overhanging upper storey. Behind its pink walls, Zübeyde, fair-haired and blue-eyed, resolutely old-fashioned and devoutly Muslim, pushes Destiny's child out into the world with one last cry of anguish, and his father, timber merchant, customs officer and administrator of Pious Foundations, leans over and whispers his name as the umbilical cord is cut. His name is to be Mustafa, the Chosen.

4

i am philothei

I am philothei an i am six eveone says wat a pritty gilr an i was
born lik that an so i am usd to it i am prittier than anyon else
but i dont bost abot it i sor ibrahim today an he was folowing
me and I wosent sposed to see him i went with drosoula who
is not pritty by ugli but she is my fren anway an ibrahim was
playign with karatavuk and mehmetçik and they were blowing
thier berdwhissles an pertendin to be berds an ibrahin sed wen
we are old we wil be maried an I sed yes proberly an he gav me
a fether an a snale shel an a pink stone with a patern on an he
tuched my arm an tomorow we are gong to eat pijjun becos it
is my name day and i will go to the curckh with the ikon of
my saynt and leve it ther al nite with candels

5

Exiled in Cephalonia, Drosoula Remembers Philothei

Philothei was my best friend, even though she was so beautiful and I was born so hideous. We were born at about the same time, but I might as well have been born in the shade. She was like the evening star, when I was like a bug.

When you are old your memory plays tricks with you. Sometimes I can't remember what I was doing five minutes ago, or where I put down the onion I was peeling, but then sometimes I can remember things that happened when I was seven years old, so clearly that it's as if I was a little girl again. I've noticed, though, that occasionally you think you remember something as if you'd witnessed it yourself, when in fact it's only that you've been told it so many times, and you've thought about it so much, that eventually you come to think that it really is your own memory when in fact it isn't. What I am saying is, that although Philothei was my best friend, I can no longer separate my own memories of her from all the stories that people liked to tell about her.

I know it's stupid to claim that one human being is special, or picked out by God, when in fact there are hundreds of millions of human beings in the world, and God knows how many millions of people long dead who have been lost to history, all of whom were probably special to someone, but I still think that Philothei was touched by an angel, and I don't suppose it matters much to you whether or not what I say is true. I am just an old woman, and you know what old women are like, going on and on about their memories, and sighing over the old days that they won't see the like of again. You don't have to pay any attention.

I remember hearing so many times about how Abdulhamid Hodja, the imam, came to visit her when she was born, and left a saintly stigma on her hand where he kissed it. I can't remember seeing it exactly, but I feel as though I did. I picture it as being red and blotchy, like those stains that you sometimes see on people's faces.

And why are you screwing up your face like that, and spitting? Because I mentioned the imam? Because I mentioned a Turk? Well, you should think before you spit, because I may be Greek now, but I was practically a Turk then, and I'm not ashamed of it either, and I'm not the only one, and this country's full of people like me who came from Anatolia because we didn't have any choice in the matter. When I came here I didn't even speak Greek, didn't you know that? I still dream in Turkish sometimes. I came here because the Christians had to leave, and they thought all the Christians like me were Greek, because the people who run the world never did and never will have any idea how complicated it really is, so if you call me a Turk you might think you're insulting me, but it's half true, and I am not ashamed. People used to call me 'Turk' when I first came here, and they didn't mean it kindly either, and they pushed in front of me and shoved me aside, and they muttered things under their breath when I passed by. I'm not like you, you see. You were brought up thinking all the Turks are devils, but you've never met one, and you probably never will, and you don't know a damned thing about it, and it's ignorant people like you who stir up all the trouble. So don't spit when I mention an imam who happened to be a Turk and a saint too, and if you don't like it I'll just talk to someone else who's got more sense. And I'll tell you something else, and I don't care if you don't like to hear it, and that is that before all the clever Christians came here from Asia Minor, you people were living like dogs and didn't have a clue about anything, and this island had almost nobody on it because anyone with any sense had left, so I'll have no more spitting when I mention the imam, and while I'm on this subject I'll just remind you of something you probably don't want to know, and that is that in all the hundreds of years of occupation the Turks never did anything to us that was half as bad as what we Greeks did to each other in the civil war, and that's something I know about, believe me.

Now I've got all worked up. One day some idiot's going to give me a heart attack. I was talking about my best friend, Philothei.

I thought she was picked out. I've had a good life, even though I lost my husband and my only son, and so I am not ungrateful to God, but I used to think that He gave my share of everything to Philothei, so that I was left with just the bare bones to gnaw upon. I wasn't bitter about it, because I too was intoxicated by how lovely she was, and even though I am old and decrepit now, I still feel a kind of gratitude that Philothei came to earth.

Philothei was vain and melodramatic, and sentimental, and unreliable and infuriating, but she was also soft-hearted and sweet-natured, and easily wounded and intelligent. She was my best friend, my heart's true friend, and I loved her because even her faults made her lovable and amusing. I followed her around as faithfully as a dog, and as shamelessly as Ibrahim, who was in love with her from the day that both of them were born. When I think back I realise that he was courting her from infancy, and that doesn't happen too often, and finally it was Ibrahim she was betrothed to, even though he was of the other faith. It did happen sometimes, so don't believe anyone who says it didn't.

If the stories are true, she was born beautiful. It was said that the imam declared her to be the most exquisite Christian child that the town had ever seen. They say that her eyes were dark as well water, so that those who leaned over the crib and looked into them had the sensation of falling and whirling. My father, for instance, I don't mind telling you that he was a brute and a drunk, and there wasn't any man ever born who was harder to love, but even he would tell us: 'When I saw her eyes I was afraid of God for the first time in my life. It was as if they belonged to someone who had lived too long and seen too much. They were an angel's eyes, and they made me think of death. I went out and drank some lemon raki to get over it, and then I went into the church to pray, and, I don't know why, but I fell down on the church steps and couldn't be raised. I lay there a long time, with the dogs licking my face, till I woke up again and went in and kissed the icon of the Virgin Mary Panagia Glykophilousa.' That is what my father said, but he was a complete sot, and my mother cursed the day she married him, and she used to go out to the taverns with a slipper in her hand and

21

F124,758

drive him home as if he were a sheep. My mother told me that he had indeed got drunk on that day, and passed out on the church steps, but that the priest – his name was Father Kristoforos – had delegated a couple of young men to carry him home. I think he would have got drunk whether he had seen the infant Philothei or not, since it needed no pretty child to provoke his drunkenness on any other day.

Philothei had very dark eyes. You couldn't even see the pupils because the iris was so dark a brown as to be black, and consequently no one ever really knew what Philothei was feeling. Normally you glean more from someone's eyes than you do from their speech, but I could read nothing at all from hers. If Philothei said something, then I just had to take her at her word, because it was impossible to look into that darkness and discover whether or not she was lying, whether or not she liked or disliked me at that moment, or whether or not she was sad. Once I pointed this out to her, I think we were about fifteen years old at the time – it was the second year of the war against the Franks, and all the boys were at Gallipoli or in the labour battalions – and she ran inside to gaze into herself in the mirror. She came back out about half an hour later, and she was quite distressed, and she said, with a tone of wonder in her voice, 'Drosoulaki, what you said is true. I can't see myself in the eyes.' Sometimes it was difficult to commune with her because of this, because words are just the vapour of the heart.

She had lovely hair too. I don't know if this is true, but it was said that she was born with a full head of hair, so black and thick and plentiful that it was like the fishing nets draped over the harbour wall in Argostoli harbour, or a flock of goats on a hill, or the tails of horses gathered and bound together. When it was first washed, so they say, her grandmother braided her hair and wound it three times about her head. This sort of thing does happen, I suppose.

I do remember her skin. It was so fine and delicate that even when she was six years old she could raise her hand against the light, and one could see the bones and veins. Mehmetçik and Karatavuk – I don't suppose I told you about them – and Ibrahim as well, they used to say, 'Philothei, Philothei, hold your hands up to the sun, we want to see, we want to see,' and she would put her hands right up to their faces so that the sun was blocked out, and they would feel sick, which is odd if you remember that in those days you could see all our ancestors' bones in the little ossuary behind the church, because there was no land for burial, and we needed the land, and in any case that was the custom. I suppose it's more horrible when you see the bones of someone who is still alive, because you don't expect it. I often think about those bones in the ossuary, and what we did with them when we left Anatolia that we loved so much and will probably mourn for ever.

But it was more than a question of hair and skin and eyes, because what one saw was more than just her beauty. You see, my father, drunkard though he was, was right when he said that she reminded you of death. When you looked at Philothei, you were reminded of a terrible truth, which is that everything decays away and is lost. Beauty is precious, you see, and the more beautiful something is, the more precious it is; and the more precious something is, the more it hurts us that it will fade away; and the more we are hurt by beauty, the more we love the world; and the more we love it, the more we are saddened that it is like finely powdered salt that runs away through the fingers, or is puffed away by the wind, or is washed away by the rain. You see, I am ugly. I have always been ugly. If I had died in my youth no one would have said, 'Look how much poorer is the world,' but to be entranced by Philothei was to receive a lesson in fate.

I was, as I have said, born hideous, and before I married I would have been better off as a goat. There was a blessing in those days which went 'May all your children be sons, and all your sheep be ewes', and the curse was 'May all your children be daughters, and all your sheep be rams'. My mother once told me that when I was born my father flew into a rage, and spat on her even as she lay exhausted on the divan, because she had inflicted another daughter upon him, who would one day have to be disposed of with a dowry.

I have always been without attractions and allure, and I still thank God that for a few years I had a husband who loved me before he was drowned. You see, I was lucky because I have had much affection and respect, and much disinterested love. Perhaps I was luckier than Philothei, whose perfection was a misfortune because she never had any peace.

There's something I think about, you know, and that is that if Philothei were still alive, then she would by now be an old crone like me, and perhaps there would be no longer anything to choose between us. It's a strange thought. How cruel God is. One old bone is as good as another for throwing to a dog, and the earth is as greedy for one corpse as it is for any other.

Sometimes I still miss the best friend of my youth, and I think of all the other things that have been lost. I lost my family, my town, my language and my earth. Perhaps it's only possible to be happy, as I am here in this foreign land that someone decided was my home, if one forgets not only the evil things, but also the very perfect ones. To forget the bad things is good. That is obvious, But sometimes one should also forget the things that were wonderful and beautiful, because if you remember them, then you have to endure the sadness of knowing that they have gone. They have gone as irrevocably as my mother, and my Anatolia, and my son who became a devil and drowned, and my sweet husband who also drowned at sea, and all those who died here in the war.

I know that all these things, all my sorrow, all my memories, all these things will disappear, and it will be as if they had never been. I ask myself why God creates all these things, only to let them go. Why does God give us a garden, and put a snake in it? What can anything mean, if all will be forgotten?

I am an old woman now. I am old and useless. I've pondered these things all my life. My flesh is not what it was, and neither are my bones. When I was young my soul seemed to be the same thing as my body. There didn't seem to be any difference, I remember that. When I needed to climb some steps, my legs just climbed, and that was all there was to it. My mind and my muscles were all one. Now when I want to climb some steps I look down at my feet and I say, 'Move, in the name of Saint Gerasimos, move!' and slowly they move, and then I stop to draw breath, and my lungs feel hard and dry, and I feel my heart fluttering in vain like the last poor starving butterfly, and this is how

I have come to know in my own way that there is a soul who is not the body, but lives inside it.

You see, I still have in me the spirit of a girl of twenty that sings when I dream of running to meet my husband when he comes back safe from the sea, or of embracing sweet Philothei when I meet her in the street, and this spirit rebels against the prison that my body has become, and my spirit is like a chrysalis that is ready to burst its shell, and when the shell bursts, it longs to be reborn in paradise, where I can touch the golden hem of the robe of the gracious, blessed, all-holy Mother of God, and it will be like washing in water at a hot day's journey's end.

And if I am reborn in Heaven, which maybe I don't deserve, then perhaps all my doubts will be answered. If I still remember those that I have loved, then I won't have lived for nothing, for what would be the point of anything, if nothing is remembered?

I am just an old woman in exile, I have no education, I am ugliness personified, but if I could break open my ribs with my bare hands, I would show you that I have a heart grown huge with love, and grief, and memory.

6

Mustafa Kemal (2)

Far away from Eskibahçe, past the Dodekanissos and across the Aegean Sea, Mustafa is growing up. He has been named after an uncle that his father killed by accident whilst an infant. He has a Negro nurse whose ancestors used to be slaves, and who sings to him.

The family of the child moves to Mount Olympus, where his father Ali Rıza Efendi is a customs officer on the new border with Greece, and where he will have the brainwave of starting a timber business.

Mustafa's mother Zübeyde wants the boy to become a hafiz, and learn the Koran by heart. She thinks that he must make the pilgrimage to Mecca and become a hodja. She wants him to go to a religious school, but Ali Rıza, who is a progressive and a liberal, wants to enrol him in the modern school of Şemsi Efendi. Zübeyde wins, and he is enrolled at the religious school, where he arrives in procession to the cheers of his new schoolmates, bearing a golden stick, and attired in white and gold.

Here the first seeds will be planted of his lifelong aversion to religion in general and Islam in particular. He thinks it stupid and pointless to learn Arabic. The classes are obliged to sit on the floor, cross-legged, but one day he stands up. 'Sit down,' says the teacher.

'I am cramped up,' explains Mustafa.

'Sit down at once,' orders the teacher.

'No,' says Mustafa. 'Infidel children don't have to sit like this. Why should we?'

'You dare disobey me?'

'Yes, I dare disobey you.'

The teacher and Mustafa glare at each other for a moment, and then the whole class rises to its feet, and says, 'We all dare disobey you.'

Shortly afterwards, perhaps at the school's behest, Ali Rıza removes his son, and enrols him in the modern and liberal establishment of Şemsi Efendi.

Now, however, Ali Rıza's timber business fails because Greek brigands, who are liberating the region by means of blackmail and extortion, menace his workers and demand protection money from him, under the threat of burning his timber. Ali Rıza gives them the money, and they burn his timber anyway. They ambush his wagons on the way to the coast, and attack his men in the forest. The commander of the gendarmerie, who is supposed to be controlling the outlaws, advises him to quit. He goes into the salt trade, fails, takes to drink, develops tuberculosis, and within three years is dead.

Zübeyde moves the family out into the country, and Mustafa and his sister happily run wild on his uncle's farm, chasing the crows from the bean crops, fighting each other, waxing strong on good food from the rusty earth, among villages where storks nest on roofs and bullocks graze the pastures.

Mustafa grows dissatisfied with his unengaged mind. To his mother he says, 'I want to go to school,' and to his uncle Hussein he says, 'I want to go to school.'

Surprisingly, they send him to the school of the local Greek priest, but he finds the language detestable and the Christian boys arrogant and tribal. He is sent to the school of the imam, but he finds the religiosity repulsive. A local woman offers her services, but he refuses to be educated by a female. He is given a tutor, but denounces him as ignorant. He is sent back to Salonika to attend the school of Kaymak Hafiz, but here he is severely beaten for fighting, and refuses to go back.

The boy yearns to go to the Military Secondary School where one can wear proper modern clothes instead of the embarrassingly old-fashioned shalwar and sash. He has a little friend called Ahmed, who looks wonderful in the military uniform. Zübeyde forbids him to go because she foresees nothing but death or perpetual absence in a military career, and in any case, if he is not to be a holy man, he could at least be a merchant and bring in some money.

Mustafa conspires with Ahmed's father, Kadri, a major in the army, and he sits the entrance exam without his mother's knowledge. He passes, and presents his mother with a fait accompli. She refuses to let him go to the school, which requires her written consent, and Mustafa tells her, 'When I was born my father gave me a sword and hung it up on the wall above my bed. Obviously he wanted me to be a soldier. I was born a soldier, and I shall die as one.'

Zübeyde is half persuaded and half dubious, but one night she is visited by a marvellous veridical dream, wherein she sees Mustafa perched on a golden tray at the very summit of a minaret. She runs to him, only to hear a voice telling her, 'If you permit your son to go to the military school, he will remain up here on high. If you do not, he shall be cast down.' One is tempted to imagine Mustafa whispering into the ears of the righteous matriarch as she slumbers.

Mustafa makes a strangely self-possessed pupil. He refuses to join in the children's games, saying that he prefers to watch. He refuses to bend his body in order to play leapfrog, demanding that others, should they wish to overleap him, must do so with him standing up. He is only twelve years old, but he turns out to be an astonishing mathematician. His teacher, also called Mustafa, puts him in charge of classes. He socialises with older boys rather than his contemporaries, and his teachers find him opinionated and difficult. He assumes equality with them.

His mother remarries, much to his alarm, jealousy and disgust, and he refuses to live in his stepfather's house, but he finds that he has an inspirational new stepbrother who is an officer in the army, who preaches to him about honour and duty, about never accepting a blow or an insult. He gives the little boy a flick knife in case some predatory man finds him too pretty for his own good, and tells him never to use it unwisely. The boy's own predilections are clearly for the fair sex, however, and it is more likely that the danger to Virtue rather derives from him.

His teacher, Mustafa, gives him a name to distinguish him from himself. The new name that he will carry all his life is 'Kemal', Perfection.

7

The Dog

The town of which I speak was finally destroyed by two earthquakes, in 1956 and 1957. It is now populated only by small
lizards and huge cicadas. Stiff grasses grow up between the stones,
and the voices of the nightingales, whose massed improvisations
at night used to drive the populace crazy with sleeplessness, now
drift out across a sea of rubble, and away over a quiet river that
has grown preoccupied and sad. The few peasants who come to
cultivate the strips of land along the banks look up at the ruins,
where their children forage for old knives and coins, and try to
imagine how it used to be. 'It should be rebuilt,' they often say,
but then someone says, 'I wouldn't live there; there are too many
ghosts.'

Not many years ago a bishop came from Rhodes, and an imam
came from Fethiye, and in the broken carapace of the Church
of Aghios Nikolaos, they prayed together for the rebirth of the
place and its community, where, side by side, there used to live
Christians who spoke only Turkish, but wrote it in the Greek
script, and Muslims who also spoke only Turkish, and also wrote
it in the Greek script. Neither God, for reasons best known to
Himself, nor the Turkish government, for cogent reasons of
expense, have answered the prayers of the bishop and the imam,
and the town of Eskibahçe, whose Greek name in the Byzantine
age was 'Paleoperiboli', slumbers on in death, without an epitaph,
and with no one to remember it.

When the town was alive, the walls of the houses were rendered
with mortar and painted jauntily in dark shades of pink. Its streets
were so narrow as to be more like alleyways, but there was no
oppressive sense of enclosure, since the buildings were stacked up
one slope of a valley, so that every dwelling received light and
air. In truth, the town seemed to have been marvellously designed
by some ancient genius whose name has been lost, and there was

probably no other place like it in all of Lydia, Caria or Lycia. Each habitation had its lowest rooms carved directly out of the rock, many of them with capacious storage spaces cut even further into the hillside, as if the earliest inhabitants had whiled away the tedium of their winters by chipping out cellars for themselves. Directly into the walls were cut niches for stoves, guns and brass cooking pots.

These lowest rooms were blessedly cool in the summers, and in the winter were commonly occupied by animals, whose natural warmth eased the chill of the room above, which itself was accessible either by a wooden ladder, or by stairs cut out of the rock. In the upper room were to be found the hearth and the divans, arranged around three sides of the room, with a fine carpet occupying the central space.

Because each house had a roof that was almost flat, this amounted to an extra room when the weather was fine, the same roof acting as a trap for rainwater, which flowed directly into a very large cistern built on to the side of the structure. Thus, for the most part of the year, the women were saved the arduous task of fetching water from the wells, or from the river that cut through the very lush flood plain immediately below, where almost everybody owned a few decares of land for cultivation. Each house also possessed a separate earth closet, which had to be emptied frequently in hot weather on account of the oppressiveness of the flies. There were those who used it only when the women were cooking, because then the insects left the closet in order to investigate the food.

Naturally, not all the buildings corresponded to this pattern, for over the centuries the population had grown a little, and there were more conventional houses on the periphery, and on the hillside opposite, that were divided into a selamlık, which was, as it were, the reception area, and the haremlık, which was the private quarters. Nonetheless, the habit of hacking extra rooms out of the rock also pertained in these buildings, and they had the same heavy walls, as thick as the length of an arm, and the same dark and tranquil interiors that had the effect of diminishing one's sense of time.

Some of the houses, it is true, were so overcrowded as to be almost hellish, for it was the custom then, as in many places it still is now, for the sons to bring their new wives into their paternal house. If there were many sons who married, and produced numerous children, then there was neither room to move nor sleep, nor was there any privacy, and there was much bad temper, especially during times of pernicious weather. Upon the death of the family patriarch, however, the sons and their families would move out to new houses where the cycle would begin again, and there would be a few years of spaciousness in one's own house, which seemed both disconcerting and marvellous.

Behind the town the scrubby hillside rolled to a gentle crest, and beyond that there was a small depression that, had it had more ambition, might have amounted to a valley. There were a few vertical rock faces, for the land had originally been laid down in flat layers that had been folded and broken by the uncompassioned northern drift of Africa and Arabia. Many of these faces had been carved into elegant façades for sepulchres in Lycian times, but one had been deeply excavated for lime, and beyond, just over another crest, was the sharp and stony incline that fell steeply down to the vivid waters where the Aegean merges into the Mediterranean Sea. It was in this waste-land between the town and the ocean, a place fit only for goats, that the man who came to be known as the Dog took up residence among the Lycian tombs, becoming a spectre even before he had properly died.

Sometimes it happens that the manner of a man's death is discernible beforehand in his face, and sometimes it is clear from the manner of a man's life. In the case of the one they named 'The Dog', it was always clear that he would die alone and in squalor, because this was what he had explicitly chosen when he undertook to lead the life that he did.

Karatavuk and Mehmetçik were very small boys at the time, but they would never forget the day that the Dog arrived. They had been sent out by their respective mothers to gather wild greens, of which there were a hundred varieties growing on the hillsides and around the edges of the pastures, all of them edible, but some of them very bitter until one was used to them and learned to perceive the delicate flavours, which might remind one of walnut or garlic or lemon. Into their goatskin satchels they had stuffed everything that they had found, and were wasting time in conspiratorial fashion in order to delay their return home, where they would probably be given yet another task. Sometimes one's mother sent one out to collect tezek, the dried dung that was used for fuel now that the trees had all been cut down and the goats had destroyed most of the shrubs. The only good thing about collecting tezek was finding the interesting and varicoloured species of beetles that inhabited it.

They were sitting on one side of the sunken track that led past the almost intact ruins of a Roman theatre, which the towns-people still used for big meetings and celebrations. They were idly tossing small stones across the track, their target a small burrow made in the opposite bank by a mouse. 'Why don't we pee in the hole?' suggested Mehmetçik. 'Then the mouse might come out, and we can catch it.'

Karatavuk frowned. 'I don't want to catch a mouse.' Karatavuk always wanted to appear more serious and adult than he really was, and it is more than likely that he would have liked to urinate in the hole to make the mouse come out, if only he had thought of it first.

'Anyway,' said Mehmetçik, 'if we pee in the mousehole, we might drown it.'

Karatavuk nodded wisely in agreement, and the two boys continued to toss their stones. Karatavuk was the second son of Iskander the Potter, and he had the handsome face of a young man even though he was only six years old, with golden skin, and shining black hair that fell across his eyes, so that frequently he had to sweep it upward with the back of his hand. He had fine lips, and when he smiled he revealed a pointed tongue and small white teeth that had no gaps, but which were just crooked enough to be charming. His mood always seemed to be more sober than it was.

Mehmetçik, who came from one of the Christian families, was shorter and stockier, and it was clear that one day he would grow up into the kind of man who can perform surprising feats of strength, the sort who can hold a heavy door in place whilst it is screwed on to its hinges. Like Karatavuk, his skin was tawny, his eyes dark brown, and his hair black and straight. They might easily have been brothers or cousins in two versions, one slim and lively, the other more solid. In fact, they were related, but in a manner tenuous enough for everyone to have forgotten how it came about. A great-great-grandfather had changed faith and married into the other family, perhaps, or a distant grand-mother had married twice, the first or perhaps the second husband being of the other family. In any case, and in one way or another, if one traced it back far enough, there was no one in that town who was not in some way a relation of everybody else, whatever the theories that Daskalos Leonidas might have propounded.

The boys compared toes, Karatavuk's thin and long, Mehmetçik's shorter and stouter. What they had in common was that they were powdery with white dust from the road, and tanned dark by the early-summer sun. Karatavuk was demon-strating that he could waggle each toe separately, and Mehmetçik was frowning with concentration in the effort to duplicate the feat, when they became aware that someone had come over the brow of the hill and was bearing down upon them.

Even before they saw him closely, they realised that he was unusual. There was something uneven and exaggerated in his stride, as if he was so used to hurrying that he was incapable of proceeding at a measured pace. Furthermore, he did not walk in a straight line, but veered slightly from one side to the other, so that his out-turned footprints in the dust left behind them the winding track of a river or a snake.

The boys sat up and watched him approach with a mixture of fascination and fear. They jumped to their feet with the single idea that they should run away, but there was something about the man's demeanour that prevented them. It was as if they were in no danger because the man did not live in the same world, and would not even see them.

Indeed, perhaps he did not see them. He was tall and very thin, with spindly legs that were nonetheless tautly muscled from his years of walking, and he was clad only in a ragged scrap of grey sheet with a hole torn out for his head, and which at front and back hardly attained the level of his knees. He had a length of ship's rope about his waist, the weight of whose knot at the front barely preserved his decency. One could see clearly the sides of his buttocks, and occasionally there were dark hints of his genitals as he walked.

His arms were as thin and sinewy as his legs, and his fingers were long and spatulate. In his right hand he grasped a quarter-staff of well-worn ash, and with this he helped to propel himself along at his unnatural speed. His left hand rested upon the neck of a black-and-white goatskin water flagon, which was suspended on a leather thong that ran diagonally down across his chest.

The tattered man was oblivious. He looked neither right nor left, with eyes that were lightest blue, like those of a Frank from the far north. His full head of disordered grey hair was knotted and matted, caked with dust, and the sweat of his brow ran down from it, leaving clean tracks across the filth that had accumulated upon his shrunken and aquiline face. With every step he groaned inarticulately, as if in conquerable pain, a groan such as one hears from a madman, or from a deaf man who has never learned to speak. These vocalisations, it seemed, were his marching song.

He swept past the two boys, and they, as of one mind, jumped to their feet and followed him, mimicking his erratic stride and giggling to each other, timidly at first, but then with greater boldness, as the man who was the object of their mirth ignored them altogether.

They approached the lower end of the town, and soon the procession grew as more children tagged along behind, in order to experience the novelty of imitating the extraordinary man. Fat little pug-nosed Drosoula, the exquisite Philothei, Ibrahim, son of Ali the Broken-Nosed, who even at that age was already following Philothei everywhere, and Gerasimos, son of the fisherman Menas, who was already feeling a fascination for Drosoula, all joined the happy ragtaggle of mockers and mimics, attracting also the town's stray dogs, which barked senselessly, prancing at the edges of the procession, which before long numbered perhaps fifteen or twenty children.

The people who had remained in the town, rather than gone to harvest tobacco, raisins and figs, came to their doors and gazed in wonder at the wild man and his retinue. Some women snatched their children away, but these were soon replaced by new ones. The men at the coffeehouses stopped their games of backgammon, and came out into the streets, their fat cigarettes clamped in their lips, and their fezzes at individual angles upon their heads. They stroked their stubble in amusement, or twisted the ends of their hyperbolical moustachios, exchanging amused smiles and wry comments, shrugging their shoulders, and then returning to their idleness. They had seen more than a few itinerant beggars in their time, although very few kept their eyes on the distance as this man did, as if he were at the helm of a ship whose crew was thirsty for land. One might think that at some time this man had been important, and had never lost his habit of lordly foresight and indifference.

Through the narrow walkways he went, pausing for nothing, even striding over the back of a recumbent camel that had obstinately blocked the route, placing his foot at the base of its neck, and causing it to grunt in protest and surprise. Dogs cowered away and chickens scattered; travelling merchants stared after him; the imam, Abdulhamid Hodja, reined in his silvery horse to let him pass; the priest, portentous and dignified in his black robes and grizzled beard, moved aside, struck suddenly by the strange and disorientating feeling that he did not exist.

People noticed that the Dog's feet were cut and bloody, as if he had walked for days, unconscious of his pain or of the danger of infection. They noticed that there was something untamed and prophetic in his demeanour, and assumed that he must be a dervish belonging to one of the many brotherhoods of Sufis. The town had not yet had a genuine saint in residence, and there were those who were struck immediately by the hope that one had at last arrived. Lovers of wonders looked forward to miracles, and traders and artisans clapped their hands together at the thought of the custom of pilgrims. Those of extreme theological sophistication, of whom, it must be admitted, there were practically none apart from the imam, were gratified that someone might have turned up who would lend their shoulder to the great cosmic wheel, directing their spiritual power to the sustention of the universe.

35

The Dog perplexed everybody on his passage through the streets by omitting to beg for anything. Onward he strode, his eyes fixed on another world, perhaps upon the past, or perhaps upon the inward turmoil of his thoughts. He passed the last houses, turning leftward and upward, surmounting the crest of the slope, standing there for a moment, his head moving mechanically from side to side as if waiting to be inspired. Suddenly, his mind made up, he headed towards the open cave from which the lime was mined. Watched by the children, who had now grown solemn and silent, some of them holding hands, he entered it, ran his fingers over the rough surface of its walls, and sniffed the atmosphere, his nostrils flaring with each breath. He smelled the sour perspiration of the generations who had hacked away at this powdery stone, he smelled the excrement of bats, and then, making the decision that he would not live in there, he left.

Still ignoring the children, he approached a pillar tomb, twenty feet high, curiously touched the Lycian script, and gazed upward, blinking against the clean light of the sky, contemplating the possibility of inhabiting the flat roof, like a latter-day Simeon Stylites. He grasped the massive stone and climbed a few feet, his muscles knotting, his fingers and toes seeking out the chips and indentations left by the ancient masons, his breath coming in rasps, and then he leapt back down, evidently uninspired.

The Dog began to explore the few sarcophagi that the centuries had left intact, followed by the children, who now began to join in the hunt, touching his elbow and pointing the way from one tomb to another. He ignored them still, peering inside each structure, caressing the carvings of warriors, lions and chimaeras. He inspected the huge slabs that made up the roofs, some of them carved in the shape of a keeled boat, but upside down, and some of them scalloped to represent the roof tiles of a house. He lay experimentally upon the stone bench inside each tomb, searching among those resting places for the couch that would be most comfortable.

Dissatisfied with the sarcophagi, realising perhaps that they were too much in the sun, he approached two large tombs that had been carved into the vertical face of a small cliff nearby. One was cut in the shape of a temple, and the other in the shape of a house. Inside each were three benches, one at the back and one at each side. The paintings upon the walls had been much defaced, partly by those who disapproved of figurative art on religious grounds, and partly because of the smoke and soot of two thousand years' worth of goatherds' fires. The Dog found these two spacious tombs to be both airy and well aspected, giving a fine view over the valley, and accordingly he laid down his quarterstaff, unslung his water flagon, and sat down on the step, between the porticos of the temple tomb. On the pediment above was inscribed in the as yet undeciphered Lycian script 'Philiste, daughter of Demetrius, built this for Moschus, whom she loved'. Underneath were written details of the fine for violation, and at the apex was carved in bas-relief a pair of open hands, the Lycian symbol for unnatural, violent and untimely death.

The Dog looked at the children for the first time, and smiled.

So horrifying was that smile that the children screamed, and ran, tumbling helter-skelter over the rocks, cutting themselves on thorns. Drosoula, Philothei, Karatavuk, Mehmetçik, Ibrahim and Gerasimos would remember that appalling sight as long as they lived, and it would haunt their nightmares for ever, sometimes coming back to them at moments when they should have been at peace.

That evening, the priest, Father Kristoforos, and the imam, Abdulhamid Hodja, encountered each other before the tomb, coincidentally but for identical reasons. Both men wished to know whether or not the newcomer was a member of his flock, and both were just as curious as the children had been, if not more so, now that the latter had told everyone about the Dog's disfigurement.

Abdulhamid Hodja reined in the spirited and exquisite Nilufer, and was tying her somewhat insecurely to an oleander bush, when Father Kristoforos came from another direction, having perspired his way up the slope in a route more direct, but steeper, than that followed by the imam and his horse.

Abdulhamid touched his right hand to his chest, to his lips, and to his forehead, saying, 'Ah, Imansız Efendi, iyi akşamlar.'

The priest smiled, returned the flowery gesture, and replied, 'And good evening to you, Apistos Efendi.' The two men had

37

for many years enjoyed the pleasantry of greeting each other as 'Infidel Efendi', the one in Turkish and the other in Greek, and had struck up a cordial relationship based upon mutual respect, somewhat tempered by an awareness that there were many of both faiths who would look askance at such a friendship. They visited each other's houses only when it was dark, and were much inclined to waste entire nights in long and occasionally heated theological discussions that enervated their families, who were trying to sleep, and always ended with one or other of them saying, 'Well, after all, we are both peoples of the Book.'

The two men presented an alarming sight to the Dog, appearing like that, both at once, at the entrance to his new accommodation. It was not often that a Christian priest, in his capacious black robes, bosky beard and lofty headdress, poked his head round one's door at the same time as an imam with his white turban, well-combed beard and green cloak. The Dog cowered, placed his arms across his forehead and eyes, as if to protect his face, and shrunk into the corner where he had been sitting, until then, in the perfect stillness of contemplation.

Abdulhamid Hodja and Father Kristoforos exchanged glances, and the latter said 'Merhaba' in the hope that such an informal and friendly greeting would reassure the trembling man. 'Salaam aleikum,' said the imam, wishing to emphasise by his greeting that they had come in peace.

'We have come to find out who you are, and whether you want anything,' he continued, subduing his voice in a spirit of gentleness.

The man lowered his arms and looked at them. Suddenly he wiped soot off the wall with one finger, and on the bench he wrote something in swirling Arabic characters that the priest did not understand. Abdulhamid Hodja noticed the priest's puzzlement, and said, 'It means "The Dog". Perhaps he is telling us that he is unclean.'

'From where do you come?' asked Abdulhamid, and the Dog dipped his finger in the soot, and wrote again. Once more the imam read it for the priest: 'It says "Hell".'

'We have come to see if we can help you,' offered Father Kristoforos, whereupon the Dog wrote 'Yalnız kalmak isterim'.

'He says, "Leave me alone,"' said Abdulhamid Hodja.

'We will bring you food and blankets,' persisted the priest, and it was then that the Dog smiled, causing both of the visitors to recoil in alarm. 'God have mercy,' exclaimed the imam.

8

I am Philothei (2)

Once when I was about eleven I heard that Ibrahim was ill, and we didn't have any candles to take into the church, so instead I stole some bread from the table, and some figs, and I took them out and went out to find a beggar, but there weren't any in the vicinity except for the one called the Blasphemer, and he was very abject because he was the most unpopular beggar in the town because he said filthy things whenever he saw a man of religion, and I didn't want to give him the bread and figs, but finally I couldn't find another beggar to give it to, and I said to the Blasphemer, 'This is because Ibrahim is unwell,' and he was aware that charity cures the sick, and so he was good about it, and he said, 'May the sick one get well, little girl, and may God make you strong as well,' and not long afterwards Ibrahim recovered, and after that I always gave alms to the Blasphemer as long as no one was looking.

This happened not long after the day of St Nicholas, when all the young men who have gone to the cities return for the feast, and so this is the best time of year for the beggars, because the young men get drunk and become generous, and the Blasphemer was the only one who had received nothing until I gave him the bread and figs.

9

Mustafa Kemal (3)

Mustafa Kemal is fourteen and has gone to the Military Training School at Manastir. It is 1898 and here beneath Mount Pelister the Greek and Slav bandit-liberators are still bringing chaos to the region, and even in the school itself there is vicious gang warfare. Greece sends irregulars to fight the Ottomans in Crete, and the Sultan declares war. The streets are crowded with soldiers, drummers, flag-wavers. Mustafa wants to run away to join the army, but the war turns out to be too short, and he will have to wait for another one.

At school Mustafa Kemal has a history teacher who enlightens him as to matters of politics, and there is a boy called Ömer Naci who writes poetry, and whose enthusiasm causes Mustafa to open his mind to literature. He learns the art of oratory, and dabbles in verse himself. He has another friend called Ali Fethi, also a Macedonian, who is crazy about French philosophy. Mustafa is ashamed of his poor French, but he knows that it is the key to European civilisation, and so he studies it in his spare time at a course run by French Dominicans. Before long he and Ali Fethi will be discussing the deliciously forbidden texts of Voltaire and Montesquieu.

At home in Salonika Mustafa's social and sexual education proceeds with even greater élan than his academic. He shuns the Muslim cafés, and goes instead to the Kristal, the Olympus, the Yonyo, where he and his friends can play backgammon for five-para coins, drink beer and stuff themselves with meze in the ribald company of Greeks. He takes dancing lessons, and goes to the cafés *chantants*, where there is music and dance performed by Jewesses, Italian girls, all the feminine exotica of the Levant, and they come and sit at his table and flirt with him. He understands that infidel girls are amusing, mettlesome and intriguing because they are allowed to be, unlike the quelled, imprisoned and uneducated women of his own race, who are only exceptionally more companionable or interesting than an ox. In the brothels, Mustafa Kemal is sometimes entertained for free, because the girls adore his fair good looks and his extraordinary blue eyes. A girl of good family, whom he is supposed to be tutoring, falls passionately in love with him.

One day Mustafa Kemal is at Salonika railway station with his poetic friend Ömer. There is more war fever, and troops are being entrained. There is a party of dervishes in their long pointed hats and voluminous robes, overblowing on their shawms and neys, crashing their cymbals and thrashing their drums, salivating, screaming, rolling their eyes. All around them the ordinary folk are falling into the contagious hysteria, crying out, swooning, in an ebullition of fanaticism.

Mustafa Kemal sees this and feels a bitter shame and embarrassment on behalf of his people. The blood rises to his cheeks, and anger to his throat. He divines clearly the advanced symptoms of spiritual and philosophical immaturity, he smells a repellent backwardness, a radical irrationality and credulity which is only just beneath the surface, and he is increasingly convinced that it is Islam that is holding his people back, locking them behind the door that separates the medieval from the modern age. He will never understand why it is that so many of them actually like to be there, locked behind that door, enwombed within their tiny horizon, perpetually consoled and reassured by their tendentious but unchanging certainties.

10

How Karatavuk and Mehmetçik Came to be Called Karatavuk and Mehmetçik

'I bet that my father is stronger than yours,' said Mehmetçik, who at that time was known to everyone by his real name, which was Nico.

'Oh do you?' replied Karatavuk, whose real name was Abdul. 'My father is stronger than your father and all your uncles put together. In fact, when there was an earthquake he stood in the doorway of the house and held it up all by himself, for two whole days.'

Mehmetçik frowned sceptically. 'What earthquake?'

'Before we were born, stupid.'

'Don't call me stupid, stupid.'

'Why not, stupid, if you are stupid?'

'My sisters are stupid,' confided Mehmetçik, 'all they do is whisper together, and then when anyone else comes into the haremlık they pretend to be busy.'

'Everyone says that your sister Philothei is very beautiful,' said Karatavuk, 'but I haven't noticed myself.'

'She's the most beautiful in the world,' replied his friend, 'and when she's grown up she's going to marry the Sultan Padishah himself, and she's going to send us money and sweets from Constantinopoli.'

'Ibrahim won't like that,' giggled Karatavuk. It was a shared joke among everybody that little Ibrahim was besotted with Philothei even though they were less than ten years old. Philothei ignored him, as though he were a stray dog hoping for a pat on the head, but she had become used to his silent and respectful adoration, feeling uncomfortable without it, should she pass from one house to another and fail to glimpse him trailing in the

43

GALWAY COUNTY LIBRARIES

distance, as often as not pretending to be poking in corners with a stick, affecting to have no interest in her whatsoever.

'Let's go and look at the Dog,' suggested Mehmetçik. 'If we take him a present he might smile.'

Karatavuk shuddered.

'Come on,' persisted Mehmetçik, 'let's.'

The children were no different from everyone else in their continued and insatiable fascination for the Dog. If the Dog had taken up residence in the Lycian tombs with the intention of living as an anchorite, then those intentions had definitely been confounded. Apart from anything else, the tombs were considered to be haunted, and even the bravest regarded them with superstitious dread. It was true that the Lycian inscriptions were said to speak of the whereabouts of hidden treasure, but only half of the alphabet was Greek, and the other letters had fallen out of use so long ago that not even Abdulhamid Hodja had any idea what their sounds were. Those who pored over the epitaphs and the other messages to posterity that were engraved on the stones came away frustrated, having been unable to concentrate in any case, on account of the fear of ghosts.

The Dog, therefore, was either wildly brave or quite insane to live in the tombs, and this added to his intrinsic and extraordinary mystique.

It had not taken long for him to become an integral part of the town's conception of itself, because the rules of hospitality were inflexibly observed. Visitors were either the responsibility of the aga, who was obliged to entertain them in his konak, or else of the entire community, in which case the guest stayed in the khan, and the men would arrive with small dishes of food, sitting afterwards, smoking their çubuks in exemplary and companionable silence, until it was time to sleep. It was bad manners indeed for a guest to be left alone even for a moment, and their resolute and stalwart hosts soon developed a mental technique for enduring hours of abject boredom with perfect equanimity.

In the case of the Dog, however, it was unclear as to whether this was a guest or a new resident, or even whether he could be considered to be a bona fide human being. Besides, nobody, however bold their disposition or generous their nature, very

44

GALWAY COUNTY LIBRARIES

much wanted to sit about with a creature of such ghastly aspect, amid the evening chill of the tombs and the emerging stars, and so it was that they arrived with their small but honourable offerings of kadınbudu köfte, green beans in olive oil and iç pilàv, and then departed, having greeted him with a quiet 'Hoş geldiniz'. Upon their return they told their wide-eyed wives and children about the grotesque and horrifying smile of the stranger, and from that time on the Dog went barely a day without a steady trickle of small gifts from those who arrived to observe him quite shamelessly, as if he were an entertainment provided for them by fate. When the aga heard about his arrival he sent a servant up with the customary sabre and loaded pistol, so that the stranger would have the capacity for self-defence. The weapons rusted in a corner of a tomb, until finally they were stolen by one of the unwashed at the time of the olive harvest.

Karatavuk and Mehmetçik scrambled through the rocks, their steps releasing the scents of oregano and thyme, and the sun causing the stones to radiate with a borrowed but mysteriously magnified heat. They passed the first of the sarcophagal tombs, whose sides were carved with serried naked warriors brandishing swords and shields, and then stopped to catch their breath and look around. The Dog had got into the habit of moving from tomb to tomb, living in one, and then another, as if he were spoiled for choice and could not make up his mind. The boys spotted him further up the hillside, and then spied on him with disgusted delight as he scraped a hole in the earth with a stone, defecated into it painfully and then covered it once again with soil. 'He does it like a cat,' whispered Karatavuk, his voice full of wonder.

'He's supposed to be a dog,' said Mehmetçik.

'Let's go and see my father working,' suggested Karatavuk, feeling guilty about having watched the Dog at a moment that should have been absolutely private. In any case, it was always wonderful to see his father shaping pots and getting splattered by mud. 'I'll race you down the hill,' said Mehmetçik, and set off at a run before his friend had had a chance to agree. 'Cheat! Cheat!' shouted Karatavuk, leaping down the hillside in Mehmetçik's wake, pulling threads out of the legs of his baggy shalwar as they caught on the thorns of the maquis.

Iskander the Potter looked up with pleasure as the two little boys thudded breathlessly to a halt in the shadow of the wicker canopy that served him as shelter for his work. Karatavuk was his favourite child, and it always gave him a thrill of pride and pleasure when his beloved son took his hand, kissed it, touched it to his forehead, and called him 'Baba'. The child never minded getting wet clay on his lips, and strained upward when his father bent down to kiss him on the top of his head, calling him 'My lion'. Karatavuk was glad of his father, and basked in such signs of affection. As far as he was concerned, his father's only short-coming, albeit a grievous one, was that he did not possess a gun, although he did have a yataghan with a heavy curved blade and engraved handle, inlaid with silver, and he did have a few equally beautiful daggers that he wore through his sash. Iskander the Potter felt the lack of a gun as keenly as his son, and was in fact producing a surplus of pots so that he could sell them in Telmessos, in order to raise the money for the smith.

Iskander was tall and wiry, with massive hands whose fingers had been worn flat and smooth by so much shaping of clay. He was burned dark by the sun, even though he worked in the shade, and the roots of his hair were just beginning to turn grey. His moustache drooped at the corners of his mouth, and when he laughed his teeth, like those of almost everyone else, were revealed to be browned and corroded by so much toping of sweetened apple tea. His legs were lean and muscular from so much kicking of the stone wheel, and for the same reason he moved with a subtle and graceful rhythm that reminded women of making love. He was fond of inventing riddles and improbable proverbs, and possessed the kind of impatient wit that showed a certain lack of resignation.

Iskander had three sets of clothes: one for working at the wheel, when he would become caked in clay, one for the tea house, and one for high days. In general he was pleased to be a potter, and therefore such a necessary man, but he was wearied by life's lack of variety. Like everyone else, he also worked his own small plot of land, in addition to another one rented from the aga in return for a proportion of his crop, and was irritated with himself because whenever he was at his pots he wished he was at his fields, and whenever he was at his fields he wished he was at his wheel.

When the two boys arrived, Iskander was making a crock large enough to hold a fair measure of water, and his hands were moving in concert up and down the surface of it, leaving behind the even spiral created by his fingers. 'Which is more useful,' he asked them, 'the sun or the moon?'

'The moon,' said Mehmetçik.

'How did you know?' asked Iskander, disappointed.

Mehmetçik rubbed his nose with his hand and replied, 'I guessed.'

'Well, you're right, but you don't know why.' He paused for effect, and said, 'The moon is more important because you need the light more at night than you do during the day when it's light.' He smiled, gratified by his pleasantry, and scratched his forehead, passing his finger under his turban, and leaving yet another dirty streak upon it. The boys looked at each other in bemusement, trying to figure the sense of the potter's answer, and Iskander asked them, 'Why is a potter second only to God?'

The boys shook their heads in unison, and Iskander explained, 'Because God created everything out of earth, air, fire and water, and these are the very same things that a potter uses to make his vessels. When a potter makes something, he acts in the image of God.'

'Are you more important than the Sultan Padishah, then?' asked Mehmetçik, astonished.

'Not on earth,' replied Iskander, 'but perhaps in paradise.' He got up from his seat and stretched, saying, 'I've made something for you, something special.' He reached into his sash and brought out two small terracotta objects, presenting one to each of the boys, one for Abdul his son, and the other for Nico.

What he gave them appeared at first sight to be a small amphora, except that he had moulded the neck so that it resembled the head of a bird, with a beak and two small holes for eyes. Out of sheer whimsy, he had given each one a small turban. Instead of a handle he had made a hollow tail whose extremity was skil-fully pierced so that it became a whistle, and he had placed two simple loops of clay upon the shoulders of the pot on either side

47

of the neck, so that they resembled wings. 'I've made you some musical birds,' he said. 'Give them back to me, and I'll show you. You half fill them with water, like this, and then you blow down the whistle.' Iskander tried some experimental puffs, emptied a little water out of each, and then blew again, placing one at each corner of his mouth. To the amazement and delight of the little boys, a torrent of birdsong cascaded out of the terracotta birds, liquid, warbling and utterly enchanting. They jumped up and down with pleasure, and, forgetting their manners, reached out their hands, impatient to receive them. 'This one,' said Iskander, 'sounds exactly like a karatavuk.' He gave it to his son, asking, 'You know the karatavuk? The one which is completely black and has the yellow beak? It goes vuk vuk vuk in the oleander to warn you away, and then it praises God at the top of the tree in the evening.' Iskander gave the other to Nico, saying, 'and this one sounds like a mehmetçik, which some people call kizilgerdan and some call the fire-nightingale.'

'It's the little one with the red breast,' said Nico, excited, but at the same time a little resentful that Abdul's produced the song of a larger bird than his.

The boys blew hard into their clay birds, and Iskander laughed. 'Gently, gently, you're blowing out the water.'

In the months that elapsed afterwards the two boys became maestros at imitating the songs of the karatavuk and mehmetçik, using the clay birds to call each other across the valleys and rocks. From time to time they became carried away, running about the hibiscus shrubs and wild pomegranates with the whistles in their mouths, flapping their arms, and wondering whether or not it might be possible to fly if only they flapped their arms enough. 'Man is a bird without wings,' Iskander told them, 'and a bird is a man without sorrows.'

Abdul begged his mother for a black shirt and waistcoat, embroidered with golden thread, and he had them before a year was out. Thereafter, because of the natural process whereby everyone in a small community ends up with a nickname, it was not long before even his mother was referring to him as Karatavuk.

Nico, soon to become Mehmetçik, interrupted his mother's labours with similar requests, until finally he obtained the red shirt and waistcoat for which he had pestered her, kissing her hand and pressing it to his cheeks. She had raised her eyes to heaven, saying, 'She who has children has torments,' but she had bought the cloth from a pedlar and made the garments in the few days before the hoeing season.

Iskander lost count of the number of times that the boys came to him, holding back their tears because they had lost their clay birds, either in a fight, or by dropping or misplacing them. He made entire batches, to sell to indulgent parents in the market at Telmessos, so that one day he would be able to afford a beautiful gun, and every time that he gave a new one to the boys he would ask, 'And who is second only to God?' withholding the toy until he had heard the correct and satisfactory answer, 'The potter, the potter, the potter.'

II

Ibrahim Gives Philothei
a Goldfinch

When Ibrahim was six years old he found a dead goldfinch in an orchard near the Letoun, where Mohammed the Leech Gatherer was wont to spend hours in the water, waiting patiently for the leeches to attach themselves to his legs. Ibrahim had been amusing himself by trying to catch lizards in his hands, a project which is altogether impossible to achieve, but is a pastime to which every child necessarily commits many oblivious hours. Catching tortoises is somewhat less of a challenge, and for this reason those creatures quickly lose their interest, unless one is simply waiting to see how long it takes a tortoise to put out its head after having been poked with a stick.

Ibrahim found the little bird because his eye was caught by the brilliant yellow markings on its wings, and the rich scarlet of the mask. It was wedged between two rocks, as if it had simply tumbled out of the sky, overtaken suddenly by death. He picked it out and turned it over in his hands, and although it had stiffened and dried into a contorted posture, he thought that it was the most pretty thing that he had ever seen. He turned it over and over in his hands, amazed by its perfect lightness and insubstantiality.

Karatavuk and Mehmetçik were swinging from a low branch of a nearby tree, and Drosoula and Philothei were sitting on a fallen pillar by the Letoun, conversing, watching Mohammed talking and grinning to himself, and throwing stiff blades of grass into the water, in order to watch them float.

Ibrahim went up to the girls, and held out his hand. 'Look what I've got,' he said.

'It's a dead bird,' said Drosoula scornfully. 'Take it away, it's horrible.'

'Oh, but it's so pretty!' exclaimed Philothei, putting her hands to her face.

'It's a kushu,' Ibrahim told her, proud of his knowledge. 'Do you like it?'

'It's so pretty!' exclaimed Philothei again.

'What are you going to do with it?' asked Drosoula, her voice still scornful.

Ibrahim ignored her, and held it out to Philothei. 'Do you want it?' he asked.

Philothei blushed with pleasure, and said, 'Oh yes. Thank you.' She put out both hands, and he laid it gently in her palms.

The little girl raised the tiny corpse to her face so that she could look more closely at it, and then quite suddenly threw it to the ground, saying, 'Öf! Öf! It stinks. It's disgusting.'

'Of course it stinks,' Ibrahim told her sensibly. 'It's dead.' Philothei stared down at the bird in continuing horror, and Ibrahim, a terrible feeling of disappointment growing in his gut, asked, 'Don't you want it, then?'

Philothei was sensitive to his feelings, even at so young an age, and she replied, diplomatically, 'Of course I want it, but not when it's stinky.'

'You're mad,' observed Drosoula, with every affectation of maturity. 'It's no use to anyone.' She would have loved it if someone had offered her such a gift, but she knew that no one ever would.

'It's pretty,' reproved Philothei.

'What if I cut the wings off, and you keep those?' asked Ibrahim. 'They're very nice, and they won't stink. Wings don't stink when you cut them off. I've got some magpie wings, and they're quite big, but they don't stink and they've never stunk.'

'I'd like the wings,' said Philothei, who did not really like the idea at all, but who was already caught up in the subtleties of the courtship that would last until the day of her death.

So it was that Philothei became the owner of a small pair of wings, black, speckled with white and golden at the leading edge. With time she was to become very fond of the curious and useless gift, and would feel a warmth in her heart, and a modest thrill of pleasure every time that she came across them in her small collection of treasures.

From that time forward, Ibrahim began to associate Philothei with birds, and he would think of her as 'the little bird'. Later on, when they were betrothed, he would refer to her by that name among his friends, without sentimentality and without embarrassment. It would also be his pet name for her during those few incandescent and illicit moments when, at the risk of their reputations, they found themselves together and alone.

12

The Proof of Innocence (1)

Polyxeni had much trouble sleeping, because that night the bulbuls were singing their hearts out, and in any case there was a full moon. She tossed restlessly on her pallet, and blinked because her eyes felt hot and dry. At about the hour before dawn she saw her mother, but afterwards was not sure whether or not she had seen her mother's ghost, or had been visited in a dream. As she told her friend later:

'It was so strange, Ayse, there she was, such a familiar shape, with her shoulders a little bent, and the grey hair poking out in wisps from the sides of her scarf, and that afflicted look in her eyes that she always had, and yet I felt nothing but peace. I said, "Mother, is that you?" and she sat on the edge of the divan and said, "Who else?" and I said, "Mother, it's been so long, what are you doing?" and she said, "The earth is weighing on my chest. Show me some light, so that I can breathe." And I lay there thinking, and I said, "Mother, it's been only three years, and you know what people have been saying." My mother says, "Well, I am innocent, and everyone can see it if you do as I ask. My bones need wine." And I say, "But Mother . . ." And she sighs and says, "Even my child suspects me," and I say, "No, no, no," and my mother says, "Just think, afterwards you can give up mourning," and I say, "I will always mourn. Your death burns me every day. Look, I am burned all over." And I hold out my arms to her. She sighs again and says, "If you do as I ask, the burning will be healed by water." And so finally I say, "I will do as you ask," and she stands up and says, "When you have done it, I would like to know. Send me a message." And I say, "Yes, Mother, I will," and I tell myself, "Polyxeni, you've got to remember this when you wake up," and then I go back to sleep, and in the morning when the azan wakes me up, I do remember it, and that's why I'm telling you about it.'

Ayse put her hand on Polyxeni's cheek, and pressed her own head against that of her friend. 'Well,' she said at last, 'I suppose it's not for me to say, really. We don't do what you people do. Our dead don't like to be molested. But in my opinion, for what it's worth, which probably isn't much, you ought to do what your mother asks.'

'I am going to do it on the day after the next psychosavato, which is only next week, but there's plenty of time to get the food ready and tell Father Kristoforos.'

Ayse pursed her lips and thought for a moment. 'Do you really think it's wise to do it so soon? I mean, I'm no one to have an opinion, if you ask me, but you know what everyone's been saying. Ever since someone started that rumour about your mother, may she rest in paradise, everyone's been saying that perhaps she made the poison that killed a lot of other people who didn't die of poison at all. This is a filthy town for gossip. I keep things to myself, you know me, but there's many who don't.'

'My mother didn't know how to make any poison,' protested Polyxeni. 'Why should she make poison to kill the family of Rustem Bey? They died of the plague that comes back from Mecca every year like a curse! She has asked me to prove her innocent, and so I will.'

'I wish you good success,' said Ayse, with a mote of scepticism in her voice, 'but I still think you should wait the full five years. And how will you send your mother a message? Can you go to her in a dream?'

'I don't know if dead people have dreams,' replied Polyxeni, knitting her brow in perplexity, 'and if they do, how can you be sure of getting into one?'

'She might come into one of yours, and then you can take advantage of the opportunity.'

'It might be a long time, though.'

'I know how you can do it,' said Ayse suddenly, tapping the side of her nose with a forefinger, in benign appreciation of her own genius.

Accordingly, Polyxeni left her friend's house by the back door, pulled on her slippers, blinked in the sunlight, which by now was growing pointed and fierce, throwing knife-edged shadows upon the pastel walls of the houses, and made her path through the alleyways down towards the meydan. She passed Iskander throwing his pots and perspiring in his little shelter, she passed the streethawkers whose cries of 'Megla! Megla!' (made in England) were universally known to be implausible, and she passed the coppersmiths whose din provided by day the racket that was provided at night by nightingales and disconsolate dogs. She arrived finally in the meydan, where she found Stamos the Birdman, selling his wares in the shade of a quince tree. He had been called Stamos because his grandfather was from Chios, and he was called the Birdman because he sold live birds in the market from the back of a venerable handcart which had belonged to his wife's father and who-knows-who-else before that. In wicker cages he stacked angry partridges upon ludicrous cockerels upon scruffy ducks, crowning the heap with a few cages containing pretty finches and robins that people bought to adorn the wall beside their front doors, so that their houses should be full of birdsong at dawn and even, and visitors would be greeted by bright, curious and friendly eyes, and a peck on the finger.

'Stamo' Efendi,' asked Polyxeni, 'can these birds fly?'

Stamos scratched his stubble and smiled slyly. 'Well, sort of yes, and sort of no.'

'Stamo' Efendi!' protested Polyxeni, 'what kind of answer is that?'

'Give them some time,' replied Stamos, 'and if they don't die, then they'll fly one of these days, God willing.'

Polyxeni realised that she was being teased, and joined in with the bantering turn of the conversation. 'So why can't they fly now, and if they live, God willing, why will they be able to fly later?'

Stamos the Birdman blinked and rubbed his nose with his hand. There was something about the sunlight of spring that made his eyes itch and his nose want to sneeze. He looked at Polyxeni and said, 'Well, the mystery is a shallow one, and not very difficult to fathom, Polyxeni Hanım. I clip their wings because most people don't want to buy a bird that might escape so that they have to sprout their own feathers in a flash and take off in hot pursuit. Most people couldn't be bothered, you see. People make odd birds; they don't fly much.'

'I want a bird that flies,' said Polyxeni, and Stamos, seeing the disappointment in her face, asked, 'Why?'

Polyxeni explained, and Stamos grew serious. 'Well, I could easily get one that isn't clipped, but it would take a few days. I think it would be after All Souls' Day, which isn't much use to you, really. Anyway, the ideal bird for that is a dove, and I don't usually have any. I think the best thing would be for you to find someone who can catch one. The red pines are full of them. You know, the ones where people climb up and tie rags to make a wish.'

'Do you know anyone?' asked Polyxeni.

Stamos rubbed his nose again, sneezed, and replied, 'Little boys.'

Polyxeni, by now a little weary of her mission, but determined nonetheless, set off in search of little boys. There seemed to be a great many, for in those days, just as in these, Anatolia was run by them. They scurried through the alleyways to borrow implements, to bear messages and to deliver brass trays laden with small cups of sweet tea. They darted like rats in and out of doorways, and they mounted resolute and incorruptible guard over packages left on camels and donkeys and in all sorts of odd places by merchants and travellers, and those who had suddenly felt the need to set off in search of a coffeehouse, a smoke and a game of backgammon – 'the only good thing the Persians left us', as people were fond of remarking.

Despite the plenitude of small boys, Polyxeni had set her mind upon two in particular, because the thought of one thing automatically inspires the thought of another, and the thought of birds naturally gave rise to the thought of her son Mehmetçik and Karatavuk, who were more easily found than most small boys thanks to the terracotta birds that Iskander made them. She heard the song of robin and blackbird on the wild slope behind the Church of St Nicholas, and found the two boys, plus Ibrahim, her daughter, Philothei, with her best friend, Drosoula, and Gerasimos, son of the fisherman, all running about in the oleanders and the Lycian tombs, leaping from rock to rock, and pretending, as usual, to be birds. Not far off, the Dog, all but naked, searched the bushes for insects to eat, and discoursed to himself with those inarticulate sobs and gulps that seemed to come from the back of the throat. The Dog, partly because of the horrible thrill caused by the ghastliness of his smile, had become the town's most preferred beggar, and if he had ever entertained notions of living in saintly solitude and poverty, he must certainly by now have abandoned them. He had been forced to settle for mere squalor and inconvenience.

Polyxeni sat nearby, panting, tired from climbing the hill, and watched the children, her heart brimming over with warmth and pleasure. Mehmetçik and Karatavuk had learned to produce a torrent of delectable noise with their whistles, and they were now jumping off rocks, flapping their arms wildly, being imitated by the other children. It looked a little mad, to be sure, but it is a child's privilege to enact the dreams that are denied to the sane. Her daughter, the lovely Philothei, waved her arms with the detached elegance with which she did almost everything, and Ibrahim flapped and pranced nearby, always in her line of sight, hoping beyond hope that she would notice how truly like a bird he was. Drosoula, pug-nosed, heavy-browed and clumsy, fluttered her arms more out of delight in the others than in any realistic attempt to fly, and Gerasimos leaped and warbled next to her. Everyone had noticed that Gerasimos was as devoted to the ugly little Drosoula as Ibrahim was to the exquisite Philothei, and it was certainly a puzzle to all concerned, but of course God does strange things, and that was all one could say about it.

Karatavuk began shouting, 'Look at me! Look at me!' and Polyxeni saw to her horror that he was about to launch himself from the flat roof of a tomb that must have been about ten feet high, at the bottom of which was a stony patch of earth. She winced at the thought of him landing on it, and she rose to her feet and called out, 'Karatavuk! Come down at once! You can't jump from there!'

He looked down at her. Diminutive as he was, he seemed magnificent and angelic, framed against the sky, the sun behind him so that a halo sparkled around the silhouette of his turban and the wisps of his hair, his black shirt making him seem even darker than the shadow that he was. 'I'm not jumping,' he said gravely, 'I'm going to fly.'

'You can't fly. Come down at once, and don't be stupid. You'll hurt yourself!'

Karatavuk bit his lip and frowned. 'I can fly,' he announced. 'I can do anything at all if I try hard enough.'

'Come down!'

Karatavuk began to flap his arms slowly, like an eagle, and closed his eyes. The other children stopped gambolling and watched him in consternation. Drosoula called, 'Karatavuk, don't!' and Polyxeni came forward and stood below, still crying out, 'Come down! Just wait till I tell your mother! Come down at once!' Philothei ran to her mother's side and clutched at her clothing, her mind seized by fearful apprehension.

Karatavuk continued to flap slowly with his eyes closed, his face utterly still from concentration. He was thinking of the snow peaks of the mountains that he had only ever seen from below, and of the great warships that sailed past on the horizon, plumed with smoke and steam. He thought of the distant countries where people dressed strangely, spoke nonsense and ate outlandish food. He imagined himself soaring to the top of the red pines and looking out over the town. He aimed towards the soft clouds that he had always longed to touch, raised one leg and hopped gently from the roof of the tomb.

Polyxeni broke his fall, but both of them tumbled over, and Karatavuk cracked a knee against a sharp stone. Polyxeni hurt the palms of her hands, and they began to sting. She frowned, and wiped them against each other to remove the embedded specks of grit. Karatavuk clutched at his knee and started to rock with pain. His face contorted slowly, and through his sudden tears he told Polyxeni, 'I hate you! I hate you! You spoiled it! I hate you!'

She gathered him in her arms and laughed. 'You don't hate me! Don't be so silly! I just saved you from a nasty fall!'

'I can fly! I can fly! You spoiled it!'

Polyxeni wiped his tears with the corner of her headscarf, and asked, 'Did you ever see a lion cry?'

Karatavuk, his face streaked, shook his head solemnly, and she said, 'Well then, my little lion, don't cry.'

'He's never seen a lion at all,' observed Drosoula, ever the realist.

'I can fly,' insisted Karatavuk, 'I can.'

'Arms aren't wings,' said Polyxeni, trying to quieten and cajole him with the softness of her voice. 'If we had wings, do you think we would suffer so much in one place? Don't you think we would fly away to paradise? Anyway, it's about birds that I want to speak to you. Stop crying and I'll tell you.' She paused, waiting for the child's curiosity to engage. 'Would you know how to catch one of the doves in the red pines, without harming it at all, so that it can still fly?'

Mehmetçik raised a hand, jealous of all the attention that Polyxeni was bestowing upon his friend and anxious to play the man in front of the others. He affected an air of lordly confidence: 'If you give us a birdcage and some corn and some string and a very long thread, we can get you a dove. It's easy.'

'If you get me a dove, I'll give you both a new knife with a brass handle and a double-edged blade.'

Gerasimos and Ibrahim gaped in disbelieving envy, and Polyxeni added, 'And you two boys . . . I'll think of something important for you to do . . . someday soon . . . and then you can have knives too.'

Gerasimos and Ibrahim scowled, but considered it beneath their dignity to make a fuss. 'Who wants a knife anyway?' demanded Philothei, in genuine puzzlement, and Drosoula shrugged, raising her shoulders so that her foreneck bulged instantly with a plump double chin. Polyxeni took the little girls' hands and descended once more into the town, leaving the boys to negotiate between themselves about who would be able to borrow the knives, and how often, and in exchange for what. 'Boys are vain and stupid, and it's very easy to get them to do what you want if only you know how,' said Polyxeni to the two small girls, confidentially passing on her hereditary feminine wisdom as they went by the church.

The next evening Polyxeni went to the graveyard bearing a cup of oil, a candle, a scrubbing brush and a jug of water. The place was already full of the other bereaved women, tending to the graves of their loved ones, and Polyxeni's heart was eased by the sight of them, even though they resembled so many gaunt and flapping crows in their black robes. She had made many intimate and comfortable friends here over the last three years, and she almost regretted that her daily excursions were about to come to an end. She had learned that women came here to cry not only over their dead, but because of their poverty, or because their husband was cruel, or because they endured pains and difficulties that they could not heal or discuss, or because they suffered from futile hopes and desires. It was easier to weep when other women were weeping. Polyxeni had become acquainted with the patterns of grief, and had seen how desolation and utter despair gradually transform themselves into philosophy. A woman who firstly lays herself wailing on the fresh-turned earth and tries to embrace her husband through it, in two years' time is cleaning his headstone in a familiar way, and telling him the latest news about the olive harvest. Later still, after the five years and its ritual, she puts on bright clothes again, and comes back across the threshold, out into the world, a woman whose ordeal by sadness has left her soul as deep and quiet as a well.

Polyxeni squatted by her mother's grave and poured water on the flowers. 'Mother,' she said, 'drink this. It won't be long now. Soon we will all see what everyone already knows.' She scrubbed the wrought-iron railing that had become a little rusty, and very much tilted askew by the settlement of the earth, and she removed the small lamp from the glass-fronted box. Carefully she filled it with the oil, inspected the wick, and went to another grave to light her candle from a lamp that was already lit. This flame she transferred to her own mother's lamp, and then she snuffed out the candle and sat back on her heels. She contemplated the grave, and found herself looking forward to the day after All Souls' Day. Behind her a woman raised her voice, and began to sing:

> 'Beloved, when will I see you?
> Where shall I wait, and how long?
> Until a garden grows beneath the sea
> Till the mountains meet
> Till the crow turns white into a dove.
> Beloved, when will I see you?
> Where shall I wait, for how long?
> If I knew, beloved, I would make you food,

I would lay out a fine good meal,
I would wash your clothes
And you could wear them on arriving,
Beloved, when will I see you?'

The woman wiped her eyes with the back of her hand, and
Polyxeni stole over to her and put an arm around her shoulder,
because this was the painful part of the lament, and Polyxeni
knew that her friend would need some help in singing it:

'If you make a meal, you must eat it yourself,
If you lay out food you will dine alone
If you wash my clothes, light a fire,
It is better to let them burn.
I will never come back, beloved,
Mother, I cannot return.'

'All these tears,' said Polyxeni, gently, 'all this scrubbing of
stones, in the end it can't bring anybody back. What can the
dead feel?'

The woman put the balls of her hands to her eyes and threw
back her head, rocking her body as tears streamed down her
cheeks. 'My son,' she cried, 'my little son!'

This woman, Polyxeni knew, still made seven meals each night,
even though there were only six to eat them. Each night she
took the extra food out to a leper and told him, 'Eat this so that
my son can eat,' and she would not leave until all the food was
gone. She had buried the child with a crown of white flowers
upon his head because he would never grow up to be a groom.

'Your son has crossed a river into a fine and beautiful place,'
said Polyxeni.

'He has married the black earth,' sobbed the woman.

'Every day,' advised Polyxeni, 'bring him water to drink. The
dead need water from home. That's what I do every day for my
mother.'

'Oh, Polyxeni, what can I do?' cried the woman. 'What can I
do to get rid of this yearning? My throat burns with it. What
can I do?'

'Come every day,' repeated Polyxeni. 'Come every day and sing, and talk with him, and pay attention to what he tells you when you dream about him, and one day you will feel your fingers unfolding and he will carry away all your pain and longing and they will be spun into yarn and made into bright clothes for him to wear in the garden across the river.'

'I wish I were a man,' said the woman. 'I could walk, and let the yearning pass.'

'Well, we're women,' said Polyxeni, 'we must sit and let it grow until one day it leaves us because we cannot contain it. And remember, because you are a woman, one day you might have another son.'

'I don't want another.'

Polyxeni patted her friend on the shoulder in a knowing way, and stood up. Her legs felt numb and tingly from so much squatting down, and for a moment she thought that she might stumble. She glanced across the cemetery with its tilting graves, its patches of dry weeds, its huddles of black-robed women, and saw Karatavuk and Mehmetçik waving to her from the far gate, reluctant to enter into a place of so much sorrow and so many women. She hurried over, washed death from her hands in the stoup of water and came out on to the pathway.

The two little boys, extremely filthy, with their clothes torn and smelling of resin, their faces scratched by twigs, their hair full of needles, their legs and hearts tired out from scrambling up trees, exhausted by fear and danger, but triumphant and vindicated, held up the birdcage for her to view. Inside, turning circles in her bewilderment, was a restless, anxious and confused grey dove with a rose-coloured breast and a pretty black ring on her neck. They had beguiled her on the same branch where Iskander the Potter had once tied a rag after the birth of the lovely Philothei, to wish the child good fortune.

13
The Proof of Innocence (2): A Bad Start

Father Kristoforos awoke suddenly in a sweat of horror. He had dreamed of coming across the distended and deliquescent corpse of once-almighty God, laid out amid the weeds of paradise, attended by tattered and impotent angels. As he awoke, the despair of the angels became the wailing of the dawn muezzin. Appalled, he crossed himself hastily several times and muttered the Jesus prayer as he did so. He rubbed his eyes and gave thanks for having awoken to the indifferent pastel light of a reassuringly chilly and ordinary sunrise as it filtered through the shutters, and understood it as an oblique refutation of what his dream had proposed. 'Kyrie eleison,' he said to himself, and shook his head and blinked several times. He rose from his pallet, went outside to relieve himself, and came back in to find his wife Lydia laying out olives and slabs of white cheese and bread on to a wooden board. He touched her on the shoulder and said, 'Wife, I have just had a very horrible dream.'

She puckered her lips sympathetically, and tutted. 'It's these pink poppies,' she said. 'Ever since the poppies started coming up pink instead of red, everyone's been having bad dreams. Anyway, you shouldn't worry. You know what they say: "Day denies the promises of night."'

Father Kristoforos tugged at his beard so that the skin on his jaw stretched pleasantly. 'Well, I'd noticed the pink poppies, but I didn't know about the bad dreams.'

'You're in another world,' said Lydia, not unkindly, but a little reprovingly nonetheless. 'I don't suppose you've been listening to all the talk. You spend your time reading the works of the Fathers, and you don't notice what's going on outside the door.'

'I like to read the Philokalia,' he said.

'Don't I know it,' she replied. 'It's me who has to go out and buy oil for the lamps.'

'Shrouds don't have pockets,' said the priest sententiously. 'You can't buy oil when you're dead, and one should read the Fathers whilst there's still some hope of salvation. And you know what they say: "The ink of the learned is equal in merit to the blood of the martyrs." '

Lydia smiled and pulled the stalks from the olives. 'You'll go to Heaven, and I'll be wandering about in Hell, looking for oil at a decent price. And anyway, anyone can quote proverbs in párdon of their own faults. And also anyway, if you know what I mean, that saying isn't one of ours.'

'I could have sworn it was one of ours. It's St Philotheos of Sinai, or Ilias the Presbyter, or someone like that.'

'Send a little boy to Abdulhamid Hodja, and he'll tell you it's one of theirs.'

'Well, I might do that, just for the curiosity.'

'If you were in the wrong, you wouldn't remember to tell me, would you?' accused Lydia, and Kristoforos patted her cheek in mock reproof. 'Probably not,' he said, adding, 'And anyway again, this is the first of the month, so, God willing, we won't go hungry for a while, so you won't have to moan about the price of oil.'

The couple sat side by side on cushions on the floor, quietly eating breakfast from the low table. They munched in happy and enjoyable silence, of the kind that grows like a vine through the long years of a good marriage, so that when everything that needs to be said has already been pronounced, it is mutually understood that there is an intimate silence that has its own loquacity.

In the first years of their espousal, Lydia had stood dutifully and modestly beside and behind him whilst he ate, her head bowed and her hands folded together before her, waiting for him to finish before she took the board away and finished the leftovers on her own, but somehow this custom had slipped unnoticed into abeyance, and now, if ever she hesitated, he simply gestured to the cushion beside him and said, 'Eat.'

It helped that they were childless, for there are no customs to keep up when one is unobserved. To begin with, Father Kristoforos had prayed fervently to St George for his wife's fertility, and both of them had tied white cloths to the rusted ironwork of the tekke of the saint. Lydia had bought one tama after another from the silversmith, and, if she had fallen pregnant, would have draped them over the icon of the Panagia Glykophilousa in the Church of St Nicholas, each tama stamped with the image of a child, but she had only been able to afford pewter ones, and sometimes she wondered whether the Virgin would have taken more notice if she had been able to offer tamata made of gold. She felt mean and unworthy, being too poor to give presents tantamount to the real worth of the Mother of God.

She had even gone to Ayse, wife of Abdulhamid Hodja, and begged her for some of the tiny slips of paper upon which Abdulhamid daily wrote verses of the Koran for the sick to eat. There were special verses, in which children were mentioned. It was an odd feeling trying to swallow them, but Lydia felt a certain glow of divine comfort when she simply placed the morsels on her tongue and kept them there until they were utterly sodden. During those times it was impossible to talk properly, for fear of dislodging the verse or accidentally spitting it out, so she would wait until she went out hoeing, or gathering wild greens. Once she had even bought a scarab beetle from an itinerant Arab quack, and eaten that. She sometimes shuddered at the memory, and wondered how on earth she had brought herself to do it, let alone buy anything from an Arab. Some people said that when God took the cart of vices around the world, He stopped for a rest in Arabia and the Arabs stole it.

No amount of praying and petitioning, and no amount of fool-proof and foul-tasting potions from the Armenian apothecary had made any difference, and so the couple had gradually ceased to preoccupy themselves. Lydia knew that behind her back she was known as 'Lydia the Barren' in order to distinguish her from the other Lydias of the town, but not many of the local nick-names were complimentary in any case, and many were much worse. Besides, there were plenty of children wandering about who needed taking care of, or who would put up with being mauled affectionately, and Lydia had enough nephews, nieces and godchildren to keep anybody busy and confused. She particu-larly liked to sit them in a semicircle and tell them gruesome stories about beheadings, and people who were ambushed in the Bey Mountains by wolves that kicked up snow in their faces in order to blind them, and then ate out their bowels. Sometimes she and the children set up a wonderful groaning to imitate the way that in autumn Mount Solyma groans in order to summon the elect to paradise, and ignorant passers-by would be thoroughly spooked, unless they heard the ensuing gales of childish laughter.

With breakfast finished, Father Kristoforos donned his cassock, his cross and his black hat. 'Is the veil at the back straight?' he asked, and Lydia came up and arranged it so that the fabric flowed neatly and symmetrically down his back. 'Your pigtail is getting tatty,' she said. 'It looks like an old bit of rope washed up on the beach.'

'Well, it can wait. We can do it this evening, before the attendance at the grave. Are you all prepared for it?'

'Well, the food is ready, except for the few things we can do today, but you know how upsetting it always is. I think that Polyxeni will be heartbroken all over again.'

'What worries me is whether Rustem Bey will turn up, on account of all the rumours.'

Lydia huffed indignantly: 'Well, those rumours were nonsense, and everyone knows them but no one believes them. That idea that her mother made poison to kill all his family! It's so stupid! Why would she do that? It's ridiculous! And who is supposed to have poured the poison down their throats? Nobody! Whoever started all that talk should have their tongue cut out. Everyone knows that they died of the plague that comes back with the haj! And we've had to make twice the amount of food because of all the people who'll turn up out of curiosity.'

Kristoforos sat on the divan whilst Lydia knelt and slipped his shoes on to his feet. Like most Christian priests, he was broad-bottomed and heavy-bellied, and it was altogether too trying to attempt the task himself. 'I am wondering why her brothers and sisters agreed to having the ceremony two years early. You must admit, it's a risk.'

'A dream's a dream,' replied Lydia, rising to her feet and tucking a stray strand of hair back under her scarf. 'If your mother comes in a dream and tells you to do something, then you have to do it. Tonight everyone will see with their own eyes that the old lady was innocent. Just you wait.'

'I just pray that nothing happens with Rustem Bey,' said the cleric, shaking his head, and with that he left, armed with two capacious bags sewn out of old kilims. He stepped forth into the early morning, in order to call in on each Christian house in turn, so that those therein might exercise their customary privilege of repaying his spiritual work with gifts less lofty but equally indispensable. Naturally there were those who were coincidentally absent every time he came to their door, and naturally there were those who thought it a suspicious thing that a priest should be coming round to collect offerings from their wives, but for the most part he was popularly esteemed, and in any case he also received quite overt offerings from Muslims who were anxious to hedge their bets with God by backing both camels.

Kristoforos himself did not like to live more or less as a beggar, and, however effusive the welcome, he inevitably experienced a flushing of his cheeks every time a door was answered. He would cross the threshold right foot first, in deference to local superstition, and would then have to munch his way through the obligatory dainties of the house. Despite his comfortable girth, he did not have much of a liking for sweet things, and he found it difficult to cope with the quantities of lokum, hoshmerim and baklava that were presented to him on brass trays by shy daughters who kissed his hands and cast their eyes to the ground. These small but cumulative hospitalities were the price he had to pay for the good loads of aubergines, tomatoes, hórta, garlic, dried beans, cockerel legs and köfte with which he would return to Lydia a few hours later. 'I feel ill,' he would complain, throwing himself down upon the divan and clutching his guts with both hands. 'I have eaten enough honey and helva to keep me bilious for a week,' to which she would reply, 'Just be thankful that there are so many good people.'

A further tribulation to the priest regularly danced attendance upon him in the form of the town's most persistently obnoxious beggar, who plagued him particularly upon the first day of the month, when he had food in his bags. This beggar, like the Dog, had arrived in the town without a history, but it was assumed that he had been cast out of his village and had wandered until he had found a home in Eskibahçe. He had the dark thin face and the remnants of clothing of a Kurd, and so it was thought that perhaps he must have drifted in from the north-east, across the measureless plains of Anatolia and through the cyclopean passes of the Taurus Mountains, in search of a climate where there was no snow in winter, so that one could live a beggar without perishing of cold. Whether he was a Muslim, or a Syrian Christian, or a Yezidi, no one ever knew, for he railed equally against all. He was known simply as 'The Blasphemer', and was quite unable to see either a priest, an imam, or a rabbi, without insulting and abusing them. It was a spontaneous and ungovernable impulse with which he had been afflicted almost as soon as he could talk. Only he knew how much he had suffered the whippings of his father, and the scoldings of his mother and aunts, whose shrill reproofs still orbited and collided inside his head every time he tried in vain to sleep. He lived in doorways, embarrassed and perplexed with himself, avoided by almost all, except by those who found in his novel kind of madness a form of amusement. Mischievous customers in the coffeehouses had been known to fetch him and push him out into the street if either Abdulhamid Hodja or Father Kristoforos were thought to be approaching.

On this occasion the Blasphemer blocked the priest's way, and the latter's heart sank. They came face to face in a steep and narrow alleyway made narrower by Ali the Snowbringer's patient donkey, which, with freezing water dripping down its flanks, was standing with one hoof poised in a dream, whilst Ali himself carried ice into an adjacent house. Kristoforos saw that peculiar grin, that curious and fanatical twitch of the eye, and shuddered as the Blasphemer grasped his hand, kissed it with what seemed like ferocious sarcasm, and then waved his scrawny arms in his face and yelled, 'A cucumber up your arse!'

'Peace! Peace!' intoned the priest, gruffly, his rubicund cheeks reddening still further, rancour and resentment rising up in his breast.

'Pastis! Anani sikeyim! Malaka!'

Kristoforos looked round to see if anyone was listening, and told the beggar: 'Look, a fart never broke any flagstones, so why don't you just keep your mouth shut? Is that so difficult?' He made to shoulder the beggar aside, his head ringing with these insults in two languages, feeling that a day that had begun with a terrifying dream had now been sullied further, when the beggar tugged at his robes, his eyes full of sorrow, and exclaimed, 'Sorry! I am sorry, Father, sorry! Son of a whore! Forgive me! Shit from the belly of a sow! Your aunt! Your mother! Forgiveness!'

Father Kristoforos made the sign of the cross over him, and looked down at him sternly. 'You poor wretch!' he growled. 'Anyone would think you'd been baptised by a priest from Cephalonia.' He reached into one of his bags and brought out a roundel of unleavened bread, a piece of hard white cheese and a tomato. 'Eat,' he said. The Blasphemer threw himself upon the food, scrabbling to take it from the priest's hands and stuffing it into his mouth.

Kristoforos proceeded on his way, reflecting that by this act of charity he had taken food out of the mouth of his wife, and wishing that the Blasphemer was more like the Dog, who lived out of the way in the Lycian tombs, or like the other idiots of the town, who just sat in a row on the wall near the meydan, grinning and pissing themselves. He wondered whether Lydia and Polyxeni and her sisters had made enough koliva to eat after the ceremony, and, sighing as he tapped upon the door of the irascible Daskalos Leonidas, he felt his heart grow heavy. He prayed to God that the old woman would be proved innocent, but there seemed little to hope for from such an ill-omened day. He noticed that a bedraggled and desiccated pink poppy was growing out of a crack where the wall of the teacher's house intersected with the cobbles of the street.

14

The Proof of Innocence (3): Mariora Returns to the Light

When the evening cooled, Polyxeni, her sisters and her friends toiled up the hill. Lydia bore candles and a flagon of red wine, and the others were bearing large baskets filled with pastries, bread and koliva, covered over with white cloth. The latter they left in the church courtyard, and then they made their way to the cemetery. On the roofs of the houses the newly arrived storks squabbled, courted, constructed nests and rattled their bills at each other, impartially confounding as usual the deathless but demonstrably false proverb that no stork will ever nest upon the roof of a Christian. High overhead a booted eagle whistled melodically as it set its course for the woody foothills of the mountains. The wild tulips of spring stood with bent heads, like cheerful but modest virgins, on the banksides, and rock roses, almost ready to flower, sprouted out of the stony earth around the orchards of olives. All day Polyxeni had been feeling eagerness, excitement and pleasure growing in her stomach, so that she began to glow inside as though she had swallowed sunlight. It was the thought of seeing her mother again after these three long years, as if her mother would be the same, and would come forth and kiss her as she used to do when Polyxeni called in on the way to the market. She had already dug up the flowers that for so long she had watered and tended faithfully, and had given them to the woman who mourned her son.

Now that the hour was drawing near, however, and the bell was ringing out sadly, she began to feel both dread and horror, horror for the obvious reason, and dread in case her dream had been a deception by the Devil or a djinn. How awful, and what a humiliation and a disaster it would be if her mother, Mariora, turned out to be guilty after all! They would have to bury her again so that Rustem Bey could not take her away and burn her.

'I feel sick,' she told Lydia the Barren, as they approached the gate of the cemetery, and she leaned on her friend's shoulder for support. 'Don't worry,' said Lydia, 'the amount you've been up here, washing her with tears and offering prayers, it's impossible that even the smallest sin remains.'

'Look at all these people!' exclaimed Polyxeni. 'I've never seen so many!' The cemetery was full of women, those in most recent mourning at the grave's edge, so that it was almost lost in flapping black sleeves and headscarves, and those in lesser mourning forming successive outer rings of less sombre colours, extending even to the low and lopsided cemetery walls, upon which sat or sprawled the little children of the town. Outside the walls stood the solemn rows of Muslim women, who would not enter the sacred ground of the infidels, but who came anyway, to serve their sisters of the other faith. Polyxeni saw her friend Ayse, wife of Abdulhamid Hodja, and raised a hand in greeting. Ayse smiled back wanly, her face full of sympathy and concern. Of the town's men, there were only Mariora's three surviving sons, standing self-consciously and uneasily among the women by the grave, feeling like mackerel who have suddenly found themselves swimming with dolphins.

The crowd parted as Polyxeni, her sister and Lydia the Barren made their way to the graveside. Lydia put down her handful of small candles and the flagon of red wine. She took the spade from one of the brothers, and the other women sat nearby on the ground or on the low kerbs of graves. Some of them began to think of their own sorrows, and others felt curiously detached, as though to keep their emotion for later. Lydia bent down, removed the oil lamp and handed it to Polyxeni, who by now was feeling so nauseous with apprehension, mounting grief, suspense and excitement, that she laid the flat of her hand to her diaphragm and tried to force herself to breathe more calmly. Lydia crossed herself, rolled up her sleeves and raised the spade a few inches above the earth. There was a moment of absolute stillness, as if the world had stopped rolling in the heavens, and then a great sigh rose from the crowd as she drove the blade down and cast aside the first spitful of soil. 'I can't bear it!' cried Polyxeni suddenly, throwing herself to the ground. Lydia drove the spade into the earth again, and one of the women outside the gate broke into ululating song:

'I had a cypress in my garden,
A cypress tall,
But the north wind blew,
And my cypress fell
And my strength was broken too.'

There was another moment of silence, broken only by the metallic slicing of iron in earth, and then the woman who mourned her son felt words move inside her, both on her own and on Polyxeni's behalf:

'Vay! Vay! Vay!
For death is the camel
The dark camel
That kneels at every door.'

Polyxeni leaned over so far to peer into the grave that Lydia had to push her gently aside. Her spade rose and fell rhythmically. She was working evenly from one end to the other, and sweat was pearling on her brow. She was hoping that Mariora had not been buried too deeply, not just because of the work, but because bodies last longer when they are deeply buried. Shameful as it might be, she was also consumed with the same violent curiosity that had attracted the large attendance of the townsfolk. She felt gravesoil working its way into her shoes and settling uncomfortably and awkwardly between her toes. From time to time she paused to draw breath and wipe her forehead. Perspiration made her clothes cling to her back and to the backs of her legs. She became so absorbed in her task that she scarcely heard the several laments that were now pouring forth simultaneously from the women around, whose passions were transporting them all the more strongly as the spade cut deeper and the heap of ochre soil rose:

'You are better off than me, even grieving,
You eat in the daylight and sleep on high . . .

Pour water, dissolve these silken threads
With which you sewed my eyes.
I want to see you. Pour water . . .
I wept for you but the tears burned
And now my face is black . . .
. . . Pour water . . .
I placed a pretty partridge in the black earth
But took out rotten quinces,
I planted a rose
And harvested bones . . .
. . . I want to see . . .
Where is our gold and silver?
All is shadow and dust and damp wood . . .
. . . Dissolve these silken threads . . .
I looked down and I understood.
I said 'Who is she that was queen?
Who was a soldier?
Who was poor?
Who is the righteous?
Who has sinned? . . .
. . . You are better off than me . . .
Give me a window for the birds,
For the nightingales,
For me to see the new leaves,
For the children to talk . . .
. . . Now my face is black . . .
I'm afraid,
For now I hear the shovel's thunder,
I hear the ring of the hoe . . .
. . . Where is our gold and silver? . . .
You gave me kisses like honey,
But the last kiss was poison and bitter,
And so was your leaving,
I kissed you, I bent over and kissed you,
I tasted the grief on your lips . . .
. . . Give me a window for the birds . . .
Bid farewell to these narrow streets,
Your little feet will never walk on them again . . .

She is married to Charos,
Rise up,
Your daughter is waiting . . .
. . . Give me a window for the birds . . .
Tell me, beloved, how did Charos receive you?
Charos the Huntsman, dressed in black,
Charos with the black horse,
He sits on my knees, his head on my chest,
When hungry he eats from my body,
When thirsty he drinks from my eyes . . .
. . . Give me a window for the birds . . . pour water . . .
Rise up,
Your daughter is waiting.
. . . I ask only a window for the birds.'

Polyxeni trembled, unable to sing at all. She crouched by the side of the grave, watching the spade's work, reaching down and picking out handfuls of soil, which she crumbled and let rain from between her fingers. She raised one handful to her nose and inhaled deeply, as if she might scent the absorption of her mother's flesh. From time to time she uttered inarticulate little exclamations, and Lydia would say, 'Sing, sister, try to sing, it will unlock your heart.' Suddenly, one of her sisters who was squatting at the other side of the grave pointed, saying, 'Look!'

Lydia stopped. She followed the line of the pointing finger, and saw the first dark brown moist fibres of rotted wood, and the blacker shade of the earth. She laid aside the spade and took up the olivewood spatula that one of Polyxeni's brothers handed to her. 'The skull first,' advised an old woman, as if Lydia did not know by now how these things were done. She began to delve carefully, and felt the implement come into contact with something hard but hollow. She scraped the soil aside, and exposed the bone just above one eye socket. Working gently, she cleared the earth all around, brushing at the relics with her fingers. Polyxeni's brothers and sisters leaned over and tossed white flowers into the grave. Lydia the Barren crossed herself, and then, very solicitously, she lifted the skull. She wiped the clagged earth off it with her fingers, loosening it from the eye sockets and shaking it out. She lifted the jawbone out of the grave, wiped that with her fingers, pushed a loosened tooth back into its bed, and located the jaw into the skull, which she then laid on a white cloth. Reverently, she held the head before her at eye level, and noted the gapped and honey-blackened teeth that were all that could be said to be reminiscent of the living Mariora. All the singing ceased. In its place there rose a wild and dreadful keening, an animal sound that could have been a herd of wounded beasts immolated in a burning wilderness. It was as if the women had expected to see Mariora as she was before. Lydia kissed the skull upon the forehead, and placed a coin upon the cloth. Finally she handed it to Polyxeni, saying, 'You have received her well.'

Polyxeni was overwhelmed. She touched it three times to her forehead, kissed it fervently and held the dead bone to her cheek as if it were her living mother. Her face contorted with sobs. Her younger sister, equally wrought, struggled to take it away from her, but she clutched on to it fiercely, exclaiming 'Alimono! Alimono! Maalesef! Maalesef!'

Finally she mastered herself, and relinquished her hold. She had devotedly embroidered a white scarf in the preceding month, and this she wrapped around the head, so that it looked like nothing so much as death's mockery of a living woman. She too placed a coin on the cloth, and then allowed the skull to be passed from hand to hand. She wanted them all to see it so that everyone would know that Mariora had been innocent in her life. The women took the skull and philosophised:

'It doesn't matter what you do, we all come to this . . .' 'This is how my mother will be too, one day she'll die and be exhumed, and this is all there'll be . . .' 'Day becomes night . . .' 'Ah, if only these bones could speak and bring us news . . .' 'We are like candles that burn in an hour . . .' 'Even the God of Death is scared of death . . .' 'Where are all her troubles now? . . .' 'Death is the veil over all things . . .' 'What use is money and a good house after all? . . .'

Polyxeni made her way through the crowd and lifted Philothei off the wall. 'Come and welcome your grandmother,' she said, leading the child to the graveside. 'Look, she is coming back to see the light for the last time, and get the weight of earth from her chest.' Philothei held her mother's hand and peered down as, bone by bone, Mariora rose from the grave. The little girl could hardly work out what to think, except that she knew that this was more serious than anything she had ever seen before. She was more fascinated and amazed than horrified, and looked up at her mother in perplexity before casting her eyes down, watching, biting her lip as Lydia lifted out the ribs one by one and placed them neatly on the white cloth that she had laid out at the side of the pit. Philothei could not make any connection between these light, soil-encrusted bones, and the woman whose face and voice she remembered but dimly, but whose affection and generosity had already entered into the annals of family myth.

Lydia toiled on, ignoring the stream of advice: 'Don't forget to count the bones . . .' '. . . don't break anything . . .' '. . . there are some bones from the hand over there, look, the little ones, don't lose them . . .' '. . . there was a gold ring . . .' '. . . there was a silver cross . . .' '. . . take out the feet bones before the leg bones, and that way you won't lose them . . .'

When the remains were perhaps half exhumed, there was a buzz in the crowd, and all faces turned towards the gate, for there stood Rustem Bey. His hair and moustache were freshly oiled, his cheeks were recently shaved, his bearing was proud, his scarlet fez was well brushed, his boots were gleaming with new polish, and in his sash he carried his silver-handled pistols, his yataghans and the knife that he had taken from Selim. There was a deep silence. Suddenly he strode forward, knowing with unthought certainty that everyone would step aside and make way. He stopped by the graveside with an abruptness and precision that was almost military, and looked down intently at the bones.

Polyxeni was incensed by a righteous rage, the rage that had eaten away at her for thirty-six months as rumours had circulated and counter-circulated. She seized the skull from the hands of the woman who nursed it, and held it aloft, above her head. She went over to the wall and paraded it back and forth before the Muslim women, strutting in a bold passion, and shouting out as if in accusation: 'Is this the head of a poisoner? Look! Only three years, and already the earth has received her! The earth has not refused her! The earth has taken her in! Only three years!'

She wheeled triumphantly and thrust the skull in the faces of the women inside the yard, hasting from one to the next. 'Do you see flesh?' she demanded. 'One scrap of skin? One wisp of hair? Do you see one trace of eyes and lips and tongue?'

With all the courage and confidence of her indignation she stopped before Rustem Bey and let him see the head, defying him. 'Clean! Clean!' she screamed, almost hysterical. 'Clean as a rock! Clean as the snow! Innocent! Innocent!'

Rustem Bey held out a hand as if to receive the skull, but Polyxeni snatched it away. He reached into his sash, and brought something out. He looked at Polyxeni levelly. 'I always knew that your mother was innocent, and for that reason I have brought this purse, as my contribution. Use it well, in memory of your mother, who was a good woman. And let us have no more bad blood.' He turned and scanned the assembled people, raising his voice: 'Wasn't it enough that I should lose all my family in the plague? Wasn't it enough that Polyxeni Hanım and her brothers and sisters should lose their mother? It's a mean-spirited and ignorant people that rubs salt and sand in other people's wounds with all these stories of poison and conspiracy! No more stories! No more bad blood!'

Rustem Bey gestured towards the grave. 'This was a good woman,' he announced, simply. He picked his way back through the crowd, and left. Now that they had been reproved by their aga, the people seemed unable to look each other in the face and think of something to say. He had called them 'mean-spirited and ignorant', and this stung like lemon in a cut. Only Polyxeni and her siblings were pleased, although they wondered why it was that an infidel pasha as important as Rustem Bey should have come to make a speech in their defence, and give them a purse of money. People had been saying that his disappointments and misfortunes had made him long for something more profound than money and domination, and perhaps this new decency was a proof.

Father Kristoforos processed slowly towards the cemetery, hoping beyond hope that the bones disinterred by his wife would have turned out to be clean. It would be a sign of God's goodness, after so many sinister omens, the pink poppies and the bad dreams, if all bitterness, suspicion and vendetta could be nipped in the bud. He stopped behind an oleander bush and surreptitiously took the precaution of spitting three times in order to avoid ill luck. In one hand he bore a great lighted candle, and in the other he swung his censer, whose fumes of frankincense spread calmness and serenity through the still air, and whose bells jingled like those that Abdulhamid Hodja tied to the neck of his horse. Kristoforos was always afraid that the charcoal in the censer would fail to light, or go out, and the tension that he felt at this moment was at least partly due to this mundane struggle with that most unreliable of the elements. He passed Rustem Bey striding down the hill, and was relieved when the latter announced curtly in passing: 'She was innocent, praise God.'

At the gate he asked one of the women: 'Are we ready yet?' and upon being answered in the affirmative, he walked with slow dignity towards the grave, casting clouds of incense all about him. The small candles were handed round, and the first one lit from the taper that the priest bore in his right hand. Soon, just as the afternoon light was beginning to fade and the Evening Star emerging, the graveyard was glistering with tiny lights.

'Everlasting be your memory, O our sister,' recited Father Kristoforos. 'Our sister who is worthy of blessedness and eternal memory. Through the orisons of the Fathers, Lord Jesus Christ Our God, have mercy and save us. Amen. Holy God, Holy Mighty, Holy Immortal, have mercy upon us.'

He received the flagon of red wine that Lydia passed him, and solemnly poured it over the skull and the heap of bones, making the sign of the cross with it three times. The wine, washing motes of soil from the bones, spread out into the white cloth like a bloodstain, and Kristoforos continued, 'You shall sprinkle me with hyssop, and I shall be clean. You shall wash me, and I will be whiter than snow. The earth is the Lord's, and the fullness thereof, the world and all that dwell therein. You are dust, and to dust you shall return.'

As the people washed their hands and left the cemetery, their ears ringing with the priest's sonorous liturgical Greek, Lydia the Barren tied the bones up into a neat bundle. She gathered it into her arms and went alone, the bones clattering and scraping together as she walked, down through the winding alleyways to the lower church, the one where the owl lived on the beams, and behind which was the ossuary. It was a simple stone structure partially excavated into the hillside. The doorway was open to the air, and at one side were steep steps leading down to a large subterranean room, where, against the back wall, were stacked the accumulated bones of the Christian dead. They rested upon each other in their cloth bundles, but at the lower layers, where the fabric had rotted away, the old bones had tumbled and mingled promiscuously together so that nobody knew any longer whose bones were whose. It smelled of damp and cold, like a cave, and candle-light flickered sorrowfully upon the darkening and softening remnants of those whose lives had passed beyond. Lydia laid down her burden in its place, adjusted Mariora's cleaned and unjointed skeleton where it lay between that of a child and that of an old man, sighed, crossed herself and left.

By the time that she returned to the churchyard of St Nicholas, most people had already received their dole of food. Small cups of red wine had been tossed down throats that only a brief time before had been constricted with emotion, and Mariora's relatives had handed round the koliva, rich with cinnamon and raisins, and the pastries and sweets. Each person licked honey from a spoon in order to sweeten away the recent bitterness of death, thinking of Mariora, and saying, 'May God forgive her.' The poorer women hovered, attempting to appear busy, waiting to take away the surplus to their families, because even the living, when they are hungry, do not despise the sweetmeats of the dead.

The close relatives and friends soon departed in a pack to the house of Polyxeni and her husband Charitos, there to be filled with coffee, raki and sweet delicacies served up on trays by Philothei and the other little children, wide-eyed with worry about whether or not they were doing it all properly. Quietly the guests conversed about the cleanness of the bones, about how well it had all gone, and about the dramatic intervention of Rustem Bey, and then they left, bidding farewell to the family, and saying, 'You have received her well, yes, very well indeed. May you live long. Patience and courage, patience and courage.'

It was agreed on going home that the exhumation had been

a good one, that the food and wine had been generous and of great quality, that the amount of money collected had been wondrous, not least because of the munificence of that infidel, Rustem Bey, and wasn't it probably wrong to accept his charity on a Christian occasion, and wasn't it an unwonted thing for an infidel to step out boldly on to Christian ground. One woman said that the corpse's shoes and graveclothes had not rotted properly, and that must mean something, and it might be because Mariora's father had died leaving debts, and may Mariora rest in paradise.

15

The Proof of Innocence (4):
The Message to Mariora

The following evening Lydia the Barren returned to the ossuary and lit a candle for Mariora. She then trudged up the hill to the graveyard, pulled a shovel out of the undergrowth where she had hidden it in a neglected corner, and began to refill the grave. Into the hole she shovelled the flesh-eating earth, along with the stubs of candles and the forlorn remains of the exhumation's flowers. 'Ah, Mariora,' she sighed, 'I wish you sunshine and good roads.' She stood and let the declining sun press its warmth into her face, promising herself that she would remember this moment because who knows when the sun will rise again.

At the same time Polyxeni, accompanied by Ayse, who had come along for moral support, was knocking on the door of Daskalos Leonidas, bearing in one hand the wicker cage in which the dove captured by the two boys was still turning in idiotic circles. They had also taken the precaution of bringing Philothei, whose prettiness, they felt sure, would be enough to make malleable the heart even of someone as stony as Daskalos Leonidas. Not far away the child Ibrahim pretended to be occupied, as always keeping his protective and proprietorial eye on Philothei. Whilst they waited for the teacher to come, the women poked their fingers into the bars of the hanging cage that held his pet goldfinch, and made sibilant twittering noises at it.

When Leonidas answered the door he suspected immediately that he was in for another ludicrous episode in which he would have to indulge the wayward ideas of these recalcitrant people. No one, it seemed, ever wanted anything sensible from him. His heart sank when he saw the two women. He hated having to speak Turkish, but in this town nobody spoke anything else, albeit larded with odd offcuts of Persian, Arabic and Greek. He dwelt in a state of perpetual longing for Smyrna, which his memory

81

and his habit of dissatisfaction had embroidered into a fantasy of great civilisation, as if it too were not teeming with every kind of Levantine and Turk. He looked down at Philothei, who was standing on one leg with her arms folded over the top of her head in one of those pointless experiments so beloved of children, and his heart did indeed soften. 'What bright eyes,' he thought to himself.

'Peace be upon you,' said the two women together, and Leonidas, as always, adjusted the spectacles on his nose and demanded, 'What do you want? I am rather busy.'

'A favour,' begged Polyxeni, 'just a favour. We have brought you something.' Ayse nudged Philothei, who held out a packet containing some of the honeyed pastries left over from the previous night, and thrust them into the teacher's hand. Leonidas almost smiled. He had recently read of the latest educational theory from Europe, which was that girls should receive some elementary education because it was mothers who were the first big influence on sons, from which it followed that pupils would be more advanced in their learning if mothers were able to begin the process before they even got to school. Leonidas was forward-thinking in these matters, and it occurred to him how charming it would be if he could teach classes of girls, as long as they were all as irresistible as Philothei. It would give him a chance, too, to teach these future mothers to speak clean Greek, and maybe that would put purer tongues in the mouths of the sons.

'As I say, I am very busy.' His voice had a crackling quality, as if his throat were full of dry leaves. 'What is it, exactly? I hope it won't take too long.' Without thinking, he reached out and patted Philothei on the crown of her head. She crossed her eyes and skipped to the other leg.

Falteringly, and with many interjections from Ayse, Polyxeni explained her mission, and even Leonidas was astonished, for this was possibly his most bizarre request yet. 'Are you serious?' he asked. 'This isn't some kind of joke? I've never heard anything like it.'

Polyxeni tried to keep her patience, astounded at what this educated man apparently did not know. 'Please, please,' she begged, 'it's not a great thing.'

'You want me to write on this dove?'

'It's only a little thing.'

Ayse and Polyxeni had been hoping to see the legendary chaos of Leonidas's house, but he disappointed them by telling them to wait at the door. He re-emerged with a pen and a jar of ink, saying, 'We can do it over here, on this wall.'

'I don't want you to write it in ink,' said Polyxeni firmly. 'I want you to do it with this.' She handed over a small, stoppered glass bottle, whose mouth and neck were moulded curiously concave on one side.

'This is water,' said Leonidas. 'I can't write messages in water.'

'Just dip your pen and write,' Polyxeni told him. She was becoming quite peeved about his obstructive attitude and vexatious manner, and her eyes were beginning to flash. 'It isn't water, it's tears.'

'Tears?'

'Yes, tears. When she was buried I went every day to the graveside and wept, and these are the tears.'

Leonidas held the diminutive bottle to the light and could not help but feel a sense of wonder. 'Holy God,' he exclaimed, 'I had no idea that people still did these kinds of things.'

'Lots of people do it,' Polyxeni informed him, 'but not many get as much tears as I did.'

'Not many are such good daughters, though they should be, if you ask me, though I'm no one to have an opinion,' added Ayse.

Shaking his head and sighing through his nose, Leonidas let himself be guided by the two women, who had removed the unfortunate dove from her cage, and had effectively immobilised her. Ayse held the bird's legs between two fingers, and Polyxeni wrapped her hands around the animal's body in order to still the wings. The dove craned her neck and peered around desperately, whilst Philothei proferred the bottle in two hands and Leonidas dipped the nib and prepared to write. Polyxeni told him: 'Say, "Beloved Mother, you can rest in peace now because everyone has seen that you are innocent. Your daughter, Polyxeni, who sends you this message and forgets you never."'

Leonidas winced, for the message was expressed in an

outrageous mixture of dog Turkish and pig Greek. It occurred to him that he could write anything at all, or indeed nothing, and the women would not be any the wiser, but he conquered his instinctive superciliousness, and, dipping the pen several times into the bottle of tears, faithfully transcribed the words on to the back of the bird, albeit somewhat schematically, given the impossibility of writing properly on feathers, and the difficulty of seeing what he had written already. 'Can your mother read?' he asked.

'No,' said Polyxeni.

'Then how shall she read this?' Leonidas twisted his mouth and raised his eyebrows condescendingly.

The two women exchanged glances, and then Polyxeni looked at him pityingly. Patiently she explained: 'In the gardens on the other side of the river there are those who can read, and one of them will read the message to her.'

'The writing will be invisible.'

'The dead can read tears.'

'I see,' said the teacher, lowering his eyebrows again, and feeling a little embarrassed. He wondered why Ayse had not thought of asking her husband to write the message, since she was married to the hodja, but he was afraid of hearing a long and complicated explanation, so he restrained his curiosity. It would not have occurred to him that she was like all women, who like to keep a side of life secret from their spouses.

After the two had departed with their captive dove, Leonidas went back inside his house and opened the packet of food. He found a small but very sticky and seductive treasure trove of lokma, tulumba tatlısı and vezir parmagi. His mouth watered, and he settled into his chair. 'It's incredible,' he thought to himself as he crammed the sweet cakes and fritters into his mouth, 'these are the heirs of Alexander, and Constantine, and Socrates! And they're no better than children!'

Ayse, Polyxeni and Philothei went back to the churchyard, and Ayse waited by the gate as the other two went over to the grave that Lydia had just filled in. Polyxeni told Philothei to open the door of the cage, and before the bird could escape she reached a hand in and carefully brought it out. 'Now look,' she said, admonishing it very seriously, eye to eye, 'don't just go straight back to the pines to see your husband and your friends. Go and find my mother, and make sure that someone reads what's written, and then you can do what you like. And I'll know if you've done it, because one day my mother will tell me in a dream, and if you haven't done it, there'll be trouble, and all your little chicks will turn out to be crows, and when you die the earth won't receive you. Fly well, pretty bird.'

She kissed the bird on the middle of its back, between the wings, and invited Philothei to do the same. The little girl was surprised, because feathers are hard and springy even though they look so soft. Polyxeni dropped her hands a little, and then flung the bird into the air. It wheeled skyward, flying higher and higher, and Ayse and Polyxeni waved it Godspeed, calling, 'Fly well! Fly well!' Polyxeni jumped up and down, and was jubilant: 'She flew east! She flew east! Did you see? She flew east!' A couple of downy breast feathers floated down, and she caught them and told Philothei to look after them, for the sake of the memory.

With Philothei hanging and swinging between them like a basket, the two friends began to walk back down the hill, chattering and sharing each other's happiness at how well it had all worked out. As they passed the house of Daskalos Leonidas, Ayse rolled her eyes and whispered, 'It's incredible! A man with that much education, and he didn't even know about how to get a message to the dead.'

16

Mustafa Kemal, Infantry Lieutenant 1474 (4)

Far away from Eskibahçe, three hundred miles across the mountains, over Denizli, over Uşak, over Bursa, across the Marmara Sea, Mustafa Kemal enrols in the War College in Harbiye, Istanbul. It is 1899 and the proud young Macedonian who, as a boy, had refused to bend down during games of leapfrog, saying, 'If you want to overleap me, you can do it with me standing up,' is now a little nobody from the provinces, as perplexed by the rowdy modernist harlotry of the Christian sector of the city, as he is by the medieval torpor and decay of the Muslim parts.

Life is hard at the college. It is accepted that sergeants can strike the cadets, as long as they address them as 'efendi', and the food is even worse than that of a British public school. No newspapers or books are allowed, Islamic piety is strictly enforced, no alcohol is allowed, and there is fasting at Ramadan. But the Christian part of the city is full of newspapers, bars and brothels. There is the Petits-Champs café, where one can get whisky, there is Yonyo's, and Stefan's and Yani's, all run and frequented by Armenians, Greeks, the improbable riff-raff of the Levant. He makes a friend of Ali Fuat, a cadet of good family, and together they go on boat trips, practise oratory, and bivouac in the woods of the islands. Ali introduces his friend to raki, and Mustafa takes one sip and says, 'What a wonderful drink this is. It makes one want to be a poet.' Raki will shape Kemal's destiny. It will help him to sleep, overcome his shyness, free his inspiration, complicate his relationships and finally kill him. Mustafa Kemal continues to read the works of the great French thinkers, and starts to develop the idea that something must be done to save his country both from the foreigners and from itself. He gets into the habit of thinking so passionately at night that he begins to be persecuted by insomnia. He becomes simultaneously an admirer of

Napoleon Bonaparte and John Stuart Mill, taking from the latter the idea that all moral and political action should tend towards the greatest happiness of the greatest number. He graduates as a lieutenant, passes on to the Staff College, and, shamelessly employing the facilities of the Department of Veterinary Science, starts a subversive newspaper whose programme is to expose corruption and abuse of power. His superior officer is detailed to apprehend him, but deliberately turns a blind eye. The Sultan has become a strangely half-baked tyrant, of such self-doubting paranoia and vacillating incompetence, such a self-defeating mixture of conciliatoriness and absolutism, that not even his own officers feel much allegiance to him any more.

He is commissioned as a captain, and he and some friends rent accommodation in an Armenian's house at Beyazit. They talk revolution, as young men do, and they accumulate forbidden European books, until one day a friend of theirs who has become one of the Sultan's vast network of spies betrays them to the police, lures them to a café, and they are arrested.

Mustafa and his friends are ill-treated, but Ali Fuat tells his interrogators with dignity and aplomb, but with a certain lack of realism, that, since he wears the Sultan's uniform, no one below the rank of Sultan is entitled to strike him. Mustafa Kemal's mother is convinced that he is going to be executed, but Mustafa contentedly spends his time in prison writing poetry and reading.

There is an inquiry, and the authorities are persuaded that Mustafa and Ali Fuat are silly boys who will grow out of their silliness and become good officers with the due passage of time. It is decreed that one should be sent to Adrianopolis and the other to Salonika, and it is left to them to agree which one will go where. They agree so quickly that the authorities find it suspicious, and send them both to Damascus. Ali Fuat and Mustafa Kemal spend their last day in Istanbul drinking whisky, and then an Austrian liner takes them to Beirut. The journey takes all of eighty days, causing one to wonder whether this Austrian liner is being propelled not by engines but by a small school of captive sardines.

17

Of Reading and Writing

Karatavuk, second son of Iskander the Potter, and Mehmetçik, son of Charitos and brother of Philothei, sat side by side on a rock above the town. They had been sent out to gather tezek, but had spent most of the time spying on the Dog, and throwing stones at a broken bottle that they had set up in the fork of a small almond tree. Now that the bottle was completely demolished, and its green fragments lay glistening and dangerous beneath the tree, the two boys took advantage of their opportunity to waste yet more time.

The boys tipped a little water from their leather bottles into their birdwhistles, and for a few minutes vied with each other to produce the longest and most elaborate cascades of birdsong. Down in the town the people paused for a few seconds to listen, and the finches and linnets in their cages hopped on their perches and cocked their heads in agitation.

Tiring of this music, Mehmetçik carefully stuffed his clay robin into his sash, and began to write in the dust at his feet with a stick.

'What have you written?' asked Karatavuk, intrigued.

'My names,' replied his friend. 'It says "Nicos", and "Mehmetçik".'

'Which one is which, then?'

'The longer one is "Mehmetçik", 'cause it's longer, stupid.'

'Stupid yourself. Why does that one say "Nicos" and that one "Mehmetçik"?'

Mehmetçik frowned. How does one explain something as simple as this? 'It just does,' he replied at last. 'These letters make "Nicos" and these ones make "Mehmetçik".'

'I wish I could read and write,' said Karatavuk.

'What do you learn at school, then? What does Abdulhamid Hodja teach you?'

'We learn about the Prophet and his three hundred authenticated miracles, and about Abraham and Isaac and Jonah and Omar and Ali and Hind and Fatima and the saints, and sometimes the big battles of Saladin against the barbarians. And we recite the Holy Koran because we have to learn al-Fatihah by heart.'

'What's that?'

'It's the beginning.'

'What's it like?'

Karatavuk closed his eyes and recited: 'Bismillah al-rahman al-rahim . . .' When he had finished he opened his eyes, and mopped his forehead. 'It's difficult,' he observed.

'I didn't understand any of it,' complained Mehmetçik. 'It sounds nice, though. Was it language?'

'Of course it was language, stupid. It's Arabic.'

'What's that, then?'

'It's what Arabs speak. And it's what God speaks, and that's why we have to learn to recite it. It's something about being merciful and the Day of Judgement and showing us the right path, and if anything is going wrong, or you're worried, or someone's sick, you just have to say al-Fatihah and everything will probably be all right.'

'I didn't know that God spoke language,' observed Mehmetçik. 'Father Kristoforos speaks to Him in Greek, but we don't understand that either.'

'What do you learn, then?'

'We learn more than you,' answered Mehmetçik self-importantly. 'We learn about Jesus Son of Mary and his miracles and St Nicholas and St Dmitri and St Menas and the saints and Abraham and Isaac and Jonah and Emperor Constantine and Alexander the Great and the Marble Emperor, and the great battles against the barbarians, and the War of Independence, and we learn reading and writing and adding up and taking away and multiplication and division.'

'Don't you learn al-Fatihah, then?'

'When things go wrong we say "Kyrie eleison", and we've got a proper prayer as well.'

'What's that like?'

Mehmetçik screwed up his eyes in unconscious imitation of

his friend, and recited: 'Pater imon, o en tois ouranis, agiasthito to onoma sou, eltheto i vasileia sou . . .'

When Mehmetçik had finished, Karatavuk asked, 'What's that about, then? Is that some kind of language?'

'It's Greek. It's what we speak to God. I don't know exactly what it means, it's something about our father who's in heaven and forgive us our daily bread, and lead us not into temptation, but it doesn't matter if we don't understand it, because God does.'

'Maybe,' pondered Karatavuk, 'Greek and Arabic are actually the same language, and that's how God understands us, like sometimes I'm Abdul and sometimes I'm Karatavuk, and sometimes you're Nico and sometimes you're Mehmetçik, but it's two names and there's only one me and there's only one you, so it might be all one language that's called Greek sometimes and Arabic sometimes.'

'I don't know,' responded Mehmetçik doubtfully. 'I suppose we'd have to ask.'

'Show me my name,' asked Karatavuk suddenly. 'Write my name in the dust.'

'Do you want "Karatavuk" or "Abdul"?'

'Put "Karatavuk".'

Mehmetçik scuffed out his own names with his foot, took the stick, and scratched the new name in the dust. Karatavuk gazed at it and felt an excitement, a curious sensation of existing more securely than he had before. He took the stick from Mehmetçik and carefully copied the letters. 'Look,' he said proudly, 'I've written my name.'

Mehmetçik inspected his work and said sceptically, 'It's not very good.'

Karatavuk was excited. 'Teach me reading and writing. Teach me those other things, that adding-up and taking-away stuff. When you come out of school you can teach me what you just learned.'

'But your school's nicer than ours,' protested Mehmetçik. 'You sit under a tree in the meydan with Abdulhamid Hodja, who is kind and makes you laugh, and we have to sit inside in the dark and scratch on our slates with Daskalos Leonidas, who hits us on the head and calls us bad names.'

'I want reading and writing,' said Karatavuk firmly. 'You Christians are always richer than us, and my father says it's all because of reading and writing and adding up and taking away, and that's why you're so good at deceiving us, and he says that we Muslims only learn what we need to get us into paradise, which is all that matters in the end, but you Christians get all the advantages on earth because you learn about all the other things as well. I want those other things too.'

Mehmetçik frowned. 'If I teach you reading and writing, I'm warning you I've got to hit you on the head and call you bad names when you're stupid, because that's how you do teaching.'

'If you hit me too hard, I'll have to hit you back, though, and you've got to promise not to tell anyone. Promise?'

'All right,' agreed Mehmetçik. He got up and searched for a short time in the maquis, returning with another stick, which he handed to his friend. 'You've got to learn the alphabet first, and then you've got to learn some new words every day, and when you've learned new words we'll do adding up to begin with because it's the easiest.'

Karatavuk watched eagerly as Mehmetçik leaned down and scratched the letter alpha into the soil. Mehmetçik straightened up, hit him lightly on the back of the head and told him to copy it. Then he hit him again and told him how to pronounce it.

18

I am Philothei (3)

I've been dying to tell you, but don't tell anyone else or I'll die. Today Ibrahim found me when I was out gathering hórta, and he just stood there looking at me, just a few paces away, and I didn't know what to say, and we just looked at each other, and then he went away, and before he went he made a little gesture of his hand, like this.

19

The Telltale Shoes

It was the shoes that did it, those accursed shoes, but it was not always the same pair of shoes. Standing there outside the door of the haremlık with his hand on the latch, the aga, Rustem Bey, would look down and behold the footwear that would, yet again, announce that his wife had a visitor so that therefore he could not enter.

Sometimes there would be dusty sandals whose leather was worn, contorted and limp. If it had been raining they would be darkened and stiffening. As time went by Rustem Bey was able to take stock of the new stitches and patches, and sometimes the new leather straps. They were neither big nor small, they were sandals that bespoke an unremarkable life, humdrum and modest, and yet Rustem Bey had come to regard them with a sharp loathing. The sight of them caused the blood to beat behind his eyes and his lips to tighten grimly.

Sometimes there would be a pretty pair of embroidered slippers that, he was absolutely sure, really belonged to his wife. He seemed to remember bringing them back from Smyrna as a gift in the early months of their marriage, and she had accepted them with a gracious lack of enthusiasm that had brought childish tears of disappointment to his eyes, which he had, with dignity and a show of indifference, held back. He had so much hoped that she would be seduced by their soft red fabric and their stitching of yellow silk and gold thread, but now she used them merely in order to pretend that she had a visitor. Once he had entertained hopes that their marriage might become more than the usual formal dance of strangers that only grows into anything better with the slow passage of time and the mutual concern for children. He knew families in Smyrna where there was a comely intimacy between man and wife, and that was what he had wanted when he married. He was a modern man, or, if he was not, that was certainly what he wanted to be. How irritating and uncomfortable it was, to feel too sophisticated at home in Eskibahçe, and yet to feel quite out of his depth in Smyrna or Constantinople; it meant that he had never found friends with whom he felt at ease. In the one case he was dealing with his peasants and tenants, and in the other he was inevitably suspicious that he was being subtly mocked. Every rural landlord that he knew suffered from the same insidious loneliness, and he had quite naively hoped that marriage with the daughter of one of them would help to fill out a life that nursed an emptiness at its core.

For Tamara, he had expanded the women's quarters from something bare and functional, but pleasant enough, into a haven of warm red drapery, cooling draughts that could be controlled by the judicious opening and closing of shutters, and smooth furniture shaped out of walnut and inlaid with satinwood. He had even bought her a bed that had arrived in pieces on the backs of two refractory camels, and he had bought chairs. Tamara had tried sleeping in the bed for a while, but finally she had lost patience with it, and reverted to the customary pallet on the floor. The beautiful bed was duly dismantled and stored in a hut that otherwise contained brooms and buckets. In the absence of a high table, the chairs too seemed curiously anomalous and redundant, and eventually they were stacked in a corner so that Tamara and her visitors could use the divans like normal people. In truth, Tamara was interested only in using the things that she had brought with her as her half of the marriage agreement, as if she could only feel at home by surrounding herself with familiar objects from her parental home near Telmessos.

Above all she prized her cezve, the tapered brass pot with the long handle, in which her mother had made coffee. Tamara's mother had been the best coffee-maker in the family, and upon her death it seemed only right that the cezve should pass to Tamara, who was the second best. When Tamara was newly wed, she would sleep with the cezve at her side, and sometimes in the night when her eyes opened and she felt the terror of the bride, she would reach out, take it and clutch it to her throat beneath the covers, as if by means of this cold metal she could feel once

94

again the dry but loving hand that had held the pot so often, and see the grey eyes that had watched so assiduously for the froth to rise. Tamara made coffee in the same way as her mother, on a little heap of white ash in the middle of the glowing charcoal, so that it brewed as slowly as possible, and sometimes she felt as if she were possessed by her mother's spirit, cut off as she was, so far from Telmessos and those she loved.

Rustem Bey, outside the women's quarters, looking down at those shoes, with his hand on the latch, knew very well who it was that Tamara loved. He knew that ever since her childhood she had adored her cousin, Selim. The family had been quite open about it, so that he would not be deceived, but they had assured him that Tamara would grow out of it, that they had persuaded her as to the unsuitability of the match, that she was dutiful and obedient and would marry the husband chosen for her in accordance with the wisdom of her elders.

Under ordinary circumstances the family would have been happy to marry Tamara to the cousin of her choice, but Selim was a human powder keg, so unreliable and ungovernable that for shame his own parents would not have consented to his marriage to anyone they respected. Tamara believed that if her mother had been alive, she might have swayed things in Selim's favour, but in that she was almost certainly mistaken. Selim was charming and handsome, but he was, even from infancy, unmistakably marked out for a bad end.

He had always been small, a little graceless in his movements, but quick and nervy. He had a dazzling smile that conveyed to a startling degree the dangerousness of his disposition, and those who saw it for the first time were always taken aback. One felt like the traveller who is approached by a dog that is wagging its tail, but which is clearly tensed for attack. When he was small, his own mother sometimes neglected to cut his hair because she was afraid that he might snatch the scissors from her, and indeed there had been occasions when his unprompted rages grew into such violent paroxysms that even his own father had felt a well-founded fear as he picked the flailing child up around the waist and carried him outdoors to be dumped unceremoniously into the cattle trough. His father would, hating himself for the brutality and necessity of it, hold him under the slimy water by the neck until imminent choking restored Selim to sanity.

The imam in Telmessos recommended attendance at the mektep in order to learn to recite some verses of the Koran, because the word of God can have a remarkably civilising effect, but Selim, who learned the mellifluous but incomprehensible Arabic with surprising facility, remained incorrigible. The Greek doctors in the city told Selim's father forthrightly that there was nothing one could do about a savage child if beating and confinement had failed. 'He will probably grow out of it,' they said, 'children often do.'

So, in fact, it almost turned out, except that Selim transformed himself slowly from a chaotic and nerve-wracking child into a young adult of fatal charm and absolute lack of principle. She had always worshipped the wayward little boy, but now it was for his youthful charm that Tamara fell, and Selim had certainly been astute enough to notice her infatuation. He had only to catch her gazing at him adoringly at the Bayram feast, and within a day he was whispering to her through the shutters at night. A sound beating from Tamara's father with the flat of a sword was Selim's last memory of Telmessos, but as he trudged away into near exile, disowned by his own family, his thoughts were concerned not with the dishonour and humiliation of having been caught out in evildoing, but instead with mulling over the sharp lesson he had just learned, namely that one should be sure of whispering through the correct window during an attempted seduction.

Tamara was devastated by Selim's dismissal, and he too felt a certain stabbing pain in the heart when he contemplated his memories of her lovely face. Her family decided to arrest her obsession and her sadness in mid-flow by finding her a suitable husband whose steadiness was beyond question. Having nothing but her happiness and prosperity in mind, they were delighted when Rustem Bey confessed his considerable interest. Rustem was the great-grandson of a tax farmer, and the wealth and land accrued by that individual had miraculously passed down intact to his descendants. The great-grandfather, like all tax farmers, had been an unsavoury, corrupt and harsh individual, but by Rustem's time the old system had been long abolished, and Rustem Bey himself was nothing if not an upright and respectable man who cared better for his tenants and his estates than was commonly expected.

Tamara knew that Rustem Bey was a better prospect than anyone had a right to hope for, and she married him out of fatalism and common sense. After their wedding night, however, Rustem Bey knew with angry resignation that much as he might invade her body, he would never touch her heart. Thus it was that he reaped nothing but heartache from his assault on happiness, and he was lonelier than he had been before, living with this lovely girl whose shoes, or those of another, were always outside the haremlık door.

Her cousin Selim was not greatly discouraged by his disgrace, and in a short while he had set himself up as a travelling mountebank, deriving a kind of exhilarated malicious pleasure from pissing into small bottles and adding sugar and a few sprigs of wild mint. These bottles he flourished in market places from Yediburun to Yaniklar; 'Selim's elixir, Selim's elixir, the water of life itself! Guaranteed against the colic and the gleet! Efficacious against the barren womb and the bad-air fever! No, I'm not saying that it restores youth, but for all I know it probably does that too! Compounded by the renowned apothecary, Gevork the Armenian of Ararat, tested and approved by Athanasios the Greek of Athens, by appointment to the Sultan Padishah himself! You, efendi, yes, you! I can see you're a little pale! Yes, you are! Isn't he, my friends? Try some, it'll do you good! Who's got a wife who's always moaning on her pallet at hoeing time? You, efendi? Give her some of this and she'll be bounding out there doing two fields a day!'

It was a hard life, trudging through the stones from one town to another all year long, in all kinds of weather, dizzy with heat in the summer and knee-deep in clinging mud in the times of rain. He learned to accept the attentions of brigands, losing his earnings over and over again to ruffians who sometimes even took all his clothes, and so it was with pleasure and relief that he had found a place in life at Eskibahçe, where he had had the good fortune to be recognised by his fair cousin, Tamara, one

97

day as he was hawking his elixir in the meydan, in the shade of the plane tree where the old men sat.

Rustem Bey, with his hand on the latch, unable to enter, knew only that someone as heavily veiled as a shia woman from Persia arrived almost every day, knocked softly, and was admitted to the haremlık by his wife, leaving those crumpled sandals outside. When it was just the embroidered slippers from Smyrna, Rustem Bey knew with bitter certainty that his wife had no visitors at all, but was merely employing a shallow ruse to keep the private quarters to herself. What he did know was that there was something not quite right about the hunched figure with bowed shoulders and head who slipped out of the haremlık and hastened away. The voice that piped a muffled 'Aleikum salaam' when greeted did not seem quite right, and neither did the bony, angular feet that slipped on the dusty sandals and pattered away down the hill past the houses where the few Armenians lived.

Rustem Bey was reduced to the shameful and shaming expedient of spying. He repeatedly tried to follow the figure through the streets, in order to find out where it lived, but was always defeated, partly because of the chaos of dogs, traders, camels and gossiping friends, but mainly because, being one of the most important men in the whole region, he was automatically waylaid by those who wished to pay their respects, or beg for alms, or a favour. He would look down on his interlocutor who had taken hold of his sleeve, and a sweat of anxiety would break out on his forehead as he tried desperately to see where the swathed figure had gone. It occurred to him that he might have the person followed by a servant, but he restrained himself. The last thing that any self-respecting man needs is to be demeaned in the eyes of his servants by involving them in skullduggery.

One evening Rustem Bey entered the haremlık after the visitor had departed, but before Tamara could put out her slippers, and asked, 'Who is that woman who comes here? Every day she is here, and I demand to know who she is.'

With studied coolness, Tamara took a morsel of lokum from the small brass tray, chewed it a while, and then looked up innocently. 'She is a friend. No one of any importance.' A little insolently, she drew the corner of her çarşaf across her mouth.

Rustem Bey felt his anger mount. 'No woman veils herself in front of her husband! Unveil yourself! I want to know who she is.'

Tamara let the çarşaf fall away, and cast her gaze modestly to the ground. 'I don't have any friends here. In the hamam they don't talk in front of me because of who my husband is, and all my relatives are in Telmessos. I need to have a friend who visits me.'

'Listen. You women do what you want. You slip in and out of each other's back doors when a man has to stand at the front and knock. Have as many friends as you like. But who is that woman?'

'She is nobody. She is my only companion in this place.'

'You have a husband. If you were less indifferent, you would have children, and the company of other women who have children.'

Tamara flushed. 'I try to do my duty.'

Rustem Bey raised his right hand in a small gesture of exasperation. 'There is no pleasure in your duty. I might as well go to a whore and couple with my eyes closed. You should know that there is more to a marriage than ignoring your husband while you idle at his expense.'

'You shouldn't talk to your wife so coarsely. It disturbs me.'

'I am disturbed,' declared Rustem Bey vehemently. 'I am disturbed that my wife has an unknown visitor almost every day. Any other husband with a wife like you would give her a beating, I swear it.'

'Beat me then,' said Tamara levelly, 'but you have no reason to be disturbed, my husband. She is an old woman called Fatima who has befriended me.'

'In this place all the women are called Fatima. Which "Fatima" is it? Who are her family? Where do they live?'

'She lives at the edge of the town. Beyond the Armenians. I have never been there. She is ashamed of her poverty, because she is a widow and all her sons have been called away on military service for ten long years. They call her "Fatima Lackluck". She comes here, and for charity I let her eat and drink a little, and ease her poor heart in talking.' Tamara gestured towards a piece of blue fabric that lay carelessly across the divan, and added, 'She has been teaching me to embroider, and I pay her a little slipper money, just a few paras. So, you see, I am not so idle.'

Rustem Bey looked into the dark eyes of his wife, but found no clue as to her veracity. He turned on his heel and left. Outside the door he paused, thought a while, lit up a fat cigarette, and then strode down the hill, past the houses and workshops of the Armenians, and began to ask around for a widow called Fatima Lackluck whose sons were all away upon military service.

The next evening, Rustem fetched a low stool and waited outside the haremlık, smoking so many cigarettes, one after the other, that a small heap of butts grew at his feet. His mouth felt as dry as summer's clay, and his heart beat so unevenly that from time to time he had to catch his breath. All day a suspicion had burned like acid into his thoughts, and a terrible agitation had taken possession of his mind, so that he knew he would not know equanimity again unless he broke a rule that in the normal course of life he held as sacred and inviolable. He knew that he might be about to disgrace himself in the eyes of his wife and the whole town, and he knew that, despite his rank, it was possible that outraged family members might arrive to take vengeance upon him, yet he knew exactly what had to be done.

Accordingly, when the bowed and veiled figure emerged from the door and closed it, Rustem Bey rose quickly to his feet, and stood in the way. 'Fatima Hanımefendi, I must speak to you.'

Fatima mumbled something indistinct, and turned away, as if in modesty, but Rustem reached out, and took hold of the corner of her veil. The woman reacted with a curious movement of her arms beneath her garment, as if she were fumbling desperately for something but failing to find it, and then, just in time, Rustem saw the flash of a blade and leapt back. From his sash he took out one of his pistols, and pointed it at his attacker. Without thought he pulled the trigger, only to recall with a mixture of impatience, panic and embarrassment that he had not carried a loaded pistol in his sash ever since an uncle of his had caused fatal damage to himself by so doing. The stranger crouched, balancing on his heels, and brandished the shining curved steel of the yataghan in his face. Rustem struck out with the pistol.

He caught his victim across the side of the temple and took advantage of the moment to draw out his own dagger, the same good weapon with which his doughty ancestors had cut off the ears and lips of rebel Serbs and Bulgarians.

Rustem thrust hard, slicing himself across the forearm on the other's weapon as he did so, and he watched dispassionately as the stranger sank slowly to the ground. He slashed downward with his yataghan, leaving a horrible gash upon the hand, and forcing it to relinquish hold of its weapon. Rustem picked the blade up, placed it carefully in his own sash, and then leaned down and tore the scarf and veil away.

He beheld a tousled head of black hair, bowed down in pain. He grasped the mop of hair and forced the head back. That handsome, fine face had malicious black eyes, a week's stubble, and a superb and glossy black moustache. Rustem saw the lips move. 'Orospu çocuğu.'

Rustem laughed bitterly. 'I am a son of a whore? Think again.' He lashed out with his left foot and sent the young man toppling sideways. The fine lips moved again, even though the eyes were dull with the nausea of approaching death: 'Cehenneme git. Kerata.'

'A cuckold I may be,' declared Rustem, 'but it will surely be you who goes to hell. You and my whore of a wife.' Rustem felt as if it were not he but someone else using his body, who was saying and doing all these things. He was both surprised and alarmed by his own efficiency in dealing with a matter so untoward and vile. He pushed open the door of the haremlık, and called, 'Wife, come out and see your whore-maker die. You shouldn't miss it.'

He had expected Tamara to emerge cowed and trembling, and was startled when she hurtled out of the door, pushed him aside, and threw herself upon the body of the dying young man. 'Selim! Selim!' she wailed, 'My aslan, my lion! What has he done? Selim! Oh God, oh God! No! No! No! My God, my eyes' light!'

She stroked Selim's cheek and with her çarşaf she dabbed at the blood and saliva that frothed at his lips. She was whimpering desperately. Suddenly she stood up and confronted her husband. He saw that her lips were trembling and that tears streamed down both cheeks even though she was not sobbing. She took off her scarf, so that her long hair fell loose about her shoulders. She swept it back with one hand, and offered him her throat. 'Now kill me,' she said.

Rustem was puzzled to find a half of himself feeling sorry for her. He even admired her defiance and her bold resignation. He saw the grief and the anger in her eyes, and realised anew how lovely she was, but by now he was caught up in a current of events from which there was no possibility of extricating himself with honour. Her lover lay dying at his feet, and before him stood an unfaithful wife. He reached out his hand and grasped a hank of her hair. 'Come with me,' he said, 'and take this opportunity to beg God for forgiveness.' With a heavy, unwilling heart but with every semblance of implacable resolution, Rustem Bey did what he knew he had to do, and dragged his wife by the hair to the meydan.

A crowd gathered almost instantaneously, as Rustem knew it would, a crowd that assembled for the lowest motives of meanness and curiosity. It was an astounding thing to see a husband revealing his wife's hair to the shame and indignity of public exposure, and such public abuse of a wife could mean only one thing. In the meydan, Rustem Bey, his voice shaking with both anger at what had been done and horror at what was about to be done, announced to the crowd: 'This woman is my wife. She is a whore and an adulteress.'

He stood aside from Tamara and watched, as calmly she placed her hair back under her scarf. He bowed his head when she looked up and said simply, 'I am guilty and I do not wish to live. Kill me, like the wolves and dogs you are in this disgusting place.'

The first stone was flung half-heartedly, almost humorously, and fell at her feet. She looked down at it and smiled. The second stone was thrown more boldly, and struck her upon the thigh. The third stone flew past her head and glanced off the trunk of one of the planes. A buzz of animal noises began to stir in the crowd, and an ugliness spiralled up in it, the evil that emanates as if from nowhere when people are permitted to act basely in a righteous cause. Women whose hearts would normally be brimming with concern and tenderness picked up stones and began to shriek as they hurled them. Children whose parents beat them for throwing stones at dogs fought each other for stones to throw at a young woman. Men for whom it was beneath their dignity to strike a woman picked up stones and bayed like hounds. Faces that were habitually calm and beneficent began to contort with gleeful cruelty, and steadily a malevolent barbarism rose up and began to feed upon itself. It was satisfying, in any case, for those lowly folk to have the opportunity to destroy a spoiled and perfumed darling from a higher walk of life.

Tamara was struck upon the head by a large cobble, and fell to her knees. The crowd drew in upon her as people hustled forward to pick up once more the stones that had already been flung. Rustem Bey sat on the low wall of the well at the foot of a plane tree, with his back to the horrible scene, feeling his heart clench within him like a fist. He heard the rabble chanting 'Orospu! Orospu! Orospu!' and put his hands over his ears. In his mind's eye he saw Tamara on their wedding night, her eyes glowing with grief in the lamplight as she turned her head aside and parted her legs as she had been warned she would have to do. He remembered her flinching, her rhythmic gasps of pain, and the sadness that had come upon him afterwards, when he had found himself wishing that he had been born to another kind of life.

The crowd were directly over her now, pelting her, those without stones resorting to savage blows with their feet. Old women and small children darted in to spit. Tamara, curiously detached from all this fury and the cruelty of the pain, began to dream of Selim.

Nobody saw Abdulhamid Hodja ride up on Nilufer, and the first thing anyone knew was that people had been thrown aside and that his horse was standing over the fallen adulteress. Abdulhamid himself was roaring at the crowd with such passion and authority that it pressed back as if pushed by invisible hands.

'Who is responsible for this?' he bellowed. 'By whose authority is this? Stand back, by God, stand back.'

Rustem Bey stood up slowly and came forward. 'It is by my authority, efendi. She is my wife and I caught her lover coming out of the haremlık. I killed him, and I am responsible for this.'

Abdulhamid glowered down at him, and Rustem added, 'She is an adulteress, and has to be stoned.'

The imam ignored him and demanded of the entire assembly, 'Don't you know the law? I know it. I am not a doctor, but I know it.' He paused, and then continued, 'The law is that . . .' He stopped suddenly and examined the faces in the crowd. 'You,' he said, pointing at Charitos. 'Come forward. I have never seen you in the mosque. You are a Christian.'

The father of the lovely Philothei stepped forward, nervously adjusting his fez upon his head. The imam pointed to other Christians, one after the other. 'Do you follow the prophet, Jesus of Nazareth, peace be upon him? Well, do you?'

Charitos and the other Christians murmured that they did, and Abdulhamid commanded, 'Go and find your priest. Ask him what it was that the prophet Jesus said when he prevented the stoning of an adulteress. Leave this place! Go and ask him. Father Kristoforos will tell you what you ought to know already. Go now, and do not condemn yourselves any further.'

The Christian men and women drifted slowly away, ashamed of themselves, but muttering to each other along the lines of 'Who does that imam think he is?' and back in the meydan Abdulhamid Hodja looked down upon the crowd and asked, 'Where are the four witnesses? Come on, I ask you, where are the four witnesses who saw this woman naked and fornicating?'

No one stepped forward except Rustem Bey, who was shaking, and attempting not to look down upon the crumpled form of Tamara where she lay beneath the horse. 'Her lover came every day, veiled as a woman, until finally I unmasked him.'

'Did you see them fornicating?'

'No, but . . .'

'Rustem Bey, a man who accuses another of adultery without being a witness of the act, and without four witnesses altogether, is sentenced to scourging with eight stripes. That is the law of God in the Holy Koran. You are fortunate that this is not a court of law and that I am not a judge.'

'I am Rustem Bey. No one scourges me.'

Abdulhamid looked down upon him sympathetically and said merely, 'Rustem Efendi, I have known you for a long time.'

The aga was to puzzle over this cryptic remark for many years, but at this moment all he could think to say was 'She admitted her guilt in front of all these people.'

'She did, she did,' murmured the crowd, whose members were by now shifting from foot to foot, anxious to escape the wrath of their prayer leader, their access of viciousness having subsided altogether.

'How many times did she admit it?'

'We heard her. She admitted it,' said Ali the Snowbringer, and others muttered in confirmation of the fact.

'How many times?' Abdulhamid looked around at the silent and embarrassed townsfolk and nodded his head sagely. 'I thought so. It was only once. Sometimes, because of their sorrows, people wish to die, and they admit things rashly. If she did not admit it four times then you have acted unlawfully and there is a grievous penalty for every one of you upon the Day of Judgement.'

Abdulhamid tapped Nilufer gently upon her neck, and she moved aside, exposing Tamara once more. The imam pointed down at her: 'See what you have done in your wickedness and ignorance? If she is alive, bring her to my wife, who will take care of her. If she is dead, bring her all the same, and we will bury her.' He turned to the aga: 'Rustem Bey, you have a wound in your arm. You ought to see to it.' With this he turned the head of the horse and clattered away along the stones, his green cloak flapping out behind him and Nilufer's bells tinkling. Her brass breastplate glinted in the declining sunlight, her blue beads rattled together, and the green ribbons fluttered in her mane, a sight whose prettiness was incongruous to such a grim occasion. The muezzins began to climb the stairs of the minarets, and a few cowed people knelt in the dust to tend to the fallen Tamara.

Rustem Bey walked home feeling as if it had been he who had been stoned. 'Nothing will ever be the same,' he repeated to himself, unable to get the words out of his mind. Outside the haremlık he overturned the corpse of Selim with his toe, and saw again how handsome and wild that young face was, even in death, even with its vacant, half-closed eyes and its lips frozen in mid-breath. He called one of the servants and gave him a heavy handful of coins, saying, 'Go and give these to the gendarmes, and keep only one of them for yourself. Tell them that there is the corpse of a stranger at my house, and I wish them to come and take it away.'

Rustem Bey put his hand on the latch and looked down at the battered sandals that would never again prevent him from entering. He picked them up, noted the shiny imprint of the feet that had worn them, and then put them down. He opened the door and entered.

Inside it was dark, but the atmosphere was warm and heavy and sweet with the intimate rituals, aromas and mysteries of disconsolate femininity. He stood for a moment and breathed it in, and then sat down upon the divan where Tamara had sat, and took up her embroidery. He looked at the blue cloth stitched with yellow tulips and red vine leaves. 'Now it will never be finished,' he thought, and he pressed it to his face and inhaled. It smelled of vanilla, rosewater, coffee and musk. It smelled of Tamara, his proud, young and self-destroying wife. He looked for the first time at the sinister gash in his forearm, and saw that it was still bleeding. He realised that it was both stinging and aching. He wrapped it tightly in the cloth. The blue grew darker, and the yellow tulips briefly glowed bright with scarlet and then turned dull. He leaned forward, placed his elbows on his knees, and began to choke with sorrow as the muezzins in the minarets sang out in harmony with each other that God is great and there is no God but God.

'Nothing will ever be the same,' thought Rustem Bey. After an hour of heartsick solitude, he went outside and picked up the telltale shoes, with the intention of putting them on the brazier and destroying them; but such small revenges seemed suddenly fatuous. It was black and chilly now, and Rustem Bey took a lamp and made his way up the alleyways until he reached the edge of town and the thorny scrubland where the Lycian tombs stood out as greater darknesses in the darkness of the stones.

He found the Dog in one of the tombs, and, shivering, he gave him the shoes.

20

Mustafa Kemal (5)

Far from Eskibahçe, past Antalya, over the Mediterranean Sea, across the island of Cyprus (where no one may go without falling in love), beyond Beirut, Mustafa Kemal, trained as an infantry officer, finds himself in 1905, with characteristic military logic, posted to the 30th Cavalry Regiment.

He is depressed and appalled by Damascus; it is a place without vivacity or pleasure, a place that endures the interminable passage from birth to death behind closed doors and shutters. It is utterly moribund, marooned, medieval, stunted and paralysed by tradition, neurotic respectability and absolutist religion. The locals are Arabs, with whom he has nothing in common and no friendships to make. They are nonetheless loyal Ottoman citizens as the British have not yet seized the chance to stir up Arab nationalism. Mustafa Kemal dresses up in civilian clothes so that he can drink in a café with Italian railway workers and listen to the enchanting and enspiriting sound of mandolins. He befriends an exiled Turkish shopkeeper called Haji Mustafa who, like Mustafa Kemal, is a Francophile who has never been to France and is steeped in French philosophy. He has been expelled from the Military Medical School for subversive activities.

At the house of Haji Mustafa a secret society is formed. It is called 'Vatan', and it is just like a hundred other secret societies that will soon be springing up all over the empire, wherever there are educated young officers who wish to reshape their country. Romantic and passionate speeches are made. Mustafa Kemal drily reminds his co-conspirators that the object is not to die for the revolution, but to live for it.

Mustafa Kemal is disgusted by the behaviour of the 5th Army of which he is a part. It is there to police an accord with the ever-troublesome Druzes, who have agreed to pay taxes in return for exemption from military service. The older officers try to prevent the younger officers from going out on field duty, and Mustafa Kemal is infuriated when he is refused permission to go out with his men. They tell him that he is in training, that he is needed back at base.

He disobeys orders and sets off to find his unit, buttonholing the officer who has been sent in his place. It turns out that in fact these expeditions are for the purposes of extortion, and the villagers are being terrorised and pillaged under the pretence of tax collection. The soldiers are paid a pittance, usually in arrears, and the tribesmen themselves are little better than bandits. The former strive to collect more tax than is due, and the latter strive not to pay any tax at all.

Mustafa Kemal develops his perverse gift for obstreperous heroism. He accepts the hostility of his senior officers, and refuses to countenance the looting. He prevents an uprising in a Circassian village because he strikes the villagers as trustworthy. One village kidnaps a major, and Mustafa Kemal turns up and harangues them until they release him. He protests about the false or exaggerated reports of victories and triumphs that are being sent back to Istanbul, saying, 'I'll have no part in a fraud.' When a friend is tempted to take his share of the looting, Mustafa asks him coldly, 'Do you want to be a man of today or of tomorrow?'

Mustafa Kemal, posted now to a marksmen's battalion in Jaffa, is determined to start the revolution, and with the connivance of Ahmet Bey, the commandant at Jaffa, absconds to Salonika via Egypt and Piraeus, finally arriving on a Greek ship. He has a forged pass which was supposed to be for Smyrna, and a friend smuggles him through the customs. His mother is appalled, fearing the wrath of the Sultan, and Mustafa himself is mildly disappointed to find that the artillery general with whom he had been hoping to conspire is a conspirator of the purely theoretical variety.

It occurs to Mustafa Kemal that he might be causing himself a few small problems with the military authorities by effectively having deserted, and so he puts on his uniform and goes to the military headquarters in Salonika, where he explains his predicament to an old friend from school, who is now a colonel. They concoct an application for sick leave, pretending that Mustafa is on the general staff rather than serving in Damascus. The ruse works admirably, and in the following four months in Salonika, Mustafa organises a Macedonian branch of his secret society, which is now called 'Fatherland and Freedom'. The conspirators are preoccupied by the obvious decline of the empire, and its intransigent political corruption and inefficiency. They feel themselves humiliated and dishonoured by the way that it is being disrupted, hamstrung and gulled by the Great Powers. The men are constitutionalists, and include Mustafa's old poetic friend Ömer Naci. Mustafa Kemal is just beginning to conceive the notion of a Turkish state within secure borders, with the accretions of empire permanently removed. Amid all the cries of 'Greece for the Greeks (Jews and Turks out)' and 'Bulgaria for the Bulgarians (Jews and Turks out)' it is hardly surprising that sooner or later someone will begin to say 'Turkey for the Turks'. One day Mustafa Kemal will say, 'Happy is the man who calls himself a Turk,' and this will be carved into hillsides all over Anatolia. It will become the truth because it was Mustafa Kemal Atatürk who said it.

He and the plotters meet at the house of an officer, newly wed, who is notorious for wearing oriental pyjamas and playing the flute. They swear allegiance to the ideals of the society upon a revolver, which they kiss reverently. Mustafa says, 'This revolver is now sacred. Keep it carefully, and one day you will pass it on to me.'

The authorities twig at last that Mustafa Kemal is in the wrong place, and they send orders for him to be arrested. Mustafa hears about it just in time, and hurries back to Jaffa, where Ahmet Bey hastens him to Beersheba, where the army is facing the British in an imperial squabble about the port of Aqaba. The commandant reports to Istanbul, implying that Kemal has been in Beersheba for months, and that the Mustafa in Salonika must therefore be a different one. The papers are shuffled about in Istanbul, heads are scratched. The documents are left in drawers and under piles, misclassified, trodden on, torn at the corners, and finally forgotten. Mustafa is promoted to adjutant major and keeps his nose temporarily clean. At last, to his joy, he is posted back to Macedonia, where he is supposed to be serving with the 3rd Army, but instead finds himself inexplicably with the general staff.

21

I am Philothei (4)

Ibrahim comes creeping up and finds me every time I go out on an errand, and I say, 'What if we get caught?' and he says, 'Who cares? We're getting married one day anyway,' and I say, 'But it's not decent!' and he just shrugs, and I am really scared about getting caught, but so far it's been all right, and it's true that our fathers have come to an agreement, and my mother is already thinking about things for the dowry box and we're going to embroider some blankets. He says, 'Now that you're twelve, you're old enough to marry,' and I say, 'But you're not,' and he says nothing, but just takes my hand and looks at me hard in the eyes, and I can see that his eyes are dark and glowing, and it makes my stomach buzz, and then he very carefully places the back of my hand first against his chest, then against his forehead, then against his lips, and finally, before he turns and leaves, back against his heart.

22

Ayse Remembers Tamara

Well, I wasn't pleased. You can imagine what I thought when my eldest son called me out of the house and said, 'Look what Baba's got us into now,' and I went out, and there were Mohammed the Leech Gatherer and Ali the Snowbringer, with Ali's donkey, and on the donkey was what I thought was a pile of rags draped across it, and I looked a bit closer and it was a body. Just imagine!

Now I've got nothing against Ali the Snowbringer or Mohammed the Leech Gatherer, but they're not the kind of people whose wives I would make friends with, if you catch my meaning. My husband, Abdulhamid Hodja, may he rest in paradise, was a very learned man, and over the years that kind of thing rubs off. A woman who marries a learned man gradually learns things, too, like a clay pot that soaks up water, and a woman who has learned things simply by having open ears doesn't necessarily want to spend her time consorting with the wives of Mohammed the Leech Gatherer and Ali the Snowbringer, although it's all one to God. Just imagine! Living in the hollow trunk of a tree! With a donkey and four children! I don't know who I felt more sorry for, the wife, the children or the donkey, but they all seemed happy enough, which is more than you can say for Rustem Bey.

Where was I? Oh yes, so there is Ali and there is Mohammed nodding their heads and wishing me peace, and delivering me a whole donkeyful of trouble without my dear husband telling me anything about it. He was in the coffeehouse sharing a waterpipe and playing backgammon with Ali the Broken-Nosed, calming himself down after all that shouting and fuss in the meydan, which I only heard about later because I missed it, being at home doing something useful unlike most other people. So Mohammed says, 'Peace be upon you, Ayse Hanımefendi, we have brought you the zina işleyen kadın.' That's what he said, those were his exact words. 'We have brought you the adulteress.' Just imagine!

'Adulteress?' I said. 'What adulteress? What do I want with an adulteress? I never asked for an adulteress. And upon you be peace.'

And Ali says, 'Ayse Hanımefendi, it was Abdulhamid Hodja himself who told us to bring her here, so that if she is alive, inshallah, she can be dealt with, and if she is dead, inshallah, she can be dealt with. So that, whatever happens, inshallah, she can be dealt with.'

And Mohammed says, 'The imam efendi told us that you would deal with her,' and Ali adds, 'Inshallah'.

So I say, 'He did?' and they nod their heads, and I say, 'So what adulteress is it, because I think I have the right to know.'

And they say, 'It is Tamara Hanım, wife of Rustem Bey,' and I am thinking, 'That husband of mine is one man who is going to get too much pepper in his food for a good long time and he'll be lucky if I sneak out into the fields with him ever again,' and they say, 'Rustem Bey killed her lover as he came out of the haremlik, and the imam stopped the rabble from stoning her,' and they exchange glances, and later I find out in the hamam that both of them were in the rabble throwing stones with everyone else, including the Christians who should have been minding their own business, as if they ever did.

So I stand there puffing my cheeks out and smiling at Ali and Mohammed even as inside I am cursing fate and my husband and Rustem Bey and his sullied wife, and I say, 'Well, perhaps you should bring her in and put her in the straw with the animals,' but neither of them want to touch her, so I say, 'Don't be foolish,' even though I didn't want to touch her either, and finally we carry her in and lay her in the part below, where Nilufer was stabled at night, snorting and farting and hinnying as horses do, so how were we supposed to sleep with all that coming up through the boards at night?

So Ali goes back to his wife and his children and his hollow tree, and Mohammed goes and catches leeches for all I know, except that it was almost night-time by now, so he probably didn't, come to think of it, and there I am in Nilufer's stable with this adulteress who may or may not be dead, these things being in God's hands, because God's the boss after all.

Well, I wasn't pleased. I was thinking, 'I hope that husband of mine, peace be upon him, cuts himself in the hand so that I can pour salt and vinegar in the wound and lemon juice and give him a good stinging, and I hope that Nilufer stands on his foot and blackens a nail,' and just then I hear the clopping of hooves, and Abdulhamid comes back on Nilufer, and swings down from the saddle, and he catches my eye and looks away again quickly because he knows I'm not much pleased and in the mood for too much pepper in his pilav, and he raises a hand as if he can make me hold my peace, and I say, 'Welcome back,' with the corners of my mouth turned down, like this.

Abdulhamid says, 'Is she alive?' and I say, 'Well, I wouldn't know because I haven't looked yet, and why would any husband want his own wife to soil her hands attending to a harlot? And why would any husband want an adulteress in the house when he has three young daughters who need protecting when harlotry is contagious like lice as everybody knows and these daughters are unmarried and pure as a new chick straight from the egg?' and Abdulhamid says, 'Where did you put her?' And he says, 'Wife, you had better watch out, because unless you attend to her I will have to do it myself, and a man is more likely to be drawn into bad deeds by a harlot than a virgin daughter is,' and of course I know he is joking because he is a virtuous man as everybody knows, and I say, 'I have enough work to do, what with making bread and hoeing and weaving . . .' and he raises his hand again, and says, 'My lale . . .' – that's what he always called me, he called me his tulip, and it always worked and he knew it did too, may he rest in paradise, and when the wild tulips came up in spring and he noticed, he used to come in and say, 'Wife, all your little sisters have arrived' – and anyway I went soft inside, and he says 'My tulip, what are the five pillars of Islam?' and I know what's coming, and I say, 'Whenever you're in the wrong you try to make out that God agrees with you,' but that doesn't stop him and he says, 'Well, charity consists of more than tossing scraps to beggars and making donations,' and I say, 'Well, I didn't know that charity consists of making more work for your wife,' and he comes back with, 'God will reward you in paradise, my tulip,' and I say, 'I'll be too worn out to make the journey if it has anything to do with you,' and anyway I go into the lower room, and I start to tend to Tamara.

I'll admit it was Rustem Bey I felt sorry for to begin with. I mean, poor man, his father goes off to Mecca on the haj, and that year all the pilgrims come back with plague, and the old man has it too, and then he dies, and then his wife dies, and then the children one by one and then half the town, and we're all trembling because it's the worst haj epidemic we've ever had in this place, and don't we get one almost every year? And quite a lot of people recover, but after all that, Rustem Bey, who's the richest man in the vilayet, has no one left in that great big house but himself and a tame partridge, and he's half dead with grief and loneliness, and then he goes and marries a cold proud woman who won't even talk to anyone else in the hamam and takes a lover who's a well-known devil, which proves that God has no respect for wealth, but some people were secretly pleased because if there's one thing that's like a gnat in the ear and a flea up the nose for most people it's when they see that someone else is doing better than they are.

But anyway, when I kneel down and start to tend to Tamara the first thing I notice is that she's alive and she's got tears just streaming out of both eyes, and I've never seen anyone cry like that before or since, without even sobbing at all, just tears streaming down as if this kind of crying is something over and above, and I wipe her cheeks with my sleeve, and my heart melts, and do you know why? It's because I see so much sorrow in that young girl's face that I just can't bear it, and when Abdulhamid calls from the door 'Is she alive?' I can hardly speak in reply, because, you know me, I'm soft, and I whisper to Tamara, 'I'm going to boil some water,' and out I go and upstairs and I call my daughters and I say, 'We've got work to do, but don't forget she's a harlot and I'm not having you catching it because if you do I'll take you to Haleb and sell you to an Arab with five wives and I mean it,' and my oldest daughter, Hasseki, you know the one, she says, 'Anneciğim, what is a harlot?' as if she didn't know, and the other two start smiling behind their hands, and I'm standing there with my hands on my hips trying to be serious, and then I smile too, and that's the end of being serious, so then we just get on with the job.

Before we start I say, 'Bismillah al-rahman al-rahim,' just to make sure that everything's fine with God, and Hasseki brings down a pallet and the other two bring down lamps and the hot water and some cords and drapes that we can arrange around her to make a kind of little room so that she doesn't have to look at Nilufer and no one can look in either, especially not Abdulhamid, and we start to undress her because we know she's been stoned and kicked, and she just lies there with her tears streaming down, and when we've undressed her, my heart begins to break, because not only does she have the big cut and the bruise on the head, but she's got broken ribs and a broken collarbone so that she can hardly breathe, and every time we move her she whimpers like a dog.

I noticed before, in the hamam, how pretty she was, she was small and slight, but her breasts were round like pomegranates, and any mother in the hamam would have wished her as a wife for the pleasure of a son, and now, even though she was bruised and cut as if she'd fallen down a cliff, I could see clearly what a lovely thing she was, and it made what had been done to her seem even more horrible because of that.

We washed her down and cleaned the wounds with raki, not that we have raki in the house, but I sent Hasseki off to borrow raki from Polyxeni, wife of Charitos, because to borrow raki from a Christian is more reputable because the rest of us aren't supposed to have it, even though we do, except in our house, and we set the collarbone as best we could, but what can you do with a collarbone? If you don't set it right in a woman then she's got one breast higher than the other till she's lying in the grave and even after, so after we've bound up her ribs we make a sort of sling with three kerchiefs so that her right hand is resting on her left shoulder, and that works, I am glad to say, and she heals up nice and square, within reason.

But what shocked us more than anything and made us shake our heads and worry about the good people of this town, and what made me less surprised about what they did to each other later, was where they'd been kicking her when she was lying there in the dust in the meydan.

It was all in the breasts and the private parts, and I think that's really disgusting.

23

Tamara's Refuge

Abdulhamid Hodja sat on a low stool with Nilufer champing straw behind him, and in front of him the drapes around the recumbent Tamara. Periodically the horse would attempt to take a mouthful out of his woollen cloak where it lay across his shoulder, and he would push Nilufer's nose away with a few gentle words of reprimand. He had not seen Tamara's face since the evening of the stoning, and had decided that it would be better not to. It was not that he placed great store by the veiling of women; no woman veiled herself in the countryside because it would have been impossible to work, and the women who covered themselves in this town, small as it was, merely did so as a point of vanity, to indicate that they enjoyed a leisuresome life. Abdulhamid, therefore, was no stranger to the sight of female faces, framed and rounded as they always were, in practical head-scarfs that kept the dust out of the hair and preserved it as something special that among men only a husband would see. The imam avoided looking at Tamara's face because her prettiness made him want to touch her, and the ineffable sadness of her eyes had the effect of filling him with an identical sadness that perturbed him. In addition, she was no older than his daughter, Hasseki, and in the light of what had happened, this also perturbed him.

'Tamara Hanım, would you like some mastika?' he asked, passing a hand through the drapes. 'It must get very tedious for you, lying in there like a carrot laid up for winter.' He felt the tickle and scrape of small fingers picking the golden crystals from his palm, and was reminded of the teeth and the soft lips of Nilufer.

'The mastika is from Chios,' he added inconsequentially. 'It's the very best, so I understand.' It was certainly difficult to make conversation, and he could not escape the feeling that he probably should not be talking to her at all. If Ayse came in, he could be sure that there would be too much pepper in his pilav that very same evening.

'I hope you are feeling better, Tamara Hanımefendi,' he said, and he listened to the sound of Tamara sucking and chewing on the resin. A small, strangled voice from behind the drapes said, 'You should have let them kill me.'

'You should not wish to undo the kind deeds of others,' riposted Abdulhamid, always happier when there was a point of principle to discuss.

'What kind of life can I have?'

'I have wondered the same thing,' confessed Abdulhamid.

'If I return to my family, they will kill me,' said Tamara. 'Am I to beg, and live in the tombs, like the Dog? And Selim is dead.'

'Remember, daughter, it is in midwinter that the almond blooms.'

'I will have no life,' said Tamara softly, 'and I will spend eternity with Satan's foot on my neck.'

Abdulhamid was shocked. 'Don't say such terrible things!'

'I am guilty,' she stated simply.

Abdulhamid clamped his hands over his ears. 'Don't say that in front of me!' he exclaimed. 'I won't hear it! I will not permit you to make me a witness! I forbid it!'

'I am guilty,' she repeated.

'I can't hear you,' said the imam quickly, and he began to sing the first popular song that came into his head:

> 'My house is a cage
> My bed is a stone
> This is my destiny
> I water you
> But you wither away
> Ama-a-a-a-a-a-n.'

The Imam stopped and removed his hands from his ears. Tamara said, 'I am . . .' But Abdulhamid quickly broke in with a new burst of wailing: 'Ama-a-a-a-a-a-a-a-a-a-a-an,' adding melismatic flourishes of which his voice was not truly capable. He stopped when he ran out of breath, and was mildly offended when he heard Tamara stifling a giggle. 'I am . . .' she said, and up started Abdulhamid: 'Ama-a-a-a-a-a-a-a-a-a-a-a-a-a-a-a-a-a-a-an.'

When he had finished and was panting to regain his breath, Tamara lay ominously silent behind the drape, and Abdulhamid realised that she was toying with him. Finally she said, 'I feel less miserable now.'

'My voice is like a nightingale, is it not?' jested the imam, and Tamara laughed.

At this point Abdulhamid Hodja realised that someone other than Nilufer was standing behind him. He glanced over his shoulder and stood up quickly. It was Rustem Bey, who had approached silently, and was stroking Nilufer's neck with the back of his right hand. In his left, he held a piece of stick with which he tapped at the sides of his high boots, and his moustache was gleaming with fresh pomade. In his sash were two silver-handled pistols and a matching yataghan, and his fez was clean and freshly brushed. He looked as dapper and proud as ever, but Abdulhamid could see that he was unconsoled.

'This horse of yours, she is very beautiful,' observed Rustem. 'I have always thought that she is a very beautiful horse. A man with a horse like this has every reason to be happy.'

'She is indeed a fine horse,' agreed Abdulhamid, 'but capricious, for which I forgive her.'

'How is Tamara Hanım?' asked Rustem, with every semblance of coolness.

'She is recovering. She is young, and in these last two weeks she has made some progress. She is still in pain.'

'When she laughed just now,' said Rustem, 'that was the first time I have ever heard her laugh.'

'She laughs prettily,' said Abdulhamid.

'I have left some coins for you on the steps,' said Rustem, 'in recompense for your troubles.'

The imam was shocked. 'There was no need for that . . .' but Rustem raised a hand and hushed him. 'We are not divorced. A man pays for his wife.' With that he caressed Nilufer's neck for one last time, said, 'Indeed, she laughs very prettily,' and left without another word. Abdulhamid watched his retreating back, and noted

119

that there was something defeated even in the conscious dignity
of his gait.

Abdulhamid sat down on his stool and drew a deep breath.
From behind the drapes came once more the small and strangled voice of Tamara, saying simply, 'That was my husband. I
know his voice.'

'He still loves you,' said Abdulhamid.

'He doesn't know anything about love,' said Tamara bitterly.

'Neither do you, daughter,' said Abdulhamid, drily, 'neither do
you.' He stood up and began to saddle Nilufer.

Meanwhile, Ayse had formulated her own plans for Tamara's
recovery. She was far from hard in the heart, but it had been a
considerable burden, caring for a fallen woman when there was
so much else to do and so little to do it with. It was not that
she particularly wanted Tamara out of the way, either, it was
merely that she wanted a return to the normal patterns and
rhythms of life, and she found it a strain maintaining an imper-
turbable front against the gossips and finger-pointers who were
joking behind their hands that the hodja was going to take Tamara
as a second wife, or hire her out to strangers.

Ayse wended her way through the clutter and chaos of the
streets and went round to the back of Polyxeni's house. She rapped
on the shutter and removed her slippers, placing them in the
nook carved out of the massive wall, along with the footwear of
all sizes and vintages that nestled together there, so that anyone
who knew the family well would know straight away who was
out and who was in.

Polyxeni poked her head out of the window and gave a little
squeal of delight, exclaiming, 'Merhaba! Merhaba!' and fluttering
her hands. She and Ayse had been friends all their lives, playing
together in the dust as children, and being bounced upon each
other's grandparents' knees. They had even nearly died together,
at the age of six, of diphtheria. The two women embraced,
breaking into the torrent of pleasurable nonsense that invariably
accompanies such reunions even if they occur almost every day,
and went indoors.

Sighing and laughing, they settled themselves into the divans
and began to crack pistachios and melon seeds, tossing the shells

into the brazier and patting the half-dozen children on the cheeks. Ayse took Philothei in her arms and hugged her so tightly that she grimaced. 'You're such a grubby little thing, my tulip,' chided Ayse indulgently, rubbing somewhat brutally at the dirt on Philothei's face with the tip of her thumb.

'She's into everything,' said Polyxeni, 'nothing but trouble, that one.'

'She's so pretty. Honestly, I've never seen such a pretty child.'

'Everyone says that,' agreed Polyxeni. 'It's because she takes after her mother.' Polyxeni adopted a smug expression and affected to be preening herself.

Ayse laughed and caressed her friend's hands. 'Of course it is, of course it is,' she said, and then renewed her affectionate assault upon the little girl. 'Ooh, she's so pretty and sweet I could just hug her to death.'

'Stop,' said Polyxeni, 'she's vain enough already. Quite the one for standing over a puddle admiring herself. God help us when she's tall enough to look in the mirror.'

'I heard that little Ibrahim's in love with her,' said Ayse. She pinched Philothei's cheek, exclaiming, 'Our little princess has an admirer!'

'That poor little boy! He's completely besotted! Wherever she goes, there he is, faithful as a shadow.'

'How sweet! One day they'll be married perhaps.'

A cough alerted Ayse to the fact that Polyxeni's ancient great-grandfather, Socrates, was propped in the darkness of the corner, as ever, completely indestructible, but capable of only one train of thought. 'Watch out,' warned Polyxeni, *sotto voce*, 'the old dog's about to do his speech again.'

'I'm ninety-four, you know,' he said, his voice cracked and wavering, his agued fingers working at his prayer beads.

Ayse approached him and kissed his cold and papery hand respectfully. 'Ah, Grandfather! Ninety-four years old! It's remarkable!'

'I've got twelve children.'

'Oh, Grandfather Socrates, it's remarkable!'

'And I've got sixty grandchildren.'

'You don't say! It's remarkable!'

'And I've got one hundred and twenty great-grandchildren.'

'Oh, Grandfather!'

'And I've even got twenty great-great-grandchildren.'

Polyxeni nudged Ayse, smiling, and whispering, 'Here it comes!' and the ancient man leaned forward, saying, 'And you know what?'

'No, Grandfather,' replied Ayse dutifully.

The old gentleman smiled seraphically, wagged his shoulders, and said, 'They're all shit.'

Ayse and Polyxeni laughed together, and the old man beamed with satisfaction, his lips with their spiky white stubble extending practically to the elongated lobes of his ears. He raised a trembling finger, with the blue prayer beads draped over it, and pointed at Polyxeni. 'She thinks I'm joking,' he said, and he retreated once more into the crepuscular world of his infinitely repeated memories.

'Poor old dog,' said Polyxeni, a little discomfited, as this was the first time that old Socrates had ever added this particular coda. From outside there came an extraordinary flurry of very loud and exuberant birdsong that could not possibly have come from birds, and Ayse raised her eyebrows. Polyxeni waved her hand towards the window, so that her bracelets jangled together as they slid back down her forearm, and said, 'It's Mehmetçik and Karatavuk, calling each other on those birdwhistles again.'

'What a pair they are,' exclaimed Ayse, 'Mehmetçik in his red shirt running around pretending to be a robin, and Karatavuk in his black shirt pretending to be a blackbird. One day one of them's going to fall over with one of those whistles in his mouth, and it'll be goodbye teeth!'

'You're better off without teeth anyway,' observed Polyxeni. 'Better to have them all out and be done with it.'

'Anyway,' said Ayse, sticking to her own train of thought, 'if you can't be raving mad when you're a child, when else will you get the chance?'

Polyxeni suddenly asked, 'And how is it with the adulteress? How soon before you're done with her? I must say, I think you're a saint. I mean, what's to be done with her?'

'There's only one place for her,' said Ayse, 'but I'm not sure she realises it yet.'

'What a fate! Still, it's no less than she deserves.'

'She's not a bad woman,' said Ayse.

'Not bad! After what she's done?'

'I mean, she has no malice. Even so, she has no choice that I can think of, and I'm dreading it that I'm the one who's got to tell her.'

Polyxeni pursed her lips and suggested, 'Well, it's more than likely she'll realise on her own, I should think.'

'Inshallah,' said Ayse hopefully, and then she asked, 'Look, can you help me out? Can you do me a little favour?'

'I don't want to come and look after that whore, if that's what you're going to ask. Don't ask me to touch her!'

'No, no. I want you to ask your Virgin Mary Panagia to do me a favour. Look, here's the money.' She fumbled in her sash and brought out a few paras. 'Buy a candle and burn it for me, and kiss the icon, and beg the Panagia to cure Tamara Hanım quickly so that I can get my life again. Between you and me, and don't tell a soul, because if you did it would kill me, it worries me that Abdulhamid talks to her so much. I can hear her laughing, and it worries me. That's how a woman wins a man's heart, by making him think that he amuses her.'

'Husbands!' exclaimed Polyxeni. 'How God must have hated wives!'

She took the meagre coins and put them on the low table next to the bowl of pistachios. 'Of course I will ask the Panagia,' she said, 'and perhaps you can tie a rag to the tekke of your saint, and beg him to stop my great-grandfather from repeating that joke.'

'You can tie a rag yourself,' said Ayse. 'Everybody does. I even saw one of the Jews doing it, you know, the one with the funny eyes who lives in the same street as the Armenians. It might even be a Christian saint for all that anybody knows.' She paused, and then adopted a pleading tone: 'Will you do it now?'

So it was that the two friends went arm in arm to the Church of St Nicholas, patron saint of virgins and children, and Ayse sat in the sunlight upon the steps outside, eating figs and looking out over the valley with its tiny river that soon disappeared into the sea. It was said that in the far past there had been a port down below, full of proud ships and merchandise, but then a sandbar had appeared in the bay, and now the river had clogged itself up and left a fine tilth to compensate for the loss of trade. Abdulhamid had a small patch of land on it, rented from Rustem Bey, and every day he went down and removed the obstinate tortoises that descended on his crops. He would ride away with them in a sack and leave them on the other side of the hill in the hope that they would not come back. Ayse reflected that it was hardly easy to be married to such a good man, because there was too much of a difference between 'good' and 'sensible', and a sensible man does not waste his time being considerate to tortoises and fallen wives.

Polyxeni went into the church and crossed herself. She kissed the icon, placed Ayse's coins in the box, and collected a wax taper, which she lit from another before she pressed it into the sand-filled silver bowl. She crossed herself again, and contemplated the icon. It was said to have been painted by St Luke himself, and to have belonged to St Nicholas, and it was so laid over with silver and gold that by now only the faces and hands of the Virgin and Child were visible in their original colours. It was a particularly tender Panagia Glykophilousa, in which a sweet-faced, brown-eyed, golden-haloed Mary propped up the Christ Child in the crook of her elbow, while the child himself was caught in the act of throwing his arms about his mother's neck. In each of the upper corners an angel prayed with its arms crossed upon its chest and a benignly inebriated expression upon its countenance. So touching was this portrait, and so many were its miracles, that it was scarcely surprising that it had inspired many centuries of devotion.

Polyxeni adored the image for a short while, until the spirit of prayer came upon her. 'Sweet Mother,' she began, 'intercede for Ayse in her troubles, even though she's an infidel, but she's a good one, and she trusts in you, so that's not bad, is it? Please find a way for Tamara Hanım to see what she has to do without Ayse having to break the news, because that would be a terrible thing, and please pray for us all, and watch over my children, and accept this kiss.'

Polyxeni leaned forward and kissed the icon again, and went back out into the sunshine. She blinked, and Ayse asked, 'Do you think she heard you?'

A fortnight later, on a Friday, Ayse led Tamara out of Nilufer's stable. Tamara was unsteady and faltering, as much from despair and foreboding as from the legacy of her injuries, but she knew that she had no other choice, and she permitted Ayse to lead her by the elbow.

Ayse looked neither to right nor left, she ignored the stares, the pointing fingers and the comments. As she and Tamara passed, people stopped what they were doing and watched. When she and Tamara had gone by, they followed in their footsteps, until the two women had a crowd of almost all the townsfolk walking behind them as if at a funeral. 'There goes Tamara Hanım,' ran the whisper. Everybody knew it was Tamara even though she wore a heavy shawl over her head that completely shielded her face as she walked slowly at Ayse's side, with her eyes cast down to the ground in shame. No one was untouched by the young woman's disgrace, and a sadness settled on the town's stones like the fine white dust in the days when the wind blew in from Arabia.

The two women and the silent crowd passed along the street where the Armenians lived, through the meydan where the old men waited under the plane trees for Grandfather Death, past the well where Rustem Bey had sat with his back turned during the stoning, past the mosque with two minarets where Abdulhamid Hodja was precentor, past the rough shelter where Iskander threw his pots, past the smallest of the Christian churches where there was an owl that perched on the beams, past the ossuary containing the wine-washed bones of the Christian dead, and beyond to where the street turned a corner sharply and ended with a final, isolated house, flat-roofed, whose façade was draped with climbing roses, and whose windows were latticed in order to conceal the dark interior.

Outside the brothel, Ayse rapped on the heavy door. The people stood silently at a respectful distance, the men observing with set lips, and the women watching with their heads turned sideways and their çarşafs drawn across their mouths as if by this gesture they could shield themselves. In the door was a tiny wrought-iron grille at head height, and suddenly it squeaked open. Drifting out of it came a heavy scent of smoke and ambergris, olibanum, oil of lemon, musk and patchouli, and a huge pair of doleful grey eyes, heavily lined with kohl, looked out. 'Welcome,' said a low voice.

'I have brought Tamara Hanım,' said Ayse, full of regret, and a hennaed finger beckoned from the grille. Tamara approached, put one hand on the door to steady herself, tried to ignore the frightening thumping of her heart, and looked beseechingly into the sympathetic grey eyes. 'What do you want, sister?' asked the low voice.

'Sanctuary,' whispered Tamara.

The prostitute sighed, and said, 'Sister, we've been expecting you.'

24

I am Philothei (5)

I went too far when I was looking for hórta, and there was almost nothing because of the time of year, and I was so busy looking that I forgot where I was and suddenly I took fright, because I heard a noise and I thought it might be Markala or some other demon because they like deserted spots, but it was only Ibrahim, and I sat down on a rock because I'd been so frightened in case it was the demon, and I had demons on my mind because it was only the day after epiphany and we'd just burned Siphotis to get rid of the evil and filth.

They tied the rope across from the door handle of my father's house over to the door handle of Iskander's house, and they sealed up the cat in the jug and hung it from the middle of the rope, and then they lit the fire of thorns and twigs at one end of the rope, and when the rope broke the jug fell and shattered, and the cat was freed, and that was how Siphotis was got rid of, and everyone danced and sang around the embers, and then the men went round with the coals and put some smoke in everyone's house and in the stables, and then the men collected gifts, and Ibrahim was tagging along with the men who came to our house to put smoke in it, and somehow he managed to put his hand against my breast when no one was looking, and I practically fainted from the possible shame.

So when he came to the rocks when I was out on the day after epiphany, I turned away and wouldn't talk. When he gave up and left, I regretted it, though, and I went to the top of a rock to watch him go, and he turned and saw me, and I was caught out and embarrassed, but he just raised his hand in that small gesture that he has, and then he went on his way.

25

Tales from the Journey to Smyrna

In May the weather can be delightful, but sometimes the days are already too hot, and the roads are beginning to generate the fine white powder that clogs the traveller's eyes and nostrils, and makes a glue of the sweat on the flanks of the horses. Dust also begins to hang over the sea, so that Rhodes becomes obscured to Carians, and those in Cilicia lose sight of Cyprus, that island where no one ventures without falling in love. At that time the spring flowers are beginning to wither, and the red-backed butcher birds have long since arrived, setting up their gibbets and larders in the trees by impaling their catch of small animals on the long spikes of thorns. The snows have undertaken the beginning of their tactical retreat to the pinnacles of the Taurus Mountains, and the few wolves that remain have returned to higher ground, along with the bandits and brigands, and the wild deer that follow the growth of fresh new grass.

In March there are still rains and cold nights, quaggy patches of red and grey mud in the roadways, and the wind known as El Hossom whipping up the equinoctial gale that blows for eight long days. In the pastures the colossal Sivas Kangal mastiffs with their iron-spiked collars do nocturnal battle with subtle lynxes and desperate wolves, and the green sandpipers have not yet returned to the marshes and woods of the north.

In April the days are bright and gentle, and the showers sweeter, so that when Rustem Bey let it be known that he was travelling with an armed retinue to the famous infidel city of Smyrna, there were many who eagerly jumped at the chance to take advantage of his protection.

In those days the provinces were full of desperadoes who were mainly deserters. The machinations of the Great Powers, and the immemorial turbulence of the Balkans, had dragged the Ottoman state from one impoverishing, bruising and demoralising war to another. Those who were conscripted found themselves serving for indefinite numbers of years in vile and hostile places hundreds of miles from home, whilst the womenfolk broke their own health in the desperate attempt to run their farms and homes alone. They were hundreds of thousands of Penelopes waiting, sometimes for ever, for the men who were blown by fate from one misfortune to another. What made it worse was that the Christians had won equal rights, and were no longer exempt from military service as they had been in the past, and so it was that the wild places of Anatolia were crawling with outlaws, most of whom had more than adequately mastered the arts of brutality, and all of whom were thieves. Harassed though these were by the gendarmerie and the occasional military expedition from Constantinople, it was still unsafe for anyone to travel the great roads alone, so that when Rustem Bey decided to go to Smyrna in the spring, there were many errands and missions that had been stored up against such an opportunity.

Rustem Bey told no one why he was going. This was not the kind of world where men unveiled their hearts to anyone, and in any case the aga had no one in whom to confide, but the truth was that Rustem Bey was looking for a woman. His brief time with Tamara had provided him with inklings of what might be between a man and a woman, and his heart, his stomach, his loins and his throat yearned for something that he could not articulate even to himself. He needed someone to meld with. He knew himself to be something like a garden where the only flowers were those of potatoes, ragweed and neglected onions, but where a true gardener would have been able to drape the trellises with vines, and coax up tulips from the earth. It would be too simple to say that Rustem Bey was looking for romantic love, because in reality he was looking for the missing part of himself, and these are not often the same quest, even though we sometimes think they are. Rustem Bey had conceived the idea that if only he could find himself a Circassian mistress, amusing in demeanour, accomplished in music, red-lipped and fair of skin, excellent and enthusiastic in the techniques of physical love, then his life would be transformed. Every night he lay sleepless, tormented by the implacable songs of the nightingales, reaching

129

out the arms of his imagination to the Circassian odalisque whose face and arms would light up his chambers like the moon. He was going to Smyrna so that he could buy himself several clocks, some patent leather shoes, some black trousers, a Stamboul frock coat of the highest quality and a new red fez. From Smyrna he was going to continue by train to Constantinople, and he was determined that when he arrived he would not be garbed like a provincial lord, in baggy shalwar, his waistcoat and sash crammed with armament. He would arrive in the capital dressed as a thoroughly modern gentleman, with a trimmed moustache, and he would return with a beauty worthy of his state, who would be the only woman in the vilayet always to know exactly what time it was. He had decided that if God should see fit to let him find a truly marvellous woman, he would build a new mosque at the southern edge of the town, and pay for its upkeep too.

Early that morning the meydan buzzed with activity as the many travellers arrived with their animals, provisions and bedrolls. Iskander the Potter, lean and sinewy, was to make the voyage on foot, as was Mohammed the Leech Gatherer, who had agreed with Ali the Snowbringer that the latter's donkey should carry his harvest of leeches in return for a small share of his takings. Ali did not have to come far for this assembly, since he and his family had taken up residence in the vast hollow of a plane tree on the square, which now boasted a roofed extension and a proper door.

Levon the Sly, Armenian, apothecary, and one of the astutest merchants of the town, arrived with three camels laden with goods that he had accumulated through half a hundred small but careful deals during the winter, which he would trade in return for drugs and potions, cosmetics and aphrodisiacs.

Stamos the Birdman, his nose red and streaming as usual, carried a cage in which he held a pair of exquisitely colourful bee-eaters. They were green, russet and yellow, with long grey beaks, breasts of Aegean blue, and eye-stripes and collars of black. He reckoned that from one of the great houses that lined the harbour at Smyrna he would be able to obtain a high price for them that would make it worth his while to spend this journey scratching in the barbarous undergrowth of the verges for insects that they could batter to death before eating. Dead insects, he had discovered, were of no great interest to the birds, and it made him smile to think of the rich people's servants having to go out looking for live ones every day as long as the birds lived.

Daskalos Leonidas was also to make the journey on foot, and was already imagining the dreadful blisters and weariness with which he would soon be afflicted. He was determined upon visiting his family, even though it was not one in which there existed much mutual affection. More importantly he was to attend a meeting of his clandestine society that devoted itself to plots of Byzantine complexity, whose ultimate aim was to restore to Greece the lands lost to the Ottomans so many centuries before. Britain no longer mourns the throne of France, Spain has no project to reclaim the Netherlands, and Portugal has no ambitions on Brazil, but there are those who are incapable of letting the past pass on, among them the Serbs who will always be obsessed by the loss of Kosovo, and the Greeks who will always be obsessed by the fall of Byzantium. Leonidas was one of these, and he was very far from alone. He was possessed by beautiful visions of Constantinople restored to its place as capital of the Greek world, and, like all who have such beautiful visions, his were predicated on the absolute belief that his own people and his own religion and his own way of life were superior to others, and should therefore have their way. Such people, even those as insignificant as Leonidas, are the motor of history, which is finally nothing but a sorry edifice constructed from hacked flesh in the name of great ideas.

There were perhaps twenty souls in this caravan, which was to be conducted in the customary manner. It would travel from khan to khan, each one day's journey apart, and it would be led by a man on a donkey, who would proceed at a regular pace whilst smoking copiously and admiring the scenery. In this case the man on the donkey was a character who went by the name of Veled the Fat. Veled was a perfectly spherical man whose short legs stuck out quite straight on either side of his donkey's flanks, and whose cratered face betrayed an early encounter with smallpox. Fortunately for his donkey, Veled was hardly more than four feet tall, so the fact that he was also four foot wide at his greatest diameter did not entail too great a burden.

After the faithful had made their prayers in response to the dawn call from the minarets, the train made ready to depart, except that very little actually happened. Veled and his donkey started off, but the first camel refused to move. Veled wheeled his donkey about, and prodded the camel's flank with his foot. 'Son of a bitch,' he exclaimed, but not in an unfriendly manner, 'what's the matter now?'

The camel eyed him sorrowfully and disdainfully, and Veled prodded it again, to no avail. 'Damned camel won't go,' he explained to the travellers, as if they may not have noticed. Veled rolled a cigarette, lit it and, with a theatrical flourish, inserted it in one corner of the camel's nostril. 'All right now, are you?' he demanded. 'Can we go?' The beast heaved itself up and sighed contentedly, inhaling the fume of the cigarette. Veled turned to the other travellers. 'It's from always walking behind me. He got used to the smoke from my cigarettes, and then he got to like it, and now he won't do anything unless I let him have a smoke first.'

'It's an expensive camel, then,' said Stamos the Birdman.

'But a good one nonetheless,' replied Veled over his shoulder as the train moved on.

'What happens when the cigarette is finished?' asked Iskander. 'Doesn't it burn his nose?'

'When it gets too hot, he sort of sneezes and blows it out. You'll see in a minute. Once he blew it out and it landed on my donkey's arse, and before I knew it I was on the ground and my donkey was a little cloud of dust in the distance. Generally it's a good donkey though.' Veled patted its neck and flicked his hand back and forth between its ears. 'There's something nice about donkeys' ears,' he observed.

The retinue began in a burst of chatter, but an hour's trudging was enough to subdue the travellers somewhat. Some of them kept their eyes on the ground, as if they might find a coin there, and some gazed around, as if seeing the Taurus Mountains, or pink poppies, or a caper plant in full flower for the first time. All of them cast glances at Rustem Bey, the aga, because by now most of the men of both faiths had been to the brothel to try out his rejected wife, Tamara. It was said that she would only consent to begin if the shutters were closed, and that the experience of being inside her was like one of those dreams where you are searching for something without knowing what it is. You came out disconcerted by those liquid, unfocused eyes that gleamed in the dark, and infected by her loneliness and stillness, and it made you nostalgic and sorrow-shot. There had been, it turned out, little satisfaction in using the wife of the landlord. People wondered if he knew what had been going on, whether he had heard about the queues for that motionless, unresponsive flesh, and whether or not any feelings about it had stirred in that proud breast.

Those walking were shifting their bags from one shoulder to another, and Daskalos Leonidas was already feeling tetchy and hard-done-by. Stamos the Birdman snatched at flies to feed to his birds, and Levon the Sly silently did mental arithmetic as he calculated over and over again the amount of profit that might be expected from this trip. At their first stop, which was by a domed water cistern, Mohammed the Leech Gatherer swigged ayran from his leather bottle, wiped his mouth with the back of his hand, and said, 'I've got an idea.'

'Oh no,' said Ali the Snowbringer, 'I know all about you and your ideas. May we be spared this one, inshallah. Your ideas ought to be strictly haram, both forbidden and punishable. I am surprised that the Prophet, peace be upon him, did not foresee the terribleness of your ideas, and forbid them in advance.'

'This is a good idea, Ali Efendi,' protested Mohammed. 'It is an idea that is both recommended and meritorious.'

'A good idea is not a good idea just because the one who has it says it is,' said Iskander, running his finger along the line where his turban lay across his forehead. This was a mannerism that he employed every time that he believed himself to have come up with a particularly good epigram.

'Doesn't anyone want to hear my idea?' demanded Mohammed.

'I'll hear it,' said Rustem Bey. 'A landlord has his duties to his tenants, after all.'

'All right. My idea is that this is going to be a long and boring and weary journey, and each one of us should tell a story to while away the time.' He looked around triumphantly, and the travellers raised their eyebrows and exchanged glances.

'It's an excellent idea,' declared Rustem Bey. 'When we reach Smyrna I shall give a new yataghan to the man with the best story.' Rustem pointed to Mohammed. 'And as it was your idea, you can be the first.'

'Me? I don't want to be first. I only had the idea.'

'It's too late,' said Ali, rubbing his hands together. 'It's been decided.'

'I won't be telling any stories,' said Leonidas, abruptly.

'We didn't expect you to,' said Rustem, 'and in any case we don't want any stories from a sour-faced infidel wretch like you. Our lives give us enough bitterness without having to listen to you.'

Leonidas set his face grimly and walked on ahead, whilst the others gathered in a knot around Mohammed, nudging and pestering him until finally he announced, 'I know a good Nasreddin Hodja story.'

'We've heard it,' said Ali and Stamos together.

'There are hundreds,' replied Mohammed, 'you might not have heard this one. It's about when Nasreddin Hodja was riding along with his donkey's saddle on his shoulders, and someone stops him and says, "Hodja, why are you riding along bareback with your donkey's saddle on your shoulder?" and the hodja says, "It's because my poor old donkey was getting tired, so I thought I'd carry the saddle for him."'

'We know that one,' said Iskander.

'Everyone knows that one,' said Ali.

'Well, you might not have.'

'It's probably the most famous one,' said Levon.

Rustem Bey was mildly outraged. 'You call that a story? When we've all heard it before and it only lasts twenty paces? At that rate we'll need a hundred thousand stories before we get to Smyrna. Hasn't anyone got a decent one?'

'I know another one about why nomads won't eat cabbage,' offered Mohammed, and the others sighed and shook their heads. 'All right, I won't tell you,' said Mohammed, much aggrieved.

'I know a story,' offered Ali the Snowbringer. 'I was told it by a dervish when he was drunk. He said it was true.'

'There's nothing like a drunken dervish for good stories,'

observed Iskander, 'except that half of them don't seem to have any meaning.' He turned to Ali. 'Give us your story, then, and let's hope it's a better one than the last.'

'Well, this one is about a good woman of Mecca. She was very rich and very respectable, and she had two hundred camels of her own because her husband had died and she was running a business, and these camels carried spices and brass pots all over the place . . .'

'What about clay pots?' demanded Iskander.

'Clay pots, too, for all I know,' said Ali, 'and dates and dried figs and fine cloths, and Korans decorated with gold, and gold jewellery for the Sultan's wives, and fine boxes made with cedar of Lebanon.'

'This is more like a proper story,' commented Rustem Bey.

'And anyway,' continued Ali, 'this woman lived in Mecca, just on the outside, and she was the very finest example of womanly chastity in the world. She had never had an unclean thought in her life, and even her shit smelled of rosewater and cinnamon.'

The company laughed, and Ali waggled his shoulders with pleasure. 'So just imagine,' he said, 'her shock and horror when one night she dreamed that she fornicated with every one of all the pilgrims who came to Mecca on the haj.'

'Every one of them?!' exclaimed Veled the Fat. 'This sounds like my kind of story! Do you happen to know where she lives exactly?'

'It was hundreds of years ago,' said Ali.

'So what happened?' asked Rustem Bey.

'Well, she woke up, and she was so ashamed and embarrassed, even though no one else knew, that she was red from head to foot all day, until she went to bed. And that night she had the same dream again, and when she woke up she was so distressed that she poured ashes over her head and went and sat on the top of a dungheap. And then the next night she had the same dream again, and it went on like that for forty days and forty nights, until she couldn't stand it any more, and finally she decided to go and see a very wise mullah who might be able to advise her.

'Now, she goes in, all in fear and trembling, and not knowing how to say it, but she veils herself and speaks in a funny voice so that the mullah won't know who she is, and she weeps a bit, and beats her own chest with her knuckles, and finally the mullah gets impatient because he has hundreds of things like this to clear up every day, and he says, "Daughter, tell me what it is, because God is merciful and forgiving, but I don't have much time," and so finally she says, "Mullah Efendi, every night I dream that I fornicate with every one of all the pilgrims who come on the haj, and I am so ashamed, and I don't know why I have such a dream, because I am a respectable woman."

'"Yes, I know you are," says the mullah, "your husband used to be a friend of mine."

'Anyway, she nearly faints with shame, and she starts to cry and flap her hands about, and then the mullah sits and thinks for a while, and he strokes his long white beard, and he drinks a cup of mint tea with a medium amount of sugar in it, and he smokes his narghile, and then he strokes his long white beard again, and then he goes out for a piss, and then he drinks another cup of tea, and then he gets a little polished stick that he keeps for the purpose, and he puts it up inside his turban and scratches his head with it, and then he says, "Daughter, I think I know what your dream means," and she says, "Mullah Efendi, take away my shame," and he says, "Daughter, it's like this. You are a good Muslim woman, and what you should know is that when a woman wants to make love with a man it's the best thing in the world for him, apart from going to paradise, inshallah. So what this dream means is that you have a great desire to do something wonderful for all the pilgrims on the haj. Now, making love makes life, and water also makes life, so in my opinion what the dream means is that you should make a well by your house so that all the pilgrims can drink from it when they come into the city."

'"Ah, yes," she says, "they always look worn out and thirsty." So anyway, she goes away and she calls some labourers, and she has them dig a well, and the well is still here today, and it's named after her, and all the pilgrims drink from it on the way in.'

'So what's the name of this well?' asked Rustem Bey.

'That I can't remember,' said Ali.

'I think it's important for the story,' advised Rustem, 'there

136

is a certain frustration in not knowing, and it spoils it some-what.'

'It was a good story, though,' said Veled. 'I know one a bit like it, except it has a judge in it.'

'Go on then,' said Rustem Bey.

'Well,' said Veled, lighting another cigarette and depositing it carefully in the left nostril of the leading camel, 'there was a married couple, and they'd been married for five years, but there weren't any children. I can't remember their names, but this is a true story, and it was told to me by a man I met in Antiphellos when I went there, but I can't remember why. But that doesn't matter. What matters is, that they'd been married for five years and they had no children, and everyone was getting at them about it. The girl's mother would arrive, and say, "Why don't you have any children?" and then the man's mother would arrive and say, "Why don't you have any children?" and then the woman's sisters would arrive and say, "Why don't you have any children?" and then the man's cousins would arrive and say, "Why don't you have any children?" and in the coffeehouse the man couldn't play backgammon without someone putting him off at a vital moment by saying, "By the way, why don't you have any children?" and in the hamam the other women would ask the poor wife, "Why don't you have any children?"

'So obviously the couple get very upset because they don't have any children, and everyone keeps asking them why, and they feel uncomfortable about going out of the house or visiting their relatives.

'One day the wife says, "Let's go and ask the advice of Ismail Hodja," and her husband replies, "What? The famous Ismail Hodja who is renowned all over the world for his wisdom?" and she says, "Yes, that one," and he says, "But I've heard that it's very hard to get to see him," and she says, "But he only lives next door," so he says, "Well, all right then, we'll give it a try."

'The husband sends a little boy to the famous judge, saying, "Can we come and see you?" and before you know it they're sitting in front of this famous judge who knows every bit of the sharia backwards, forwards and sideways, and is notoriously full of common sense as well, and the husband strokes his moustache and says, "Kadi Efendi, we have come to see you because we don't have any children, and it is beginning to upset us when so many people ask us why not."

'The kadi blinks his eyes and he says, "What have you been doing about it?" and the husband says, "About what?"

'"About making children."

'The husband and wife look at each other, and she says, "What do you mean, 'making' them?"

'"Well, you have to make them," says the kadi, "or they don't arrive."

'"Really?" exclaims the husband. "Are you sure?"

'"Of course I'm sure," says the kadi, and the husband turns to his wife and says, "Did you know anything about this?" and she shrugs and lifts her hands, and so anyway it turns out that the couple didn't know anything about how to make children because no one had ever told them, and they'd never worked it out for themselves, and the wife says to the kadi, "Perhaps you could give us some hints."

'So the kadi stands up and lifts his robe, and he shows them his kamiş, and it's about a foot long and hard as a rock, with a great bulging purple tip like an aubergine . . .'

'Spare us the details,' said Rustem Bey.

'. . . and it's standing up like a soldier, and the wife says, "God save us," and the kadi says to the husband, "Does yours ever get like this?" and he replies, "Well, yes, it does, but mine's more like a carrot than a cucumber," and the kadi says, "Well, that's an advantage, because not many women can cope with one like this," and he turns to the wife and he says, "You've probably noticed that you've got one mouth in your face and another one elsewhere in the darker regions. Well, the one in your face is for eating food, and the other one is for swallowing one of these, but you're only allowed to use it to eat your husband's, and you'll both find fairly quickly that you like it, and that's how you make children."

'The husband says, "But what if she bites it off? How am I going to piss?" and the kadi replies, "Don't worry, because it doesn't have teeth, and when you come out you find there isn't any damage."

'The woman is still looking at the kadi's gigantic kamiş with her eyes popping out like this and her mouth open, but the kadi puts it away, and then they all make their salaams, and off they go, and lo and behold a few months later they've got a child, and they call it after the kadi, even though it's a girl, and that's why in Antiphellos there was once a girl called Osman, who was the only girl with that name in the entire known world.'

Stamos the Birdman sighed and said, 'You can always rely on Veled to come up with something filthy.'

'It's a true story, I swear it,' protested Veled.

'Does anyone know a story that isn't filthy?' asked Rustem Bey. 'I ask just out of curiosity, and not with much hope.' He looked around at the company and caught the eye of the potter. 'Ah, Iskander Efendi, I am prepared to bet that you don't tell such tales.'

'I don't know any proper stories,' said Iskander the Potter, 'but I like to tell people things that really did happen. Perhaps you would like to know the story of why I am coming to Smyrna for the fourth time, when I don't even have anything to sell and I don't know anyone who lives there.'

'Somebody must have told you about the brothel on the waterfront,' suggested Veled the Fat, and some of the others laughed.

Iskander pursed his lips and raised his eyes to the heavens, and Rustem Bey said, 'Ignore him.'

'Everyone else does,' said Mohammed, who was still somewhat prickled after the poor reception of his Nasreddin Hodja story.

'Well, I'll tell you if you're interested,' said Iskander, and he paused before commencing, as if to gather his thoughts. 'As you know, one of my sons is called Karatavuk because once I made him a whistle that sounded like a blackbird, and he started to make a big pretence of being a blackbird, and he put on a black shirt and liked to have black things, and he would run about flapping his arms and leaping about on the rocks behind the town where the old tombs are, with that whistle in his mouth.

'Well, Karatavuk has a friend, one of the Christian boys, and I made him a whistle too, that sounded like a robin. With these whistles it's really a matter of luck what they sound like, and you never know until you've tried it what it's going to resemble.

Sometimes they sound like a bulbul, for example, or a song thrush.

'Karatavuk's little Christian friend, he's the son of Polyxeni and Charitos, you know them, and that pretty girl Philothei is one of his sisters, well, he's a strong boy, and anyway he decided to call himself Mehmetçik because if Karatavuk is a blackbird, he thought, "Well then, I am a robin."'

'So now we have two little boys who are running around pretending to be birds, and when they're not pretending to be birds they're often with me, because they like to mess around with the clay, and sometimes I let them make things out of it, and sometimes they come with me to dig the clay, and sometimes they get into the big tank of sludge and help Blind Old Dimos to get the stones out . . .'

'I've often wondered about that,' said Ali. 'Why do you have a blind old man walking up and down in a tank of clay, getting all filthy and coming out looking like a cross between a leper and a demon and a corpse, all caked up?'

'Well,' said Iskander, 'it's because freshly dug clay is full of stones and grit and little bits of wood, and God knows what else, so you put it in a tank and stir it up with lots of water. As it settles, all the grit and stones sink to the bottom, and then someone walks about in it, picking it up between his toes. When you've got it all out you draw the slush out from a hole in the tank that's a little bit higher than the bottom, and then you can dry it out and you've got clean clay that won't explode or get big holes in it when you fire it in the kiln. Anyway, you don't need eyes in order to walk up and down in a tank, and even blind people need work, and blind people get very sensitive with their sense of touch, and so I pay Blind Old Dimos to do it.'

'Don't you think it's bad luck to have a Christian walking up and down in your clay, though?' asked Ali. 'I mean, it doesn't seem right for a Muslim pot to have had Christian feet in it.'

Iskander laughed. 'Feet are only feet, and in any case Blind Old Dimos is married to one of my wife's aunt's cousins, and I do it for charity, and I've never heard that charity should only go to those of one's own kind. And in any case I sell my pots to anyone. Levon the Sly here has several, and I've sold them to the Jews, and even to the Devil Worshippers. Money has no religion except itself.'

Ali nodded doubtfully, and Iskander said, 'Where was I?'

'You were telling us why you were going to Smyrna for the fourth time even though you have nothing to sell and you don't know anyone who lives there,' said Rustem Bey, 'but for some reason you were telling us about your son who pretends to be a bird, and then we got on to an old Christian who walks up and down in a tank of wet clay.'

'Ah, yes,' said Iskander, 'now I remember. The thing about stories is that they are like bindweeds that have to wind round and round and creep all over the place before they get to the top of the pole. Let me see . . . Yes, this little boy Mehmetçik, one day he says to my son Karatavuk, "How come your baba doesn't have a gun?" and my son says, "I don't know," and Mehmetçik says, "I expect he can't afford one," and my son says, "Yes he can," and Mehmetçik says, "No he can't!" And my son says, "Yes he can," and Mehmetçik says, "No he can't!" You know what little boys are like. And Mehmetçik says, "My baba's got a gun," and, "My baba's better than your baba," and so my son Karatavuk gets very angry and he swipes Mehmetçik and gives him a black eye, and then Mehmetçik starts to cry and gives my son a good kick in the shins, and so my son is howling, and that's when Abdulhamid Hodja comes by and grabs them both by the scruff of the neck and twists their ears for fighting in the street, and brings them along to me, and I get the story out of them.

'So, the odd thing is that after a while I begin to think about this gun that I don't have. I say to myself, 'I don't need a gun. It's a waste of money, what do I want a gun for?" And then there's this other voice in my ear, saying, "Yes, but you'd like one really, wouldn't you?" and the first voice says, "Don't be stupid," whereupon the second voice says, "Every man has a gun, and in fact no man is a proper man unless he's got a gun."'

'That's right,' interrupted Stamos, 'that's perfectly true. That's why I've got one. It's probably more important than having balls and a whole clutch of children.'

'Anyway,' continued Iskander, 'these voices keep on and on at me, until finally I can't even sleep at night because of them quarrelling with each other and ruling each other out, and abusing each other, and it's worse than when the nightingales won't shut up. Finally, I am at my wheel one day, and I am making a plate, which isn't easy at the best of times, and suddenly it goes wobbly and collapses, and I get really irritated, and I pick up the spoiled plate and squash it in my hands and fling it back into the bucket of clay, because I have realised that I can't even concentrate on my work any more because I am thinking about this damned gun that I don't have. I decide there and then that the only way out is to get myself a gun, and then I can be at peace.'

'An excellent decision,' agreed Mohammed. 'That's what I would have done.'

'So,' continued Iskander, 'I decided to go on the next caravan to Smyrna and get myself a gun. I had some trouble with my wife, who said it was a waste of money, and we were too poor, and all those sorts of things, but then I said I would bring her back a silver bracelet, and suddenly we had plenty of money, and wasn't it all a wonderful idea, and a gun would be bound to come in useful eventually. I worked day and night to make enough pots, but there weren't enough people to sell them to, until a party of Yörük nomads passed by, and they'd been selling carpets in Aleppo, and had lots of money, and it so happened that they needed pots. So I was lucky.

'I had some trouble in Smyrna because it's such a big place, and there are so many people, and I was quite lost, and people kept giving me instructions and directions that I couldn't follow, and half the time people spoke in languages I couldn't even recognise, and I slept down on the wharf to save money, which wasn't funny, because at night the rats come out, and I hate rats, and it's also where the cheapest whores go and fornicate on the coiled heaps of rope with all the foreign sailors, so you can say that I didn't sleep much.

'The day after I arrived I met a man who had a beautiful pistol in his sash, and I said, "Salaam aleikum, and please excuse me for molesting you, but please may I ask where you got that beautiful pistol? Because I am looking for something like it."

'He tells me about Abdul Chrysostomos the Gunsmith, and points me in the direction of the Turkish quarter, where it joins up with the Armenian quarter, and he says, "I am warning you, it isn't a simple thing to get any sense out of Abdul Chrysostomos. You'll end up with a beautiful gun, but don't expect results too fast."

'After a little difficulty I find this Abdul Chrysostomos and he is definitely a peculiar character. He is like a Jew crossed with a Greek, crossed with an Armenian, crossed with an Arab, crossed with a Bulgarian, crossed with a Negro and a mad dog too. He speaks with an accent that's like a donkey, if a donkey could speak, and he's got his head shaved except for in the top of the middle of his head, and that's made into a plait, and he's got a gold ring through one nostril, and four or five gold rings in each ear. He's got great big lips that spread from ear to ear when he smiles, and in one of his front teeth he's had a diamond set in, so that it flashes all the time and it makes him hard to talk to, because you keep having this diamond flashing at you.

'He works in a shop that's full of burning coals and furnaces and it stinks of hot metal, and it's just like a picture of Hell, and everything is covered with soot, including Abdul Chrysostomos, so I still don't know whether or not he's a black man or an Arab or any of those other things.

'This gunsmith shows me all the different models that he makes, and the difference between a Damascus barrel and a bored barrel, and he tells me that he can make me a rifled barrel if I want and if I keep quiet about it, because it's supposed to be illegal, and he says that actually a smooth barrel is more versatile, even though it's less accurate, and he shows me all the beautiful inlay in ivory or silver or mother-of-pearl that he might or might not put into the stock, which might or might not be made of walnut or birch or whatever, and he talks to me about whether or not the gun will be muzzle-loading or breech-loading, and whether or not it will be single-shot or provided with a revolving chamber, until finally, I am clutching my head in my hands, and I say, "Abdul Efendi, you are giving me so much choice that I am completely confused, and I think my brain has just stopped working."

'He says, "Well, let's just start from the beginning. Do you want a pistol or something to fire from the shoulder?"

'This is a difficult one in itself, because I had thought I wanted a nice pistol to wear in my sash, but now I begin to think, "A bigger gun might be nicer." I think about the expense, and this devil inside my head starts to say, "Who cares?" and I say, "Actually, I want one of each," and his face lights up because I am the kind of customer he likes. Anyway, we finally decide that I am going to have a smooth-bored single-shot breech-loading pistol with a nice plain birchwood handle, and a rifled single-shot breech-loading hunting gun with a plain birchwood stock. You can see I was trying to be sensible in the midst of all my folly, because the guns would be practical and useful, but not too fancy or expensive. We haggle over the price, and even though it's a lot, it's not too much, and you can always hope for another party of nomads. They break a lot of pots because they travel so much, and their route to the south passes through our town, so there's always plenty of trade. Abdul Chrysostomos says to me, "Come back in a couple of months, and they'll be ready."

'Naturally, I am in a ferment of looking-forward, and I can hardly concentrate on anything, and every pot I make falls to pieces between my fingers, and then finally I travel back with the next caravan, and I find myself in the shop of Abdul Chrysostomos, and he remembers me, and he says, "Ah, Iskander Efendi, how good to see you. You'll be pleased to know that your weapons are ready, and I am sure you will be delighted with them." Even so, he has a sheepish expression, and I soon find out why. First of all, the pistol has a walnut handle inlaid with silver filigree, and he's given it four muzzle-loaded barrels, and these barrels are splayed out like the fingers of a hand, and I say, "Abdul Efendi, what on earth is this?" and he says, "It's a mutiny pistol, a very classic design. You can kill four people with one pull of the trigger, as long as they are standing side by side."

'"Abdul Efendi," I say, "it's beautiful, but I don't need to put down any mutinies. In fact, I have never been on a ship and I've never been in the sea, and I am not a captain who needs to keep any order. I am a potter who needs a pistol to put in my sash when I walk about the town and when I celebrate the holy days."

'Abdul looks very crestfallen, and says, "Don't you want it then? I thought it was very fine, and that you'd be pleased."

'"Abdul Efendi," I say, "it's absolutely beautiful, but it isn't what I asked for, and I bet it's more expensive too."

'He puts on this voice like a little child, and his bottom lip begins to quiver, and a tear runs down one cheek, and this great big brute of a man starts to cry, and he says, "I thought you'd like it. I worked so hard, I made it with so much love, and it only costs twice as much."

'I try to comfort him, and I say, "Abdul, it's a masterpiece, and you should send it as a gift to the Sultan Padishah himself, because it is worthy of the Royal Armoury, but it is too good for me, and I can't afford it. Have you got the rifle?"

'Abdul Chrysostomos wipes his face with the back of his hand, so that it's smeared with wet soot, and he fetches the rifle, and I look at it, and I can hardly believe my eyes, because this one has six barrels all joined together, and when you pull the trigger they revolve one at a time. The stock is made of ebony, and it's inlaid with mother-of-pearl, and it's very beautiful, and it's so heavy because of all the barrels that I actually can't lift it to my shoulder. Abdul smiles and says proudly, "It's my newest design."

'I say, "Abdul Efendi, this is another one for the Sultan Padishah. It's exquisite, but it's too heavy to lift, and it isn't what I ordered."

'He looks at me as if I have just informed him of the death of his mother, and the long and short of it is that finally I agree to come back in another couple of months with the next caravan.

'So I come back the third time, and now he's made me a pistol with a rifled barrel and a revolving chamber that takes seven bullets, and the calibre of it is so huge that it would knock over the wall of a house with a single shot. Honestly, I could get my first finger up the barrel. And he's made a rifle that has a barrel six feet long because he says that it's more accurate and with a barrel like that you could hit a single ball of rabbit shit from a thousand yards. We go through the whole process again, and he starts crying, and he says he's an artist and he can't help being carried away by his creative impulses, and I say, "Well, you could say that I am an artist too, but when someone commissions a pot, they get what they ask for, and I do it as well as I can, because the art is just as much in the making as in the conceiving, and a thing doesn't have to be complicated to be finely made."'

Iskander paused. 'Now I'm going back, for the fourth time, in the hope that finally I'll get the pistol and rifle I asked for, and I've been through all this trouble and inconvenience just because my son had a fight with his friend and made me feel bad about having no gun. I think I have been a fool.' He pointed to the sky. 'I think that God is probably up there laughing at me.'

'Nonetheless,' Ali comforted him, 'a man needs a gun to feel completely himself. That's just the way it is. When you go back your wife will have greater respect for you, and your sons will be proud of you, and when you stroll around the town in the evening, you will be feeling as important as Rustem Bey himself.'

Rustem Bey smiled at this implied flattery, and Iskander admitted, 'I do feel a certain excitement already.'

Stamos wiped his nose with his sleeve, and said, 'That's a story without an ending. I don't feel satisfied. You will have to tell us what happens next when we make the return.'

'I liked the bit where you described the gunsmith,' said Mohammed. 'I could just imagine him, with all those gold rings and the plait.' He looked around at his fellows, and asked, 'Who's next?'

Levon the Sly raised his right hand. 'I know the one about the Forty Viziers.'

'Now that's the longest story in the world,' exclaimed Iskander.

'It is if you can remember all of it,' said Levon. 'I fear that many of the tales will escape my memory.'

'I expect we can remind you,' said Stamos.

So it was that for two days Levon the Sly related the lengthiest story that has ever been composed about the trickery and perfidy of women. Everyone laughed, and no one took the misogyny too seriously, except for Rustem Bey, who fell silent and unhappy, and curiously ashamed. Nonetheless, it was Levon the Sly who won the yataghan, which was perhaps a little ironical, since the Armenian merchant was the only infidel who told a story, and he was the only storyteller there who had no interest in weapons whatsoever.

26

Mustafa Kemal (6)

Far away from Eskibahçe, past the Dodekanissos and across the Aegean Sea, it is 1907, and Mustafa Kemal is at last back in Salonika, the town of his birth. He finds to his frustration and irritation that his exile in Damascus has spoiled his chances of becoming a leader of the revolutionaries. There is a new Committee of Union and Progress, consisting of people like Talât Bey, Çemal and Ali Fethi. They meet in Masonic secrecy, swear oaths on swords and the Koran, and will one day soon become widely known as 'The Young Turks'. They are suspicious of Mustafa Kemal, who finds all the hocus-pocus very tedious, and whose Fatherland and Freedom Society becomes absorbed into the new entity. He spends his time inspecting the Macedonian railways, excluded from the seat of action.

The Sultan sends two commissions to deal with the Committee of Union and Progress, and the leader of the first is shot and wounded. The second apparently seeks conciliation, but there is a young and dashing major who, instead of going to Istanbul to parley, takes his men to the hills. This man is Enver, who is shortly joined by another officer who is an expert in guerrilla warfare. The revolution is openly proclaimed at last, and the Sultan sends troops to deal with it, but they join the revolution instead. The Sultan is forced to restore the old liberal constitution of 1876. The handsome Enver appears on the balcony of the Olympus Palace Hotel, and proclaims the new policy of Ottomanism. There will be no more special privileges for particular ethnic and religious groups, and from now on all obligations and rights are the same for everybody. There is euphoria in Salonika. Rabbis and imams embrace, political prisoners emerge, astonished, into the light. Agents of the Sultan are murdered, and the bodies are spat upon in the streets.

Enver is just the sort of man that Kemal dislikes. He is a good and respectable Muslim who neither smokes nor drinks, and he is vain and punctilious. Kemal is also envious of his leadership and success, and sees no good coming from it. He sees that Enver is a fine officer in the field, but detects no other quality to redeem him. Mustafa Kemal chafes because he is keenly aware of his own superiority.

The revolution is a half-baked affair. It has no real plan and no real ideology beyond the intention to restore the empire to its previous strength. The revolutionaries do not comprehend the power and seduction of the new nationalisms. The Christians are not necessarily pleased at having earned the right to do compulsory military service and become free Ottoman citizens, and very soon the Young Turks find that they have accelerated the disintegration of the empire instead of arresting it. Bulgaria declares independence. Crete declares union with Greece. Austria illegally and opportunistically annexes Bosnia and Herzegovina, thereby setting in train the dismal events that will distort the entire course of European history for more than a hundred years.

Mustafa Kemal sees the chaos, and is more than disgruntled. In the Kristal café, in the White Tower café, in the Olympus café, he complains loudly and bitterly to his brother officers. The Committee of Union and Progress decides to pack him off to Tripoli in order to sort out some local business and Kemal reluctantly agrees to go.

On the way he disembarks in Sicily, and the local children bombard him with lemon peel and mock his Ottoman fez. He suddenly sees for the first time that the fez epitomises all that makes the empire ridiculous in the eyes of foreigners, and he begins to conceive a hatred of it. One day, when he is dictator of Turkey, he will outlaw it in a fit of illiberality.

In Tripoli, Mustafa Kemal has to deal both with fractious Arabs and old-fashioned Ottomans who do not acknowledge the authority of the CUP. He browbeats the local pasha, and, characteristically and unfailingly heroic, he goes to the courtyard of a mosque that is the headquarters of Arabs who are planning to abduct him. He addresses the hostile crowds and ladles patriotism and religion over their heads. He threatens them implicitly by emphasising the power of the CUP, but comforts them by promising that this power is for their protection only.

Mustafa Kemal impresses a sceptical Arab sheikh by tearing up his own papers of accreditation, announcing that his own word is enough and that he has no need of papers, whereupon the sheikh releases from prison the three previous emissaries who had mistakenly relied too heavily upon their own such letters.

In Binghazi, Sheikh Mansour has overborne the local Ottoman authorities, and Mustafa Kemal thinks up a ruse to defeat him. He gathers the local troops together in the barracks, and proposes to the officers that he should lead them in an exercise. He tells them that they are to imagine that they are an infantry regiment marching to confront an enemy upon the left, but which then receives notice to wheel about and face an enemy on the right.

In this way, and without anyone suspecting it in advance, Mustafa Kemal surrounds the house of Sheikh Mansour, who is obliged to send out an emissary with a white flag, and a parley is set up. Mustafa Kemal lectures him upon the nature and intentions of the CUP, and in his turn the sheikh gets Mustafa Kemal to swear upon the Koran that he will not harm the Sultan, the Lord Caliph. It is doubtful in the extreme that Mustafa Kemal would have invested any great seriousness in a Koranic oath, but nonetheless honour is satisfied and order is restored. Mustafa Kemal, his mission entirely accomplished, returns in triumph to Salonika, only to find that the revolution has run aground.

27

The Tyranny of Honour

Yusuf the Tall loved all his children equally, with a passionate adoration that, when he thought about it, sometimes made him lachrymose. If his life were like a garden, then his daughters would be like the roses growing alongside its walls, and his sons would be like young trees that formed a palisade against the world. When they were small he devoted happy hours to their entertainment, and when they grew older he hugged them until their eyes bulged and they thought that their ribs would crack. He had grown to love his wife too, partly because this is what happens when a wife is well chosen, and partly because from her loins had sprung these brooks and becks of happiness.

But now Yusuf the Tall did not know what to do with his hands. It seemed as though they were behaving on their own. The thumb and middle finger of his left hand stroked across his eyeballs, meeting at the bridge of his nose. It was comforting, perhaps, for a scintilla of time. There was no comfort longer than that in this terrible situation. Sometimes his hands lay side by side on his face, the tips of his thumbs touching the lobes of his ears. He had thrown off his fez so that they could stroke his hair backwards, coming to rest on the back of his neck. The maroon fez lay in a corner on its side, so that his wife Kaya kept glancing at it. Despite this awful emergency, and the drama in which she was caught up, her instinct was to tidy it away, even if it were only to set it upright. She sat on the low divan, kneading her fingers, biting her lip and looking up at her husband. She was as helpless as one who stands before the throne of God.

Yusuf the Tall strode up and down the room, waving his hands, protesting and expostulating, sometimes burying his face in his hands. Kaya had not seen him so anguished and begrieved since the death of his mother three years before. He had painted the tulip on the headstone with his own hands, and had taken bread and olives so that he could eat at the graveside, imagining his mother underneath the stones, but unable to picture her as anything but living and intact.

Yusuf had passed the stage of anger. The time had gone when these patrollings of the room had been accompanied by obscenities so fearful that Kaya and her children had had to flee the house with their hands over their ears, their heads ringing with his curses against his daughter and the Christian: 'Orospu çocuğu! Orospu çocuğu! Piç!'

By now, however, Yusuf the Tall was in that state of grief which foreknew in its full import the horror of what was inescapably to come. His face glistened with anticipatory tears, and when he threw his head back and opened his mouth to groan, thick saliva strung itself across his teeth.

Overtaken, finally, by weariness, Kaya had given up pleading with him, partly because she herself could see no other way to deal with what had occurred. If it had been a Muslim, perhaps they could have married her to him, or perhaps they could have repeated what had been done with Tamara Hanım. Perhaps they could have kept her concealed in the house, unmarried for ever, and perhaps the child could have been given away. Perhaps they could have left it at the gates of a monastery. Perhaps they could have sent her away in disgrace, to fend for herself and suffer whatever indignities fate and divine malice should rain upon her head. It had not been a Muslim, however, it had been an infidel.

Yusuf was an implacable and undeviating adherent to his faith. Originally from Konya, he was not like the other Muslims of this mongrel town who seemed to be neither one thing nor the other, getting converted when they married, drinking wine with Christians either overtly or in secret, begging favours in their prayers from Mary Mother of Jesus, not asking what the white meat was when they shared a meal, and being buried with a silver cross wrapped in a scrap of the Koran enfolded in their hands, just because it was wise to back both camels in salvation's race. Yusuf the Tall regarded such people with disdain. Moreover, it is one of the greatest curses of religion that it takes only the very slightest twist of a knife tip in the cloth of a shirt to turn neighbours who have loved each other into bitter enemies. He had lived serenely among Christians for most of his life, but now that she had despoiled and defiled herself with an infidel, this was the worst in all that tormented him.

Yusuf stopped pacing the room, and at last called his sons together. His other daughters assembled too, standing silent and cowed at the back of the darkened room.

When his sons were before him, Yusuf took his pistol from his sash, weighed it in his hand, took it by the barrel, and handed it to his second son, Sadettin. Sadettin took it by the butt, and looked at it in disbelief. At first his voice seemed to fail him. 'Baba, not me,' he said.

'I have tried,' said Yusuf, 'and I can't. I am ashamed, but I can't.'

'Not me, Baba. Why me?'

'You have courage. Great courage. And you are obedient. This is my command.'

'Baba!'

Yusuf beheld the spiritual and moral agony of his second son, and the surprise, but he would not relent.

'It should be Ekrem,' pleaded his second son, gesturing towards the first-born. 'Ekrem is oldest.' Ekrem held out his hands as if to push his brother away, shaking his head vigorously.

'Ekrem will take my place when your mother dies,' said Yusuf. 'He is the first-born. You are all used to obeying him. He will be head of the family. It is you who must do this thing.' He paused. 'I command it.'

Father and second son looked at each other for a long moment. 'I command it,' repeated Yusuf the Tall.

'I would rather kill myself,' said Sadettin at last.

'I have other sons.' Yusuf placed his hand on Sadettin's shoulder. 'I am your father.'

'I will never forgive you,' replied his second son.

'I know. Nonetheless, it is my decision. Sometimes . . .' and here he hesitated, trying to name whatever it is that takes our choices away, '. . . sometimes we are defeated.'

Yusuf and Sadettin stood facing each other silently, and at the back of the room one of the girls began to sob. Sadettin appealed to his mother; kneeling before her and taking her hands in his, 'Anneciğim! Anneciğim!'

Kaya removed her hands from his grasp, and raised them in a small gesture of impotence. She seemed suddenly like an old woman who has turned her back on life.

'I command you,' said Yusuf the Tall.

'It will be on your head,' exclaimed Sadettin angrily, rising to his feet.

'On my head,' repeated Yusuf.

Sadettin entered the haremlık. It was dark because the shutters were closed, and it smelled comfortingly of things feminine and mysterious. In the corner, glowing and glittering with terror in the half-light, he saw the eyes of his sweet sister, Bezmialem, of all his sisters the most gentle, and the one he loved the best.

'Sadettin,' she murmured, her soft voice full of resignation. 'I thought it would be Ekrem.'

'I thought it would be him,' said Sadettin.

She glanced at the pistol, placed her hand on her stomach and looked down. 'You will kill both of us.'

'Yes.'

'The child is innocent.'

Sadettin felt the pistol grow heavier in his hand. To himself he thought, 'I won't defile my right hand,' and he transferred it to his left.

'I am innocent,' said Sadettin.

'We are all innocent,' replied Bezmialem.

'You are not.' He felt a sudden surge of anger. He blamed her for bringing down the shame, and for shutting him in this trap.

'I found something better than honour,' she said, her eyes momentarily shining with happy remembrance.

'What is better than honour?'

'I don't know the name of it. But it is better. It makes me innocent.'

Sadettin took his sister's right hand in his, knelt before her, and touched it to his heart, his lips and his forehead. He kissed it. He tried to suppress his pain, and he bowed his head. 'It is not me who does this thing,' he managed to say at last. He said

153

it as quickly as he could, so that the words would not be throttled by sorrow and die in his throat.

'It is our father who does this,' said his sister. 'The injustice isn't yours.'

'May God receive you in paradise,' said Sadettin.

'May I see you there,' replied Bezmialem.

'May the angels carry you.'

'And you when the time comes.'

Sadettin raised himself up and realised that after all he would have to defile his right hand. He transferred the pistol, threw his left arm around his sister's neck and embraced her. They stood together, trembling. Softly she put her arms around him, as if he were a lover. He felt the soft pulse of her breath on his neck. He placed the muzzle of his pistol against her heart, clenched his eyes shut, muttered, 'In the name of God . . .' and fired. He held Bezmialem to him as she choked and the spasms and convulsions overcame her. He thought that they would never end, and the dread came over him that he might have to go out, reload the pistol and shoot her again. For a desperate few seconds he wondered if it might not be possible to take her to a surgeon and save her. At last her head fell on his shoulder, and finally he let her down gently to the floor. He knelt and kissed her, the arc of his motion so familiar because so akin to the rituals of the mosque, and then he rested his forehead on hers.

When Sadettin emerged into the selamlık, his shirt was glistening with the dark blood that his sister had coughed up, and it was as if he had become another man. He threw the gun down at his father's feet in a brutal gesture of contempt, held his father's gaze, and wiped his hands so roughly together that they made a sound like clapping. 'I have defiled my right hand because of you. I am finished with you all,' he said.

'Where will you go?' asked his father.

'Where do the birds go?' asked Sadettin. He gestured in the direction of the Taurus Mountains, rising up from the Elysian coastal plain like a vast and sombre fortress. Behind them stretched the grim plains of the east, where a hard and uncouth people sat silently in the dark for months, doing nothing whilst they waited for the winter snows to melt.

'I am an outlaw,' he said. 'That is where I will be. With God's help, I shall not live long.'

Sadettin left, taking nothing with him but a musket, and without kissing his father's hand, or touching it to his forehead, or to his heart.

Shortly afterwards Yusuf the Tall emerged from the house with the pistol restored to his sash, his fez brushed and restored to his head. A small and anxious crowd of people had gathered outside, wondering about the meaning of the shot. They had seen Sadettin leave in a fury, with his musket over his shoulder and the blood on his shirt, and his air of one who would never be able to bear a human touch again.

Ignoring these people, Yusuf set off down the steep and teeming alleyways.

He was affronted by the normality of the town. He stepped over the sleeping dogs, and skirted the kneeling camels. In the distance he could hear the Blasphemer railing against the priest. Little Philothei was being followed as usual by Ibrahim. Her friend Drosoula, as usual, had the devoted Gerasimos in tow. Abdulhamid Hodja rode by on Nilufer, her bells tinkling and her ribbons fluttering. Under his awning, Iskander the Potter worked at his wheel, and raised a lazy clay-caked hand in greeting. The goldfinch of Leonidas twittered in its cage outside the teacher's door. Ali the Snowbringer led his donkey by, its flanks wet and glistening from the melting packs of ice. Karatavuk in his black shirt, and Mehmetçik in his red, played with stones under a fig tree. To Yusuf, all this ordinariness was like the mockery of God.

He found the two gendarmes playing backgammon together on a table in the shade of the plane trees of the meydan. As the day had grown warmer, so more of the buttons of their tunics had become undone. Both of them were in urgent need of the weekly shave that they would take that evening before Friday began. They looked up, not unduly pleased to be interrupted in their duty to the holy game of backgammon, and pronounced 'Hoş geldiniz' in reluctant unison.

'Hoş bulduk,' replied Yusuf, adding, 'I am sorry to disturb you.' He drew the pistol from his sash, and laid it down gently on the board, so that he would not disturb the pieces. The gendarmes looked up at him in puzzlement and expectation.

'I am a murderer,' declared Yusuf gently, 'and I have come to offer myself for arrest.'

28

The Humiliation of Levon the Armenian

Ever since the year 1189 in the Muslim calendar, which was 1774 in the Christian, the Russian Empire had exercised a policy of religious expurgation every time that it expanded into newly conquered lands. In the Crimea, in the Caucasus, in southern Ukraine, in Azerbaijan, Kars-Ardahan and Laz, the Russians massacred and displaced the Muslim populations, swamping the Ottoman Empire with refugees with which it could not cope. It is impossible to calculate the number of deaths, or to reimagine the manner in which these murders were perpetrated. It was a perduring holocaust, but, unlike the more famous one of the Second World War, it is uncommemorated by the world because it received no publicity at the time or afterwards. No monuments have been raised, no dates of commemoration have entered the calendars, no religious services have been held, and no hindsighted pieties have been repeated for our edification. The Russians replaced these slaughtered populations with Christians, preferably of Slav origin, but in the absence of Slavs they made do with Ukrainians and Armenians.

It is curious that the Russians, calling themselves Christians, and like so many other nominal Christians throughout history, took no notice whatsoever of the key parable of Jesus Christ himself, which taught that you shall love your neighbour as yourself, and that even those you have despised and hated are your neighbours. This has never made any difference to Christians, since the primary epiphenomena of any religion's foundation are the production and flourishment of hypocrisy, megalomania and psychopathy, and the first casualties of a religion's establishment are the intentions of its founder. One can imagine Jesus and Mohammed glumly comparing notes in paradise, scratching their heads and bemoaning their vain expense of effort and suffering, which resulted only in the construction of two monumental whited sepulchres.

Unsurprisingly, but unfortunately for themselves, orthodox Armenians were often seduced by their own religious affiliations into supporting the Russians against their fellow Ottomans, and many joined the Russian armies. Consequently, the tides of war carried opportunist Armenian settlers into territories freshly emptied of Muslims. Unsurprisingly, to Ottoman ears the word 'Armenian' became virtually synonymous with 'traitor', and thus was life made arduous or dangerous for those hundreds of thousands of Armenians scattered throughout the empire and living side by side with Ottomans of other denominations and races, who could not distinguish between one type of Armenian and another, and who would not have lowered a raised fist just because a particular Armenian was in fact a Protestant or a Catholic, or a loyal subject of the Sultan.

It was in the year 1331 by the Islamic calendar, and 1912 by the Christian, the year in which Greece, Bulgaria and Serbia attacked the empire in the hope of expansion and the liberation of their brethren, that Drosoula's father, Constantinos, was accidentally jostled in the meydan by Levon the Armenian. The latter was walking with his eyes squinting against the sun because he was idly looking at a vulture that had appeared high over the western end of the town, and because of this inattention his shoulder struck that of Constantinos, who was passing the other way.

Constantinos was a notorious and inveterate drunk who began each day with a poisonous hangover and ended it by vomiting in the gutter. There were those who plied him with raki deliberately, in order to enjoy the chaos that he generated and the shameful displays in which he indulged. It was a miracle to many that he managed to be drunk even when he had no money with which to buy the alcohol, and it seemed that he was capable of becoming inebriated even when he had had very little to drink.

On this particular morning the bright sunshine was making his head throb even more agonisingly than usual, and he was clenching his eyes and grimacing in the attempt to ease the suffering of it. He was sweating as if in a fever, his gait was unsteady, and his eyes drifted in and out of focus, causing his mind to feel as if it had become remote and tangential, as though it was operating his body by a system of levers. He was already in a state of irritation because the Blasphemer was also in the meydan, and had been yelling insults at Abdulhamid Hodja as he rode by on Nilufer. These cries and curses had hurt his brain almost as much as if a nail had been driven through it, and his jaws ached so badly that it was hard for him to tell where the pain originated.

The jolt he received from Levon was therefore a most unwelcome and disorientating intervention in the turbid stream of his consciousness, and his immediate and unthinking reaction was to lash out. 'Haydi! Haydi! Haydi!' he shouted, pushing the Armenian in the sternum, and forcing him backwards. 'Filthy shit! What do you think you're doing? Pig!'

Levon, often known as 'Levon the Sly' because of his astute business sense, was an apothecary and general merchant, and, whilst he had experienced some abuse in his life, he had never experienced any direct violence. He was at that time only thirty-two years old, and had three pretty little daughters whom everybody expected to become beautiful in the fullness of time. Owing to his frequent business in Smyrna, he prided himself, like Rustem Bey, upon being a thoroughly modern man, and there was certainly nothing about his outward appearance that would have marked him out as an Armenian. His well-brushed crimson fez, his abundant black moustache, his satin sash, his black waistcoat embroidered with gold thread, his high boots, all bespoke a man at peace with himself and well off in the world. He was much admired for knowing the entire story of the Forty Viziers, which made him a great asset on long evenings, and he mixed freely with the notables of the town. He was not, however, in the least equipped for the onslaught of an angry drunk with a vile headache and a short temper. Unlike Rustem Bey, he was not robustly built, for he had thrived on his ingenuity rather than his physique, and was not the sort of man who was accustomed to hard riding and days out in the hills hunting.

His initial reaction was one of astonishment, and his mouth fell open. He said something inarticulate, and Constantinos merely thrust at him in the chest again. 'Pig! Filthy Armenian! Traitor pig!'

There was a dog asleep in the dust, and as Levon stepped

backwards, he came up against it and fell over, his arms flailing. The dog yelped, leapt up and hurried away, its tail between its legs, looking over its shoulder in fear of further trouble.

As Levon tried to sit up, the drunk began to kick him in the thighs, and the other people in the meydan were attracted to the brouhaha. Constantinos repeated his insults, and spat in the Armenian's face. 'Pig! Pig!'

If there had been any notables in the meydan, or if the gendarmes had been playing backgammon there as usual, then it is more than likely that the sot would have been dragged off his victim, and reprimanded. But there was no one there with any authority, and the plebeians were of the sort who enjoyed a spectacle, particularly when someone cleverer or more fortunate than themselves was degraded. There had probably been nothing as good as this since Tamara Hanım had been dragged out into the streets by the hair.

There was not a single one of those there who would not have helped Levon if they had found him injured by the side of the road, but as a mob they were individually not a wit superior to hyenas.

So it was that a laughing and mocking crowd of people surrounded the terrified man, and egged on his assailant, who continued to kick and spit.

'Go on, Constantin', get him, get him!' cried Veled the Fat, and his yells of encouragement were taken up by the likes of Stamos the Birdman, Mohammed the Leech Gatherer, Iskander the Potter, Ali the Broken-Nosed, Charitos, father of Philothei and Mehmetçik, and any number of others who happened to be there at the time. The women too were not to be held back, and Ayse, Polyxeni, Lydia the Barren and Hasseki, daughter of Ayse, were among those who pressed themselves into the throng in order to howl gleefully with the rest. An unknown but uncouth hand squeezed Hasseki's virginal backside, however, and she squealed and backed out.

Spurred on by the crowd and by his own pain and rage, Constantinos began to kick at the fallen man's ribs. Levon instinctively huddled into a foetal position and tried to protect his chest with his arms.

'Look at the coward!' exclaimed Iskander, and people laughed.

'He's not a man, he's a dog!' shouted Charitos, to more laughter.

'Kick him, kick him!' cried the women, like an intoxicated chorus of maenads.

'Traitor pig, Armenian son of a whore!' cursed Constantinos, rhythmically swinging his right foot into the recumbent and cowering body.

Constantinos raised his foot high, and suddenly everyone fell silent. It was clear that he was about to bring his foot down and stamp on the man's head. It was the crucial point at which the game might overleap itself into murder. No one was able to say anything, and nobody moved.

The hush continued for what seemed like minutes, as Constantinos stood there with one foot raised high, swaying lightly back and forth as the terrible deed germinated in his intention.

The injured man whimpered, and out of the fallen bundle came the words, faint but completely clear: 'I am a loyal Ottoman. Long live the Sultan Padishah. I am an Ottoman. Long live the Sultan. Long live the Empire.'

Constantinos lowered his foot carefully to the ground, and placed it beside the other. He swayed a little, and then suddenly wheeled round and faced the silent and appalled crowd of people. He waved his arms drunkenly, embracing them all by his gesture, and then pointed at them accusingly. He announced in a voice that was slurred but full of anger and contempt: 'You! You're all shits! You're all shits and pigs like this son of a whore, and you're all sluts and slutsons. Fuck you all, fuck you all, and may you all rot in the earth with your whore mothers and your whore-begotten fathers!' He spat on to the ground, and wiped his hands together as if brushing off the dust.

With this, he composed himself as best he drunkenly could, and lurched purposefully away in the direction of the Church of St Nicholas. Iskander the Potter leaned down and touched the arm of Levon the Armenian. Idiotically, he asked, 'Levon Efendi, are you all right?'

Levon moaned and began the slow, painful process of trying to stand up. He was covered in white filth, and his fine clothes were torn and disarrayed. Ali the Broken-Nosed picked up the man's fez, brushed it off with his fingers and handed it to him. Such was the pain in Levon's sides that he could hardly breathe if he stood upright. Nonetheless, he forced himself erect, and looked at the people who surrounded him, concern on their faces where only moments before there had been malevolent pleasure. There was a long moment of silence, and then Levon said softly, but with great dignity, 'Shame. Shame on you all.'

With that he turned and began to walk very slowly and with the utmost difficulty in the direction of the Armenian quarter. Charitos, father of Philothei, full of regret and the very shame that Levon had wished upon him, impulsively went forward to take his arm and help him away. The rest of the people looked at each other and shrugged, and then went quietly about their business, as if there were someone asleep nearby, whom they did not wish to wake.

29

I am Philothei (6)

One year when I was quite little we had been fortunate, and
it was decided that we would perform a kurban, and sacrifice a ram on my father's saint's day, and so he bought a big
Karaman ram, and that was the kind we all preferred because of
there being so much fat in the tail, the kind that we cooked with
honey to make the Panagia's food. It was a very beautiful ram,
and it was washed, and we tied it with ribbons and flowers, and
I put my hand into its wool, and it felt wonderful, and I began
to have feelings of affection for it.

On the evening before, my father sharpened the knife, and my
mother and I went into the church and cleaned it so well that
everything sparkled for lack of dust. In the morning my little
brother Mehmetçik, whose real name was Nicos, had to lead the
ram to the church and tie it up at the gate, but the ram was
obstinate and it wasn't easy, and everyone was laughing to see
him struggling so hard, but he managed in the end, and so the
onlookers applauded, and then Father Kristoforos arrived to read
the gospel to the ram, and bless it.

Then at the time of the doxology my father Charitos untied
the ram and led it round the altar three times, and then he
turned the head of the animal to face the east, and he pressed
it up against the altar, and then the stone was moved under
the ram's neck, and with the knife my father made the sign of
the cross three times at its throat, and I was so horrified that
I was watching through my fingers and then my father said,
'May this be acceptable to God,' and I saw him cut the animal's
throat. Then the blood flowed out into the dish of the stone,
and the ram kicked a few times, and Father Kristoforos swung
the incense over it, because incense makes the dead happy, and
so the ram would forgive us. When the throat was cut and the
ram kicked, I started to cry because I had loved the ram, and

163

my mother told me to be quiet and not be so silly, it was only a ram.

But I was very upset, and afterwards I hit my own father because I was angry, and fortunately he only laughed, and we decked ourselves with flowers and we children were given our little branches hung with fruit, and the Patrikos went ahead of us crying out the message about the feast, and we went down to the meydan, and I sat with my brother Mehmetçik in the meydan where the sacrifice was roasting, and I was still crying and didn't want to talk to anyone, and people were saying, 'She has a tender heart, this little pretty one, all covered with flowers.'

And when the meal was being served with rice, and everyone was feeling merry, my mouth was watering, but I wouldn't accept any food, and everyone found this very amusing, and then finally my brother whispered in my ear and said, 'If you don't eat any, someone will die,' and I said, 'Who?' and he whispered, 'Ibrahim', and I didn't really believe him, but because I was unsure I had to eat the meat anyway, just in case, because my anxiety was greater for Ibrahim than it was for the sheep, and it was only afterwards that Mehmetçik admitted he'd been lying, and so I got revenge by putting a dead beetle in his rice, and he ate it because it was dark by then, and it wasn't till the following Christmas that I asked my father Charitos to forgive me for hitting him.

One day I would like to tell Ibrahim this story.

30

Mustafa Kemal, His Own Policeman (7)

The Young Turks' plans to root out corruption and nepotism, to improve education, to update the armed forces, all come to nothing in the face of old habits, opportunistic vendettas and tribal loyalties. The vast majority of the population are deeply conservative, because for them the Sultan is chief of all the Muslims, the Shadow of God on Earth. To rebel against him or to contest with him is tantamount to sacrilege. Officials appointed under the *ancien régime* find themselves undermined and operating under ambiguous loyalties. The deputies in the new parliament, Turks, Greeks, Arabs, Albanians, Jews, Serbs, Armenians, Bulgarians and a Vlach, prove themselves incapable of any ideal higher than ethnic self-interest. Unrest grows in the army as officers promoted from the ranks see their chances of further promotion diminished. Military units become fractious because of being transferred away from Istanbul on the grounds of their dubious loyalty. A Mohammedan Union arises to combat the secularism of the Young Turks, to fight for the adoption of the sharia law, and for the exemption of religious students from military service in the event of their failing their religious exams. The press, which now has freedom under the reinstated constitution, begins to agitate vociferously, like a dog that barks with no clear intention at the moon. An opposition journalist is murdered on the Galata Bridge, and his funeral becomes a mass protest.

In April 1909 there is a mutiny among troops sent to Istanbul under the assumption that they would be loyal. They are joined by Islamic students and teachers, and they march on parliament, chanting 'We want the Holy Law' and killing a naval officer and two politicians who had been mistaken for someone else. From Salonika the Young Turks send soldiers, among them Mustafa Kemal in charge of a division, and the mutiny is suppressed. The

Sultan is deposed, fainting into the arms of his chief eunuch when he is informed that he is to be sent to Salonika, and his trepidatious, pliable brother is released from thirty years' house arrest in order to be enthroned in his place. Eighty counter-revolutionaries are hanged, including the leader of the Moham-medan Union, and even the unfortunate who used to blend the Sultan's tobacco. In Adana, the hot-headed and nominally Christian Archbishop Moushegh encourages his fellow Armenians to acquire arms and kill Muslims, causing a backlash that leads to the burning of the town and the massacre of twenty thou-sand Armenians and two thousand Muslims. Çemal Pasha arrives and quells the disturbances, executing forty-seven guilty Muslims and one Armenian.

Mustafa Kemal begins to argue that it is necessary to keep the army out of politics. He says that members of the Committee of Union and Progress should decide whether or not they want to be politicians or soldiers, and to forswear political activity alto-gether should they opt for the latter. This does not prove popular with politicised officers such as the handsome and respectable Enver Pasha. Mustafa Kemal's assassination is set in train, but the latter suspects the young man who has been sent to talk to him, and he places a revolver before him on the desk. His revolver, coupled with his cool eloquence, so impress the young man that he confesses to his mission, and announces a change of heart. Now the party arranges for Yakup Cemil to kill Mustafa Kemal, but the former has much admiration for the latter, refuses the mission and warns him in advance. One dark night Kemal ducks into a doorway and draws his revolver because he senses that he is being followed. The man who passes by is Enver Pasha's uncle. Kemal boasts, 'I am my own policeman.'

31

The Circassian Mistress (1)

It is said that in those days one could hear seventy languages in the streets of Istanbul. The vast Ottoman Empire, shrunken and weakened though it now was, had made it normal and natural for Greeks to inhabit Egypt, Persians to settle in Arabia and Albanians to live with Slavs. Christians and Muslims of all sects, Alevis, Zoroastrians, Jews, worshippers of the Peacock Angel, subsisted side by side and in the most improbable places and combinations. There were Muslim Greeks, Catholic Armenians, Arab Christians and Serbian Jews. Istanbul was the hub of this broken-felloed wheel, and there could be found epitomised the fantastical bedlam and babel, which, although no one realised it at the time, was destined to be the model and precursor of all the world's great metropoles a hundred years hence, by which time Istanbul itself would, paradoxically, have lost its cosmopolitan brilliance entirely. It would be destined, perhaps, one day to find it again, if only the devilish false idols of nationalism, that specious patriotism of the morally stunted, might finally be toppled in the century to come.

At the time of Rustem Bey's arrival, Istanbul was still the latest living incarnation of Constantinople and Byzantium, whereby names and rulers had changed, but customs, institutions and habits had not. His first plunge into this teeming and colourful chaos was necessarily at the railway station, kindly donated by the Germans (whose Kaiser had proclaimed himself protector of the world's Muslims) and which was predictably equipped with towers that made it look like a fort.

Infidel Smyrna had been good practice for the ordeal of coping with Istanbul's extraordinary confusion, but since then Rustem Bey had had to endure the railway journey between the two cities, and he was not in the best of tempers. He possessed little aptitude for Islamic fatalism, so that by the time the train had ground and jolted its laborious way through more mountains than it seemed reasonable for God to have created, and by the time that it had reached Eskişehir, he was already beyond all patience. The train had inexplicably halted for up to two hours at a time, in the full heat of the day, so that perspiration dripped down his forehead and into his eyes, before making its way down to the tips of his moustache and falling into his lap. Four times the train had actually gone backwards for considerable distances. More than once he had been unable to prevent himself from exclaiming, 'By God, it would have been quicker to walk!' Once, when the view was so beautiful that it had almost calmed him down, he had put his head out of the window and had collected a large smut in his left eye, projected there with uncanny accuracy by the slipstream. His servants' concerned dabbing at the sooty water with kerchiefs had added injury to what seemed like the locomotive's personal insult. Furthermore, despite his efforts to secure private and comfortable seating, the carriages had inexorably filled up until they were bursting at the rivets. Opportunistic travellers congregated at the points where the gradient forced the train to a snail's pace, and leapt on, often accompanied by goats, babies, rolls of carpet and huge copper pots. At the legitimate stops it seemed that no one got off, but a great many more got on. Outside, the çay-sellers with their prodigious samovars kept up a constant supply of sweet tea, and little boys ran back and forth bearing dusty rings of unleavened bread threaded through a stick.

Rustem Bey found himself crammed into a corner beneath a sweaty heap of the most diverse forms of humanity. On his lap was a birdcage containing two pretty hawfinches of unknown ownership, and between his feet was a mastiff puppy that chewed at the new patent leather of his boots. People were smoking at strange angles so as not to burn the clothes of their neighbours, and the air had grown thick, heavy and blue, the smoke settling in gently wreathing horizontal bands. The passengers, unable to resist the temptation to share each other's parcels of food and to tell each other the stories of their lives, and their relatives' lives, and even the lives of those they had never heard of, turned the compartment into a kind of ferocious indoor picnic. A very old long-faced Kurd with hypnotic eyes, a filthy white turban and no teeth, regaled

Rustem Bey for three hours with Karagiosiz and Temel stories, in an eastern dialect of which he understood barely one word.

When he arrived in Istanbul therefore, Rustem Bey was in a state of irritable disrepair. Both his eyes were red and stinging, the left much more than the other. His new boots bore small toothmarks, and his nose was itching on account of the birds. His new Stamboul frock coat was dusty and creased, his new crimson fez was impregnated with cigarette ash, his moustache felt like a rodent that had adhered to his upper lip and died, and there were saliva stains on his trousers where the ancient Kurd had dribbled on him, having fallen asleep in an upright position, jammed between a dejected soldier and a crook-backed Jewish tailor. Rustem Bey had become more and more strongly aware that the musty and stale smell that had been tormenting him for several hours was in fact emanating from himself.

As he waited on the platform for his servants to disembark his baggage, Rustem Bey surveyed the press of people and listened to the hubbub, wondering whether in fact he was about to make a complete fool of himself. He was suffering from severe misgivings about the whole project, dimly aware that there was something self-defeating about it, something to which he could not adduce a precise analysis. Nonetheless, he also knew that he was an obstinate man, and that once he had made a decision, he would stick to it. This was why he had never given in to the suspicions aroused by the rumours that Mariora, mother of Polyxeni, had, quite without motive, been the cause of the deaths of all his family. Rumours are the great seducers of reason, but, once he had decided that they were simply malicious gossip such as infect all small towns, he had steadfastly stuck to that decision and had not once allowed himself to be tempted to believe otherwise. He had felt as vindicated as Polyxeni herself when Mariora's bones turned out to be clean, even though he set no store by such Christian superstition.

At that time there were about 180 khans in Istanbul, endowed by philanthropic Muslims, where one could arrive with one's own bedroll and sleep in peace in the upper rooms whilst the horses occupied the stables below. Some were famous, such as the Valideh Khan and the Yeni Khan, with their courtyards of trees and fountains, and their fireproof storerooms for merchandise, but even the modest ones were pleasant and clean. They were unfurnished, and were therefore easily swept free of fleas, lice and bedbugs, so that even travellers as demoralised as Rustem Bey could make themselves comfortable and quickly recover their *beaux esprits*. Rustem Bey directed one of his servants to hire one of the many stray errand boys to lead them to the nearest one, since it was almost dusk, and another of his servants to hire four hamals to transport their luggage. After so many hours of discomfort in the train, he decided not to hire a sedan chair for himself, feeling that a walk would loosen his limbs and do him good.

The hamals in those days were Armenians from Lake Van, who had formed themselves into a union in order to monopolise the trade in porterage. These immanitous men were single-handedly capable of carrying pianos uphill on their necks, in the full fire of the sun, with nothing but a cushion by way of assistance. There was a rumour, believed by almost everybody, and widely disseminated by the hamals themselves, that it was only possible to maintain the enormous strength necessary for the job if one lived solely on cucumbers and water, and it was by this means that they discouraged others from taking up the trade.

Thanks to these formidable gentlemen, Rustem Bey was soon installed above a calm courtyard that was washed with the gentle noise of a fountain and the sweet smell of figs. Longing for cleanliness with a desperation that was akin to a thirst in a foundry, he set out for the hamam that was attached to the local mosque, having sent a servant ahead to inform the bath attendants that an important personage was about to arrive, and that this personage did not take kindly to homoerotic suggestions. After having bathed and made certain enquiries of the masseurs at the hamam, he would find a barber to shave away the journey's stubble, and to massage its horrors out of his neck. Like all barbers, this one entertained him with gossip about the Sultan and his courtiers, and then helpfully informed him that a foolproof way to avoid insect bites for a whole twelve months was to say 'Nevruz suyu' on the Persian new year. Rustem Bey raised his eyebrows, the quantity of balderdash presented as indisputable fact never ceasing to amaze him.

32

The Circassian Mistress (2)

Despite the cacophonous and diligent howling of the city's tribes of dogs, Rustem Bey slept well, and quite early next morning he breakfasted on bread, honey, yogurt, olives and sweet coffee. It being Friday, he then made his way to the mosque near the hamam where he had bathed the previous evening. He was not by any means devout or punctilious in his religious observance, but, like most people who are brought up in a faith, his natural impulse in difficult or testing times was to enlist the assistance of God. In this he was perhaps, from the Deity's point of view, rather like those old friends who suddenly remember their affections when they have run out of money, or when one has suddenly become famous, or been appointed to a position of influence.

He washed himself at the fountain outside, left his boots at the door, and entered. In his right hand, draped over his fingers, he held the fine, heavy tespih that he had inherited from his grandfather. The thirty-three beads were made of polished onyx, its string and embellishments were made of silver, and between the eleventh and twelfth beads, and the twenty-second and twenty-third, were twin silver discs cut to resemble flowers. With his eyes closed, and his thumbnail flicking the beads, he named the name of God thirty-three times. He recited internally the first sura of the Koran, the Arabic phrases lining up in his head quite automatically, even though he would have been quite unable to translate them. Then he knelt and touched his forehead to the carpet, hoping that God would look down and hold out His hand in blessing on his enterprise.

Out in the sunlight, he stood on the steps of the mosque and slipped the prayer beads into the inside pocket of his new coat. For a moment he watched the crowds, the red fezzes of the men, with their black tassles, reminding him of the wheat fields full of

poppies at home, before they had all turned pink. A group of
Mevlevi dervishes walked past together, clad in their great skirts
and their hats that looked like tombstones. A hamal strode by,
bearing a cast-iron cauldron upon his head. A Jewess was borne
past, her sedan chair inlaid with nacre and ivory. Behind her came
a letter-writer, bearing his pens and scrolls, an accidental ink mark
slanting across his cheek like a scar. A mixed party of Muslims
and Christians took their first steps towards Ephesus, making
pilgrimage together to the house of the Virgin Mary. Two gypsy
women with babies at their backs walked hand in hand with two
capuchin monkeys. A portly Orthodox priest sweated behind a
party of bedouins draped in white cloaks, and after them a
golden-vested Greek merchant rode side by side with a merchant
from Italy, discussing prices in French. Four more hamals appeared,
bearing between them a small dead camel that hung forlornly
from two poles that rested upon their shoulders, then came
another, laden with a black tin trunk. Clutching a pink silk
parasol, the dainty wife of one of the European ambassadors
tripped along, flanked by four black servants and a grotesque
eunuch from Ethiopia. A small group of Maltese nuns, whispering and giggling together, pattered along with parcels of medicines in their hands, whilst a group of Persians jostled with a
band of Albanians, armed to the teeth and dressed entirely in
white. Two young Greek women with scarlet skullcaps, their
black hair flowing down over their shoulders, caught Rustem
Bey's eye and nudged one another. A solemn Turk on a small
ass led twelve ludicrously pompous camels, strung together, their
halters hung with large azure prayer beads. Such was the normality
of Istanbul, and none of these people found anything remarkable
in such heterogeneity.

All this mommixity and foofaraw was compressed into a street
no more than three paces wide, and was further complicated by
the dogs who, exhausted by their nocturnal serenades and excursions, slept promiscuously in the paths and alleyways. Their
numbers had begun to decline rapidly because of the advent of
wheeled vehicles, since for centuries they had merely been stepped
over, and had never been obliged to develop any ideas about
getting out of anyone's way. At this time, however, they yet

populated the city in numbers equal to the humans, and fouled it to about the same degree. The Muslims were very fond of them, fed them, and even left them money in their wills, but at night the Greeks left them poison. This was because, although they were sweet-natured with humans, the dogs themselves were tribal, and had divided the city between them into small canine republics, devoting much of their energy to assaulting dogs that strayed in from foreign neighbourhoods. This made it impossible for Christians to keep dogs as pets, since Christian house-dogs were considered to be interlopers and were routinely set upon. Muslims, fond as they might be of the street-dogs, never adopted them as household pets because the Koran declares them to be unclean, and hence their concern was only for the ones that lived in the streets, pleading for alms with their big brown eyes. So it was that the followers of Christ poisoned the freebooting Muslim dogs so that they could keep captive Christian ones. Situations analogous to this, involving humans rather than animals, but just as hard to explain, are not unknown to this day in the nearby regions of the Balkans.

Stepping over these somnolent Islamic mutts, and avoiding as best he could the press and shove of the crowds, he sidestepped the open sewage channels with their varied but uniformly loathsome flotsam, holding to his nose a kerchief soaked in lemon cologne. He pressed small coins into the hands or turbans of the wonderfully distorted cripples and beggars that loomed up to bar his passage, and worked his way back towards the railway station, because from the waterfront nearby he would be able to take a boat across the Bosporus. At the khan he would collect two of his servants, because he was about to venture over to Galata where no sensible outsider, however brave or strong, would hazard himself without a bodyguard, a place so infamous that it had even been heard of back home in Eskibahçe.

As the day warmed up and the sun brightened they dipped past the Kızkalesi Tower, where once upon a time a tragic princess had been immured, in order to preserve her from a prophesied death by snakebite, only to be killed by a serpent hauled up to the windows in a basket of fruit. Rustem Bey trailed his hand in the black water and marvelled at what he saw. He wondered

173

how he might have described it to the people back home in Lycia. He felt both exhilarated and discomfited by the splendour, diversity and cacophony of it all. The channel was clogged with caiques, rowing boats, skiffs and barques of all shapes and sizes and in all states of repair, some propelled by sail, but most of them by brawn. The air seemed crowded by the hollow knock of hulls, the creaking of rowlocks, the shrieks of seagulls, and the hoarse shouts of the boatmen as they called insults to each other and jested in their impenetrable patois. Before him on the southern side of the Golden Horn rose the imposing walls of the Topkapı Palace, and on its northern side, those of the Galata Tower. Beneath him on the seabed, he fancied, shivering a little at the thought, bobbed the corpses of those discarded wives and concubines of past sultans, which were popularly supposed to have been disposed of in weighted sacks.

Rustem Bey found it hard to concentrate on the sights around him, because his boatman was engaged in the sort of inconsequential monologue that everywhere in the world passes for friendly conversation among such people, rendered curiously stilted and unbalanced by the deep breaths that he drew before each stroke of the oars. The boatman himself had the shoulders and arms of a titan, the skin of a disused waterbag, the moustache of a hog, and the pointed ochre teeth of an inveterate smoker and drinker of highly sugared tea. His black eyes squinted out from beneath beetling eyebrows, and his nose, which must at some time have been flattened in a fight, was like a small aubergine that has been bruised by a passing mule and left in the road for the birds.

'. . . so,' he was saying, 'this is my uncle, this is, he goes into his neighbour's house and he says, "I feel dizzy, I'm so hungry, you couldn't spare me a little nibble, could you? My wife's out and I don't know where she keeps the food," and so this neighbour says, "How about a bit of chicken?" and so my uncle says, "That'll be fine," and so he eats two legs of chicken, and the neighbour says, "How about some potatoes?" and my uncle says, "That'll be fine," and so eats this heap of potatoes, and then the neighbour says, "How about some bread?" and my uncle says, "That'll be fine," and he eats three or four pieces, and then the neighbour says, "How about some baklava?" and my uncle gets all annoyed and says, "Do you think I'm a pig or something? I said I only wanted a nibble." Well, that's my uncle for you, that is, that's just what he's like, he's a cantankerous ungrateful old piç, and that's for sure, and my father says he doesn't know why God punished him with such a brother . . .'

'Yes, yes, how interesting,' interjected Rustem Bey at appropriate points, as the boatman changed seamlessly from one topic to another.

'. . . so there's this old lady and she's up in court testifying, and the kadi is trying to work out what date she's talking about, and he asks her, "When did this happen, exactly?" and she says, "I can't be sure, but I do know that we were eating okra," so the judge says, "Well, it must have been July or August then," and she says, "Well, I'm not sure about that," and he says, "Well, it must have been; are you sure it was okra?" so she says, "Yes, I'm sure it was okra," so he says, "Well then, it must have been July or August because that's when the okra comes in," and she scratches her head and says, "Yes, but this okra was pickled," so anyway, they never did get that one sorted out.'

'How interesting,' repeated Rustem Bey, beginning to feel nervous and dubious about what he was about to do when he got to the other side. It was impossible to collect himself whilst enduring the boatman's disorientating verbal bombardment. Finally he leaned forward and asked, 'If I pay you twice the fee we agreed, would you be quiet for the rest of the trip?'

It was useless, however, for after a few moments' silence he was told a story about a Greek who ate a lethal herb, which expanded in his stomach so greatly that ultimately he exploded and died, although apparently not before bidding a philosophical farewell to his relatives, and dictating a will in which he forgave his wife for serving him the lethal herb, since it had been a genuine accident, but even so the wife committed suicide because of the remorse.

As soon as they had scrambled up the ladder to the quay on the other side, Rustem Bey and his servants found themselves besieged by a ragged horde of street urchins. Some fifteen smutty-faced and snotty-nosed gypsy children swooped upon them like a flock of jackdaws upon a carcase, clamouring for coins or for errands to run. Rustem Bey kept his hands firmly upon his purse and, through the thicket of waving hands, searched for one face that looked open and honest. Finally he pointed: 'You,' he said.

The appointed child, a twelve-year-old boy with a confident air and a rent in his shirt that was pulled together with a zigzag of string, led them away from the harbour. Rustem addressed his servants: 'Keep your eyes open. Keep your hands on your knives. Don't look nervous. Puff out your chests. Walk slowly. Look people in the eye but don't hold their gaze too long. Don't smile.'

Rustem Bey himself kept his left hand upon the inlaid hilt of one of the pistols that he had placed conspicuously in his sash, and with the forefinger of his right hand he smoothed his moustache, as if in thought. Thus he overlaid his inner anxiety with a thick carapace of outer calm.

They entered the lowly streets of Galata. The respectable Muslims of Scutari, on the other side of the water, used to like to whisper in prurient and self-righteous tones that in Galata there lived the worst kinds of Greeks. Here there were pimps and whores, card-sharps, confidence tricksters, counterfeiters, cutpurses and pickpockets, one-legged blind alcoholics, opium addicts, unemployable sailors, abortionists, charlatans, fortune tellers, sexual deviants, poison-makers, false prophets, beggars with sham disabilities, prodigal sons and dissolute daughters, deserters, contract murderers, illegal distillers, foul-mouthed sluts, footpads, procurers, tax officials and thieves.

The boy led the three men through streets so squalid that Rustem Bey once more felt impelled to pour lemon cologne upon his handkerchief and walk with it held to his nose. Emaciated dogs squabbled with naked infants and pigs over heaps of rubbish, offal and excrement. Prostitutes, filthy, flaunting and inebriated, howled and catcalled from the doorways and balconies. Tattered chickens with bleeding rumps scratched in the gutters. A dead cat lay swelling on the cobbles, circled by crows. Rats preened their whiskers in the cornerways. Shutters and doors sagged from their rotting frames on broken hinges, roofs patched with packing case and cardboard caved gently in upon their beams, and dead-eyed drunks swerved along the straitened alleyways or slept stupefied in the gutters, their mouths working soundlessly, their chins flecked with spittle. 'At least,' thought Rustem Bey, 'there is no one here who will have to endure the pains and troubles of growing old,' but it was so grim that he found himself thinking that there was nothing to do with such a place, except burn it to the ground and start again. He gave thanks to God that it had not been his destiny to live in such a hell of desperation, filth and iniquity, but it did not yet strike him as paradoxical that he had come here in order to seek his happiness.

33

The Circassian Mistress (3)

The gypsy boy led them down a tight alleyway, and pointed wordlessly to a doorway that was partially sunken below the level of the stones outside. Rustem Bey looked at the building, and noticed that although the walls were particoloured, and pocked with what appeared to be bullet holes, it was in better condition than those that neighboured it. A musky odour seemed to emanate from it, and from within there came the cheerful sound of someone plucking an oud. He heard the laughter of a young woman, and the tinkle of something brassy being dropped to the floor.

Wordlessly, the boy held out a grubby hand, palm upward, and Rustem Bey pressed a coin into it. 'Stay here,' he said, 'I will need you to guide us back.'

On the door was a knocker in the shape of a small hand holding a ball, and he raised it on its hinge with some trepidation. Back home only the Armenians had door knockers, and having to use one gave him the same kind of misgivings that one might have upon mounting a horse for the first time.

The grille opened, and a pair of dark eyes peered out, heavily made up with kohl. 'Who is it?' demanded a curiously strangulated voice. 'I'm very busy just now, and I can't go wasting my time.'

'I have come about . . . something,' said Rustem Bey, his cheeks colouring.

'Everyone comes about something, my aga. What might this little something be?'

Rustem had the distinct impression that he was being teased. 'I was recommended to come to you by one of the attendants in the hamam. He said I was sure to find . . . what I was after.'

'Oh, those hamam boys, they're just so mischievous,' said the voice, and the eyes rolled theatrically, framed as they were by the grille. 'The things I could tell you! Still, I don't know what we'd do without them.' The eyes examined him for a moment, and then the strange voice said, 'Oh well, I suppose you look like a reasonably decent proposition. You wouldn't believe the dreadful riff-raff we get turning up here sometimes. You'd better come in.'

The bolt was drawn back, and Rustem Bey told his servants and the gypsy boy to stay where they were. Down the steps he went, holding on to his new fez so that it was not knocked off by the lintel, and found himself in a surprisingly well-appointed room whose walls were hung with heavily made carpets of no mean manufacture. Oil lamps fixed to the walls spilled a dim, reddened light, and in the centre of the floor stood an ornate brass brazier which gave off the scent of charcoal and olibanum. The floor was thick underfoot with kilims laid across each other more or less at random, and cushions and low divans lay about the floor in a kind of ordered abandon. A large and ornate narghile stood by the brazier, with four tubes inserted into its bowl.

Rustem Bey removed his boots and placed them carefully by the steps, alongside three small pairs of Moroccan slippers, and one pair that seemed absolutely enormous.

This latter pair belonged without doubt to the creature who stood before him. This epicene person was stupendously tall and thin, and was garbed in richly embroidered robes of green and crimson, and an oversized white turban pinned at the front with an enamelled golden brooch in the form of a peacock. The face was pale but heavily rouged, and the thin lips were painted bright scarlet, in such a way as to make them seem fuller than they were. The eyebrows were plucked, and just at the point of showing stubble where they were beginning to regrow. What struck Rustem Bey particularly was a very large and prominent Adam's apple that seemed quite out of place in one whose every care was quite clearly to manifest and emphasise the trappings of femininity.

'Do sit down,' she said, 'I shall just nip inside and alert the girls. They'll be so excited, I can't tell you. Mind you, they always are.'

179

When she returned she stood for a moment looking at her guest, with her hands folded and her lips pursed. Then she produced a pouch from the folds of her robes and bent down to fill the bowl of the narghile, saying, 'I expect you'd like a smoke, wouldn't you? It's quite a trip on those horrid boats, and as for these streets, well, horrid's not the word, is it? I don't know how I bring myself to live here, I really don't. I used to be in Scutari, but the local people, what prigs! Honestly, it was impossible. They'd be banging on the shutters, throwing stones, they were such animals. And I'll tell you something else, those very same people banging and throwing stones in daylight were the ones who came back at night hoping for a dip into one of my girls. The hypocrisy! It makes you sick. At least the scum around here know that that's what they are, so that's a good thing, isn't it? I do hope you're not a hypocrite, my aga, because if you are, I can't be doing with you.'

Rustem Bey was much disconcerted by this bizarre and garrulous stranger. He was used to a stiff and carefully patterned formality in his dealings, and always felt uncomfortable to find that there were other worlds than his. He fumbled in the pockets of his Stamboul frock coat, and found the amber mouthpiece that he carried with him. He inserted it into one of the tubes, and sucked as, with a pair of small tongs, his host held a glowing coal to the bowl of tobacco. 'Well, that's something,' she said, 'a real gentleman always brings his own mouthpiece. You'll be surprised at the number of slovens who turn up here and expect us to let them slobber on ours. Makes you sick, it really does. I like to call myself "Kardelen", by the way. It's such a pretty little flower, and I was born right at the end of winter, and when you see them peeping out you always know that spring's not too far off.' She added, 'Where I come from, anyway.'

'It is indeed a lovely name, Kardelen Hanım,' agreed Rustem Bey, who had never seen a snowdrop in his life, and had not a clue as to what she was talking about. He puffed on the pipe, and detected a taste that was unfamiliar, but not unpleasant. His head began to swim a little, and he blinked his eyes.

One wall of this room was a false one, and behind the hanging carpets three young women, stifling their giggles, listened, whispered excitedly and watched through three strategically placed holes.

Kardelen threw herself with some dramatic skill down on to a divan, and smiled playfully at Rustem Bey. 'Tell me about yourself. You are rich, I hope. I never allow my girls to be taken into poverty. Their welfare is always uppermost in my mind, you know. One gets so fond of them, they become like one's own daughters, and it would break my heart, it so much would, if any of them ended up in the gutter, or in a brothel, God help us.'

'I have a very large amount of land,' Rustem Bey told her, embarrassed by the reference to brothels, 'I have many servants, and I employ a considerable number of people in my town.' He paused and added, 'I have a great number of clocks.'

'And where would your town be, my aga?'

'Beyond Smyrna. The nearest large town is Telmessos, but my town is large enough. We have everything. It is very peaceful.'

'Not too peaceful, I hope. None of my girls cope with boredom, you know. Too much peace can be so tedious, don't you think? Absolute peace is altogether too much like death, in my opinion.'

'It's a town like any other. It's very old, it's mainly on a hillside, we have a river below in the valley, and the sea is just over the hill. Let me see. There is a beautiful pine forest that you ride through when you approach it, and we Muslims bury our dead among the trees. It's a nice thing to see those whitewashed graves among the trees. When you see them you feel you have at last come home.'

Kardelen shuddered archly. 'Oh no, don't. Please let's not talk about graves. It makes me feel so . . . so mortal. What else is there, apart from graves?'

Rustem Bey struggled to think. 'Well, we have lots of Christians, you know, the Greek kind, but they're quite harmless, and most of them don't even speak Greek, and we have some Jews doing the usual things that Jews do, and we have some Armenians – the apothecary is Armenian – and we have nomads at harvest time, and all the pedlars who go to Telmessos come to us too. We have a fine mosque.' Here Rustem Bey hesitated. 'I have sworn an oath that if I find a good woman here, I will build another mosque.'

'Forgive me,' said Kardelen, delicately, 'but it strikes me as surprising that you don't have a wife. I mean, a man in your position . . .'

'I have a wife,' said Rustem, 'but I have put her aside. She was a slut.'

'My aga, a good slut is not to be sniffed at,' said Kardelen, and before Rustem Bey could think about this, she asked, 'You are divorced?'

'No, but I have put her aside.'

'And your family have found you no one else?'

'My family are all dead. It was the fever that comes back with the haj.' At this moment a young black woman appeared as if from nowhere with a tray upon which there were two small glasses of coffee. She placed it on the low table between them, and vanished just as neatly as she had arrived.

'Oh yes,' observed Kardelen drily, 'God reaps a goodly harvest from the haj. Every year He looks around paradise and finds literally thousands of new recruits, all in green turbans. So becoming.'

'Who was that?' asked Rustem Bey, ignoring Kardelen's last remark, and tossing his chin in the direction that the girl had taken.

'One of my girls. So, tell me, what exactly have you come here for?'

Rustem Bey flushed, reached for his glass of coffee and, avoiding Kardelen's gaze, said, 'I have heard very good things of Circassian women.'

The black girl behind the carpet pouted and whispered, 'He won't want me then. Damn, he's so sweet!'

'He's too serious!' whispered the Arab girl with the merry face. 'You need a man who laughs.'

'But he's so lovely,' whispered the ebony girl with the satin skin. 'I could go all night with him! Every night, believe me!' She rolled her eyes and puffed out her cheeks.

The two other girls put their hands to their mouths and pretended to be shocked. 'You're such a little fitchet,' said the one with porcelain skin and long black hair, 'you'd probably make him die of exhaustion.'

The black girl put her finger to her lips, and they nudged each other and stifled their laughter as they continued to eavesdrop.

'Circassian women,' repeated Kardelen. 'Round faces, pale as the moon. I suppose you know that story about why so many women wear the veil? It's rather droll.'

'I might have heard it,' replied Rustem Bey, 'but it escapes my memory.'

'Oh, it's such fun!' Kardelen leaned forward, as if imparting a confidence. 'The story is that when the capital was still at Bursa there was a positive invasion of Circassians because those Russians, dreadful people, such rapists and drunks, were persecuting Muslims again, and anyway they all arrived in Bursa seeking sanctuary, and the women were so beautiful that all the local men fell in love with them, and every night there were such brawls and arguments and murders because of the men squabbling over the beautiful Circassians! So one day the Sultan, I forget which one, they're all equally mad, summons the leader of the Circassians, and says to him, "You've got to tell your women to cover up their faces, because they're so beautiful that there isn't any peace around here any more." So the leader tells the women to cover up because the Sultan Padishah wants all the fighting to stop. So the women cover up, and then all the other women cover up too, and do you know why? It's out of vanity! It's because they want everyone to think that they're beautiful as well! So all the old hags start to wander about in the market places pretending to be too beautiful to show their faces! It makes you laugh, it really does. Still, it has spared us from having to look at all the ugly women all this time, so some good came out of it after all. Where were we?'

Rustem Bey had listened to the end of this story with some unease, since he had had direct experience of what ugliness might be hidden beneath a veil, and was not sure what to say next. Finally he offered, 'I think I might have heard that story before, but I had forgotten it.'

('He's so solemn!' whispered the Arab girl behind the hanging carpet.)

Kardelen sipped her coffee coyly, and continued. 'Of course, there probably isn't one little iota of truth in it. The best stories are always lies, I find.'

(The white-skinned girl sighed, and whispered, 'I think he might be just what I need. He's so handsome! And gentle too!'

'You're so lucky,' whispered the black girl.

'If he chooses me.'

'He couldn't resist you,' said the Arab girl, 'nobody can.'

The fair one pulled a grimace. 'That last one was a nightmare. If he ever finds me, I'm going to kill myself.')

Kardelen sipped at her coffee again, adopted a confiding expression, and said, 'I do happen to have a Circassian girl.'

('Completely brazen!' whispered the black girl.)

'It's such a sad story too,' said Kardelen.

('Hark at this!' whispered the Arab.)

'Her father was a bandit, quite a notorious one, and you know what these Circassian bandits are like. They keep their sons and teach them to be brigands, and the daughters they give away to be brought up by someone else, and then they come back for them when they're ready to get married off. Well, in this case the bandit got killed by the gendarmes, and no one ever came back for poor little Leyla.'

('Leyla?' repeated the fair one. 'Is that what I've got to call myself?'

'Well, you can't call yourself Ioanna if you're going to be Circassian,' whispered the Arab.)

'Poor little Leyla!' continued Kardelen, emotionally. 'Fragrant as a rose, sweeter than the apples of Nevsehir! Intoxicating as the honey of Pontus!'

('Brilliant!' whispered the black girl.)

Rustem Bey began to feel even more strange, and wondered if there was something odd about the tobacco. He was experiencing a pleasant but disorientating light-headedness, a kind of unbalanced serenity. 'Might I see the young woman concerned?' he asked.

Kardelen leaned forward and touched his knee with her hand. 'If only you saw her naked . . .'

'Is such a thing possible?' asked Rustem Bey, much to his own surprise. He was abruptly overcome with such shame that he looked about the room, as if to check whether anybody else had been witness to it. Stronger than his shame, however, was his animal instinct, and stronger even than that was the common-sense determination that if he was going to disburse an enormous sum of money to this loquacious androgyne, he would make very sure that the goods were worth the expense.

Behind the hanging carpet, the fair one with the black hair cursed under her breath and whispered vehemently, 'God, I hate it when I have to do this! I never get enough warning!' She slipped away as silently as she could, and the other two girls exchanged glances of amused complicity.

'It so happens that Leyla likes to be naked when she's in her room,' said Kardelen, raising one eyebrow and shaking her head salaciously, 'and I happen to know where there's a little chink in the hangings.' She took Rustem Bey's hand, and he found that he was unable to resist her. It was as if he had been mesmerised into docility. He stumbled after her, still holding on to her bony fingers, and shortly afterwards found himself most uncomfortably bent double, peering into a poorly lit but richly furnished chamber through a knot-hole in the planking.

Inside, he beheld the marble-white form of a young naked woman, reclining on her cushions, apparently absorbed in combing out her long, shining black hair. Occasionally she puffed delicately on a very slim cigarette that she held to her lips by means of a small pair of ornate silver tongs. Languidly the young woman moved, and Rustem saw her round plump breasts, the gentle mound of her stomach (whose navel was embellished with a blood-red garnet set in silver), the graceful curve of her neck, and the sensual tapering of her thighs. Conquering his better inclinations, he tried to see what there was at the apex of her legs, but her pose and the shadows made it impossible. He felt short of breath. He had never seen his own wife Tamara as naked as this. He had never really seen her naked at all. He suddenly realised, with a sense of profound wonder, that he had never appreciated before how beautiful a woman was, and how strange and unlike anything else this beauty was. He found himself wondering with a pang whether Tamara had been beautiful like this. He was borne in upon by a disturbing sense of the sacred.

The young woman moved on to her belly in order to polish her nails, and Rustem took in the pert roundness of her backside and the quick contours of her back. He saw how small her feet were, and that she had a gold chain about one of her ankles, but most of all he saw how full of life she was, how much she seemed to glow with inner light, how little she was akin to the oxen-like women who worked in his field and drudged away their unavailing lives in Eskibahçe. He backed away from the wall and returned silently to the antechamber.

'Sit down,' said Kardelen, and Rustem Bey sat down. 'I have seen what I should not have seen,' he said, his voice weak and uncertain.

'You poor thing,' drawled Kardelen, her voice expressing both sympathy and sarcasm. She always found it very tiresome when people's niceties and scruples got in the way of pleasures or beauty, but she realised that Rustem Bey was in a state of some perplexity.

'As you can see,' said Kardelen, suddenly becoming businesslike, 'she is the ideal of beauty. Her face is slightly oval, her skin is very fine and white, her eyebrows are black and meet in the middle, her lips are very red and fresh. She is neither tall nor squat. Furthermore, she plays the oud very delightfully, and she sings. She makes coffee as well as any girl I have ever known. She is educated reasonably well, and I have myself taught her everything she could possibly need to know about how to please a man.'

Rustem Bey looked worried. 'She is a virgin?'

Kardelen smiled indulgently. 'Well, naturally she is a virgin, my aga. She is as virgin as the day she was born, and no one can be more virgin than that, not even Mary Mother of Jesus, may she rest in paradise. I have told her everything she needs to know, in very great detail, I may say, but she has had no direct experience of it.'

(Ioanna, soon to be renamed Leyla, but still naked, had by now rejoined the two girls who were observing these proceedings, and the Arabess put her hand to Leyla's ear and whispered, 'Guess what? You're a virgin again!'

Ioanna bit her lower lip and wagged her head. 'Again!' she exclaimed. 'Our dear Kardelen works so many miracles with chicken blood.')

'And how old is she?'

'She is fifteen years old, just at the very beginning of what will be a long period of beauty, in my estimation.'

('You've got young again!' whispered the Negress, her white teeth sparkling in her suppressed mirth.)

'And how much are you selling her for?' asked Rustem Bey.

Kardelen bridled visibly. 'She is not for sale. I sell nobody, and there have been no slaves in Istanbul for more than fifty years. You must know that, surely.'

'How do I . . . acquire her, then?' asked Rustem Bey.

'This is what happens,' said Kardelen. 'I take in these poor girls who are orphans, or fugitives, or whatever, and have no one to care for them. Clearly they have nothing of their own, and I am by no means rich, and so the poor things have no dowry, so marriage is difficult or out of the question, although not always impossible. When they reach the age of attractiveness I find men for them who are seeking another kind of arrangement, but I do it with the utmost care. My girls are such darlings, and I grow fond of them. We have a happy time here, and I don't like to let them go at all, to tell the truth, but naturally one needs the money.'

'The money?' repeated Rustem Bey.

'The money,' said Kardelen. 'The money is to recompense me for the time and toil that I have put into their education, their clothing, their feeding, and suchlike. Naturally the money must be sufficient for me to be able to begin again with a new girl.' Kardelen paused portentously, and then announced rather quickly, 'In the case of Leyla, who is exceptional, the recompense will have to be sixty thousand piastres.'

Rustem Bey winced. 'Do you have any other girls?'

'I have a fine young Abyssinian who was abducted from her master in Alexandria (not by me, I hasten to say) and abandoned in Adrianopolis, and I have a plump little Arabess from Lebanon, who is a complete sweetheart. Neither of them is Circassian, by any stretch of the imagination, since one is black and the other is golden.'

'Sixty thousand piastres is far more than I have come with,' said Rustem Bey, who by now had set his heart upon having the

Circassian, mainly because he thought he saw her slipping out of his grasp.

'If she likes you, I might drop the price,' said Kardelen. 'Perhaps you will excuse me for a few minutes.' She got up with great dignity and swept out of the room, as if disgusted by Rustem Bey's ungentlemanly stinginess.

Kardelen, Ioanna and the other two girls convened in the kitchen, and chattered excitedly to each other. 'What do you think?' asked Kardelen.

'He's gorgeous,' exclaimed the Negress, 'you're so lucky!'

'He is handsome,' agreed Ioanna, 'and his clothes are very smart. And his accent is so sweet and funny! Do they all talk like that in the south?'

'He must be quite rich,' said the Arabess, adding, 'Don't you think he looks sad, though?'

'The point is, do you think you would enjoy pleasing him?' asked Kardelen, and Ioanna smiled coyly. 'I think I would. For a while, anyway. You know me.'

'You mustn't run away again and get me into even more trouble,' said Kardelen, her voice full of mock reproach. 'I can't tell you what a horror it was having to move everything at such short notice. Twice! I could have killed you.'

'I was bored with him,' Ioanna excused herself, 'and he was mean, and he was a pig. At least I've earned you money twice over. The best thing about this one is that he comes from so far away that no one will ever find me.' She paused, and then a thought occurred to her. 'Do I really have to be Leyla? Don't you think he'll realise I'm a Greek?'

'He wouldn't know a real Circassian if one fell out of his back-side,' said Kardelen. 'They don't have any in the south, and anyway, you're not any old shitty Greek from a hole in the ground. You're practically Italian, darling. Come along, put your clothes on and make us some coffee.'

'And I get half the money?'

'Of course you do, sweetie, but I don't think I'll get sixty thousand, so don't expect too much.'

'What if I have to go in the mosque?' asked Ioanna, but Kardelen had already left. She re-entered the selamlık, her hips swaying perhaps a little too much, and folded her long limbs and bony ankles beneath her on the divan. Rustem Bey extracted his mouthpiece from the narghile, and put it back in his pocket. He was feeling even more light-headed, and a little sick. 'I can offer you thirty thousand piastres,' he said. Kardelen merely raised her eyebrows and smiled condescendingly.

'There are conditions,' said Kardelen.

'Conditions?'

'One: you cannot hire Leyla out to anyone else, and you cannot sell her or pass her on without her consent. If, after twelve years, she wants her freedom, you must grant it, and make provision for her. If she declines it, you must keep her as before. If you marry her, she must be the equal of any other wife, and if she has children they must be cared for as your own. And, by the way, thirty thousand piastres is quite out of the question. I might possibly consider fifty thousand.'

'How do you enforce these conditions?' asked Rustem Bey, genuinely puzzled.

'Enforce them? I only allow my girls to go to honourable men, and so I make them promise. You would have to promise. You are an honourable man?'

'Of course.'

'And do you promise?'

Rustem Bey felt confused. The strange tobacco and the heavy atmosphere of the room had fuddled his intellect. 'What were those conditions again?'

The gynandrous Kardelen repeated them, again adding, 'Do you promise?'

'I promise,' said Rustem Bey at last.

'Very well. Tomorrow you must return with fifty thousand piastres and a couple of hamals, and Leyla will be packed and ready, inshallah. Not that she's ever on time for anything, in my experience.'

Rustem Bey emerged into the polluted sunlight with his head thumping, and gripped himself hard across the temples between the thumb and forefinger of his right hand. He stood with his head bowed, screwing up his eyes. Finally he lifted his head, shook it as if to clear away its buzz of disconnected thoughts and impressions, and signalled his servants and guide to walk ahead. The suspicion occurred to him quite instanter that the somewhat intersexual Kardelen might have been a deviant man rather than a masculine woman, if indeed she was either, and he was brushed simultaneously by an uncomfortable intuition that the flow of his destiny had veered off course. He braced himself for whatever was to come, and took a caique back to Scutari, where he made his way to the Ayazma Mosque, to pray once more to the Deity whose unaccustomed aid he had so recently thought to enlist. As he touched his forehead to the prayer mat, he had the distinct impression that no one was listening, and when he emerged back into the meydan, he felt as though he had begun to inhabit a life other than his own.

34

Rustem Bey and Leyla Hanım

Rustem Bey sits smoking in the selamlık of his konak and listens to the clocks. He has collected so many of them, because this is a country where it is hard to think of things to buy, and this is how in any case the rich display their wealth. As time has passed, the clocks have surreptitiously synchronised their beat, and in quiet times, when the bustle of the town has ceased, or when the bulbuls have fallen silent, the steady tick of the clocks resounds through the almost empty house like the pulse of a great mechanical heart that registers succinctly the falling away of life. When the hours are struck, the house is filled with a strange but beautiful disharmony that is never twice the same. Tamara Hanım once asked the servants to switch off the chimes, and Rustem had found the silence so oppressive that he had got up in the middle of the night, lit an oil lamp, and gone round the rooms returning the levers to the chime.

Rustem Bey senses that his life has been taken off course, but he does not care. Despite his better judgement, he finds every-thing about Leyla refreshing and enchanting, and he regrets only that his own manner is too formal to match her own exuber-ance and *savoir vivre*. At this moment she is in the haremlık, happily ordering the servants to put this there, take that away, move this a little. She is delighted with the bed that Tamara rejected, and it has been reassembled and polished with walnut oil scented with oil of lavender. She lolls on its thickly stuffed mattress, eating loukoúmi and combing her hair, and when he tells her that she's lazy, she adopts an arch expression, laughs, and says, 'Me? I'm not lazy, I'm just passionate about leisure.'

He recalls his arrival back at Kardelen's residence, as agreed, accompanied by his servants and two particularly gigantic hamals, to find the narrow alleyway crammed and heaped with Leyla's possessions. There are carpets, bulging boxes of clothes whose lids are unfastenable, sacks of shoes, slippers and parasols. He wonders how she has managed to accumulate so much. Whilst Leyla is busy, Kardelen takes him aside and tells him very seriously, 'Now, you mustn't mind me saying this, but you won't get anywhere with Leyla if you try to hurry her. Let her come to you in her own time, and she will be the best mistress in the world, I promise you. If you force things . . .' and here Kardelen shudders theatrically and rolls her eyes, '. . . well, it'll be a disaster. Remember she's a virgin, and she's a mistress, not a wife, so don't treat her like one. I trust you know what I mean? A wife is a cross between a slave and a brood mare, but a mistress is the smell of a rose that comes in through the shutters on a summer night. Think of her as semi-divine.' Kardelen flutters her hands, as if in intimation of divinity. She pauses, and enquires, 'Do you know what is the most difficult thing in the world?'

Rustem Bey scratches the side of his nose, and replies, 'Stalking a pigeon.'

Kardelen looks at him as if he has gone mad, and the aga explains, 'They always see you, and they always fly off.'

'I see,' says Kardelen, curling her lip. 'I suppose I wouldn't know about such . . . country matters.' She pauses for rhetorical effect, and says, 'The hardest thing in the world is to learn how to become irresistible to a woman, so that you don't have to force the issue, if you take my meaning. Do you want my advice?'

'I feel that you are going to give it,' says Rustem drily.

'Indeed I am. You should simply accept as an inevitable fact that Leyla will come to adore you and will give herself to you sooner or later. It's a question of faith.'

'Faith?'

'Oh yes, faith moves women like nothing else.'

It is true that he has been wondering how to approach this delicate issue. He has not been able to sleep because of remembering her nakedness, and longing to see it again. His throat aches from desire, and alarming and unprecedented tingles travel through his body. He imagines making love to her, and wonders how such a thing can come about. He is not by nature a violator, and he feels a mild relief that effectively Leyla's body is to be left in Leyla's gift, but he also feels a mild irritation that he has come so far, spent so much money, and done so much, only to achieve a bargain with no guarantee. He resents it that this freakish creature can give him advice with so much natural authority, when she is so much below him in the order of the world. He does not know that Kardelen has sternly warned Leyla not to delay too long in delivering her favours, '. . . or there'll be another fiasco, you can be sure of it, and I'm not going to bale you out again. And don't forget the little bottle.'

On top of the pile of Leyla's belongings there is a large wicker birdcage containing not a bird, but a cat. 'What's this?' demands Rustem Bey.

'It's a cat,' says Leyla.

'I reckoned on no cat,' says Rustem Bey.

'This is Pamuk. This is my cat.'

'I reckoned on no cat,' repeats Rustem Bey. He has never liked cats and has never seen the point of them. Their yeowling and fighting at night causes almost as much sleeplessness as the nightingales. 'I have a tame partridge,' adds Rustem Bey.

'We'll keep them separate,' says Leyla, brightly.

Kardelen intervenes. 'She wouldn't be happy without the cat.' She raises her eyebrows and nods significantly. She seems to be telling Rustem Bey that the resentment of being without the cat will cause her to be especially reluctant to bestow her favours. He looks at the animal. It is a white angora, with a fluffy tail that is thin at the base. It has one yellow eye and one blue eye, and it is plainly indignant. It objects to Rustem Bey looking at it, and it opens its mouth and hisses. Rustem Bey feels insulted. 'I don't like cats,' he says. Nonetheless, he has lost the argument.

The clocks chime, and Rustem Bey remembers how they got to the quayside and were just about to get into the boat, when suddenly Leyla panics. 'I've forgotten my medicine!' she cries. 'My medicine! We've got to go back! We've got to go back!'

'Medicine? You are ill? What medicine?'

'My medicine, Kardelen Hanım's got my medicine!'

'We can get more medicine,' says Rustem Bey, who is anxious to get on with the journey.

'No! No! No!' wails Leyla. 'I've got to have my medicine!'

193

She begins to show alarming signs of hysteria, and her tears are irresistible.

It is useless to try to placate her or put her off. Two servants are dispatched back to Kardelen's house, and return shortly with a small brown bottle that is corked and sealed with wax. Rustem Bey inspects it, shakes it, looks at it against the light. It is a dark, viscous liquid. He hands it to Leyla, whose face is white with anxiety. She takes it. 'What is your illness?' demands Rustem Bey. He is not pleased to have acquired a woman who might be sick. Women have an infinite capacity for lying around groaning. She looks up at him, and recognises the command in his voice. She looks away and says, 'It is a woman's matter. It's nothing. It passes.'

'A woman's matter,' he repeats, and shrugs. His mother and sisters were always referring in hushed tones to 'women's matters'. He knows that further enquiry will be fruitless. It is as forbidden to know about women's matters as it is to go into the hamam when the women are in it. He remembers himself and his friends as little boys, speculating salaciously about what it might be like to be able to see a whole hamam full of naked women. If only one could have drilled a little hole in the wall.

Rustem Bey remembers their journey back to Smyrna on a small Italian boat, she keeping to the women's quarters, and he to the men's. He has not been able to face another train journey like the last, and has preferred a slower journey in greater comfort. In the daytime they sit awkwardly side by side on the deck. He makes phatic observations about the weather and the state of the sea, and points to places on shore that might be this town or another. In Smyrna they shop for fabrics, for draughts and potions, cosmetics and liniments and lotions, for things that she insists she must have, and of most of which he has never heard. He buys her a string of gold coins to wear about her forehead, and she is so pleased and grateful that she touches his face with her hand. He loves it when she speaks, because her accent is endearing. She likes his accent too, but wishes he were less grave.

They hear how the young Greek men in this city are out of the control of their elders, are getting overbold and impudent, knocking the fezzes off the heads of respectable old men, jerking at the veils of pious women and, in their infidel script, daubing slogans on walls about Greater Greece. Rustem Bey grows angry, sucks harder on his cigarette, and asks, 'Why doesn't the governor execute a few more of them? What good can come of it?' But this is a city where most of the population are Greek, it is they who have the money and the influence, and they get away with everything. He has to admit to himself that Smyrna is also a city that is much more amusing than his own little town. Its Levantine exuberance always raises his morale. He loves the busy harbour lined with ships from places with unimaginably romantic names like Buenos Aires and Liverpool, and he admires the majestic houses of the merchants that overlook them. He likes the way that the Greek women, their eyes made up heavily with kohl, sit still by their shutters so that they can keep a watch on life while being admired. He likes the way that some of the men of the Greek lowlife shave their heads except for a long pigtail at the nape. Smyrna, he thinks, is a place where one might have an ambition to live. He cannot conceive of anyone becoming lonely or bored in Smyrna.

'You can't do anything about Greeks,' says Leyla, apropos of nothing in particular, and smiling ironically to herself.

Rustem Bey visits the gunsmith, Abdul Chrysostomos. He wants powder and birdshot for his fowling piece, and has to resist the gunsmith's attempts to interest him in his new invention, a bolt-action rifle with a ten-foot barrel that fires a bullet like a small cannon shell, and is uncannily accurate at an extraordinary range. It has a spring-loaded magazine that holds ten bullets, and it is too heavy to lift. When Rustem Bey says, 'I have no ambition to shoot elephants and camels from a great distance,' tears of genuine sadness come unbidden to Abdul's eyes. It is bitter to be a genius and yet to be so frequently rejected. It is not two years since he has invented a concave mirror that focuses the sun's rays into a spot so hot that it can burn a wooden ship off the water, and has informed the Sultan by means of a letter written with the aid of a street-scribe. The War Minister's secretary has finally written to him advising him that the Padishah's armed forces currently have no use for such a device, at least not until the focus is adjustable. Two years is a long time to wait, when one is only to be disappointed. Nonetheless, he is already working out how to adjust the mirror, and his mind is awhirl with systems of levers and fulcra, and the street-scribes are writing to all and sundry in order to enquire as to whether there is any such thing as flexible silvered glass.

Rustem Bey and Leyla stay in the Turkish quarter, because the aga feels more at home there and the food is better. In the Greek quarter they cook things too long, and they don't know how to use spices. Rustem Bey finds a place where they can eat together in a private room, and to their mutual relief they discover that they are both garlic lovers. They ask the proprietor of the lokanta to lace everything with it. 'Everything?' asks the patron, and he brings a jug of water with a clove floating on top. Leyla puts her hand to her mouth and laughs, and in a moment Rustem Bey too has overcome his natural solemnity. Leyla says, 'One day I am going to make you a meal which has so much garlic in it that it will cause a shortage in the whole vilayet.' Afterwards, somewhat afflated, they go to his customary accommodation, a small khan with a courtyard shaded by figs and planted with rosemary and roses. The rooms are bare and swept meticulously clean, so that no one will pick up bedbugs or fleas. Leyla is in the women's quarters with her rancorous cat, and Rustem Bey is in the company of the men. He watches Leyla from the balcony as she supervises the toilet of her cat among the flower beds, encouraging it and showering it with endearments. The scene is touching, and she is unaware of being observed. Later he asks her, 'Why do you talk to your cat in Greek?'

Leyla is momentarily dumbfounded. 'Do I?' she asks.

'Yes. I heard you in the courtyard.'

She looks around, as if for a means of escape. 'Greek is the language of cats,' says Leyla at last.

'On the contrary,' replies Rustem Bey, 'Turkish is the language of cats. I have heard of a cat that could say "granny" and "grandmother".'

'Why would it say that?'

'I don't know. Perhaps somebody taught it.'

They look at each other in silence, and then he says, 'I didn't know you could speak Greek.'

'Everyone can speak Greek,' replies Leyla. The colour is rising to her cheeks, and trouble appears in her dark eyes.

'Can they? In my town even the Greeks speak Turkish.'

'Greek is the universal language of these parts.'

'I thought it was Italian.'

'Do you speak Italian?'

'No.'

'Well,' she says, 'I can speak some Italian too.' She has the air of having trumped him, and whilst he is considering this information, she wanders away to the balcony and leans over. It is not until a long while later that he realises that she still has not told him why she can speak Greek.

The journey home is hardly a pleasure. There are other men in the caravan, who ride donkeys whilst their women walk behind them, or who ride camels whilst their women ride donkeys behind them, but Rustem Bey knows without further thought that Leyla will never walk for several days in the wake of an animal, and will not be content with a donkey. It is odd how trepidatious he feels with respect to her. He worries about her reactions, her discomforts and pleasures, in a way that he never would have done with Tamara, who was only his wife. He hires a small and pretty camel for her, and a large one for himself. For her luggage he is obliged to hire several donkeys and a drover.

Despite the trouble taken for her comfort, Leyla is refractory for the entire journey. Lurching and swaying about on the top of a camel for several days is hardly her idea of luxury, even though she enjoys the feeling of superiority that comes from being mounted on an animal. The sun is implacable and oppressive, despite her parasol, and it is awful to have to spend so much time sitting upright when her natural propensity is for the horizontal. She has forgotten to buy mastika, so instead she chews toasted melon seeds irascibly, and spits the husks out on to the hot road. She has the town dweller's horror of peasants, those who subsist on a starvation diet of cracked wheat, yogurt and outlandish fatalism, whom now she encounters with disturbing frequency, their gnarled hands and nut-brown faces betokening the grinding labour that she finds impossible to contemplate without horror. Except for those moments when she is suddenly struck by the majesty of the Taurus Mountains, she successfully maintains a bad temper for the whole journey, as does the cat Pamuk, who is affronted and appalled by the entire experience, hissing at shepherd mastiffs from the safety of the birdcage that has been lashed behind Leyla's perch.

Near Eskibahçe, or Paleoperiboli as it was called by the Greeks, Rustem Bey points out that for some reason all the poppies have come up pink, a piece of information that Leyla receives with absolute lack of interest. Here the road dips suddenly down into the calm and scented slopes of a pine wood, and at the precise moment that one enters it, one feels a sensation of peace, and of the earth's sanctity. One's donkey's feet tread softly upon pine needles instead of stones, the sunlight is broken up into dapples and the birds sing.

Because of its great tranquillity, this is the place where the Muslims bury their dead, in whitewashed tombs scattered about among the trees. Rustem Bey turns about on his camel, resting his right hand on its croup, and says to Leyla, 'This is where we will lie when we are dead.'

She looks at the pretty graves, the old ones subsiding and slipping at abandoned angles, the new ones upright and pristine, painted with a turban for the men and a tulip for the women, and she feels a pang. She has never bothered much about her faith. She was born a Christian, something that she must henceforth conceal, but she knows nothing about it, and her beliefs have never consisted of anything more than the usual superstitions. Like Kardelen and her fellow odalisques, she is sure that religion has nothing at all to do with life. She finds priests and imams equally otiose. Now, however, she feels an inexplicable dread of being buried among Muslims, which she quickly dismisses from her mind, thinking, 'I'm not dead yet,' and, 'Who knows what will happen in the end?' She wonders how long she will be able to keep up the pretence of being a Circassian and a Muslim. She glances over at Rustem Bey, and a small flower of affection begins to open up inside her. She also feels a twinge of fear. She knows that one day she will want to please him.

At the further end of the Elysian pine wood, there lie the ruins of a temple that once was sacred to Leto, Artemis and Apollo.

No one knows this now, except for the British archaeologists who came twenty years before with sailors and dragomen, waving a firman from the governor that no one could read, and took away the statues and carvings in wooden crates. What remains of the marble temple has sunk on account of earthquakes, and now it is thigh-deep in clear green water, in which terrapins and frogs lead oblivious lives. Above it there flit swallows and maroon- and crimson-coloured damselflies. Rustem Bey and Leyla see Mohammed the Leech Gatherer, in his grubby turban, dripping wet, standing nearby on a sheet that he has spread upon the stiff grasses. Leyla gasps and cries out in alarm, because, adhering to his bare legs like the fur of a faun, are dozens of glistening, sparkling black leeches. Mohammed raises his hand in greeting, and calls, 'Salaam aleikum.' He will wait until the leeches have gorged themselves on his blood, and have dropped off on to the sheet. He will keep them wrapped in damp cloth, and when he has enough he will take them for sale to the Greek doctors in Smyrna. Karatavuk and Mehmetçik are bending down at the water's edge, filling their birdwhistles with water. Drosoula and Philothei, holding hands, are watching. Philothei smiles at Leyla, who seems to her to be the most wonderfully beautiful woman she has ever seen, and Leyla's heart melts.

Beyond the temple and the remains of the Roman theatre, one comes out suddenly beneath the town, and there it is, rising up the hillside in an intimate jumble of homes and alleyways. Leyla sees the houses, painted gaily in pinks and blues, she sees the white minarets of the mosque and the golden dome of the Church of St Nicholas, she hears the cries of the vendors and artisans, and she feels happy. She is back where she belongs, amid the softness of civilisation.

That evening, when they have eaten, and are reclining on opposite divans, except for Pamuk who is hiding beneath the low table, she tells Rustem Bey, 'I am going to need a servant.'

'I have a great many servants,' observes the aga reasonably.

'I mean my own servant, a maid. I would like a girl who is very pretty and young. I need someone who is pretty, otherwise my eyes will be in a bad mood all the time.' She pops a piece of rose-scented lokum into her mouth, chews it, swallows, and says, 'Do you remember that little girl who was by the water? Not the ugly one. The very pretty one? That's the one I want.'

Rustem Bey looks at her, and she smiles back, her beauty glowing around her face like a nimbus. He says, 'The ugly one and the pretty one are always together. I have been wondering if they are sisters.' He pauses. 'We have an Armenian here. His name is Levon. He has three very pretty daughters, but they are older, so they might be more useful than the child.' It occurs to him all over again that to have a mistress is not an inexpensive thing.

'No,' says Leyla, 'I want the pretty child.'

On the far side of the town, Father Kristoforos has dozed off after his meal, and now he wakes suddenly and shakes his head. He has had another one of his disturbing dreams about witnessing the funeral of God, except that this time the angels are dumb, and the coffin is so minute that it would scarcely hold a babe.

In the aga's konak the clocks in synchrony tick away the time.

In the half-light of the brothel Tamara weeps silently as she cradles in her arms the hundred-fathered syphilitic child to which she has just given birth. The disease has ravaged the empire ever since the introduction of compulsory military service, and the child is white-faced and distorted. Its eye sockets are empty, and it scarcely breathes. On one side of her sits a divorcee, and on the other a widow, both of them driven into the profession by poverty. The widow has been a prostitute for a long time, and she says, 'Don't worry, sister, it can't live.'

Tamara's face runs with fresh tears, she feels as if her heart will burst, and the divorcee puts her arm around her, and says, 'Don't worry, sister, sooner or later you stop conceiving at all.'

35

I am Philothei (7)

I have told no one about this, apart from Drosoula and Leyla Hanım.

My mother had been making reçel, and I was a little sick from eating so much of it. She used more grapes than most people, and extra sugar, and I'd put a lot of it on to bread, because that day there was new baking, and that's why I was queasy.

I went outside to breathe away the sickness and it was getting dark, and it was just about to rain so that everyone else had gone indoors and was wondering whether or not it was dark enough to warrant lighting the lamps, and the nightingales were starting to sing, and there were only cats in the street, when suddenly Ibrahim arrived at my side, and I was very surprised, and he said, 'Quick, let me kiss your hand,' and I said, 'It's got jam on it,' and so he looked swiftly to all sides, and then he took my hand and licked the jam from my fingers with his tongue, and afterwards I was trembling and I wasn't normal for hours, and I couldn't wash my hands because I couldn't bear to wash away the traces of his tongue.

36

A Cure for Toothache

It was after dark, and most of the town was asleep. Father Kristoforos was adrift in his dreams, in which he was conversing with the Archangel Gabriel, who was refusing to show his face. 'If I show you my face, you will die,' asseverated the archangel. 'The light will burn you up completely and you will arrive in paradise in flakes of ash,' whereupon Kristoforos pleaded, 'Just one glimpse, just the smallest glimpse!'

'I will show you one feather of my wing,' said the archangel, and in his dreaming Kristoforos saw a vast white feather, stretching as far as all possible horizons, filling up the entire heaven, and glowing like the autumn moon.

As Father Kristoforos lay stupefied in holy wonder, the drunken Constantinos walked unsurely through the alleyways of the Armenian quarter, trying to make the most of the minimal light of the oil lamps whose residual glow seeped out of the chinks of the shutters. Some of the time he ran his hands along the walls of the houses so that he could be sure of keeping to the way, and every now and then he would come up against the slumbering form of a dog or a donkey, so that he and the animal concerned would recoil with alarm. The town's cats yeowled their threats and love songs on walls and roofs, and from the almond trees the operatic nightingales and bulbuls projected into the night their medleys of arias and cantatas. Far off, Leyla Hanım's clear voice could be heard, as she plucked at her oud and sang to Rustem Bey the night's last lullaby, which was in reality addressed to the child she wished she had, and which she sang in Greek.

Constantinos was not so intoxicated as to be infirm of purpose, or incapable of finding the house for which he searched. He knew that it had a brass door knocker in the shape of a hand holding a ball, and he was therefore very carefully running his hands over each door in order to find the knocker and see what shape it was. The style of door knocker was quite common, and so he was looking for the third one on the right-hand side of this particular alleyway.

When he found it he dropped his head forward and rested it on the door, as if reflecting on his mission, or perhaps wearily summoning up his resources. He sighed, breathed heavily once or twice, and then knocked. He heard the sound echo in the room behind, and put his ear to the wooden planks of the door in order to be able to hear the approach of a servant.

Somehow the servant approached quite noiselessly, however, and Constantinos suffered the embarrassment of having the door opened when he was still crouching with his ear to it. He almost lost his balance, and sprang upright with the exaggerated alert-ness of the drunk who is trying to appear otherwise.

The servant was bearing an oil lamp in one hand, and he stood there with a dim yellow glow casting his face into shadows. He held out the lamp to shed light upon the visitor's face, and then withdrew it again. 'Yes?' he said.

'I have come to see the Armenian,' said Constantinos, with some effort.

'Come back in the morning. The master has gone to bed, and the house is closed.'

'I can't come back. Not in the light. I must see him.'

'It's impossible.'

'Please ask him.'

The servant was impressed by the urgency of the request, which had been expressed in a tone of voice that was halfway between pleading and desperation, and he was hesitating in the doorway, when Levon himself, dressed for the night, appeared at his shoulder. 'What's going on?' he demanded. 'Who is knocking so late at night?'

'It's a townsman,' said the servant, and Constantinos stepped forward and said, 'It's me. I must speak with you.'

Levon started when he saw his erstwhile attacker, and stepped back. 'I have no wish to speak to you. I must ask you to leave.'

Constantinos ignored the request, asking, 'Are you all right? Are you much injured?'

'I have trouble in breathing, and a great deal of pain. I don't know why you think you can come here like this, after what you have done. In your position one would surely be ashamed.'

Constantinos cast his eyes down and conceded, 'I am ashamed.' He paused, looked up, and said, 'I know you are not a traitor. I know you are not the things I said.'

'I have given your wife medicines at cost price,' said Levon stiffly, 'because of your poverty. Look how you repaid me.'

'I know, I know, efendi.'

'It's very late. Are you drunk again?'

'Of course I am drunk. I have come here because I am always drunk.'

'To make yourself ridiculous is one thing,' said Levon contemptuously, 'but to allow yourself to stoop to violence is another.'

'I am drunk because I am always drunk,' said Constantinos, marshalling his thoughts.

'So everyone sees,' said Levon.

'And I am always drunk because I am always drinking.'

'Evidently.'

'And I am always drinking because of the teeth.'

'The teeth?'

'Yes, efendi. Because of the teeth.'

'I am sorry, I don't follow.'

Constantinos tapped the side of his mouth with his hand. 'My teeth,' he said. 'I have such pain, such terrible pain. It goes on all day and all night. It has been a torment all my life. I have never known peace for more than an hour. It was all because of my teeth.'

Levon thought that he almost heard a sob of self-pity in his interlocutor's voice, and was suddenly struck by how much one's understanding of people can be amiss. 'Toothache,' he reflected, 'the universal torture of all mankind. How sweet life would be without it.'

'I have often thought of death,' continued Constantinos, 'but it would be a sin.'

'And that is why you drink?'

Constantinos nodded slowly and miserably, and Levon added, 'You drink to dull the pain?'

'That's why I am drunk. That's why I live in poverty and that's why my wife and daughter hate me, and that's why everybody despises me.'

'Why have you done nothing about it? Why have you never explained yourself?'

'I am a man. A man endures pain, and doesn't complain.'

'You should have your teeth pulled. Don't you know which tooth it is?'

'The pain fills all my head, and it goes into my ears and down into my throat. I don't know which one it is. It could be all of them for all I know. I can't eat, and so I get drunk quicker, and a tooth-puller costs money. When the tooth-puller comes he asks to be paid before the teeth are pulled, and he sees that I am drunk and he knows that I have no money. What am I supposed to do?'

'There is no one more heartless than a drawtooth,' said the Armenian. 'Have you tried opium? I sell it, and it's very effective.'

'I have no money.'

'Just as well, perhaps. Some get addicted to it, and finally they go crazy. The lunatic asylums are full of them. Sometimes I refuse to sell it to certain people; I say I don't have any left, though I would be a lot richer if I was less scrupulous.'

'Does this man have to be standing here?' asked Constantinos, nodding in the direction of the servant. 'Does he have to listen to all of this? Don't I have enough to bear?'

'If he goes, he will have to give me the light, and then he won't have a light to find his way back to his pallet. If he takes the light with him, then we two will be talking in the dark.'

'I don't follow,' said Constantinos. 'I would probably follow if I wasn't pissed.'

'Anyway,' said the merchant, 'I will do you a favour, even though you don't deserve it.'

'A favour?'

'A favour, yes. I will pay for your teeth to be pulled.'

'You'll give me money? After my misdeed?' Constantinos was incredulous.

'No, I won't give you money, because you'll only drink it. What I will do is send a servant for you next time the drawtooth comes from Telmessos. I will pay him directly, and he will pull the rotten teeth. Then you will have less pain, and perhaps you will not need to drink so much.'

Constantinos raised his face, and affected a pitiful tone of voice. 'Have you got a drink, Levon Efendi? A little glass of raki? I am beginning to need one.'

'Stay here,' said the Armenian, and he took the lamp from his servant and disappeared into the house.

'If I was him,' confided the servant, in his master's absence, 'I'd have your throat cut.'

'Well, you can just fuck off,' replied Constantinos. 'If I could see you, I'd knock your head off.'

'Pisshead,' said the servant contemptuously.

Oblivious to this uncouth exchange, Levon returned bearing a half-bottle of amber liquid. It had foreign writing on it, in Roman script, and there was a picture of a bird on the label that looked somewhat like a partridge. He handed it to Constantinos, who inspected it suspiciously, swaying on his feet as he tried to concentrate. 'Is it alcohol?'

'Yes. It's called Scotch, and in the absence of a drawtooth, it's the best possible treatment for toothache.'

'Better than raki?'

'Well, I think so. If you use it correctly it can kill a toothache for a couple of days. I get it in Smyrna, and it's very precious. It comes from a place called Scotland, which is a Frankish country somewhere a very long way in the north.' Levon gestured in a vaguely northerly direction. 'It's so far north that it's exceedingly cold. I've heard it said that in Scotland you can sometimes go hunting by just picking the birds out of the branches, because their feet freeze to the twigs at night, and they say that the people are marvellously hairy, so that they can keep warm, and the women have an extra breast under each arm. They make this drink as a cure for toothache and many other ills.'

'Extra breasts? That's quite something.' Constantinos opened the bottle and sniffed it. 'Smells good.'

'What you have to do is take a sip, and swill the stuff back and forth through your teeth. It might hurt quite a lot at first. Then you keep the stuff in your mouth, swilling it back and forth, back and forth, for as long as you possibly can, and you keep doing it until you find that you have to speak to someone, and so you have to swallow it.'

Constantinos took a mouthful and did as he was advised, watched with interest by the master and servant. There was an initial rush of lancinating pain, and he grimaced and winced, but then he began to feel the working of the panacea. He waved the bottle at Levon and pointed to it with his other hand, as if poking at it appreciatively. He tried to grunt, but Levon said, 'Don't speak. Just keep swilling.'

'Nggggggg,' said Constantinos.

'I hope you can find your way home,' said Levon. 'I'm going to bed. I wish you a very good night.'

'Ngggggg,' repeated Constantinos, sucking the whisky through his teeth, and waving the bottle to signal his farewells.

The servant closed the door, and said, 'If I were you, master, I'd have his throat cut.'

Levon demurred, 'No doubt you would, but really he's just another unfortunate. The raki will kill him soon enough, whether his teeth are cured or not, and that'll be another poor useless nobody under the earth, with no one to regret him. I doubt if any of those Greeks will even dig his bones up to wash them.'

As they proceeded back into the house, Levon shook his head and said, 'There's altogether too much affliction in this world. And I have just given away a most precious bottle of medicine that's as rare as a feathered goat. I must be mad.'

37

Mustafa Kemal (8)

Mustafa Kemal decides to follow his own precepts, and gets out of politics. He will be a soldier, *tout court*. He joins the Training Command of the 3rd Army, and initially antagonises the old-fashioned types with his newfangled ideas and his trenchant criticisms, but he impresses his pupils by his lucid teaching, and his unnatural ability to arrive fresh and early each morning, despite his long nocturnal bouts of crapulence. Adjutant Major Mustafa Kemal is scornful of anyone above his own rank.

The Germans are donating their military expertise to the Ottomans, and Mustafa Kemal neither likes nor trusts them. He does, however, think that they are wonderful soldiers, and he sets out to learn as much from them as he can. He translates a military manual by General Litzman, and he impresses Marshal von der Goltz when the latter comes to supervise an exercise for which Kemal has devised the general scheme. He conducts more and more exercises, with himself in charge. On exercises where he is not in charge, he prepares his own plans and orders, and then compares them to the ones actually used. During debriefs he is unstinting in his criticisms, and pernickety about details.

He is still vexatious to his superiors, and they put him in charge of a regiment in the hope that the great theoretician will make a fool of himself in practice. During an Albanian uprising Kemal draws up a plan for the capture of a crucial pass, and it is taken without the loss of one soldier. The uprising is crushed. At the celebratory dinner in Salonika, Mustafa Kemal prophesies that one day there will be a Turkish, not an Ottoman army, and that it will save the nation. He tells Colonel von Anderten that the Turkish army will not have done its duty until it has also saved Turkey from its own backwardness.

Mustafa Kemal goes to Paris with a military delegation, and before he goes he buys himself a hat and a suit that he thinks are Western. When he arrives, his friend Fethi meets him at the station, and mocks him delightedly because the hat is too jaunty and the suit is green. Mustafa Kemal and Fethi go out to buy him another suit that Parisians might take seriously. During the military discussions, when he is in uniform, Kemal makes himself conspicuous by vociferously advocating his own plans during the manoeuvres, and a French officer tells him that no matter how brilliant he is, no one will take him seriously as long as he wears a kalpak on his head. One day, when he is dictator of Turkey, the kalpak will go the way of the turban and the fez, Mustafa Kemal having become the only dictator in the history of the world with a profound grasp of the semiotics of headwear.

Back in Salonika, Kemal becomes disillusioned and depressed. There has been no promotion and there seems to be no future. He tells a friend that he is resigning his commission, but after an encouraging drinking bout at the White Tower, he changes his mind.

He also seems to have changed his mind about staying out of politics. He has become frustrated, and when out drinking likes to tell his friends of the government offices to which he will one day appoint them. Fethi, who is Kemal's putative roaming ambassador, starts to tease him by calling him 'Mustafa Kemal, the drunken Sultan'.

Mustafa Kemal is frustrated because he knows that he is destined for greatness, but does not see how it will come about. He is not in charge of the revolution, and his fellow revolutionaries are bar-room theoreticians, talkers and dreamers. They operate within gratifyingly elaborate systems of secrecy, a world of passwords and arcane oaths, and they devote much of their time to conspiring against each other. Mustafa Kemal wants things to be clear and direct, he wants specific goals to be set, and he wants unerring action to be taken in achieving them. Mustafa Kemal wants to reform the whole political system, and he has clearly understood, as his future career will demonstrate, exactly what Rousseau meant when he said that a people must be forced to be free.

Mustafa Kemal has to conceal his agnosticism from his respectably Muslim co-conspirators, but everyone knows of it, just as they know of his promiscuity and his bibulousness.

Nonetheless, there are those who incline towards Kemal's ideas; Islam is gradually being replaced by Turkish nationalism, and the argument is going to be about the nature of this nationalism. There is in Salonika a revolutionary professor who bears upon his forehead the romantic cruciform scars of a failed suicide, who animadverts that Turks should revert to their pre-Islamic ways, but Mustafa Kemal is of the opinion that Turkey should become a modern Western state. Gradually he is finding people who agree with him, and the authorities are becoming suspicious again. They transfer him from his regimental command, and install him at the office of the general staff in Istanbul, where they can keep a close eye on him.

Fate intervenes in the form of the imperial Western powers, which are at the height of their weening self-confidence. They are generously bringing Western civilisation to the unenlightened lesser breeds, whether the latter wish it or not, and with the notable omission of the democratic institutions that are precisely what make Western civilisation worth having. Germany seizes Agadir, whereupon the French become indignant, and it is ultimately agreed with the Germans that France shall have Morocco, and Germany shall have some of the Congo. The Italians, piqued at not having been invited to the party, seize Cyrenaica and Tripolitania, which are, inconveniently, but pertinently to the progress of Mustafa Kemal, Ottoman possessions.

Accordingly, the empire has to go to war, and the handsome, romantic, but unintellectual Enver Pasha is duly dispatched to Tripoli with a dashing contingent of officers. Mustafa Kemal does not really care about North Africa, since Turks do not live there, and in any case the Balkans are a far more present danger, but he seizes the chance to attain a little glory, and, disguised as a journalist, bearing false papers, off he sails on a Russian ship, accompanied by the poetic Ömer Naci. Also with him, much to his irritation, comes Yakup Cemil, his former would-be assassin. He has had to raise the money for the journey all by himself.

Whilst he is in Libya, his native town, his beloved Salonika, is taken by the Greeks, and he will never see it again. The Greeks demolish the mosques one by one, and those Turks who have the means to do so contrive to leave. The great fire of 1917 will further obliterate the town of his youth, and the remnants of the Turks will be forcibly deported at the end of this story, during the catastrophic events of 1923. For the moment the ancient colony of Spanish-speaking Hebrews are permitted to remain, only to disappear twenty years later, when the Nazis in their turn will have taken Salonika from the Greeks.

38

Exiled in Cephalonia, Drosoula Remembers Leyla and Philothei

Well, as I've always said, you have your mother's prettiness, God rest her soul, but do you want to know how to be beautiful, koritsimou? No, no, don't pretend to modesty you don't have. I've seen you preening yourself often enough. 'Make the most of it' is what I say; make the most of it whilst you're young and you've still got it. You can't be pretty for ever, you know that? But you can always be beautiful. At least, that's what Leyla Hanım said to me and Philothei.

You must excuse an old woman her memories, and who am I to talk about beauty after all, but we women have secrets and a duty to pass them on, don't you think? I'm too far gone to be beautiful, I always was, unlike most, but I can tell you what Leyla Hanım said to Philothei and me.

Let me see, it was not long after Yusuf the Tall murdered his daughter and was taken away by the gendarmes, and Sadettin left for the mountains. Everyone was still talking about it. I was standing with Philothei by the pool with the ruins in it, and who should pass by but Rustem Bey on a camel, and a small caravan of donkeys. Just behind him on a pert little camel was a woman. She was very pretty – the woman that is, not the camel – and there was something about her that made the corners of your mouth lift when you saw her. You could tell she had a good heart. She had a veil of course, she came from a town, you see, but it was so thin that she may as well not have bothered. It was just a little bit of gauze. More to do with encouraging temptation than preventing it. Anyway, she had the kind of eyebrows that arch over in a very nice curve and just about meet in the middle. She had dark eyes that sparkled, and they were made up with kohl. People used kohl very heavily in those days, at least in those parts. God knows what was going on back then, here in Cephalonia; I expect you were all still in the caves. Apart from your father, of course; he was still at sea, learning to be a doctor from those books of his, no doubt. No, he would have been a little boy. He's the same age as me! How stupid I'm becoming! What was I talking about? Oh yes, Leyla Hanım. Her lips were very red. I remember she had lovely clothes, they were everyone's envy, and she wore gold, lots of it, so that she rattled in a dull sort of way every time she moved. She had a chain of gold coins that she wore around her forehead, the kind that you used to borrow from your relatives when you got married.

Anyway, she spotted Philothei as she passed into the town for the first time, standing by the sunken temple, and she and Philothei smiled at each other. I remember it well, because it was as if those two recognised something in each other. The curse of beauty, or the blessing of it, I suppose, and she asked Rustem Bey if she could have her as a maid, which is why Rustem Bey sent a servant to call in on Charitos. Well, we all heard that Polyxeni kicked up a fuss, not least from Polyxeni herself, saying things like, 'I'm not sending my little girl to be the servant of a rich man's whore, and an infidel into the bargain,' but the fact is that you didn't refuse a request from the aga back in those days. It wasn't that Rustem Bey was a bad man. Most people respected him, and a lot of people liked him, but it's just that you don't refuse the man who owns all the land as far as you can walk in every direction, and who everyone depends on. Charitos said something like, 'She isn't a whore, she's a mistress,' though I don't suppose that Polyxeni saw any difference, and pointed out that the aga was offering a good sum for Philothei's hire. It wasn't as if he was trying to abduct Philothei or anything, and so Polyxeni had to give in. I'm sure that Polyxeni wasn't averse to the money either, though she wouldn't have said so, and anyway, as everyone knows, the servants of a rich man find ways of sneaking nice things out of the house, and that's one of the attractions of being a servant. It's like being a wife who's happy to serve her husband a meal and stand behind him humbly whilst he's eating it, because unbeknownst to him she's eaten all the best bits in the kitchen when she was preparing it. Leyla Hanım once told me that there were two kinds of wives, the stupid ones, and the ones who ate the best bits in the kitchen. She used to say lots of things like that. She once said that if you were lazy, the only way not to get bored was to work hard at it.

We were just little girls, and we didn't know anything about anything, so it didn't occur to me that I wasn't supposed to go along with Philothei when she reported for work at the aga's konak. We went around to the back door and took off our shoes, and just went in. In those days Ibrahim was already following Philothei, and Gerasimos was following me, we were still young enough for it to be innocent, you see, and we had to leave them outside. Sometimes they would wait for hours together, drawing in the sand with a stick, or trying to catch crickets, but as far as I know they never said a word to each other. Isn't that odd? They weren't like Karatavuk and Mehmetçik who spent all their time pretending to be birds and getting up to mischief. I suppose it was because they were there for us rather than for each other.

What I remember about the aga's house is that it was full of clocks that ticked together, but chimed out of tune with each other. Some of them were very beautiful and complicated. The walls were hung with very nice carpets, most of them red, and there were red carpets on the floor too. The place smelled of tobacco smoke, frankincense and rosewater. It was dark but very calm and peaceful; you wouldn't have believed that so much drama had happened there, what with the business of the aga's unfaithful wife, and all his family dying at once of the fever that comes back from the haj.

We were wondering what to do, just standing there inside the door, when Leyla Hanım herself came out of the haremlık, and when she saw us she gave a little cry of delight. In her hand she had an amazingly long cigarette holder, it was as long as your arm, and in the end was smouldering one of those tiny slim cigarettes that she used to roll for herself. I think the idea was that you don't get yellow stains on your hair or your hands. She kissed Philothei on the cheeks, and then she leaned back and looked down on me. 'I never expected two of you,' she said. I think she must have seen the look in my face, and I'll always remember this as a demonstration of her good heart, because suddenly she leaned down, took my face in her hands, and kissed me on the cheeks as well, ugly and unwanted as I was. Her lips were so soft, and she smelled of something that made your head reel as if you'd been drinking wine. In retrospect I can quite see why Rustem Bey besought her.

She took each of us by the hand, and led us into the haremlık to show us round. She was the first person in that town to have a bed, and we girls were enormously impressed by it. It's the bed that I remember the most. Once the news spread, of course, it wasn't very long before all sorts of people started to think that they wanted a bed too. We slept just as well on a bedroll on the floor, though. At least with a bedroll you just roll it up in the daytime, and that makes more space, doesn't it? It's because of all these beds that people want big houses nowadays. Most of us had houses that were one room up and one room down, and in the winter you had your animals downstairs so that the heat came up. It was lovely and warm, and the smell wasn't as bad as you'd think. Sometimes it was quite nice, in fact. Only meat-eaters' dung smells bad.

Anyway, Leyla Hanım said something in a foreign language, and we just stood there dumbly and looked back at her. Then she said, 'I thought you people were Greek.' We didn't know what she was getting at, and we felt uneasy, and then she said, 'Doesn't anybody speak Greek?' Philothei said, 'Daskalos Leonidas does. He tries to teach it to the boys. And Father Kristoforos, he does.'

'What a shame,' said Leyla Hanım. 'I'd been looking forward to speaking Greek.' She looked quite wistful. Then she said to Philothei, 'Do you know why I've hired you, little one?'

Philothei didn't know she'd been hired. Why should she know anything? She just knew that from then on she was going to be with Leyla Hanım for much of the time. She shook her head, and Leyla Hanım said, 'It's because you're so pretty. Having you about the place will make me feel . . . lighter. And I don't mind if you bring your little friend sometimes, but I don't think Rustem Bey will pay anything.' She laughed, and added, 'You can only get so much out of a man, even a good one.'

Now, I don't remember Philothei having to do anything in particular whilst she was Leyla Hanım's servant. They went together to the hamam on ladies' afternoons, and they would both come out so exhausted they could hardly walk from the steaming and pummelling you got in there, and their faces would be glowing like lamps. It was lovely in the hamam. It was only a small one, but it was about five hundred years old, and it looked like a tiny little mosque, with white walls and a dome and everything, and when you got inside you poured water over yourself from a brass dish, and you just sat and sweated in the steam room until it was your turn to get scrubbed and battered by the masseuses. In the old days it was shiny black ugly eunuchs from Ethiopia, so they said. I'll never forget, they used to fill a muslin bag with olive-oil soap suds, and blow in it till it frothed, and waft the bag up and down you. It was lovely. And then they'd scrub you with a mitt made of that rough string. You wouldn't believe how much filthy skin got sloughed off. Anyway, it was a lovely place to go, and all the women could just sit around naked, huffing and puffing in the heat, laughing and gossiping, knowing that no one's husband was ever going to come in and ask for his dinner. I'll tell you something else. The older women used to go in there to select the nicest young girls to be wives for their sons. Don't laugh! It's true! They'd look out for nice round breasts and thighs, a decent bit of fat, and hips big enough for babies, and they'd get an idea of what the girl was like, because there's nothing like being in a hamam with no clothes on for getting to know someone, and I'll tell you something else, just between you and me, and that is that when a girl took a fancy to any boy in particular she'd make a special point of fussing over the mother in the hamam. I know several cases where it worked like a charm.

Anyway, Leyla Hanım used to go to the hamam with Philothei, and even though some of the women wouldn't talk to Leyla because they said she was a whore, Leyla never noticed or took offence because she always had Philothei to laugh with.

I've forgotten what it was I was telling you about. Oh yes, it was about being beautiful. Anyway, one day we had all come back from the hamam, all glowing and scented with rosewater, feeling on top of the world, and we were back in Leyla's haremlık, and she was brushing Philothei's hair to get out the tangles. Suddenly she asked, 'Do you think I'm beautiful?'

It was a surprising question, but Philothei said straight away, 'Oh yes.'

'Truly beautiful?'

'Truly, truly, truly,' said Philothei, who was sitting on her knee. You see, Philothei and Leyla loved each other, I am sure of that, and if you love someone they become beautiful, even if they aren't. And Leyla Hanım leaned forward and whispered, 'Well, I'll tell you a secret.' She put her finger to her lips and made a conspirator's face.

'What, what, what?' chanted Philothei. 'What secret?'

'Promise you won't tell anyone?'

'Promise.'

She looked at me. 'Do you promise too?'

'Promise,' I said.

'Promise by the Beard of the Prophet and the Hem of the Virgin's Gown?'

'Promise!'

'All right,' she said, 'my secret is that I'm not really beautiful at all.' She looked at us a bit wryly and waited for a response. We just sat there open-mouthed, because it wasn't true, but anyway, we half believed her just because she'd said it, and we couldn't understand how we'd been wrong. You can tell children almost anything and they'll take it seriously.

'My real secret is that the secret of being beautiful is to make people believe that you are, until you believe in it yourself, and then it becomes true.' She saw that we didn't understand, and she smiled to herself. 'I'll tell you about being a beautiful woman.

'The first thing is that being beautiful is like having a job. You know, if you're a man you can be a peasant, or an apothecary, or a soldier. If you're a woman you can be a mother or a servant or something, but you can also be beautiful. If you're beautiful it's better than working, even if you have to work at it, because you can always get what you want sooner or later. It's like having money, except more fun, because having a job is work, and being beautiful is a game.

'And it's more than money. It's a weapon. What's a weapon for, unless it's for getting what you want? If a beautiful woman smiles at a man, it's like giving him a gift, it's a reward, you can make

217

him happy for a whole day. If a beautiful woman scowls at a man, it's like a stab in the heart. You can make him miserable for a whole day. What a power that is! That's where the pleasure is! A man becomes a prince or a leper, just depending on how you look at him. It's true! And there's another thing . . .' She leaned and whispered something in Philothei's ear, and then they both looked at me and giggled. Afterwards I asked Philothei what it was, and she refused to tell me. I kept asking her right up to the time we left Anatolia altogether, and she still never told me, so I still don't know what it was. She just said, 'It's better if you don't know, honestly. Anyway, it's not important, and if it was, I'd probably tell you, except that Leyla Hanım made me promise not to, and anyway it wouldn't do you any good, so I'd better not.' So it's always remained a mystery, even though I nagged and nagged and nagged, and sometimes I still wonder what it was.

Leyla Hanım said, 'I'll tell you some bad things about being beautiful. You know, if you're beautiful it's easy to forget other people. It's probably like being rich, or being the Sultan. There's always someone else who wants to know you, and so no one ever matters very much, so you tend to lose even the ones you're fond of. And another thing is, that if you're beautiful, you always have to be suspicious. If Rustem Bey says that he loves me, how do I know that it isn't because he wants to avail himself? Sometimes you wonder why people are being nice to you, and sometimes you know that your beauty is the reason that some people want to be horrible to you. People think that they want to know you, but really they are fascinated by a mask.' Leyla ran her fingernails over her face. 'You know what? If I tore the skin off my face to the thickness of a piece of paper, I would be the ugliest and most horrible thing in the world, and everyone who used to think they wanted to know me would put their hands over their eyes and run away.' Philothei and I felt a bit sick after she said this. We were both wide-eyed with horror at the thought of Leyla Hanım's face being flayed. 'If you are beautiful,' added Leyla, 'you never know how real is the friendliness of your friends. You have to keep testing them, and then sometimes you go too far, and that way you lose them. It's a kind of loneliness that you never escape, but if you don't want anyone to know you, to know you as you really are, then beauty is the perfect protection. You get solitude. Freedom.

'I am going to tell you things that you don't need to know,' said Leyla, 'because you two will grow up and get married and be ordinary people, faithful little wives. But when you're old, and you remember me, I want you to understand a little bit about who I was, because I want you to remember me as something better than what people might be saying.

'You know, when a man wins a beautiful woman, to begin with he feels very proud and pleased with himself. But then he feels scared that he is going to lose her, and he gets jealous. It's so pathetic! You don't know whether to laugh or cry, despise him or be pleased! And sometimes *he* gets cantankerous, and sometimes he tries to spoil you to keep you sweet. And, between you and me, if he doesn't spoil you quite enough, you start to get annoyed. And if you're beautiful, and . . . and . . . well, if you're the kind of woman I am, then you can have any man you want, more or less, so every time you try to find a man who's better than the last. It makes you fickle. Sometimes I think that I won't be content until I know I've found someone who's better than me, someone who makes me feel more beautiful every day just because he's mine. Rustem Bey . . . who knows . . . perhaps . . .' Leyla fell silent for a short time, and then she smiled and said, 'You know, if you let yourself get ugly on the inside, then you get ugly on the outside too. The beauty doesn't last. If you don't try and keep your spirit beautiful, it soon starts to show, and people won't want you any more.

'But it's not all bad! Who wants to be beautiful?' She raised a finger, and so did Philothei. I hesitated, and then raised my finger too. 'Ah, beauty,' she said, smiling and shaking her head, 'it's like opium, it's an addiction, you've got to have more and more of it, it's like a great heat in the heart that expands and expands and expands and fills you up – like having a sun inside. I just want to get more and more and more beautiful all the time, and I want everything around me to get more beautiful. I'm beauty's slave. Really.'

I suppose that we girls might have been looking a bit mysti-fied – did I tell you that she had a slightly strange accent when she spoke, and that it made her seem even more exotic, like a princess? – and so she turned towards the mirror and put Philothei beside her. There wasn't room for three faces side by side in the mirror, so I just stood at the side and watched. 'I don't let Rustem Bey see me in the morning, and I don't go out at all, until I've made sure that I'm beautiful,' she said. 'I've got to do the magic so that no one but me ever knows that really I'm not beautiful at all, apart from you two girls. Do you want to see the magic?'

We did, as you can imagine.

'Well, you just sit quietly in front of the mirror, and you concentrate very hard, and you just look and look at yourself until you're sure that you're beautiful again, and getting more and more beautiful. Philothei and I'll do it first, and then you can change places with Philothei, Drosoulakimou.' It was the first time that anyone had ever called me that, and it wasn't till years later that I remembered it and realised that it was Greek. Where she got that bit of Greek from, I can't imagine. One of the curious things about her was that she was always looking for someone to speak Greek to. She tried most of the women in the hamam, but really she might just as well have asked it of a cow.

Anyway, she and Philothei sat side by side gazing at themselves in the mirror. It was fascinating to watch. They went into a sort of hypnosis. Philothei was breathing so hard with concentration that I could see her nostrils flaring a little with every breath. Her cheeks flushed and her eyes got blacker and brighter. Her lips got a little redder. The same sort of thing was happening with Leyla Hanım. They were both just sitting there, sort of composing their faces, willing them to get more lovely, absolutely mesmerised by whatever it was that they were doing. I felt a definite chill of fear running up and down my back, but I couldn't break away in case it disturbed them. It was a kind of magic, as Leyla Hanım said. I bet you that if the Holy Patriarch in Constantinople found out about it, or even Father Arsenios, he'd try to forbid it.

They must have gazed at themselves for a good half-hour. You know, I think that that time, and all the times afterwards that they did it together, they were making use of each other, borrowing each other's power. How can I explain it? It's as if two beautiful people side by side doing that in the mirror, doing that magic, end up with the beauty of four people rather than two. It's the mathematics of angels. What I do know is that from then on Philothei's beauty almost got out of control and started to make for difficulties. Maybe I'll tell you about that another time.

Anyway, at the end, they sighed at the same moment, and shook their heads, as if to come back to the world. I couldn't possibly put my finger on the precise reasons, but they both looked more beautiful than they had before, and I'm not making that up. It's true, and I saw it myself, not just then, but many more times too. Maybe you should try it, even though you're probably too pretty for your own good already.

Did I try it? Well, Leyla Hanım asked me to come to the mirror, but I was ashamed, and I shook my head. Later on I went down to the pool at the sunken temple, where Mohammed the Leech Gatherer used to catch his leeches, and I knelt down to study myself in the water. We didn't have a mirror at home, thank God, because of our poverty, and anyway, I didn't want anyone to see me. Gerasimos wasn't there, or I wouldn't have tried it, I know.

Well, I took one look at that great ugly moonface looking back out at me, and I knew straight away that it was hopeless.

39

The Seduction of Rustem Bey

Rustem Bey had been placed in an invidious position. The promises extracted from him by Kardelen, and the conditions imposed, were quite unreasonable, and before long he was beginning to feel that he had been put upon. He had expended much time, parted with a very large sum of money, had been generous and patient afterwards, and as yet had enjoyed no embraces from his mistress at all. It was as if he were looking after a very expensive sister. If it were not for the fact that he felt obscurely that everything was as it should be, he would have become much more irritated than he did. He was not the kind of man who could have brought himself to impose upon a reluctant subject, a solution that would have cut the Gordian knot (but left him afterwards with a perpetually resentful woman), and so he knew that his alternatives were either to wait, or to repudiate. He appreciated that she was not like a wife, whose lot is simply to cooperate and resign, and he had grown fond of her too, so, despite many moments when he contemplated sending her back to Istanbul, he lay awake each night listening to the bulbuls, his imagination and his loins burning, steeling himself to be perseverant. In any case, he felt a distinct pleasure in having her in the house, and he often reminded himself that he was happier than he had been before, even though it had become remarkably less easy to accumulate wealth. Unlike Tamara Hanım, Leyla had an unending list of expensive requirements of which Rustem Bey had never previously heard. She had brought about a small boom in trade for everyone from Levon the Armenian Apothecary to Ali the Snowbringer to Iskander the Potter. On the other hand, unlike Tamara, who had often had the air of a cowed and frightened rabbit, she brought a certain joy to the house, with her oud music, her laughter and her pleasure in appetite. Rustem Bey had even grown fond of her obstreperous cat, Pamuk, who had fortunately shown no interest at all in his pet partridge.

Leyla watched Rustem Bey carefully, knowing that she could not afford to keep him waiting too long. It gave her a kind of teasing pleasure to do so, however, and besides, she felt that she had the right, even though she would not have been able to say precisely why. She was a woman with a strong sense of right timing, and she was herself waiting with longing and impatience. When she lay with him she wanted it to be natural and whole-hearted, because she had had enough of struggle and pretence in that past which Rustem Bey must never know.

One night in midsummer, just before the time when many of the populace move out of town and up into the mountain pastures, she found that she could not sleep. The clocks kept her awake instead of soothing her, and the nightingales' battles of song cut the air into jagged slices instead of smoothing it out. She had woken from a dream in which she had been making love to Rustem Bey among the graves of the Muslims in the pine woods, and she was sweating, agitated and lubricious. She rose from her bed and went to the window, throwing open the shutters even though the common wisdom was that it was the night air of summer that caused malaria. She leaned on the sill and looked out. Everything was divided sharply between eerie silver light and blackest shadow. She saw the dim yellow glow of Daskalos Leonidas's olive-oil lamp as he wrote through the small hours. A cat yeowled and a couple of dogs barked point-lessly. She felt her belly stirring, thinking that she had never known such peace and contentment in her life. She wondered whether she still missed Kardelen and the girls, wondered what had become of them in the time since she had left, and decided that she did not miss them at all. They were as part of another life. 'This is where I am,' she thought. 'This funny little place that is nowhere at all, is where I am.' With her fingers she smoothed her hair back so that it rested momentarily behind her ears, and she shook her head in a kind of bewilderment at herself. She was an impostor in half a dozen ways, and yet it seemed that God had smiled.

Leyla left her room softly and, with her hand against the wall, found her way to the room where her master lay sleeping. She hesitated a moment in the doorway, trying to locate herself in the semi-darkness, and then she approached the form that slept upon the low divan.

But Rustem Bey was not asleep at all, for the same reasons as had kept his mistress wakeful. He heard her come to the door, smelled the scent of musk and rosewater that always preceded her, and pretended to be asleep. He knew that there was about to be some sort of enchantment and, although his heart knocked in his chest, he lay absolutely still.

Leyla knelt down beside his divan, and her hair lightly brushed his cheek. He felt her very gently laying the side of her face against his. Her soft breath played across his ear. He could both hear it and feel it. She held herself there motionless, and suddenly he felt something very hot and wet slide from her face on to his. She had shed a tear that ran down his cheek and into the corner of his mouth. He tasted that wondrous alien salt on his tongue. 'Why is she crying?' he thought, even though he seemed to know the reason intuitively. She lifted her head and he felt the back of her hand delicately stroking his temple. 'My lion,' she whispered, 'my lion, my beautiful lion, my strong and beautiful lion.' The words were like a spell, binding him to be the thing she named. She bent forward once more and kissed him softly on the temple. Her lips were warm and lingering.

Leyla sat back on her haunches, and then was gone. Rustem Bey remained absolutely still for a moment, and then thought of following her, but knew instinctively that it would have been a mistake. He turned on to his back and thought about her sweet accent whispering 'My lion, my lion, my beautiful lion, my strong and beautiful lion'. Happiness awoke in his bowels and spread outwards down his legs, up into his lungs and into his throat. Tears prickled in his eyes, but he suppressed them. For some reason Tamara came into his mind and a small sadness and bitterness flowered where wonder and gratitude had been, but then his thoughts turned back to the mysterious and vibrant creature that he had all but bought and almost won. Once again, his life appeared to his inward eye to be a road at a forking of the ways, and he knew that there was a destiny that he had chosen himself, but which took away his choice. 'Master and slave,' he thought, without quite knowing why, 'master and slave.'

Outside, the bulbuls and nightingales dissected the night with their swords of song, and in his cluttered room, by the light of a stinking wick, Daskalos Leonidas wrote his endless vehement screeds about Freedom and the Great Idea, and Greater Greece, one more propagandist for a war that was yet to come, whose atrocity and wastefulness, like so many others, he would fail to foresee.

A woman wailed somewhere out in the streets, and those who were awake shuddered. There had been a time when everyone had believed that the wailing woman was a ghost, but eventually it had transpired that it was just someone who had lost all her sons in the wars that the imperilled empire had been fighting year upon year. So many conscripted sons had been lost that at night the town consented to let the maddened woman wail for all of them. These days there were not enough men to bring in the harvest or build the houses, there were not enough men to make bridegrooms, no one to make the music for the weddings, no one to father the babies for sacrifice in future wars.

In the morning Leyla came to life with an energy that no one who knew her would have believed possible. She had much to do. Before she forgot it, she made sure that Kardelen's small brown bottle of chicken blood was safely to hand, so that at the opportune moment she could reclaim her virginity to Rustem Bey's satisfaction. Him she told that she was preparing a special treat for the evening, and that he should stay away from the kitchens, the haremlik and the inner court. 'There was never a man so treated in his own house,' he thought, unable to believe how tractable he had become under her tutelage, but he could tell from her happy and conspiratorial mien that it was to his profit to indulge her. He mounted his horse and went to inspect some of his lands to the west. Leyla sent Philothei out with an urgent message to all the children of the town, offering rewards, and causing Karatavuk and Mehmetçik, Ibrahim, Gerasimos and Drosoula to spend a day in the heat of the hillside, scared of the Dog as they were, becoming more and more grubby, scratched and parched as they searched amid the stony maquis and filled their sacks. Leyla sent out the servants to bully the town's traders into selling her their entire stock of candles, and to smallholders for their bulbs of garlic, sending others to raid the vegetable plots of Rustem Bey's own land.

Leyla took over the kitchen, causing some initial disgruntlement to the cook. This amiable and portly fellow was a native of the vilayet of Bolu, the area by Lake Abant where marvellous chefs spring up like mushrooms, only to be enticed away by the rich. Rustem Bey's cook had done his ten years of apprenticeship and had earned his sash and his silver watch, and it is doubtful if there was another cook as good as him in the whole of the south-west. He had long been won over by Leyla's unbounded enthusiasm for his cuisine, however, and like so many others, he had also fallen for her vivaciousness and charm, and so it was with surprising ease that she won him over to her plan, the creation of a magnificent feast of the flavour that she and Rustem Bey loved the best. It was to be an orgy of garlic. Leyla took two aubergines and charred them over the brazier, leaving them until they became soft enough to mash up with lemon juice, garlic and olive oil. She boiled potatoes until they were utterly soft, and mashed them up with the same ingredients, adding the olive oil drip by drip. She made cacik with mint and yogurt, garlic and cucumber. She prepared humus so that the chickpeas would provide an aphrodisiac, and she mixed a marvellous and exotic drink of camel's milk with honey, cinnamon, nutmeg and cardamom, with the same aim in mind. She made a paste of yellow lentils, in order that happiness and laughter should come into the house. The cook took cubes of lamb, made a small slot in each, and hid a small clove of garlic in every one. He browned them over a quick flame and then simmered them at almost indiscernible heat for the whole day, in a ratatouille of parsley, tomatoes, onions and pepper. He would add the remaining flavours at the last minute so that they would be full in the mouth. He made Smyrna meatballs and Adana kebabs. In honour of Leyla he created Circassian chicken, rich with tarragon, cloves, paprika, walnuts, garlic and walnut oil. He laid it out on a great flat dish so that it would be as white and round and lovely as the face of the Circassian maid that she purported to be.

All morning they laboured, filling the street outside with odours that caused a knot of beggars to congregate, and passers-by to salivate with envy. Then Leyla went to the hamam in order to steam every grain of dirt from her skin. She lolled, oblivious in the stifling humidity, chewing mastika to sweeten her breath, calculating and weighing all the lovely and poetic things that she would say once she was in her master's arms. Her stomach contracted with nervousness and often she closed her eyes and forced herself to be calm. It was not as if she was in *terra incognita*, but this time she wanted it all to be as perfect as God and providence might allow. When finally she emerged, she had quietened the doubts and quelled the anxieties. She foresaw the success of the night so clearly and strongly that she could no longer doubt it. Nevertheless, she bought a tama depicting a woman, and sneaked into the Church of St Nicholas when she thought that there was no one inside, in order to hang it over the icon of the Panagia Glykophilousa. Polyxeni was in there, however, lighting a candle to place in the bowl of sand, and she didn't know what to think, and neither did the rest of the town when the gossip spread.

Leyla practised a while on her oud, until she grew bored with being unable to concentrate, and then combed the long white hair of her cat Pamuk, who, as usual, became wild-eyed, carried away by the ecstasy, and started to kick and bite when she was grooming its stomach. 'Gentle, gentle,' reproached Leyla. 'I don't want any scratches and holes in my hands tonight. You and I have got to be beautiful, both of us.' She went and sat in front of her mirror, mesmerising herself until she was dizzy with the effort. Finally she blinked her eyes, and told her reflection, 'This is as beautiful as we shall ever be.' She and her image smiled confidingly at each other. She placed a kiss upon her fingers and touched them to the kiss on the fingers of her reflection. 'Wish me luck,' the two of them said, adding 'Nazar deymesin' in case there was anyone about with the evil eye.

She supervised the setting out of the low table and the cushions in the inner courtyard, and then she went to the room where she could inspect the results of the children's hunt on the hillside. She set a servant, albeit one mightily bemused by the task, to dealing with the business of the candles. It was all very satisfactory; the nearer that it came to the time, the more confident she grew, and the more triumphant in advance.

Leyla returned to the mirror and carefully outlined her eyes in kohl. She dabbed rouge on each cheek, combed her eyelashes and eyebrows, put musk on her wrists and neck, and sprinkled rosewater on the clothing that she had laid out on the bed. She undressed, sat on the side of the bed, and carefully trimmed her dark wedge of pubic hair neatly with a small pair of scissors, not too much, and just enough. It was important that nothing should seem unnatural. She stroked herself a little to make sure that it felt soft and inviting to the hand, finding that it did. She put a little musk on the insides of her thighs, where the soft flesh begins, just above the knees. She stood in front of the mirror and massaged something milky and sweet into her flesh, kneading her breasts, relishing the cool slipperiness of the lotion and the sensations that rippled down to her belly.

Finding that she had an hour or two to kill, she lay down and dozed, forcing herself to sleep a little so that later she would have the vivacity to face a long night. Pamuk settled on her bosom and purred too loudly. The cat had a habit of dribbling when it was happy, and Leyla tolerated this with some displeasure. The worst thing was getting a drop of saliva down your ear when you were sleeping on your side at night.

The sun fell behind the hill, and Rustem Bey came home to his konak at the appointed hour, unsure of what was in store, but with good presentiment. Leyla met him in the selamlık as he came in, and he stopped dead when he saw her. Not only did she smell delicious, but never before had he seen her looking so free and so lovely. She was dressed very lightly in loose baggy shirt and shalwar, scarlet, with a lilac-coloured sash around her waist. Her waistcoat was of black velvet with embroidery of heavy gold thread, and her slippers were of the same design and material. Her fingers were heavy with silver rings. Her black hair was superbly brushed and shining, and her eyes seemed huge and infinitely dark. They glittered in the half-light. Across her forehead glowed the string of gold coins that he had bought for her in Smyrna on their travels, and from the lobes of her ears hung more gold coins, in descending order of size. 'Hanım, there is a beautiful moon tonight,' said Rustem Bey. 'One can see in the dark quite clearly.'

'Like last night,' said Leyla Hanım.

'You too are very beautiful,' he said awkwardly, after a hesitation.

She held out her hand, took his, placed it to her heart, kissed it and then touched it to her forehead. 'My beauty, if I have any . . . it's for you,' she said. 'Come, I have something to show you.'

Rustem Bey allowed himself to be led by the sleeve. When they reached the door to the inner courtyard, Leyla Hanım said, 'Close your eyes.'

A few steps later she said, 'Open them.'

Rustem Bey beheld something so marvellous, so unwonted, that he fell speechless. He put one hand to his forehead, and laughed out loud with delight. Finally he asked, 'What have you done? Have I come to paradise?'

The inner court was a sea of glimmering, moving golden-yellow lights. There was no pattern to it. Some of the flames were momentarily still, and others were travelling, meandering slowly among the lemon trees, the pots of pelargonium, oregano, mint and rose. It was as if the stars had been captured from Heaven and been set in motion there in that small square of the lower world. Leyla laughed with pleasure to see him so amazed. 'I did it for you,' she exclaimed. 'I did it for you.'

Rustem Bey stepped forward and bent down to look. 'By the Prophet!' he exclaimed. Each light was the flame of a candle, and each candle was borne upon the back of an animal. 'It's wonderful,' he said. 'Where on earth did you find so many tortoises?'

'The children,' said Leyla. 'I got the children to go out and find them.'

'It's wonderful,' repeated Rustem Bey. 'I have never seen anything so pretty in all my life. You did this for me?'

'Yes, my lion.'

'My lion,' he repeated. 'You have never called me that before.'

'I have,' she replied, softly, 'but not so as you would hear.'

'I might have heard.'

They stood facing each other, looking into each other's eyes, the emotion of this encounter transporting them somewhere new and strange. 'Come and eat,' she said at last. 'I have prepared a feast.'

Outside the kitchen Rustem Bey found a low table, decorated with tiny lamps, set up with a mezze of small dishes. 'Sit down,' said Leyla, her hand upon his shoulder.

Leyla knelt beside him, breaking bread and dipping the pieces by turn in the humus, the cacik, the yellow lentil, the patlican salatasi. These she fed into the mouth of Rustem Bey as if he were a child or someone sick. 'Eat, my lion,' she encouraged him, 'eat.'

Rustem Bey closed his eyes and let the flavours overwhelm him. 'So much garlic,' he said, over and over again, 'I have never eaten so much garlic.'

The bulbuls and nightingales set themselves to song, and in the distance the bereaved woman wailed for her slaughtered sons. An owl shrieked, and another whooped. The moon, just at the beginning of the wane, was like a swan adrift on a dark lake. The myriad candle flames wandered slowly about the courtyard, disorientating the senses.

With her right hand Leyla fed the morsels of lamb into her master's mouth, chanting, 'Eat, my lion, eat.' The fumes of garlic filled his head and intoxicated him. Leyla gave him tumblers of water mixed with lemon juice to clean his palate between mouthfuls. She gave him the glasses of spiced and honeyed camel's milk, and made sure that he drank it. 'This is strange, a strange taste indeed,' he said. Pamuk sat expectantly nearby, patiently waiting for scraps to be handed down.

A servant brought forth a small clay dish, and lifted the lid. The steam cleared, and Rustem Bey exclaimed, 'An entire head? A whole head of garlic!'

'Baked with olive oil, with its clothes on,' said Leyla. She broke off a clove and squeezed the soft sweet pulp out of the crisp golden skin and on to a sliver of bread. 'Eat,' she said.

Rustem Bey chewed, and shook his head. 'It's astounding. I have never had such a feast in my life, not even at a wedding.'

'Eat,' said Leyla, 'there are no sweets afterwards, so that the taste will not be spoiled. This is all there is. Eat.'

When Rustem Bey had tried all the dishes and was replete, Leyla disappeared to the kitchen. On the embers of the brazier she placed the small brass cezve. She waited for the magical moment when the foam began to rise off the coffee, and just when it was about to overflow the rim she took it off and let it settle. Then she put it back on to the embers and waited for it to rise again. Only then did she tip it carefully into a small cup, and take it out to Rustem Bey. A servant brought out the narghile, along with an ember in a pair of tongs. Rustem Bey sipped at the coffee and inhaled the cool smoke, which had a flavour, heady and rich, that he had not encountered before. He felt as though adrift. A servant brought out a copper with a few hot cinders in it. From a linen bag Leyla drew out handfuls of the skins from the heads of garlic that they had consumed. 'Smell this,' she said, tossing them a few at a time into the dish, and Rustem Bey leaned over and caught the rich but delicate incense in his nostrils. It was exquisite. He looked up at the stars, at the moon, around at the errant candlelight, and then at Leyla. He caught her intently watching his face.

'All my life, hanım,' he said, 'all of it that is granted to remain, I shall remember this night, this feast, these pretty lights, you, your great beauty. What is better, after this? After this, there is only death.'

'I will sing,' said Leyla. She clapped her hands, and a servant brought out her oud. She sat cross-legged on the cushions, took the instrument, tuned it, and began to pick out the notes with a long plectrum shaved from cherrywood. When she had established the melody with its little rushes and hesitations, its melismas and its small sadnesses, she set to singing, all the while gazing into the face of her companion, as if to hypnotise him:

> 'My lion, when I kissed you it was night.
> Who saw?
> The night stars saw, and the moon saw,
> And the moon told the sea,
> And the sea told the oar,
> And the oar told the sailor.

When you kissed me my lipstick was on your lips,
Who saw?
The eagle saw, and went in search
Of an equal shade of red,
And the eagle found it
On the lips of a princess.

Let's light the lantern
And go down to the shore.
What if the waves are too big
And carry us far away?
We'll turn ourselves both into boats,
And our hands will become the oars.'

'Sing something sad,' said Rustem Bey. 'If there is too much
happiness in one night, someone will give us the evil eye.'

Leyla stroked the strings, composed herself, and sang, her voice
deepening with sorrow:

'As death approaches,
My only wish
Is to die in the place
Where I was born.
Life is painful,
But on it goes.'

She stopped quite suddenly, and Rustem Bey looked at her.
She smiled back, but he asked, 'Why are you crying? You have
tears in your eyes.'

'I can't help it. It's the sad song.' She wiped her eyes with the
back of her sleeve, and added, 'I will never again see the place
where I was born.' She sang again:

'Where can I plant you, my red rose?
I fear the sailors
If it's by the shore.
I fear the cold
If it's out upon the mountains.

I'll plant you by a mosque,
I'll plant you by a church,
By a beautiful sainted tomb,
Between two apple trees,
By two bitter-orange trees,
So that all their blossom and
All their fruit will fall
On you, my red rose,
And by your root,
There will I lie asleep.'

Her warm voice, full of passion and melancholy, carried out over the town and echoed among the ruins of the Lycian tombs, where the Dog lay on a slab and listened. 'Have you noticed?' said Rustem Bey. 'The nightingales have stopped.'

They sat silently for a moment. Out in the town the puritanical women and rigid men, decent and narrow, good Muslims and Christians all, tutted in their little rooms and said, 'I don't know what's happened to our Rustem Bey. First he gets himself a whore, and then he lets her play an oud like a man, and sing. It's a disgrace, it isn't right, it's not respectable, and we've got to sit here and listen to it, whatever is the world coming to?'

Leyla and Rustem Bey looked into each other's faces obliviously. The world had become very small. Very tentatively Leyla leaned forward and placed a soft kiss on Rustem's lips. She took up her oud and, the corners of her mouth curling upward in the slightest of smiles, sang softly, delicately, salaciously:

'My lips are sugar,
My cheeks an apple,
My breasts paradise, and
My body is a lily.
O, my lion,
I wait for you
To kiss the sugar,
To bite the apple,
To open paradise, and
Possess the lily.'

233

An owl hooted in the momentary silence, and Rustem Bey felt a kind of drunkenness come over him. Leyla carefully laid the oud upon a cushion. She stood up, shook her hair back, and held out her hand. 'Come,' she said, 'it's time. The night is warm and good. The eagle must fly at last to his nest.'

40

The Veiling of Philothei

There were many who believed that Ali the Snowbringer was so called because his profession was to bring ice down from the mountains, but the truth was that he had earned this sobriquet because, on the night of his birth, it had snowed for the first time in seventy-five years.

All day long, an unnatural stillness and a dry cold had settled upon the coastal plain. People stamped their feet and grumbled, because this was a place where permanently fair weather had left the inhabitants softer than those from the Anatolian vastness. Only the hunters and shepherds up on the slopes had ever experienced anything quite as penetratingly icy as this. In the late evening the air stirred, and the poyraz wind sprang up from the north-east. Old men of apocalyptic disposition muttered ominously that at this time of year there were supposed to be gales from the south, and that a knife-edged wind at such an odd time could bode the world no good. Dull and heavy clouds gathered above, and the cold intensified as the twilight grew suddenly black.

It was with wonderment that, as the birth-cries of Ali's mother died away, the people ran out of the houses and beheld the white flakes begin to descend upon their town. The dogs barked and yelped, bounding up on their hind legs and shaking their heads as they attempted to catch the snowflakes in their teeth, and the townsfolk gathered outdoors, dark and cold as it was, to marvel at the eerily silent descent. 'Çok güzel, çok güzel!' they exclaimed, this people innocent of snow, enchanted by its pristine novelty even as they shivered, and the children caught it on their tongues, or scooped it up and crammed it into their mouths.

It fell only to half a hand's depth, and by the following mid-morning it had gone, leaving behind it only a new child, and a communal memory that had the savour of those stories that tell of lost Edens and magical lands. Ali amounted to that memory made physical, and therefore, throughout his life, he had the good fortune to be aware of himself as someone special, someone marked out significantly by providence, and this despite the fact that in his whole life he did nothing remarkable until his one noble deed at the time of the exodus. He would explain to people that not only was his donkey a proper Muslim donkey because it was brown all over and had no cross upon its shoulders, but that he spent his life bringing ice down from the mountains because he was Ali the Snowbringer, but he was not Ali the Snowbringer because he brought ice from the mountains.

He did, however, play a small part in the little drama that was Philothei's life, for by the time that she was fourteen, as oblivious as anyone else to an outside world that was poised upon the brink of the first technologised mass slaughter in history, she had flowered into a prettiness so irresistible and adorable that it was impossible for any man of the town to remain at ease.

Shaped by nature and by Leyla Hanım's careful and loving tutelage, she had grown in physical loveliness day by day, until she had become as luminous as Selene. Even Leyla, generous in spirit as she was, began to find that Philothei's presence, however enchanting, was causing her anxiety. She perceived that often the sad eyes of Rustem Bey rested upon her companion rather than upon herself, she saw the glittering of his momentary pangs of delight and pleasure, and she felt the points of sexual jealousy pricking at the back of her throat, repress them though she tried.

It would be easy to say that Philothei was supremely beautiful, but, even though many people certainly thought that she was, such would be an oversimplification. Some women are ugly, but in their presence men become dry-mouthed with desire. Some women are neither ugly nor beautiful, but a light shines out of their faces that causes them to become beloved. Sometimes a woman is objectively beautiful, but no man desires her, because there is no light. In Philothei's case it was the high spirit that shone out of her face that made her captivating. It was a matter of intelligence and good humour, and consequently it would be unprofitable to taxonomise her beauties, to dwell upon the shape of her mouth, or the arc of her eyebrows, or the line of her nose.

She was a pretty girl made beautiful by her youth, her sweet nature and her manner.

All through his childhood Ibrahim had dogged her faithfully, sure of his destiny as her husband, but now other men began to find her populating their daydreams. When she passed, men in conversation would fall silent and watch her until she had gone. Others knew the times that she went to Leyla Hanım, and arranged to be by the window or the front door, or in the meydan. Even the Dog came down more often from his anchoritic home in the tombs, terrifying Philothei with his ghastly smile as he sidled by her and tried to catch her eye. For his part, Ali the Snowbringer started to neglect his work in order to follow her.

He would straggle behind, pathetically trying to look as if he were about his business, ambling from door to door, or flitting up an alleyway so that he could descend by another and greet her coming the other way, his expression full of longing and shame. Philothei, entirely oblivious to him, proceeded on her way as if he did not exist, but Ibrahim noticed, and so did many others.

Thus it was that in the hamam one day, Safiye, wife of Ali the Snowbringer, plonked herself down on the slab next to Ayse, wife of Abdulhamid Hodja, sighed portentously, and began, 'Peace upon you, Ayse Efendim.'

'And upon you,' replied Ayse, even though she heartily wished otherwise. As far as she was concerned the hamam was a sacred place in which one accomplished the essence of nothing, and she resented having to speak in that infernal paradise of steam, olive-oil soap and perspiration. Least of all did she wish to speak to Safiye, who lived in the hollow trunk of an admittedly large tree with her husband, four children and a donkey, and who was, moreover, rather unprepossessing in appearance. Ayse liked to look upon the young women, with the fat shining on their thighs and hips, their round breasts and their sparkling brown eyes. She particularly liked to see Leyla Hanım, even though she was a Circassian whore. Leyla's good living left her plumper and more at ease in her skin with every day that passed. Ayse took no pleasure in the older women, however, whose breasts pointed downwards, and in this she was, of course, a hypocrite, who, like all hypocrites, would have been the last to realise that that was what she was. The two middle-aged women, identically pendulous, sat side by side in the stupendous humidity whilst Safiye explained her problem.

Ayse listened wide-eyed, wiped the sweat futilely from her brow, and protested, 'Are you serious? You want my husband to do something about it?'

'Oh please, Ayse Efendim, you must ask him to speak to the father of Philothei.'

'It's not Philothei's fault if your husband has become silly,' replied Ayse. 'Why should my husband have anything to do with it?'

'You don't understand, it's because your husband is an important man, and the father of Philothei will listen to him. You don't know what it's like! My husband has not brought down any ice for two weeks. We don't have one para left! He just follows Philothei. I know it, because I followed him myself. He's bewitched.'

'You followed him?'

'What else can a woman do, a poor wife like me?'

'Why don't you speak to Philothei's mother? Surely you know Polyxeni?'

'I don't know her. We've never spoken. She's Christian, and her family is richer than us.'

'Never spoken? A lifetime in the same town, and you've never spoken?'

'I never needed to,' replied Safiye, miserably. 'I don't know how to speak to her.'

Ayse rolled her eyes impatiently. 'Do you think that a Christian would bite your nose off?'

'Well, they aren't like us.'

'They're not so different either,' Ayse told her, 'and a mother is a mother whatever she is. Would you like me to speak to her?'

'No. I want Abdulhamid Hodja to speak to her father. Abdulhamid Hodja is wise, and will know what to say.'

Ayse bristled with indignation. 'Safiye Efendim, are you saying that I am not wise?'

'Oh no, Ayse Efendim. I want someone to speak to her father, because he has more authority, and you can't speak to him, can you? It wouldn't be decent.'

Ayse saw the sense of this observation, and accordingly mentioned the matter to Abdulhamid Hodja that evening after prayers. She relayed Safiye's request with some scorn and sarcasm, adding, 'Whatever next! What a ridiculous thing, not that my opinion ever counts for anything. Not that anyone ever listens to me.'

Abdulhamid, reverend and sensible as he was, had also been suffering some private discomfort on account of Philothei, and therefore had more insight into the nature of the problem than he might have wished his wife to realise. There was nothing like a young woman's beauty for sowing discord in the world, and everyone knew many tragical stories concerning it.

So it was that he found himself in the improbable position of having to approach Charitos, father of Philothei, in the coffee-house and having to talk quietly to him whilst they played abstractedly at backgammon, that game which mirrors life by being composed half of calculation and half of luck, with the luck, good or bad, mainly occurring in the second half. Charitos drew on the waterpipe that they shared, drank his coffee and listened, twisting the ends of his moustache and frowning.

'I suggest,' concluded Abdulhamid, having explained the nature of the quandary, and listened sympathetically to Charitos's protestations of his daughter's absolute innocence, 'that you do as the Sultan once did when the capital was still in Bursa.'

'What was that?' asked Charitos, the response for which Abdulhamid Hodja had neatly angled.

'There was an influx of Circassian refugees. More persecution by the Russians, no doubt. The Circassian women were so beautiful that the local men began to fight about them, and so, in order to restore the peace, the Sultan summoned the leader of the Circassians, and told him to veil the women. This was done, and the fighting finished.'

'You want me to veil my daughter? With us, this isn't done. How can I do that? Not even your women veil themselves round here. Everyone will think she has become an infidel from somewhere else!'

'"Infidel" is a word that should be picked up from a safe distance with tongs,' reproved Abdulhamid. 'To you I am an infidel, and to me you are an infidel. So, neither one of us is an infidel, or we both are. The Angel commanded the Prophet, peace be upon him, to write that for every nation there is a messenger, and for every nation there is an appointed time, and to write that for each God has appointed a divine law and a predetermined way. We are commanded to vie with one another in good works, and when we all return, God will inform us of the things wherein we differ. Your prophet, Jesus Son of Mary, peace be upon him, commanded his disciples to go out among the Gentiles. So we will have no more talk of infidels. And you forget that Philothei has been long betrothed to Ibrahim, and obviously she will become a Muslim when they marry. Will she then be an infidel?'

'She will be a Christian Muslim,' protested Charitos, who, like most of us, was quickly wearied by preaching and was paying little attention to his own words.

Abdulhamid paused, smiling to himself, because this was a theoretical impossibility that was daily experienced as a practical reality, and said, 'I am not talking about veiling her, exactly. Let her hide her face more. Let her wear her scarf so that her face is more in shadow. She might pull her scarf across her face when she is out in the street or in the meydan, that's all. She must adopt greater modesty. It will be for the better peace of all.'

Philothei was horrified when she heard the news that she must adopt such forced modesty, and she ran first to Drosoula's house, crying, 'Drosoulaki, Drosoulaki!' The two girls went together in a rush to the konak of Rustem Bey, hurrying through the steep narrow alleyways, negotiating their way past the crush of hawkers, donkeys, dogs and camels. They left their slippers in disorder outside the door of the haremlık, and entered, Philothei throwing herself down on the divan, wiping the angry tears from her face whilst Drosoula stood slightly awkwardly, making sympathetic faces and toying with the leaves of the basil plant that had been left on the sill to keep the mosquitoes away. The room was quite dark, on account of the shutters being semi-closed, and the heavy red carpets hanging from the walls. A brass coffee pot was beginning to raise its froth on the ashes of the brazier, and Leyla, clad in shalwar the colour of lapis lazuli, was reclining on her bed, popping syrupy morsels of tulumba tatlısı into her mouth, in between smoking a tightly rolled little cigarette from her unfeasibly long silver cigarette holder, and caressing the cat Pamuk, who was purring stertorously, kneading the covers with her claws, and dribbling. Leyla picked up her oud and ran a long, languid nail across the strings. She let the thoughtful chord ring and fade, put the instrument down again, and went to sit next to her tearful handmaiden on the divan. She put her arms around her neck and kissed her fondly. 'My little partridge! Tell me all about it, come on.'

Philothei was much comforted in those plump and maternal arms, breathing in the scents of amber and frankincense, cinnamon and rosewater. She calmed down a little, and related the awful news, whereupon Leyla clapped her hands with delight, and cried, 'It's the best thing I've ever heard! Oh, it's so marvellous, and I'm so pleased for you!'

'Pleased for me?' repeated Philothei. 'Have you been listening? Is there something wrong with you? They want me to cover my face.'

'But it's only in public, and just think what it means! It means that you're too beautiful! What more could you possibly want? Everyone will know that you are too beautiful! God knows, I wish I could have such luck.' She looked up at Drosoula with a conspiratorial expression that seemed to mean 'Isn't that what we'd all want?' She took Philothei's face between her hands and kissed away her tears for sheer vicarious happiness.

Philothei, who was not entirely without vanity, began suddenly to come round to Leyla's point of view. Leyla threw the damask covering off her trunk of clothes, and burrowed eagerly in its depths. She rummaged for handfuls of silks, satins, gauzes and finely woven cottons, and threw them on to the divan. Standing behind Philothei in front of a mirror, Leyla reached over her head with the veils as they tried first one, then another, then the first again, giggling and exclaiming, until they had settled on a selection that would set off Philothei's prettiness to the best advantage.

241

Drosoula watched these proceedings with regret and resignation in her breast. She too was fourteen years old, and she had already developed into one of those perplexing creatures as ugly as the mythical wife of Antiphates, of whom the poet wrote that she was 'a monstrous woman whose ill-aspect struck men with horror'. She was moon-faced, great-girthed and hairy, but she was an amiable and good-natured girl, whom fate had deprived of a pretext for becoming vain. The feminine games, the frivolous pleasures in which Leyla and Philothei so naturally engaged, were of a world from which nature had excluded her, and she watched them with a pleasure that was both generous and sad. 'Try this one,' she would say, or, 'You look better in that one, but the other one was nice too,' but there was never a moment when she felt she might try a veil upon herself. She could not conceive of what it might be like to have to conceal one's beauty, and so for her Leyla and Philothei were magical creatures whose pretty ways she felt privileged to observe, through the invisible but palpable gauze that separated herself from them. She felt a yearning, a kind of nostalgia for that which has never happened.

That evening Philothei proudly returned home to the house of her parents, wearing an exiguous veil so finely woven that it was almost transparent, embroidered with tiny golden stars and crescent moons. When Ibrahim saw her in the meydan his heart leapt in his chest even more violently than usual, and he turned to Gerasimos beside him and said, 'It's time that I spoke to my mother so that she can speak to my father.' He was referring to the marriage that everyone knew to be foreordained. Philothei was fourteen, two years past the age when many girls married, her parents had very deliberately not left an empty bottle on their roof to signify that a girl of marriageable age was available within, and now it seemed that there was no more point in waiting. Gerasimos, who had watched over Drosoula for as many years and as faithfully as Ibrahim had watched over Philothei, also decided to speak to his mother. He wondered what opposition he might meet, and braced himself for it in advance. Not only was his beloved ugly, but her father was a shameless drunk, and there would be little dowry to speak of, in return for the goats and the household goods that would come from his own folk.

In the meantime, the upshot of it all was that Philothei grew somewhat in coquettishness. Leyla supplied her all that she needed to conceal her features to an extent that was exactly tantalising, and taught her to adopt a disingenuously modest mien that merely exacerbated her desirability. Ali the Snowbringer, lovesick though he might have been, reverted soon enough to his profession through sheer pressure of poverty and wifely remonstrance, and Ibrahim came to know the delicious pleasure of having the veil lifted solely for himself whenever he and Philothei chanced to find themselves alone in the township's extraordinary maze of tiny alleys.

Inevitably, the same thing happened in Eskibahçe as had happened in Bursa in the days of the Circassian refugees and the Sultan's intervention. The novelty caught on, and almost all the women, including the ugly and the indifferent ones, who nonetheless lacked neither astuteness nor vanity, took to wearing veils in public in order to imply that they likewise were too beautiful to be safely gazed upon. In Telmessos the people started to make jokes about the presumption and silliness of the women of Eskibahçe, but of course the fashion briefly caught on there as well.

One day Abdulhamid Hodja composed a song that was about the ways in which one's plans can be confounded, on an evening when for some reason he was reminded of his futile mission in the matter of Philothei. As he cleared away into sacks the tortoises that raided his vegetables at dusk, the words just came into his head, and he sang:

> 'I wanted to go fishing
> And I needed a mouse for bait
> So I sent out the cat to fetch one
> And back he came with a moth.'

There are people on the coastal plain who sing it still.

41

An Embarrassing Question

'You're so lazy,' said Rustem Bey, leaning over her where she reclined on the divan in the haremlık, 'you just lie around all day doing nothing, only getting up to be fed.'

She blinked up at him with an expression that seemed to proclaim that he was completely mad, and he touched a finger to her cheek. 'And what's more, everywhere that you've been sleeping you leave patches of hair and grit. So much grit! Where does it come from? Why don't you wash? Have you no self-respect?'

'She doesn't care about how much grit there is,' said Leyla Hanım, who was reclining equally lazily upon the bed, 'as long as someone comes and sweeps it away.' She popped a piece of pink lokum into her mouth, and continued, 'When I remember how much you didn't want to bring the cat along when you took me from Istanbul, it makes me laugh. I remember your face. You said, "I reckoned on no cat!"' Leyla giggled at the memory, the end of her nose wrinkling up with mirth, in the manner that he had always found very fetching.

'Pamuk and I are good friends now,' said Rustem Bey. 'She hasn't eaten my partridge, and she is very good to talk with.'

'You love her more than you love me,' replied Leyla, pouting and rolling over on to her stomach. She kicked her heels in the air, and smiled coquettishly at Rustem, licking the sugar off her fingers.

'There's nothing to choose between you,' observed Rustem. 'You're both completely idle and you're both getting plump.'

'She's not completely idle! She goes out at night and has fights, and yeowls along with the best of them. I'm much lazier than she is.'

'You say that with pride, it seems.'

'I've worked very hard to get as lazy as this. At night I can't go out and fight and yeowl because my master wants to lie with me, and besides, I'm tired from all the lying about I have to do. Anyway, don't you like me plump? You don't think I eat like this just to please myself?'

'Well, of course you do. But I like you plump anyway.'

'More to enjoy?' suggested Leyla salaciously.

'More to enjoy.' Rustem stroked his moustache, and asked, 'Why do you think Pamuk has never had kittens?'

'God decreed otherwise,' said Leyla. 'I've never got pregnant myself, and I wonder why. If we were married I would be afraid that you'd divorce me.'

'Has Philothei gone home?' asked Rustem Bey, and when she nodded he sat beside her on the bed and stroked her face in much the same way as he had been stroking the cheek of the cat. 'I want to ask you something.'

'Yes?'

'It's been intriguing me for a long time, but I never got round to asking.'

'Yes?'

'When we are together . . . at night . . .' he smiled shyly, 'you say things, you know, when we are . . .'

'Together?'

'Yes. When we are in pleasure together.'

'What things?'

'You say things that sound like "s'agapo" and "agapi mou".'

'Do I?'

'Yes. What do they mean?'

'Mean? They mean nothing.'

'Nothing?'

'They are little words I like to say . . . endearments . . . to show my pleasure.' Leyla was by now feeling very embarrassed and awkward. She could feel her cheeks begin to flush, and that knowledge made them flush even more. Her brain whirled as she tried to think of an explanation.

'What language are they?' demanded Rustem Bey.

'What language?'

'Yes.' And then Rustem saved her unintentionally by saying, 'I always supposed that they're Circassian.'

Much relieved, Leyla said, 'Yes, they're Circassian. Of course.' She held out her arms and summoned him by beckoning with all of her fingers at once, her painted nails glowing in the light of the brazier. 'Come, my eagle,' she said, 'Philothei's gone home and so has her sweet but ugly little friend. I'm suddenly not feeling quite so lazy.'

Rustem Bey hesitated, but then he acquiesced.

42

Mustafa Kemal (9)

It is 1911, and the Ottoman state begins its Great War. From now on, caught up in other people's imperial wars, and with only one year unblooded, it will be sloughing off its sons continuously until 1923. Mustafa Kemal will be busy indeed.

Mustafa Kemal passes through Egypt, which is in the hands of the British, and is not spotted by them even though he is obviously not an Egyptian. He is fair-haired and blue-eyed, he walks proudly with a military mien. He gains an audience with the Khedive, who promises him support, and recruits Arabs to send to Benghazi.

It is as an Arab that he disguises himself for the train journey to the east. He has with him an Egyptian guide, a Turkish gunner and an Arabic interpreter. An Egyptian officer searches the train, with instructions to arrest the Turkish officers on board, and Kemal realises that the game is up. He therefore reveals his identity and harangues the officer. 'This is a holy war,' he declaims, 'it is a war of Muslim against infidel. It is not for you to stand in the way of God.' Rhetorically masterful, eloquent and persuasive, he cynically but brilliantly persuades the officer of what he himself cannot believe, and the following day all but the Turkish gunner are released.

Well provided for by their Egyptian agents, Kemal and his party of picaresques ride off across the lunar desert on their camels. They reach what they think is the border, and change into their Turkish uniforms, only to be confronted by a unit of the British army. Mustafa Kemal once more brings to bear his prodigious powers of bluster. 'This is Ottoman territory,' he tells the British, 'and you are trespassing upon it.'

'Old chap, you are misinformed,' say the British. 'The borders have lately been changed.'

'Nonsense,' says Mustafa Kemal. 'If you do not withdraw at

once, we shall be obliged to open fire upon you and remove you by force.'

The British officers laugh, because they are well armed and many, and Kemal's men are pitifully few, but they enjoy and admire Kemal's swashbuckling gasconade, and they let his party pass.

At Tobruk the Italians occupy all the best positions, and Enver Pasha has been busy trying to seduce the Senussi Arabs into resistance. Glamorously engaged to a niece of the Sultan, he is now, however, disguised as a sheikh, is issuing his own currency, signed by himself, and is ensconced in a finely caparisoned tent, whence he has been doling out Turkish gold, but without so far managing to persuade anyone to fight the Italians.

Kemal also disguises himself as a sheikh, perhaps in the spirit of competition, and makes a survey of the military dispositions. He invites the tribesmen and their sheikhs to a pourparler, and finds them to be a shabby crowd of ruffians armed with clubs and muskets. He plays the Islamic card, previously so successful, but finds that they are unimpressed. He insults the honour of the truculent Sheikh Mebre by stating that he knows him to be an Italian spy, and adding that from now on he will only give money and assistance to other tribes.

The bluff works, and in the morning the proud chieftain announces that he will attack the Italians with his own men alone. Armed with Turkish rifles, and summarily trained in their use, the tribesmen attack the Italians at dawn and destroy some seventy guns, bringing back two hundred Italians, who, like their sons after them, prove to have no great liking for imperial desert wars, and gleefully surrender. Enver Pasha and Mustafa Kemal cannot think of what to do with them all, so they release them in the desert near the Egyptian border, and let them find their own way home.

The Turks have only one active warship, and the Italians have complete control of the sea, so it is impossible for the Ottoman troops to displace them from Tobruk. It is equally impossible for the Italians to take control of the desert hinterland, where there is no water, but a great many hostile tribesmen. Enver Pasha, however, has romantic dreams of conquest, and over many attacks he futilely expends his troops by the hundred. Mustafa Kémal, horrified, but unwilling to cause a split in the command of such a small expeditionary force, holds his tongue and bides his time. He is struck down by an eye infection that temporarily blinds his left eye. He finds that his Arab tribesmen come and go as they please, and he never knows quite how many soldiers he has under his command at any one time. They are paid two piastres apiece for each day's work, and consequently they avoid combat as much as possible in order to prolong the war. The Turkish officers are amazed by the fact that from the age of three years, the Arab women are not allowed out at all. Nuri Bey writes: 'We lead ascetic lives like the monks of Mount Athos. If we go on from here, our next stop will surely be paradise.'

The Italians bomb Beirut, shell the forts that line the Dardanelles, and occupy Rhodes and other islands of the Dodecanese. They send torpedo boats in the direction of Istanbul.

Back in Istanbul the revolutionary government that once promised so much has declined into chaotic tyranny. It dissolves parliament and packs the infamous sopalı seçim election in its own favour. Just as the Committee of Union and Progress had once acted against the despotism of the Sultan's government, now a similar group of young officers is acting against the despotism of the Committee. Paradoxically, they demand the withdrawal of the military from all political activity and the restoration of a freely enfranchised parliament.

They succeed in establishing a new liberal government just as the Balkan nations, incited by the Russians, for the first and only time in their history manage to concoct a collective conspiracy, and actually cooperate to implement it. Serbia aspires to the Adriatic coast, and Bulgaria to the Mediterranean, whilst Greece wants Thrace. All three want what they can get of Macedonia. Bulgaria and Greece both want Thrace. The Balkan states combine in a military 'exercise'. In the meantime, 120 Ottoman battalions in the Balkans have been demobilised as an imprudent gesture of conciliation. Suddenly the King of Montenegro declares war on the Ottoman Empire on 8 October 1912, and the Serbs, the Greeks and the Bulgarians join in shortly after. Eleftherios Venizelos, the Greek Prime Minister, makes a proclamation calling his people to come to the' aid of downtrodden Christians. The Muslim populations in the path of the invaders begin to suffer an unimaginably horrible but entirely unremembered holocaust, as they become refugees, demented with terror and exhaustion, pushed hither and thither between equally malevolent and efficiently vicious armies of looters and rapists. There are terrible massacres of Muslims, particularly in the path of the Bulgarians. Many of the fleeing will find their way to Istanbul, where, in the courtyards of the mosques, they will die by the thousand of winter cold, disease and starvation. One day Mustafa Kemal will chance upon his mother and sister just in time, and find a place for them to live.

The Ottoman government makes rapid peace with Italy, and Mustafa Kemal has to wend home from Africa via Italy, Austria, Hungary and Romania. In Vienna he has his infected eye treated by Austrian doctors. Monastir falls to the Serbs. It is at the Egyptian border, at the beginning of his homeward odyssey, that a British officer recognises him, saying, 'I know you; you're Mustafa Kemal. You may go anywhere you like in this damned country.'

43

I am Philothei (8)

Every time there was a harvest, we would give the first-fruit to a neighbour, and it so happened that since I was betrothed to Ibrahim, his family would give things to us and we would give things to them, and fortunately they often sent Ibrahim with the gifts, and so I would know that if I was in the right place Ibrahim would pass by, and in this way I would be sure of seeing him. This is how I got to see him on the first baking of the new wheat, and on the day of St Theodoros when he came round with lokma, and on the afternoon of the Holy Cross when we broke the fast with grapes and olives and koliva.

And this is how I saw him on Holy Thursday, when some of the Muslims joined us and sent yeast, salt, eggs and bread to the church, because Jesus Son of Mary and Mary herself are also theirs as well as ours, and these things were placed by the icon and then Father Kristoforos would read the gospel over them and then we had to fetch them home again, and we threw the salt into our larders, and the yeast we put back with the yeast, and the eggs we put among our own icons for the sake of Easter, and we all ate a little of the bread and kept the rest in tiny portions so that we could eat of them when an animal was sick and needed a cure. I saw Ibrahim during all these errands.

I remember there was one night when Ibrahim showed how great his love was. It was at three o'clock in the morning on the night of the service for the Resurrection, and the town crier had come round and roused us by knocking on our doors, and we said the Jesus Prayer, and we were going to the church in the dark, and out of the corner of my eye I saw something moving in the shadows of an almond tree, and it was Ibrahim who had got up in the coldness of three o'clock in the morning on Resurrection Day even though he was a Muslim, and he did it

GALWAY COUNTY LIBRARIES

just to catch a glimpse of me in the dark, and that is how much he loved me.

All in all I was grateful to God for ordaining us so many feasts and obligations, because that was one way in which I often saw my beloved.

GALWAY COUNTY LIBRARIES

44

In Which a Playful Conversation
Takes a Bad Turn

One evening Rustem Bey sat relaxing on cushions in the selamlık with a narghile before him whilst Leyla played to him on the oud. Pamuk lay curled up on the divan with her tail over her nose, snoring lightly, and the charcoal in the brazier glowed, giving off warmth and the deliciously incensuous smell generated by the garlic skins that Leyla periodically tossed upon them. Drosoula had called round to ask for her friend, and Leyla had allowed Philothei to leave her work and go home to her parents. The house had been cleaned that day, because it was a Wednesday, and Leyla Hanım said that this was the day on which the Sultan's harem was cleaned. The brass ornaments sparkled and glowed in the gentle light of the oil lamps. Leyla Hanım played a song in Greek, in which a sailor was promising the Panagia that if she saved him from the storm he would silver-plate her icon, and Rustem Bey, who did not understand the words at all, was marvelling once again that she knew so many songs in two languages, and was wondering how it came about that she had learned them. The music did not seem to be going very well, however, and Leyla ceased her singing and frowned. 'What's the matter?' enquired Rustem Bey.

'It's this plectrum,' she replied. 'It's new. The old one became thin and frayed, but on this one they've cut the cherrywood too thick, and now it doesn't play on the strings as it should. It needs to be thinned down at the tip.'

'Go and cut it down then, my partridge,' said Rustem Bey, contentedly puffing out a cloud of sweetly scented smoke.

She stood up and went into the kitchen, where she carefully removed some very thin shavings with the blade of a knife, held at ninety degrees so that it would scrape rather than pare. Rustem Bey could hear the dull rattle of her bracelets on the chopping board. He reflected upon how happy he was, and also upon the undeniable fact that there was something in his soul that troubled him.

When Leyla returned she tried the plectrum briefly and then set the instrument down beside her. She looked at her lover archly. 'You'll never guess,' she said, 'what people are saying.'

He raised his eyebrows in silent enquiry.

'They're saying that you are a bad master to me because you don't beat me. I have heard women in the hamam saying it, and remarking how I never have any bruises.'

Rustem Bey looked at her in amusement. 'They have a saying around here that a woman is like an olive tree. She bears the best fruit when well thrashed.'

'Do they? I have never heard of anyone thrashing an olive tree.'

'Neither have I. If anyone really thrashed an olive tree, he would be thought mad.'

Leyla crawled on all fours from her cushions to his, and lay down with the back of her head on his lap. She reached up a hand and placed it on the nape of his neck. 'Kiss me, my lion,' she said.

Rustem Bey leaned down, but stopped halfway. 'I can't,' he said. 'Either I am too fat or too inflexible.'

'Why don't you beat me?'

'I don't feel like it. Perhaps if I felt like it, I would. Anyway, you don't do anything to be beaten for.'

'Some men beat their wives every week, on a Friday, just to ensure good behaviour,' she said teasingly.

'These are not modern men,' replied Rustem Bey, impatiently. 'This is all old stuff. Do you think that in France, in modern places, men still beat the women? Do you want to be beaten? Do you think it would do you good?'

Leyla shuddered, and rolled her eyes in mock horror. 'Certainly not. I only brought it up because it was amusing. If you beat me I would run away.'

'Well, I couldn't be bothered to beat you.'

'Don't you care for me then?'

'I don't beat my servants, I don't beat my horses, I don't beat my dogs, I don't beat my olive trees. I care for all of them, and all of them are perfectly good. I don't even beat Pamuk when she sticks her claws in my leg or leaves the guts of mice on the floor.'

'Everyone beats their servants,' observed Leyla, 'everyone but you.' She laughed mischievously, and suggested, 'Why don't we open the shutters, and you can pretend to beat me, and you can beat the doorpost and the divan with a belt or something, and you can shout and I'll scream, and then everyone will know that you treat me right after all.'

'I do believe you're serious,' he said, amazed.

'It would be fun, just to fool the neighbours, and hear the story spreading from mouth to ear. It would be wonderful, honestly. Go on. Let's do it.' She jumped up, and her eyes glistened with a childish excitement and anticipation.

Rustem Bey let himself admire her joy and her beauty for a moment, before saying, 'If you don't stop talking about this, I might beat you after all. You are spoiling the enjoyment of smoking, and if we were to do as you suggest, it would undoubtedly frighten the cat, and I don't believe it would truly improve my reputation.' There was a long silence, and Leyla bent forward and kissed his face, dabbing her lips upon his eyes and his cheeks and his mouth. The aga was still unused to such affection even after so much time, and his reaction was always the same; he sat very stiffly and behaved as if she were doing nothing at all. He inhaled the scent of rosewater from her hair, and the musk and amber that she caressed into her neck and between her breasts.

'I have never beaten anyone, but I killed someone once,' said Rustem Bey suddenly, 'but it was in self-defence, and he deserved it.'

Leyla drew back. 'I know. I heard about it.'

'In the hamam?'

'Where else?' There was a long pause, and then she said, very tentatively, 'From time to time I see your wife. In the hamam.'

Rustem Bey did not respond.

'She asks after you. Her health is very bad.'

There was still no response, but his face was darkening with displeasure. Finally he said sharply, 'Do you talk with prostitutes in the hamam?'

Leyla sat up abruptly and went over to where she had been sitting before. She rolled herself a very thin cigarette of Latakia tobacco, took it up in a long, delicate pair of golden tongs, lit it from the brazier and put it to her lips. She let the smoke curl out of her mouth, and finally replied, 'Who do you think I sit with, when I am in the hamam? Who else do you think would let me sit beside them? According to the people of this town, I am anyway nothing but a whore.'

There was anger and bitterness in her voice, and he repented and said softly, 'You are my chosen one,' but she ignored the pacifying hand that he held outstretched, and went out, leaving him to feel ashamed.

45

The Humiliation of Daskalos Leonidas

Allow me to introduce myself, although you won't have heard of me unless you have approached Eskibahçe from the lower end, where the road emerges from the pine forest that has all the Muslim graves in it, and where you would have found on your left the ruins of a pump house with constantly running water. It was modest enough, but it served to water both men and horses when they arrived, and was a very welcome addition to the amenities of the town, especially in high summer. What could be better than to enter a shady, cool and dignified little building of neoclassical design in order to drink water and wash your face after a long journey? Above the door you can still read, in Greek script, 'Constructed for the Benefit of All, by Georgio P. Theodorou, 1919'.

That's me. I am Georgio P. Theodorou, at your service, ladies and gentlemen, and I wasn't even a citizen of that town, but I did belong to one of the societies in Smyrna who engaged in little works of philanthropy aimed at improving the lives of our people in the more obscure places. I was a merchant, you see; you name it, I obtained it and sold it on at a profit. Smyrna was the ideal place for a port, halfway to Africa, halfway to Europe, and, apart from that, it was a delightful city altogether, before it was burned down, a real cosmopolis. I built that little pump house in Eskibahçe with funds I earned from supplying the Ottoman authorities with a few essential items during the Great War, and my connection with that town was that Leonidas the teacher lived there.

I can say, with some truth, that I did know Daskalos Leonidas quite well, and was one of the few people that liked him. Most people thought he was a pain in the proctol aperture, as a medical friend of mine used to say. He was the son of another friend, a merchant like me, and so I watched Leonidas grow up. You could say that I was like an uncle to him. It was me who listened to him when he started to get big ideas as a teenager. Even then he was scrawny and dry-voiced, and if he laughed or smiled it gave you a sense of present discomfort and imminent unpleasantness. Nonetheless, he was very intelligent, and what made me sympathise with him was that he always suffered in his soul. I felt sorry for him in the same way as one feels sorry for an aged athlete or an overladen donkey, or a dedicated artist who is never quite good enough to sell any paintings.

I remember one night when I was at his father's house, and Leonidas was about twenty years old. We were at dinner when he mentioned quite casually that he had joined the local Philiki Etairia, knowing perfectly well that his father would throw a fit. He always was courageous, you can say that for him, and was always prepared to stand up to his father. In this respect he was quite out of the ordinary, because in those days everyone knew what was what, and you didn't contradict your father. If he'd been my son I would have thrashed him I should think, but as he was someone else's I was able to admire his independence of spirit.

'What?' shouted his father, practically expelling a mouthful of meatballs. 'You've joined the Philiki Etairia? Are you stupid or something? Do you want to get us arrested? Do you want your mother and me to be thrown in prison?' He glared at his son and gestured around at the walls, richly decorated as they were, with the carved furniture, the heavy carpets, and the silver candlesticks and samovar. 'Do you want us to lose everything?'

Leonidas paled under his father's rage, but said simply, 'It's for Greece.'

Perhaps I should explain that the Philiki Etairia were secret societies formed to bring about the reunification of Greece, because there were many who said that Thrace, the Black Sea coast, the west coast of Turkey, and, of course, Constantinople, were historically Greek, and mainly populated by Greeks, and ought to be Greek again. It was all about reconstructing Byzantium and turning Haghia Sophia back into a cathedral, and bringing about 'Greater Greece', and having a King Constantine back on the throne, and the whole caboodle was known as 'The Big Idea'. For all I know there may be those who call it so still.

'Those idiots with their Big Idea!' bawled his father. 'They have no idea! Can Greece win a war against the Turks? Do you know how many of them there are? You're crazy! You want to be ruled from Athens? Have you ever been to Athens? It's a shitty little village, that's what! A shitty little provincial village with some ruins and no theatre worth going to, and the people with no education and no culture, and the houses with all the paint peeled off, and they can't even speak Greek properly! Is that what you want? You're a fool.'

Leonidas tried to defend himself: 'The new Greece would be ruled from Constantinople, Father, just as the old Greece was.'

'We are already ruled from Constantinople,' replied his father. 'By Turks.'

'Well, why should we care, precisely? Here in Smyrna we have the most pleasant and delightful city in the world. We are all prosperous. We don't have to give a damn about what happens in the capital. We Greeks occupy all the most important and powerful positions. We virtually make our own laws. We are in paradise, and you and your friends want to mess it up with your stupid Big Idea, for God's sake! It's nostalgia, pure and simple! Do you want us all to go to the wall for the sake of nostalgia?'

'We are governed by Turks,' replied Leonidas, with some dignity. 'They are inferior to us in every way, and it cannot be natural. They breed like rabbits, and soon there'll be no room for all of us to live.'

'We are all Ottomans now. Times have changed. Anyway, look at all my servants. What are they? They are all Turks. Look at Georgio's servants. They are all Turks. Who digs the roads and carries away the night-soil? Turks. Who slaves in the fields to grow the produce that we sell on? Turks. Don't tell me we are governed by Turks, when the evidence to the contrary is right in front of your eyes. What would we do without them? How can a son of mine be so stupid? That's what I want to know! And you want to destroy everything we are!'

'Greece was great once,' replied Leonidas, his voice rising. 'Some of us have more ambition for Greece! Greece was the light of the world! At one time you couldn't be called civilised if you didn't speak Greek. Why do you think the Turks call us

Romans? Because eventually even the Romans spoke Greek! We are the greatest race in the world, and look what we've come down to, Father. Our time must come again. All it needs is our determination, and perhaps a new Alexander.'

'Alexander?' sneered his father. 'Spreading our culture and civilisation all over the world? Well, forgive me my heterodoxy, but he did it by spreading slaughter and destruction from Macedonia to India. How many weeping widows and raped virgins went and thanked him for his culture, do you suppose? Don't you know what inevitably arrives in the wake of glorious military conquest? Famine and disease, famine and disease.'

'It was worth it,' replied Leonidas. 'The naturally superior must rise to the top by any means, because their superiority legitimates the means.'

'I'll tell you something, my son,' said his father, jabbing in his direction with a fork. 'I'd have more respect for Alexander and you and your friends if you were bright enough to understand that it's money and enterprise and brains that make the world turn round. All these military campaigns, and revolutions, and conspiracies, and talk about racial this and racial that . . . What do they bring? Bloodshed and disaster. If you want to be any use in the world, put money in your pocket.'

Leonidas looked at his father pityingly, and the latter repeated, 'Put money in your pocket.'

'Money won't restore Greece,' said Leonidas.

'Idiot! It's the only thing that will. You should be like Georgio here! Make a lot of money and spend it on useful little works of philanthropy. That way you'll live usefully and die respected. It's simple.'

'I'm talking about dignity, the national soul. I am not talking about being fat and complacent.'

'Fat and complacent! Fat and complacent! Your head is full of dogfart! All the money I spent on your education, and you learned nothing! You're no son of mine. Your mother must have been with someone else.'

Leonidas's mother scowled at her husband, but maintained her composure. She was quite used to this particular rhetorical flourish, which was not to a standard that matched the general quality of his intellect. All of their sons and daughters had been accused at one time or another of not being children of his, and she used to remark drily that if she had had as many lovers as he sometimes supposed, she would have had an eventful and exhausting life indeed.

I mention this conversation, which was typical of many, because it reflects a general tendency at the time. We Asia Minor Greeks were caught between the hot-headed idealists and nationalists who wanted to turn the world upside down in the name of a beautiful vision of Byzantium, and the sensible fellows like me and Leonidas's father, who wanted a nice comfortable life trading in commodities and getting whatever we wanted because we were clever and rich enough to get it. I do remember that in those days everyone thought they were entitled to an empire, and perhaps Leonidas and his friends were just a symptom of the times, like Mussolini. Personally, I liked the idea of a new Greater Greece, in theory, but I couldn't see the point of risking anything for it, and I couldn't stop thinking of the mainlanders as at worst a bunch of crazy foreigners, or at best like embarrassing cousins with too many halfwits in the family. I wasn't in any kind of mood to die for them, and no one was more surprised than me when they decided to come over and die for us. I can't say I was very surprised, however, when the fiasco concluded with all of us losing everything, and it was we who died for them.

I also mention that conversation because it shows why Leonidas ended up as a teacher in an insignificant little town, rather than as a merchant like the rest of us. He defied his father firmly, and went to Eskibahçe to try and educate the Greeks back into being Greeks. He wanted to knock the Turkishness out of them. He wanted them to speak Greek instead of Turkish, and learn about the classical past. He wanted to fire them up about the War of Independence, and the struggles in Crete. He wanted to tell them about heroic women who hurled their children over precipices rather than yield them to the Turks. He wanted them to understand the church services, instead of listening to all that rolling ecclesiastical liturgy in dumb and uncomprehending awe.

It was hard to like Leonidas, but I'll say one thing for him: he might have been a romantic, but he really did manage to get the

Christians to send their children to his little school. He lived off practically nothing, endured ingratitude and ridicule, and spent his nights writing fiery tracts that got stuck up crooked on walls, and which no one could be bothered to read. I read them of course, because he always sent me copies, much to my consternation. I shudder to think how much oil and wakefulness he wasted. As I know from poring over my accounts late at night, it leaves you feeling disorientated and unhealthy. What I would like to add is that, just as we sensible types feared all along, the romantic enthusiasms of people like Leonidas ended up with peaceable fellows like me drowning in harbours whilst their cities burned.

In that little town Leonidas suffered much humiliation, and to be honest, I would guess it was mostly his own fault. He had that sense of personal superiority that automatically puts people's backs up, and which no merchant would dare to express publicly because he would lose half his customers. Just imagine what would have happened if I'd told my Jewish or Armenian clients what I really thought of them! Or the Turkish officials! Commercial catastrophe, that's what. Give me nice polite hypocrisy any time, which is something all of us could profitably learn from the English, I'd say.

Anyway, there came a time when I had to go to Eskibahçe because I had heard that there was a very good potter there who worked hard and made excellent things. I had seen the little clay whistles that he made in the shape of various birds, which you half filled with water, and then they warbled like a bird when you blew into them. Such toys were very common of course, but his were definitely a cut above the rest because of the quality of the design and decoration, and because they always sounded like the bird they represented, which was by no means usual with other people's. I wanted to visit this Iskander the Potter because it occurred to me that I could probably make four hundred per cent profit by selling his wares to the Italians, whilst at the same time doubling the profits that he took for himself. The man concerned turned out to be an amiable, grubby-turbaned fellow with a disconcerting habit of speaking in proverbs that he seemed to have invented himself, but we struck a good deal, and there was something for everyone, which is what it's all about when it comes down to it. He had a blind old man walking up and down in his great tank of clay, picking out the stones between his toes, an arrangement that struck me as peculiarly inspired, since it was the ideal job for a blind old man, and no doubt the exercise kept him robust in his senescence.

Because I knew that Leonidas was in that town, I sent a message to say that I would come and stay with him, but that he wasn't to go to any trouble, and a week later I turned up. I sent my bodyguards and servants to stay in the khan, which was very clean and comfortable, and I went to stay in Leonidas's house, which very much wasn't, and I saw that indeed he had conscientiously honoured my request, and not gone to any trouble at all.

I must say, though, that I took a fancy to that town the moment I saw it. What a lovely place! I can quite see why it was called Paleoperiboli in ancient times. I arrived in the early evening when the swallows had come down for the flies and the tortoises had clattered out for their daily peripato. From the minaret of the mosque the muezzin was calling the azan at the top of his lungs, and the resound of it was echoing with half a second's delay from the hillside behind. Like many Christians I always found the azan both irritating and exciting.

You approach the town through a lovely shady pine wood that, here and there, shelters the lopsided whitewashed tombs of the Muslims, some of them freshly sparkling and others so dilapidated, grey and subsiding as to have become part of the natural scree of the forest floor. A perfect spot to rest, I would say, at any rate somewhat superior to being cremated in your own house or shredded by crabs in the mud at the bottom of a harbour. Amid the sand and rock, thick with pine needles, grew little shrubs of holly, and in the clearings I saw groups of euphorbia and indigo wild delphinium. In one place there were deep red hibiscus, and chickens roosting in the trees. The smell of figs was intoxicating, and I leaned over from my horse and picked one that was scarlet and slightly overripe, and tasted of coconut. At the ingress to the town there were two dogs, forgive me for mentioning it, hopelessly knotted together after the sexual act, going round in circles and being taunted by other dogs who wanted to get at the bitch. I felt that was a good metaphor for something, but I couldn't think what. There was also a small house, outside which a Muslim woman was sitting in the shade of a vine, rolling thin unleavened bread on a lapboard with a slim rolling pin, the very image of domestic contentment. From her I bought a salty glass of ayran, because I prefer it to the sweet kind, drank it whilst I observed the unfortunate dogs, and felt infinitely refreshed. Opposite this house, a little trickle of water came out of the hillside and ran across the road, which is what inspired me to build a pump house there, with a trough and a drinking fountain. As I was dusty and thirsty from travel, I was surprised that no one had thought of it before. A man who does well in this world has to put something back in, I say, and, let's face it, it never does a man any commercial harm to generate some goodwill with the occasional act of generosity.

I noticed, oddly· enough, that the poppies that grew in the stones were all pink instead of red, and I remember that my uncle used to say that women were like poppies; they fall away to nothing as soon as they are plucked, or words to that effect. There were swathes of prostrate capers, with their delicate and strange lilac swirls of stamen inside their cups of four white petals, crowding out of the walls and verges, alongside those dark blue bells of convolvulus. There was a knot of scruffy little children plucking the flowers and blowing into them until they popped loudly. I tried it myself later on, when no one was about, and it was curiously satisfying and amusing.

On my right, below the road, was a great pool full of ancient ruins, a temple I suppose, that had about it an aura of femininity. It was decorated, as it were, by crimson damselflies, martens perched sideways on reeds and little flotillas of ducks. Frogs squelched and yelped like rubber cats, and turtles glided about beneath the water from one stone to another. In the centre of the pool stood a still and silent man with his shalwar rolled up above his knees, who very much resembled a heron, and was clearly a leech gatherer.

The town itself rose up to the left-hand side, occupying a concave hillside that was like a vast amphitheatre. In it our ances-tors could have built the biggest theatre in the world, had the idea occurred to them, because down at the bottom was the meydan, which might have been a natural stage. In the meydan, and I swear this is not some mischievous traveller's tale, there was actually a family living with an asthmatic donkey in the hollowed trunk of an enormous tree. More than anything else this illustrates how quickly civilised standards tailed away the further you got from Smyrna. This was the kind of place where you might find beehives actually inside people's houses, and people making cattle food in their kitchens, consisting of cakes made of apricot and walnut leaves. There was a small group of people there who had turned Turk because they had got fed up with the exactions of Lent, and it wasn't uncommon for Turks to go into churches and light candles. Sometimes they even went to observe the services, and would stand at the back of the church with their arms folded, in the perfect attitude of interested scepticism. Apparently they particularly enjoyed the service on Resurrection Day.

Once I was in the town in a time of drought, and the townswomen were busy making rain. I was astonished to see it.

There was a woman wearing a cow's forehead and horns on her own head, all bedecked with ribbons and beads, and all the women were quaintly dressed in rags and wildflowers and herbs, and they pranced and danced and sang from house to house, and the people in the houses would give them nuts and chickpeas and raisins, and they sang a song which went.

'May May my Constantine
Give rain here and mud there
To our meadows
To our water pots
Seven times
Seven times
Once here, once there
Once in Charon's yard.'

I remember this in particular, because when I saw it there was a marvellously ugly little girl in the procession who was accompanied by one who was marvellously pretty, and I couldn't help noticing the anomaly of it.

The town was a bafflingly intractable labyrinth, but at the same time it was, in my opinion, very well thought out. Streets wide enough only for the passing of two camels radiated up the hillside and twisted almost horizontally along its contours, so that houses and courtyards were connected to each other in the most surprising ways, all of them eventually converging upon the Church of St Nicholas, with its famous nine chandeliers, its exterior walls cleverly rendered to appear like stone, its efficacious and benefacient icon of the Panagia Glykophilousa, and its mosaicked courtyard of chevrons, roundels and squares, all executed beautifully in fragments of marble, maroon and white and black, with the number '1910' set in to commemorate its recent renovation. In this church, strange to report, and much to my astonishment, some of the Christians lit their candles and placed them in the sandbox as you might expect, but then knelt down and prayed whilst making Muslim prostrations. Behind the church was its ossuary, perhaps two metres deep, and from that dank cave emanated the disconsolate odour of mouldering rags and slowly decomposing bones. Because it was a church of St Nicholas, the olive tree outside it was tied with rags put there by barren women. There was a woman who tied many rags there, and she was apparently the wife of the priest. This woman was sometimes called upon to cure children who were late to learn how to speak, and she cured them by pressing the crosspiece of the church key against their lips. Whether it worked or not, I have no idea.

I thought the construction of the houses wonderfully sensible, for they were made in stone with a system of terracotta guttering that replenished large cisterns that were invariably built on to the side of every house. This must have reduced enormously the difficulties one often has with a shortage of water in the summer, and must have saved the women from making many arduous trips to the wells, whose stonework was deeply grooved from so many centuries of raising and lowering the buckets. On another outside corner of every house was a small but decent round-roofed earth closet with a proper door and a comfortably made seat, and a little window high up to carry off any unpleasant miasma.

Many of the houses had wooden platforms slotted into their sides in order to increase space, surmounted by gaily coloured

266

canopies to reduce the oppression of the sun. The chimney tops were of a most practical design, resembling small houses with pitched roofs, and windows cut into the sides to let out the smoke. The fireplaces themselves were always on the upper floor, since it was customary to keep animals below in winter, so that their warmth could rise up and supplement the effects of the fires. One's impression of the interiors was dominated by the fact that everyone painted their woodwork in a most jolly shade of cornflower blue. The exteriors, on the other hand, were painted in gentle pinks, blues and yellows, and each one had a songbird in a small cage suspended outside a window or the front door, so that the town not only presented a very pretty and homely picture indeed as it rose higgledy-piggledy up the hillside, but was always rich in competitive birdsong.

There was a lower church at the bottom of the town, a modest but pleasant building dedicated to St Minas, who had a great following in those parts. It had its own ossuary round the back, protected by a wrought-iron grille, and its floor was cleverly but cheaply made out of black and white pebbles carefully arranged to resemble a big star surrounded by an entwinement of vine tendrils. What particularly struck me about this church was that an owl was permitted to live in it unmolested, spending its days perched on a beam, occasionally opening its eyes to inspect scornfully those who stood below and disturbed its repose. A cloth was placed on the floor beneath its perch, for obvious reasons.

Because the town was built on the side of a hill whose other side slopes down to a cliff above the sea, there is a constant wind that deflects off the rocks above and produces a sound like thunder. This booming is so regular and perpetual that very quickly one ceases to notice it. I climbed and wended up those steep, rough-stoned, stepped pathways to the top of the town, where there is a broken Byzantine watch tower and a tiny white chapel, and found that nearby there is a cleft where a deliciously cool wind blows through and preserves the town from the bad air disease in summer, when God in His infinite perversity decrees that the hardest work must be done at the hottest time of the year. Cut into the ground is a deep lime quarry full of hidey-holes, where sometimes the children play in the evenings.

I walked along the ridge above the town and saw that there were many old tombs. There was a dumb man living there as a sort of hermit of unknown provenance, though some thought that he might have been a Kalandar dervish, whose smile was so hideous that no one could bear to behold it. When I saw it I received such a shock that I recoiled violently and fell over, knocking my head on a rock and grazing my hand. It was said that he must at some time have had his lips pinned back and been forced to bite down upon a large red-hot iron that caused unspeakable damage to his teeth, his gums and his tongue. He was a harmless lost soul, known by everyone as the Dog, and was a frequent object of charity, whose spirit in the town he helped to nourish by his presence.

I also saw the 'tekke of the saint', as they called it, which was a tomb that had a small hole drilled in the lid and another beneath. The custom was that anyone of any faith would pour olive oil through the top hole so that it would wash over the bones before emerging from the bottom hole, to be used as a general panacea. No one knew anything about this saint, except that he was one, although it looked to me as though the tomb must greatly predate the time of Christ. Certainly he must have been the saint with the oiliest bones in the world, and I collected a small phial of this oil just in case it turned out to be of any use. I employed it on a small patch of dry skin, with efficacious results.

The rocky wilderness above the town was rich in peppery oregano, thyme, stunted melissa, mountain tea, figs, exuberantly coloured beetles and wonderful charcoal-coloured crickets that flashed red wings when they jumped. It was a fine thing to sit up there at dusk as the sun descended behind me, watching the smoke rise up from the braziers, and seeing the gold leaf of the minaret of the mosque sparkling ruby in the day's last rays.

Where was I? I've forgotten what I was supposed to be talking about. I think I must have digressed somewhat. Ah, yes, well, it was Leonidas. I do apologise. You will have realised that I was enthusiastic about this town and its amenities, not least because it was one of the very few I have ever visited that provided the comfort and consolation of a public urinal. It is a poignant experience to see that forsaken paradise now, mainly reduced to rubble, looted, uninhabited except by ghosts, lizards and the traces of ancient memory.

Yes, I loved that town, enough to build it a pump house at my own expense, but I was considerably less keen on the dwelling of Leonidas. He lived in the most appalling and abject disorder in a house that would have been eminently pleasant had it been occupied by anyone else. Leonidas, however, had visited upon it an apocalypse of dust, scattered papers and books heaped up in tottering columns. God alone knows how he subsisted, because I encountered no food in his house, and nothing that I would dignify with the name of bedding. I regretted greatly that my servants and bodyguards were in the khan without me, but found that I could not decently leave immediately because Leonidas himself was in a terrible state. His hands were shaking, he could barely walk, and he was incoherent with rage and fright, despite the events which had upset him having occurred two days before. He had dark rings round his eyes, his hair was dishevelled and his face was white with shock.

When I came into his house he threw his arms around my neck and kissed me on both cheeks, which was most uncharacteristic behaviour, since he was normally as reserved as a German, and then, even more uncharacteristically, he began to sob, his shoulders heaving as he took in great gulps of air. I was somewhat disconcerted.

Leonidas told me that he had had to endure a series of humiliations, the least of which was that whenever he bought a songbird to put in the little cage outside his window, someone would immediately replace it with a sparrow, and the greatest of which was that he had been abducted and abased in front of a substantial proportion of the townsmen.

It's a complicated story, but it appears that it was all because a substantial minority of the townspeople were Alevis, the people who believe in the twelve imams and that Mohammed passed on special knowledge to Ali. Don't ask me to explain it all, I'm a Christian, or perhaps I should say that I was supposed to be one, and it's all mysterious to me. I just know that there are an awful lot of Alevis, they're different from other Muslims, and you can scratch your head wondering, should you feel so inclined, whether they're really Muslims at all. A lot of the men there were called Ali, if that is of any interest.

These Alevis, it transpired, used to have secret drinking parties called 'muhabbets', and because of the general confusion of the population in that place, all the intermarriage and changing of faiths and so on, a lot of people who weren't Alevis at all, or maybe just a bit Alevi, used to get to go to these parties. The puritanical Leonidas was disgusted that so many Christians were there, acting like infidels, but it seemed to me to be perfectly understandable that all sorts of people should like to gather together and get paralysed with drink and hilarity. It's the sort of thing I used to do myself when I was young and silly, which Leonidas unfortunately never was.

At these muhabbets there was always someone who was in charge, who would order people to start drinking raki, and would then order people to drink more. If you defied him or left the table without his permission, you were fined a bottle of raki and a cockerel, an imposition that for some reason they called a Gabriel.

The party in question had been going for some time, and they had drunk a great deal whilst listening to drinking songs and tragic dirges about the death of Ali, when the inebriated conversation of the men turned to deciding upon who was the most unpleasant and least popular person in the town, and, I regret to say (although I am not surprised to find myself saying it), that Leonidas was elected unanimously.

What happened was that two strong young men were sent out to bring him in, and he was dragged in his night attire through the streets, struggling and shouting, witnessed by all those who came to their doors and did nothing to intervene. He was hauled into the house where the muhabbet was taking place, thrown down on the floor, and heartily mocked and abused. Then he was ordered to drink raki, which he refused, so it was poured down his throat whilst he was forced to his knees and his head held back by the hair. Then the saki ordered him to dance, and when he failed to comply they started to stamp on his toes so that he would have to dance in order to avoid his feet being crushed. He was forced alternately to drink and dance until he could barely stand, so he said, and his heart was thumping so hard that he thought he was going to die. With a pistol at his head they made him recite lists of dreadful insults against himself, and then someone fetched a donkey's pack saddle, saddled him with it, and forced him to dance and drink and vomit until he was so insensible that they disposed of him simply by throwing him out in the street, still besaddled, where he crawled a short way before falling unconscious, and where at dawn he was found in a pool of his own effluents by the imam, who fetched two Christians to carry him home. Before long someone called Ali the Snowbringer, stupendously drunk, turned up and without the slightest hint of compunction reclaimed the saddle.

Naturally I was horrified by this history of assault, but I did try to explain to Leonidas that he had probably helped to bring it upon himself by his intolerant and supercilious manner. This provoked an argument, as you might imagine, even though I was much his senior, and I came imminently to understand why his own father had disowned him. He called me a traitor and a heathen and a philistine and a vulgar materialist and a Turkish Dog and an Ottoman Lackey, and a False Greek. He hurled an inkpot at my head with serendipitous inaccuracy, and demanded somewhat hysterically that I should leave, which I confess that I did with some relief, because by then I had been offended quite enough, and had legitimate excuse to stay in the khan rather than in his dreadful little house.

I never saw Leonidas again, and nor did I ever want to, even though I came quite often to the town to develop my trade with it. Like his father, I decided that he was a lost cause, and avoided his quarter quite conscientiously. I took pleasure in seeing other people instead. Iskander the Potter became almost a friend despite our differences of station. I liked the imam too, a magnificent, white-bearded, green-turbaned fellow who rode around on a coquettish white mare that was decorated with ribbons and little brass bells. Sometimes I would see that prettiest girl, happily walking arm in arm with that plainest. I always thought that that, too, was a metaphor for something, but I never decided what.

I wonder what became of them all.

46

Mustafa Kemal (10)

By the time that Mustafa Kemal reaches Istanbul, the war is already all but lost. The supplies of the Ottoman troops always seem to have gone to the wrong places, and they cannot work out how to operate the wonderful modern weapons with which the Germans have supplied them. They are outnumbered almost two to one. A German battleship has moved the Sultan and his wives to the Asiatic side of the Bosporus. Macedonia has been lost, and Salonika is occupied first by Greek and then by Bulgarian troops. The Albanians suddenly find themselves cut off from the empire by various Balkan armies, and take the opportunity to declare independence.

Istanbul is well defended, and Adrianopolis is still holding out against siege. The empire's only battleship, the antique *Hamidiye*, in despite of a large hole in her side, has slipped past the Greek fleet in the Dardanelles, and is single-handedly and quixotically sinking Greek cargo boats and bombarding Greek towns. Its crew and its improbable commander are becoming national heroes.

The government decides to sue for peace, and the Grand Vizier considers ceding Adrianopolis and Thrace to the enemy, but the romantic, handsome and unintellectual Enver Pasha persuades the Committee of Union and Progress that Adrianopolis must not be given up. At the head of a patriotic crowd he enters the council chambers of the Sublime Porte. The Minister of War, a cigarette dangling lackadaisically from the corner of his mouth, admits Enver, but the former's bodyguard shoots one of the intruders, and so someone immediately shoots the Minister, who falls down to the ground, exclaiming 'The dogs have done me in!'

The Grand Vizier gives up his job with no apparent regret, remarking laconically, 'I suppose you want the Grand Seal.'

Enver Pasha and his comrades assume absolute power, thus completing the usual trajectory of the revolutionary, who begins as a liberator and ends up the same as, or worse than, the tyrants he has displaced in the name of his liberal ideal.

Mustafa Kemal is dismayed and disgusted, but for the moment the coup is a popular one. Enver has a dashing scheme for saving Adrianopolis, which includes encircling the Bulgarian army via the Gallipoli peninsula, where Mustafa Kemal is Director of Operations. The attack is a shambles, and breaks down amid the mutual recriminations of its commanding officers, including Mustafa Kemal, who resigns. Adrianopolis falls, not least because a Serbian army has arrived, and inside its walls there are large numbers of Greeks and Bulgarians who are able to subvert its defences. Enver is forced to accept the very conditions that his coup was intended to prevent, whereupon his new War Minister is promptly assassinated. At Adrianopolis, the conquering Serbs and Bulgarians put 20,000 captured Ottoman troops on the island of Sarayiçi, where they die of disease and starvation.

Enver forms a triumvirate military dictatorship, and sets about hanging his rivals. Most fortunately for him, but inevitably and predictably, since they have never done anything else, the Balkan states start to quarrel and fall out over the carving up of the conquered territories. Bulgaria declares war on her Allies, the tide of refugees begins to flow again, and Enver is able to take advantage of the mayhem. His armies retake eastern Thrace, and he enters Adrianopolis in triumph at the head of a unit of cavalry, thus deeply irritating Mustafa Kemal and the other commanders who have actually done all the fighting and planning. Enver preens himself as the hero of the hour. He finally marries the Sultan's niece, and goes to live in a palace on the Bosporus. In the meantime, Greece and Serbia have joyously divided between them what was taken from the Bulgarians. The latter sign a treaty with the Ottomans, arranging for an exchange of populations, supposedly of Turks and Bulgarians only, but Enver's government takes the opportunity to expel 100,000 Greeks at the same time. Shortly afterwards they will take the further opportunity of expelling 200,000 Greeks from the Aegean coast. All is quiet until the assassination of the Austrian Archduke in Sarajevo in June of 1914. Salonika remains in Greek hands, and becomes Thessaloníki. Mustafa Kemal says to his brother officers, 'How could you leave Salonika, that beautiful home of ours? Why did you hand it over to the enemy and come here?' He will always be angry and ashamed that it was surrendered to the Greeks without a shot being fired.

Mustafa Kemal and his friend Fethi are exasperated by Enver and his regime. Mustafa is too blunt and truthful to be a success under such circumstances. He writes anonymous pamphlets attacking Enver. He and Fethi want to dispense with the paid terrorists who operate under the auspices of the Committee of Union and Progress, and consequently it seems likely that they themselves will become candidates for disposal. Their lives are probably saved by an offer that neither of them is in a position to refuse, and they are both posted to Sofia. Mustafa Kemal has to leave behind his friend Corinne, the Italian widow of an old comrade. Whether they were lovers or not is a matter known only to them, but it is certain that in her charming and interesting salon his admiration and love for Western culture became ever deeper. In Sofia this love cannot but grow, and Mustafa Kemal begins to envisage that one day opera houses and orchestras will spring up in Ankara and Istanbul.

47

I am Philothei (9)

I was once out working on the hillside, expecting Ibrahim to creep up on me at any time, when what should happen but his dog Kopek arrived instead.

Kopek was a nice dog except to strangers, but even so I was frightened of him because he was practically the size of a donkey, and he had a metal collar with spikes round his neck, and his teeth were like big white daggers, and when he came to find me I jumped up on a rock. I was thinking, 'Oh God, I hope he doesn't bite me in my face, not in my face,' but Kopek wasn't interested in biting anyone on that occasion.

He kept coming up to me and then turning round to go, and then he'd look back over his shoulder, and it was obvious that he wanted me to follow him, and he wouldn't give in, so finally it was me who gave in, and I followed him, and he kept looking over his shoulder to make sure I was there.

That was how I found Ibrahim with his foot trapped in the narrow space between two big boulders, and he couldn't get it out. I laughed at him and said, 'How did you do that?' and he said, 'I don't know. Just stop laughing and go and get help.'

I said, 'How can I tell anyone I've been with you up here? What about the disgrace?' and he said, 'Tell your brother, and make him swear it was him who found me.'

So that is what I did. I told Mehmetçik that I had come across Ibrahim accidentally, and please not to tell anyone because of the talk, and he agreed, and so it was that a whole party of men had to go up and bash at the rocks and dig round them, and finally when Ibrahim got free he was very badly bruised and was limping for days.

Next time I saw him he said, 'Now I suppose you think I am very stupid,' and I said, 'No, I've discovered that Kopek is very clever, that's all.'

Of course I did think that Ibrahim was stupid to get his foot trapped like that, but Leyla Hanım once told me that if you make a man feel stupid he starts to hate you, so I took her advice and kept quiet about it.

48

Of Righteousness and Wrongdoing

Rustem Bey walked slowly through the narrow streets, dodging the hawkers and beggars, and pushing past recumbent camels and overburdened donkeys. His head was aching, and he was feeling demoralised and unwell. Frequently he passed his hands over his eyes, as if he could wipe away the oppression of his mood. He noticed that the poppies that grew out of the interstices of the walls and pavements were at last beginning to come up red rather than pink, and he beheld them with that small but happy sense of recognition that one always experiences upon coming across something forgotten but familiar.

He came to the front door of Abdulhamid Hodja's house, and was about to knock when he heard the imam's voice chanting softly in the lower part where he kept his horse, Nilufer, and where Tamara Hanım had lain in the straw after the stoning. He stopped and listened, realising that the old man was extemporising a prayer to protect his mare from the evil eye. It was not such a peculiar thing to do, for, despite her advancing age, Nilufer was still the most beautiful horse in the region, more beautiful even than any of those owned by Rustem Bey, and there were many who openly regarded her with envy. Besides, everyone knew that there were women in the town who could cast the evil eye without even intending it. Rustem Bey leaned on the door jamb, reassured by the sweet musty smell of horse and hay, unwilling to interrupt the verse, which struck him as quite intimately beautiful, and he watched with a kind of indulgent affection as Abdulhamid unselfconsciously braided the blue beads into the horse's mane. 'Nazar deymesin,' repeated the imam,

> 'Nazar deymesin.
> May these beads divert the evil eye,
> May it never look upon you.

My eyes, my soul, my heart,
May I always keep you to myself.
How beautiful you are.
Let me wipe your eyes with the corners of my robe.
Let me smooth your body with my sleeve.
I am poor, my antelope, yet I raised you in my dwelling
As if you were a child.
I have never beaten nor chided you.
I have always caressed you fondly.
How sweet is your breath, scented with hay and with herbs.
How deep and brown are your eyes, like those of a maid.
God preserve you, beloved.
You are lovely.
How soft and white is your mane.
How gentle and rich is your soul.
How beautiful you are.
My dolphin,
God defend you from envious eyes.
Nazar deymesin.'

Abdulhamid Hodja, on account of that instinct that all of us have, suddenly became aware that there was someone present, and turned his head quickly. He caught sight of the interloper and exclaimed, 'Salaam aleikum, salaam aleikum! I do believe you have just caught me talking to my horse. It's the madness of old age. You should ignore it, out of charity.'

'It's all right,' replied Rustem Bey, 'sometimes I talk to my partridge, and lately I have been finding myself confiding in a cat.'

'Ah yes, the white cat with the one yellow eye and the one blue eye. What's its name?'

'Pamuk.'

'Ah yes, Pamuk. Fortunately it is quite reasonable to confide in an animal. It's when you do it to trees and stones that people call you mad.'

Rustem Bey smiled. 'And when you talk to your horse, efendi, does she say anything sensible in return?'

Abdulhamid waggled his head as if in thought, shrugged, and said, 'Well, she flares her lips and bares her teeth and gums, and tosses her head and rolls her eyes. I have found that this is all she has to say about pretty much anything. She finds it eloquence enough for most purposes, and the odd thing is that I usually know what she means.'

'Pamuk has many more things to say,' observed Rustem Bey. 'So many chirrups and miaows. She seems quite certain that I understand her.'

'And what about you? What do you have to say?' asked Abdulhamid. 'Did you want something? Anything I can help with?'

Rustem Bey was silent for a moment, and then said, 'I have heard that there's going to be a war.'

'Another one? God help us! What is it this time?'

'A matter of battleships. Apparently the British sold us some battleships, and now, because of their own war, they are keeping them back from us. You remember, the money was raised by public subscription, and so everyone is very angry.'

The two men looked at one another for a few moments, and Abdulhamid Hodja finally broke the silence: 'But, Aga Efendi, you didn't come here to talk to me about a war, and I am sure that I've paid the rent on my land.'

'No,' agreed Rustem Bey, 'I didn't want to talk about the war.' He breathed deeply and said abruptly, 'Efendi, how does one know when one has done something wrong?'

'Something wrong? How does one know?' The imam paused for reflection, furrowing his brow and stroking his white beard. 'Well, you must understand that some things can only be understood with reference to some kind of opposite. Night, for example, is only night because it stands against day, and male is only male because it stands against female. Do you follow me?'

Rustem Bey nodded seriously.

'So wrongdoing must be understood by standing it against righteousness,' explained Abdulhamid, holding out his hands, 'like right against left.' He turned one hand over and then the other.

He paused to take note of whether Rustem Bey was still with him. 'Righteousness is good morality, but it is also that about which the soul feels tranquil and the heart feels tranquil. This is what the Prophet said to Wabisa ibn Mabad.

'As for wrongdoing, Nawwas ibn Saman said that he overheard the Prophet saying that wrongdoing is that which wavers in the soul and which you dislike people finding out about, and Wabisa ibn Mabad said that he heard the Prophet say that wrongdoing is that which wavers in the soul and moves to and fro in the breast, even though people again and again have given you their legal opinion in its favour.

'Both of these traditions came from imams with a good chain of authorities, one from Imam Ahmad ibn Hanbal, and the other from Imam ad-Darimi, may God be pleased with them both, so no doubt these things are what was said by the Prophet, peace be upon him.'

Abdulhamid, initially pleased by this impressive display of erudition, then looked Rustem Bey in the face and saw the trouble and distress in his dark eyes. He placed his hand on the aga's forearm, shook it gently, and in a voice full of compassion enquired, 'Rustem Beyefendi, do you feel a wavering in your soul? Let us say, even though everyone agrees you were in the right?'

Rustem Bey looked away, as if expecting something to appear on the horizon, and then cast his eyes down to the ground, scuffing at a stone with the toe of his boot. He hung his head, and said, 'I feel a terrible wavering in my soul.'

49

Mustafa Kemal (11)

It is November 1913, and it is the first time that Mustafa Kemal has lived in a European capital, and he is enchanted. In Sofia there are wide boulevards, and parks. Life is orderly, there are dinners and salons, there is sparkling conversation with intelligent and cultivated ladies. Sofia is like Vienna on a more intimate scale.

It takes time for Mustafa Kemal to adapt. He has to learn to become a European, he has to acquire the nuances of manners, he has to bring himself to make small talk, he has to drink his alcohol with a little less virile gusto. He becomes adept at the tango and the waltz, and the ladies find him intriguingly attractive. He goes to the opera, is introduced to King 'Foxy' Ferdinand, and afterwards, enthused by the opera rather than the monarch, is too excited to go to sleep.

He writes frequently to Corinne, sometimes in clumsy French, and sometimes in Turkish written in Roman letters. He likes to assure her that there are no beautiful or attractive women that have caught his attention.

He has the Justice Minister to dinner, and this leads to a dinner with his erstwhile enemy, the Bulgarian Minister of War, General Kovatchev, who had fought against Kemal in the second Balkan War. He and Kemal become close friends, and talk the nights away in reminiscence and in discussion of military affairs. The general has a pretty daughter, Dimitrina, and Kemal begins to notice her.

The general is Kemal's entrée to high society, and soon he is courted by everyone who is anyone. He becomes an habitué of the drawing room of Sultana Ratcho Petrova, Sofia's most sought-after hostess. He receives the congratulations of King Ferdinand for having the best fancy-dress outfit at a masked ball. He has sent an orderly away to Istanbul to borrow a janizary uniform from a museum. He has the spectacular headdress, and a sword that sparkles with jewels, and he is a sensation. The King gives him a silver cigarette case. Years later, when Ferdinand's foxiness has run out, and he is in exile, Mustafa Kemal will remember the compliment, and send him a gold one.

Mustafa Kemal tours Bulgaria to see for himself how the Turkish minority lives. He is surprised but gratified to find them running businesses and industries, becoming rich by their own efforts, sending their children to schools where there are proper curricula, and not merely the recitation of the Koran in Arabic. The women are unveiled. Mustafa Kemal becomes ever clearer about what he wants for Turkey. He attends the Bulgarian parliament in order to witness the modern practice of politics. He involves himself with more or less clandestine projects involving the Turkish community. However, the most impressive thing is how far the ordinary Bulgarians have advanced in the few years since they threw off the Ottoman yoke. Once upon a time they were regarded as savages, but now they have forged ahead.

Kemal is disappointed in love, perhaps, but only he and Dimitrina know the truth. Perhaps he has fallen for her, this pretty daughter of his friend General Kovatchev. He dances with her all night at a ball, and they talk of music. Then he speaks passionately to her of his ambitions for Turkey, of how women will be unveiled, about how their marriages will no longer be an enslavement, of how they will become as captivating and free and educated as Dimitrina herself. It is said that Mustafa Kemal sounds out how the general would feel about a proposal of marriage, and is discouraged. The general pointedly but politely refuses an invitation to a ball at the embassy. In any case, Mustafa Kemal will never see the sweet Dimitrina again, though equally she will never forget him.

Enver and his companions are enjoying the salad days of power, and they are doing unexpectedly well. Enver has been promoted from major to colonel to brigadier within nineteen days, and he has ousted the War Minister and taken his place. 'It is impossible!' exclaims the Sultan. 'He is much too young.' With marvellous energy Enver is reforming the armed services, allegedly purging the old-fashioned ignorant time-servers among the officer corps, but apparently sacking every influential officer equal to or above his own rank. Enver gives over the reform of the army to the Germans, and General Liman von Sanders arrives with a large number of officers who will take control of all sorts of vital commands. The Germans find that the Ottoman soldiers are barefoot and in rags, that their destitute families have to eat in military canteens, that there is no care for the men on the part of the officers, that military hospitals are squalid, and that the horses and mules are sick and useless. Von Sanders and his men set about their Herculean task, and all goes well.

Only hindsight will reveal what a catastrophe this dependence on Germany will bring in its train. The Archduke Ferdinand has been assassinated in Sarajevo, and now Enver and an inner cabal of the Cabinet have agreed a secret treaty with Germany, with the intention of presenting a united front against Russia, the eternal enemy and arch-devil. All attempts to seek assistance and assurances from Great Britain and France have failed, and the Germans had seemed the obvious last resort. Enver keeps the Great Powers in the dark about his agreement, until he is ready to take the offensive.

Mustafa Kemal thinks that the Germans will probably not win, and in any case he mistrusts them. He sees great danger coming from the Bulgarians, who have allied with Austria and still have dreams of a Greater Bulgaria. Enver, however, is enthusiastic and impulsive. By means of public subscription the empire has commissioned two battleships from the British, and the British are withholding them because Churchill has not been deceived about Enver's intentions as war breaks out. The Ottoman public is outraged and two German battleships synchronicitously turn up, having gallantly run the gauntlet of the British fleet. The Germans generously, but not entirely disinterestedly, sell the ships to Enver, the sailors exchange their caps for fezzes, and Germany becomes ever more popular with the Turkish people.

Enver is convinced that he can get the entire Muslim world behind him by playing the Islamic card, thus disabling much of the Russian, British and French empires. Unfortunately the Kaiser believes the same thing. Enver thinks that a war might be a very fine and profitable enterprise, and so, without telling anyone else, he arranges for the two new battleships plus the valiant old *Hamidiye* to enter the Black Sea. In his pocket the German admiral has a secret order, which states: 'The Turkish fleet should gain mastery of the Black Sea by force. Seek out the Russian fleet, and attack her wherever you find her, without declaration of war.' They bombard the Russian ports of Odessa, Novorossik and Sevastopol, and sink some Russian warships.

Enver's colleagues are appalled and amazed by what he has done behind their backs. The Grand Vizier tries to resign, but the Sultan begs him to remain so that he has at least one reliable person in the government who is not insane. He and the Sultan are weeping together when the French and British ambassadors arrive to request their passports.

Thanks to Enver's idiotic adventurism the Ottoman Empire is now at war with Russia, which is at war with Germany and Austria–Hungary. As if this were not bad enough, because Russia herself has Allies, the Ottoman Empire is now at war with Britain and France as well. The reluctant Sultan, who also has the misfortune to be the head of the Muslim world, is persuaded to declare the war a holy one. This he does in the great hall of the Topkapı Palace where the relics of the Prophet are kept. It is expected that the declaration of jihad will be received with much public enthusiasm, but in this case the empire is inexplicably siding with some Christian countries against some other Christian countries, and not many Muslims can make any sense of it. The Arabs in particular will prove disloyal and useless. At the Battle of Shuaiba they will hold back from the fight so that they can pillage whichever side is the loser, causing their Turkish commander to shoot himself in his disillusionment, anger and despair.

Enver tells Mustafa Kemal to stay in Sofia, and Kemal is frustrated. He thinks that the war is a foolish one because it has no military object, but he still wants to be in it. He sets about trying to ensure that Bulgaria will come in on the side of the empire, but he chafes in his exile. He writes to Enver demanding to know whether the latter considers him an incompetent soldier, and he even considers leaving his post and enlisting as a private soldier, but, just in time, he is finally summoned home to be commander of the 19th Division.

50

The Exchange

A tremor of consternation ran through the town. Many of the young men felt excited, even elated, but some felt dread and foreboding rise up in the pit of the stomach. Mothers and sisters put their hands to their mouths and opened their eyes wide with anxiety. Widows in penury reflected that they had nothing left to lose, and wives foresaw the same inevitability for themselves and their children.

It was the beginning of November, a warm and gentle keşişleme breeze was blowing from Cyprus and Arabia. The people of the town had heard that some ships had been built for the Sultan by the Frankish folk called 'British', with money raised by public subscription, and then the British had gone to war and kept the ships for themselves. Everyone in the empire was furious about the betrayal, and there had been much bold and angry rhetoric in all the meydans and coffeehouses. The people had not, however, yet heard the news that the kind Frankish people called 'Germans' had donated battleships of their own, and that these had opened fire on the Black Sea bases of the Russian Empire. They did not know that Enver Pasha, effectively the military dictator, had ordered the bombardment of these bases without consulting the Sultan, the Grand Vizier, or the majority of the other ministers, four of whom had consequently resigned in disgust. They did not know that Enver Pasha had a great vision to pursue, of expanding the Ottoman Empire to the east, to include all the Turkic peoples. This was the age when everyone wanted an empire and felt entitled to one, days of innocence perhaps, before the world realised, if it yet has, that empires were pointless and expensive, and their subject peoples rancorous and ungrateful. Perhaps it galled Enver Pasha that over the previous ninety years the empire had repeatedly and relentlessly been under malicious and opportunist attack from its neighbours and former territories.

Where does it all begin? History has no beginnings, for everything that happens becomes the cause or pretext for what occurs afterwards, and this chain of cause and pretext stretches back to the palaeolithic age, when the first Cain of one tribe murdered the first Abel of another. All war is fratricide, and there is therefore an infinite chain of blame that winds its circuitous route back and forth across the path and under the feet of every people and every nation, so that a people who are the victims of one time become the victimisers a generation later, and newly liberated nations resort immediately to the means of their former oppressors. The triple contagions of nationalism, utopianism and religious absolutism effervesce together into an acid that corrodes the moral metal of a race, and it shamelessly and even proudly performs deeds that it would deem vile if they were done by any other.

There was between 1821 and 1913 a prolonged and atrocious holocaust which we have chosen to forget, and from which we have learned absolutely nothing. In 1821, between 26 March and Easter Sunday, in the name of liberty, the southern Greek Christians tortured and massacred 15,000 Greek Muslim civilians, looted their possessions, and burned their dwellings. The Greek hero, Kolokotronis, boasted without qualm that so many were the corpses that his horse's hooves never had to touch the ground between the town gates of Athens and the citadel. In the Peloponnese many thousands of Muslims, mainly women and children, were rounded up and butchered. Thousands of shrines and mosques were destroyed, so that even now there are only one or two left in the whole of Greece.

During the 1820s, as a result of war against Serbia and Russia, 20,000 Muslims were expelled from Serbia.

In 1875, Orthodox Bosnian Serb Christians began a campaign of assassination against Muslims in general and Ottoman officials in particular.

In 1876, Bulgarian Christians massacred an unknown number of peasants of Turkish origin.

In 1877, Russia attempted to impose humiliating concessions on the Ottomans, and as a result of their refusal, declared war. Using tactics invented for use against Muslims in the Caucasus,

Cossacks assisted by Bulgarian revolutionaries and peasants seized all the property of Muslims. Cossacks would surround the villages to prevent any escape, disarm the inhabitants and send the Bulgarians in to slaughter them. Sometimes the villages were simply obliterated by artillery. Sometimes the inhabitants were sold into slavery. European diplomats recorded that this episode was remarkable for the systematic manner in which new ways were invented to torture women to death as slowly as possible.

As a consequence of this campaign of extermination, a vast swarm of half a million starving Muslim refugees of one religion but of all ethnic backgrounds took to the roads, driven hither and thither without rest by bandits, guerrillas and soldiers. In Edirne one hundred of them died each day of typhus. In Istanbul's great church of Aya Sofya, then a mosque, there huddled four thousand hopeless souls, of whom thirty died every day, only to be replaced by others. Alongside and among these Muslims, almost unnoticed by history, suffered and died the Jews, because the common cry of the liberating heroes in those days was 'Jews and Turks Out!'

The Montenegrins killed or expelled their entire Muslim population.

By 1879, one-third of all the Muslims of Bosnia–Herzogovina had either emigrated or been killed.

Sir Henry Layard, British Ambassador to the Sublime Porte, wrote that the policy of the Russians in the region was to eliminate the Muslims and replace them with Slavs.

In 1912, Bulgaria, Serbia, Montenegro and Greece all declared war on the Ottoman Empire with the intention of seizing more Ottoman territory and bringing about more forced migration. To the tactics described above was added the technique of herding Muslims into coffeehouses and barns, and then burning them down. As before, civilian men were killed quickly, but women were tortured to death as slowly as possible. Captured Ottoman soldiers were treated with particular brutality. In Edirne the defeated soldiers were put on to an island and starved to death. The history books coyly declare that the details of the horrors that were perpetrated are too gruesome to report.

The main tactic was for irregular shock troops, called komitadjis, who might otherwise be described as guerrillas, bandits, brigands or liberating heroes, motivated by hatred and the desire for loot (otherwise known as patriotism), to attack the villages and force the inhabitants on to the roads. Montenegrins devastated Albania. The Turkish refugees of Thrace were driven eastwards by the Greeks, and then driven back again by the Bulgarians marching south, and back once more. Their misery and desperation is unimaginable. The Bulgarian army left behind it eighty miles of ruined villages. After their victory, the Bulgarians, Greeks and Serbians all claimed Macedonia, and the two latter went to war with the former, with Romania joining the party shortly afterwards. The Ottomans took advantage of the squabble between the Christian liberators, and retook Edirne and eastern Thrace.

It is impossible to know how many Muslim, Jewish and Turkish civilians died during the Balkan Wars, nor how many soldiers, but it is known that the Ottomans had to take in about half a million new refugees. The constant fighting and the never-ending influx of refugees crippled the economy. Also ruined was the Ottoman Empire's greatest achievement, the millet system which guaranteed religious liberty for all. Despite some lapses, for almost all of its history the empire had protected the different denominations, allowing them to administer their own affairs and follow their own laws, which is the reason that the Greek Orthodox Church was able to survive intact, as an arm of the Ottoman state, carrying with it the Greek language, and the culture and religion of the Byzantines, just as the sultans had taken over the administrative system of the Byzantines and left it unchanged. Now, however, the hell's broth of religious and nationalist hatred had been stirred up by a multitude of village Hitlers, and the Balkans were irreparably changed for the worse.

It is possible that on 29 October 1914, when he either agreed or gave the order for the bombardment of those Russian bases by German sailors dressed in Turkish uniform, manning German battleships with Turkish names, Enver Pasha was thinking that he had no choice but to side with Germany.

It was very simple. Britain and France were old yet exacting friends of the empire, but they were allied with Russia, and every Turk suspected that Russia wanted Turkey in its empire, preferably without any Turks left alive in it. An Allied victory would have been a sanguinary catastrophe for the Turks, and a satisfying final solution for the Russians. It must have been clear to Enver Pasha that his enemy's enemy was his friend, and he had no choice but to gamble on a German victory. Apart from that, there was a century of disaster to make up for, and no one can know how much he was motivated by injured pride on behalf of his own people. If so, it was an irony that his own incompetence and ambition should result in yet more disaster for his country, for instead of fighting a sensible defensive war, he went straight into the attack against the Russians in north-eastern Anatolia, through impassable mountains, and snow that was sometimes twenty feet deep. Within two months 75,000 of an army of 95,000 were dead, and he had lost all his machine guns and artillery.

It was as part of this sorry concatenation of events that in November 1914 there occurred the arrival in Eskibahçe of Sergeant Osman, along with a Jewish clerk, a donkey laden with ledgers, and four dusty and disgruntled gendarmes.

Sergeant Osman was an artilleryman of long service and fierce disposition. Unlike the gendarmes, the donkey and the Jew, Osman had managed to remain reasonably smart after the long and exhausting trek from Telmessos. He had a moustache waxed elegantly to upturn at the tips, he had blue and red epaulettes, a crimson fez, and red stripes at the bottom of his sleeves. Around his neck he wore the whistle that he once had employed for shrilling out the coded orders that took the place of shouting when in the heat of battle. Sergeant Osman had a romantic sabre scar across his left cheek, his face was dark and leathery from living a hard life in all weathers, and he was tough in the way that only Turkish soldiers can be. He was the kind of man who could march five hundred miles with a band of captives, and be genuinely puzzled at the end of it as to why all his prisoners had died on the way. He had not seen his wife and children for a year, and he had seen such terrible things in Thrace that much of the time he concentrated upon keeping his mind resolutely blank. Despite this, he could not repress one image of the Balkan War that recurred frequently and unpredictably, sometimes making him wake up at night with his eyes staring and his heart thumping

289

painfully in his chest. It was of a field of stupendous carnage in Thrace in which only one building remained partially intact, and on the wooden door of that building hung a naked little girl who had been crucified and disembowelled. He could not forget the sweetness and innocence of that bowed little head with its tumbling shaggy locks of hair falling about its face. He could not forget that face with its open mouth and its little pink tongue and its two rows of tiny milk teeth. He could not forget reaching out and touching the child's neck, realising as he did so that she was freshly dead. Worst of all was the crimson cavity of the stomach, disgorging its multicoloured and glistening cascade of entrails, piled up as if from the ground, that was already abuzz with flies. Sergeant Osman was not a philosophically sophisticated man, and so he was neither amazed nor outraged by the sacrilege that the retreating Greeks had perpetrated in visiting upon a child the same death as had been suffered by their own innocent Lord. In any case this crucifixion of children by Christians was quite a common thing in his experience, and the shock of it eventually wore off. What struck Osman as he touched the child's neck was that it looked just like one of his own daughters at the same age, and so it was that in the nightmares and flashbacks of later years, it was his own child that he saw disembowelled and nailed to a door in Thrace. Sergeant Osman seldom thought of the vile things that he himself had done whilst in the baresark rage of victory or revenge, because it was all wiped out and cancelled by this one scene that overtopped and outplayed them all.

Sergeant Osman had been so repeatedly wounded that he now found himself limping from town to town and village to village, accompanied by four gendarmes, a donkey and a Jew, in order to call up the reserve and recruit new troops. It caused him much frustration and bitterness that he had thus been apparently demoted, and in every place where there was a letter-writer he caused a letter to be written to Enver Pasha and the Sultan himself, begging to be allowed back into the front line with his regiment, this being in addition to the many written on his behalf by the patient and long-suffering Jew. Osman had a sense of his destiny, and he knew that this job was not a part of it, so that occasionally he became irascible in the prosecution of it.

Upon arrival in the town Osman went for a shave, and then, refreshed and smelling of lemon cologne, he set up office under a plane tree in the meydan and sent out the gendarmes with the clerk to fetch in the empire's new soldiers.

Thus it was that Iskander was in the shade of his tatty awning happily fashioning birdwhistles for Mr Theodorou's export business in Smyrna, when he became aware of the four unfamiliar gendarmes and the clerk standing by his side waiting for him to finish the particular one which he was making. His initial reaction was to wonder what he had done wrong, and he felt a pang of fear. The clerk pushed his spectacles further up his nose and asked, 'You are Iskander, a potter of this town?'

'I am Iskander, yes. Peace be with you.'

'And with you,' replied the clerk drily, scratching his forehead with a pencil, and tipping back his fez, 'although I fear it may not be as much peace as you might have wished.'

Iskander looked at him for a moment, and then the clerk said, 'There has been a general mobilisation, and you have been called up again. I am sorry if this is an inconvenience, but there is no choice in the matter, I am afraid.'

Iskander paled. 'I've done my service. I was in Arabia. You can check. I've done my service.'

'I know, I know,' said the clerk, 'but you must realise that you are still in the ihtiyat. You remain in the active reserve for six years, and you have only done five years and nine months.'

'It's nearly six,' replied Iskander, aghast. 'What will happen to my family? How will they live?'

'What will happen to us? How will we live?' wailed Nermin when her distraught but stoical husband came indoors to tell her the news. 'What about the children? What will we do for money? We'll starve. There'll be no one to save us. It'll be like it was when you were in Arabia. We were skeletons. What if you die? I can't go through it all again. Oh God! Oh God! Oh God!' She rocked miserably where she sat, and wiped her eyes with the back of her sleeve.

'It's a holy war,' said Iskander resignedly. 'It's been declared a holy war. God will provide, God willing. What can I do? I've got to go. The Franks have declared war with us, and tomorrow I've got to go. If I die I go to paradise, God willing.'

'What use are you in paradise?' demanded Nermin tearfully.

At this point Karatavuk stepped out of the shadow and knelt before his father, touching his father's hand to his lips and forehead. 'Baba,' he said, 'let me go in your place.'

Iskander looked down at his son and said, 'You're only fifteen.'

'I'm strong. I can fight. I have courage. Let me go. They'll call me up anyway before too long. So let me go now. For the sake of my brothers and sisters, and for Mother's sake.'

Iskander stood speechless, looking down at his favourite son. He knew that there was nothing he could say. If he said 'yes' then he would feel that he had been a coward who was prepared to send his son into danger. If he said 'no' then his wife and family would have no means to live. Nermin also found nothing to say. She went on her knees beside her son, and took his hands in hers, kissing them and pressing them to her cheek so that he could feel the warm trickle of her tears.

'I will not give you permission,' said Iskander at last, as pride conquered his common sense. 'I have to do my duty. It's a holy war, and I don't have the choice. God will protect His own.'

Karatavuk stood up to protest, and his father silenced him with one hand raised. 'Enough,' said Iskander. 'God will surely remember what you have offered to do, as I will remember it. You are a most excellent son.'

So it was that shortly afterwards Karatavuk went to find his friend Mehmetçik, and the two went together to see Sergeant Osman and the clerk at their desk under the plane tree in the meydan. The sergeant, standing at ease with his fingers linked behind his back, raised his eyebrows in enquiry as their turn in the queue came up, and scanned them sceptically.

'We've come to volunteer,' said Mehmetçik.

'Why?' asked the sergeant bluntly.

'For the empire and the Sultan Padishah,' replied Mehmetçik.

'How old are you?'

'I am eighteen,' lied Mehmetçik.

'Your name?'

'Mehmetçik.'

'Son of?'

'Charitos.'

'So, you are Mehmetçik, son of Charitos? So Mehmetçik, I suppose, is a nickname?'

'Yes, beyefendi, my real name is Nico.'

'That's a shame. Mehmetçik is obviously such a good name for a soldier. You and your father are Christian, then?'

'Yes, beyefendi. But I still want to go and fight, as long as I can stay with Karatavuk. For the empire and the Sultan Padishah.'

An expression of puzzlement passed over the sergeant's face. 'Who is this blackbird that you want to stay with?'

'It's my nickname,' said Karatavuk, stepping forward. 'My real name is Abdul.'

The sergeant assessed the boy: dark-eyed, golden-skinned, a little taller than the norm. 'This business of nicknames is an irritation,' he exclaimed at last, waving his hand in a small gesture of exasperation. 'Everyone seems to have one even though the Prophet expressly forbids it. Who are you the son of?'

'Iskander the Potter.'

'I see,' said the sergeant. 'But let's do this one at a time.' He returned to Mehmetçik, stockier and shorter than his friend, but oddly similar nonetheless. 'So you are Nico, son of Charitos, and you say you are eighteen. And a Christian, yes?'

'Yes, beyefendi. But nowadays Christians aren't exempt.'

'I know. Obviously I know. I am a soldier, you see. I have a tendency to know about these things. But haven't you heard that this is a holy war? Haven't you heard that we are fighting the Franks, and that the Franks are Christians? Didn't you hear about the ships, and how they cheated us?'

'I am an Ottoman,' replied Mehmetçik proudly, 'and one of the Frankish peoples is with us. I have heard that they are called "Almanca".'

'Yes, the Germans are with us, but still it's a holy war, and you can't expect us to trust Christians in the army in case they turn against us. It's only natural common sense. If you want to join up you will have to go to one of the labour battalions.'

'Labour battalions?'

'Roads, bridges, things like that,' said the sergeant.

'I want to fight,' said Mehmetçik scornfully, 'not dig holes.'

'You'd better not volunteer, then,' replied the sergeant, with a glint of humour in his eyes. 'We'll come and get you sometime anyway, and then you'll go in a labour battalion. Probably when you really are as old as you say you are. In any case, much of a soldier's life does consist of digging holes. You would just be digging holes without being shot at, which is slightly safer.'

Mehmetçik's eyes glowed with disappointed anger, but he could think of nothing to say, except, 'I don't want to be safer.'

'I am sorry, young man,' said Osman sympathetically. 'In my opinion we'll need all the soldiers we can get, and as a matter of fact one of my grandfathers was Christian, he was from Serbia, but it's not up to me to decide these things. You'll have to wait and see if the rules are changed. In the meantime, if you really want to help the Sultan Padishah and the empire, the best thing you can do is grow food and breed mules.'

'As for you,' said the sergeant, turning to Karatavuk, 'you are a son of Iskander the Potter. You are not on our list. Your father is, however.' He turned to the clerk. 'You have already spoken to him, haven't you, Solomon Efendi?'

'I have.'

'I am offering myself in my father's place,' said Karatavuk, 'according to the tradition.'

'According to the tradition,' repeated the sergeant, regarding Karatavuk with particular respect. 'Do you have your father's permission to go in his place?'

'Yes,' declared Karatavuk, avoiding looking directly in the sergeant's face. 'It's for the sake of my mother and my brothers and sisters.'

'You're lying,' observed the sergeant, 'but fortunately I have not noticed it.'

'Thank you, beyefendi,' said Karatavuk, repeating, 'It's for the sake of my mother and my brothers and sisters. Without my father they won't live. Without me they will have more chance. I am strong. I can fight.'

'You are a good son,' observed the sergeant. 'A man would be proud to have a son like you.'

Karatavuk's shoulders seemed visibly to broaden beneath this praise. 'Do you accept me, beyefendi?'

The sergeant sighed wearily. He had seen so many young sons making this sacrifice. It was always both moving and depressing. He wondered how many of the fine youngsters would ever see their mother's face again. 'Very well, you may come in your father's place, according to the tradition. Let it be on your conscience and not mine for deceiving your father, and may God forgive you for it.'

'Thank you, beyefendi, and, beyefendi, please don't tell my father.'

The sergeant nodded. 'I'll send a message to your father to tell him that after all he has been exempted. He won't know why. You must be here tomorrow in his place.'

As the two boys walked away, Mehmetçik cursed softly under his breath. He had tears of anger in his eyes. 'Grow food and breed mules!' he repeated bitterly, and Karatavuk put his arm round his shoulder in sympathy. 'They'll probably change the rules,' he said, 'if the war gets bad enough.'

'Let's hope that it does, then,' said Mehmetçik shortly. They stopped by Abdulhamid Hodja's house, and Mehmetçik took his leather purse out of his sash. He removed a few paras from it, which he folded back into his sash, and then leaned down and scraped up a handful of earth. He tipped it into the purse, repeated the action, and then drew the string tight. He held it out to his friend. 'Wherever you go,' he said, 'take this with you, and don't empty it out until you return, and when you come back make sure you tip it back in exactly this place.'

Karatavuk took the purse and loosened the drawstring. He sniffed at the soil and sighed. 'The earth of home. It has a partic-ular smell. Have you ever noticed it? When I am far away I shall be able put this to my nose and be reminded.' He closed the purse, put it to his lips and kissed it. He placed it in his own sash, and then he put his arms around his best friend and dropped his forehead on his shoulder for a moment. He felt his throat constrict, and was overcome with an emotion that he could not name, because it was a mixture of so many. 'Ah, my friend, my friend,' he said, drawing back and thumping his chest, 'I have a heavy feeling in here. I feel as if I have a stone in my heart. I wonder what'll become of us all.'

'I think we'll be divided,' said Mehmetçik sadly. 'Suddenly it matters that I am a Christian, where it mattered only a little before.'

'We won't be divided,' replied Karatavuk firmly. 'We have always been friends. We have always been together. You have taught me to read and write.'

'I don't know how much use that will be,' said Mehmetçik. 'When it comes down to it, there's nothing to read, and in other places I hear that all the writing is a different sort, like that writing on the mosque that only Abdulhamid Hodja understands.'

Karatavuk reached once more into his sash and took out his birdwhistle. 'I'm taking this with me. If I break it I will write to my father and ask him to send me another one. When I return you'll hear it and you'll know I'm back.'

'God bring the day,' said Mehmetçik.

'Do you remember,' asked Karatavuk, 'when we were little boys, and we decided not to piss down mouseholes in case the mice drowned? Well, now I've got to go out and put bullets through other men.'

'At least a mouse is innocent,' observed Mehmetçik.

'I wonder what it feels like,' said Karatavuk.

51

The Sadness of Rustem Bey

'Why are you unhappy, my lion?' asked Leyla Hanım, coming up beside Rustem Bey, and placing a hand on his shoulder. It was early evening, and he was seated on a low wall that surrounded a flower bed in the courtyard, his hands limp in his lap, and a stricken look on his face. Pamuk the white cat lay curled up in her favourite place beneath the orange tree. She had lain in the same place so much over the years that she had created a cat-shaped declivity in the gritty soil. Near his feet a large tortoise crawled laboriously by, its shell draped in lava flows of solidified white wax, because Leyla had at some time in the recent past employed it as one of her romantic mobile candelabra.

'I am not so much unhappy, as sad,' he replied.

'There's a difference?'

'I feel there is one, but it might be hard to explain.'

'What is it that saddens you, then?'

Rustem Bey gestured inarticulately. 'It's the war. I ought to be in it, and I have bad feelings about it.'

'You've done all your military service,' said Leyla, appalled at the thought that he might be leaving. She added, somewhat thoughtlessly, 'Aren't you too old?'

Fortunately Rustem Bey was not in the mood for taking offence. 'I have a great deal of experience, and a man is not too old unless he is no longer strong. I daresay I am stronger than most boys who go to war.'

'Of course you are,' agreed Leyla, meaning it quite sincerely. This was a man who disappeared for days at a time to hunt in the mountains. He could lift the dead deer up on to his horse's back as if they were made of stuffed felt.

'I would go,' said Rustem Bey. 'In fact, I made enquiries with my old regiment as soon as war seemed likely. However, I have had a message from the governor asking me to raise a militia and maintain law and order. It seems that most of the gendarmerie will be called to the front.'

'A militia?'

'Old men and little boys and cripples,' said Rustem Bey, 'and as soon as the little boys are old enough, they'll be off to the front too, and then I will have to go and look for more little boys to replace them.'

'So you will stay?'

'Yes, I will stay. But not without some guilt and regret.'

'Oh, thank God,' she said. 'Without you here I couldn't live.' She knew that his presence in the town was the only reason for which she was treated with any consideration or respect.

'I am also sad just because there is a war,' said Rustem Bey, ignoring her, and speaking as if to himself. 'In the first place, we are now at war with France, and France is the civilisation towards which everyone like me naturally aspires. In my regiment the officers all learned French and tried to speak it to each other. In the second place, we are at war with Britain, which has excellent soldiers and sailors, and the biggest empire in the history of the world, and which used to be our best friend, and in the third place, we are at war with Russia, which has always hated us and obstructed us and wanted to take Istanbul from us. On our side we have Austria–Hungary, about which I know very little, and Germany, about which I know less, except that she seems to be extremely good from a military point of view.'

'We have Enver Pasha,' said Leyla, wondering which side the Greeks would take, and wondering who, in her case, 'we' really were.

Rustem snorted. 'Enver Pasha has grown great by taking advantage of good luck and by taking the credit for what has really been achieved by other people. He is certainly ambitious.'

'Well, I don't know about these things,' sighed Leyla. Military and political matters did not interest her very greatly. What really concerned her was that she should not lose Rustem Bey.

'Another thing,' continued Rustem Bey, as if no one were listening, 'I have seen battlefields strewn with the bodies of young men, and old ones too. I have smelled the corpses when there wasn't enough time to bury them before they began to rot. I've

298

seen what happens to the women and the children. The Sultan Padishah has declared it a holy war.'

Rustem Bey paused and Leyla wondered what it signified. 'A holy war?'

'Yes, a holy war. The Sultan Padishah has never been on a burial party when the corpses have been left too long. I will say this to you, my tulip, but I would not say it to anyone else because of what it would do to my reputation . . . do you promise never to repeat this?'

'Repeat what?'

'What I am about to say.'

'I won't repeat it if you don't want me to. Who would I repeat it to anyway? Pamuk?'

'You like to talk with Philothei and Drosoula. Sometimes you do it for hours. I have no doubt that what gets said here is repeated in the town.'

'But what is it that I am not to repeat? And I promise I won't repeat it to them or even to Pamuk.'

'I have an opinion about holy war, which in general I must keep to myself. I have no wish to be known as a heretic. It is . . . that if a war can be holy, then God cannot. At best, a war can only be necessary.'

'Oh,' said Leyla, realising that she would have to think about this before its full import would sink in.

Rustem Bey stood up and faced her. He touched a hand tenderly to her cheek and smiled ironically. 'You shouldn't assume I'll survive, you know. Every time there's a war, the countryside fills up with outlaws and bandits because all the dregs of the armies take the first opportunity to desert, and take their weapons with them. I'll be out there after them with my invincible squads of cripples, old men and little boys.'

'I want you to survive,' said Leyla, her eyes beginning to brim.

'Maybe I'd better leave the invincible squads behind and go after them on my own, then,' said Rustem Bey. 'I suppose I had better start to get something organised.' He touched her face again, and went back into the house. Leyla took his place on the wall, wondering what might come, and fearing for Rustem Bey and herself.

52

A Small Act of Kindness

Polyxeni hurried through the alleyways with a pot in her hands, and was struck all over again by how much more quiet the place had become since so many of the men had been called away. It had only been a few days, and the town already had a hollow feel, everything one saw had the air of being a backdrop to an absence. There were so many faces missing, so many shadows uncast, so many deep or raucous voices unechoed by the walls. The air missed its usual smells of sweat and tobacco, and the tables of the coffeehouse seemed uneasy without their workshy habitués bent over the backgammon boards. There was no news from the war. In this empire, so vast and disorganised, so besieged on all sides, so crippled by perpetual attack, one often only knew whether one's husband or son was dead when there was no news of them for years.

Polyxeni kicked off her shoes at the back door of Nermin's house, knocked, did not wait for a reply, and entered. She found Nermin peeling onions in the semi-darkness, and for that reason was not sure what she was crying about. 'You should do them under water,' advised Polyxeni, 'and that way you don't weep so much.'

'If it wasn't onions . . .' replied Nermin, shrugging.

'How are you?'

'Two of my sons have gone,' said Nermin. 'Karatavuk went in place of his father, and now Iskander's in a fury. He says he was lied to by his own son.'

'It was a noble lie.'

'Yes, it was good. But who knows if he will ever come back? The Sultan calls, and the men go away and die, and we women, we are left to eat the dust and drink tears.'

'Mehmetçik's in a fury too. They wouldn't let him go with Karatavuk.' Polyxeni touched her friend's arm. 'Everything is in

God's hands. God arranges everything and we don't know the plan, but God knows it. God knows where every sparrow falls, and to what place every grain of sand is carried by the wind.'

'God gives us hardship and sorrow. I want to ask God, "Why do we deserve it?" Did I tell you that Karatavuk says he will write letters to us? I asked him how, thinking that he would find a comrade to write for him, and he told me then that Mehmetçik taught him to read and write when they were boys, writing in the dust with sticks. I knew nothing about it. I was amazed, and then I was happy, and then I thought, "But how will I read them?"'

'You will find someone to read them for you.'

'I often thought,' replied Nermin, 'what would happen if we learned to read and write? I thought, "Who cares?" Reading is not for us. What is there to read? What is our life? We hoe, we make food, we give birth, what's the use of reading? What is there to know?' She paused. 'Now that my sons have gone, I know the use.'

The two women looked at each other for a moment, and then Polyxeni held out the pot she had been carrying. Nermin recognised her own husband's handiwork, and briefly felt a warm glow in the pit of her stomach. 'For you,' said Polyxeni.

'What is it?' Nermin took it, lifted the lid, and peered inside.

'Olives. In my family we have a tree, and we believe that if you eat olives from this tree when your loved ones are away, it makes them come back safely. It's always worked for us, so maybe it'll work for you too. You should eat one a day, and your sons will come back.'

Nermin was touched. 'Oh,' she said, 'but shouldn't you keep them? One day they'll come for Mehmetçik, for the labour battalions. That's what Karatavuk said.'

'It's a good tree,' said Polyxeni. 'We have a lot of olives. We save them up and don't eat them unless someone is away. If you run out, I'll give you some more. But when your sons return, can I have the pot back? It's a good pot, and I haven't got so many. Iskander made it.'

'I know,' said Nermin. 'When I hold one of his pots in my hands, it is very like holding his hands. It gives me the feeling of being comforted. I can feel the strength of his fingers.'

'I must go,' said Polyxeni. 'There's nothing to eat, and I have to go and invent something out of thin air as usual.'

'Take one of these onions,' said Nermin, 'and can I ask you one more thing?'

'Yes?'

'Thank you for the olives. But can you kiss the icon and ask your Panagia to watch over my Karatavuk?'

'I'll slip into the church on my way past,' agreed Polyxeni. 'Have courage.'

Nermin raised a hand and smiled weakly in return. She reminded herself to tell her husband to go and tie another rag to the red pine, and it occurred to her that she should go to the tomb of the saint and collect some olive oil that had run over the bones, in case a son came home wounded and needed a salve. Outside the back door Polyxeni slid her feet into her shoes, and turned to go back out into the unnatural peace of the town.

53

The Removal

For many decades there had been troubles in the east of Anatolia. Living separate lives in separate villages, Armenians and other tribesmen had been assiduously at each other's throats, committing against each other the banal but vile atrocities so frequently rehearsed by those who are deeply addicted to the orgasmic pleasures of extreme mutual hatred. Relations were particularly bad between Kurds and Armenians, both convinced of the superiority of their own race and religion. The Kurds were fanatically Islamic, even though it is doubtful that any of them had ever read a word of the Koran, and in the case of the Armenians there was the strong belief that they were the descendants of Noah, and that this made them special. A reasonably attentive reading of the Bible would have revealed the obvious fact that if its account is true, then absolutely everyone is a descendant of Noah. Many Armenians desired an autonomous land for themselves, aspiring to situate it even in places where they were not in the majority. The Kurds were at that time still more or less loyal to the state, and the state itself was too chaotic to impose tolerance or order on these far-flung and undeveloped places, where life had become equally perilous and abject for all races. To this day the Kurds of that region and the descendants of the Armenians will tell identical stories against each other, perhaps the most common being that one had to disguise one's little girls as boys, and women as men. Armenian guerrillas were armed through the charitable efforts of Russian Armenians, and encouraged by Great Britain, whose politicians calculated that an independent Armenian state would constitute an excellent buffer to keep out the Russians.

There had been for years a campaign of brutal brigandage between the various parties, accompanied by predictable literatures of hatred, which inevitably polarised populations that had

for centuries lived side by side. The empire now officially operated a policy known as 'Ottomanisation', whereby all races had
equal rights, liberties and duties. Among the latter was included
the duty of military service, and the only way out of it was to
pay a special tax, which applied equally to all. As a consequence
the armies of the empire were now filled with reluctant conscripts
whose families had been too poor to pay the tax. There were
thus a great many Armenian soldiers in the Ottoman army, whose
natural aspiration was towards an independent Armenian state.

The first step that led the Armenian people into their great
tragedy came about when the Ottomans were at war with the
Russians on the eastern front, and a deputy of the assembly at
Erzurum named Garo Pastermadjian led most of the Armenian
officers and men of the 3rd Army over to the Russian side,
returning with them in their campaign of pillage and rapine
through the Muslim villages in their path.

The Ottomans, seething with indignation over what from their
point of view was high treason, removed all remaining Armenian
officers and men from the 3rd Army, and put them to work in
labour battalions, where conditions were so bad that there was a
wave of desertions. Soon there were bands of roaming *francs-tireurs*
behind the Ottoman lines, sometimes officered by Russians, and
whether one calls them terrorists, bandits or freedom fighters is
in a sense beside the point, as they quite easily managed to be
all three simultaneously. Telegraph lines and bridges were cut,
ammunition and supply columns were attacked, as well as cara-
vans of the wounded coming back from the front. Their campaigns
against Kurdish and Circassian villages were greatly facilitated by
the fact that all able-bodied men had been called up.

On 2 May 1915, Enver Pasha sent a fatal telegram to Tâlat Bey,
the Minister for the Interior, proposing that the only way to deal
with an intolerable situation was to remove all Armenians from
behind Ottoman lines, and replace them with Muslim refugees
from elsewhere. Over the next few months this policy began to
be implemented, with many directives coming out of Istanbul that
there should be no ill treatment. The plan was to auction the
possessions of each family and give them the money when they
arrived at their destinations, so that they could start life afresh.

The policy of removal and compensation may have seemed like the obvious solution, but the government could not control what actually happened at such great distances in places where there were virtually no systems of communication or of command and control. There was no proper organisation, no transport, no medical assistance, no food, no money, and very little pity. The straggling columns of refugees fell victim to epidemics, they died of thirst, exhaustion and hunger, and they were easy targets for brigands and for the vengefulness and cruelty of the troops that escorted them and considered them to be traitors. These troops were often not proper soldiers, since those were at the fronts, but Kurdish irregulars, recruited from wild and ignorant tribesmen who had every reason to loathe and despise those whom they were escorting.

It is not possible to calculate how many Armenians died on the forced marches. In 1915 the number was thought to be 300,000, a figure which has been progressively increased ever since, thanks to the efforts of angry propagandists. To argue about whether it was 300,000 or 2,000,000 is in a sense irrelevant and distasteful, however, since both numbers are great enough to be equally distressing, and the suffering of individual victims in their trajectory towards death is in both cases immeasurable.

It is sometimes alleged that Tâlat Bey was colluding in a deliberate campaign of extermination without the knowledge of other government members. This is for others to argue about. What is decidedly strange is that many Armenians were deported even from places where they were not immediately behind the lines of the army, depending, it seems, upon the enthusiasms of local governors.

This can be the only explanation for the arrival of a band of irregulars in Eskibahçe, who came to remove the small number of Armenians resident there, including the only one with whom we have become acquainted, Levon Krikorian, apothecary, husband of Gadar, father of three young girls, and sometimes known as 'the Sly'.

Ever since it had become known that bands of Armenians had effectively started a civil war behind the lines on the Russian front, Levon Krikorian and his family had had to put up with small insults. He sometimes heard the words 'vatan haini' muttered as he passed by, and once there had been stones thrown against his shutters at night. He and the womenfolk had become anxious and worried, but not yet frightened.

The gendarmes in the meydan were initially puzzled when a nefarious-looking band of mounted and armed irregulars turned up and interrupted their lifelong games of backgammon, demanding in unfamiliar accents to know where the traitors' quarter was, and brandishing an order from the governor that in fact no one was able to read. The gendarmes were impressed by the official-looking seals and flourishes, and, once they had understood that the traitors were the Armenians, accompanied the troops to their quarter, which consisted of no more than a few pleasant and spacious houses along one side of a small street up one flank of the hillside.

What occurred there that day did not seem particularly sinister. Whilst the troops lounged about in the meydan, their sergeant went from door to door in the company of one of the gendarmes, informing the occupants that they were to be relocated in the interests of the Sultan Caliph and for their own protection. They were to gather in the meydan at dawn, bringing with them only their most valuable possessions, so that these could be sold at their destination in order to help them begin a new life. They were also to compile a complete inventory of all possessions left behind, so that they could be compensated upon arrival with goods to a similar value.

The unexpected news almost struck people dumb, and it was only slowly that the reality of the situation began to sink in.

'We can't just leave everything behind,' said Gadar, wife of the apothecary. 'Why should we go? We don't need protecting. No one will hurt us here.'

'How far have we got to walk?' asked Anoush, and her sisters Sirvart and Sossy wanted to know if they were going to Telmessos or somewhere nice like that. The girls were very typical of their race, with fair skin and dramatic black hair and heavy eyebrows. No doubt they would all grow up to be beautiful for as long as time condescended to bestow its conditional generosity.

Levon went down to the meydan to make enquiries, and found

every other paterfamilias already there, asking the same questions. When he saw the troops he grew pale and agitated, and hurried back to his house. He ushered his wife into the back room and told her, 'Gadar, it's very bad. They've sent Hamidiye to get us. Hamidiye! Can you imagine? God knows where they got them from! It can't be from anywhere here! It's not good, it's not good at all.'

'Hamidiye! God and the saints help us! Hamidiye!'

'Don't tell the girls. We don't want to alarm them.'

'Husband, we can't go with them. We'd be better off in a pit of serpents. We should run away now, whilst there's time.'

'Where could we go? They've got a document promising to protect us.' Levon did not believe in his own words, but he tried to comfort her: 'It's signed by the governor.'

'Who would protect us now? Everyone calls us traitors. No one wants us any more!'

'Calm yourself, Gadar, calm yourself.'

'How can I be calm? What about the girls? What about the girls? Tell me that!'

Levon knew in his heart that she was right, and could think of no convincing reply. 'I'm going out for a while,' he said. 'You and the girls carry on getting ready.'

He took a flask of oil and a small cup from the kitchen, left the house and made his way up the hillside, through the maquis and past the Lycian tombs where the Dog eked out his anchoritic life. At the tomb of the saint he knelt down and prayed sincerely for protection, and then he poured the oil through the small hole in the top of the lid. He knelt once more and collected the oil from the hole underneath, whence it now made its leisurely exit, having passed over the holy bones. He anointed his own brow with a little oil, and then made his way home to do likewise to his wife and daughters. The oil that was left he sealed in its flask, and placed in his sash.

The family was wealthy by most people's standards, but did not in truth have a great many valuables, and once these were collected together, they sat in their selamlik wondering what to say and do next. After a little while Gadar left the room silently and went out through the door into the street.

She made her way through the lifeless alleyways down to the aga's konak, knocked on the haremlık door, slipped off her shoes and went in. She found Leyla Hanım lounging on a divan with Pamuk on her lap, alternately polishing her fingernails and eating pistachio nuts.

'Leyla Hanım,' she said, kneeling before her, 'please save us.'

Leyla was astonished and a little amused, having heard nothing of the day's alarms. 'Save you? From what? When did I start being worth praying to?'

'They've sent Hamidiye to take us all away. Please ask Rustem Bey to save us.'

'But, Gadar Hanım, what are Hamidiye? Some kind of soldier?'

'Our families came here all the way from Van thirty years ago, just to get away from people like them. They're tribesmen, horsemen, Kurds. They're savages, and they hate us.'

'I've never heard of them,' said Leyla, who thought that things could not really be so bad.

'They're not from here. Why should you have heard of them? Please ask Rustem Bey to save us.'

Leyla Hanım made a small gesture of helplessness. 'He's not here. He went to Telmessos, and he's expected back sometime tomorrow.'

'When, though, when?'

'I don't know. Really, I don't know.'

Gadar put her hands to her face and began to wail, 'Oh God, Oh God, Oh God! My girls, my poor girls!' Leyla Hanım knelt down on the floor and put her arms around her to comfort her. This felt very strange to Gadar. Like everyone else in the town her opinion of Leyla Hanım had always been that she was merely a whore, albeit the whore of the aga, and it did not feel quite right to be embraced by her. Nonetheless, Leyla's body was soft and motherly, and she smelled of warm perfumes and rosewater, and Gadar allowed herself to weep in Leyla's arms for a while. When finally she stood up, she dried her eyes with the back of her hand, and said, 'My last hope is gone. God be with you, Leyla Hanım.'

'And with you,' said Leyla, who by now was feeling tearful herself. Gadar raised her right hand a little and let it fall. 'All we wanted,' she said, 'was to live in peace and earn an honest living. Everything was very good.'

Impulsively, Leyla removed a gold bracelet from her wrist and presented it to Gadar. 'Take and sell it,' she said. 'I won't miss it. I have others.'

'Thank you, Leyla Hanım. I take it in God's name, out of necessity, and I am truly sorry,' said Gadar.

'Sorry? Sorry for what?'

'For all the things that have been said about you.' With this she turned and left, leaving Leyla's ears burning with shame and indignation, even though she knew that Gadar had meant no offence. She took up her oud and played on it until her equable mood returned.

It so happened that Rustem Bey did return just before the column of the dispossessed took the fork that led southward. It was mid-afternoon, it was stultifyingly hot, and the walkers had had no food or water since dawn. Three old people who had been unable to continue had already been bludgeoned to death with rifle butts in order to save on bullets, and anyone with good footwear had had it taken from them and installed on the feet of their escorts. The stones were excruciatingly hot, and people's soles were burned and bleeding. The women of the column had set up a continuous low moaning and keening, and the men blinked against the sweat in their eyes, muttered prayers to the ever empty sky and longed for it all to be over. Most had already been beaten at least once, and within half an hour's march had been forced to hand over the valuables that they had been told to bring with them.

Rustem Bey heard the eerie moaning from some considerable distance, and was astonished when finally his horse brought him up to the column. He was even more astonished when he recognised the faces of people who had been notable in the town only the day before. He could scarcely credit how abject they had become in such a short time.

Rustem Bey realised immediately what had happened. He had heard about the deportations, and in principle was not at all sympathetic to the victims. He had been as outraged as everyone else by the treachery and perfidy of these citizens who had turned

309

against the Sultan, deserted the army and then attacked it from behind. He had found himself scowling at every Armenian he passed in the street, resenting them suddenly for the first time in his life. However, he was intelligent enough to know that none of these particular Armenians had ever been near the front, and none of them had ever attacked anyone, from behind or otherwise. Indeed, Levon Krikorian had been stalwart in the event of each of his few illnesses, advising the aga on remedies that had often worked.

As his horse drew up to the stationary column, Rustem Bey became aware of a forest of hands raised up to him in supplication. He looked down at all those agonised faces, and heard their desperate, inarticulate cries for help. He was confused and paralysed for an instant, but then he spurred his horse over to the sergeant who was obviously in charge and summoned up his courage. Assuming a lordly air of great importance, which was, after all, merely the reflection of a reality, he asked very directly, 'By whose authority do you take these people?'

The sergeant, intimidated and surprised, dug into his sash and produced the firman. 'By the authority of the governor, efendi,' he replied. Rustem Bey took the document and pretended to read it. The elaborate official calligraphy and fantastically convoluted wording would have made it all but unreadable even to the literate, among whose number Rustem Bey did not in fact find himself. Nonetheless, the governor's official seal was very familiar to him, and he knew that the document was a valid one. Silently, he handed it back to the sergeant.

A woman took hold of his leg and looked up at him, pleading, 'Save us, save us, Rustem Beyefendi, for the love of God save us.'

'The order is from the governor,' said the aga. 'I can't do anything about it. Otherwise, by God's will, I would save you.' He looked down at that small sea of upturned and hopeless faces, and shook his head sadly. 'These are evil times,' he said. 'Satan is abroad in the world.'

He looked around at the ruffianly and narrow faces of the Hamidiye, and was suddenly surprised when he noticed that, ludicrously, they were all draped with expensive women's jewellery. He addressed them directly. 'I know the governor,' he informed them. 'If these people are mistreated, you will all be shot. Each one of your turbans will be without a head, each one of your horses will be without a rider, and each one of your bodies will rot on the surface of the earth without a shroud. I shall obtain a fatwa and each one of your souls shall be locked out of paradise for ever.'

The tribesmen were genuinely cowed by this impressive threat, and there was a moment's silence during which it became clear why the column had been stationary when he had drawn up to it. From behind a clump of trees nearby came suddenly the sound of screaming. Now Levon Krikorian clasped his leg, and cried, 'My girls, my girls! My girls, efendi, my girls!'

Rustem Bey kicked the sides of his horse, and rapidly circled the trees, at the other side of which he found a party of five cavalrymen, who, having thrown the girls to the ground, were tearing gleefully at the clothes of all three of Levon's daughters, preparatory to a rape in which, no doubt, all the troops had been hoping to take their turn. The girls were struggling hysterically, and had managed to begin screaming because they had somehow loosened the gags from their mouths.

Feeling that he had no choice, or as if he had been taken over by some valiant spirit that was not his own, Rustem Bey took his silver-handled pistol from his sash, drew near, and declared loudly, 'In the name of the Sultan Padishah, terror of the world!'

Surprised and a little bewildered, the tribesmen stopped and looked up at him, and the girls remained dishevelled on the ground, staring at him with huge and desperate eyes.

'In the name of the Sultan,' repeated Rustem Bey.

There was a long silence, during which Rustem Bey assessed the degree of stupidity of the rapists, and they in their turn assessed his importance. It was very clear that he was not only rich and distinguished, but a man of great authority. His boots shone, his breeches were of fine cloth, his sash was of red silk, his fez was beautifully brushed and his fine moustache was waxed. His pistol sparkled in the afternoon sun, as did the handle and sheath of his yataghan, and he rode a fine and spirited bay horse that made their own mounts seem paltry by comparison. Every one of the troopers had the same thought, namely that here would be a gentleman well worth robbing. None of them felt quite daring enough, however, especially as Rustem Bey held his revolver in his right hand, which rested on his horse's neck, and was quite casually pointing in their direction.

Rustem Bey assessed their degree of stupidity as quite high, and he told them, 'You can't have these women. They are already taken.'

'Taken, efendi?' said one of the men.

'Yes. It was all arranged, and they have been removed by mistake. As they are mine, I have come to take them back.' He looked at the girls and silently begged them to say nothing.

The troopers exchanged glances, unsure what to make of this.

'One of them is to be my wife, and the other two have been betrothed to my brothers,' said Rustem Bey firmly.

'Three brothers with infidel wives?' said another of the troopers. 'All sisters?'

'They will become Muslim when they marry,' asserted Rustem Bey.

'This one is only about ten,' said the first man, indicating Sossy. 'How can she be married?'

'If she is old enough to rape, she is old enough to marry,' replied Rustem Bey. 'You were about to rape my betrothed wife and the betrothed wives of my brothers.' He raised his pistol a little and said, 'You must know the penalty for rape. And I am well acquainted with the governor. You should be grateful that I have saved you from this crime and the punishment that would have followed from it.'

The troopers calculated that Rustem Bey very probably did know the governor, and very probably could have them stoned to death. Besides, their sadistic sexual ardour had cooled completely thanks to the appearance of the aga and the ensuing confrontation. Rustem Bey looked at their faces, realised that he had won, and said imperiously, 'Go back to your comrades.' He told the girls, 'Stay here until I come back.'

He rode back to the column, accompanied by the perplexed and baulked troopers, and looked for Levon's face in the crowd, beckoning to him to come over. He leaned down from his horse and said softly, 'I have saved your daughters. But I can't save you all.'

'Keep them safe, Rustem Beyefendi,' begged Levon tearfully, taking his hand and kissing it.

'I promise you by my honour,' said Rustem Bey.

The aga trudged into town that evening, exhausted and dusty, still shaking a little, and still disbelievingly impressed by his own bluster. He was also still upset by having found on the road the corpses of the old folk who had been battered to death, and whom he had known since boyhood. The three miserable young girls sat in a row astride his equally exhausted horse, as they had rapidly become unable to walk. The girls he consigned to the haremlık, and the horse he tended to himself, since the remains of all of his grooms had long since begun to dissolve beneath the dank earth of the Russian front.

After she had nobly forced herself to overcome her initial jealousy and her suspicions of Rustem Bey's motives, Leyla Hanım washed the young sisters and gave them perfume and new clothes. She persuaded them to eat a little food, and played the oud, sitting with them, and singing sad half-remembered Greek lullabies whilst they shook with fright and clung to each other late into the night.

54

Olives

Nermin began to wonder if now it was more probable that her sons would never return. Over the next few days the feeling of unease grew so great that finally she decided to go and see her friend.

She found Polyxeni outside the back of her house, breaking up twigs for use in her brazier. Nermin felt ashamed to be asking for something directly, and Polyxeni perceived her confusion. Nermin was fiddling with a pot that she held in her hands, rotating it, and putting her fingers inside it, not knowing where to look with her eyes. Polyxeni knew straight away what Nermin wanted, because of the pot, but she teased her friend a little anyway. She said, 'You know you can say what you want! Come on, what is it?'

'Oh, Polyxeni,' exclaimed Nermin at last, 'Polyxeni, I've finished the last of the lucky olives you gave me, and I ate one every day, as you said, and everything felt good, but now I've eaten the last one, and I worry that now my luck will run out, and my sons won't return. I am sorry to ask, normally I would never ask, but do you have any left? Without them I don't feel lucky any more. And I brought Iskander's pot back, just as you asked.'

Polyxeni laughed. 'Is that all?' She took the pot and went inside and filled it. When she came back out she gave the pot to Nermin, and said, 'I haven't heard from Mehmetçik since they took all the Christian boys for the labour battalions.'

Nermin looked at her tearfully. 'Will you have enough lucky olives for both of us?'

'Pray for a good harvest,' said Polyxeni.

The two women embraced before Nermin left. On the way home she ate one lucky olive for each day that she had missed.

55

Mustafa Kemal (12)

Enver Pasha, young, respectable, handsome, dashing, nephew-in-law to the Sultan, sets off on an egregiously Napoleonic misadventure. Mustafa Kemal has already turned down the command of one of Enver's madder schemes, to send three regiments through Persia to India, in order to raise a rebellion among the Muslims there. Enver has sent someone to Afghanistan as well, who is quite nonplussed about how to raise the people in revolt, and eventually returns home, having distributed much gold to Afghan warlords who then mysteriously disappear.

Now Enver wishes to attack Russia. He has long dreamed of expanding the empire to the east, a dream that he will never relinquish, and which will be the main reason for the loss of the war, and he also wants an immediate offensive in the south.

General Liman von Sanders tells him that the eastern campaign is a very bad idea, that the armed forces need a long period of training, re-equipping and consolidation, but Enver puts himself in command of the expedition, and blithely departs across the Caucasus Mountains in the direction of Russia. The Allahuekber range is three thousand metres high, the temperature is -26°, the snow is in places six metres deep, and it snows all the time. Most of the soldiers freeze to death, the remnant is defeated by the Russians at Sarikamiş, and the 10,000 who manage to return are all but wiped out by typhus. It is a disaster of almost unimaginable proportions.

In the south, an army of 18,000 is led across Sinai, and the Suez Canal is assaulted. Six hundred manage to get across it, but they are repelled by the British. The Muslims of Egypt do not rebel against their colonial masters, and the master plan necessarily fails. The army returns to Palestine, its roll-call now numbering three thousand fewer. The British vigorously set about reinforcing the defences along the Suez Canal, and put it permanently beyond attack.

When Mustafa Kemal sees Enver in Istanbul, he finds him pale and shaken. Enver is vague about Kemal's appointment, and advises him to enquire at the offices of the general staff, who, embarrassingly, do not seem to have heard either of Mustafa Kemal or of the 19th Division to whose command he has been appointed. Finally the confusion is sorted out, and he departs for Maydos, on the Gallipoli peninsula. Maydos is a charming little harbour town, and there are many wealthy Greeks there who live in big and airy houses. There are also a great many craftsmen jewellers. After the war, after the Greeks have gone, the little town will be renamed Eceabat. It will sport several statues of Mustafa Kemal Atatürk, and the optimistic locals will never cease their sanguine excavations in search of the jewels and money that the Greeks are supposed to have cached in gardens, walls and cellars.

Now, however, Mustafa Kemal has with him the 57th Regiment, which is undermanned, ill-trained and ill-equipped. His troops will have to endure heavy bombardment, and resist many incursions by small Allied landing parties who are intent upon destroying the defences. The 72nd and 77th Regiments arrive, but they are not the units that Mustafa Kemal expected. They are mainly Arabs, many are opposed to the war, and they have not been trained. Mustafa Kemal stiffly requests proper Turkish troops, and is refused.

Karatavuk arrives in Maydos; he has been hurriedly initiated into the military arts, and has proved a naturally good shot. He is incandescent with enthusiasm for the jihad, and he is looking forward to meeting the Prophet in his own garden in paradise. Furthermore, he is thrilled by the natural beauty of the Gallipoli peninsula, and he writes to his mother in a strange ecstasy:

My dear Mother,
    You are proud to have given birth to two soldiers. It was a delight to my heart to receive the letter that you caused to be written to me with a neighbour's pen. It was so full of advice. When it was given to me I was sitting under a

pear tree nearby a stream in the middle of Divrin Plain, so beautiful and green. My soul was enchanted already by the sweetness of the land . . .

56

The Letter from Karatavuk

Iskander kicked at his wheel to set it spinning, gave it a few surplus kicks as if to inform it of his intention to get a decent amount of work done, wet his hands in the bowl that he kept on a stool at his side, and picked up a large ball of clay. He frequently did not know what he was going to make until he had started to make it. This was a kind of courtesy to his material, which seemed often to have preconceived ideas about what it wanted to become. Sometimes it would wobble about, or collapse, if he tried to make a bowl out of clay that wanted to be a pot, or vice versa, and it was best just to mould it in the fingers for a short while, get the feel of it and then watch it grow into something. 'Take your time,' he would say to himself, 'if the cat's in a hurry, she has peculiar kittens.'

Iskander made pots these days partly to take the world off his mind. His sons had gone to war, his wife and daughters were having to do the men's work in the fields as well as their own, and they kept falling ill, which was one of the natural hazards of being female, it seemed. It was entirely possible that one of these days he too would have to go to fight, if the authorities remembered his existence, since one was in the reserve for half a lifetime after one's national service. He remembered his five years in the army with a shudder, even though he had made unforgettable friends, and had learned that the most terrible things can be endured. It was true that this war was a jihad, and therefore he would be bound to die gladly for the love of God, but all the same it was puzzling to the faith when one learned that the Arabs had sided with the British, as had the Muslims from the other side of Persia. It seemed that only Turks took the jihad seriously. 'I am a Turk,' he thought, rolling the idea around his mind, remembering the days when the word 'Turk' implied something almost shameful, a barbarian out of the East. Nowadays, instead of saying, 'We are Osmanlis,' or 'We are Ottomans,' people were saying, 'Yes, we are Turks.' How strange that the world should change because of words, and words change because of the world. 'Iskander the Turk,' he said to himself, internally scrutinising the strange and novel sensation of possessing a deeper identity, of being something beyond himself. Some people said that the word 'Turk' meant 'strength'. He squeezed the clay with extra force, and it sprouted upward between his fingers. 'Ah, a candlestick,' said Iskander.

'Salaam aleikum,' said a voice very nearby, and Iskander, lost so deeply in his thoughts, started with almost comic surprise. He looked up, placing a hand over his heart to still the shock, and the stranger bowed his head a little, both as greeting and apology. Iskander beheld a round, friendly and deeply sunburned face capped by a battered and dusty fez, and realised from the man's clothes that he had once been wealthy, but had fallen on harder times. His accent was that of a man from further south, perhaps from Kıbrıs. 'Forgive me,' he said, 'but are you Iskander the Potter?' The man nodded towards the wheel, adding, 'I have reason to suspect that you might be. I am sorry to disturb you at your work. He who works hard is the equal of he who fights in the holy war, so they say.'

'A good proverb seasons the speech,' said Iskander, 'and a neat lie satisfies more than a sloppy truth. But I have sons in the war, and I think that their work is greater than making pots.'

'These are precarious times,' said the stranger. 'There is a great battle in the north.'

'My sons are there,' sighed Iskander, 'at Gallipoli. War is easier to watch when soldiers are other people's sons.'

'Perhaps I bring consolation,' said the stranger, burrowing among the pistols and yataghans that were stuffed into his sash, until eventually he produced a very battered envelope. It had clearly been passed from hand to hand over a period of some weeks, and bore traces of several people who must have held it. There was soot from a forge, honey from somebody's table, grease that was probably from the axle of a cart, a circle of olive oil that had left a transparent patch in the paper, and a smell of patchouli. 'I am sorry it's so mangled,' said the stranger, 'but a letter arrives by any means that it may. I was given it in Telmessos when it was heard that I was coming this way. I wish you well of its news.'

Iskander turned the letter over in his hands, covering it with wet clay in his excitement. He had never received a letter before, and it gave him both a sense of enormous importance, and a sense of dread. 'Çay?' he asked the traveller. 'May I offer you tea?'

'God forgive me,' replied the stranger, 'but I had çay the moment I got here – I was tired and hot, and I should have come to find you first of all, but the flesh is weak. So, I have had some tea, but I thank you all the same. I am going to Knidos, I don't have much time, and I am going down to the sea to find out if there are any fishing boats that can drop me along the coast. My feet and I have had quite enough of walking.'

'Only with travel can a man ripen,' observed Iskander, who had travelled nowhere further than Smyrna for some fifteen years.

The stranger grinned, but gave a bitter and knowing laugh. 'Every journey is a little bit of hell. Remain well.'

'Go well,' called Iskander after him, and he sat at his wheel wondering what to do with his letter, which he turned over and over in his hands, marking it with more buff-coloured splodges of clay. What if it held bad news? What if one of his sons, or both of them, were dead? What if it was a letter saying that he too had to go to war? What if it was from somebody who wanted money? Still, as they always say, when the messenger is slow, then the news is good, and this letter had clearly been a long time in the coming.

Iskander stepped out of the shade of his potting stall, and was stroked by the heat of the sun. It was May, and in two months' time the sun would strike like a wooden mallet. Iskander wondered whether anyone would be going up to the yaylas this year; everything was in chaos, with so many of the men missing, so how could the journey be managed? And everybody was always waiting for news, which would never arrive if they were up in the high pastures. But on the other hand, the heat would be insufferable, and would bring illnesses and vile, tormenting insects if the people remained. But if the women took the cattle and pets and children up to the high ground, would the old men be able to protect them from opportunists and brigands? Who would prevent them from spending too much money buying carpets from nomads?

These were problems for all to consider before too long, but just now the weather was perfect and all the wild flowers had come out, succeeding the bulbs, which had died back, leaving fat seed-heads, and desiccated stalks and leaves. Poppies of darkest scarlet embellished the fields of wheat down in the river valley, and ox-eye daisies, huge blue-bearded irises and white orchids blew in the grasses of the verges. Iskander walked to his house, enjoying the loveliness of the world at the same time as he worried about the possible burden of the letter, which became more and more portentous as he passed it from hand to hand, looking down at the strange swirls that he was unable to read. It occurred to him that the writing probably said something like 'Iskander the Potter at Eskibahçe, not far from Telmessos'. For the first time in his life it struck him that it might be a very useful thing to be able to read, and now he understood why Karatavuk had persuaded Mehmetçik to teach him. It was true that the Christians always had the advantage, they learned to read and write, and do complicated things with numbers, and that was why you always had to be suspicious of them, and that was why they made you feel stupid, but it was also why you depended upon them so often for help. Iskander had gone to the mektep when he was a child, and had learned nothing except to recite by heart the holy verses of the Koran. The Arabic phrases still rolled off his tongue, but he knew not what they might mean, and yes, he would go to paradise, but it was Jews and Christians who organised the world. 'Fortunately,' thought Iskander, 'for the bird that cannot soar, God has provided low branches.'

He removed his muddy shoes, placed them in the niche in the wall outside his back door, and entered the house. His wife had become so expert at indicating her disapproval of all the clay dust that he brought in with him that he barely dared to touch anything, or even exist at all, until he had changed into his clean clothes. He feared the oppression of her pursed lips, the click of her tongue, the furrowing of her brow, the busy air that she adopted as she cleaned things, so that her whole body seemed to be the veritable incarnation and epitome of uncomplaining complaint. He found her slicing onions on the table, wiping her eyes with the back of her hand and shaking her head against the smarting.

'I have a letter,' Iskander told her, holding it out to show her.

'A letter,' she repeated, having troubled thoughts that exactly echoed those of her husband. 'Who is it from? What can it be? Who will read it for us? I pray God that the news is good.'

There was something about his wife's anxiety that strengthened Iskander. They had been together for so long now that he could not imagine life without her, even though at times he had heartily detested her. It had been a struggle to maintain his dignity and self-respect in the face of her clear but unspoken belief that she might have married a better man, but he knew that after all this time they had grown to suit each other, just as a boot and a foot change shape to accommodate the pressure of each other's forms. 'Every woman,' he used to say to console himself, 'thinks that she could have married the Sultan if only she had not been married to her husband first.'

'I think I should ask Abdulhamid Hodja to read it,' said Iskander, and his wife's face brightened. He was pleased that she thought he was right. 'I will come back afterwards, and if the news concerns you, I will tell you what it is.'

She nodded, and cut another slice off the onion. 'Be back soon,' she said.

It was seldom difficult to find Abdulhamid Hodja, who was either conspicuous upon the back of Nilufer (who was now approaching the end of her days), or was tending his vegetables in the large patch that he cultivated, halfway down to the river, and not far from the sunken temple of Leto.

Iskander found Abdulhamid wandering about amid his plants, bending down and putting things into a large sack. He watched the imam for a while, so absorbed in his work, and reflected that the hodja must now be about sixty years old. His beard had become completely white, and his cheeks had imperceptibly sunken over the years. Thickets of stout grey hairs had sprouted out of his nose and ears, and his glinting eyes seemed to have receded further into his head with the passing of time. Nonetheless, he was still strong and virile, and it was touching to see the way

322

that he did everything with as much absorption and concern as he always had. If Nilufer was lame, which she often was now that she was old and tired, then the hodja led her about by a rope until she got better, saying that the exercise would do her good, but refusing to ride her. He still braided her mane, tying it up with green ribbons and bells, and he still polished her brass breastplate, so that it glinted in the sun even though the engraved verses of the Koran were wearing away. 'Nilufer still believes that she is young and beautiful,' he used to say, 'and who am I to disabuse her?'

'Salaam aleikum,' said Iskander, startling the imam just as he had himself been startled by the stranger with the letter.

'I'm too old to be crept up on,' protested the cleric, remembering to add 'aleikum salaam' as an afterthought. Iskander took his hand and kissed it, pressing it afterwards to his forehead. 'I'm too old for so much respect, as well,' added the imam a little testily. 'Sooner or later one wearies of it.'

'Respect can only be earned,' said Iskander, adopting a learned air, 'and the same is true of disrespect.'

'Well then, well then, I shall have to do some disgraceful and disreputable things,' replied the imam. 'What can I do for you, anyway? I don't suppose that you came to find me merely in order to make me jump out of my skin.'

'I need to learn to read,' said Iskander. 'I've just received a letter.'

'It takes more than a few minutes, you know,' said the imam. 'In fact, it takes months of work, and even then you are still learning how to do it for the rest of your life.'

'Perhaps you could read it,' said Iskander hopefully, 'and tell me what it says. Otherwise it tells me as little as the songs of the birds.'

Abdulhamid took the grubby envelope and read: 'To Nermin, wife of Iskander the Potter, in the town of Eskibahçe, two or three days' journey from Telmessos.' He looked up. 'It's for your wife.'

'If you read it to me I can tell her what it says,' said Iskander, adding, 'A wife's letters are not a secret from her husband.'

'Of course, of course,' said the imam, unsealing the envelope and pulling out two sheets of unbleached paper covered in writing. 'Ah,' he said, 'I'm afraid I can't read this.'

'You can't read it?' repeated Iskander, perplexed. He raised his hands in puzzlement, and the imam waved the sheets of paper. 'Look,' he said, 'it's written in Greek. I don't know Greek.'

'I thought you knew all languages,' said Iskander, mildly disappointed to discover that the imam was not, after all, omniscient.

'I know Persian, Arabic and Turkic, but these letters are Greek. If you don't believe me, go and look at the letters on the old tombs. Some of them are the same as this.'

'But you read the envelope,' protested Iskander.

The imam showed him the envelope and poked at the writing with his finger. 'This,' he said, 'is written in Arabic script, but in our language. Whoever wrote the letter knew that the address had to be in Arabic script, or else it might never arrive; our Christian friends are not too popular with the rest of us these days. No doubt the address was written by somebody else, just to make sure that it reached here.'

'My son learned how to write the Greek letters,' said Iskander. 'Mehmetçik taught him, even though at first I forbade it.'

'You were right; much harm can come from writing,' said the imam, 'perhaps even more than comes from speaking. So the letter might be from Karatavuk? That would be a very happy thing.'

'What shall I do?' asked Iskander.

'You will have to ask the troublemaker,' said the imam.

'Leonidas the Greek? He wouldn't do anything for anyone.'

'I can't think of anyone else, can you? Perhaps you should take him a present to soften him up. The thing is, I can't tell from looking at this whether it's Turkic written in Greek letters, or Greek written in Greek letters. The quickest way to find out is to ask Leonidas, obnoxious as he might be.'

Iskander's eye was suddenly distracted. 'Excuse me,' he said, 'but I just noticed something moving about inside your sack.'

Abdulhamid Hodja, a little abashed, opened the neck of the sack and showed Iskander the contents. Iskander peered in and saw a heap of what at first appeared to be clods of earth, or rocks. 'Tortoises,' explained the hodja. 'They wreak havoc among the vegetables, but I don't have the heart to kill them. So I collect them up and go for a ride on Nilufer. When we find a nice place out of harm's way, I let them all go.' He reached into the sack and brought out a very large one. 'Look at this monster,' he said proudly. The tortoise popped its head out of its shell, opened its mouth and hissed vehemently. 'That's courage for you,' said the imam. 'It's like me: too old to be frightened of anything.'

Iskander regarded the petulant beast, and raised his eyebrows. The imam's saintly eccentricity was inexhaustibly surprising. He tapped the heavily ridged shell, and the animal hissed again. 'Bad temper, bad marriage,' said the imam, reproaching it.

It was with reluctance and with severe reservations that Iskander tapped upon the door of Daskalos Leonidas. He had always despised the Greek, whose ability to foster division and rancour was quite unsurpassed. Additionally, Iskander doubted that the teacher had ever forgiven him for having abetted in his humiliation at the muhabbet so many years before. Moreover, Iskander found himself feeling awkward, and clumsy of speech, when dealing with a Christian bookworm.

Whilst he waited, he noticed that there was something odd about the songbird that occupied the cage by the door. Almost everyone had a finch, or a nightingale, or a yellowhammer, or a robin, so that at dawn and dusk, at the same time as the muezzin called from the minaret of the mosque, the birds would fill the town with their own call to prayer. The bird in Daskalos Leonidas's cage, however, was very much like the teacher himself. It was scrawny, drab, depressed, and had the air of knowing a great deal about nothing.

Iskander was looking at it in astonishment when Leonidas opened the door, irritated at having been interrupted just when he was writing to another member of the secret society in Smyrna. It concerned matters of some confidentiality, and a knock on his door when no one was expected was enough to cause him a small attack of panic. He lived in constant fear of arrest, and had no illusions as to his treatment in the event. Certainly he was prepared to suffer and to die for Greece, but he knew that he was not made naturally in the heroic mould. His life was a kind of martyrdom, believing so much in a great ideal and an historic mission, but at the same time knowing perfectly well that he was no Agamemnon or Achilles.

'Yes?' said Leonidas when he saw Iskander standing humbly at his doorstep.

'Peace upon you,' said Iskander.

'What do you want?' asked Leonidas. 'I am rather busy.'

'I have a letter,' said Iskander, holding it out, 'and I can't read it.' Iskander tried to look past Leonidas into his house. It was said to be an extraordinary and stupendous chaos of books, papers, cobwebs and dust. It was said that Leonidas did not know how to cook, and was too miserly to pay anyone else to do it, so he lived off bread and olives. They said he was such a miser that he regretted having to shit.

Leonidas took the letter grudgingly, and peered through his spectacles at it. 'It's in Turkish,' he said, 'really I don't care to read it. It jars on the tongue.' The teacher's voice was like the creaking of a wheel.

Iskander did not know whether to be angry or wistful. 'The letters are Greek,' he said, advancing the fact as a mitigating circumstance.

'Indeed, indeed,' agreed Leonidas, adding, 'It is a letter to your wife, you know.'

'If you read it to me, I will remember it, and tell her. I have an excellent memory for words, even if I can't write them.'

Leonidas read the letter to himself, and his attitude seemed to mollify. 'This is from your son,' he said. 'I have to admit it has a certain beauty. It's quite remarkable, really. I wouldn't have thought that such a one would have had it in him.'

'Please read it,' begged Iskander.

'You should fetch your wife, I think,' said Leonidas. 'Really you should both hear it.'

'I will hear it, and then decide,' insisted Iskander.

'Oh, very well, then,' said Leonidas impatiently; these small-town Turks were nothing if not obtuse. 'The letter was, incidentally, written about a month ago.'

'Thank you, thank you,' said Iskander, and Leonidas began to read: 'Valideciğim, Iki asker doğurmakla müftehir . . .'

My dear Mother,

You are proud to have given birth to two soldiers. It was a delight to my heart to receive the letter that you caused to be written to me with a neighbour's pen. It was so full of advice. When it was given to me I was sitting under a pear tree nearby a stream in the middle of Divrin Plain, so beautiful and green. My soul was enchanted already by the sweetness of the land, and my enchantment was increased on account of your words. I read it, and whilst I read it I learned the lessons that you wrote in it. I read it again. I was glad to do the task of reading your letter, because the task was beautiful and holy. I opened my eyes and looked far away. The green wheat bending with the wind was as though in salutation to the letter of my mother. The wheat and the trees were bending towards me as congratulation for the letter of my mother.

I looked towards the right side; the mighty pine trees at the bottom of the slope were greeting me with their proper sound. I looked towards the left side, and the stream was chattering and smiling and playing and foaming because of the letter of my mother. I raised my head and I looked at the leaves of the tree above the place where I was resting. All of the leaves were dancing and sharing my happiness so that I should feel it even more myself. I looked to a branch in the tree, and a nightingale was greeting me, and its watery sweet voice was sharing my feelings in its throat.

During this moment, my friend came, and said, 'Here is some tea.'

'This is good,' I said, and I took the cup and looked, and it was tea with milk, and I asked him: 'Fikret, from where did you get this milk?' and he said, 'Do you know the flock that goes by the stream?' and I said, 'Yes, I love to see it,' and he said, 'I bought it from the shepherd for ten paras.' Dear Mother, it was pure milk, without water in it, for ten paras, coming from a sheep. I took it and drank. But I was thinking, 'My mother has no milk to drink. Is this possible? Why is it so?' and the nightingale was singing, 'What can we do? It is your mother's fate. If she were a man she could drink this milk, smell these flowers, see these crops bending, and see the slow flight of the stream and listen to its voice.'

Please do not worry about my brother. Perhaps he too will see beautiful things.

Dear Mother, don't be sorry. One day I will bring you here and show you how beautiful it is.

On the green side of this gentle meadow the soldiers are washing their clothes.

Someone with a voice of angels was calling the faithful to prayer.

O God, how beautiful was his voice echoing over the plain. Even the birds stopped singing. The wheat fell still, and the stream also was still. Everybody was silent, all creatures and all things, attending to the voice.

The azan was over, and I washed myself in the waters of the stream. Together we prayed, kneeling down on the fresh grass. When my forehead touched the ground I smelled the musk of the earth. I forgot the tumult and the glory of the world. I raised my hands and looked up, and these words came out of my mouth: 'O mighty God of the Turks, creator of the singing bird, of the bleating sheep, of the worshipping wheat and grass and the mountains of majesty; You gave all these things to the Turks. Permit us to keep them. For such loveliness is proper to the Turks, we who praise You, we who believe in the mercy and strength and truth of our God.

'O God, the sole wish of these soldiers is to make Your name known to the Franks. Accept the honourable wish of the soldiers. Make sharp our bayonets and scatter the Franks.'

Dear Mother, when I raised myself up, no one could imagine how my heart was full.

This is the loveliest place in the world, but here there aren't any weddings. When I come home I think I would like to marry. Soon the enemy will make a landing, and afterwards there might be a time for weddings.

Dear Mother, please don't send me any money. I don't need underwear. I promise that I will not cut my toenails and my fingernails on the same day, and I won't cut my fingernails at night. If I die, remember that death is a mule; mount it, and it takes you to paradise. If I die, don't grieve.

Tell the mother of Mehmetçik to tell Mehmetçik that I have the birdwhistle, and that I remember him.

I kiss my father's hands, and on my knees I kiss your hands, and I carry your face in my heart.

Your son Karatavuk.

When Daskalos Leonidas had finished, both men were deeply moved, and neither spoke. Iskander was astonished by the power of Karatavuk's devotion for his mother. The potter had truly never realised how strong it was, and he even felt a pang of wistful jealousy that a father cannot be loved in such a deep and over-whelming way. 'A woman is not loved until she has a son, and then she is loved absolutely,' he thought.

Leonidas, on the other hand, was engaged in an inner struggle; he had spent so many years and expended so much energy on cultivating his sense of superiority to the Turks that it came as a shock to disencrypt the tender soul of Karatavuk. Much as he despised the young man's faith, he could not but be affected by its beauty and sincerity. 'It's a fine letter,' he said at length, 'it has poetry. A fine letter indeed.'

'If I bring my wife, will you read it again?' asked Iskander. 'I didn't know that she had caused a letter to be written. I will bring you something. Perhaps candlesticks? Or a bowl, or a vase of some sort? To express my gratitude.'

'By all means,' said Leonidas, still softened and disconcerted, and it was not until Iskander had gone that he noticed that some prankster had taken his goldfinch and replaced it with a sparrow. The metallic taste of disdain returned reassuringly to his tongue.

57

Karatavuk at Gallipoli:
Karatavuk Remembers (1)

I will not relate what happened during my training. It was hard and I was more miserable even than when I was at war in the winter, but at least it was over quickly, which was because we were needed urgently at the front. Also, we were all indignant about the way the Franks had cheated us out of the battleships, and our anger carried us through. One good thing was that I did well, I learned very quickly, and this was noticed by my superiors, and they thought it all the more remarkable because I was so young, and they esteemed me because I had volunteered to come in the place of my father. One of the things I remember is that we had a kind of grenade thrower that you operated when lying on the ground, and we practised with rocks of the correct weight, and I could hit anything with it. I was a master with that weapon, and who would have guessed that one day I would use such a weapon for hurling cans of bully beef? I also became a very good shot with a rifle, and because of this I arrived at my regiment with a recommendation that I would make a good sniper, and this recommendation is probably why I am alive today whilst most of my comrades are dead, because there came a time when I was creeping about doing sniping duties whilst my comrades were sitting in the trench, and many of them were suddenly killed by a mine that had been put in a sap underneath.

When I think back to those early days, the first thing I recall was that all of us believed it was a holy war. We were told this over and over again, and every unit had an imam who repeated it to us, and the Sultan himself declared that it was a jihad. As the first fighting broke out on the Feast of the Sacrifice, we all understood that it was we who were the lambs. I will say now that I doubt if there is any such thing as a holy war, because war is unholy by nature, just as a dog is a dog by nature, and I will say now, since no one will read these lines until I am dead, that in my opinion there is no God either. I think this because I have seen too many evil things and I have done too many evil things even when I believed in Him, and I think that if there was a God He would have prevented all these evil things. These are thoughts that I have not dared to say to anyone, and every Friday I go to the mosque like everyone else, and I move the beads on my tespih. I observe the fast at ramadan, and I touch my forehead to the ground when I make my salats, but all the time I am wondering how many of those doing the same things around me are respectable hypocrites like me. I will say that if there is no God, then everything is inexplicable, and that would be very hard for us, but if there is God, then He is not good. Now that the years have passed by I will say that the war was sacred for a different reason, and this reason is that it caused Turkey to be born out of the empire, which was mother of it, and gave birth to it as it lay dying.

But at that time not one of us doubted that it was a holy war, and all of us were intoxicated with the idea of martyrdom, and the imams told us that if we died in a holy war, then we would meet the Prophet himself in the garden where he abides, and we would be carried there by the green birds of paradise that come only for martyrs, and we knew that God had promised us success, and we knew that it is hard to get to Heaven and easy to get to Hell, and we were being given a chance to go straight to Heaven with no questions asked. It made us feel very good. If we shed a drop of blood, it would wash away our sins on the instant, God would not judge us, and on the day of resurrection each of us would have the privilege of naming seventy people who we wished to enter paradise with us, and they would enter it, and so all our family and our friends would be there with us, and the best thing was that when we reached paradise we would have seventy-two virgins to wait on us and do our pleasure. When we were in a coarse mood we often talked about the seventy-two virgins, and if you are a young man, what more could you want in your imagination? For us there was a wavering between this world and the next, and we were joyful because eternal bliss was at our fingertips and the wall between us and bliss was as thin as this paper on which I write, and as easy to tear asunder. Many of us took the oath of martyrdom with one hand on the Koran, and I was one of them, but even then I thought there was something not quite right, but I did come to understand why they would not let Christians come and fight, because the Christians would have doubted that it was a holy war and they might have dampened our enthusiasm, because doubt, when it is spilt, spreads like water. I do remember that I fought like a mastiff with a wolf, because I thought that the war was holy, and I fought thinking that with God alongside me I was invincible. To tell the truth, I often enjoyed the fighting. There is a wild excitement that takes you over when the attacks begin, and the fear and trembling has been overruled by action. Sometimes I feel sad when I remember the enthusiasm of those days, because I was never happier than when I had those beliefs and thought I was doing God's work. I smile when I think of how I envied the men of the 57th Regiment, who were all wiped out in one battle, right at the beginning, when Mustafa Kemal commanded them all not only to fight, but to die, telling them that in the time they took to die, reinforcements would have time to arrive, and so it was that all of them died, including the imam and the water boy. But now I am glad I was not in that regiment but in another. Certainly I will never forget what it was like when we put our ladders up against the parapet, and the standard bearer would unfurl the white flag with the red crescent moon and star on it, and we would call on the name of God, and climb the ladders, and pour out of the trenches, and charge the enemy. All of us knew we would go to paradise. Of course, the standard bearer was always the first to get killed.

My heart sinks at the thought of describing my eight years of chaos and destruction in two separate wars. How can I describe all the things I learned, and how quickly I learned them?

I was assigned to the 5th Army, and so I arrived at Maydos in the early spring, or the late winter if that is how you would prefer to say it. It is a place where the olive trees and the pines are the same size. At that time there was cistus growing in the rocks, and poppies redder than pigeon's blood, lilac and pink mallows, little orchids, ox-eye daisies, oregano as sharp and strong

332

as pepper, and tiny red flowers with black at the centre. There were old men and little boys in the streets, selling bread on sticks. With the other recruits I had marched for days, and now I come to think of it, I must have marched far enough in my time as a soldier to go three times round the world. There was never any transport, and we marched the length and breadth of the earth. I am surprised that my legs were not worn down to stumps from all that marching, and I cannot count the number of pairs of boots I must have used up. Anyone who has been a soldier understands the value of boots. One of the things you look forward to, when somebody is killed, is the prospect of finding a better pair of boots, and we took them equally from the dead enemy and our own comrades, but it was often enough that we were reduced to fighting with nothing on our feet at all. Sometimes if you had a special comrade with good boots, he would let it be known who was to inherit them when he was killed. I had a comrade called Fikret who was killed, but before he was wounded we had an agreement like that. I said to him, 'If I am killed first, I would like you to have my boots,' and he said, 'If you are killed first, I would rather have your seventy-two virgins, so perhaps you could send them down from paradise,' and we both laughed, but it was *he* who was killed first, and I got his belt, which was better than mine, and I took what remained of his ammunition, and with it I killed fifteen Franks by sniping, and that is how I avenged him.

At first I didn't have a proper uniform. I was wearing bits and pieces of the white summer uniform that was abolished, and I was wearing a fez on my head instead of a proper enverieh. The corporal who was my first corporal made me rub it with mud to take away the brightness of it, and laughed at me when I was reluctant, and anyway it was blown off my head in the naval bombardment, and I never found it again.

Maydos was a pretty town by the water's side. It had rough streets paved with heavy stones, and there were soft-eyed dogs asleep on steps and in doorways. There were figs and vines, and the sparrows were very noisy in the eves. There were goats making idiot noise, and mournful cows lowing, and cockerels crowing in competition. There was a wealthy street taken up with

Greek jewellers. There was an old man selling fish that were threaded on to string through the gills. I remember that we were sent almost immediately to Divrin Plain, and there I wrote a long letter to my mother, because she had managed to send one to me, and I told her of how beautiful the place was, and how my mother's letter had given it enchantment. I think I told her that when I got home I would like to get married. I wonder what happened to the letter, because I cannot imagine that my mother would have thrown it away. After that I was not allowed to write any more, and in any case the great Frankish battleships were coming, and there was fighting to be done almost immediately.

I was sent straight away to assist the field artillery, because the big ships were coming, and it was their intention to get through the minefield so that Istanbul could be taken, but they couldn't get their big ships through until the mines were cleared, and they couldn't get the minesweepers in until the big ships had knocked out our guns, but the big ships couldn't knock out our guns until the mines were cleared. So it was a difficult situation for the Franks.

I have never seen anything like those big ships. I think there were about sixteen of them. I can't explain to you in words how vast they were. They were like islands. They filled the heavens with black smoke, and they had guns so enormous that it was impossible to imagine how these were made by human hands. When we saw them filling the sea our hearts sank and we felt that it was all hopeless, but the officers seemed confident, and they kept us very occupied, and so we drew hope from them.

Do you know the strangest thing about being a soldier? It is that you are repeatedly ordered to commit suicide, and you obey. So it was lucky that so many of us wanted to get to paradise. Almost all of the attacks were frontal assaults on well-defended positions. This was true of the Frankish attacks and of our own, and when we saw the heaps of Frankish dead in front of our trenches, we began to feel sorry for them. I wonder if they felt sorry for us when they saw our dead heaped up in front of theirs. There were times when the dead lay three-deep, all mixed up with the wounded.

Before I arrived, the Franks had already demolished the fort at Seddülbahir with battleships, and also the fort at Kumkale, and they sent soldiers ashore to occupy them and destroy them completely, but after our soliders had withdrawn, they came back again, and drove the Franks out. This is how we did everything in that campaign. If we withdrew, we always came back. There was a soldier called Mehmet whose gun jammed, and he attacked a Frankish sailor with stones. Mustafa Kemal held him up to us as an example, and now the incident is famous all over Turkey, and that is why, I think, everyone these days refers to a soldier as a Mehmetçik. Of course, when I hear the name, I think mainly of my old friend, and I wonder where he is and if he has survived.

We still had very big guns at Çanakkale, across the other side of the water from where we were, and we had big guns at Kilitbahir, where there were forts. The Franks demolished the forts and the big guns in them, but they couldn't do very much about our field guns and howitzers, which were mobile. We had torpedo tubes as well. I was near Kilitbahir, which is not far from Maydos, but I was glad not to be in the fort itself, because the big ships were dropping shells on it by the hundred. Imagine big holes opening up in the ground, and pieces of rock and lumps of earth hurtling past your head, and no enemy to get your hands on directly. Imagine a noise like the end of the world, like the roll of thunder and the crack of lightning, and whistling noises, and whirring noises, and pinging noises, and strange intervals of absolute silence. Imagine the groans and gurgles of the wounded, and all the different kinds of screams, from low and musical ones, to shrieks that cut the brain. Imagine being covered with filth and being so soaked in sweat that the filth clings to you and cakes on to your body. Imagine being full of cuts so that the daub of filth has dark patches of blood in it. Imagine your throat so dry with thirst that it feels as though it has swallowed dried leaves and swollen up enough to stop the breath. Later on, when the Frankish ships bombarded our trenches, they used shrapnel which burst harmlessly, because we covered our trenches over. If they had used high explosive we would have been defeated, but they cannot have had any left. We too ran out of shells at different times. The curious thing about the Frankish high explosive was that it made you turn yellow, and you would be as yellow as a serin finch.

My particular job on the day of the great bombardment was to commit suicide by setting off smoke bombs that would draw enemy fire, hoping that the enemy would think they were real guns. I was told not to set off too many in any one place, and so I ran from rock to rock, setting off smoke bombs and waiting to be shelled. If I was shelled, this would signify my success. In the meantime, the howitzers would be dragged from place to place by their crews, and there weren't enough horses, so they had to use teams of buffalo, and the idea was to knock out the Frankish minesweepers, and it was important to keep moving so as not to be destroyed by return fire. I had never seen such frantic activity, and neither had I ever heard such a quantity of obscenities, because the lot of the gunners was even worse than my lot. This is one of the consolations of the soldier, that when you are in shit up to the chest, there are always others who are in shit up to the neck. The gunners were clever people, because they hid their howitzers just below the crests of the hills, on the side where they could not be seen, and in such a way that the trajectory of their shells would fall on the ships, but the shells from the ships would have to pass over them without touching them. It was then that I realised that much of war depends not upon courage and strength, but upon cleverness. The Franks never had enough howitzers, or high-explosive shells, or trench mortars, or proper grenades, and without these there can be no success in the trenches. It is surprising that the Franks were not clever enough to realise this, when they were clever enough to make such big ships. Only the French Franks had proper mortars, and these dropped a bomb that we called the Black Cat, and we were appalled by them. They made a noise like a steam train, and they came vertically down out of the sky. We called the French Franks 'Tangos', and they also had the most lethal artillery.

Sometime after midday we thought we had lost, because we were exhausted and we had taken too much damage, and used up most of our ammunition, but for some reason several of the ships that had been bombarding us from close by began to withdraw, and then one of them hit a mine on the other side of the

336

bay, and it sank in two minutes before our unbelieving eyes. Some minesweepers came in, but they lost courage, and then, maybe two hours after the first ship sank, another two ships also struck mines, and one of them drifted so close that it was easy to shell it. Later on, both of these ships sank, and it made us sad to know of it, because those ships were magnificent, and it was like when a bull is slaughtered, and one is glad of the meat but sorry for the death of the great bull.

At the end of that day we knew we had won a victory, and no one was more surprised than us. We wandered about in the smoke and the chaos and the carnage, with a great thirst, and we smiled at each other and gave thanks to God.

All the same, we knew that we stood no chance at all when the enemy came back with his ships in the morning. Our towns were devastated completely, our forts had all but gone. We knew that soon the big ships would be in the harbours of Istanbul, and the war would be lost.

That night we ate melons and drank raki with water in it, and you know what raki does. You don't want to go home, and you love everybody, and it gives you serenity. On that occasion it reconciled us to death in the morning.

The next day we rose up prepared for martyrdom, and we talked about the green birds that would take us to paradise, and the virgins that awaited us, and some people were elated because they would soon meet the Prophet in his own garden. We waited and waited for the ships to come back, but they did not come back either that day or in the days after.

The triumph swelled our chests and we felt like giants, and we who had believed that God was with us, believed it now even more than before, and those who had not believed it began to do so, because the fact is that the artillery at the narrows had only thirty shells left, and the Franks could have sailed straight past us in the morning.

58

Karatavuk at Gallipoli: Karatavuk Remembers (2)

It was another month before the Franks returned, and in the meantime a very great deal happened.

In the first place I discovered something that confused us all, which was that some of the Franks were on our side. We were confused because of the proverb that 'Unbelief is one nation', and now it appeared that it was not, and there were some Franks who were on the side of the House of Islam, and not the House of War. These Franks were called Germans, and most surprisingly they were Christians. They had an emperor who had declared himself the protector of the Muslims, and it was they who supplied us with the new battleships that replaced the ones that were withheld by the other Franks called British. I had not been aware that the Franks were divided among themselves, and I thought it strange, as I still do, that these German Franks were fighting alongside us when our own Christians were forbidden to do so. All the more strange was that these German Franks were in positions of great power, and we were commanded by one such who was called Liman von Sanders, who was a very great general for us. Sometimes you saw him with his ADCs, walking about the lines, and sometimes he was on a horse, and often he wore a Turkish uniform and not a Frankish one. There were many other of these German Frank officers, and they gave advice and orders to our Turkish officers, and they conversed with our officers in a language which was neither German nor Turkish, but it was another Frankish language called French. I will confuse you, as we were confused, when I tell you that the French people who actually originated this language were among our enemies who invaded us, and were the ones we called 'Tangos'. My lieutenant, who was called Orhan, explained to me that he spoke French with the German officers because French is the universal language of civilisation.

In the second place I was forbidden to write any more letters to my mother, and I was treated very harshly because of the writing.

It was not expected that a soldier would know how to write, and therefore I fell under suspicion. One morning after the prayer, when I was just about to set out with a labour detail, I was seized suddenly by two soldiers and taken to see my company commander. On the way I was kicked and beaten by the soldiers, who were military policemen, and I was struck with a rifle butt. Everybody hates the military police, and they in return have a hatred of proper soldiers. These two men were very big, and they had stupid faces, and they smelled of raki. By the time that I got to see the commander, I was bleeding from a wound in my cheek, and I had difficulty marching in before him, because I had been kicked in the knee.

The company commander looked up at me when I saluted, and moved some papers on his desk, and he said, 'At ease.' He then confirmed my name and my unit, and he showed me a letter, saying, 'Did you write this, Abdul Nefer?' and I took the letter, which was the second one to my mother, and looked at it, and I said, 'This is the second letter I have written to my mother.'

The commander said, 'Read it.'

I did not want to read it, because it was to my mother, but I realised that one does not refuse a company commander who gives a direct order, and so I began to read: 'My dear Mother, I am sitting once more under a pear tree, and everything is more beautiful even than it was before. My soul is enchanted yet more greatly by the sweetness of the land . . .'

It was something like that. When I wrote to my mother, the thought of her made me inspired, and I wrote more tenderly than when I write this, and I told her no bad things that would make her concerned. I read it from start to finish, knowing the terrible shame of having a private thing exposed to strangers, and then I handed it back to the major. He said, 'How do we know that it says this?'

I pointed to the paper, and said, 'Because it is written.'

He said, 'The characters are Greek.'

I said, 'The words are Turk.'

The commander looked at me and said, 'Not long ago the Greeks were at war with us, and before long they may well be again. They did terrible things to us in Thrace. I know, because I was there. I have seen little children disembowelled and nailed to doors. We don't want Greeks among us here, not in the army. The danger of espionage is obvious.'

'I am not a Greek, sir,' I replied.

'You are not a Christian?'

'I am Muslim, sir. I am not an infidel.'

The commander said, 'The imam of your unit assures me that you are a Muslim, but then it is easy to impersonate a Muslim. Please explain this letter.'

'It is a letter to my mother, sir.'

'Yes, yes, it is a letter to your mother, but why is it in Greek?'

'It is not in Greek, sir,' I repeated, 'it is Turk, and only the letters are Greek. I was taught by my friend because I was anxious to learn.'

'How does this come about?' asked the commander, as if to no one in particular, and at that point Lieutenant Orhan, who was standing behind him and to one side, leaned over, and said, 'If I may, sir.' He took the letter and looked at it, and said, 'There are places where Turkish is spoken and written in Greek, I have heard that is quite common on the west coast, and in particular in the south-west where this soldier comes from. The people are sometimes called Karamanlids.'

The commander said, 'How can we check this?' and the lieutenant replied, 'We do have a great many Greek doctors,' and the commander said, 'Fetch me one.'

So it was that shortly afterwards a Greek doctor from a medical detachment came and looked at the letter, and said, 'The letters are Greek, but the language is Turkish. No Greek would understand this unless he were also a Turkish speaker.' I remember that many of us were opposed to having Greek doctors, because we thought that they did not care to treat us properly when we were ill or wounded, but all that was to come later, and this particular doctor was a good thing for me without a doubt.

When he heard that it really was Turkish, the commander dismissed the doctor, and he spoke to Lieutenant Orhan, of whom

340

I will speak later, and who was my platoon commander, and he said, 'Is this a good soldier?' whereupon Lieutenant Orhan said, 'He volunteered in place of his father, and he distinguished himself in the naval attack. I have every confidence in him as a soldier, and I have thought of recommending that he should be promoted to corporal. I would like to say, sir, that I object to him being beaten for no reason by the military police.'

The commander sighed, and he stood up and said to the two military policeman who had brought me in, 'Was it you that struck this soldier so that his face bleeds?' and they said, 'Yes, sir, it was us.' And the commander asked, 'And was it because he resisted arrest?' and the military police said, 'No, sir.'

I have always thought that this shows how stupid the military police are, because they should have said 'Yes', but anyway the commander told them to stand to attention. He drew his pistol from his holster, and he struck each one of them across the cheek with the barrel of his pistol, so that they bled as I did. They stood there at attention, bleeding, and said nothing. Afterwards the commander turned to me and said, 'You will write no more letters in Greek script. I have enough to worry about without the censors coming to me with their stupid problems. Do you understand?'

I said, 'Yes, sir,' and he said, 'You are dismissed,' so I came to attention, saluted and left, and limped with Lieutenant Orhan back towards my platoon, and it is for this reason that my mother heard nothing of me for the next three years.

Lieutenant Orhan once said to us, 'I think we have been lucky in having such a stupid enemy, so we should take heart.' He said this because the Franks always gave us plenty of time to prepare our defences. Four months before the big battle I have just described, they sent in ships to bombard the forts at Kumkale and Seddülbahir, and a magazine exploded, killing eight-six men, and so we knew that we had to fortify the narrows, and then two months later a Frankish submarine sank our battleship *Messudieh*, and so we knew to lay mines and submarine nets.

When we were walking back to my unit, and a gentle rain had begun to fall, Lieutenant Orhan said to me, 'You interest me very much.'

I did not know how to reply, and said nothing, because a soldier does not normally converse with an officer, and then he turned and explained: 'You are the only soldier I have ever had under my command who was able to read and write.' He paused, and then continued, 'And the odd thing about it is that what you have learned is almost useless. To write Turkish with Greek letters is like growing a new fruit that is partly a lemon and partly a fig, which no one will ever eat.'

'What should I do then, sir?' I asked him, and he said, 'The first thing is to survive the war. However, I have heard Mustafa Kemal say that we should write in Roman letters, like the Franks, so if he has his way, one day you might have to learn those instead of the Greek ones.'

'I expect we will win the war, inshallah,' I said, because to say or think otherwise was unacceptable, 'and afterwards I can go back to writing things down.'

'We have been fortunate,' said Lieutenant Orhan. 'The Germans have great military skills that we are learning, and the British and the French have been unaccountably stupid in giving us so much time in which to prepare ourselves. I think it is very probable that we will defeat them. Also, we have Colonel Mustafa Kemal in charge of the reserve.'

'What should I do?' I asked him, and he said, 'Keep your bayonet sharp, enjoy everything you do as if it were the last time you are ever going to do it, and when you have to dig, dig deeply and dig well.'

Lieutenant Orhan was the best of the three officers we had, and before an attack we would always hear him sharpening his sword, making the blade sing with a rhythm like marching feet, and when we went into attack he would go before us with his sword in his hand, and we would watch for the moment when he raised his sword, and he would cry out 'God is Great', and at that moment we would begin the charge, and we would all cry out 'God is Great' and feel the wild courage rising up inside us. Lieutenant Orhan was like an angel to us, and it was a terrible grief to us when he was killed. I think this was at the second battle of Krithia. After the Franks fell back, I crept out between the lines to look for him at dawn, because I had seen him fall, and I had the idea that he might still be alive, but when I found him he was already bloating, and his blood was black in his wounds, and he was covered in the eggs of corpse flies. I prised open his fingers and I took his sword, and when I brought it back, we few survivors of the battle took turns to kiss it. I don't know what happened to the sword in the end.

I often think about Lieutenant Orhan, and now that I am older, if I doze off in the early afternoon, seated under the plane trees in the meydan, I dream that he and my comrades come, one by one, and clasp my shoulders in their hands, and kiss my cheeks in greeting.

59

Karatavuk at Gallipoli: Karatavuk Remembers (3)

We all knew that the Franks would return with an army as well as ships, and many people grew fearful, but I had the fate of being commanded by Mustafa Kemal, and so I and my comrades were among the lucky ones.

You know how it is. Sometimes there is someone who is special and stands out among all others. I think that Abdulhamid Hodja was like that, and also Rustem Bey. Sometimes there is someone who is selected to be a lion or an eagle when the rest of us are selected to be sheep and sparrows, and this someone is not caught up by destiny, but makes destiny for themselves, as if they have a greater knowledge of what must be done, and an understanding of the direction in which the world must go.

I know that Mustafa Kemal is now the President, and anyone would be ignorant indeed who has not heard of him, and I know that for all of us now he is the greatest Turk of all, and those like me who have met him personally shine with some of his glory for ever afterwards, but back then he was just an officer, and none of us knew how he would grow to be great. Even so, we knew he was the best commander to have, and we soldiers were grateful to serve under him rather than someone else, because we had confidence in him. This was because he was a serious officer, and not somebody who was just passing his life away in a uniform, and he had served in that region before, and therefore knew it very well. He would go forward and spy on the Franks with his binoculars, and risk getting shot, like a proper soldier, and he would stride about in the battle and never get hit, as if he were protected. It was said that when he commanded the 38th Regiment, he had made it perfect, and this knowledge strengthened us. Mustafa Kemal knew how to read the intentions of the enemy, and so he was able to confound them, and

344

most of his attacks were successful, but nowadays, when I think back, I have to admit that I have grown doubtful. As I have said, all the attacks were frontal assaults, and several times Mustafa Kemal sacrificed thousands of us in one day. He inspired us, and anyway we were prepared to die, but now it strikes me as wasteful. A soldier is a kind of ammunition, and we were always told not to waste ammunition. In my opinion, looking back after all these years, there was no need for us to make any attacks or counter-attacks at all. All we had to do was wait for the Franks to exterminate themselves by attacking us, because all the casualties for both sides were caused by attacks and not by defence.

Because the peninsula was so large, and the armies small, and not big enough to defend every landing place, it was decided to create a mobile reserve, and this was the 19th Division, and I was in it, and we were encamped near Bigalı. This was the best place for the reserve because we could go in one direction to support the 7th Division, or in another to support the 9th. At Bigalı, Mustafa Kemal was in a house. This house was a peaceful one, and it had a balcony and balustrades, and a courtyard, and heavy tiles on the roof, and in the garden were roses and mint, and for some reason there were no windows at the back of the house. Every time we saw this peaceful house, we felt better because Mustafa Kemal and Major Izzettin were in it, making plans.

During the month before the Franks returned, five more divisions were moved in, and we spent the time in two ways, and there was not a moment's rest. We laid barbed wire until our hands bled and our uniforms were in shreds, and we did this until the wire ran out. We dug ramparts and foxholes, and filled sandbags to make little strongpoints with them, and we cleared trees and shrubs to make better lines of fire. We made trenches covered over with planks and earth, to keep us safe from shells. Mustafa Kemal made us train continually, and he marched us at high speed all over the peninsula so that we would be strengthened and know the terrain, which twisted and turned and was very confusing. There were many deep water courses that were dry in the summer, and ravines and gullies that meandered about and went nowhere, and the land was very unsuitable for proper battles, because there were very thick thorny bushes which meant

345

that soldiers had to go in file along tiny goat tracks rather than advance, properly spread out, and consequently it was very easy to train machine guns on to the goat tracks and get any soldiers who came along them. Also, when you advanced, you got lost almost straight away, and lost contact with the rest of your unit, and every unit lost touch with every other unit, and so every attack degenerated into chaos.

It was a place where the land constantly changes. By the sea there are steep and stony cliffs covered with spiky shrubs, and in places there is beautiful soft farmland, and there are woods of small pine trees, full of yellow singing birds, and in places there are the deep gullies and ravines that I just mentioned, and there are hills which are rocky and also covered in spiky shrubs. There were no roads, and so we marched everywhere across country, making the tracks as we went, and everything had to be carried by animals and men, and not in carts, and sometimes the horses were so hungry that they were trying to eat the paint off the buildings. At that time of year it was spring, and it was very beautiful, with flowers growing everywhere as if they did not know there was a war. The shepherds' dogs had rounded ears and spiked collars. There were tortoises clattering about in the stones of the forts, and little lizards that lived beneath the rims of the wells. There were beetles with tan backs, and big beetles that walked backwards dragging leaves, and tiny turquoise damselflies, and big brown whirring dragonflies. There were black ants that made their own little roads, and very big ants that carried away caterpillars. There were big snakes with golden-brown heads. Out on the jetties there were cormorants hanging out their wings to dry, and in the skies there were magpies and ravens. These are the things that a soldier notices, because he lives close to the earth, and these are his companions, and he becomes interested in them because there is often very little to do, and they make him think about what it is to live, and about the many types of life. He remembers these things long after the details of the battles have faded away. Of course, as the seasons changed, we realised more and more that the place was not for long the paradise that it was in the spring.

Mustafa Kemal thought that the attack would come from the

south, but the Frankish German general thought it would come at Bolayır, and so we were marching from one place to another, staging mock attacks and practising movement at night and by day, and we learned how to use the bayonet, because at close quarters a bayonet is less dangerous to your own comrades than a bullet, since a bullet can go straight through an enemy and strike a friend. We learned for ourselves, however, after the battles had begun, that it was best not to bayonet someone in the ribs, because the ribs are like springs, and they clamp down on the bayonet, and you can't get it out unless you pull it out with your foot on the man's chest, and this is not a good thing to have to do, since it is very cruel to a dying man, and he clutches at the bayonet with his hands, and you have to look in his face, and you remember this face for a long time, and his eyes, and the blood that he coughs up, and this comes up in your dreams, and so it is difficult to sleep, even when you are exhausted. Also, if a bayonet is stuck between someone's ribs, you might be bayoneted yourself whilst trying to pull it out. The other thing is that sometimes you can fight an entire battle with bayonets, without firing a single shot. It happened when we had no ammunition, and sometimes even when we did. I often thought we would have been better off with swords, because, if you think about it, a rifle with a bayonet is just like a dagger on a stick, or maybe a short spear that you can't throw, or like a stabbing sword, as opposed to a sabre. In my opinion we all should have had swords, and not just the officers. This opinion is made stronger by the fact that the Franks had some little men called Gurkhas. These Gurkhas were the fiercest and bravest of the soldiers, and they had heavy knives that were bent in shape, and the bottom half had a big bulge, and with these they could cut off your head or your arm with one stroke, and they were very effective in the trenches. I have one of these knives that I took from a dead Gurkha, and I keep it on the wall of my house.

We in Mustafa Kemal's division considered that we were the best troops of all after the month was over, and we also thought we had the best commander, because he was always going from one place to another, examining everything through his binoculars, and thinking seriously. He had blond hair and blue eyes, which made him strangely fascinating to us, who were not like him at all, and these blue eyes shone with light and cleverness, and when he stopped to talk to you, you felt as honoured as if it were the Sultan Padishah himself. He had a doctor with him who gave him injections from time to time, but I don't know why, and the doctor's name was Hussein Bey.

When the Frankish landing happened, it was the day after we had finished all our preparations. The fields of fire were cleared, the big guns were ranged and the sights of our rifles were zeroed. It was like when a wedding is arranged, and the guests arrive just as you are putting out the food.

60

Mustafa Kemal (13)

Mustafa Kemal develops a curious relationship with the German commander, Otto Liman von Sanders. Von Sanders is an intelligent and determined officer who seldom makes mistakes, and has placed Germans rather than Turks in positions of command in most of the crucial places, causing much animosity among Ottoman officers. Unlike Sir Ian Hamilton, the British commander, von Sanders is always willing to sack incompetent officers. Kemal is openly anti-German, and tells the general to his face that he thinks that Germany will lose the war. Kemal is irritatingly convinced of the correctness of his own opinions in all things strategic and tactical, and he disagrees with the general about the probable site of the Allied landings. In time, von Sanders will overcome his annoyance with the obstreperous and opinionated Kemal, and will entrust him with more and more responsibility. Kemal turns out to be right about the landings, but the general has organised his divisions so that only a small number of soldiers are distributed around the coast, and the remainder are concentrated so as to be able to be deployed as soon as Allied intentions become clear, and their diversions only fool him for one day.

Kemal is given the command of the reserves, and on the morning of the invasion, he is awakened by the distant sound of naval bombardment. He sends a cavalry squadron to reconnoitre, and is informed that a small enemy force is heading for high ground that would give them complete dominance of the peninsula. Accordingly, he takes matters into his own hands, acts without authority – something which he does very often, and always gets away with – and departs with the entire 57th Regiment and a mountain battery. By serendipitous coincidence the 57th Regiment is kitted up and ready to go, on account of exercises that have already been scheduled. Fortunately for Kemal and the

Ottoman Empire, he has read the Allied intentions correctly. If he had not, he would have led the reserves to the wrong place and the campaign would have been lost immediately.

Kemal leaves his regiment to recover from the rapid march, and goes forward through the scrubland. He sees the enemy ships scattered about the ocean. Ottoman troops are fleeing towards him, and Kemal asks, 'Why are you running?' and they reply 'They're coming! They're coming!'

'Who is?' demands Kemal.

'The enemy, sir.'

'Where?'

'Over there!'

Sure enough, a line of Australian troops is advancing towards Çonk Bayırı, the crucial high ground that is destined to be the objective with which the Allied commanders will become most obsessed.

'You must not retreat,' Kemal tells them.

'But we have no ammunition left!'

Kemal realises that the Australians are a lot closer to him than his own troops are. He needs to buy time, and is nudged by a providential inspiration. 'Fix bayonets and lie down,' he commands. They do as he says, and the Australians think they are about to be fired upon, and they too lie down, and prepare for a firefight. An officer is dispatched to fetch the 57th Regiment.

Kemal reminds the regiment that they have the disgraceful losses of the Balkan Wars to redeem. He issues the famous statement: 'I am not ordering you to attack, I am ordering you to die. By the time that we are dead, other units and other commanders will arrive to take our place.' Kemal personally helps to shoulder the batteries into position, and controls the battle from the skyline. Miraculously, he is not hit. Inspired by Kemal, inspired by jihad, the 57th Regiment manages to hold the Australian advance, and is almost completely wiped out. Within a short time, even the imam and the water boy will be dead, and the 57th Regiment will enter into Turkish myth for ever. On the following day, however, the Arab 77th Regiment flees in panic, deepening the general contempt for Arab soldiers that is increasingly taking hold in the Ottoman army, but within five days the position is stabilised, and after a catastrophic counter-offensive by the 5th Division, the lines at Anzac are more or less permanently entrenched. Mustafa Kemal is awarded the Ottoman Order of Imtiyaz, and his divisional headquarters acquires the nickname 'Kemalyeri'. Liman von Sanders sends a German officer to be Kemal's chief of staff, and Kemal pointedly sends him away and retains the faithful Major Izzettin.

One day Mustafa Kemal stops and speaks briefly with Karatavuk. He takes Karatavuk's rifle and inspects it, easing the bolt and peering down the barrel, and then commends Karatavuk for his attention to it. Karatavuk will remember this proudly for the rest of his life, but will be unable to recall precisely what was said.

61

I am Philothei (10)

When I was about thirteen two very funny things happened. The first was that somebody thought up the idea that I should wear a veil, because my prettiness was upsetting the men in the town. It was when Ali the Snowbringer was following me around gaping at me when he was supposed to be collecting ice. He used to appear in front of me at all times of day, rather like Ibrahim did, and he would be practically salivating. I sort of liked it but it also made me feel annoyed. It was like being persecuted. When he did it, I was annoyed, and when he didn't do it, I was also put out a bit, and I would think, 'Oh, maybe I'm not so pretty any more,' so when he reappeared I felt relieved as well as annoyed, because at least it showed that I hadn't lost my looks.

Don't tell anyone, because I'd die, and I've never told this to anyone else, so it's a secret and you really must keep it to yourself, but sometimes I would guess where Ali the Snowbringer was likely to be, and that's where I'd go, and I did it just to tease him. I hope you don't think I'm too awful, I know I'm bad without you having to tell me.

What happened after a while was that all the other women started to veil themselves to show how pretty they were. It didn't last long, though.

The other thing that happened was that the bleeding came upon me quite suddenly, and I hadn't expected it, and didn't even know what it was, so I was very frightened and thought I must be dying of something. Fortunately I was at the aga's konak at the time, and Leyla Hanım had been brushing my hair after I'd done hers, and Drosoula was brushing the cat Pamuk, and Pamuk was biting her because of the ecstasy.

Anyway, I had to go to the little room outside to relieve myself, and that was when I realised that I was bleeding, and I came running back in and I was weeping and throwing myself around and wailing and acting as if the world was about to end, and finally Leyla Hanım took hold of my arms to keep me still, and then she managed to force it out of me, and I said, 'Leyla Han im, I'm bleeding,' and at first she says, 'Where? Where? Have you cut yourself?' and then finally she twigged, and she put her hand to her mouth and laughed. She had a nice laugh, it was silvery, like this . . .

Anyway, she called Drosoula over, who was also bleeding but on her hands because of the cat, and she asked her if she had started a woman's bleeding yet, and Drosoula just looked puzzled, so that way Leyla Hanım knew that she hadn't started yet.

Leyla said, 'When blood comes out from between your legs it just means that you're old enough to have babies. It lasts a few days every month, and you've just got to put up with it, because there isn't any choice, so there's no point in complaining.' She said, 'I suppose you both want babies?' and Drosoula and I both said yes, it would be a good thing, and Leyla said, 'I have been sad because of not having babies,' and her eyes started to shine a bit. She showed us how to fold a cloth to keep us from leaving drips on the floor, which was how she put it, which wasn't very nice really.

She said, 'And do you know how it's done?' and we said, 'How what's done, Leyla Hanım?' and she said, 'Making babies,' and we said no we didn't know.

Then Leyla tried to explain and she got very flustered and embarrassed, and she put it so poetically and she praised it so much that we didn't really understand at all. It was another couple of years before I really understood, and until that time Drosoula and I really did think it was something to do with pomegranates and plums and cucumbers, and we'd always wondered why she thought that all that business with fruit was so much fun.

62

The Letter to Karatavuk

I do not know the correct manner of addressing someone such as yourself, never before having had to write to the son of a potter, and one of the infidel persuasion at that, and so I beg your indulgence for beginning this letter with no greeting at all. I suspect that, given these trying circumstances, letters such as this are unlikely to arrive at their destinations in any case, especially when one considers that often they did not arrive even in times of peace. One also has to consider whether, as in this case, a letter's recipient will be alive to read it, since you are a soldier, and there are many mishaps in war. I have found myself in the irksome situation of becoming your parents' amanuensis, since the other letter-writers of the town, those that have remained at any rate, customarily write in the Ottoman script, which, I understand, you are unable to read. I must say I was very surprised when I was told by your parents that you have learned to read and write Turkish in the Greek script, apparently taught by one of my own erstwhile pupils. I had become accustomed to believing that Turks are intellectually idle to the last degree, and it was salutary to discover that there is at least one among you with both brains and initiative, causing me to speculate as to whether the backwardness of your race is more explicable in terms of deficient education than natural inability. I have always thought it odd that this education consists entirely in uselessly memorising pages in Arabic that no one can understand.

I have to tell you that it sits very ill with me, having to write to you in Turkish using the Greek script, which I would prefer to remain unsullied and unadulterated, although I know that this is an ingrained habit in many places around here, presumably where the original Greeks have been degraded by mingling for too many hundreds of years with their interloping Turkish neighbours. I have not had to read such stuff before, let alone write it, and it is indeed difficult to locate myself within a discourse whose rules and grammar are unknown, since they have never hitherto been laid down by scholars. One has to invent spellings for oneself, according to a system of guesses and approximations. For me it is like having to use a golden spoon to clear out a drain, since my own language and my manner of writing are so much superior to yours in every manner of expression. I concede, however, that the letter you wrote to your parents, and which I have had to read to them, much against my initial inclination, did possess some considerable poetic force, and I was moved by it, somewhat against my will.

I write to you then, reluctantly, at great expense to my time and patience, but at the insistence of your parents, who are most unrelenting. Your father has presented me with various pots, and so I am obliged to him, and your mother is tearful, which is also hard to endure. Your father has in addition given me one of those birdwhistles with which you and your friends used to torment the town, as if we did not have bulbuls and nightingales enough to keep us awake at night. He advised me to pass it on to any child of which I might be fond, whereupon I declared that, since I am a schoolmaster, there are no longer any such.

Your parents instruct me to write:

We pray to God that He and His Angels watch over you and keep you from the bullets and the darkness of the Devil. We pray that there is an angel that spreads his wings above you and around you and protects you. We pray that no bad djinn comes by you. We pray that danger sees you and looks the other way and passes on the other side. We pray that you are well, and not ill, and that you are rewarded with sleep when weary. We pray that you have food for your stomach and water for your throat. We pray that Mary Mother of Jesus also watches over you. We pray that amid hardship you find peace and whatever joy is to be found within it.

We pray that if death finds you, there will be a white shroud to carry you to paradise, and a green turban, and that you will be at the gates of paradise to meet us when we come. We pray that no harm will happen to your companions. We pray that you remember us, and do not forget us, and pray for us in this hard and unforgiving world. We pray that God forgives you for the deception of your father, as we have forgiven you, because now we are able to carry on. We pray that the Sultan himself rewards you, and God also, as we will reward you when you return. We pray that if things go well for you, you will not suffer the evil eye.

There is much trouble in this place. We who had nothing now have even less. Everything that was bad is now worse. Nothing is mended, no good things arrive by road or sea. We are lucky if there is one onion to eat, the tradesmen have no one to trade with.

The good thing is that Leyla Hanım plays the oud, and the sound of the strings floats out over us and brings us peace. Another good thing is that we of this town have seen an aeroplane for the first time, which flew over our heads making a great clattering noise, and all of us ran outdoors, and some people were most afraid, and the dogs were going mad with barking and jumping up and down. But Rustem Bey knew what it was, and explained that it was a machine that flies with a man in it, and when we looked we saw the man, who waved to us, and he flew once or twice around the town and over our heads, and we have been talking a great deal of this because it is like a miracle, and none of us knows who the man was. I expect that by now you will have seen an aeroplane also, and we wonder what you think of such things. We are not sure that they are good, because God gave it to birds to fly and to us to walk. If we are to become like birds, what will the birds become? What if a man flies so high that he reaches Heaven? What will God do?

A very bad thing is that the gendarmes have arrived and taken away many of the Christian boys who were forbidden to fight because of the jihad, and there were scenes of the greatest sorrow and alarm because it was all so sudden, and it was said that the boys were taken for labour battalions, who will build roads and bridges and dig holes and put up buildings. We have heard that the life is very bad in the labour battalions because the Christians have been turned against, and they are being worked almost to death and are living in terrible places. Your friend Mehmetçik who taught you to read has been one of the taken, even though he requested to be a soldier, and his mother and father are frightened by it and say that there is no hope, but we have tried to comfort them, and they us, because we are all losing our sons. Now the girls and women that are left are performing the men's work, and many are thin and ill from the work and the lack of food.

Another very bad thing is that people have been here from the Sultan taking our animals. They have taken many mules, donkeys and horses, saying that the army needs them in the jihad against the infidels, but how do we know who these people are? They give us papers that we cannot read, and tell us that when we present these papers at a later time we will get our animals back, or animals that are equal. Some say that these men are outlaws and thieves and come not from the Sultan at all. People hid their mules when they heard what was happening and so thank God Ali the Snowbringer still has his mule, but it was most terrible for Abdulhamid Hodja, who has lost his Nilufer. You know how much he loved and defended that horse. She was old but she was still strong, and she was the most beautiful silver horse of all, more beautiful even than the horses of Rustem Bey. It was wonderful to see her with her mane braided, and the green ribbons in her mane and the brass bells, and the brass breastplate engraved with verses, and the Yörük saddle that he bought from the unwashed. And it was wonderful how proud and lovely it was to see Abdulhamid Hodja mounted upon it. When the people from the Sultan saw the horse and the imam upon it, they roughly bade him dismount, even though he is venerable and a hafiz, and they made him part with the horse, and he threw his arms around the neck of the horse and lamented so that everyone heard it and everyone was sorry beyond reason, and he called upon God to spare him the horse but they tore his arms from around the neck of the horse and he fell to the ground, but he stood up and embraced her again and recited in her ears and the horse pricked her ears and stamped her feet, and then two of the people held the imam until Nilufer was led away, and he was shouting and weeping.

Now Abdulhamid Hodja is very ill on account of despair and sorrow, because he loved the horse, and a horse is a most important thing to anyone that has one, especially if it is good. He says that Nilufer will be worked to death and the army starves such horses until they eat the paint from carts and houses, and he remembers this from when he was a soldier. Now Abdulhamid is on his pallet and will not eat, and he has pains in his sides and says that he will not be long for us in this world, and his wife says that he cannot pass water, so God knows if he will recover. There are no doctors here now because they were all Christians and they have gone to look after the soldiers even though no Christian is allowed to fight, and we are helpless if we are ill except for the cures passed down to us. Abdulhamid Hodja says that he will never see Nilufer again, and that the earth has opened before his feet so that he might lie down in it. Ayse Hanım wrings her hands and weeps, but there is nothing to be done. Abdulhamid Hodja lies upon his pallet and recites the Holy Koran, and he says that when he has finished it and spoken every word that is in it, then he will close his eyes and put on the white shroud and be laid down in the earth among the pines. And if he dies, who will lead our prayers?

Another thing that has happened is that we thought we had a ghost, because every night there would be crying and wailing after midnight, and it would wake us all up, and we would listen on our pallets shaking with fear, and the wailing would go through the streets and not stop for hours. The dogs would bark and the owls would fall silent and so would the nightingales. We were all talking and wondering what it means, and then Rustem Bey went out at night because he has authority and duty, and he went with Father Kristoforos the priest, but not with Abdulhamid Hodja because he was very ill and in despair, and Father Kristoforos had holy oil and water and an icon and other such Christian things, and there were two servants with them and Rustem Bey had a pistol. It turned out that the ghost was a woman who had lost her husband a few years ago in Macedonia, and now she has lost all her sons in Mesopotamia, and she has gone drunk with grief, and was wandering at night, and so there was no ghost after all, but it was very frightening whilst we thought there was. Now the woman is tied to her doorpost at night to stop her going out, and in the morning she is untied, and she wails and grieves inside her house, so that there is less noise in the streets. You will remember that in the last war there was another woman who was the same.

Your father says that a soldier is like one of the fingers of a potter and his comrades are the other fingers, and the soldiers of the enemy are the fingers of the other hand, and they work in opposition because no pot was ever well made with one hand, and the potter is God, and God moulds the world like clay by means of soldiers, so he says you should be proud to be one of God's fingers, and if not proud, resigned. Your mother says that it is important to wash your clothes whenever possible or else your skin will become itchy and inflamed. And she says that she wishes you were a child once more and did not have to go away to war.

This concludes the letter of your parents, which has caused me much inconvenience and trouble to transcribe, since both of them talk at once on different topics in a language which unfailingly grates upon the ear and intellect. I have left out much of your mother's advice and many of her exhortations, since I am sure that you will already have them by heart, having heard them so often repeated whilst you were still among us. It is clear to me that they hold you very dearly in their hearts, suffering much anxiety as to your safety, and so it would be well for them if you were able to write back soon, even though this would no doubt cause me further travail and perplexity.

I would like to add that I have long been aware that it was you and your friend Mehmetçik who used to steal the linnets and finches from my birdcage, and replace them with sparrows. I also know that it was you two who stole everybody's shoes from the niches outside their back doors, and swapped them round, causing such confusion and bother. Therefore I say that life is quieter and more equable without you, but I do not say that it is better.

Leonidas, Schoolmaster.

63

Karatavuk at Gallipoli: Karatavuk Remembers (4)

Every soldier has a comrade who stands out above the others. If your comrade is killed, you find another after a while, but there is still only one comrade that you remember in particular, and you think of him as being above all other comrades. This is because, after the great comrade has been killed, the wound in your heart makes it impossible to have such a comrade again.

I will write of Fikret. He was from Pera, and his slogan was 'I am from Pera, so I don't give a shit'. He was built like a stevedore, and the reason for this is that he had been working as a stevedore in the docks at Istanbul. I am not saying that he was big, because he was no taller than I am, but he had the powerful deep chest, and the thick, strong arms and legs of a man who has learned to lift and carry the heaviest things. I know personally that he was very strong, because he was the one who lifted the beams into place when we were making covered trenches, and he was stronger than anyone when we were collecting the wounded during the ceasefires. He could make us laugh by clenching the muscles of his neck, and they would all stand out and make him look grotesque. If you bumped into him accidentally, it was like walking into a tree.

Fikret was ugly. He had the hooked nose of an Arab, and a loose lower lip. His eyes were not set equally on his face, he had a moustache like the frayed end of a wire hawser, and he was covered with a thick stubble only a couple of hours after shaving. He smelled like a goat much of the time, as did we all, but the goatishness of his smell was on a greater scale than any of the rest of us could manage even after days of furious fighting in the trenches. In the trenches, what you smell is in this order: corpses, cordite, shit, piss, sweat. After a couple of days in action, Fikret's smell came in between the cordite and the shit.

What was good about Fikret was the honesty of his badness. To begin with he was always in trouble. He told the imam that he didn't give a shit about God, and he didn't give a shit if the war was holy or not, because all that mattered was that it needed fighting, and all of us were outraged by what he said, and the imam reported him so that he was in trouble for conduct likely to demoralise his comrades and undermine the state. He was given extra labour fatigues, and he said afterwards, 'I don't give a shit; I am from Pera.' If Lieutenant Orhan had not intervened, I think he would have been shot. Lieutenant Orhan told him to keep his opinions to himself, and fortunately he had more respect for the lieutenant than he did for the imam or even God Himself, so he confined himself to all the other topics he didn't give a shit about.

Fikret was dependably foul-mouthed as well. If you asked him where to put something, or if he knew where someone was, he would always reply, 'Up your mother's cunt.' Normally anyone who said this would expect to get a knife in the throat, but he would say it in a very friendly manner, just as if he were being genuinely helpful, and in any case soldiers quickly adapt to the worst behaviour of their friends. 'I am from Pera, so I don't give a shit' became the slogan of all of us, even though Fikret was the only one who was really from Pera, and soon even the most pious of us was replying 'Up your mother's cunt' when anyone asked where anything was. To this day I still have to catch myself out, and prevent myself from saying it.

Fikret liked to put on the appearance of being very lazy and apathetic, but when there was something to be done he worked very methodically. He didn't work fast, but he never needed a rest. He always fought at my side, and we looked out for each other. I don't know why this happened, because there was no reason for us to be friends.

I first got to know him because he showed me how to delouse my clothing. It didn't get washed very often anyway, but even a good washing does not kill the lice. One day when I was itching, Fikret told me to take off my uniform, and not be modest about it, because no one has to be modest in the presence of lice. We sat in the sun and he showed me how to get the lice out of the seams of the uniform, and crack them with the thumbnail against the side of the first finger. Fikret knew a lot about lice, because he said the louse was the number-one animal in Pera. There are three kinds of lice. One of them is the parting keepsake of a whore, one is on the head, so that you have to shave it, and the third is the kind that puts pinpricks in your armpits and thighs and belly, and makes you itch so much that you scratch its shit into your skin with your dirty nails, and that's how you make yourself ill. It is worse if you are hairy, because the eggs are laid on to the hairs. At Çanakkale we had lice in two sizes, and they were grey or white, unless they were purple from drinking blood. When we went for our relief days behind the lines, we always deloused, except for the kind of ignorant peasant who has always had them anyway. When I first made friends with Fikret, he took my jacket and showed me how to search through the seams, looking on both sides. Up until then I had avoided him, because the things he said were shocking to me, but it was this concern of his about my lice that made me realise that he was not entirely a bad man.

One day when we were behind the lines at the resting point, Lieutenant Orhan came up to me and ordered me to put my shirt on an anthill that was nearby. I didn't dare to question the order, and so I did it, and a few hours later Lieutenant Orhan returned, and he picked up the shirt carefully, and shook all the ants off, and he showed the shirt to me, and he said, 'Just as I thought. Check this shirt for lice, Abdul Nefer.' There weren't any lice at all. It turned out that he had been watching the Franks through his binoculars, and had seen them doing this trick with anthills. I don't know if the ants eat the lice, or kill them, or just drive them away, but my hint for all soldiers who try this is to make sure you get all the ants off before you put the shirt on, because the sting of an ant is very much more painful than the bite of a louse. I also advise all soldiers never to put up their head suddenly over the parapet of a trench, because the sudden movement attracts attention. Always put your head up as slowly as you can possibly manage, even though this takes a lot of nerve. My advice to snipers is that you can cause machine-gun emplace-ments to collapse by careful shooting. What you do is stitch a row of shots side by side vertically down the sides of the supporting sandbags. This causes the bags to break in half and lose their sand, and the emplacements can sometimes collapse quite suddenly. You do this mainly for entertainment, and the enemy always rebuilds the emplacement during the night.

One day Fikret had the idea that we should collect all our lice into tins, without killing them, and toss these tins into the Frankish trenches. We had the opportunity to do this, because our trenches at one time were only five paces apart. We were laughing about this, when we heard a Frank shouting, 'Hey, Abdul,' and the tin came back with a turd in it. The Franks always called us 'Abdul', which was strange to me, as it is my real name and Karatavuk is only a nickname, and sometimes they threw over chocolate, which I had never had before and which I liked a great deal, and we would throw back sweets and cigarettes, which were much better than theirs, and sometimes grapes. We shouted 'Haydi, Johnny' when we threw things. The Franks were living off small round hard pieces of unleavened bread that were called biscuit, and also a kind of meat in tins that was called bully beef. After a time they were fed up with eating it, and they would throw it into our trenches. One time I was hit on the head by a can and I had a big bruise. We opened the tins with our bayonets. There came a time when we were fed up with eating it ourselves, because in the hot weather the fat in it melted and it poured out of the tin like slime, and we got Lieutenant Orhan to write a note in French and we tied it to a can and we threw the can back. The note said: 'No more bully beef, please, but milk yes.' As for us, when we were in the trench we lived on bulghur wheat and olives and bits of bread. The Franks were lucky, because Greek traders arrived and set up stalls on their beaches, and didn't care about the shrapnel shells bursting all around them. We had very few Greek traders coming to us, because we had no money anyway. This trading with the Franks made many of us hate the Greeks, because we were sure that many of them were from Ottoman lands. Greeks will trade with anyone, even the murderers of their own mothers.

People would be surprised if they knew that we and the Franks threw each other gifts, as well as bombs. It came about because we got to know our enemies. To begin with we did not take prisoners at all. We hated them, and they hated us, and we bayo-neted them because the extra merit in killing infidels would get us to paradise more easily. Lieutenant Orhan always told us not to kill prisoners or the wounded, because they might have useful information, and, in addition, troops who know they will be killed are much less inclined to surrender, but sometimes we killed them anyway when he wasn't looking or when the killing lust was up.

There comes a time when you are satiated with killing, however, and you get lazy about it, and it starts to disgust you. You look into the eyes of the enemy and you don't see an infidel any more, and there is no more hatred. In any case, something happened that changed everything.

It was early on in the campaign, no more than a month after the beginning. The days were getting hot, but the nights were still very cold. We were facing the Franks who were called Australian and New Zealander. They were tall and proud men who fought as fiercely as the little men called Gurkhas, and they had fought their way up a steep slope from the beach, and we couldn't dislodge them from the gullies. Later we found that the best way to destroy them was to let them attack. Generally, they were very big indeed and made easy targets. They would be uncontrollably enthusiastic and they would carry on too far, and then we could isolate them in little groups, and slaughter them. We found out that they called themselves Anzac, which was very puzzling to us. When the weather grew hot these soldiers fought only in their boots and shorts, and their bodies grew dark, and they had tattoos on their bodies which were pictures of monsters, and women with almost no clothes on. They had a strange war cry which was 'Imshi yallah' and we thought it was perhaps 'inshallah' in their language.

We put in the biggest attack that it is possible to imagine. We were 40,000 and we attacked them at dawn. We were so closely packed and there were so many of us, that every bullet must have killed several men. I think that most people do not know that bullets normally go right through a body. I was fighting with Fikret at my side, and I could smell him. The Franks had many machine guns that cut us down like grass.

365

By midday 10,000 of us were dead, and I doubt if we killed many of the Franks. The attack was called off, and Fikret and I crawled back to our trench.

By the next noonday, the stink of the 10,000 in the hot sun was so bad that we couldn't bear it. It was sweet and loathsome. What was worse was that none of the wounded had been collected, and they were dying of thirst and agony, crying out and whimpering between the lines. Fikret wept to hear it, and all of us were utterly grief-stricken by it, because the pity had risen up in our hearts. We were saying to God, 'Please let there be a cease-fire.'

From the Frankish trench a Red Cross flag was sent up, and we had a burst of hope. But straight away one of our snipers shot the flag down, and the hope sank. But then Lieutenant Orhan said, 'Wish me luck,' and climbed out of the trench. He ran out towards the enemy with his hands raised, and quickly our own men raised the Red Crescent flag. Lieutenant Orhan had gone to apologise to the Franks for the shooting down of the Red Cross flag.

We came out of the trenches with our stretchers, and collected the wounded, working alongside the Australian and New Zealander Franks. They nodded to us and looked down from their great height, and said, 'Good day, Abdul.' It was strange to be working peacefully at a merciful task alongside those who had been killing us. Some of us swapped badges and cigarettes with the Franks.

It was arranged that the dead would be buried four days later, by which time the air was so vile that it was making us vomit. Our chief prayer after such battles was for the wind to blow westward and let the stench carry over the enemy's lines instead of our own.

It was when we were burying the dead that everything changed between us and the Australian and New Zealander Franks. The British Franks sent a special officer who spoke Turkish and Arabic, and his name was Honourable Herbert. This officer was the only one who could coordinate what all of us were doing, and so we Turks took orders from him, and so did the Australian and New Zealander Franks. Honourable Herbert gave us receipts for money and other things that were found on the dead.

I will tell you about the dead. There had been fighting for one month, and the dead had never been collected. The bodies were of different ages, and so they were all in different stages of decomposition. Some bodies were swollen up, and some were black, and they were seething with maggots, and others were turning to green slime, and others were fully rotted and shrivelling up so that the bones stuck out through the skin. A lot of them were built into the parapets and fortifications, so that you might say they were being employed as sandbags. Most of the dead at that time were ours.

When they were being buried, there were sentries posted by both sides, and these sentries stood at ease with bayonets fixed, and we chose the biggest man there was to stand with the white flag, and the Franks also chose their biggest soldier, and so there were two enormous giants standing there with their white flags, and we had flags fixed in the ground by both sides to show how far it was permissible to go. They told us not to take photographs, but only officers have cameras, and they took photographs anyway, because the Frankish officers were also taking photographs. Their officers talked to our officers, and I think it must have been French, because Lieutenant Orhan knew how to speak it, and I heard him speaking. We exchanged cigarettes, and the Franks liked to shake our hands, so we had to accustom ourselves to it.

All the time we were slaving in the sun, and we were sweating as if we were steaming in a hamam, and our backs were aching from lifting. The original idea was that a white line of cloth was laid halfway between our lines, and we would carry all the Frankish bodies and put them in their half, and the Franks would carry all the Ottoman bodies and put them in our half. But this was impossible because the older bodies fell to pieces when you tried to move them, and the meathooks and broomsticks were ineffective, and sometimes the bodies that were swollen up exploded, so finally we agreed to bury the bodies where they lay. We were covered in corpse slime, and the corpses were covered in green corpse flies. We got the corpse slime from our hands by picking up handfuls of earth and rubbing the slime away. We buried the many thousands in shallow graves, barely covered with earth, knowing that many of them would soon come back to the surface when the shelling started again. I had the nausea in my nostrils for weeks afterwards, and sometimes it still comes back upon me when I dream. It was after this burial that the dysentery began to take hold.

In the early evening we had to finish our work, and the British Frank, Honourable Herbert, who had been commanding us, said, 'Tomorrow you can shoot me,' and we all said, 'May God prevent it.' He came to our trenches and some other Franks came, and they shook hands with us, and the Franks looked down on us and said, 'Bye-bye, Abdul,' and when they went we all gave them a salaam. The firing resumed almost immediately, but after this we did not hate each other any more, and I never again shot a Frank who was not engaged directly in a military activity. We had realised that they, too, were men whose hearts had been left behind in the fields about their homes, and after this the war became less holy. All the same, we continued to hear the stories of how the martyrs had come back from the dead, wearing the green turban of the haj, in order to fight again, some of them carrying their heads under their arms. It was said that they had begged God to send them back to earth so that they could be martyred all over again.

We heard that if we accidentally charged over a ravine, we would float down to safety. These kinds of stories were always being told to us, and even in the height of summer we heard that a company of the enemy had charged, and a cloud came down, and when the fog lifted, the company had completely disappeared. As for me, I became interested in small miracles, and I collected a lot of bullets that had collided with each other in the air, and they had interpenetrated and made crosses. I have ones which are made out of every type of bullet that was used. I also have a bullet that has gone into the middle of a ball of shrapnel.

It was good that we were able to throw gifts to each other, but it was generally bad to have the trenches so close together. It was impossible to sleep because of the grenades. The Franks did not have proper grenades, and they made their own with tin cans that had nails and stones in them. They didn't kill us, but they filled our skin with nasty fragments, and they were bad for our peace of mind. We had proper grenades that were round like balls. You had to light a fuse first. At times we ran out of these grenades, and made our own, very similar to the Frankish ones.

These grenades were turned against us, because some of the Franks, but not the French Franks, would catch them and toss them back at us. We never knew how this was possible until we realised from observing the Franks on the beach that they had a game which involved waving a plank, running backwards and forwards, and frequently throwing and catching a ball. The consequence of this was that all the Franks, except for the French Tangos, were very good at catching and throwing, and I believe that they had men on the alert whose job was to catch the grenades as they came in, or scoop them up straight away and throw them back. After a time we got wise to this and we let the fuses burn for longer before we threw them. They still threw them back, but the game became more dangerous for all of us. The best thing to do with grenades is to drop a sandbag on them. The Franks had another game which consisted of kicking a large ball around on the beach. They did this stark naked, and every now and then they would jump up and down and cheer for no reason, and if a shell fell among them, they would just clear away the dead and wounded, and carry on playing the game. Also, they would throw bread on the water, and wait for fish, and then throw a grenade among them, and then collect the fish. They were naked when they did this too, and often they swam naked together in the water, so when people say that the Franks are shameless and immodest, I know personally that this is true.

The other bad thing about having trenches close together is that it was easier to dig under each other's lines and plant high explosives. Sometimes our saps would coincide with theirs, and we would meet underground, and we would be stabbing each other in the dark. This was the most terrifying and horrible fighting of all, and I am glad that it only happened to me once. It was similar in midsummer, however, because by then we had covered our trenches over completely, and were shooting out of embrasures and loopholes, and when the Franks attacked, they pulled parts of the covering aside and dropped down among us, and then we were all hacking and punching and kicking each other in the dark until we all fell with exhaustion, and lay among the heaps of wounded and dead, and I have no idea how many people I killed with my bayonet, and how many were Turks and how many were Franks, and I don't know if it was a Frank or a Turk who gave me the stab wound whose scar I still have in my thigh.

One thing that happened to us was that we got moved around a great deal, and were often not in one place with our particular unit. They split us up and spread us about so that one day we were a proper regiment, and the next day we were part of another unit that consisted of men from different regiments. This was done according to where the officers thought that reinforcements were needed the most, so we who survived got to know all of the sectors. I will tell you about some of the enemy that I have not mentioned yet.

The French Tangos were partly white men and partly black men. The black men carried machetes, and these were almost as bad as the bent knives of the Gurkhas, but the officers wore red trousers, kepis and dark blue coats. With the black French soldiers, all we had to do was shoot the officers, and then the black men would lose heart and turn round and run away. Obviously we always shot the officers first when there was an attack, and it was lucky for us that they were dressed up like peacocks. The British officers had special belts and service hats, and they had revolvers instead of rifles, and they wore their insignia on their cuffs, so it was easy to shoot them as well. When I was sniping I always tried to shoot the officers, but by the end of the campaign the Frankish officers were no longer wearing their insignia, so that we snipers no longer had any advantage. We used to shoot messengers and signallers as well. I remember that I did not shoot those who were trying to rescue the wounded. There was a man with a donkey that we saw very often, and he would collect the wounded on his donkey, and we often talked about him, but one day one of our snipers shot him anyway. When I went out sniping I would disguise myself as a bush, all tied up with branches and leaves, and I would have to move very slowly, and I would take a long time between shots, so that no one could locate me. There was one of us who disguised himself as a pig, and we didn't like this, and thought it was unclean, but the imam said it was not unclean to disguise yourself as a pig, it was only unclean to touch a real one. In the long boring days in the trenches when nothing was happening, the Franks played a game with us. They would hold up a piece of white board on a pole, and wave it back and forth slowly, and we would try to hit it. If we missed they would raise another board that said 'miss', and if we hit it they would raise a board that said 'hit'. Sometimes there were duels, when one of us and one of them would stand up on the parapets whilst the rest of us watched, and these two men would shoot at each other until one of them was hit.

The French Tangos liked to be shelled by the big guns on the other side of the water, because after it was over, the white officers would go to the big holes made by the shells, and look for ancient things. They even went to look for ancient things when we were still shelling them, and many of them got killed like this. In the big battles it was the black French Franks in the far south whose line always gave way, and consequently we were able to enfilade the rest of the Franks, so they all had to fall back. This is one of the reasons that the Franks could not defeat us. The French Franks had the Black Cat mortar that I mentioned before, and also the 75mm guns that were just as bad for us, because those 75s could fire twenty rounds a minute, and every time we attacked the French Franks we were cut to pieces in the open ground before we could advance any distance at all. You could say, therefore, that on the one side the French Franks were no good at attack, but on the other it was impossible to defeat them by attacking.

The British Franks were south of the Australian and New Zealand Franks, and they fought very much the same. They were smaller, and they were discouraged when you shot their officers, whereas this did not affect the Australian and New Zealand Franks. The British Franks had a strange policy of attacking in the middle of the morning, just as the heat of the day was coming upon them, after we had eaten our breakfast and had time to get everything prepared. For this reason they hardly ever surprised us, they were quickly exhausted by the sun and the terrible thirst that it brings, and we slaughtered them very easily. They once did an attack at ten in the morning, three days running, immediately after a very light bombardment that alerted us to the fact that they were imminently arriving, and we heaped their bodies high before us. Everyone knows that you should attack by stealth at dawn.

There were also some other Franks, and I will tell you a little story about them. They were from a place called India, and they had big beards and turbans, so naturally we thought they were Muslims. They fought like devils. We couldn't understand why Muslims would be fighting against us when this was a jihad. Anyway, one day a scheme was hatched out, at a time when it was known that the ordinary Franks were to be replaced by these men with beards and turbans. By the way, there was another kind of Frank with a beard, who was British, and who was really a sailor who was fighting as a soldier, and they were called Royal Naval Division, but it is not those that I mean, as those ones did not have turbans.

Now the idea was that we would creep up to the trench as the ordinary troops were leaving, and drop down into it to greet the Muslims when they arrived, and persuade them to desert to our side. In this way we would take the trench without blood-shed, and win many extra troops.

The plan went surprisingly well, as none of us expected even to reach the trench. But we reached it, and dropped down, and we held our rifles in our left hands, pointing upwards, and when the Indians approached, looking at us as if we were mad, we salaamed, and said, 'Salaam aleikum,' expecting them to say 'Aleikum salaam' and greet us like brothers. It seems that they thought we were trying to surrender, so instead of greeting us they tried to take our rifles, and we had little struggles with them, but no shots were fired. Then Lieutenant Orhan suddenly said, 'That's enough! Come on, men,' and we climbed out of the trench and ran back to our own lines, doubled over, but no one took a shot at us, and we reached our trench. After he had recovered his breath, Lieutenant Orhan said, 'Maybe not everyone who looks like a Muslim is one.' This was true, because it turned out those soldiers were called Sikh, and were not Muslim at all, and it is also true that for a long time we thought the Gurkhas were Muslim, and we sent them messages and greetings and invitations, but it turned out that they were of another religion completely, and it so happened that it was Muslims that they hated the most in the whole world.

Sometimes those of our officers who could speak English or French would shout out orders to the Frankish troops, and it was a ruse that often worked. Sometimes the bravest ones would infiltrate the Frankish trenches, and in the darkness of the middle of the night they would ask to see the officer in charge, and then they would shoot him and make their escape.

I will tell you a curious thing about the Franks. When we took them prisoner they believed that we were going to castrate them.

64

Mustafa Kemal (14)

The pattern of the Gallipoli campaign becomes established on almost every front of the war. Whoever attacks loses spectacular numbers of soldiers. Not even Kemal's night attack works, and neither do the assaults in overwhelming numbers that are tried by other commanders.

Kemal is appointed full colonel, and receives battle medals from the Sultan. Kaiser Wilhelm gives him an Iron Cross, and King Ferdinand of Bulgaria creates him Commander of the Order of St Alexander. He has another falling-out with Enver Pasha, who opposes Kemal's plans for an attack. The attack fails, as Enver had predicted, and Kemal resigns, blaming Enver for his interference, but after Enver has returned to Istanbul, Kemal is persuaded to stay by Liman von Sanders. Enver offers Kemal a command in Tripolitania, a considerably less important theatre of the war, and Kemal says he will think about it, but nothing comes of it.

Kemal remains quarrelsome. He fires off letters demanding better defence of his positions, and disputing the command structure in his sector. He is seldom guilty of subtle and tactful diplomacy, and he makes a vocation of antagonising important people.

The corps commander comes to see him, and Kemal explains to him how the enemy will circle round from Suvla Bay. Essad Pasha looks at the difficulty of the terrain, and says, 'Don't worry, beyefendi, they can't possibly do it.' Of course, and perhaps irritatingly, Mustafa Kemal turns out to be right again, and in midsummer the enemy attack occurs exactly as he had predicted. The empire is saved only because the new landing and the assault are grotesquely mismanaged.

Kemal longs for the sweet company of Corinne Lütfü, and corresponds with her regularly. He asks her advice about which novels he should read, and explains to her why it is that Turkish soldiers fight so well. He says that if they survive they think they will become Ghazis, and if not, they will go to paradise and spend eternity in the arms of a vast number of houris. Kemal does not believe in any of this, but he is always quite willing to take advantage of the naive spiritual strength of his men. Either he is cynical, or he is like Plato's philosopher king, who acquiesces in a noble lie in order to consolidate the greater good.

65

Karatavuk at Gallipoli:
Karatavuk Remembers (5)

I will tell you about something that happened with Fikret. There was once a battle at Çonk Bayırı, and then there was a cease-fire, and the dead were collected, and then the ceasefire was over, but the battle had not yet begun again.

Not long after, terrible cries came from in between our lines. I do not know any English, and so I do not know what the man was calling out, but obviously he was wounded and was in very great pain. The sun was growing hot, and the thirst and burning that this brings inevitably increases the agony of wounds. Often there were also ants that attacked the wounds. In fact, the Franks always suffered from thirst, and if you were to capture one, or rescue one who was wounded, he always begged for water, and his tongue might be blackened and swollen up in his mouth, and 'su' was the first word in Turkish that he learned. I remember one summer day when Lieutenant Orhan had been watching the Franks through his binoculars, and as he came past us he said, 'I've just seen any number of Franks drinking their own piss.' The Franks had few wells behind their lines, but we had plenty of them, and water was brought in on mules and then carried to us by water boys. Our water boy for some months was an old man called Irfan, and he was half crazy, and every morning he would hang his washing out on a bush, but no Frank ever shot at him, because he was old and mad.

The Frank continued to cry out in a most pitiful way, and we tried to seal our ears against it. Normally a wounded man even-tually passes out or becomes too weak to cry out, and normally we would let him die, because if we had come out of our trench, we would have been shot. So we would just listen to the dying man, and wonder if this would also be our fate, and whether the rewards of martyrdom would be any compensation. But I will

376

tell you a secret, which is that almost no soldier truly believes that he will be killed. This is because it is impossible for the human being to imagine that he is dead, and this is because he is always alive and present in the act of imagining. This inconceivability of death is what makes it possible for a soldier to fight. He sees his comrades die, but he thinks himself immune, and this fatal lack in his nature makes him a good fighter. Even a man who has decided to die on purpose and become a martyr does not really believe in his own death.

Fikret was leaning with his forehead against the parapet, and he was muttering obscenities every time that the Frank cried out, and the sounds of the crying were cutting into our souls and hurting our hearts, and we all wanted to do something about it, even if it was only to go out and shoot the soldier, but none of us would move.

Then Fikret turned round and bent down, and started to rummage in his knapsack. He pulled out some white underwear. He fixed his bayonet in his rifle, and he impaled the underwear on it, and then he began to wave his rifle above the trench.

A strange thing happened, because the shooting in our sector suddenly stopped. Fikret took a ladder and started to climb out of the trench, and I was very stupid, and I caught hold of his leg and said, 'Where are you going?' and he said, 'Up your mother's cunt,' and I said, 'You'll be killed,' and he looked down at me and said, 'I am from Pera, so I don't give a shit.'

He put his hands up to show he was unarmed, and he walked to where the man was crying. He bent down and took the man up in his arms, and he carried him to the Frankish trench and laid him down at the edge of the parapet. Then, very slowly and carefully, walking upright, wiping his forehead on his sleeve, he came back, and the Frankish soldiers were cheering him.

When he had dropped back down among us, we were astonished by what he had done, and we just looked at him. He went to his rifle and plucked the underwear from his bayonet, and he showed us the rent it had made, and he just said, 'Another damned hole,' and then he stuffed the underwear back into his knapsack, and said, 'Fortunately, I don't give a shit.'

The odd thing about this act of heroism and compassion is

that often I had seen Fikret coldly dispatching the wounded with his bayonet, and joyfully killing prisoners. When I asked him why he had unexpectedly turned into an angel, he looked guilty, and cast his eyes down, and said, 'Sometimes a man suddenly feels like doing something decent for a change.'

From then on, whenever he said, 'I am from Pera, I don't give a shit,' we no longer believed him.

66

Karatavuk at Gallipoli: Fikret and the Goat (6)

Generally, we had two days in the trench at a time, and at least a day behind the lines. Then we could wash and delouse, and eat better food, and sleep. Because the trenches were full of shit and flies and corpses, it made the beautiful places behind the lines seem even more beautiful. The Franks had no areas behind the lines, because their bridgehead was very small, so they cannot have had any good rests as we did, as we could always shoot or shell them wherever they were. It would have been very bad to have been a Frank.

There was a village where we stayed that was a Greek village, but the Christians had mostly gone because of what happened to their women. In this village there was a well that had no wall around it. It was just a hole in the ground, and one day a goat fell in.

The first thing we knew was that we heard echoey bleating coming up from it, and Fikret went to have a look, and he called us over, and we saw the goat very dimly down below, swimming and kicking out at the sides, as if it thought it could climb them. I went to fetch Lieutenant Orhan, and he came and looked over the side, and he said, 'If it dies down there, it'll poison the water, and anyway, this is a good milking goat.' He looked at us, and said, 'I need a volunteer,' and he looked at each one of us, and we tried to avoid his eyes without looking as if that was what we were doing, and he said to Fikret, 'It's you.'

Fikret came to attention and said, 'I don't give a shit, sir, and I am happy to volunteer.'

'Good man,' said Lieutenant Orhan.

So it was that we lowered Fikret down on a rope, and there were about ten of us on the rope, so it wasn't too difficult, and Fikret had the rope around his chest and under his armpits, but not very tight.

It was a fairly small goat, but Fikret had a lot of trouble grab-bing hold of it because it was dark and because the animal was in a panic and did not want to be lifted up. It took a long time, and the goat was bleating, and there was great splashing, and Fikret was saying, 'Son of a whore, son of a bitch, Iblis fuck your mother's cunt, and your mother's mother's cunt and the cunt of every cunt of every mother's cunt,' and we were looking down and making it all worse by bleating like the goat and laughing at Fikret. Fikret's curses and all the laughter and bleating echoed in the well and made a booming sound.

Finally he got the goat round the body and held it under one arm, and started walking up the side of the well as we hauled on the rope. He was still cursing as he came up, and when he arrived at the top he threw the goat over the rim, and just as he did so, the goat shat, and the shit fell down into the water. Then the goat bleated and ran off. The bleating reminded me of the various kinds of bleats that Ibrahim used to mimic, such as 'the bleat of a goat with nothing to say', and I had a pang of home-sickness.

When Fikret came up over the edge he was panting from the effort and soaking wet, and you could see that he was bleeding and bruised all over from where the goat was kicking out with its sharp little hooves. Fikret complained, 'That son of a bitch kicked me in the balls.'

Lieutenant Orhan called Fikret to attention, and said to him, 'Now go down and collect the shit, Fikret Nefer,' and a look of outrage passed over Fikret's ugly face, and he said, 'Permission to speak, sir,' and the lieutenant said, 'Permission granted,' and Fikret said, 'Why me, sir? Not that I give a shit, sir,' and the lieutenant said, 'Because there is no point in anyone else getting wet, and partly because you don't give a shit, but most of all because it was an order.'

So Fikret went down the well again, and Lieutenant Orhan said, 'Men, we just have to hope that goatshit floats.'

So Fikret came back up, absolutely soaked, with his pockets full of shining black pellets of goatshit, and ceremoniously laid them at the lieutenant's feet in a crescent pattern, and then he stood up, dripping with water, and saluted. Lieutenant Orhan saluted him back, and the two men looked at each other, and the lieutenant said, 'Fikret Nefer, if there were a medal for rescuing goats and goatshit, and thereby securing the purity of our water supply, I would recommend you for it.'

'Thank you, sir,' said Fikret.

'But fortunately, you don't give a shit,' said the lieutenant.

'No, sir,' agreed Fikret.

'Do you want to know why it was you who volunteered?' asked Orhan.

'No, sir,' answered Fikret, according to his time-honoured principle of not giving a shit.

'Well, it was because you smell exactly the same as a goat, and I thought that she would be less frightened if I sent you down rather than someone else. Also, I thought you would be pleased to get your hands on something female, even if it was only a goat.'

Fikret looked genuinely pleased, as if he had received a compliment, and said, 'Thank you, sir,' and then he saluted, and Lieutenant Orhan smiled very slightly, and saluted him back, and said, 'Dismiss,' and he was still smiling when he walked away.

Later on Fikret turned to me when we were eating cheese and olives under a lemon tree, and we could hear the big guns thumping in the distance, and he tapped the side of his nose, and said to me, 'That lieutenant and me, we really understand each other.'

67

Karatavuk at Gallipoli:
The Death of Fikret (7)

One of the odd things about being at war is that you are exposed to all sorts of miracles, such as when you bend down, and suddenly a ball of shrapnel smacks into the trench wall just behind you where your head had just been, or you are on the latrine when a karakedi mortar shell comes down and explodes in the bit of the trench where you had been posted, or a hand grenade lands next to you, but it doesn't go off, or it lands next to you just when you are shifting a sandbag, and all you have to do is drop the sandbag on the top of the grenade. These small things make you feel that God is looking after you.

Speaking for myself, I would say that what I found most miraculous was seeing aeroplanes in the sky. The first time I saw one, I could not believe my eyes. Obviously your first impression is that it is a huge and strange bird that makes a coughing and droning noise, but you realise very quickly that it is not, and everyone says, 'Look, an aeroplane!' and they wave, and if the plane is low, the pilot waves back. I asked everybody how they worked, but no one seemed to know. Of course there is an engine, which is something I now understand, but instead of flapping its wings like a true bird, the aeroplane has a propeller at the front which goes round very quickly and eats the air in front of the plane and throws it behind. The German Franks had brought with them a plane called the Taube, which means 'dove' in their language, and it was a monoplane, and the wings really were shaped to be exactly like a bird, and the tailplane was shaped to be like tail feathers. It contained two men, and it was the most beautiful and elegant of all the planes that I saw. The Taube used to drop little steel arrows on to the enemy, and these were called 'flechettes'. I have one that I pulled from a tree after the campaign was over. Unfortunately, the Taube was bombed by the Franks when it was in its hangar at Çonk. We also had a plane, called the Aviatik, but it wasn't beautiful. The Franks had a lot of planes, at least eighteen, and I used to be able to recognise all of them. We men took great pride in being able to identify enemy aircraft, just as we had a pride in being able to identify their ships and know the names of their regiments. They had Farmans, Sopwith Tabloids and BE2s. The Farman looked like a skeleton held together with wires, but the Tabloid and the BE2s were very pretty, though not as pretty as the Taube. The Franks used to drop little bombs on us, a few at a time, and when that happened you could hear the Frankish soldiers cheering in their trenches. I think the planes were good for reconnaissance and taking photographs, but I don't think they will ever be much use for attacking. They did cause panic every time they appeared over-head, but the damage was never very great. Anyway, of the things I remember with pleasure, the aeroplanes are the best, and in my opinion they are the greatest miracle of the world. If I was as rich as Rustem Bey, I would buy one, and fly out over the sea like an osprey and look down at the ships, and I would fly into the mountains like an eagle and look down on the valleys, and every day it would be like a new miracle.

The imam was always announcing miracles. He was a mean man who fulfilled the proverb that my father Iskander liked so much, the one that said 'You might as well expect tears from a corpse as alms from an imam', but anyway he had a great ability to perceive miracles, which shows that anyone who believes in them will think that they see a great many, and it is true that many times we could have been defeated if only the Franks had realised their opportunities. We cheered and praised God when we sank the *Bouvet*, the *Goliath*, and the *Triumph*, and the *Majestic*, which were great ships, but naturally we didn't praise Him when the *Guj Djemal* was sunk with six thousand new troops on board. We praised God when Enver Pasha announced that the Sultan Padishah had been pronounced a Ghazi. We praised God when there was a break that allowed us to bring up ten new divisions, and when there was an attack by the Frankish Australian Light Horse. On that occasion their bombardment stopped several minutes before the attack, which gave us time to reoccupy our positions, and we massacred them completely, without taking a single casualty ourselves. There was also an attack by the King's Own Scottish Borderers, and we praised God because they forgot to clear the communications trenches when they advanced, and so our men were able to rise up and shoot them from behind. We praised God for the miracle that the Frankish invasion began on the very night when Mustafa Kemal had all of us marching about on a night exercise, so we were already fully kitted up and mobile when it happened. We also praised God in spring when the enemy aeroplanes bombed an encampment behind the lines, and so our troops had to be moved up to the front early, and this turned out to be just in time to meet an attack. We didn't praise God when the Frankish ships managed to fire right over the peninsula by means of using observation balloons, and sank some of our ships. We praised God when we heard the Frankish bugler announcing the imminent arrival of a shell from our giant gun on the other side of the water. This bugler would watch out for the flash, and every French Tango would know that he had twenty-eight seconds in which to hide. We did not praise God when the Gurkhas took the top of the hill at Çonk, which gave them a big advantage, but we did praise God when the Frankish big guns stupidly opened fire on them and wiped them out, so that all we had to do was wait a little while, and then charge them and finish them off. That was when I took the bent Gurkha knife that I now have on my wall. After this the Franks brought up new troops, and there was a terrible battle in which count-less thousands of us died. We were fighting like the mad, with our teeth, and with stones, as much as with our bayonets, and we did not praise God for that, even though we did praise Him when finally we were left in possession of the top of the hill. We praised God when the enemy landed at Suvla, and for some reason gave our German Frankish Major Wilmer time to bring up three battalions.

If you are a soldier, you are forced to think about God more than those who are at home. All around you is death and devas-tation. You look at a disembowelled body, and you see that man consists of coils of slime inside, and yet he is smooth and beauti-ful on the outside. You look at a body and you see that it is not a man because the spirit has fled, and so the body does not fill you with grief. You believe that God caused every second of your destiny to be written on the fortieth day after conception, and so you do not complain about hardship and horror, and you know that every single little thing that happens is because God wills it. This is a great comfort, knowing that God carries us in the palm of His hand, just as a man might carry a fledgling in the palm of his hand. You realise that there is no point in resisting the will of God, and so you recite the martyr's prayer for the hundredth time, and so you say to yourself and your comrades 'Allah koruson', and you go over the trench parapet shouting the name of God, knowing that whatever horror comes upon you, it is only the first difficult step to paradise. There are very few people, and I was one, who begin to wonder why God wishes such cruelty and suffering upon His flock, and, when people say 'God is merciful', feel perplexity and a contrary feeling stealing over them. It is only people like me who wonder why God does not do just one good miracle, and make the world perfect in an instant.

It is very possible to believe it a miracle from God when you duck down and thereby miss a bullet in the head, but then why does God decree a week later that you will die of dysentery?

The dysentery came upon us when the hot weather arrived. Çanakkale was perfect in the spring and autumn, but in the winter it was cold beyond imagination, and in the height of summer it was like being in a bread oven along with the loaves. All the green plants turned brown, all the flowers vanished away, the birds sat on the branches with their beaks open, and the sun made the skin shrink and the eyes ache, and the lips crack, and dizziness overwhelms. There was so much thirst that the water boys couldn't keep up with us. You couldn't touch anything made of metal, and you couldn't touch the stones. The sweat would pour down our faces and down our chests, and pour off the backs of our necks and down our spines and between the buttocks, and our uniforms would have thick wavy lines of white where the salt had dried out of the sweat. We would sit in our trenches longing for the night, and when the night arrived, the relief of it was like being caressed by the hand of an angel, and then, of course, it quickly became too cold.

Much worse than the heat itself was what it brought with it. All the thousands of unburied corpses rotted so violently that the stink drifted over us at every movement of a breeze. It was such a stink that you got used to vomiting from it. If you want to know what it was like, you should kill a dog in midsummer, leave it in the sun for a few days until it swells up, cut open its belly, and thrust your head inside and breathe deeply. Sometimes the corpses would swell up so much in front of the trenches that they would obstruct our view, and so we would shoot at them and the gases would escape with a hissing sound, and the smell of sulphur would come over us. But no matter how many times you deflated a corpse, it would always blow up again, and I never understood why, because you would think that the holes would prevent it.

The other thing was that the corpses made millions of maggots, which were very big, and had shrewd-looking eyes, and black heads, and these maggots were crawling everywhere. Sometimes you saw what looked like a puddle of maggots, and you realised that it was because there was a corpse buried very shallowly, and the maggots were coming up to the surface. I had a comrade who was terrified of the maggots. His name was Ocak, and he was from Van, and he was otherwise very courageous, but he was so horrified by the maggots that one day he refused to advance over some ground where there were corpses full of maggots, and so the officer shot him, and it wasn't long before he was full of maggots too, and we would say, 'Look at poor Ocak, he must have got used to the maggots by now.'

The violent rotting and the stink brought in the corpse flies, which were very big, and bright green. These flies were so numerous that they covered the world, and you would look around and everything seemed to be moving and shimmering, and a kind of desperate madness tried to overtake you, because the flies were so persistent that all you wanted to do was run away for ever, or run down to the sea and sink beneath the water. It was useless killing the flies, because it would have been like counting grains of sand, and if you did kill them, there were other very tiny flies that laid eggs on their bodies and made tiny maggots. The corpse flies went in and out of the mouths of corpses, because when

386

you die your mouth falls open, and they were attracted to open wounds.

The corpse flies landed on your food when you were eating, and it was impossible to eat at all without eating the corpse flies. They landed on your cup when you were drinking, and you could not drink without drinking corpse flies. The corpse flies were as desperate for moisture as we were, and they would try to drink from our eyes, and they would cling to our lips so that we would have to pull them off by force. One day I fell asleep with my mouth open, and when I awoke my mouth was full of the corpse flies. After that I cut a corner from the white shroud that my mother had sent me in the event of my martyrdom, and I put this corner over my face whenever I wanted to sleep. As time went by I cut more bits off for my comrades, on condition that they would be gathered up and sewn back together if I was killed, but the truth is that you never know where the bodies of your comrades are, and so I never got the pieces back, and it was lucky I wasn't killed, and now I have a new shroud waiting for me, that was made by my wife, and no doubt she looks forward to the day when she can wrap me in it.

It was because of the corpse flies that diseases came upon us. The flies were full of the filth of the putrid corpses, and they transferred this filth to us when we ate and drank them. Some people got a disease called enteric fever, and this disease gave you an unbearable headache and a sweating fever, and a cough deep in the chest, and pains in the stomach, and big spots, and it also gave you the shits. Some people got malaria if they came from places where malaria was bad, because when they got weak and unhealthy with the bad conditions at the front, the malaria would come back upon them, and this killed some people, and some people were made helpless for days at a time. Other soldiers got an illness where the heart stopped working properly. All of us became very thin and weak, and it became difficult even to lift a rifle or walk.

The very worst thing was dysentery, and it is hard to explain the horror of it. It comes upon you very suddenly, and you have to run to the latrine, and to begin with you are shitting proper shit. Soon afterwards you become more and more desperate to shit, but all you can shit is slime and blood, and it oozes out of you, and in your stomach you feel cramps and spasms that make you double over and clutch your stomach and cry out with pain and misery. The fever comes over you, and the sweat pours from you, and you can't make sense, and you are longing for water with a terrible thirst, and your tongue in your head turns white and yellow, and one of the worst things is that you can't piss, however much you want to.

It happened to Fikret and me at the same time, and we spent whole nights asleep on the latrine between shitting blood and slime, and there were uncountable others like us, and there were many who died at the latrine because they were so ill that they died shitting out entrails, and fell into the latrine, and if they were not quite dead, then they drowned in the shit and blood, which were also covered with corpse flies, and they were so ill and wretched beyond measure that they were glad to die by drowning in shit and blood, and the shit and blood in the latrine was also heaving and buzzing with flies. Afterwards, you have to wipe yourself with your hands and then clean your hands with earth, but your hands never felt clean. One of the small satisfactions of life was to throw sand down into the latrines and bury the flies. I don't know how many soldiers died of dysentery or left as invalids, but I think it was very many thousands. Fikret nearly died, and so did I, and the field hospital had so many cases that the doctors couldn't help us, and we just lay there in a fever, shitting blood and slime, with our lives and our will to live pouring out between our legs. I missed many battles, and at one point it seemed I would never go back to the lines. Whenever I think of the military glory that we won at Çanakkale, and my throat swells with pride, I also remind myself of the inglory of groaning and sweating and shitting blood and slime, and not being able to piss, which is also a part of the military life. I remember our second officer, who was very smart and correct when he arrived, with his boots polished, and with a neat waxed moustache and the smell about him of lemon cologne, but soon he was crawling on his hands and knees among the corpses, crying out like a wounded dog, with blood soaking into the seat of his breeches, and we pitied him for the loss of his dignity, and then finally he shot himself because of the indignity.

After a while Fikret and I were moved to a hospital that had been set up further behind the lines, near Maydos. We were taken on a cart pulled by a little donkey, and the cart was full of men, and the road was very bad, and you could tell that the donkey was being worked to death, its ribs stuck out against the skin, it was blind in one eye and was covered in scars, and out of pity some of the wounded got out of the cart and stumbled along at the back of it, half pushing it and half being held up by it.

One good thing I remember about the hospital was a nurse who took an interest in Fikret and me. The military nurses were like angels or ghosts, dressed completely in robes of white with only their faces showing, and they went silently from man to man, and spoke in modest voices, but they could be very strong when it was necessary, such as when a man was in a delirium or in too much agony. It seems strange now that I should have been tended and cleaned up by women who were not from my family, and touched me, but spoke to me as a mother does. I was too ill to let it concern me back then, and everybody knows that in time of war all the rules are changed, and it is like a man who eats the flesh of a pig because he is starving and there is nothing else to eat, and therefore he is forgiven.

The nurse who was very good to Fikret and me spoke Turkish badly, with an odd accent that we couldn't identify, and she had a Frankish name, which was 'Georgina', and she had an extra name. Instead of being 'Georgina, daughter of so-and-so', she had an extra name which was 'Iliff'. I said, 'What does it mean?' and she answered, 'I'm told it means "long life",' and Fikret, who was feeling not so bad by then, said, 'Are you sure it's not ilik?'★ and she laughed because she was very pretty, and she made a deep impression, and it was a good compliment, and after a time she became very like a sister to us, and it is acceptable to be familiar with a sister. I looked at her blue eyes and fair complexion and pink cheeks, and I said, 'Are you a Frank? Or are you Circassian?' and she said, 'I am Irish,' and I said, 'Is that a kind of Frank?' and

★ 'Ilik' means 'delicious' in Turkish.

she said, 'I suppose so,' and I said, 'Are you a Christian?' and she said, 'Yes, I am,' and Fikret said, 'Even so, I am going to marry you when I get out of here, and you won't even have to convert,' and she said, 'The bride price is very high, and in any case my husband would object,' and we wondered what kind of a man it was who let his wife work with men, and be in contact with them, and we concluded that he must be an infidel, and it turned out that her husband was a diplomat who had married this Georgina in England before being recalled when the war began. We said, 'Is your husband an infidel?' and she was puzzled at first, and then said, 'He's an Ottoman, and his mother is from Serbia and his father is from Smyrna.' Fikret said, 'Why are you here in the hospital?' and she sighed and said, 'Because I didn't want to be useless.' This Georgina made us mint tea with a great deal of sugar in it, and I am sure it was a good medicine for dysentery, and she said we should eat salt, and she gave us ayran with salt in it if there was any ayran to be had. That good nurse is one of the excellent memories that I have of the war, and it also saddened me because it reminded me of the sisters and mother I had left behind in Eskibahçe. When I left, I gave her one of my miracles that I had picked up at the front. It was a German bullet perfectly penetrated through the middle by a French bullet, so that it made the shape of a cross, and Georgina Iliff was very pleased with it, and she said she would have it made into a brooch, but I don't know if she ever did.

Fikret and I were back in the lines for the big attack that happened in late summer, when the heat is at its worst. We were both very weak, and probably we should not have gone back, and I think that if we had not been so weak, then perhaps Fikret would have survived his wound. We believed that we should prove ourselves men, and not let down our comrades, and we pretended to the Greek doctors that we were better than we were.

The Franks began their bombardment in the afternoon, and there was no air to breathe and no wind, and so when the shells exploded they threw up great clouds of dust that hung in the air and made the world invisible, and the world was shaking and vibrating all around us because of the explosions, and I remember this in particular because at the time I had a toothache, and the vibrating of every explosion made it much worse, and sent pain through my head with every impact. It was like the continuous roaring of a storm when you are standing by the sea, but much louder.

About an hour and a half after the bombardment began, we realised that the British Frankish troops were coming, even though we couldn't see them, and our guns opened fire on the space between the lines, hoping to kill the Franks as they advanced. When we were able to see the British Franks, we shot them down. As a result of this, their attack failed. In another part of the line the Australian and New Zealander Franks managed to capture a trench after two days of fighting in the darkness, and it was said that we lost five thousand men. At the same time there was an attack from Suvla Bay, but it was no good, and the Franks were beaten.

Because it was high summer all the bushes were very dry, and because of the guns these bushes caught fire. As a result, the Frankish soldiers who fell wounded were burned to death, or suffocated, and most often their ammunition pouches exploded, and that killed them even if the fires did not, and that was just as well, because otherwise the ants would attack the wounds and the burns of the wounded, which was an agony, and the thirst of dying out in the stones among the burning bushes was also an agony, and we could hear them crying out for hours. There was a very big fire in the other attack that was taking place not far from us, and the sky was full of smoke and dust, and the smell of charring meat, and the bullets were whistling like birds.

In this battle Fikret stood up on a ladder to get a better field of fire, and there did not seem to be much danger because it was we who were mowing down the Franks, and not them us. Suddenly he fell back from the ladder, and for a moment I thought he must have been hit in the head. I was torn between tending to him and continuing to shoot down the British Franks, and I knew my duty was to shoot the Franks, so I had to leave Fikret. I kept turning to look at him, and he seemed not too bad. He was just sitting with his legs out before him, staring at the opposite wall of the trench, and trying to say something.

Fortunately the attack of the British Franks ended, and as soon as I was sure that no more were coming upon us, I came down from the firing step and knelt down beside him at his left side, saying, 'Where are you hit, my friend, where are you hit?' and with his left arm he reached round and pointed to his right arm, but said nothing.

I looked and I saw that a bullet had gone through his arm above the elbow, and completely shattered the bones, and the rest of his arm was just hanging there as if it belonged to no one, and there was scarlet blood pouring down it and dripping to the end of the fingers, which had no life in them. He also had a bullet through his belly, and the dark bloodstains were swelling out into his tunic both at the front and the back, and I realised that this would be the wound that would kill him, because the blood just fills the belly.

Fikret turned his head very slowly, and his eyes had the look of a dead man, and he said, 'Is your bayonet sharp?' and I said, 'Yes, my friend, very sharp,' and I thought he was going to ask me to kill him.

He gestured again with his left hand and pointed to his right arm, and said, 'You'd better cut it off.'

'Cut it off?' I repeated, feeling a sickness coming over me.

'It's no good. I want it cut off.'

'I can't,' I said.

'If you love me, cut it off. It offends me. If you honour me, cut it off.'

So I took my bayonet, and made sure it was sharp. I went round to his right side, and I knelt beside him, and I prayed, and first I cut through the cloth of his uniform, and then I held the lower arm in my left hand, and I said, 'In the name of God,' and with the bayonet in my right hand began to cut through the muscles and tendons that were full of shining white fragments of bone. Fikret was a strong man, and he had big muscles. When I was cutting him, it was like cutting meat off a sheep, and made a crunching sound, and he was moaning softly, and I was weeping, with tears that ran down my cheeks and fell on to him. I wept so that I had to keep wiping my eyes with my sleeves, because otherwise I wouldn't have been able to see, and because I was weeping I could not speak to him.

When I had cut away the arm, and laid it gently down beside him, he said, 'Tie something round the stump,' so I took the piece of sleeve I had cut off, and cut it into strips, and the strips were just long enough to tie around the stump, and when I had done this, the bleeding was much less. With his left hand Fikret picked up his right arm, and hefted it in his hand, and he said, 'I didn't know my own arm was so heavy,' and I thought it strange that he was holding his own right arm and couldn't move the fingers of the hand any more because it was just meat. He put the arm down, and then held hands with it, feeling the fingers with his fingers. Fikret said, 'It was a good arm,' but I thought it didn't look as though it belonged to anyone at all, it was just an object. He said, 'How the whores of Pera are going to miss these fingers.'

All this time some of my comrades had been standing watching, because there is a fascination in these things, and for the ones who see the dead and wounded there is always the thought that is secretly in their head, which is 'Thank God it wasn't me'. One of them kept saying, 'Be strong, Fikret, God's the boss,' and then finally Fikret just looked at him, and you could tell that Fikret's look was saying 'Go and fuck your mother's cunt', and so the soldier shut up.

Fikret said, 'I would like a cigarette,' but mine were all finished, and no one else had one either, and the imam wouldn't give me any, so I went to the officer, who was not Orhan, because Orhan had been killed some time before. This officer was a Turk from Bosnia, and he was good, and he had a Bosnian accent. I said to him, 'Permission to speak, sir,' and he said, 'What is it, Abdul Nefer?' and I said, 'Fikret Nefer has had his arm shot off, and he has requested a cigarette, sir.'

So the officer took out his silver cigarette case, which he had taken from a dead Frankish officer along with his watch, and he gave me not one, but five cigarettes. He said, 'If Fikret Nefer dies before he finishes them, please return the surplus ones to me.'

I saluted him and he saluted back, and I took the cigarettes to Fikret and laid them on his left side where he could pick them up.

When Fikret started to smoke, he proved that his character had not changed, because he blew out the first puff, and said, 'By God, that's almost as good as a cunt.'

'We should get you to the field hospital,' I said, and he blew out more smoke and replied, 'No. This is it.' He smoked some more, and said, 'Why are you weeping, stupid son of a bitch?' and I didn't know till then that I was weeping.

I sat beside him as he smoked, first one cigarette, and then two, and by the third cigarette his head was beginning to fall and his eyes to close. I put my head close to his face, and he said, 'This time I'm really fucked. I've got no blood left.'

He managed to smoke another cigarette, but mostly it smouldered between his fingers. When I realised he was truly dying, I was seized by a certain curiosity, and I said, 'Fikret, Fikret, can you see the green birds?'

Very slowly and quietly and sadly he said, 'There are no green birds.'

I wanted to say something light, so I said, 'Will you send me your spare virgins?' and he smiled a very little and shook his head to say no, and then he sighed very deeply and died. I took his cigarette from between his fingers and finished it for him. I looked at him, and saw how beaten down he was. His uniform was patched with pieces of hessian taken from sandbags, and his boots were different sizes because they had been taken from different corpses. He looked like a beggar. For a long time I looked at the profile of his face, the Arab nose, the loose lower lip, and felt a coldness coming over me. I was shocked by how little I felt, by how quickly I got bored sitting next to his corpse and wanted to do something else. It was only later that the grief began to trickle out of my hidden heart and into my veins, when I remembered the conversations that we had for many hours on many nights under the stars, when we discussed everything that there was to discuss, and we talked of our homes and our memories, and the plans, and he would say, 'Now you describe every olive tree in your home town, and then I will describe every Greek harlot and every Greek café in Pera,' and that's what we did, until we had talked about everything that ever was, and we smoked and laughed and talked of coarse things the way that soldiers do, and in the daytime we set up little battles between, say, a scorpion and an ant-lion, or an ant-lion and a beetle, and he would support one insect and I would support the other, and we would be crouching down in the stones cheering our insect on, and we would do a little dance of triumph if our insect won, and we'd never felt so careless in our lives.

I took Fikret's ammunition, and with it I killed fifteen Franks over the next few days, but just then, for the sake of something to do, I took the spare cigarette back to the officer, but he glanced at the blood on it and said, 'Smoke it yourself, Abdul Nefer,' so I took it, and I sat next to Fikret, whose head had dropped to his chest, and I leaned up against him, and I smoked the cigarette, thinking about the great preciousness of tobacco, with his blood congealing and darkening on my bayonet and on my hands, and the field guns falling silent, and the corpse flies buzzing and diving.

68

Mustafa Kemal (15)

When the botched Allied attack occurs, Kemal is given charge of six divisions, and he is elated, partly because Destiny has finally agreed with his assessment of himself as a man thereof, but mainly because he no longer has to stay in one place where the stench of corpses has become overwhelming. The attack gives him some fresh air for a change. He has not slept for three nights, but he rides about from place to place, upbraiding lazy or incompetent commanders, and assuming control in all areas. Fortunately, the Allied attack is a miserable fiasco, and their troops perish in the fires among the scrubland and are cut down by Kemal's sharpshooters. Kemal displays his normal foolhardy courage, and does not even leave the track when an enemy aircraft bears down upon him and his mounted group of officers. After two divisional commanders are killed, and armed with a whip, he personally leads the dawn attack on the high ground of Çonk Bayırı, which has tantalised the Allies from the start, and which now they have finally attained. A ball of shrapnel smacks into his chest, but his heart is saved by a watch in his breast pocket. Later on he will give this watch to Liman von Sanders as a souvenir, and the latter will give him a gold watch in return, engraved with the von Sanders coat of arms. Mustafa Kemal will have a huge and painful bruise on his chest for weeks after the Allies are driven off the crucial peak. Mustafa Kemal's dawn attack works, and the exhausted British soldiers are overwhelmed by sheer numbers. Up on the hill the Ottoman troops are subjected to an apocalyptic bombardment by the British navy, and the ground erupts into crater and flame, but all the Allied assaults are beaten off, and trench warfare predictably establishes itself on the new front. Kemal's extraordinary luck and his rigid disregard for personal safety continue to burnish his legend among the troops.

Squabbling in the high command resumes with the same

predictability as trench warfare, as the Germans tighten their control over essential commands. Mustafa Kemal coninues to suffer severe attacks of malaria and, coincidentally, the Allied commander, Sir Ian Hamilton, continues to go down with debilitating attacks of dysentery. Kemal becomes extremely bad-tempered, and is insulted once again by Enver Pasha, who fails to visit him on an official tour. Kemal resigns all over again, and resists all blandishments to make him change his mind. It is entirely possible that he is really angling to go and fight on the new fronts opened up by Bulgaria's opportunistic entry into the war on the German side. Kemal's hopes of going to Macedonia are confounded, however, by an appointment to go and command the armies in Mesopotamia, where the British have occupied Kut during a shambolic campaign that appears to have no precise objective. Ibrahim the Goatherd, exhausted in limb and spirit, is at this moment marching to confront them, his mind filled only with the desire to go home and marry Philothei at last.

The Macedonian plan does not work out, however, and a German general takes command in Mesopotamia. Kemal stays on the Gallipoli peninsula, and resumes his personal war with anyone in authority. He refuses to accept any German officers in his sector, sending away the new commander of the 11th Division, and von Sanders agrees not to send any more of them. An Ottoman officer declines to accept an order from a German superior, and Kemal similarly refuses an order to hand him over. Liman von Sanders, highly embarrassed, sends Mustafa Kemal back to Istanbul, on 'medical grounds', and the truth is that Kemal is quite happy to go. He is indeed quite ill, and utterly weary, and he is tired of having his opinions ignored. People who know him are alarmed by his ravaged appearance. He goes to live with his mother and sister, for ever exiled from their comfortable pink house in Salonika, and again he seeks out the seductive company of Corinne Lütfü. Ten days after his departure, the Allies also leave Gallipoli, and Mustafa Kemal says that he knew they would, all along.

It is quite likely that without Mustafa Kemal the Ottomans would have lost the campaign at Gallipoli, which would have saved the whole world a great deal of trouble. There would

have been no Russian Revolution and no Cold War, and the
Great War might have ended a year sooner, but Mustafa Kemal
does not believe in saving anyone any trouble, and in Istanbul he
continues to harass the authorities without pity.

69

Karatavuk at Gallipoli:
The End of the Campaign (8)

As I might have told you, in places the lines were so close together that it was easy to dig saps underneath each other. Sometimes the sappers met each other in the dark and fought like rats. Sometimes the trench floor would collapse into a sap, and sometimes a dead body would fall on the sappers because of all the corpses buried in the floors of the trenches, and sometimes a sap would accidentally come out into the side of a trench, and you would sit very quietly, listening to the crunch of the spades and picks, and the voices of the miners, and as soon as a hole appeared, you said, 'Haydi, Johnny,' and you threw in a grenade. If a sap was successful, a mine would go off underneath the trenches, and it would cause great damage and a big shock, and very many deaths. Mostly we and the Franks spent the time improving the trench systems, making it more and more impossible for any attacks to succeed, and we would advance our trenches underground and make a new front line until in some sectors we and the Franks were within a few paces of each other. People like me spent their time creeping about, sniping. The Franks developed a way of sniping using a special wooden frame and a periscope, so that the sniper was safe. This meant that I had to try to shoot the periscopes, and that way I never got bored. After a time I stopped climbing trees when I was sniping, because the Franks would rake each tree with machine guns quite regularly. It was also less tedious when the ducks began to migrate south, and we and the Franks shot them out of the sky by the thousand, and for once we had good meat to eat, even though it was tough, and by then our teeth were rotten and our gums were bleeding, and we all had toothache which is almost as bad as dysentery for making you unable to think. After the campaign I noticed that the following year there were no more ducks flying over at that time.

The next big thing that happened was in the late autumn and early winter, when it suddenly seemed as if God Himself had got bored, and He threw the weather at us for four days. One evening there was a tempest of rain so violent that I have never experienced the like of it before or since. The air was solid with water, the rain fell in huge lumps, and it would have been possible for fish to swim in it. I swear there has never been rain like it anywhere. It roared like wild beasts, and it came down so swiftly that the trenches filled instantly with water, and a wall of water swept down on us, and many of us drowned, and I was only saved because a comrade scrambled out of the trench and held out his rifle, and I grasped it and he pulled me out just in time. I lay above the trench and watched it collapse in on itself, and I was as wet as if I were lying under the sea, and I saw the drowned bodies of my comrades floating past below me, and a dead mule, and old corpses that had floated up out of the floor of the trench, and old bones, and packages of supplies, and knapsacks, and I saw the water getting deeper and deeper, and we who had survived lay on the mud in the falling water, and prayed, and wondered if this was the end of the world, and we could hardly see an arm's length in front of us, and our clothes were heavy and sticking to us, and we were as miserable as the damned, and the winds picked up ground sheets and blankets and whirled them about in the air like giant birds afflicted by madness.

In the morning the water had subsided to a rifle's depth, but we couldn't go back down into the trenches, and there was nothing to eat, and we were still soaked. Fortunately the Franks had suffered the same as us, and they did not shoot as many of us as they could have.

In the evening the wind turned round and came from the north. It didn't often do this, and when it did the stench of corpses was carried to Çanakkale for a change. The north wind was always cold, though, and this time it was colder than I had ever known, and it began to snow. Snow is very beautiful, and I remember the story of Ali the Snowbringer, who was given that name because it snowed on the day he was born, but on this day it was so cold that the snow was not beautiful, it was like a knife stuck into the bone and twisted. After the rain it was like someone coming back to kill your father and brothers the day after he has slaughtered your mother and sisters. We huddled in the mud above the parapets of the trenches, with the snow settling on our bodies and our rifles and our equipment, shaking and trembling, our stomachs crying for something hot to eat, and I was thinking of all the times back home when we used to complain that the days were too hot in late summer, and I was thinking that if I ever got too hot again, I would praise God for it.

It was as if God heard me and decided to play a trick, because he took the snow and multiplied it, and he took the wind and multiplied it, and he took the cold and multiplied it, and it became a blizzard. I had heard of blizzards from those who had been up in the mountains in winter, but I had never been able to imagine what it is like to have the bones aching from the inside with a pain as if they had been broken, to have the fingers immovable and without feeling, to have the jaws clattering their teeth together, and to feel the lungs hardening with every frozen breath. We did not have any winter clothing prepared, because winter had not been expected yet, and all our spare clothing was down in the trenches, buried under the mud and the snow that fell on top of it. Some people managed to light bonfires, they achieved the impossible, but what use was it when the wind whipped the heat away? When we stood in futility around the bonfires, stamping our feet and swinging our arms, the Franks did not shoot at us, nor we at them.

I believe that the rain was worse for the Franks because they were on lower ground, and the torrent had swept through their trenches after leaving ours, but the snow and the wind and the cold were worse for us because we were on higher ground. There was nothing we could do, except huddle together. Eight men of my platoon, including myself, decided to lie in a heap together, to keep the warmth in and the cold out, and it is true that the lower you are, the less the wind is. We lay on the muddy stones, up against each other, our hands inside our clothes, the wind eating at our flesh, the snow piling up on our bodies, our mouths tasting of metal, and that way we endured until daybreak, when we discovered that, on account of our wet clothing, some of us had frozen to the ground and were unable to get up. Three of us were dead, and of the rest of us, four lost fingers and toes, and one man had to have his ears removed. I lost one toe on my left foot and I nearly lost the tips of three fingers, but I was lucky in the end, even though I have no feeling in those fingers any more. Our imam was found dead, with his knees and toes and forehead frozen to the ground in the act of prayer, and we found a sentry who had frozen to death on the firing step of the trench, clasping his rifle, upright in the correct position. Those who suffered the least bodily damage were those who had forced themselves to walk about all night, and those who suffered the most were those who had fallen with exhaustion. All of us were so wounded by the cold that we had to be withdrawn from the line, and replaced, and only two of us recovered enough to return. This was the worst calamity I have ever been through, and after being so nearly swallowed by death, I live each day in a state of surprise and wonderment. I will never forget the pain that went through me when I began to thaw out, the tingling and throbbing of it, and I would say that this pain was as bad as being frozen in the first place. The one thing about the freeze that was God's insult to us was that when our clothing unfroze after three days, the lice that had been in there all came back to life as if they had never been frozen. The one good thing was that we were able to eat the mules and donkeys that had died, and the meat was good after so many months of olives and bread and bulghur wheat.

One astonishing thing happened as a result of the blizzard. Afterwards there was no more dysentery. From then on, no one would be groaning with stomach cramps, shitting his life out on the latrine along with blood and slime. Afterwards the weather became beautiful again, and the sun set over Mount Athos and Samothráki as if we had never known anything but peace.

It was not long after this that the Anzacs and the soldiers at Suvla vanished overnight. They disappeared like ghosts. They left rifles that fired at us on their own, because water or sand dripped into cans that were tied to triggers, and when the can was full, the trigger was pulled. They also left a huge mine that exploded early in the morning in a sap under the trenches where we had massacred the Australian Light Horse, and they left many traps that exploded in their trenches when we went into them. All this was an unnecessary unkindness. They blew up their stores on the beach, but there was still enough equipment left for we who remained to take two years to collect it all. This included the bully beef that neither we nor they liked very much. In their trenches some soldiers had left tricks for us, such as rum bottles filled with paraffin, but others had left meals for us, set out on plates, and they left messages for us. Obviously I couldn't read them, but I was told that they said things like 'Goodbye, Johnny Turk, thank you for respecting the Red Cross, and remember that it was us who left, it wasn't you who pushed us out.' I have a piece of paper that is now very old and yellow, and apparently it says, 'Goodbye, Abdul.'

We half expected the British and French Franks in the south to pull out in the same way, and the spare divisions were moved there quickly from Gaba Tepe and Ariburnu, but the Franks took us by surprise all over again. There were more storms and gales, and they managed to make it seem that they were all still there, and they even repelled an attack on the night they left. On this attack we carried planks to cross the Frankish trenches with, and we had inflammable things so that we could set fire to their boats, but, I am ashamed to say, even though there had been a very long and violent bombardment, since we had new German guns supporting us, many of us refused to go forward, and the officers started to beat us with the flats of their sabres, and our cries of 'Allah, Allah' dried on our lips, and the Franks mowed us down where we stood paralysed above the parapets of our trenches. This also happened on another occasion, about a month before. I have often thought about this, and wondered why it happened, but the truth is that for months we had lived off little but olives and bread, we had frozen in ice and cooked in the sun, we had marched back and forth, back and forth, we had finally heard enough about martyrdom, we had faced death and agony unnumbered times, we had been treated like slaves and dogs, we had been beaten and shouted at, and finally we were too weary to throw ourselves once more into the hailstorms of singing bullets and the thorn-thickets of sharpened bayonets. We were worn out and we wouldn't go on. What upsets me now when I remember this is the dishonour that we brought upon ourselves in the eyes of the Frankish soldiers who saw it. I also know that many of our men had been deserting, and crawling over to the Frankish lines to give themselves up. Nobody needs that kind of man anyway, and their dishonour makes them contemptible, and I don't think of them as Turks. I expect they were Armenians, or Arabs or Bosnians, but not Turks.

When they went they also blew up all their ammunition on the beach, and it made a very great roaring, a huge red cloud shaped like a mushroom. It was the loudest noise and the greatest fire ever seen.

I will tell you a sad thing about the leaving of the Franks, which affected me very much. When we went down to the beaches we found all the mules and horses that they had left behind. They were well-fed, big animals, and they were combed and brushed and beautiful, with fine markings, and they were tethered on the beach in a line. But the Franks had not been able to take them away with them, and so, to prevent us from having them, and even though they obviously cared for them, the Franks had sacrificed them all, with love in their hearts, and had cut their throats or shot them after feeding and combing them. Some Frankish soldiers disobeyed the order, however, as we would find donkeys hidden away in the bushes with a big bag of hay, and this is what happens in war, which is that out of all the vileness, a small light still shines.

The good thing about the leaving of the Franks was that they left a great deal of food among the abandoned stores. The sentries couldn't hold us back, and we carried away many jars of sticky fruit in glass jars that was extremely sweet, and I ate so much of it that I felt very strange, as if I was drifting, and it hurt my teeth. There was a marvellous quantity of flour. Also, they left a great deal of useful cloth and pieces of clothing, so for some time many of us who had been dressed in rags wore new breeches made of Frankish flags, and we put Australian hats on our heads, and we made belts out of their puttees, and we looked very colourful and strange, and our officers were not pleased as we did not appear military, but they knew very well that there was no choice because we never received new uniforms. My new officer was killed when he opened the firebox of a steam traction engine that had been left behind, and that had been booby-trapped with melinite.

After the Franks left I felt bereavement, because they had been the whole purpose of my life and my sufferings for many months. I had killed a very large number of them by sniping, usually through the head, even at great distances, and they had killed most of my comrades, including my best comrade, Fikret. After the hatred at first, and the merciless killing, we and the Franks had got to know each other a little, and I think that, strange as it may sound, we had come to like each other. Speaking for myself, I had discovered that infidels are not necessarily devils, which I should have known already because, after all, I grew up in a town among many different kinds of them, except that they weren't Frankish. I still remember with a smile how the Frankish soldiers used to catapult their tins of bully beef over to us, and we would fill them with stones and put messages inside, saying things like 'We're going to miss you when you go. See you at Suez', and we would catapult them back again, and I still remember how they and we would cut little slots in the shells of tortoises, and put folded messages in the slots, and prod the tortoises in the direction of the enemy lines, and I still remember how if a mouse or a rat appeared between the lines, it would be shot at from both sides, for the sport of it, and when it was dead, only then would we go back to taking shots at each other.

Most of the men on the peninsula were reassigned to other theatres of war, but I stayed with the garrison. It took almost two years to clear up everything that the Franks had left behind.

I couldn't find where we had buried Fikret, even though I looked whenever I had the time. The land came back to life so quickly that it soon became hard to recognise even the most familiar places. We didn't mark graves the way the Franks did, and often the dead were tipped into pits or buried in trenches. We never did get rid of corpses as efficiently as them, and I remember living and fighting among the dead almost all the time. We just put up with them. When we took Frankish prisoners and led them through our trenches, they were always horrified, and at the time we took it as a sign of weakness.

There were many who believed that if you were not buried in a white shroud, you would not be admitted to paradise. If that is true, there must be many ghosts wandering at Çanakkale. It became customary for me to walk everywhere among the decomposing and shrivelling corpses that had been left on the surface, all dressed in shreds of uniform and lying in strange twisted positions, and I would find rifles and bayonets rusting in the spring rains, and in the turpentine pines the yellow birds sang in the sunlight as if nothing had ever happened. I would often look at the bodies and wonder which of these Franks I had killed myself, when I was sniping, and I would look to see which of the corpses had been shot in the head. I lost count of my kills because I got weary of counting, but it must have been two or three hundred.

I was frustrated by being left behind with the garrison. I wanted to carry on fighting. I loved the fighting, the excitement of it, the way that my soul seemed to lift out of my body and watch what my body was doing, the rushing of the blood in the veins, the joy and intoxication of chanting 'Allah, Allah' all together as we followed the banner over the parapets and charged to maryrdom. It was only a long time afterwards that I began to reflect on the killing that I did. Of course there were more wars and more fighting to come, but back then I didn't know it, and I felt as though the taste of life had fallen dull on my tongue. I thought, 'How can I go home, now, and get married, and make children, and live mildly, and make pots, and grow aubergines, as if I had never been to war?' Without the Franks I felt lonely. I felt sad as I did my patrols and my guard duties and my training in that place. The night sky did not seem correct without the parachute flares and Very lights that lit up no man's land at night and made the world stand out in perfect white light and perfect black shadow; and rockets and star shells, the brief glimmers of shells as they landed and the howitzers as they fired, the bright spark and sparkle of bullets as they ricocheted from the stones. The air was not correct without the stench of cordite, shit, piss, sweat and rottenness, the buzzing of bullets, the whistle and thump of incoming shells, the miaowing of the high-explosive fragments and the grunting of the sixty-pounders, the coughing of aeroplanes, the screams and wails of the wounded, and the laughter and songs coming over from the Frankish trenches, those odd jerky melodies that I can still remember and whose words I never understood. My shoulder did not feel correct without the constant reliable bruise from the recoil of my Mauser, and my forefinger did not feel correct with no trigger to fold itself around. It did not feel correct that there were no more tiny whirlwinds made of dust, skipping away from the impact of a shell. It did not feel correct that I no longer spent my days up trees, or crawling about in the stones with twigs and branches tied around me. It did not feel correct that Mustafa Kemal was no longer there, getting thinner and paler, and more bright-eyed and hoarse-voiced and courageous every day, crawling in the dark along the parapets of the trenches to encourage us before an attack, whispering, 'Follow me, and don't charge until I raise my sword,' and his being always there in the worst of the fighting, and always being by a miracle in the right place with his troops at the right time, and never once being struck except for the ball of shrapnel that hit his watch.

In the deserted trenches and ragged trees I heard constantly the voice of Fikret, saying, 'I am from Pera and I don't give a shit,' and I caught glimpses of the faces of comrades that I thought I had forgotten, and the faces of Franks that I had killed. Sometimes I would wake up suddenly, my heart thudding with eagerness, and make a grab for my rifle, because I hoped there was an attack.

The huge cloud of angry shit-coloured dust that had hung over us for months, laden with the sweet smell of rottenness, finally began to disperse. The sides of the trenches began to fall in, and everywhere the dead lay in strange poses as they forgot about their senses and their flesh. In the Frankish trenches we found by the hundred the entrenching tools that we had been so short of and which we always carried away in raids, and which we didn't need now that there were so many of them to be had for no effort. The oleander, the myrtle and thyme sprang up among them in the stones, and in spring the poppies came up and covered the battlefields, and the hillside of Achi Baba turned scarlet red, because disturbed ground throws up poppies like a corpse makes maggots. I imagined that each poppy was a message from a soldier, and each poppy was scarlet because of a soldier's blood, and I remembered all those years back home when for some reason all the poppies came up pink, and people used to remark on it and wonder what it meant.

Now, as the great Frankish ships rusted on the beach, and the great Frankish armies went to fight elsewhere, the goatherds returned with their savage round-eared dogs, the farmers began to collect the military barbed wire for their own fences, townspeople from Maydos came to scavenge among the shrivelling corpses for watches and rings and coins and cigarette cases, tortoises clattered about once more among the ruins of the fortresses, and again the frogs and crickets set up their croaking and sawing. Yellow flowers sprang up in the woods, and yellow birds sang again in the pines, and in this beautiful peace I was covered up in sadness and in solitude.

70

Tamara Receives a Visitor

It was the summer of 1916, one year after the deportation of Levon and the other Armenians, and just a few months after the Frankish Allies had crept off the Gallipoli peninsula in the dark of a winter's night. Karatavuk was still there with the occupying garrison, but Mehmetçik had escaped his labour battalion to live precariously as an outlaw in the uncompromising Taurus Mountains. Levon and his wife were dead of exhaustion, cruelty, starvation and despair somewhere on the ossuarial road to Syria Deserta.

Little remained the same. In Eskibahçe the work was being done by children, the women, the very old, and the few men who had returned crippled from active service. All the towns-folk were half starved, and most of them were desperate. The stock was regularly rustled by gangs of deserters, and there were those who stole from their neighbours' fields, even though the punishment for being caught was absolute and condign. There were no camels left, no horses except those of Rustem Bey, and but few goats and donkeys.

The town evidenced its economic and moral decline in its very appearance. The dilapidated streets remained uncleaned, broken shutters hung at drunken angles from torn window frames, and the cheerful pastel paintwork of walls and woodwork had long since begun to peel away. The stray dogs, no longer benignly supplied with crusts of bread by the kind-hearted, died in the streets and rotted there, filling the air with the same pervasive, sweet and rich stink of death that had supplanted the scent of satisfied earth and wild flowers all across the disfigured fields of Europe. The row of idiots who used to sit on the walls together, laughing and gesticulating, now sat there in rags, all the pleasures and disinhibitions of insanity done away with by the dejection of hunger. They had ceased to be entertainment either to them-selves or to anyone else.

The few shops that opened had almost nothing to sell, and no one had any money with which to buy. Some of the ones that used to belong to the Armenians had been looted. The wonderfully varied stalls that used to make the meydan almost impassable were sagging on their trestles, unused and unmaintained. Stamos the Birdman was not to be found there, since nowadays his pretty little finches were barbecued on sticks and eaten, bones and all, by himself and his family. Neither was Mehmet the Tinsman ever there, because his tin was no longer arriving from the far and exotic land of Cornwall, and in any case, the pots were wearing out more slowly for lack of the wherewithal to cook in them. Neither was Ali the Broken-Nosed there, because he had no goats' milk to sell now that most of his flock had been taken by brigands. Ali the Snowbringer, still living with his wife and four children in the hollowed trunk of a mighty tree, did not pass through the meydan with his dripping sacks, because no one had a few paras to spare for ice. He counted himself lucky that he and his donkey had been out on the mountainsides when the gendarmerie had arrived to requisition the pack animals. Equally lucky was Gerasimos, now happily married to Drosoula. He had been out in his boat when the gendarmerie had arrived to take away the young Christian men for the labour battalions, and these days he slept down on the beach, near his boat, in case they returned, and on good days he brought fish to the town. He was one of the very few who was richer than he had been before, not least because there was no longer anything to buy, and so his coins merely accumulated. No strong men came to the town any more, with their cannons and striped pantaloons, and neither were there acrobats and jugglers. Abdulhamid Hodja was no longer seen there, because he was already beginning to die, and only the two gendarmes continued to play backgammon in the shade of the planes.

Only a few things remained the same. Leonidas, thinner and more cantankerous, continued to write his subversive political tracts at night, by the stinking wick of an olive-oil lamp, and persisted in sending his writings to his few accomplices in Smyrna, undeterred by the undoubtedly inconvenient truth that it was only mainland Greeks who really wanted Greece to expand into Anatolia and fulfil 'The Great Idea'. Drosoula's father, Constantinos, jaundiced and delirious, still drank away the agony of toothache, and as usual incurred the obloquy of all. The Blasphemer, now skeletal and more mad, still cursed God and His representatives in the streets. The Dog still lived obliviously among the Lycian tombs, occasionally wearing the remains of Selim's telltale shoes, and apparently thriving on locusts. Iskander still made pots and birdwhistles, and Mohammed the Leech Gatherer still stood heron-like in the pool of the Letoun, because leeches were still required by the doctors of Smyrna. Leyla Hanım still sang to her oud at night, sending sad lullabies in mis-remembered Greek out over the roofs. She had turned temp-orarily into a housewife, since most of the male servants had gone to war, and she had taken to improvising meals out of the few things that Rustem Bey shot on the mountainsides, or that she could find in the market. Nowadays she went out like any other woman, to look for wild greens, and it is true to say that the change had done her good. Sometimes she looked at the dried skin of her hands, with their ingrained dirt and scuffed nails, and even felt a little proud of herself. She no longer had that enjoyable but nonetheless guilty sense of wasting her life on frippery and idleness, and she most usually glowed with good humour in spite of the many unwonted difficulties of life in wartime. She still employed Philothei, and together they went out frequently to gather wild food, accompanied by a sleepy and very elderly retainer, who had been armed with a musket for their protection. Unlike Drosoula, Philothei had been unable to marry on time, and now she waited for Ibrahim to come back from the front. There had been no news for months, and if it had not been for the cheerful company of Leyla Hanım, she would have suffered a great deal more from the constant fear and worry. At night in Eskibahçe the bulbuls and nightin-gales still kept light sleepers irritably awake.

It was on one such bird-struck night that a figure slipped out of one of the richer homes at the top corner of the town, and vanished into the darkened alleyways. He was wrapped so heavily in a black cloak as to be almost invisible, and it was obvious that he was being deliberately furtive. He stood still for a while, accustoming his eyes to the darkness, and then he set off. He stumbled occasionally against rocks that protruded through the cobbles, and was brushed by the sweet-smelling leaves of the figs that grew from the interstice of wall and road. Even in that darkness, it was clear that he knew where he was going, and there was something in his manner that betrayed great purpose.

He passed the former houses of the few Armenians, and the mosque, with its two minarets and silenced fountain. He passed through the meydan, and the Church of St Nicholas, with its icon by St Luke of the Virgin Sweet-and-Loving. He passed the lower church, where there was still an owl that perched on the beams, and where the ossuary was that contained the wine-washed bones of the Christian dead. He came to where the street turned a corner sharply, and ended with a final, isolated house, flat-roofed, whose façade was draped with climbing roses, and whose windows were latticed in order to conceal the dark interior.

He rapped on the heavy door, in which there was a tiny wrought-iron grille at head height. Suddenly it squeaked open, and, drifting out, came a heavy scent of smoke and ambergris, olibanum, oil of lemon, musk and patchouli. A huge pair of doleful grey eyes, heavily lined with kohl, looked out. 'Welcome,' said a low voice. 'What do you want?'

The stranger put one hand on the door to steady himself, tried to ignore the frightening thumping of his heart, and looked beseechingly into the sympathetic grey eyes. 'I have come to see Tamara Hanım,' he whispered. The prostitute sighed, and pulled back the latches to let him in.

He had never been in the place before, and at first he found the dark pink light almost too dim, even though he had just come in out of utter darkness. He was in a room that in its respectable days would have been the selamlık, but which was now divided into smaller chambers by large kilims hanging across it on cords. In each chamber there were cushions and in some there were divans. In most of the chambers he could just discern the figures of thinly clad women, lolling, their faces unnaturally white, their lips painted thickly in scarlet, and their eyes kohled into huge circles. Some of them beckoned to him with poorly simulated salacity, saying, 'Come to me, my lion, to me, to me.

Let it be me, my lion,' and others, their eyes large and empty, sucked deeply on waterpipes and scarcely registered his presence at all, blowing clouds of smoke out of their mouths with a pleasure that seemed both profound and melancholy. 'I had no idea there were so many here,' said the man to the doorkeeper, who was still accompanying him. 'Well, you haven't been here before,' came the soft answer. In the background were the sounds of a woman in the agony of childbirth, of another woman sobbing, and of a man approaching a noisy climax. To the visitor's ear the frenzied voice sounded somewhat like that of Ali the Broken-Nosed.

Tamara Hanım was in what used to be the haremlık, in a similar small chamber composed of hanging carpets, cushions and a divan. She was simply sitting motionless and timeless on the divan, with her hands between her knees, and her head bowed. He recognised something about her immediately, her outline, or perhaps her atmosphere, even though he had not seen her now for many years. 'Tamara,' he said, and the doorkeeper silently left.

She looked up, unbelieving. He loosened his cloak and folded it on his arm before laying it on the floor by one of the cushions. She saw the sash with the familiar silver-handled pistols and the yataghan, and she raised her eyes to see his face. He was thinner and older, but he had scarcely changed, except that his eyes had in them less pride and more kindness than before. 'It's you,' she said at last.

'It's me.'

'Why?'

He gestured confusedly. 'I had to come.' He tapped his chest with the knuckles of his right hand, and said, 'It was in here. Like a voice. I have ignored it for years, but finally I have listened. And so, as you see, I have come at last.'

Tamara began to weep silently, and tears rolled down her cheeks, splashing on to the hands that were now trembling in her lap. 'You've come,' she said.

He gestured again. 'I had to.'

'Sit down if you like,' she said, and he sat down at the other end of the divan. She put her head into her hands and wept more noisily now, her shoulders heaving with sobs, uttering little cries that reminded him of a whipped puppy. He could think of nothing to do or say, and he watched in anxious alarm as the tears emerged from between her fingers and ran down the backs of her hands.

After a long interval she stopped, removed her hands from her face, and smiled wanly. 'I am sorry,' she said, 'these are women's tears.'

'They are not just a woman's tears,' he said quietly. 'These tears are yours.'

'I am very rich when it comes to tears,' she said, but without any bitterness in her voice. 'It doesn't matter how many I spend, I always have more and I never run out. If I had as many coins as I have tears, I could buy the world from the Devil.'

'I am sorry for your tears,' he said soberly.

She dabbed her eyes and looked at him. 'Are you well?'

'I am very well,' he replied.

'You seem thinner.'

'I have a lot of exercise. I spend a great deal of time out hunting, for days at a time. Otherwise it is hard to eat.'

'Even for you?'

'Yes, even for us.'

'Do you still have a tame partridge to tempt the other birds, so that you can shoot them?'

'Yes, I still have a partridge.'

'I liked the partridge. It was very pretty, and sometimes it had funny ways. Some men call their wives and daughters "My little partridge". Did you know that?'

He nodded. 'I once heard my father say it to my mother, when he thought that there was no one there. I was quite surprised. He was a hard man, as far as I knew.' There was a long pause, and then he asked, 'Do you have enough to eat?'

She looked him straight in the eye, and shook her head. 'No. We are all starving. There are no young men any more, and the old ones are too poor. Some of us use opium to take away the cramps and the faintness.'

'Is that what this heavy smell is?'

She nodded. 'Yes.'

'But you don't use it?'

'They do it mostly to forget, but I don't want to forget. I want to remember. And in any case it either kills them or sends them mad.' She smiled wryly and continued, almost to herself alone, as if she were merely voicing a repetitive old thought, 'But that's how you leave this place anyway, I suppose. You go to the asylum or you go to the earth. I might as well smoke opium, but I just don't. I am going to the earth in my own time, and I am sure that it won't be long.'

'I can bring you food,' he said.

'Why should you do that?'

'I have the desire, that's all.'

'I would like food,' she said.

'I heard that you were all starving,' he said. 'I brought you this.' He reached into his sash and brought out a package wrapped in a cloth. He handed it to her and she took it. 'I'll eat it when you've gone,' she said.

'It has a lot of good things in it,' he said.

'May giving it do you as much good as I will get from receiving it,' she said, very formally. After another long pause she said, 'I sometimes hear news of you from Leyla Hanım.'

'She tells me news of you,' said Rustem Bey. 'She told me you were ill.'

'The respectable women won't sit with her in the hamam, and so she comes and sits with us,' said Tamara scornfully. 'I hate those women. If I was a man who was married to one of them, I would wade out into the sea and drown. They are as sour as wild cherries and as dry as leather, and their hearts and bellies are full of grave dust and ground glass. They say that Leyla Hanım is just a concubine, and so they don't sit with her.'

'I have heard Leyla Hanım's complaints,' he said.

Tamara wanted to reply 'And so have we heard them', but she restrained herself for Leyla's sake.

'I have heard from Leyla Hanım that you have had children,' he said, with obvious pain in his voice.

'They are all dead. I had four, but now they're dead. I buried them under the stones, among the tombs where the Dog lives, and near the tomb of the saint. I don't think I'll have any more.'

415

She fell silent, and then she demanded suddenly, 'Why haven't you divorced me?'

He was much taken aback by the directness of the question, and he hung his head to ponder it. At last he replied, 'It was for the sake of something that I can't explain. Well, perhaps I can explain it, but to most people the explanation would make very little sense.' He glanced up. 'I don't talk to anyone about these things. I am not practised in this kind of talk.'

'I am glad to see you,' she replied. 'Try to explain it anyway.'

'Do you remember when I discovered you with Selim, and I killed him, and I dragged you out to be stoned, and the people started to stone you?'

'You dragged me out by the hair, and turned your back whilst they attacked me in the meydan, and started to kill me. Your hands had been bleeding, and you had Selim's blood on you, and your blood and his blood were on me, and I was thinking when they attacked me that your blood and his blood were mixing up with mine.'

'I did it because I thought it was right, and for the sake of my honour. I not only thought it was right, but I knew it. It says in the Holy Koran that adulterers shall be stoned. It's the custom, and it's the sharia. I knew it was right. I did it because there was no question.

'But even then the certainty was too uncertain. When I had my back to you, it was only shame that prevented me from rising up and whipping away those vermin that surrounded you. I was wishing that I had not dragged you out. The longing for justice and vengeance became less than my longing to save you and take you away. The revenge tasted like copper and vinegar in my mouth, and all the sweetness and satisfaction of it vanished away. It was only the shame that stopped me . . . and then when Abdulhamid Hodja arrived and saved you, my heart was singing with relief even at the same time as I should have killed him for taking away my just revenge. If I had killed him, no one would have found me guilty.'

'Abdulhamid Hodja will surely rest for ever in paradise,' said Tamara Hanım softly.

'I didn't divorce you, because you had suffered enough shame.'

'It would have been less shame than this,' she said, indicating her surroundings with a small wave of her hand. 'Do you think that divorce would have been any shame to me at all, compared to this?'

He looked at her a little guiltily. 'I did suffer,' he said.

'Your suffering was like a dewdrop compared to the ocean,' she said.

'Sometimes the dewdrop believes itself to be an ocean.'

'It believes mistakenly.'

'I went to Abdulhamid Hodja. We have often talked about this. He asked me if I have wavering in my soul, because in a righteous man this is the consciousness of wrongdoing.'

'What did you say?'

'I told him that I have a terrible wavering in my soul.'

'Do you?' she asked.

'Even though every good opinion is on my side, I have always felt a terrible wavering in my soul about what was done to you, and about what I did. Because of this wavering I did not divorce you, even though it was a great scandal and still is. You are still my wife, and when you die you will still be my wife, and I will provide the white shroud and the grave, and the headstone in the shape of a tulip, should you be the first to die. This is nothing perhaps, but it reduces the wavering in my soul.'

'If you don't divorce me, you can't marry Leyla Hanım.'

'A man can have more than one wife. Look how many the Prophet had.'

'But you are a modern man. You are like the people in Smyrna. You like to dress in Frankish clothes, and have only one wife.'

'Yes, I can only have one wife.'

'What about Leyla Hanım?'

'Leyla Hanım is a hetaira. She might want to be a wife, but she would be like a bird that sits and sings with its feet tied to a branch, and finally tears out its own feathers and bleeds to death. She would be a bad wife, but she is an excellent concubine. If I made her into a wife it would be like chaining up a dog and expecting it to bleat and give milk.'

'She wants to be a wife. I know it. You misjudge her. And if you are not married to her and you are still married to me, then you are an adulterer when you lie with her.'

417

He laughed ironically. 'Then I should be stoned by the rabble in the meydan, no doubt.'

'You would never be stoned. You are not a wife as I was. You are not a young woman who is easy to stone. You are a lion and the rabble are like little dogs. If you roared, they would run away.'

He smiled at her. 'You have changed a great deal. There was a time when you would have been too timid and too humble to talk to me like this. Now you talk to me directly, as Leyla Hanım does. It is a very unusual thing in a woman.'

Tamara bridled a little. 'I knew my place. I knew what was expected. I was respectable. Leyla Hanım and I are not respectable, and so we speak as we see.'

He added, as if in afterthought, as if returning to a previous train of thought, 'I have only one wife.'

'I am no use as a wife,' she said.

He summoned up his courage and then told her, more directly than he had intended, 'Tamara Hanım, I want to lie with you again.'

She looked at him in astonishment, and repeated, 'Lie with me again?'

'Yes.'

'After all that I have been? After all that has happened? What about the daughters of Levon the Armenian that I have heard you rescued? Aren't they very beautiful? What about Leyla Hanım? Isn't she a good mistress?'

'The daughters of the Armenian are very beautiful, but they are under my protection. I saved them from dishonour, and therefore I cannot dishonour them myself. They are like you when you first came to me. They are frightened and unhappy and bewildered, and so I have sheltered them under my wing. As for Leyla Hanım, she has been very good. But the time has passed by and at last I can no longer forget myself with her. There was always a doubt in my mind, and the pleasure is still very great, but it is not the kind of drunkenness it was. She has become my companion, and we live together because it is very pleasant and we have become like two vines that have twisted together. And despite this, I have also begun to be alone. For a long time I didn't feel that. She banished it, but now it has come back.'

'All the same, it sounds very good, being with her,' observed Tamara.

'It is very good. I remember that when I went to Istanbul to find her, I went to a mosque first, and it was a Friday morning. I told the beads of my tespih, and made a promise to God.'

'A promise to God?'

'Yes. I promised Him that if I found a woman who would bring me all that I wanted in a woman, then I would build Him a mosque. Well, I was just beginning the mosque when the war with the Franks broke out, and the young men were taken away, and so the mosque only has some trenches for the foundations, and these are slowly being filled in with plants and falls of earth.'

'God doesn't want His mosque, then,' said Tamara.

'The odd thing is that when I made the promise, I had the feeling that I was promising it to no one, that no one was listening. I started to build it anyway, because I had made the promise.' He raised his eyebrows and sighed. The wails of the woman in childbirth suddenly ended, and they waited for the infant's cry, but none came.

'Another dead one,' said Tamara.

'I have never forgotten you,' he exclaimed suddenly, 'I have always had you in my mind, you are like someone who waves to me from a distant ridge, who cries out and whose voice it takes me a little while to recognise. In the short time that you were with me you also planted a seed, and that seed continued to grow even though most of the time I was unaware of it, and now I have realised that that seed is also a vine that has entwined with my vine. I have missed you, and I want to lie with you again, even though . . .'

'I have become a whore?'

'No.'

'Even though I was unskilled and very poor entertainment?'

His lack of response signalled that this was precisely what he had meant, and she said, 'I am still unskilled, and very poor entertainment. I have never made any pretence as I should have done to earn my keep. I am among the poorest of these poor whores.'

'Sometimes it is not entertainment that one wants. With us, something has been sundered, like a pot that has fallen on the floor and broken into two pieces. Sometimes, if you haven't thrown away the pieces, you pick them up and fit them together, and look at how good the fit is, and see whether or not there are little chips missing, and your heart wishes that they could be joined once more. Sometimes when I am lying with Leyla Hanım I see her face in the dark and my mind changes her face and her body into yours.'

'This is a kind of infidelity,' said Tamara, 'but no one can stone you for it, I suppose.' She looked down at her hands, as if they were not hers, and watched her fingers twisting together nervously. When she looked up, there were tears running down her cheeks again. 'I can't lie with you. I have too many diseases.'

'Diseases?'

'Yes, diseases. That is what killed my babies. If I lie with you, you will become diseased, and you will give the sicknesses to Leyla Hanım, and you might go mad, as many of these whores do, and certainly you will both die too soon, as I will. For this reason I will only lie with worthless people.'

'You don't think me worthless then?'

'I have thought many things of you, but I have never once thought you worthless. I have become worthless, and so I can lie with the worthless. Their worthlessness and my worthlessness is what gives me permission, and excuses what I do.'

'I once knew that you were worthless,' he said, 'but even when I knew it, I didn't believe it, and now I think that I was mistaken. My knowledge came from what I knew as common knowledge, but not from what I knew in here.' He tapped his chest once more with the knuckles of his right hand. He changed the subject. 'Can these diseases be cured?'

'Now that Levon the Armenian has been taken away, there is no apothecary, and the doctor who looked after us out of kindness was also Armenian.'

'What if I took you to Smyrna? There must be doctors there who can cure you.'

'There are no cures, or none that anyone has heard of. The cures that they offer make you just as sick, and I think that none of them is any good.'

'I would like to send you to Smyrna to be cured.'

Very calmly she said, 'I am happy to die too soon. This life is just death's selamlık, and I have no pleasure. Even if I was cured, I would have no happiness, and I would still be waiting to die. Besides,' she continued, 'these poor women in here are my companions. We care for each other, after a fashion. These women are divorced, or widowed, or dishonoured, and I am pleased to keep them as my sisters and mothers until it is my turn to be buried near my babies.'

'Nonetheless, when I next go to Smyrna, I shall enquire of the doctors.'

'You can enquire,' she said.

Rustem Bey stood up, as if to leave, and began to wrap himself once more in his copious black cloak. 'If you were not diseased, and I had asked you, would you have lain with me again?'

She gazed at him very sincerely. 'Yes, my lion, I would have done, and afterwards I would have wept again, and perhaps I never would have stopped.'

He approached more closely and put his hands on her head, as if in benediction. He tried to tip her head back a little. 'Let me look at your face again. Let me look at your eyes that used to look at me so sadly when you were young.'

She pulled herself away. 'No, don't look at me! Why do you think we keep the light so dim? If you look at me you will see the diseases, and you will see that I am under a curse, and you will not be able to think of me.' She let her head fall, put her hands to her face, and clenched the muscles of her shoulders to resist him.

He stepped back, and his hands fell to his sides. 'I will bring you food and money whenever I can.'

'Will you tell Leyla Hanım that you came?'

'No.'

Tamara nodded, and he said, as if trying to lighten the conversation and ease the farewells, 'The woman who let me in is very strange. She is quite beautiful in an ugly sort of way, and she has a low voice, and is very tall, and has hands like a man. I once came across a woman like that in Istanbul. It gives me an uncomfortable feeling.'

Tamara smiled at his innocence. 'He's a eunuch,' she said. 'Some men come here specially for him.'

421

After he had gone, Tamara undid the package and found olives, cheese, bread and cooked chicken. She also found a pair of earrings made out of gold coins, and a pair of embroidered slippers that she recognised as a gift that he had brought back from Smyrna in the early months of their marriage, and which she had accepted graciously, but without enthusiasm or gratitude. She remembered that she used to put these embroidered slippers outside her door in order to make him think that she had a visitor.

71

The Death of Abdulhamid Hodja

After the battle of Gallipoli, Karatavuk was spared any further military action until the invasion of the Greeks some years later, as he was detailed to remain with the Ottoman garrison on the peninsula, chafing with boredom, and longing to return to battle. The time was passed in an endless round of drill, guard duty and tinkering with the defences. The fact that he was an accomplished sniper with expertise in concealment meant, however, that he was able to spend many a contemplative day hidden in various remote spots, watching for anything suspicious. In these places he was the only living creature in the midst of silent hordes of contorted and decomposing dead. He became used to them, and even lost his curiosity. The carrion birds departed, and the rats starved and ate each other.

The task of disposing of so many corpses was too great for the military authorities to contemplate, and so it was that armies of soldiers lay undisturbed except by the grasses and shrubs that grew through their bones until, after the war, Allied authorities would arrive to try to identify thousand upon thousand of clean skeletons, most still clad in the remnants of their uniforms. Without a uniform, it is impossible to tell the nationality of a soldier's frame, and many an unidentifiable, incomplete and anonymous heap of fractured bones ended up in co-interment with those of former enemies, near monuments speciously engraved with the sentiment that 'Their Name Liveth For Evermore'.

In deference to such spectacular carnage it is perhaps perverse to dwell upon one person's death, but we are creatures so constituted that the passing of one friend or one acquaintance has a profounder effect than that of 100,000 strangers. If there is any metaphorical truth in the Jewish proverb that he who saves one life saves the whole world, then there is equal metaphorical truth in the proposition that when one person dies, the whole world dies with them.

Abdulhamid Hodja began to fall ill at roughly the time when the Allies were withdrawing from Gallipoli, but no one had seriously thought that he had only a few months in which to live.

On a day when new flowers were forcing themselves out of the land, Ayse Hanım, ragged and thin, made her way through streets that were eerily uncluttered, and came to the back door of Polyxeni's house, where she put her shoes into the niche in the wall. They were nearly worn out, and more often than not these days Ayse went barefoot in order to conserve them. She opened the door, called softly, and slipped inside.

Polyxeni, also thin and worn, was seated on the divan where the light from the window could illuminate her work. She was sewing a patch into a pair of shalwar. She gave a soft coo of pleasure, and said, 'Merhaba, merhaba,' without even looking up.

Ayse sat down near her old friend, and said, 'I am sorry, I have nothing to bring you, or I would have brought something.'

'No one has anything,' said Polyxeni. 'We are all living off thin air and hope. I don't even have a melon seed. If it wasn't for Philothei bringing things back from Rustem Bey, I don't know what we'd do.'

From the darkness of a corner, Great-Grandfather Socrates said, 'I'm ninety-four, you know.' In response to his croaking voice, Ayse got to her feet and went to kiss his hand, saying, 'Ah, Grandfather Socrates, may you be ninety-four for ever!'

'I think he always has been ninety-four,' observed Polyxeni. 'He has been for as long as I can remember. The shame of it is that he has so many memories, but nowadays he can't remember any of them. He is like an iron chest full of treasure, and the key's been lost.'

'It's good to live long,' said Ayse, sitting down and hanging her head. Polyxeni looked up from her stitching, and realised from the shaking of Ayse's shoulders that she was weeping. 'Oh, Ayse, what is it?' she asked, moving to put a comforting arm around her friend. 'What's happened?'

'The hodja,' said Ayse. 'My poor husband.'

'The hodja? Why, what is it?'

424

'He won't live long.'

'But he's not old!'

'There are many who died younger than him, and I don't just mean the soldiers.'

'A lot of women giving birth,' agreed Polyxeni, 'but not the men.'

'Oh, Polyxeni, he is very ill. I know it. What am I going to do?'

'What's the matter, though? He hasn't looked well for a long time, but you didn't say anything!'

'It's not an easy thing to say. He was never the same after they took the horse.'

'He's not dying because they took the horse?' Polyxeni was astounded. She had never heard of anyone dying of despair over a horse.

'Oh no, Polyxeni, it's much worse than that.'

'Tell me, Ayse, you must tell me.'

'It's embarrassing.'

'Embarrassing?'

'Oh, Polyxeni, please don't tell anyone, but it's . . . it's . . . the hodja can't piss.'

'He can't piss?'

'It's killing him. He is in such pain that the tears roll down his face all the time, but he won't cry out. His belly is swollen like a waterskin.'

'How long has he been like this?'

'It's just a few days, but it began a long time ago. He'd go out, and then come back in and say, "I don't seem to be able to get it all out," and then it got a bit worse, and he couldn't get it started, and he used to go out for hours and he'd just have to stand there trying to get a few drops out, and then he'd come back in and a few minutes later he'd have to go back out and try all over again. He'd say to me, "Wife, this is very tedious, I am becoming an old man," and he tried to laugh about it, but it wasn't funny. He tried drinking lots of water to sort of push the old water out, but it didn't work, and now he's even worse. I said to him, "Maybe someone's put a curse on you," and he said, "I have used every verse in the Koran that I can think of, I've written out the first sura and placed it on my belly, I've taken oil from the tomb of the saint and rubbed it in, but I still can't piss." He said, "God has decided that it's time," and I said, "You have served God faithfully all your life, so why is He giving you so much pain?" and the hodja didn't know what to say for a moment, and then he said, "I have been wondering the same thing. I think I have become unbeloved."'

Ayse held out her hand. 'Polyxeni, please, I want you to put this in front of the icon and ask the Mother of Jesus to help us. If God won't listen to the hodja and me, maybe He will listen to Mary Mother of Jesus.' Polyxeni saw that Ayse was offering her a small silver coin.

Polyxeni felt herself stabbed by the pain of compassion. She took the little mite and then gave it back to Ayse. 'The Mother doesn't need any coins,' she said gently, 'the Mother knows that you need this more than she does. In Heaven nobody spends any coins, and even the Mother can't spend it. The Mother will know that you wanted to give her the coin. I'll go to the church and kiss the icon, and ask her to help you, and the Mother will consider that you wanted to give her the coin.'

'Thank you,' said Ayse, her eyes full of tears. 'But are you sure? What if the Mother doesn't listen?'

'We should find a doctor,' said Polyxeni. 'Wouldn't a doctor know what to do?'

'All the doctors have gone. There is no one left. And they were all Christians, and I couldn't have paid them.'

'Perhaps there's a doctor in Smyrna.'

'It'll be too late, the hodja is already dying. He would die on the journey, and if we went to fetch someone he would be dead before we got back. Oh, Polyxeni, you would weep if you saw him. He is babbling, and his skin is turning yellow, and there are white crystals like salt all over it that I have to wipe off when his sweat dries, and his breath is foul and smells of piss, and . . . and . . .' Ayse hid her face in her hands.

'What, Ayse? What?'

'His eyes are bleeding. They were so kind and beautiful, everyone said so, but now they are full of blood.'

'I've got twelve children,' said Grandfather Socrates, and the women sighed and ignored him.

426

'What about Levon the Armenian? He is an apothecary, he will know exactly what to do.'

'He was taken away. They took all the Armenians away. You know they did.'

'Oh, I'd forgotten for a moment. Who could have known how it would be without them?'

Abdulhamid Hodja lay on his palliasse, drifting in and out of consciousness, the usual clarity of his mind obliterated by waves of agony. In truth, he had suffered more than his wife knew, because his was not a querulous and complaining nature, but a stoical one. All his life he had accepted that anything that happens is the will of God, and therefore one must learn acceptance, but in the face of his afflictions he had discovered a certain rebelliousness. He had questioned God a great deal in his moments of lucidity. He had endured headaches that were like red-hot rods inserted into the back of his head and his neck. He had become drowsy and disorientated, but unable to sleep. He had undergone a fit of convulsions that had utterly terrified him, and a recurring delusion of being eaten slowly by the Archangel Azrael that was even worse. Sometimes he had suddenly been unable to breathe at night, and had sat up quickly, fighting for breath as if there were no more air in the world. It was like having the invisible hands of demons around his throat. Sometimes his fingers had lost all feeling, and sometimes there were cramps that he could not dispel by any amount of twisting and contorting. Every now and then he had been blind and deaf for hours at a time, and had undergone the indignity of sudden and frequent diarrhoea. In these last hours, the pressure from the distension of his abdomen had caused him such extreme pain that he had decided to fight no longer. The torment from within his body was so appalling that if anyone had branded him on the face with an iron, he would not even have noticed it, and he began to fall in love with the prospect of death.

When Ayse returned from Polyxeni's house, and Polyxeni had gone to the church to talk to the Panagia, she found Abdulhamid Hodja very weak and very near the end. His face had sunken in over the bones, making his hooked nose seem greatly bigger than it was, and his face was like yellow paper. Ayse knelt beside him, along with her daughter Hasseki, who was rubbing her father's hands and sobbing softly. 'Ah, my tulip,' whispered the hodja. He lifted his hand feebly and beckoned to Ayse to draw close. She put her ear next to his lips, and he said, 'God has chosen me a vile and horrible death. I am sorry . . . that you have to see it.' He fell silent, and Ayse talked to him, sure that he was listening. 'If our sons come back from the war, I will give them your blessing,' she said.

'Ah, my tulip,' whispered the hodja.

'My husband,' said Ayse suddenly, 'is it true what some people say, that a woman has no soul and can't go to paradise?' She had been troubled by this question ever since it had become clear that her husband was fading away. She realised that she could not bear the thought of spending a separate eternity.

The hodja smiled weakly with his eyes closed, and squeezed her hand very lightly. 'Without you . . . it would not . . . it could not be paradise,' he whispered.

Ayse and Hasseki watched disbelievingly and with desolate hearts as he visibly began to die. They took one of his hands each, and kissed them. He spoke only one more time, when he briefly opened his blood-filled eyes: 'Hasseki,' he said, 'you have been a most excellent daughter.' To Ayse he said, 'Tulip, tulip, you are the best of all women. I shall go and tell it to God.'

Listening to him groan with agony, Ayse and Hasseki had the same thoughts, remembering Abdulhamid Hodja in his prime, when he wore his green cloak and the white turban wound about his fez, and a silver yataghan in his sash, when his beard was combed, and his black eyes were sharp like a bird's. They thought of him proudly riding about on the silvery Nilufer, with her polished brass breastplate engraved with a verse from the Koran, and the green ribbons with the tiny bells braided into her mane. 'He was a great horseman,' said Ayse softly. 'He was like no other. I am glad that I was put beside him in this life.'

Hasseki laughed tearfully. 'He collected tortoises in a sack and took them away from the vegetables. Who else would have done it?'

'We will have to do it,' said Ayse, 'and it will always remind us.'

Abdulhamid Hodja had sunk swiftly into a coma, and the women were watching him leaving. His breaths became more and more infrequent, and they held their own breath in agonised sympathy. As the intervals grew longer they could scarcely believe that any more would come. The suspense was unbearable. Then there was at last no more breath, and a low gurgling sound came from the hodja's throat.

'He's gone,' said Hasseki.

'Yes,' said Ayse. She seemed quite calm as she got to her feet, and then she went to the door and out into the evening. The nightingales and bulbuls had just begun to sing. Ayse numbly thought that she was going to be all right, but then the waves of grief began to surge up inside and push rhythmically at her guts. They were very like the contractions of birth. She held them back for a moment, but then could do so no longer. Out in the narrow street, clutching her head between her hands, she began to howl and wail, her clear and dolorous voice carrying over the rooftops and up the hillside, proclaiming her wretched-ness and misery to the empty sky. Up among the ancient tombs, the Dog cocked his head and listened, understanding that there must have been a death.

Two hours later Polyxeni called in at the house of Iskander the Potter, and spoke to his wife Nermin, asking her to request a favour of Iskander. The latter was virtually the only able-bodied Muslim man remaining in the town, and the message to him was that Ayse and Hasseki had been trying to dig a grave for Abdulhamid Hodja on their own. They had been defeated by the exhaustion of malnourishment, by stones, by darkness, by sorrow and by tree roots, and had gone home to sleep until dawn, when they intended to finish the grave and put the hodja's body into it, as decreed by law. Polyxeni had heard Ayse's cries, recog-nised her friend's voice, and arrived immediately to try to be of comfort, but Ayse had not wanted her to help in the digging of the grave, because it did not seem quite right for a Christian. Polyxeni had sat nearby, singing to them as they hacked at the hard earth of the forest floor, and now that they had given up for the night, she had conceived the idea of asking Iskander to help.

Iskander listened to the message that he received via his wife, and reflected that, much as he was reluctant to venture out, it would be an honour to dig the imam's grave. He reflected in addition that the merit would be greater if no one were told that he had dug it, and so he asked Nermin to tell Polyxeni that she should say nothing to Ayse.

Accordingly, he took a spade and an axe and went down by bright moonlight into the pine woods, returning two hours later, filthy, tired and satisfied.

Amazed and even frightened by the miracle of the fully excavated grave, Ayse and Hasseki wrapped Abdulhamid Hodja's wasted body in a white shroud, and carried it down on a litter, burying him with his Koran folded into his hands and Nilufer's brass breastplate under his head. After the war, when the stonemasons returned, a headstone was carved and painted in the form of a white turban wrapped about a fez.

There is some argument about whether or not it involved the intervention of angels, but there are still stories in that region about an imam who was such a saint that his grave dug itself in the night, and this story and the headstone are the only traces that remain.

72

Mustafa Kemal (16)

Mustafa Kemal believes that Germany is dragging the empire down into ruin, requisitioning troops and supplies that are desperately needed at home, and plotting to make Turkey into a colony. He believes that Enver Pasha has become a German poodle, and he writes furious and detailed letters to the Grand Vizier. He lectures the Minister of Foreign Affairs, denouncing German hegemony on the general staff. He goes to Sofia for a break, but returns to Adrianople to take command of the 16th Army Corps, a unit withdrawn from Gallipoli, and destined for the Caucasus in order to salvage Enver's disastrous campaign against the Russians. In Adrianople he receives a hero's welcome from the populace, who have been primed by his old comrade, Major Izzettin. Back in Istanbul, Mustafa Kemal's achievements at Gallipoli are sedulously left unmentioned and unlauded during the victory celebrations.

The new command is not the greatest job in the world, but at least Kemal has now been promoted to brigadier general, and become a pasha. He finds the armies at Diyarbekir in a desperate state, diseased and unsupplied, anarchic and miserable, and his requests to Istanbul are ignored. The Russians attack before he can get properly organised, and he is obliged to take part in a vicious battle in which he fights with the bayonet alongside his men. On his own initiative he then orders a retreat, gambling that the Russians will not follow. By the summer, his troops have been so transformed that they take Bitlis and Muş within five days, and drive the Russians out. He receives the Order of the Golden Sword. He writes to Corinne Lütfü, saying, 'What a pleasure it is to face fire and death among those that one esteems.' Then the Russians retake Muş.

That winter the situation of the troops once more becomes hopeless. They have no food or supplies for the ironical reason that they are operating in an area from which the Armenian population has been deported. There are no farmers, craftsmen or tradesmen left, and the place is a desert. To compound the situation, the Russian armies have driven before them several hundred thousand famished Muslim refugees, many of them Kurds. The Armenians and the Kurds have loathed each other for centuries, and, owing to the fact that there are many Armenian units and commanders in the Russian army, the same banal atrocities have been committed against the Kurds that the latter have always enjoyed committing against Armenians.

That winter, dressed in the rags of their summer uniforms, with their feet bound up in shreds of rags, Kemal's soldiers perish in blizzards and freeze to death in caves. The men are on one-third of normal rations, and there is nothing for the animals.

Mustafa Kemal is promoted again, and then his ragged army is saved by the Russian Revolution. The front stabilises, and the Russian army disintegrates under the management of proletarian soldiers' committees which churn out idiotic, pompous and turgidly prolix orders, and demote the officers to the ranks.

It is on this front that Kemal makes friends with Colonel Ismet, who will accompany Kemal for the rest of his career, and become President after him. Ismet is so opposite to Kemal in temperament as to be indispensable, but to begin with they get on very badly.

Now that the fighting on the Russian front has ceased, Mustafa Kemal establishes high standards in the officers' mess, and turns every mealtime into a symposium in which he can talk brilliantly and at length in his customary style. He starts to work out his thoughts on the emancipation of women, which he believes will have an improving effect on men. Meanwhile, a plot to overthrow Enver Pasha has been uncovered in Istanbul, and suspicion of complicity falls upon Mustafa Kemal, but it is unlikely that he has anything to do with it. Enver very shrewdly decides to send Kemal to take command in the Hejaz, where the British have successfully encouraged the Emir of Mecca to raise the Arabs in revolt and declare himself King of the Arabs. Enver and Kemal and the local commander decide, however, that Medina is strategically useless, and prepare to give it up, but this is vetoed in

Istanbul by the Grand Vizier, because the Caliphate cannot afford the disgrace of giving up Islam's second-most holy city. In any case, it is quite likely that T. E. Lawrence's Arabs will destroy the Turkish forces as they try to retreat. The plan is abandoned, and the Turkish commander in Medina devoutly refuses to withdraw, whatever happens. The Ottoman forces remain entrenched there until long after the war is over, refusing to give it up, and eating the animals which would have been their sole means of transport out of it.

In Istanbul, a plotter by the name of Yakup Cemil confesses under interrogation that the empire can only be saved if Enver Pasha is deposed and replaced by Mustafa Kemal as Minister of War and Commander-in-Chief. Upon hearing of this, the latter remarks, 'I would have accepted the two posts, but I would have had Yakup Cemil hanged first. I am not the type to come to power with the backing of such people.'

In Mesopotamia the British begin a series of spectacular successes under Generals Maude and Allenby, and Kut and Baghdad fall. Allenby pulls off some exceptionally brilliant and elaborate deceptions. Mustafa Kemal agrees to take command of the 7th Army under Marshal Falkenhayn, but it is clear that his intention is to obstruct Falkenhayn whenever possible, because he believes that the Germans ultimately want to oust the Ottomans from the Middle East, and take control of it themselves. He makes himself as awkward and quarrelsome as only he knows how, and insists upon taking command of all operations himself, with the Germans serving under him. Enver Pasha attempts compromises, but Kemal refuses even to meet the German commander, and angrily resigns, returning to him a sum in gold with which he says the German has been attempting to bribe him. Because he is penniless and needs money to get home, he sells his horses to his friend Çemal Pasha.

Back in Istanbul he refuses an appointment to command the 2nd Army, and installs himself in the Pera Palace Hotel. General Allenby takes Jerusalem, and the Ottomans retreat to a line north of Jaffa and Jericho. There is an apocryphal story that Enver and Kemal have an argument so violent that it nearly leads to a gunfight. Mustafa Kemal is asked to accompany the heir to the throne on an official visit to meet the Kaiser. He finds the Prince dreamy and strange, and has serious doubts as to his competence as future Sultan. Nonetheless, it occurs to him that he might be able to influence him, and tries to persuade him that the Germans will not win the war. The Prince receives his suggestions luke-warmly.

Mustafa Kemal meets the Kaiser, wrongly addressing him as 'Your Excellency', and manages to be his usual perverse, blunt and prickly self when dealing with the Germans. Back home in Istanbul he falls ill with a kidney infection, and the war has to go on without him. The Ottomans reinvade areas of the east that had been taken by Russia, partly to prevent Armenian massacres of Muslims. The Sultan dies, and is succeeded by the vague Prince, whilst Mustafa Kemal is being treated in a clinic in Vienna. His thoughts turn once again to the emancipation of women, and he writes that he is determined to bring the Turkish people up to his own level, rather than compromise by sinking to theirs. Before he is well, he is summoned back to Istanbul, but is delayed by an attack of the Spanish flu.

He has three audiences with the new Sultan Mehmet, and tries to persuade him to take over the army, but he demurs, and appoints Kemal to the command of the 7th Army in Palestine, where he will once again be under his Gallipoli commander, Otto Liman von Sanders. He finds his new army in a pitiable condition; there are British spies everywhere, and he frankly acknowledges that the local population can hardly wait for the British to arrive and drive out the Ottomans. He himself continues to be prostrated by his kidney infection.

General Allenby brilliantly defeats the 8th Army, and Kemal's 7th Army is forced to retreat as a consequence. The Ottoman army has by now become so demoralised that there are 300,000 deserters. The men have no summer clothes for the unbearable tempera-tures of the Jordan valley, and as usual their diet is execrable. Perhaps most terrible of all, the cherished myth of Islamic unity has been broken apart for ever, even though it will perhaps always survive as the ingenuous ghost of a conventional piety. The Ottoman soldiers find that the Arabs, now that they know who is going to win, have completely switched their loyalty to the British, and the

Bedouins descend ferociously upon them, committing the same incomprehensibly malicious atrocities against them as they had against everyone else when employed by the Sultan. Arabs have turned out to be not merely undependable, but treacherous.

Liman von Sanders attempts to reorganise and regroup, but it is impossible. Australian cavalry take Damascus, and naively install an Arab government that immediately provokes ungovernable riots. Von Sanders pays the savage Druzes to allow free passage to Germans fleeing north, and Kemal decides to go to Aleppo. It is impossible to organise the retreat of armies that no longer exist, and Kemal fulminates against everyone except himself. There is vicious streetfighting, and Mustafa Kemal beats off angry Arab attackers with his whip. He finds it ironic that he is being attacked by those he seeks to defend, and soon organises for his machine-gunners to thin the crowds, with dramatic and immediate efficacity. On his retreat from that town, the Arabs go on a looting spree, neighbour against neighbour, whooping and firing *feux de joie* into the air. Mustafa Kemal successfully defeats a series of British attacks as he withdraws, in what will be the very last engagements of the war.

He replaces Liman von Sanders as overall commander of the southern front. He is only thirty-seven years old, and the loyal core of his troops is still in place, battered and famished, guarding the long frontier that will mark the boundary of a new country. Among them is Ibrahim the Goatherd, who will one day be known as Ibrahim the Mad. He has marched thousands of miles, and has survived heat and cold, wounds, famine, disease, despair and shells. He is the spectre of his former self, emaciated and weak, his gums bleeding, and not a shred of his former uniform remaining. On his feet he wears the remains of a pair of boots that he took from an Indian soldier after the siege of Kut. He is unaware that in so doing he condemned that soldier to death, because the prisoners of war were subsequently to be marched by Arab and Kurdish escorts for two thousand miles in implacable heat, without transport, food, clothing or water. It was to be an exact recapitulation of what was happening to the Armenians, and in this case half of the prisoners would die en route, for the same reasons.

Ibrahim has often thought of deserting, but he does not know the way home, and in any case his sense of honour is too great. He has been profoundly disquieted to realise that it was not, after all, enough to be a Muslim, but he feels a new strength in the idea that now he is above all things a Turk. As peace descends upon the suddenly useless trench on the heights behind Aleppo, and the men take to sleeping above the parados, he dreams only of returning home and marrying Philothei, with whom he has had the misfortune to be in love since childhood, and who has been promised to him, and who has always been his destiny. He has a heavy necklace made of gold coins that he looted from an abandoned Armenian house, which he means to give to her. He has carried it for months, and never sold it even when he was starving. He does not know if Philothei is still alive, and she in her turn has had no news of her fiancé for four years.

She is still employed by Leyla Hanım, and these days she is capable of sitting in perfect stillness during empty hours, having perfected the kismetic art of waiting. All around her, Rustem Bey's extraordinary collection of clocks are synchronously effacing time, striking away the hours and ticking away the months. She is still beautiful, but these days her eyes glow with melancholy rather than ardour, and no longer does she sit in front of the mirror, as Leyla taught her, composing her face into ever greater forms of beauty. Nowadays, her inward eye is straining to envision things beyond the exiguous black horizon of sight.

73

I am Philothei (11)

I remember once that Ibrahim came to me and recited a verse that he had made, and he said that he had remembered it badly from a trader that came from Crete, and so he had had to change it to make it whole again. He recited it, and it went

> I kissed your red lips and my own turned red
> And I wiped my lips and my kerchief was dyed red
> And I washed it in the river and the river turned red
> And the red spread
> To the farthest shore and
> To the middle of the sea
> And an eagle flew down to drink it
> And his wings were dyed red
> And away he flew
> And he painted the sun
> And the whole moon.

He shrugged and said, 'It's an explanation of dawn and sunset.'
Then he said, 'Little bird, I have another verse for you, but it has to be whispered,' and I said, 'Whisper it then,' and he leaned towards me and he whispered another verse in my ear, and I closed my eyes, and I could feel his lips against my ear and the softness of them, and the gentleness of his breath, and this verse was

> Your lips are like sugar
> And your cheeks an apple
> Your breasts are paradise
> And your body a lily.
> O, to kiss the sugar
> To bite the apple

To reveal paradise
And open the lily.

I stood there with my eyes closed, hearing only the doves in the red pines, and it was only after a few moments that I understood the verse properly, and when I did, I felt the blood and the blushing rush to my face and my ears.

I was astonished that he had recited such a thing, and when I opened my eyes he had already gone, and I felt as if my whole body was burning, and I had to sit down.

74

Lieutenant Granitola's Occupation (1)

The column of soldiers marched wearily and out of step into Eskibahçe. At their head perspired Lieutenant Gofredo Granitola, distant relation of a distinguished Sicilian family, and late veteran of the battles of Isonzo and Caporetto. He and his men had tramped for several days, all the way from Telmessos, and they were not in the mood either for flirting or playing football, or, indeed, for playing mandolins and singing choruses from operas. They had been given a map that was not even notionally accurate, and had had the greatest difficulty in asking anyone directions. In the first place, not one of the soldiers knew any Turkish, and in the second place the civilian population ran away and hid at their every approach. On account of mass desertion from both the army and the labour battalions, the countryside was now plagued with bands of outlaws, Greeks, Circassians, Armenians and Turks happily competing in brigandage. As a consequence the people had learned to dread the very sight of an armed man, especially one in the remnants of a uniform. For lack of sensible advice, the soldiers had marched many unnecessary miles, and were by now hungry, blistered, thirsty, filthy, stinging with sunburn and more than disgruntled. 'This place had better be important,' observed Lieutenant Granitola to Sergeant Oliva, more than once, 'because if it turns out to be another little fleapit, I swear by the Virgin that I am going to have to shoot someone.'

They had been sent to Eskibahçe on the grounds that it looked like an important town on the map, and therefore ought to have a garrison in order to partake fully in the rights and privileges of a proper Italian occupation, and it was, then, with a sense of relief and pleasure that they passed the tilting whitewashed graves of the Muslims and emerged from the pine forest to behold, at the entrance to the town, the neoclassical drinking fountain and watering house newly and munificently bestowed upon the town in 1919 by Georgio P. Theodorou, for the relief and benefit of all.

The troops smiled with benign fatigue at an old woman in the shade of her doorway, who, petrified with consternation, suddenly stopped whirling her pancake around its stick, and let it fall to the floor. She picked it up, ran inside the house and out of the back door. Into the meydan she went, pancake still in hand, spreading word of the invasion.

'Halt the men and fall them out,' Granitola instructed his sergeant. 'We'll take half an hour.'

The men came to a shambolic and exhausted halt, and stood at ease whilst the sergeant issued his instructions: half an hour only, drink plenty of water, have a wash, and no wandering off, or, by the Virgin, he would come down on them like a thunderbolt from God His Very Self, and he'd send them home to their mothers with their balls torn off and stuffed up their arses. These threats from Sergeant Pietro Oliva were taken in good part by the men. He was a tall man with humorous dark brown eyes, black hair that receded from a high forehead and the learned air of a Florentine priest.

A bellyful of water and half an hour's rest on the hillside above the pines restored the men's morale to the point where they felt revived, and by then it was almost unnecessary to take them into the town, because the town had come to them. They found themselves surrounded by a silent and intensely curious group of old men and tiny children, as well as a few women who, for decency's sake, were holding their scarves across their noses and mouths. There were also the distorted shapes of a few younger men, those who had been maimed in the war, and been fortunate or resolute enough to find their way home. Dozens of pairs of brown eyes watched the soldiers intently and unblinkingly, with much the same pointless attention with which people watch dogs copulating.

Word had got about that some proper soldiers had arrived, who were not brigands at all, and in truth the townspeople were glad to see them. All but two of their gendarmes had been called up during the war, many of them to fight with resolution and success at Gallipoli, and since then it had been very difficult to get any protection from outlaws. Iskander the Potter had been called out many a time, on account of his ownership of the magnificent gun made for him in Smyrna by Abdul Chrysostomos, but much to his frustration, it had always been too late, and he had never actually had the opportunity to shoot anyone with it. Thus far he had used it for hunting, and, after every firing of his kiln, he had also had the satisfaction of setting up the cracked or otherwise failed pots upon the wall, and blasting them to fragments. If there was an outlaw to be shot, it seemed that Rustem Bey always got there first, as if luck had a snobbish deference for rank.

Granitola surveyed the onlookers and ordered his sergeant: 'Make them go away. They make me feel like something grotesque in a museum.'

Sergeant Oliva got up from the shade of his thorn oak, and waved his arms in the faces of the people, exclaiming '*Via! Via! Vaffanculo!* Sons of whores! Bitches! Pigpricks!'

The people, who could clearly discern Oliva's good nature, in spite of his attempt at ferocity, moved back a little, but stirred no further. 'They think you're swatting flies,' observed Lieutenant Granitola, drily, 'and I feel that they don't understand your pleasantries and compliments.' With an air of dutiful resignation the Lieutenant got to his feet, and told the sergeant to call the men together and form ranks, so that he could address them.

'Right, men,' he said, walking up and down with his hands behind his back, 'listen in. We are going to go into the centre of the town to occupy the square, after which we will have to set about finding billets and organising supplies. From this point you will march smartly and in a proper military manner, in order to create the correct military impression. The correct impression is one of implacable efficiency, undeviating purpose and indomitable courage. You will not look from side to side, you will not gawp at sights of interest, and when we arrive in the square you will halt smartly and ground arms smartly. Everything must be done to create the impression of soldiers with a decisive air of good order, who mean business. I am not expecting any trouble, but you must be on the watch for it, so I am expecting you to be on the alert at all times. Any questions?'

441

There were no questions forthcoming, and so he nodded to Sergeant Oliva, who bawled '*Attenti!*' and forthwith the soldiers were marched into the town followed by rangy dogs, prancing children who sloped sticks over their shoulders in ape of rifles, and old folk and *blessés de guerre* who tried to keep up.

The meydan turned out to be only a few yards away, around the next corner at the bottom of the town, whilst the rest of the town spread up the natural amphitheatre formed by the hillsides. Consequently, the soldiers arrived under the planes with the disappointing and anti-climactic feeling of not having had a chance to create the proper military impression. They stood at ease listening to the lieutenant telling them to wait under the planes whilst he got things sorted out, aware that he did not really have any idea what he was supposed to do next, and enjoying his confident display of bluff. It is always a pleasure for the common soldier to observe the discomfiture of officers.

As the men fell out and began their occupation by occupying the stone benches under the trees, Sergeant Oliva approached Lieutenant Granitola and said, 'Permission to speak, sir.'

'Permission granted, Sergeant.'

'There are two armed gendarmes approaching, sir. Shall we shoot them?' He asked this question with mischievous serious-ness, knowing quite well that Granitola would say what he did, which was: 'Certainly not, Sergeant. Our instructions are to work with the normal civil authorities as much as possible. We will make them welcome.'

'As you say, sir,' responded the sergeant, affecting surprise at such signal lack of bellicosity.

The two gendarmes, the weakest and oldest of the town's former detachment, who consequently had been spared call-up, were feeling outnumbered and trepidatious, although no one had ever doubted their courage. They had no idea who these troops were, and had certainly received no information or instructions from the governor or anyone else. They had not even heard that the Italians had occupied Antalya.

'What shall we do?' the old one was asking the even older, who replied through gritted teeth, 'Clench your arse, and don't even fart, in case you shit yourself.'

When the two gendarmes came face to face with the two Italians, there was an initial mismatch of manners, for the Turks performed a respectful Ottoman salute, and the Italians held out their hands to be shaken. When these manoeuvres failed, the situation was reversed, and the Italians attempted clumsy versions of the Ottoman salute, whilst the Turks awkwardly held out their hands. This led, of course, to laughter, and in this way the ice was providentially broken. Before long there was fraternisation, and from the time that the Italians arrived to the time that they left, the two gendarmes had not a clue as to who the invaders were, knowing only that they were proper soldiers and were quite friendly, and were very good shots.

The initial point of contact occurred when professional interest caused the gendarmes to want to take a look at the weapons of the Italian soldiers, and the Italian soldiers to want to take a look at the pistols of the gendarmes. There was much resort to dumb-show as instructions about operation were exchanged, and from then on there was never any trouble between them.

One of the gendarmes had the very good idea of sending a small boy to fetch their aga, Rustem Bey, who would surely know what to do about the new arrivals. The latter was in the haremlık of his house, cleaning his hunting rifle whilst Leyla Hanım sang to him a lullaby which she had composed on the oud. She had recently come to realise that she would probably never have children, and so she sang her new song with a certain affecting lachrimosity. 'It would be good if that music could be written down,' said Rustem Bey, 'otherwise it will be forgotten, and that would be a shame.'

Rustem Bey was much thinner than he had been in the years before the Great War, because times were hard even for him, and he still spent much of his time out in the mountains hunting, an occupation that was nowadays especially dangerous because of all the bandits that infested them. Nonetheless, he created an instantly striking impression upon the Italians when he came down into the meydan. He was dressed in a very well-cut suit that had been made for him by a Greek tailor in Smyrna, and to this Western garb he had added a red satin sash to accommodate his silver pistols and yataghan. In his right hand he carried a silver-topped cane. He wore polished knee-high riding boots, and on his head he wore a maroon fez, well brushed. With the exception of his waxed moustache, he was clean-shaven, and smelled of new lemon cologne. Despite this refined appearance, he was also very sunburned, had a soldierly bearing, and was clearly strong and fit. He was every inch a fine Ottoman gentleman, and Lieutenant Granitola immediately felt both respectful of him and at ease.

Rustem Bey conscientiously shook hands first with Lieutenant Granitola, then with Sergeant Oliva and the two corporals, then with every one of the thirty soldiers, greeting each with a polite 'Hoş geldiniz'. All of them felt as though they had been cere-moniously honoured, and wished that they knew how to reply.

Watched by nearly everyone in the town, Rustem Bey conducted a kind of negotiation with Granitola. 'Who are you?' he asked, in Turkish, and receiving no response other than perplexity, he said, 'Ismim Rustem Beyefendi.' He tapped his chest as he told them his name, repeating it, 'Rustem Beyefendi.'

'Ah!' exclaimed Granitola. 'Your name is Rustem Beyefendi? Ah, yes, very good. My name is Lieutenant Gofredo Granitola, Lieutenant Gofredo Granitola. *Capisci?*'

'Capisci,' repeated Rustem Bey.

'No, no, not capisci. Lieutenant Gofredo Granitola.'

'Granitola?'

'*Si, si,* Granitola.'

'Ah, Granitola.' Rustem Bey beamed with enlightenment.

The sergeant pointed to his own chest, and said, 'Oliva,' sensibly sparing the details of his rank and his other names. 'Oliva,' repeated Rustem Bey, who then went through the same ritual with every one of the soldiers. He then stood back and, pointing to each soldier in turn, repeated their names from memory.

'The man is a phenomenon, Sergeant,' whispered Granitola.

'Certainly is, sir,' said Oliva, who, like all the other soldiers, was profoundly impressed by this mnemonic feat.

'You should have been a diplomat,' said Granitola to Rustem Bey, knowing perfectly well that the latter would not understand.

'Are you Greek?' asked Rustem Bey. He used the Turkish word 'Yunanlı', however, and received no intelligent response. He pointed to himself and said, 'Ottoman', and then changed this to

444

'Turk'. He swept his hand to indicate the assembled soldiers, and then raised both hands in an interrogatory gesture of surmise.

'Ah,' exclaimed Sergeant Oliva, who had suddenly understood the question, '*Italiani.*'

'*Italiani,*' repeated Rustem Bey, enlightened but at the same time mystified. He was wondering what on earth a platoon of Italian soldiers was doing in Eskibahçe. It did give him a way forward, however. '*Est-ce que vous parlez français?*' he enquired.

This produced an extraordinary effect on Granitola who suddenly perceived that all of his difficulties were about to be relieved. '*Mais oui, je parle français,*' he said, adding snobbishly, '*tout le monde parle français.*'

'*C'est la langue universelle de la civilisation, n'est-ce pas?*' said Rustem Bey drily, raising an eloquent eyebrow. '*Je l'ai appris un peu pendant le service militaire. J'étais officier, et c'était plus ou moins obligatoire.*'

In truth, neither man spoke very good French. Rustem Bey had had the misadventure of being taught by someone with a very strong southern accent, so that all the 'n' sounds arrived with the addition of a hard 'g'. '*Je reviens lendemain*' would come out as '*je revieng lendemeng*', and all the vowels would arrive in the fresh air appropriately and correspondingly modified. Similarly, Granitola had never advanced beyond the pleasantries necessary for attending officers' parties with one's allies, and both men had forgotten most of what they had learned. Over the months of their friendship, the two men succeeded in engendering a private language which both of them sincerely believed to be French, and for the rest of his life Granitola would horrify occasional French interlocutors with the fluent but bizarre jargon rendered in the heavy Provençal accent that he had unwittingly co-generated with Rustem Bey.

Leyla Hanım, of course, actually could speak some Italian, since dialects of it were known in the Ionian islands of her birth, but she was never able to employ it. As a matter of policy she sedulously avoided any indication that she was not from the Caucasus. She seethed with longing and frustration, and was only relieved of it when the Italians finally departed.

On this night, however, Rustem Bey led the Italian soldiers to the town's khan, a pleasant square of bare rooms surrounding a shady courtyard. It was eminently suitable as a temporary barracks, its only inconvenience being that travellers expected to be able to use it as usual, and could not be dissuaded from unpacking their bedrolls and settling down to snore the night away even in the midst of rooms full of soldiers. The latter, however, enjoyed the custom of sharing food with travellers, and many savoury items passed their lips that they would remember with pleasure, and try to induce their wives to recreate.

Because it was the first night, Rustem Bey did his duty, and had waterpipes and foodstuffs that he could not truly spare sent down from his house. Because it was the custom with new arrivals, Rustem Bey doggedly sat in silence among the soldiers, fulfilling the obligations of hospitality, and they in their turn sat doggedly and waited for him to go, fulfilling equally their side of the obligation. The waterpipes went round and round, and eventually even those who were frightened of Turkish microbes had a few puffs on it. They noticed that Rustem Bey had his own mouthpiece, which he inserted into the pipe after removing the communal one. The smoke was cool, sweet and aromatic, it filled one with a gentle pleasure, and by mid-evening it was impossible for the weary men to remain awake any longer. No one saw Rustem Bey leave, because he did not depart until all the foreigners had nodded off.

He went home proud of having done his duty, proud of having lived up to the town's expectations of him, proud of having been able to use his French, and pleased to have had an interesting day. He turfed the uncomplaining Pamuk off the bed, and woke Leyla Hanım by tickling her lips and eyelashes with a feather. They made love languidly, and afterwards, as he lay listening to the nightingales, he said to Leyla, 'I am going to have to get more mouthpieces for the waterpipes, to present to the soldiers.'

A little while later, apropos of nothing, and not even sure that Leyla was awake to hear him, he said, 'I am mostly a happy man.' It was the first time he had ever thought it or said it.

75

Mustafa Kemal (17)

Karatavuk in Gallipoli and Ibrahim in Aleppo share the strange
limbo that descends upon an army that is still in existence
but whose government has surrendered. Military routine continues, but no one knows what it is all for any more, and some
soldiers cannot look each other in the eye, as if suspecting themselves of guilt for the defeat. Others start to chafe, carrying out
orders sloppily, and losing their fear of their officers. They talk
about going home, about how this might be accomplished, about
whether or not there might be transport. There is a steady trickle
of desertion now that it has become pointless to be a soldier, and
much of the army demobilises haphazardly and unofficially. Many
of those taking their weapons with them will simply become
bandits in the interior, further exacerbating the misery of the
population. Pay is not coming through, and the diet continues
to be meagre beyond endurance. Some soldiers steal from the
civilian population, and others beg.

The collapse of the Ottoman Empire has been brought about
by the defeat of Bulgaria, because this has opened up the possibility of an easy Allied invasion on a long front, whilst the bulk
of the army is still irretrievably far away in the Caucasus and in
Syria. The Grand Vizier, Tâlat Pasha, announces, 'We've eaten
shit,' and resigns. The government of Enver Pasha and the 'Young
Turks' falls at last, and Mustafa Kemal is disappointed not to be
appointed to the new Cabinet. The British impose harsh conditions upon the new government, and Enver and his former
colleagues escape to Germany. The Ottomans realise too late that
the British do not share their assumption that there will be no
military advances into Ottoman territory, and Mosul is occupied,
breaking an agreement that the British had made two days previously. This is the new era of the fight for Turkish independence,
because the commander of the Ottoman 6th Army begins secretly

to accumulate weapons and supplies when he realises what is happening. In Syria, Mustafa Kemal finds that he is in charge of a border that does not officially exist on any modern maps, since it is defined by the ancient and indefinable border of the kingdom of Cilicia. The British announce that they intend to occupy Aleppo, and Mustafa Kemal takes steps to resist any incursion into İskenderun. He is not pleased when told to desist by the government, and is recalled to Istanbul. In the meantime, he too has started to make preparations for resistance. His successor sets about removing essential supplies into the interior, where the Allies cannot sequester them. On every front, Ottoman commanders, as if knowing what is to come, set about gathering and organising supplies and munitions.

The French occupy Adana, in late 1918, and immediately set the cat among the pigeons. The Ottoman Empire has asked for an armistice, but it has not surrendered. It is weary and economically ruined, it is inconceivable that it has any fight left in it, but the victors have yet to become fully cognisant of the fantastic obstinacy of the Turks. Now that foreign troops are beginning to occupy its territory, it is inevitable that resistance will be organised, and a pattern begins to emerge: as the authorities of the empire progressively capitulate, and accede more and more to the Allies' demands, resistance originates more and more from a loose coterie of dissident army officers. The empire begins to divide, but it will take a while for Mustafa Kemal and his brother officers to fire up the abject population. In this they are greatly helped by the French, who unleash detachments of Armenian volunteers upon the population of Adana. These volunteers set about exacting revenge upon the locals, and resistance predictably commences. All over Anatolia, Ottoman weapons stores that are under Allied guard begin to have armaments smuggled out of them.

In Istanbul, Mustafa Kemal surveys the Allied warships in the harbours and becomes depressed. He had suffered months of insomnia and sacrificed tens of thousands of men at Gallipoli in order to prevent this very thing. He is downcast, but at the same time entertains the hope that one day soon he will be head of a government that will put all this to rights and end the succession of humiliations. He rents a house from an Armenian at Osmanbey, conveniently close to the nexus of political life, and conveniently far from his mother.

The occupying French and British troops freely antagonise each other and the local population in Istanbul. The French are just setting into motion a petulant foreign policy which has remained steadfastly unchanged ever since, and whose sole object is to obstruct and irritate the Anglo-Saxon world as much as possible, even when that is against French interests. The Italian troops are pleasant to everyone, but the Italian government is plotting to frustrate Greek ambitions to reclaim territory that was anciently Greek. The British and French have a vague under-standing with the Greeks that lends wings to this ambition. There are Greek troops in Istanbul, who have been ecstatically welcomed by the vast Greek population. For those such as Mustafa Kemal, this is most worrying of all, because everyone knows that the Greeks yearn to regain the ancient capital of Byzantium.

Astute Turkish politicians, however, begin to appreciate just how war-weary the Allies are, and how easy it might be to exploit their divisions. Mustafa Kemal throws himself into full-time manoeuvring, but because the politicians are incapable of mutual cooperation, it is in fact the general staff of the armed forces that becomes the focus of resistance to the Allies, and in particular that group of nationalist officers of whom Mustafa Kemal is to become the leader.

The Greek Prime Minister, Eleftherios Venizelos, submits a memorandum in which Greece lays claim to Thrace and to western Anatolia. He proposes a voluntary exchange of Turkish and Greek populations. The idea seems terribly sensible, as if it is a perfectly acceptable idea that the lives of hundreds of thou-sands of innocent individuals should be arbitrarily disrupted in the interests of nation-building. In Istanbul, the Greek Orthodox patriarch announces on behalf of the Greek population that it is no longer Ottoman, and declares union with Greece. Unsurprisingly, Turkish societies for the defence of national rights begin to proliferate all over Turkey. The Italians decide to frustrate the Greeks, and land troops in Antalya. Uniquely among the Allies, the Italian policy is to butter up the Turkish population at every possible opportunity, and treat respectfully with Ottoman emissaries.

Under Allied authority the Greek government sends soldiers to occupy Smyrna, and ultimately another war will be sparked off. Instead of going home, Karatavuk and Ibrahim will find themselves embroiled in a campaign which will be marked particularly by its dishonour and viciousness. Back in Eskibahçe, where there is now a small detachment of Italian troops, the lovely Philothei, more melancholy than ever, still yearns for the return of her fiancé, believing, as so many girls do, that life does not truly begin until one is a bride. She knows that when he returns she will have to become a Muslim, but this prospect has little meaning for her, as she will still be able to leave little offerings in front of the icon of the Panagia Glykophilousa, and it has always been the pattern for a woman to take her husband's faith, and there have been certain Muslim and Christian families in Eskibahçe that have customarily intermarried since memory began. She is comforted by Drosoula, who talks of nothing but hope, and by Leyla Hanım, who tries to force her to learn to play the oud, thrusting it into her hands and explaining how to use the cherrywood plectrum. Philothei resolutely refuses, forbidden by her own gentleness from explaining that in common opinion hereabouts, the only kind of woman who plays the oud is a whore.

Philothei has long ago ceased to wear a veil, because unhappiness has reduced the joys of vanity and, apart from the tatterdemalion Italian soldiers who awake from their perpetual siesta under the plane trees of the meydan in order to blow her kisses that she scornfully disdains, there are no men left in the place who might become quarrelsome on account of her beauty.

The Allied occupation of Istanbul proceeds with comic effect. The British and the French continue to irritate both each other and the populace, and the Italians continue to be kind to everyone. The latter have been promised the Smyrna region, but they know from bitter experience in Libya that it isn't easy to occupy Ottoman territory. It takes fewer men and less trouble just to establish a zone of influence, and they astutely choose the role of protecting the Turks against Greek ambition, which is to take the western coast, and create Greater Greece. The Ottoman government is alarmed by the presence of Greek troops and warships in Istanbul, where a very substantial proportion of the population is Greek.

Mustafa Kemal throws himself into the demoralising and complicated machinations required to lever him into a position of power. He is convinced that only he can lead the Turks to national independence. He exploits contacts in the press, and has fruitless interviews with the Sultan. He plots to obstruct the appointment of a new and uncongenial Grand Vizier.

The British persuade the Ottoman government to take action against those officials and officers who have been implicated in war crimes, such as the death marches of Armenians and British prisoners of war, and the deportations of west-coast Greeks in 1914. This is a good opportunity to get rid of Enver Pasha's old cronies from the Committee of Union and Progress, the Young Turks who are not quite so young any more, and many of whom have blood on their hands. Mustafa Kemal is not arrested, and the Italian ambassador offers to protect him, should the British decide to exile him. In any case, he has never been implicated in any war crimes, and his military career has been nothing but distinguished. The Sultan checks the legal validity of the death sentences with the Sheikulislam, and the executions begin. Mustafa Kemal enters into full-time plotting with other nationalist officers; their plan is to get rid of the Allies in the entire Turkish heartland.

The nationalists contrive to obstruct the demobilisation and disarmament of the Ottoman army, and to retain sympathisers in high office. The gendarmerie mysteriously gets bigger as the army gets smaller. An officer named Kâzim Karabekir, another child of Destiny, calls in on Mustafa Kemal to sound him out about the idea of forming a national government in eastern Anatolia, in defiance, if necessary, of the government in Istanbul. 'It's an idea,' says Kemal. There are dozens of like-minded officers waiting for the right moment.

The Italians move in on western Anatolia, officially in order to put an end to brigandage, but really to get there before the Greeks. Ottoman Societies for the Defence of National Rights spring up like toadstools, and violence increases between rival ethnicities. Prince Abdürrahim sets off on a conciliation mission, and is welcomed by Muslims in Smyrna. In Antalya and Konya the cynical Italians, who also happen to be the only occupying force with any sense, turn out their own soldiers to greet him with full honours. Whilst the Prince is there, news comes in of the Greek landing at Smyrna. The royal attempts at peacemaking are boycotted everywhere by Christians, who do not want peace. In Pontus, on the south coast of the Black Sea, where the disappeared Armenians are being replaced by Greek refugees from communist Russia, the Greeks are demanding independence. The Muslims, many of them also refugees from Russia and the Caucasus, would rather die fighting than submit to Greeks and Armenians. Their bandit chiefs inaugurate a campaign of terror against the local Christians. The British make token efforts to restore order, but they lack the will to do it properly. They are beginning the long process of realising that to be the world's police force and to have the largest empire in the history of the world is expensive, tiresome and unrewarding.

Mustafa Kemal is appointed by the Sultan to investigate Greek complaints and prevent the formation of soviets in the 9th Army. His powers are so great that the Sultan has effectively appointed him the military and civil commander of eastern Anatolia. Nothing could be better for Mustafa Kemal. The 9th Army is large, powerful, well equipped, a long way from Istanbul and in exactly the right place. The Sultan presents him with a gold watch. Kemal is just about to go, when the Greeks land at Smyrna.

The Greeks have been given permission to do so by Presidents Wilson and Clemenceau, and Prime Minister Lloyd George. The Allied intention is to use one Ally, Greece, to frustrate another Ally, the Italians. Venizelos, the Greek Prime Minister, really wants to annex western Anatolia permanently, to accomplish what the Greeks have always referred to as 'The Big Idea'. It almost amounts to the rebuilding of Byzantium. In the British government, Lloyd George, sanguine and ignorant, is the only one who thinks that the Greek landing is a good thing.

The landing goes disastrously wrong, and within a few days many Turks have been killed by Greek troops and rioting Greek civilians. After a few days Aristeides Stergiadis arrives and takes control. He is a tough and principled man with an extraordinary sense of fair play, so that local Greeks routinely accuse him of being pro-Turk, but even he cannot control the Bashi-Bazouks and renegade soldiers in the interior, nor repair the intercommunal damage done by the fiasco of the landing. Stergiadis offends the local bigwigs mainly by refusing to go to their dinner parties. He has to cope with an anomalous situation in which a British general in Istanbul is technically in command of the Greek army, even though he isn't, in a place which is technically still under the sovereignty of the Sultan, but is actually under Greek rule.

The Allies inform the Ottoman government of the landing only the day before it happens, and Mustafa Kemal finds everyone in a state of outraged disbelief. An Italian occupation might have been acceptable, but a Greek one is intolerable. It puts steel into the hearts of Mustafa Kemal and everyone like him. The British hesitate before granting him a travel permit.

Before he goes, his ship is inspected for smuggled goods, and Mustafa Kemal says, 'We are not taking contraband or weapons, but faith and determination.'

Back in Eskibahçe, a little strength and determination is rekindling in the inhabitants, along with the return of some of its menfolk, who are beginning to arrive from all directions, starving, ragged and bootless. Many of them are deserters, and others are from units that have somehow dissolved in the general chaos. Some of them say that they can't stay long, they've got to find Mustafa Kemal. Karatavuk's brother comes back, provoking wails of joy from their mother, Nermin, who immediately runs to tell Ayse and Polyxeni.

Ayse has been reduced to penury by the death of Abdulhamid Hodja. She does not have his skill in cultivation, and, worse than this, she has very little hope. 'I am waiting to die,' she says, 'and I pray it might be soon.' She has been living off the charity of her friends, who also have nothing. Even Ayse, however, is affected by the arrival of the long lost, and casts around for something positive to do. She finds a pot of whitewash in the corner of Nilufer's empty stable, and she has a good idea. She collects twenty large stones and paints them white.

One by one she takes them down to Abdulhamid's grave, and lays them around it to make a border.

She has another idea. She goes to fetch the brass ornaments and the blue beads and the green ribbons. She rubs the verdigris off the brass with vinegar, and takes Abdulhamid's spade from its hook on the wall.

She overturns a few spadefuls of earth, and buries Nilufer's accoutrements in her husband's grave. She stands over it for a few moments, leaning on the spade to catch her breath, feeling weak and dizzy. She reflects that by now Abdulhamid must be nothing other than ochre bones. When she has recovered she kneels down and whispers into the earth so that he can hear her clearly. 'My lion,' she says. She thinks about how she is going to continue, because one has to be economical when addressing the deceased. 'I expect that Nilufer is dead by now,' she says. 'I've brought you her things, and now you can ride her in Heaven.'

Ayse puts her ear to the earth, and listens.

76

Lieutenant Granitola's Occupation (2)

Whilst the war between Greece and the rebel forces of Mustafa Kemal unrolled elsewhere, Lieutenant Granitola's platoon of Italians settled into their occupation of Eskibahçe.

The Lieutenant was initially much vexed by the problem of how he was supposed to communicate with headquarters, which was at a great distance, at the end of a very bad road that was infested with bandits. It was not good to feel so completely cut off from the rest of the army, without the slightest idea of what was happening in the great world, without a telephone line, and no assurance of supplies.

Rustem Bey solved this problem by proposing that tradesmen and other citizens wishing to travel back and forth to Telmessos should guide and feed a section of the occupying soldiers, in return for their protection on the journey. Upon arrival, the soldiers would report to base, collect pay, orders and supplies, and then escort the traders and travellers back again. The problem with this system was that pack animals had been conscripted and killed at the same rate as human beings during the Great War, and there was an intractable shortage of camels and mules. There were not enough left from which to breed, and those which had been bred in the war's aftermath were only just maturing to the age when they could be usefully employed. The only person in the town who still had a donkey was Ali the Snowbringer, and since it was at present impossible to go safely to the mountains to fetch ice, he and his donkey now found a new role which certainly saved his family from desperate straits. Similarly it was now possible for Mohammed the Leech Gatherer and Stamos the Birdman to resume their vocations, although there were few doctors left to purchase leeches, and few folk who could afford to splash out on anything as frivolous as a pet bird. Rustem Bey lent two old but serviceable horses to the trains, and often went on the journeys himself, since he liked to ride, and enjoyed the adventures that were often entailed. In addition, although he was a modernising Turk, he still had ancient mores deeply ingrained in his psyche, and he felt morally obliged to protect those who were beneath him. There was perhaps also a part of him that realistically knew that his position of privilege could not endure unless he was seen very publicly to deserve it, and those such as Ali the Snowbringer certainly felt great relief if they heard that Rustem Bey was to be part of the escort.

For Rustem Bey the Italian occupation was probably the golden age of his life, because for the first time he had a friend in the town who assumed equality with him. Whereas Leyla Hanım had filled out more than one half of what was missing in his life, in Lieutenant Granitola he found a true comrade. Granitola was himself a snob, and it was natural and inevitable for him to befriend unselfconsciously the most important person he could find in the whole community.

Lieutenant Gofredo Granitola was a slim man of average height, but his habit of authority made him seem taller than he really was. He wore an exiguous military moustache, and on his left cheek he bore the neatly angled scar of a bayonet wound that gave him the romantic air of a gentleman pirate. He liked to be smart at all times, believing that this was good for the morale of his men, and had achieved some notoriety in the Austrian campaign for shaving punctiliously at dawn even under shellfire, when expecting an imminent assault. He had kept his boots polished even when the soles had detached themselves. He had been decorated for gallantry twice, and been presented to the King, but he had failed to be promoted on account of his sedulous cultivation of the art of offending military superiors that he considered to be socially otherwise. If not for this, he could by now have expected to have become a lieutenant colonel. He had, however, no intention of staying in the army after the death of his father and the entailment of the family estates, but envisaged for himself a career in politics. He did indeed join the Fascist Party in 1926, only to secede quietly from it in 1930, having scotched his prospects by being scornfully rude to Roberto

456

Farinacci at a ball. Thereafter he made wine, travelled to stay with Rustem Bey in the new republic of Turkey, and had children with a variety of mistresses until his life was abbreviated by a misdirected Allied bomb in 1943.

Initially, the friendship between Granitola and Rustem Bey came about because of the necessity of feeding the Italian soldiers, who for a while were obliged to live off bulghur wheat and olives, supplemented by the few fish that they could purchase from Gerasimos the Fisherman, husband of Drosoula, and father of Mandras. Granitola mentioned the problem of meat to Rustem Bey one evening when they were sharing a waterpipe in the khan, and the latter proposed that the only solution was to go hunting. Granitola had already created a small flock of military chickens by giving the escorts money to buy them in the market at Telmessos. These chickens, each with a name and a rank, now lived by pecking about in the courtyard of the khan, which they quickly reduced to an inglorious dust bath.

Eggs were not quite enough to keep the men happy, however, and so it was that Rustem Bey and Granitola set out into the wilderness very early one morning armed with two scatterguns, and with Rustem Bey's pet partridge dangling from his saddle in a wickerwork cage. Granitola had never experienced this method of hunting before, and he was very intrigued when Rustem Bey tied the bird to a bush in the middle of a relatively clear space, scattered some seed for it to browse on, scattered more seed at a safe distance from it, and then retired to a place of concealment. 'Please don't shoot the tame partridge,' Rustem Bey told him. 'They are hard to replace, and I am quite fond of it.'

The method certainly worked, since one could often get two or three birds at once by waiting for them to bunch up. However, it was rare to get very many birds, and certainly not enough to feed a whole platoon, so Granitola had to introduce a rota system. This naturally led to the kind of griping so enjoyed by soldiers, since soldier B would complain of being given a pigeon when soldier A had been given a partridge the week before.

More of a problem from Granitola's point of view was that the patient Turkish method was too boring. He ached with tedium as he and Rustem Bey waited motionless, often prone upon the ground, covered over with brush, for hours at a time. One day he proposed to Rustem Bey that they should try the Italian method.

'*Et qu'est-ce que c'est, la méthode italieng?*' asked Rustem Bey in his egregious Provençal accent.

'We walk about, keeping ourselves fairly well concealed, and when the birds fly overhead, we shoot them down.'

'It isn't possible to shoot flying birds,' said Rustem Bey firmly. 'Nobody does that.'

'In Italy, that's how we do it.'

'I find it impossible to believe. Why would anyone choose a method so difficult?'

'But it isn't difficult. It's just a technique.'

'I would like to see it,' said Rustem Bey sceptically.

Rustem Bey did see it shortly afterwards. Lieutenant Granitola spotted a duck flying towards them, and dropped it out of the sky with such precision that it landed at their feet, stone dead.

Rustem Bey's reaction was initially a curious one. He became angry. It seemed to him to be very bad manners to controvert one's host so curtly. He felt that Granitola should have had the good manners to miss a couple of times first. He also felt a childish fury at having been proved wrong at all; since he was the aga, he did not inhabit a world where it was possible for him to be wrong with any great frequency, and being wrong was not something he was ever likely to have to get used to. He walked away suddenly, and vehemently smoked a cigarette with his back turned to Granitola, who was by now feeling frightened and disturbed. All that Granitola could think was 'Holy Maria, I've offended a Turk.' He knew that one can fight with Turks, but one seldom gets away with offending them.

When the cigarette was finished, Rustem Bey ground the stub into the stones with his foot, paused a minute, and turned about. He was clearly still angry, because his face was glassy with hostility, and his eyes were glittering. He had managed to conquer himself, however, and said curtly, 'I would like you to instruct me.'

'You were a soldier, weren't you?' asked Granitola.

'Yes, but a bird moves faster than a running man, and more often that not you miss a running man in any case.'

'The principle is the same,' said Granitola, 'but with birdshot it is much easier, because the shot spreads out as it flies. You aim in front of the bird, and experience teaches you how far in front it should be. You have to remember to keep the gun swinging at the same pace as the bird, until after you've fired. It's no good keeping the gun still and hoping to pull the trigger at the right time. It never works.'

'How far in front should you shoot? I need to have an idea.'

'Well, really it depends on the speed and distance. I can assure you it becomes instinctive.'

Rustem Bey did not risk losing further face. He waited until he could go out on his own, and eventually succeeded in bagging two pigeons. Thereafter he shot a partridge, a duck and another pigeon. He shot three seagulls just for the practice, and then resumed his trips with Granitola, acquitting himself so well that the latter was astonished by his proficiency at something which only shortly before he had deemed impossible. In his turn, Rustem Bey found himself in a position to educate the Italian in the art of stalking deer and wild goat, and how to ride a horse with a Turkish saddle, and so it came about that they achieved and maintained that equality of authority and esteem that is essential to the friendship of two proud men, perhaps especially when those men may have a twenty-five-year discrepancy in their ages.

As for the rest of the soldiers, Granitola ensured that Sergeant Oliva kept them very busy, believing that idleness is disastrous for morale and performance. They marched hither and thither, staged high-spirited section and platoon attacks, and charged with wild screams and bayonets fixed at ranks of hostile sandbags suspended from the branches of olive trees. Those of peasant origin were detailed to grow vegetables, the sergeant carefully checking the straightness of the drills with pieces of string. Those who could not swim were taught to do so by those who could, and the chickens were removed to the ruins of the ancient Greek amphitheatre. There also were staged entertainments that repeated the same acts that the soldiers had put on for each other a hundred times before, and which always concluded with the singing of patriotic anthems and the unstopping of flasks of wine. The locals regarded them with a mixture of admiration and perplexity, and

459

they in their turn developed a taste for raki, and for roasting and steaming in the hamam. Fortunately for their own health, they never made the discovery that the town had its own brothel, whose sick and pathetic inhabitants were by now on the verge of starvation from lack of clientele, so that it had become more like a convent of Poor Clares than a house of licence.

What consolidated the relationship between the soldiers and the populace was the determination of the two gendarmes to teach the former how to play backgammon. Sergeant Oliva began the downward spiral into addiction as he had become fascinated by watching the gendarmes playing it in the meydan. He was the first to be taught the game, and consequently the first to become addicted, to be followed hierarchically by the corporals and then the privates, so that it spread through the ranks like one of the diseases that they might have acquired in the brothel, had they known of its existence. Extra backgammon boards were sent for from Telmessos. Each evening the meydan rattled to the sound of dice and counter, and cries either of despair or triumph could be heard until well after dark. Backgammon is a game in which the first half consists of skill, and the second half of luck, so it appeals both to the cunning and the reckless, but it is always skill that wins. Tournaments and championships were inaugurated, with prizes being presented either by Rustem Bey or Lieutenant Granitola, and contestants including more and more of the townsmen, so that eventually even Iskander the Potter and Ali the Broken-Nosed were participants, but no one was ever able to beat the two gendarmes, who had devoted a lifetime to playing it whilst waiting for something to happen.

Few of the Christian men joined in, however, and it is a curious fact that still puzzles and vexes Greeks to this day, that the Italians got on much better with the Muslims than with the Orthodox Christians, and tended to side with them. This they hold to be evidence that the Italians cannot be proper Christians and are perfidious and unreasonable. It is true that Italian government policy at that time was explicitly to frustrate Greek aspirations, but it is also true that in the occupied territory the mutual dislike on the ground came about because of the attitude of the Orthodox clergy, whose power over their congregations was absolute.

Kristoforos was still plagued by his grotesque dreams of the funeral of God, and he and Lydia had had their share of suffering in the war. Most of the younger males in his congregation had disappeared into the labour battalions, never to reappear, and consequently the tillage was left entirely to desperate widows and unmarriageable daughters. On his weekly round to collect the offerings of his flock, he found that he was necessarily receiving less and less as time passed, and by and by he and Lydia ever more had to resort to practical measures. Lydia stayed out all day collecting wild greens, and Kristoforos even learned to lay lines from the rocks, thus achieving a neat reversal of Christ's project to convert fishermen into fishers of men. He became more like an imam in his style of life.

The Italians had brought no chaplain with them, and found no Roman Catholic church in the town. Naturally they assumed that they could use the Orthodox ones, of which there were two. It was not that they had any intention of attending services, it was simply that a church was where one went for moments of prayer or solitude, and to indulge those occasions when a fit of religiousness descends upon the psyche.

There was much in the churches that was strange, such as the unreadable Greek lettering, the Byzantine style of decoration, and the depiction of saints such as St Menas, of whom they had never heard, but there was much that was absolutely familiar, such as the candles, the incense and the fact that there was so much iconography. There were even the same mass-produced pious old ladies dressed from toe to head in black, crossing themselves, lighting tapers and finding things that needed tidying.

Sergeant Pietro Oliva was a good Catholic. He liked to go into a church and cross himself, genuflect to the altar, and then settle down to a little prayer and contemplation, savouring the coolness, the heavy odours, the darkness, and the sensation of being soaked in the atmosphere of centuries' worth of devotion that hung in the tenebrous and golden air of churches. He liked to request the Virgin to watch over his wife and two little children, and to check the well-being of his parents in Florence. He took a particular liking to the icon of the Virgin Glykophilousa, and wished that somewhere he could find a copy of it to take home.

He was crossing himself before it one day early in the occupation, when he had the astonishing experience of being assaulted from behind by what seemed at first to be a very large and infuriated bat. As he put his arms up to protect his head, he realised that he was being attacked by a very angry Orthodox priest, who was battering him about the head with a holy book, and cursing him in language that he did not understand, but which was undoubtedly vehement and picturesque. Kristoforos's eyes were glittering, he was so enraged that he spat with each curse, and his beard was quivering.

Sergeant Oliva ran swiftly out of the church with his hands protecting his head, with Father Kristoforos in full hue and cry, still cursing and denouncing him, and that was the last time that he or any of the other Italians went into either of the churches.

The dramatic pursuit of Sergeant Oliva through the alleyways by Father Kristoforos soon became the talk of the town, as did his subsequent visits to the homes of Christians.

It was initially a relief to these Christians that Kristoforos was not asking for alms, but they were subjected instead to what amounted to a strict set of orders. His first port of call was the house of Charitos and Polyxeni. After they had kissed his hand, he said, 'I have come to tell you strictly that you must have nothing to do with the Italians.'

'Nothing, Patir?' repeated Charitos.

'Nothing at all. If one of them touches you, you must go and wash immediately. If one of them talks to you, you must ignore him. You must avoid all contamination.'

'But why, Father, if I may respectfully ask?'

Kristoforos drew a deep breath, almost unable to conceptualise the loathing and disgust that was overwhelming him. 'They are agents of the Devil,' he said at last.

'Aren't they Christians, Father?' asked Polyxeni. 'I've seen them crossing themselves.'

'They are the Devil's Christians. They don't even cross themselves correctly. You must avoid them at all costs.'

'Does the Devil have Christians?' asked Charitos, genuinely perplexed.

'The Devil disguises himself as a Christian whenever it suits

him,' said Kristoforos, with authority. 'These people are schismatics and heretics.'

'Yes?' said Charitos, and he exchanged glances with his wife,
since neither of them understood these terms with any clarity.
Kristoforos perceived their puzzlement, and explained, 'They split
away from the true Church. It was the worst crime against God.'

'Worse than murder?' asked Charitos, slightly awed by the
concept of a worst crime against God.

'Worse than murder,' confirmed Kristoforos. 'It was like a murder
of the faith.'

'What did they do, Father?' asked Polyxeni.

The priest drew himself up to his full height, and inhaled
portentously: 'They put "and from the Son" into the Nicene
Creed.' His eyes sparkled once again with disdain and disgust.
'And they use unleavened bread for the Eucharist!'

The heinousness of these offences was quite lost on the two
Christians, and Charitos said very hesitantly, 'And this is very
serious, Father?'

'It couldn't be more serious. This is the reason that we are
irreconcilable. They will burn for it when God sends fire down
the rivers at the Last Day. This is why you must take it on my
authority that you shall have nothing to do with them at any
time, to preserve yourself from the same danger of burning at
the Last Day. These Roman Catholics have a false patriarch in
Rome who is nothing but an Antichrist.'

The word 'Antichrist' held no particular meaning for Polyxeni
and her husband, but they were nonetheless very impressed by
it. It rang in their heads with truly satanic resonance.

Father Kristoforos gave similar warnings to the inhabitants of
every Christian household, and even interrupted his services to
repeat them before the congregation. Every Friday he went down
to the meydan to pronounce anathemas upon any Italians who
might be there playing backgammon with the gendarmes, and as
time went by perfected a reliable tirade in fairly inaccurate biblical
Greek. Whilst the backgammon players raised their eyebrows,
sighed and shook their heads, Kristoforos boomed out prophe-
cies and curses along the lines of:

'Schismatics of Rome, children of Christ who weeps for thee,

463

pawns of tyrants, ye who are unjust, ye who are filthy, ye who are unrighteous, ye who are dogs and whoremongers, sorcerers and idolaters, ye whose hearts are unlit by the sun, ye that have no temple within, ye that shall not be saved, ye that work abominations, ye that defile the Virgin, ye that cannot drink the truth whatever thy thirst; ye are corrupt and have done nothing good, ye have done iniquity, ye have eaten my people like bread, ye have not called upon God, ye have encamped against our cities, ye have been put to shame and God hath despised thee and scattered thy bones. Behold the Lord shall give ear to the words of my mouth, for He is my helper, He is with them who uphold my soul, He shall reward evils unto mine enemies, He shall cut them off in His truth, for strangers are risen up against my people, oppressors seek after our trees of olive and our maidens, wickedness is in the midst of them. My soul is among lions, and I lie even with them that are set on fire, even the sons of men, whose teeth are spears and arrows, and their tongue a sharp sword.

'Yea, in your heart ye work wickedness, ye weigh the violence of your hands upon the earth, ye are estranged from the womb, ye go astray as soon as ye be born, speaking lies, thy poison is like the poison of the serpent, ye are like the deaf adder that stoppeth her ear.

'Schismatics of Rome, the Lord hath prepared a pit! He hath laid up a net to thy steps! Calamities shall overpass thee! Satan shall be loosed from his prison, and Gog and Magog shall go out to deceive the nations that are in the four quarters of the earth, to gather them together in battle; the number of them is as the sands of the sea, and fire shall come out of Heaven above the beloved city, and devour thee, and thou shalt be cast, yea, even the innocent and those as pure as babes, into the lake of oil and brimstone where the beast and the false prophet are, and thy flesh shall be divided from thy bones, for ye have not been found written in the book of life, and shall be cast into the flame!'

From this grandiloquent beginning Father Kristoforos was perfectly capable of improvising a good hour's worth of pyrotechnics. When he felt his voice beginning to crack he would resort to shaking his fists, grimacing, and thrusting out towards them the silver cross that he wore about his neck. It is true to say that he derived very great satisfaction from this holy pursuit, and slept better than he ever had before in life. Lydia thought him much more serene and gentle in the home, and the congregation found his new publicly fiery behaviour very impressive indeed, so that his status among them was considerably elevated.

In those days, whenever the Christians discussed the presence of the Italians in the town, one would hear sentiments such as:

'Well, you never would have believed it, if Father Kristoforos hadn't warned us.'

'Yes, they seem so nice, don't they?'

'It just goes to show, doesn't it?'

'The Antichrist, just fancy.'

'Terrible, isn't it? They put something into the Creed when they shouldn't have.'

'Well, I passed one yesterday, and I spat at his feet, and he gave me a look like the Devil, I can tell you.'

The Italians, of necessity at first, and then by inclination, fraternised solely with the non-Christians. The backgammon players moved their venue first to the courtyard of the khan, and then when Kristoforos found them, back to the meydan, and then down to the amphitheatre, and then to the Letoun.

Then, one day, after a very long and tedious rant from the priest which none but he could have understood, one of the gendarmes finally lost patience, leapt to his feet, turned about and pulled out his pistol.

He pointed it straight at the priest's chest. For one petrifying moment Kristoforos thought that he was going to be killed, and words failed him altogether. Everyone in the meydan froze, and watched helplessly as they waited for the seemingly inevitable horror that was about to come to pass. The Italian soldiers, who had left their weapons locked up in the khan, wondered whether or not they should intervene, and Sergeant Oliva got to his feet with the reluctant intention of doing so.

Then the gendarme slowly lowered the weapon, and put it back into its holster. Grim-faced and still shaking with rage, he turned his back on the priest, and sat down to resume the game.

The priest stood still for a moment, and then realised that he was violently trembling. Suddenly humiliated by his own fear, dry in the mouth and dizzy, urgently aware that he was going to have to empty his bowels and bladder, he turned and left, perturbed and ashamed by the way in which his faith and determination had suddenly deserted him when faced by imminent martyrdom.

From that time Kristoforos sensibly left the Italians alone, but he never relented in his warnings to his flock. His troubled sleep returned, as did his disheartening dreams. His redemption would wait upon another day.

77
I am Philothei (12)

When Ibrahim was young he was very funny. My little brother Mehmetçik and his friend Karatavuk could perfectly imitate robins and blackbirds on their birdwhistles, and this was very admirable, and this was how they called to each other, but my beloved could imitate all the different bleats of goats. I think it was because he was a goatherd, and he came to recognise all of these bleats as he became more experienced. Once he very nearly got into trouble for bleating when Abdulhamid Hodja was speaking, and fortunately Abdulhamid forgave him just in time to prevent a beating.

I have forgotten the names of some of these bleats, but they were things like the bleat of a goat who is looking for its kid, the bleat of a goat that has accidentally bitten on a stone, and the bleat of a goat that is unable to fart. He used to do these bleats for the entertainment of his parents' visitors, and for anyone else who asked. He wasn't shy about doing them.

As time went by he started to do bleats which were more and more absurd. The bleat of a goat that is thinking of becoming a Christian. The bleat of a goat that wishes to go to Telmessos and buy a waterpipe for its grandmother. The bleat of a goat that is too stupid to know how stupid it is. The bleat of a goat that had a good idea the day before and can't remember what it was.

The best bleat of all was the bleat of a goat with nothing to say. I can't describe it, but it's a bleat that anyone would recognise straight away, because it's the kind of bleat that goats do when they're all together munching away among the rocks, and there really is nothing to say, but they bleat anyway. Ibrahim used to say that what the bleat probably meant was 'It's me'.

Ibrahim could do this bleat and just exaggerate it enough to make it very ridiculous, and he could do it in all sorts of versions and variants, and people never tired of hearing him do it, and it always made them laugh.

I used to go out and harvest wild plants at about the same time every day, and Ibrahim knew this, and he would leave the goats in the charge of his dog Kopek, and he would scramble over the rocks, and I would know that he was coming because he had a version of the bleat that was just for me, and his game was that he would try to get as close as he could before I could spot him, and then he would pop up from behind a rock or a thorny oak and do the bleat very loudly, and the expression on his face when he did it was really just like a goat's.

It's a miracle that we were never caught in all those years. The disgrace would have been unbearable, and I lived in a state of great nervousness. Quite often I went out to gather greens with Drosoula, and we trusted her not to tell anyone.

What I loved about Ibrahim was that he always could make me laugh, and because of this it didn't matter that he was only a goatherd. I also loved it when I heard him playing the kaval.

These years of war have been utterly wearisome, and I can't wait for the time when my beloved returns, and I hear the kaval again, and he pops up from behind a rock and bleats the bleat of a goat with nothing to say.

78

Mustafa Kemal (18)

General Liman von Sanders once remarked that it was impossible to get Turkish officers to cooperate with each other because of their rivalries. In Samsun, nonetheless, Mustafa Kemal begins the difficult process of trying to bring about the impossible. The British catch on too late to what he is really up to.

Kemal's task is to take advantage of Muslim anxieties. In the east, Kurds are worried about Armenians, as is the population of French-occupied Cilicia, to which Armenians are returning, intent upon revenge after their ill treatment during the Great War. In the west, Muslim refugees from the Balkan Wars, who have been rehoused in the homes of Greeks displaced in 1914, are now under threat from the return of those same Greek refugees. So many winds have been sown by previous stupidities and injustices on all sides that Mustafa Kemal now has several whirlwinds to reap. A British captain, L. H. Hurst, is sent to keep an eye on him, and Mustafa Kemal treats him politely but does not allay his suspicions. The British induce the government to recall Mustafa Kemal to Istanbul. He doesn't go. He spends his time exploiting the country's excellent telegraph system in order to set up the necessary contacts, and his activities become more political than military. He begins liaison with irregular bands, which one might describe either as terrorists, bandits or freedom fighters, according to one's own prejudices and inclinations. They were certainly not the kind of folk to be invited to the Pera Palace Hotel to meet one's maiden aunt.

Armed resistance to the Greeks begins in the west, in response to the havoc and economic ruin brought about by the occupying Greek forces. A crucial point is approaching, as it is becoming more and more clear that the government in Istanbul is incapable of standing up to the Allies and defending Turkish interests. Sooner or later a new nationalist government has to be formed elsewhere. Kemal defies a ban by the government on his use of the telegraph system, and threatens any uncooperative telegraphist with court martial. The turning point comes when Kemal and his fellow officers and dignitaries set up congresses in Erzurum and Sivas. The process begins of exploiting Bolshevik Russia's hostility to the Allies, while remaining independent of it. The Istanbul government finds that it is powerless to remove him. He receives a missive from the Sultan, who says that he understands that Kemal is motivated solely by patriotism, that he doesn't want to dismiss him, and perhaps he should take a couple of months' leave. On 5 July 1919, Mustafa Kemal informs the War Minister that he is no longer serving the Istanbul government, but the nation.

On 9 July, the War Minister and Mustafa Kemal spend hours on the telegraph, and the latter resigns from the army as the War Minister simultaneously cashiers him. Kâzim Karabekir is appointed in his place as inspector of the 3rd Army, but stands by his comrade, and at a meeting of important leaders it is agreed that all should continue to take their orders from Mustafa Kemal even though he has been dismissed. Nonetheless, Kemal descends into despair because he feels he has lost his legitimacy, but this is abruptly relieved when Kâzim Karabekir arrives, salutes him, and informs him that he is still the commander. Karabekir has brought a cavalry escort and a car with him in order to prove his point. 'Pasha, we are all at your service,' declares Karabekir.

There is a congress in Erzurum, and Kemal and Karabekir go to it together. A sheep is sacrificed, prayers are said, and democratic politics begin. Kemal is elected chairman, and he exercises his oratorical powers to good effect, talking of the state of the nation and its unjust subjection to the Allies. There are statements of loyalty to the Sultan, and already splits are appearing between modernisers and traditionalists. He borrows civilian clothes from the governor, in response to objections to having the chairman dressed as a general. The congress concludes with a charter which amounts to a declaration of independence.

Kemal is not pleased to have to work with such 'miserable people' as the leader of a Kurdish tribe and a Nakşibendi dervish sheikh, but he intends to use the committee for his own ends, of whomsoever it might consist. In Istanbul, the government progressively weakens as it fails to win any points over the Allies at the Paris Peace Conference.

Another congress takes place in Sivas, and Mustafa Kemal has to borrow a retired major's life savings in order to be able to afford to go to it. He leaves accompanied by a machine-gun detachment, and has a machine gun mounted on the leading car. He and the Nakşibendi dervish sheikh have to travel through territory controlled by the Dersim Kurds, who have only three principles. One is greed, the other is violence, and the third is to have no principles other than these two.

At the conference it is resolved not to revive the Committee of Union and Progress, and not to be partisan to any political party. The era of the Young Turks is over. The conference confirms that it wants national independence within the lines set out at the armistice; in other words it wants to get rid of the Arab lands. The Arabs either fought badly in the Great War or defected to the British side, and the Turks want nothing more to do with them. Kemal and his comrades have fully embraced the principles set forth by President Wilson concerning national self-determination. There is talk of an American mandate whilst the country recovers, but Mustafa Kemal prefers help to hegemony. He will accept aid from anyone, as long as nobody tries to tell him what to do.

The new War Minister in Istanbul decides to send a detachment of Kurdish cavalry to arrest Mustafa Kemal, and the British seek to exploit Kurdish nationalism in order to disrupt Kemal's plans. Nothing comes of it, because Kemal has managed to befriend Kurdish chieftains, and anyway, organising Kurds is like trying to keep kittens in a box. Typically, they go home as soon as they have as much plunder as they can carry. Kemal suspects the Sultan of plotting against him, but keeps quiet about it. Nationalists begin to seize civil control almost everywhere. The British begin withdrawing in order to avoid clashes with them, and to prevent the Ottoman government from taking action, so as to forestall a civil war. The government is in an impossible position, and the Grand Vizier resigns. In Sivas it is becoming increasingly clear that Mustafa Kemal is accumulating powers tantamount to dictatorship, and there are many who do not like it.

Kemal discovers that one cannot govern in chaotic times and keep one's hands clean. He raises taxes to fund his operations, but it amounts to banditry. He does not in any case hesitate to employ bandits. There is dissent and plot and counterplot, among officers and throughout the nation, against a background of national elections.

In the meantime, there are wars to prosecute. Kemal cannot afford direct confrontations with the Allies, so he sends irregulars against the French, commanded by a gentleman who takes 'Ali the Sword' as his *nom de guerre*. The French find themselves not only confronting Arabs and Turkish nationalists, but also having to cope with the embarrassing misbehaviour of their own Armenian legionaries, and the plans, plots and ambitions of the British. Clemenceau loses the French election, and it is clear that things are going to change.

It is decided to move the nationalist headquarters from Sivas to Ankara, and Kemal borrows petrol and tyres from the headmistress of a local American school for Armenians. The Sivas branch of the Ottoman Bank is besieged for a week by a colleague of Kemal's until the manager stops pretending to be ill and comes up with a loan.

Kemal is welcomed in Ankara, a town ruined economically by a fire and by the expulsion of the Armenians who had made it prosperous. There have been national elections, and Kemal himself has become a member of parliament, but he remains in Ankara. Parliament in Istanbul is now packed with his supporters. The government returns his decorations and revokes his cashiering from the Ottoman army, but Kemal is still uncooperative. He declares his intention of driving the Greeks from the region of Smyrna, and is shortly joined in Ankara by Colonel Ismet, another of the new country's men of Destiny.

Kemal and Ismet realise that they cannot rely indefinitely upon irregulars, whose actions are frequently barbaric, capricious and counter-productive, and so the build-up of the regular army proceeds apace. In the meantime, Kemal has to face off the British. They are interfering in government and trying to dictate

472

who should be in the Cabinet. Kemal orders his officials country-wide to be prepared to arrest British control officers. He steps up military pressure against the French in Cilicia, and an astoundingly daring guerrilla band raids a French arms depot in Gallipoli, and empties it out.

Kemal begins to feel marginalised in Ankara. Nationalist politics are going ahead without him in Istanbul. An interesting thing happens, however; whereas the word 'Turkey' has been in common usage for centuries in countries outside the Ottoman Empire, it is now used for the first time in an official document in Istanbul. The use of the word signifies that the Turks are beginning to see themselves as the inhabitants of the Anatolian heartland. They are no longer thinking of themselves as Ottoman, and so they are losing their affinity with their co-religionists in Arabia, or anywhere else in the former empire. When 'Turkey' becomes a word used by Turks, it really means the end of the ulema, the pan-Islamic dream of Muslim idealists, a fantasy just as fantastic as the Greek dream of Greater Greece.

The Allies of the Paris Peace Conference become enmired in confusion. They have contradictory ideas as to how to deal with Turkey. The Italians leak information to the nationalists, and Kemal has the confidence of the commander of the French detachment in Ankara. The British occupy Istanbul in a clumsy and bloody operation. They arrest the nationalist leadership there and send them to Malta.

This is the most marvellous thing that Kemal could have hoped for. The British have removed the legitimate government and ensured that he is the only important nationalist leader left. Kemal declares that the Ottoman state is finished. He says, 'Today the Turkish nation is called to defend its capacity for civilisation, its right to life and independence, its entire future.' He orders the arrest of British officers, and these effectively become hostages. The Istanbul parliament resigns in protest against the British action, and Kemal organises new elections, whose deputies duly arrive in Ankara. Nationalist intellectuals and activists go to Ankara in a steady stream. Once he has won over the commander of the 12th Corps, all real power in unoccupied Turkey has effectively devolved upon Mustafa Kemal.

Back in Eskibahçe, no one has been able to follow these events. News percolates slowly into the countryside from the big towns, and by the time it has arrived, it has undergone a whole series of mutations.

The current preoccupation in these parts is with the ever more virulent plagues of outlaws and bandits. Rustem Bey is in charge of tracking them down, and has seen some vicious fighting in the mountains, as bad as anything he experienced when he was in the army. This amounts to guerrilla war, a nervy chaos of ambushes, long and fruitless treks through unfamiliar country, terrifying surprises, single shots from indeterminable directions that ricochet among the rocks, and short and brutal engagements. Rustem Bey has become thin and dark-skinned, and his riding boots are so scuffed that there is little point in polishing them any more. Instead he rubs them with fat. He has a bullet hole through his fez, and a long scar from a sabre on his right arm. Leyla Hanım weeps with anxiety whenever he departs, and weeps again with joy when he returns.

His militia consists of old men, little boys, the mildly disabled and those, like Iskander the Potter, who have somehow escaped from military service. Iskander is an enthusiastic outlaw-hunter, as he likes to seize any opportunity to use the pistol and hunting rifle that he bought from Abdul Chrysostomos. He enjoys the long marches out into the countryside and the roasting of birds in the ashes of campfires. Unfortunately, Iskander is a poor shot, he is hasty at the trigger and is slightly short-sighted, so that his contributions have consisted merely of adding to the general din of the skirmishes.

He has once had a chance to shoot Red Wolf, the notorious outlaw whose trademark was always to wear a scarlet shirt, when the latter was scrambling away up a hillside, but the bullet was a dud, and by the time that he had cleared the breech it was too late.

Iskander takes pride in his prowess, and regrets only that he has not yet managed to prove it. He says, 'The patient hunter gets his reward.' He sometimes wonders whether Abdul Chrysostomos made the barrel straight, or whether all his bullets might be defective, but the fact is that Rustem Bey once tried out the rifle, to satisfy his own curiosity, and knocked a bottle off a wall at 150 yards. When Iskander tried it, he knocked chips out of a stone two paces away.

79

I am Philothei (13)

I remember once I was out gathering figs and I had gone quite a long way, and I had picked a lot of them because I needed them both for my father's house and for Rustem Bey's house. Then Ibrahim appeared. He had done the bleat of a goat that had nothing to say, and so I knew he was coming.

When he popped up from behind a bush, he made me laugh as usual. Then he came out and took my hand and kissed it, and said, 'My little bird,' and I said, 'Why do you always call me little bird?' and he said, 'Because you are delicate and beautiful, and you sing when you are working, and I have always thought of you as a little bird. When a thought of you suddenly comes into my mind, I think, "Oh, it's the little bird."'

I said, 'Do you remember when Karatavuk and Mehmetçik my brother tried to fly and ran around flapping their arms, and it never worked?' and he thought about it and said, 'I think it's because arms don't have feathers.'

I said, 'If we had feathers on our arms, do you think we could fly?' and he said, 'Maybe not. If that was possible, someone would have done it by now,' and I said, 'Think how free we would be. We could fly to the top of a mountain and there would be no one to tell us to be ashamed, and no one would see us.'

Next time I saw him he said, 'I had a dream about flying, and when I woke up I had verses in my head.'

I said, 'Verses? Can you remember them?' and he recited:

'Don't pity the eagle
Who can climb the sky and fly
But for the little wingless bird
Cry.

Fire will be found by
Birds that fly too high
And all his feathers burn
And he'll fall down and die.

What bird has two nests
Only one shall remain
And his wings burn
And he'll not fly again.

What if I make a high nest
But the branch sinks low?
They will take my little bird
And I will die of woe.

Oh my little bird
Who will chase you?
Who will put you in a cage
And tenderly embrace you?

It's not possible to light a
Candle that doesn't drip,
And it's not possible to love
And never weep.'

And I said, 'Oh, Ibrahim, where did these words come from?'
and he said, 'They were given to me by the night,' and I said,
'With words like these you could become famous, if only you
were known in the Sultan's court.'

He said, 'I will never be known in the Sultan's court. Sometimes
I feel I am like an eagle. I feel I am strong and whole in the
heart, I feel as if I could accomplish anything. I could look down
on the earth and beyond it, and I would be lord of the earth
because I am lord of the air. But I have been tied to the ground.
I will be scratching dust for ever, like a chicken.'

Then he paused and turned away from me, and said, 'I would
be an eagle, but God has clipped my wings.'

I said, 'What kind of a bird would I be?'

He thought for a few moments, and said, 'A partridge.'

80

Mustafa Kemal (19)

A virtual state of civil war exists between Kemal loyalists and those loyal to the Sultan, particularly between Circassian factions. The Sheikulislam issues a fatwa stating that nationalists are infidels and must be killed. The mufti of Ankara issues a counter-fatwa signed by 250 colleagues, stating that since the Sultan Caliph is a prisoner of the infidels, fatwas issued under duress have no validity.

Kemal very cleverly, and no doubt cynically, allays the fears of religious and political conservatives by ensuring that the opening of the Ankara parliament on a good Muslim Friday is preceded by recitations from the Koran and the Hadith. The Prophet's banner and a hair from his beard are processed. Sheep are sacrificed, prayers are offered for the safety of the Sultan Caliph. Similar ceremonies are organised by nationalists all over the country, and there are plenty of enthusiasts to shout 'God is Great'. When he is elected President, Kemal declares his hope that the Sultan will rule for ever, free of foreign interference. Mustafa Kemal knows how to dissemble.

The day after, Kemal begins the seduction of the Bolsheviks in Moscow, asking for arms, ammunition and five million roubles, and speaking to them in their jargon. Then he sends a telegram to the Sultan, declaring his loyalty. Then he sends out expeditions against the Sultan's loyalists, easily defeating them and hanging their leaders. Many of the enemy desert and change sides. The British bomb Kemal's troops to keep them away from the capital. The British urgently need new Allied troops, and only the Greeks are near enough. The Greek Prime Minister, Eleftherios Venizelos, seizes the opportunity.

Venizelos has been warned that if he goes to war with Turkey he will get no support, but now he offers a division to help out the British, and in return he gets permission for a concerted action in the region of Smyrna. He takes this as carte blanche to undertake a full-scale invasion, convinced that ultimately the British will support him and hoping to establish a fait accompli. Greek troops advance beyond the boundary laid down for them, and move east and north. They occupy the Aegean coast, and the southern coast of Marmara. The Turkish troops are away, suppressing rebellions elsewhere. The Greeks take Bursa and advance two hundred miles to Uşak. Far away in eastern Thrace they overrun the Ottoman garrisons, and occupy Adrianople. In Ankara, Kemal reacts to the anger of the assembly by declaring a jihad. A turbulent Circassian warlord is dispatched against the Greeks, and his irregular forces drive the Greeks from Demirici.

There is an anti-nationalist rebellion in Konya, the centre of Islamic orthodoxy. Kurdish nationalists in the south-east rise in rebellion, but are incapable of cooperating with each other. Kemal suppresses them. The Allies force the desperate Sultan to accede to a treaty at Sèvres in which he agrees to the total dismemberment of his kingdom. In order to be legal, however, the treaty has to be ratified by the Ottoman parliament, which no longer exists. It is obvious to everyone in Istanbul, including the Sultan, that the nationalists are the sole hope for Turkey, and all official action against them ceases.

Kemal has to deal with the east before he can deal with the Greeks in the west. The Soviets take Azerbaijan, and it looks as though they will take Armenia, where the Armenians have driven out the Muslims and the army is controlled by officers from the old Tsarist army.

Kemal needs to take advantage of both the Soviets and the British by pretending to be going along with them. He starts his own Bolshevik party and, much to their surprise, appoints his own friends to its offices. No communist activity is permitted except under its auspices. Simultaneously, he forestalls Soviet ambitions in Armenia by unleashing Kâzim Karabekir, who takes Kars. Two thousand Armenian troops are killed, and only nine Turkish. Ultimately, Karabekir pushes the Armenians beyond Mount Ararat, their sacred mountain, and a treaty is signed that fixes the border at the place where it still stands. Soon the remainder of Armenia will be taken by the Bolsheviks and it will sink into unendurable twilight behind the Iron Curtain, with its holy mountain in sight, but heartbreakingly out of reach. President Wilson's arbitration concerning the extent of Armenia, issued four days later, is made ridiculous by these events, and remains unpublished. Turkish and Soviet borders now coincide, and it is considerably easier for Kemal to get his weapons, gold and medical supplies.

In the south, in Cilicia, Kemal's men confront the French, often with great success. There is one incident when the French commander is deluded into thinking that he faces 15,000 troops, and so he surrenders five hundred soldiers to a little band of villagers armed with bird guns. The French are really interested in holding on to Syria, and they wait to see how the Kemalists will fare against the Greeks.

Before he can engage the Hellenic invaders, Kemal neutralises the bands of irregulars who are a law unto themselves, disobeying orders, taking independent action and making strategy difficult. He brings the adorable Fikriye from Istanbul to be his companion. She is twenty-three years old, a good musician, she is not in good health, but she is ladylike and uncomplaining. For the time being Mustafa Kemal remains happily unmarried to her.

It is at this point that Fritz and Moritz accidentally change the course of history.

81

Fritz and Moritz Accidentally Change History

King Alexander is as handsome as a film star. He is honest-eyed and elegant. Enhanced by a military moustache, and arrayed in his military uniforms, he gazes humorously out of old photographs looking exactly like those poorly remembered great-uncles who were killed in some time-lost war, leaving behind them their fiancées, no doubt, and motorcycles that remain in the garden shed for seventeen years. It is 17 September 1920, and Greece is at war with the Ottoman Turks, taking advantage of their post-war weakness in the hope of regaining anciently Greek Constantinople and the western parts of Anatolia. Prime Minister Venizelos, ambitious on his own account, and ill-advised by the irrepressibly unwise Lloyd George, has freshly ordered the Greek army to move out of its positions in Smyrna. Included in the improvised Turkish army that faces them are Ibrahim and Karatavuk, two unfortunate nobodies in these great imperial games. The Greek attempt to expand their territory eastwards will be as disastrous as Enver Pasha's attempts to achieve the same thing for the Ottomans during the Great War, but in the week of the young King's death that particular nemesis is yet a long way off, and all the old dreams of the Greeks are intact. At the same time, the Turks are beginning to nurture the vision of a brand new land that will rise full-fledged out of the embers of the old empire.

King Alexander is about to die, and he will leave behind one and a half wives. His first wife is Greece, whom he loves, and his second wife is Aspasia, an upper-class Greek who is as beautiful as he is. He married her morganatically earlier in the year, against his parents' wishes, and the state will not recognise the marriage as legitimate until two years after his death. At this moment Aspasia is five months pregnant with a child whose sex will

481

preclude it from inheriting the throne. The child is destined to marry King Peter of Serbia, in 1944, confirming our suspicion that there is something ineluctably and essentially tragic about being born to the blood royal. King Alexander has married Aspasia because he loves her, and anyway, he notes sourly, if he had followed his parents' wishes and married a foreign princess, it would have made foreign policy that much more complicated to determine, since his wife would undoubtedly have wished to interfere.

King Alexander is twenty-seven years old. He is charismatic, he is high-spirited, and the war with Turkey has not yet gone disastrously wrong. Greece is warmly supported by Great Britain, who greatly approves of the new King, even though she violently disliked and distrusted his father, now exiled and deposed.

The King gets up early and exercises in his gymnasium on a day when autumn hovers at the far edge of the horizon, and the birds are still singing. He throws a ball for his favourite dog, the German shepherd, the faithful and impulsive Fritz. Not only does he love his dog, but he is also cathartically in love with the internal combustion engine, like so many young men before and since, and today he is intending to ride his motorcycle in the grounds of the Tatoi Palace, accompanied by his hounds. He has an entire morning free, but at one o'clock he is due for lunch in Kifissia with Aspasia and his friend, Zalokostas.

He rides with the dogs barking behind him, and revels in the speed of his machine. He reflects on the unfortunate fact that just recently Fritz accidentally cracked a mirror, and feels a shiver at ill fortune's apprehension. He recalls that (worse by far) he and Aspasia were yesterday on a British warship when the captain had lit all three of their cigarettes from one match. 'One of us three will die,' thinks the King, with unanticipated bitterness, and he remembers saying to Aspasia, 'It would have been better if the ship had sunk.'

(With the first flame of a match Charos the Huntsman, Charos dressed in black, Charos with the black horse, knows you are present, with the second he takes aim and cocks the gun, and with the third he fires).

The King rides his motorcycle in the woods, and in the fields where the grapes are grown for Dekeleia wine. His brother, Prince Christopher, describes him as the unhappiest man in Greece, because he is lonely, his family is in exile, and he agonises about the legitimacy of his reign when his father has not even renounced the throne. He does not know whether he is a king or a regent, but he does know that his elder brother George has a better claim than he does. He wants to forget the pro- and anti-Venizelist factions that bedevil his reign, he is frustrated by his powerlessness, he worries about the progress of the new war. For a king, hope has fewer feathers than for anyone else on earth. The dogs bark, and the motorcycle coughs. He plays with the advance and retard lever to get a better spark.

He is nearing the home of the palace vet, Herr Sturm, and remembers that Sturm has many interesting foreign magazines full of information about the latest cars. The temptation is too great, he simply must go and see if there are any new magazines, but he realises at the same time that he has managed to lose Fritz. He dismounts and calls to the dog, walking towards the villa of the vet.

Where is Fritz? The monarch calls to him, but he does not appear. The pines ring with the clear voice of the King.

Suddenly King Alexander hears barking and screaming. He breaks into a run, and finds his dog in a frenzy, attempting to devour a Barbary ape that is tied to a chain near the house of the vet. According to one account, the two Barbary apes which concern us were presented by Prince Christopher to a tavern owner who gave them to the vet. According to Prince Christopher, however, the apes belonged to a vineyard keeper whose vineyard the King happened to be passing. Thus is the impossibility of historical accuracy neatly exemplified, and one can only be certain that the grapes of the vineyard, if it was really a vineyard, and if it was really there, and if the King was really passing it, would have been producing grapes for Dekeleia wine, since in that area no other kind of grape was grown.

What is also certain is that the Barbary ape is fast, courageous, clever, and well toothed. It is the only ape that is native to Europe, so it is perhaps a comfort that the King is not to be killed by an outright outsider, from Africa perhaps, or South America.

Valiantly the young King intervenes, grabbing at the two animals in order to separate them. Unfortunately, the ape is a female, and her mate, Moritz, is nearby. Moritz gallantly hastens to defend his beloved, and charges up, shrieking. He sinks his teeth into the left calf of the King, allegorically re-enacting the fate of many a monarch at the hands and teeth of his people, and begins to savage it.

Alexander attempts to fend off the infuriated Moritz, and is bitten on the hand, at which point Sturm appears, and the four combatants are shortly separated with Teutonic firmness.

The King is in great pain, and he is helped, bleeding, into the palace, where he telephones his friend Stefanos Metaxas, saying that it is nothing serious, but asking him to bring a doctor and some bandages. He decides that there should be no publicity about the event, because he wishes to avoid ridicule. Metaxas assumes that his friend must have tumbled from his motorcycle, and calls the eminent physician, Constantinos Mermingas, instructing him to bring equipment for a broken leg. In the meantime, Alexander calls his beloved Aspasia, asking her to come to the palace.

Dr Mermingas lays aside the splints and plaster that he has brought in vain, examines the wound, and finds that there are seven bites, with a particularly deep one at the centre. He considers the wounds to be ghastly, but not necessarily serious. He washes the wounds in alcohol, and then asks for petrol. There is none in the palace, and so Stefanos Metaxas goes outside and drains some from his car, bringing it back carefully in a bowl. The doctor declares that the muscle of the calf has been completely crushed, and he washes it in the petrol and then daubs it with iodine. One winces at the thought of the stinging pains that the King must have had to endure. Dr Mermingas binds the wound with bandages.

Aspasia arrives with Zalokostas, with whom they had intended to take lunch, and Zalokostas tries to comfort her. She is super-stitious, and she remembers with dread the lighting of the three cigarettes on the British warship. King Alexander calms her, repeating that he wishes to avoid publicity, for it is beneath the dignity of a king to have been bitten in a battle with an ape.

484

The King passes a bad night but feels reasonably well upon the morrow. The doctor changes the bandages and finds the wound to be inflamed. He looks for pus, finding none, but nonetheless advises the King to cancel his appointments.

After three nights the King's temperature has reached thirty-nine degrees, but there is still no pus.

After five nights there is a great quantity of pus, and the government begins to worry. Prime Minister Venizelos, who has devoted his entire political career to attempting to frustrate the monarchy and wrest its power away, is particularly concerned. He is, after all, very fond of this king, even though he was responsible for the spectacular fall of his father, the ill-fated King Constantine. It is impossible not to be fond of the handsome young man, even if you are a republican. Venizelos orders the creation of a council of eight doctors, thus unsagely yielding to the politician's inveterate propensity to create committees that are paralysed by the clamour of dissent and the dead hand of caution.

The eight doctors issue daily bulletins that are accurate but optimistic. The King has a local infection, but the situation is not unduly grave. Dr Savas, the eminent microbiologist, takes a culture from the leg wound and detects the presence of streptococcus. The swelling becomes greatly worse, and the wound enlarges. The King's temperature reaches forty degrees. The surgeon, Gerasimos Fokas, pronounces that the swelling is not just a phlegmon, it is septicaemia. He is a formidable expert in war wounds, and he states that the only solution is amputation, for only amputation will save the royal life. In this he is undoubtedly correct, but the rest of the committee are horrified, and veto it, most probably because they cannot conceive of cutting off the leg of a king, even though others in the past have been but little bequalmed about cutting off their heads.

Zalokostas goes to Prime Minister Venizelos, who has taken to his bed with influenza, and for the first time the politician finds out exactly how serious the situation is. He masters his fever sufficiently to summon a specialist from Paris. George Ferdinand Widal, expert in intractable inflammations, will find a Greek warship waiting for him at Brindisi, and he will arrive on the

485

thirteenth day, three days after the infection reaches Alexander's stomach, causing him to vomit and to lose weight.

Her beloved begins to turn yellow, and the lovely Aspasia dutifully, but perhaps unimaginatively, dons a nurse's uniform. She is in attendance always, she holds his hands, and between them there pass the most intense and touching scenes of connubial devotion.

The whole country now knows the truth, and services take place in the churches. Telegrams begin to arrive from all over the world. Wild rumours begin to circulate, to the effect that the different doctors are treating the King according to their own political inclinations, with the royalist ones trying to save him (apart from Savas, who, on account of having been Queen Sophia's physician, is still loyal to the old King), and the Venizelist ones trying to kill him.

Venizelos and the exiled royal family are at loggerheads. He sends them a telegram every day, but he heartlessly refuses Queen Sophia's pleas to let her come to her son's bedside, bizarrely advising her to address her requests to the Greek embassy in Zurich. Venizelos is surprised that she sends only two telegrams in eighteen days, but Prince Christopher is to recall that she was heartbroken at ever having been separated from her son, and that Venizelos deliberately blocked her attempts to communicate with him. Sophia disapproves of Aspasia, and so it is unlikely that her presence would in any case soothe her son. Venizelos permits Olga, the Queen Dowager, to come instead of Sophia, but she arrives two days too late, on account of rough seas. In the meantime, Venizelos goes to the Tatoi Palace every other day to chat with the King, but does not discuss politics, since it is indecent to discuss politics with a dying man.

The newspaper *New Day* reports that Prime Minister Venizelos had ordered Moritz the monkey to be infected with rabies, in order that he might fatally bite the King, and the Prime Minister initiates litigation against it, for libel.

On the twelfth day Alexander becomes delirious at night, but improves slightly during the day. All remain optimistic, except for the cleaning lady, Kyria Eleni. She has read dire and ominous portents in the coffee grounds, and she understands the significance of Fritz breaking the mirror. She tells Aspasia, the doctors and the Prime Minister that she can, if they are willing, and even though she is only a cleaning lady, perform an act of iatrosophia for them. All she needs them to do is kill Fritz the dog, and bring her his liver so that she can make an ointment with it. They express gratitude for her advice, but her offer is declined by the doctors, who place more confidence in the efficaciousness of their own iatrosophia.

That night King Alexander begins to call out, 'Oh Father, oh Father,' and 'Mother, Mother, save me.' In a moment of clarity he tells the desolate Aspasia to go and take some rest.

Dr Widal administers a vaccine to the King, and estimates that he has four more days to live. A new doctor arrives. He is Pierre Delbet, whose ship has deposited him near the Corinth Canal. He is driven to the palace at stupendous speed, in a Panhard racing car which the stricken King would have loved to have driven himself, had the patient been someone other than himself. Dr Delbet finds the patient coughing blood, and a new lethal microbe is found. The doctors return to the subject of amputation, but they know that at this stage it is too late. Alexander falls into a coma, and when he finally wakes he asks to embrace the beautiful Aspasia.

The King is delirious again, and he tries to speak. He dreams that he is standing at the edge of a great river, and on the opposite bank there stands the familiar figure of his beloved grandfather, the late King George, who calls to him, saying, 'Come, my child, the time has come for me to take you.'

Alexander cries out, 'Yes, Grandfather, I am coming, but first I want you to meet Aspasia.' Hearing this, Aspasia swoons away.

A priest is called, and he is placed behind a screen. Aspasia does not want to perturb her husband, so she has the priest recite *sotto voce*, and she serves the communion wine to Alexander on a spoon, telling him that it is medicine. He sleeps heroically, dreaming of victory in Thrace. He calls, 'We are winning, we are winning!' He asks, 'Where is Melas? Bring me the latest reports.'

Melas, his aide-de-camp, is summoned, and instructed to make something up for the sake of the King's peace of mind. The King's breathing becomes stertorous, and he is clearly about to die. He calls Aspasia by her pet name. 'Bika,' he says, 'I want to see Mitsos.'

The royal chauffeur is called, and he heaves his vast bulk into the chamber. The giant is grief-stricken and unsure of himself. Aspasia bends down and tells her husband: 'Mitsos is here.'

'Mitsos,' says Alexander, 'is my car ready?'

'It's always ready, Your Majesty,' replies Mitsos with a certain professional pride in his voice, which implies that, were the circumstances otherwise, he would have been wounded at the suggestion that he was not always perfectly prepared.

'Mitsos, are the lights working properly?'

Mitsos looks at Aspasia in puzzlement, and she indicates that he should say that the lights are fine.

'Mitsos, prepare the car for a long journey. You drive. I'm exhausted.'

At three thirty the young King says, 'Bika,' and dies. He is buried next to the tomb of his grandfather, King George, who has so recently appeared in his dreams in order to summon him to the other side of the Styx.

Thus the headstrong German shepherd dog, Fritz, and Moritz, the Barbary ape, innocently and gallantly defending his mate, plunge Greece into a political void. The country is at war, the King is dead and new elections are due. Some people wonder whether Venizelos is going to proclaim a republic.

Instead, he asks Prince Paul if he would be King, but Paul is still very young and has an older brother and a father with better claim than he, and he refuses. Venizelos summons parliament, and Admiral Koundouriotis is appointed temporary viceroy.

Venizelos waits confidently for the elections of November, and is astounded when he loses heavily. Perhaps the Greeks are weary after so much war, or perhaps they are simply capricious. Certainly they have suddenly forgotten their relief when King Constantine was disgraced and deposed after obstinately and unpopularly supporting the losers in the Great War. The presence of the venerable Queen Olga reminds them suddenly that they loved the old set-up all along. The equally venerable new Prime Minister goes to the Tatoi Palace to beg the old Queen to accept the regency. He weeps with joy as he kneels before her, and when he refuses to rise, she kneels with him so that they can weep together, and then they struggle to rise with mutual aid.

King Constantine is asked to return to the throne, but sour experience has left him suspicious, and he asks for a plebiscite, which he wins overwhelmingly.

The return of the royal family is accomplished amid scenes of some chaos. Princes Andrew and Christopher arrive with Princess Mary, and they are deposited near the Corinth Canal by an Italian ship from Brindisi. They are awakened at dawn by a startling volley of gunfire, and emerge on deck to find a torpedo boat coming to fetch them. It is commanded by Admiral Ioannides and a crew of sailors who are lachrymose with joy. Princess Mary and the admiral eye each other with discreet interest, and are married some time later.

The Corinthians turn out with flowers and flags, waving pictures of King Constantine that they must previously have kept hidden in drawers. The royals are pelted with flowers by people running alongside the banks of the canal. The harbour of Piraeus is filled with boats of all descriptions, crammed to the gunwhales with enthusiastic plebeians who are shouting themselves hoarse whilst factory sirens wail and church bells ring. Queen Olga appears in the royal launch, then, when they all get ashore, it takes them three-quarters of an hour to reach their car, which is a mere forty metres away. Their hands are shaken until they are bruised, they are kissed on the cheeks, and there is a hyperbolical babble of laughing, crying and shouting. Queen Olga has to be surrounded by bodyguards to prevent her from being crushed. The crowd tears the running boards and the mudguards from the royal car, and somehow the clutch is disenabled. A rescue car is sent in by the army.

The car inches its way towards Athens, but there the people throw themselves to the ground before it, calling on the occupants to get out. Prince Christopher turns to Prince Andrew and says, 'I think we're going to have to make the sacrifice.'

Each of them is carried the four miles to the palace on the shoulders of the populace. Their royal flesh, unaccustomed to public adoration and the rough treatment that it entails, is so bruised that none of them can walk for a week afterwards. Prince

Christopher finds one of his legs being pulled in one direction by a woman in a mauve suit, and the other being pulled in another direction by a mechanic clad in his work overalls. He has a fanatical hairstyle. 'Bring my legs back!' cries Prince Christopher. Prince Andrew struggles valiantly to prevent his garters being purloined by his souvenir-seeking admirers, and fails.

It is very like riding all day on a camel. Prince Christopher is set down at the palace by his bearers, but the titanic and fanatic mechanic will not release him, and picks him up again to carry him indoors on his back, despite the struggles and howls of his cargo. The mechanic tries to carry the Prince upstairs, but the ancient Prime Minister intervenes, thrashing the mechanic with his walking stick, and crying, 'Let His Royal Highness down at once!' The mechanic fanatic drops the Prince and hurls the Prime Minister into a corner, enabling two soldiers to frogmarch the Prince away whilst the mechanic is distracted.

Unable to go out because of the crowds, the remainder of the royal party wait until dark and then steal out like spies, in order to go to the Tatoi Palace. They drive through villages festooned with flags, flowers and pictures of the King. The entourage has gifts of vegetables and game heaped upon it. In their cars rabbits and aubergines pile up around their feet. The bells peal, and the people shout, 'Erxetai! Erxetai!'

When the King does arrive at last, the scenes are even wilder. Of the one million who voted in the referendum, only ten thousand have voted against his return. Venizelos has fled the country, and the new old King is welcomed at the railway station by ecstatic crowds who clamber all over the carriages. He is carried straight to the cathedral, where the archbishop offers up prayers of thanksgiving.

Fritz bit Moritz and Moritz bit the King and the King died, and so there is a new king, who happens to be a previously deposed one who is detested vehemently by all the Allies. The loss of Allied support means the loss of the war.

Moritz, the Barbary ape, and Fritz, the German shepherd dog, will have successfully altered the entire course of Greek and Turkish history, but they themselves will retire modestly into oblivion and obscurity. They will leave neither simian nor canine memoirs explaining their side of the story. No one will know what happened to either of them in the end, or what would have happened if Moritz had not bitten the King.

82

Mustafa Kemal (20)

The Allies are disgusted by the re-enthronement of the old King. There had been a national schism in Greece because of his determination to keep Greece out of the Great War. He is Kaiser Wilhelm's brother-in-law, and he is universally thought to be Germanophile. France and Italy withdraw all support for Greece. These days they are both selling arms to Mustafa Kemal, effectively having changed sides. Even Britain notifies Greece that there will be no further financial assistance. In Greece, the war is already creating desperate economic problems.

Prime Minister Venizelos has flown into exile, and the war was, after all, Venizelos's pet project. This is an ideal opportunity to take Greece out of the war with dignity. King Constantine simply takes it over, however, and royalist officers are appointed to replace the Venizelist ones. The new general, Papoulas, scores a victory at Inönü, but retreats because he thinks the Turks are more numerous than they really are. Colonel Ismet, who will later take the surname 'Inönü' when Mustafa Kemal takes that of 'Atatürk', is mightily surprised by the Greek withdrawal, and reoccupies his old positions. He is promoted to brigadier general and is entitled to be addressed as 'Pasha'.

Mustafa Kemal sends a delegation to the London Conference, in tandem with one from the Istanbul government. The Italians considerately provide a warship for transport. The conference is relatively pointless, however, because the Turks are demanding Greek withdrawal from Thrace and Anatolia, whereas the Greeks still think they can win. The Turks make agreements on the side with the French and the Italians, and only Lloyd George holds out for a Greek presence in Anatolia. From now on, however, the Allies have made it known that they will be neutral in any conflict between Greece and Turkey. At the other end of Europe, the Bolshevik Russians agree to supply Kemal with a stupendous quantity of arms in return for leaving them to occupy Georgia.

General Papoulas attacks again at Inönü, and again the Turks retreat, only to return victoriously after some desperate moments. Ismet Pasha adds new lustre to his star. In the south the Greeks are forced out of Afyon Karahisar, but now the Greek line is a straight and much more invulnerable one. The French and the British send unofficial officials to Ankara to negotiate their future terms of reference.

Mustafa Kemal sets up his own political party, which means that epiphenomenally he has created his own opposition in parliament. He will always be a dictator who has a democratic future for his country in mind, and this is not the only time that he will set up his own opposition.

The Sultan's grandson arrives to join the nationalist cause, but Kemal politely sends him back to Istanbul.

King Constantine arrives in Smyrna, symbolically landing in the place once used by crusaders, rather than in the port. The reference is not lost on local Muslims. Massive Greek reinforcements arrive, and a new offensive takes place, with considerable Greek success. They win decisively at Kütahya, partly because of chaotic Turkish organisation. Only five divisions are actually fighting, whilst thirteen are marching about with no definite plan. Mustafa Kemal hurries to the front and consults with Ismet Pasha.

The Turks counter-attack, but fail. More chaos ensues. The Turks lose Eskişehir, and some 48,000 Turkish soldiers desert, fleeing along the railway line with the civilian refugees.

Mustafa Kemal orders a retreat to the Sakarya River, and this causes a crisis in parliament and among the civilian population. Sakarya is rather close to Ankara, and evacuation to Kayseri is planned. Parliament demands the resignation of the military commanders responsible for the disaster, and the Prime Minister, Fevzi Bey, responds boldly that solely he is responsible. Mustafa Kemal gives all his money to the wife of a colleague so that she can flee with her children. A rapid recruitment drive is inaugurated, and new troops are dispatched to Sakarya. The assembly persuades Mustafa Kemal to take command of the armed forces

GALWAY COUNTY LIBRARIES

personally. He is suspicious that this is really because his political opponents want someone to blame in the event of failure, and he worries about being away from the centre of power. He agrees to take command for three months.

The Russians send new supplies of weapons and ammunition, and much of this is driven to the front by peasant women in ox-carts. They are the heroines of the Turkish War of Independence, and without them it probably would not have been won.

Mustafa Kemal requisitions from every household one pair of boots and one set of underwear, and forty per cent of all stocks of candles, soap, flour, leather and cloth. All vehicle owners have to provide one hundred kilometres' worth of free transport every month. All civilians must disarm and send their weapons to the army. All horse-drawn vehicles are to be given up. The massive resentment that this causes among civilians can only possibly be assuaged by victory.

Kemal's command is delayed for five days when he falls off a horse and breaks a rib, but he is at the front in time for the new Greek offensive. In his headquarters he is joined by Halide Edip, the first truly notable Turkish feminist. She has been made a corporal, and she is impressed to see Kemal at work, although she does not enjoy the rough conditions. Kemal has periods of despair in between his times of superhuman determination.

The Greeks are superior in numbers, and better armed, and at once they succeed in capturing Mount Mangal and several other hills, but the Turks nearly capture General Papoulas and the King's brother, Prince Andrew – he who once bragged that he had paved his courtyard with Muslim tombstones. The Greek success has the effect of shortening the Turkish line, making it both stronger and easier to control. The Greeks finally capture Mount Çal, which everybody considers to be the most crucial objective. It looks as if the Turks have lost.

The Greek troops, however, are utterly exhausted by the heat, the lack of food and the losses. They have few supplies because the Turks have large numbers of cavalry who are moving about and constantly raiding behind their lines.

Mustafa Kemal endures more despair, and it is a curious irony that both the Greeks and the Turks are contemplating withdrawal.

GALWAY COUNTY LIBRARIES

General Papoulas is the first to lose his nerve, and the Turks, heartened by his withdrawal, immediately go into attack. They regain Mount Çal and the banks of the Sakarya River, but they are too exhausted to go on, and in any case they have no motorised transport. Only the cavalry can pursue the Greeks, and during one raid they succeed in capturing General Papoulas's medals. Mustafa Kemal breaks the terms of the armistice and orders a general mobilisation. He becomes a marshal, and is awarded the honorific 'Ghazi'.

He is now Ghazi Mustafa Kemal Pasha, Saviour of the Nation.

Back in Eskibahçe, Rustem Bey has become the saviour of the town. His campaigns against the brigands have made it almost impossible for them to operate in the locality, and they are seeking their fortunes elsewhere. It has become common for people to say: 'Thank God we have Rustem Bey as aga, and not one of the usual bastards.'

In Rustem Bey's house, Philothei grows more pale and listless as she waits for the return of Ibrahim, and Leyla whiles away the time playing the oud and working out ways to cook what little there is. Pamuk lazes under the orange tree in the courtyard.

In his unkempt house Daskalos Leonidas writes through the night in exultant celebration of the imminent restoration of Byzantium, whilst not far off Father Kristoforos sleeps beside Lydia, dreaming of the saints in Heaven playing backgammon, gambling with their robes and golden crowns. Some of them have been reduced to nakedness, but Kristoforos is unable to identify them. He thinks they must be the Catholic ones. In the brothel Tamara gazes into a mirror, and contemplates its story of infection, hunger, misuse and decay. She has achieved the sad detachment of an anchoress who expects nothing, and is there-fore never disappointed by it. The bulbuls and nightingales sing through the night as if there were no catastrophes.

One day Mehmet the Coppersmith arrives on his quarterly mission to tin everybody's pans, and he is bearing a message for Iskander the Potter from Georgio P. Theodorou in Smyrna. Iskander has to take it to Leonidas to be read, and it transpires that Theodorou would like five hundred more clay birdwhistles for export to Italy. He is offering a good price, but Iskander is appalled by the prospect of all that repetition, and resolves to make twenty a day, so that he will also have time to make more interesting things.

Ayse is amazed one morning when she is standing outside her house and a pigeon flies straight past her head and crashes into the wall. She takes the dying bird in her hands and feels the softness and stiffness of the feathers. It has blood dripping out of its mouth. It is a gift from Heaven, and later, when she is cooking it on a skewer, she is still incredulous, exhilarated by the tiny miracle. She leaves one leg, and later covers it with honey, and takes it to Polyxeni as a little treat.

83

Lieutenant Granitola Takes His Leave

'These have been three very enjoyable years,' said Granitola. It was early evening, and he was sitting on cushions facing Rustem Bey. Between them was a small beaten brass table on to which had been engraved allegorical animals, and pieties from the Koran in Arabic. Upon the table there was a large waterpipe which the two men were sharing, and the room was heavy with cool and aromatic smoke. On the walls around them Rustem Bey's formidable collection of clocks ticked synchronously.

'I am very sorry you are leaving,' said Rustem Bey. 'You have become one of us. I was fully expecting to have to find you a wife and a little bit of land. I had in mind a pleasant meadow and orchard down by the river.'

'A very pretty dream indeed,' said Granitola.

'I hope you will return,' said Rustem Bey. Granitola looked a little surprised and concerned, but then his face opened up into a wide smile and he said, 'It hadn't actually occurred to me, but now that you suggest it, I will certainly do so. I have been an occupier and I hadn't thought that I might simply return as a guest.'

'I think you can easily get a boat from Rhodes,' said Rustem Bey, 'and within a short time there will be motor vehicles here. I fully intend to get one myself. I have seen them in Smyrna, and I find them very impressive. I think they will become the thing of the future.'

'I doubt if they will ever replace the horse,' said Granitola, sagely. 'Horses can go anywhere more or less, and motor vehicles require not only petrol and expert knowledge, but reasonably wide and level surfaces.'

'Well, you might be right. In any case, I shall look forward with pleasure to your return. May I ask you a question?'

'Of course, my friend, of course.'

'Why do you think that your occupation has been so peaceful around here, when the French had nothing but disaster in Cilicia?'

'Well, we didn't bring Armenian troops in to cause havoc and wreak revenge . . . and we have always treated Mustafa Kemal with sensible respect, and we were good to all the Muslim refugees from the Greek sector. And we allowed the Turkish chettas to operate from our territory.'

'Why? Surely the Greeks were Allies?'

'Allies don't stick together after victories. It was a thing between us and the Greeks. It's a question of who dominates in the eastern Mediterranean. The French don't like the Greeks either, especially with the old King back on the throne, and now the British have the big embarrassment of being the only people left who are reluctantly supporting them.'

'Does anyone know why the French left?'

Granitola laughed. 'I understand that they decided to be the first to break ranks because they came up with an excellent commercial deal with Mustafa Kemal.'

'So why are you leaving?'

'Because I've been recalled, my friend. I'm afraid I have no choice at all.'

'No, I mean why are all of you leaving? Why has Italy recalled you?'

'I suspect it might be something similar. On top of that, it's obvious that Mustafa Kemal is going to win, and why should we face up to him when there's nothing to be gained by it? We've had a lovely time here, and now it's time to go, and the important thing was to prevent the Greeks from getting anything we might have wanted for ourselves.'

'I heard that the Greeks are in full retreat,' said Rustem Bey. 'I just hope they don't burn Smyrna if they leave. I have a lot of friends there, and that's where all my money's in the bank.'

'They've burned everything else, I am sorry to say, but, speaking as a soldier, there would be no point in burning Smyrna because one only burns towns to make them useless to an advancing enemy. It slows him up a great deal because then he can't supply or accommodate himself locally. Once the Greeks are at sea,

Mustafa Kemal will have no reason to follow them any further, and there would be no point in burning it. Personally I am more worried about what Kemal's troops are going to do when they get the freedom of the Armenian quarter.'

'Mustafa Kemal is becoming a giant,' observed Rustem Bey, his thoughts looping away on a different track. Then, returning to the subject, he asked, 'If you and the Greeks are both leaving, am I right in thinking that only the British will still be here?'

'Well, yes. They control Istanbul and the Dardanelles. Whether or not Mustafa Kemal will turn on them after the Greeks have gone, I wouldn't care to say. The British will be the last of the Allies, allied in the end to no one at all. Not an enviable position.'

'Surely Mustafa Kemal wouldn't dare take on the British? He doesn't even have a navy.'

Granitola laughed and shook his head. 'You're a Turk. What would you do in his place?'

'I think I would threaten the British and see what happens. Like a cat that bushes up its tail to frighten a dog.'

'As an Italian, I think I would do the same.'

'I shall miss our discussions,' said Rustem Bey.

'We have sorted out the world so much that now it cannot help but become absolutely perfect.' Granitola looked at his watch, twisted his mouth into a wry expression, and continued: 'But unfortunately I really must go and make ready. We leave very early in the morning.'

'I shall come down to the meydan to see you off.'

As he left, Granitola kissed Rustem Bey on each cheek, according to the custom that he had quite unconsciously acquired, and then he said, 'Did you know that the sergeant of the gendarmes has given Sergeant Oliva his backgammon set as a farewell present?'

Rustem Bey laughed. 'I have never heard of a Turk making such a terrible sacrifice.'

'Apparently he was weeping when he handed it over, but I don't know whether it was on account of parting with Sergeant Oliva or the backgammon set.'

'It was probably both,' said Rustem Bey, adding, 'When you go back to Italy I doubt if you will be able to carry on wearing that fez.'

Lieutenant Granitola took it off his head, looked at it, and then replaced it. 'I doubt it too. It isn't yet standard issue in the army, I believe, and is unlikely to become so. Even so, I shall wear it in the evenings as I sit in my study and contemplate, and I shall feel briefly like a Turk.'

'Wait a minute,' said Rustem Bey, and he went into the house and came back bearing his waterpipe. 'You must take this,' he said, holding it out. 'No, please, I have another. Smoke it in the evenings with the fez on your head.'

84
Mustafa Kemal (21)

Mustafa Kemal moves to a house bought for him by public subscription, and, in accordance with his long-standing determination both to be and to appear to be incorruptible, he promptly transfers the deeds to the army. He has a piano and a billiard table. He makes agreements with the Russians and the French. The latter are leaving Cilicia, but are to retain İskenderun, and they agree to sell their abandoned military materiel for a pittance, so that Kemal can use it against the Greeks. The Turks regain their territory in the south as the French leave, taking with them those Armenians who had previously returned. The Italians also leave behind them plenty of materiel, and more is illicitly sold to Kemal by both the Italians and the French. Weapons are smuggled out of caches in Istanbul, where they are supposedly under guard.

It is at this juncture that the Greeks entirely lose the sympathy of the rest of the world. They make the mistake of committing atrocities too near to Istanbul, where everybody will notice. As they retreat they destroy everything left behind, so that towns, villages and countryside are reduced to smoking desert. Greek irregulars, calling themselves 'Black Fate', make a career of murdering Turkish civilians.

Turkish atrocities are less noticeable since they occur in places where Allied observers have left. Nurettin Pasha viciously suppresses a Kurdish rebellion. In the Pontus, on the Black Sea coast, a Greek battleship bombards Ankara's feeder port, Inebolu. The Greek population of Pontus is enormous, swollen by Greek refugees from Russia, and to prevent an uprising Nurettin Pasha recommends that all Greek men between the ages of fifteen and fifty should be deported to the interior. Kemal accepts the idea, and what follows is an exact repetition of the death marches of Aegean Greeks in 1914, the death marches of Armenians in 1915, and the death marches of British prisoners of war after the fall of Kut. In Samsun the Turks execute those suspected of being Greek or Armenian leaders. A notorious Turkish guerrilla leader named Lame Osman does his worst, and the Greeks make it all worse still by bombarding the port of Samsun from the sea.

For some months Mustafa Kemal devotes himself to consolidating his own power and resisting other people's attempts to moderate it. He has to deal with the peacock pride of his own officers, who are always jostling for prestige and precedence.

The Allies propose a peace treaty, and the Greeks accept it, even though its terms are mostly favourable to the Turks. Kemal delays, however, because he realises that he is winning the war. General Papoulas has resigned and is replaced by General Hazianestis, a man widely considered to be mad, who sometimes thinks that his legs are made of glass or sugar. Hazianestis is sanguine about the chances of success, and does not even establish a second line of defence behind his army, which is stretched out almost in single file along an impossibly long front of four hundred miles. Hazianestis has his headquarters in a ship anchored in Smyrna harbour, which is about as far from the front as it is possible to be, short of going back to Greece. He moves large numbers of his men to Thrace. The Greeks have a new plan to take Thrace and occupy Istanbul, thinking that this will end the war.

When the British and the French find out, they inform Athens that they will resist any such plan by force of arms. British and French troops are sent to man the borders, and the British fleet puts to sea.

Kemal and Ismet realise that one cannot attack the Greeks along an entire front that is four hundred miles long, and so they pick one place in which to attack in force. This is the Afyon salient. Preparations are carried out in the utmost secrecy, mainly at night.

The attack is initially slow to succeed. There is one heroic but tragic commander who promises Mustafa Kemal that he will take Mount Çiğiltepe within half an hour. Before long Kemal receives Colonel Reşat's suicide note, saying, 'I have decided to finish my life because I have failed to keep my word.' Colonel Reşat is an old comrade of Kemal's from the Great War.

On the second day the Turks break through, and their cavalry appears in the rear of the Greek line. The Greek 1st Corps retreats in a hurry, leaving behind its stores. Communications break down altogether, and General Hazianestis issues an order to counter-attack which he might as well have addressed to thin air.

Mustafa Kemal risks sending his men in pursuit of the fleeing Greeks, even though there are intact Greek formations elsewhere. The attack is successful, and the Greek 1st and 2nd Corps disintegrate completely. The 3rd Corps in the north, which has so far stayed out of the fighting, prepares to retreat to Marmara because it is now vulnerable from the south. Kemal issues the famous order: 'Armies! Your objective is the Mediterranean. Forward!'

The Turks take thousands of captives, ambushing them as they descend from the slopes of Mount Murat. Mustafa Kemal has the delightfully ironic task of informing the captured General Trikoupis that he has just received information that the latter has been appointed commander of the entire Greek front.

The Greeks wreak havoc on their retreat, and everything is laid waste without sense or pity. The Greek army sidesteps Smyrna, and leaves it defenceless against a Turkish army that has advanced through the desolation, becoming more astonished with outrage at every pace. The Turkish soldiers heading for the city are commanded by Nurettin Pasha, its former governor, and victor against the Kurds. Mustafa Kemal has issued orders that the civilian population of Smyrna must be treated with respect, and that any soldiers violating this code will be hanged, but the Pasha is a prickly character who dislikes and envies Mustafa Kemal, and disobeys him whenever possible. He has a well-earned reputation for shameless brutality.

It is one of history's little ironies that in one century the Greeks should have fought a war of independence against the Turks, and in the following century the Turks should have fought a war of independence against the Greeks. In the final battle of this last war, the Greeks lost 70,000 men, and the Turks 13,000.

In Smyrna the last great catastrophe of the war takes place. It is now time for the Christian population to become the mirror of the Muslim one. Having seen what the Greek troops did to Anatolia, the Turkish troops are in the mood for revenge.

Nurettin Pasha summons Archbishop Chrysostom, the hell-raising cleric who originally got the pasha dismissed from his job in Smyrna in 1919. He hands the archbishop over to the Turkish mob, who mutilate him mercilessly until finally a sympathiser puts him out of his misery and shoots him. A French patrol nearby does nothing to intervene.

The Armenian quarter is set alight, and soon the European and Greek quarters are completely destroyed. The Turks say that the Greeks did this to prevent them from having it. After all, the Greeks burned everything else as they retreated. However, in this case the Greek army had already departed some days before. Some say that Armenians started the fire in order to prevent the Turks from having it. Some say that the fire was started because there were Armenian snipers in some of the houses, and it is common military practice to burn out snipers. Some say that Turkish soldiers started it on purpose to disguise what they had done to the Armenian civilians who lay eviscerated and raped inside the houses, or to make sure that they would have to leave and never come back. Some blame Mustafa Kemal, others Nurettin Pasha, who was a rabble-rouser and demagogue. Some blame Turkish regular troops, and others blame the uncontrollable irregulars who came along for the ride. In other words, everybody has someone else to blame and to despise for what happened to the fairest and happiest and most prosperous port on the Levant. In the end the blame really lies with Venizelos and the Allies, and in particular with David Lloyd George.

Out in the harbour the crews of Allied warships watch as the city becomes an inferno and the desperate Christian population crowds on to the quays. The ships are there to evacuate their compatriots, not to help the locals. At first both Turkish and Allied patrol boats prevent them getting out to the ships, but finally the captains and crews of the warships can take this cruelty no longer, and begin to allow them on board. In the end they save about 200,000 people, but there are many who have never forgiven them for waiting so long.

Beneath the oily water, thrown out of a boat and shot, it is too late for Georgio P. Theodorou, dealer in commodities and general merchandise, frequenter of Rosa's cathouse, philanthropist, creator and donor of the fine neoclassical pump house at Eskibahçe.

85

I am Georgio P. Theodorou

Yes, it's me again, Georgio P. Theodorou, at your service, merchant and philanthropist. Should you have forgotten, it was me who erected the pump house at the entrance of Eskibahçe, and it was me who regaled you with a somewhat overlong description of the town, and related to you the events surrounding the humiliation of Daskalos Leonidas, when he was made to wear a pack saddle. I wonder what happened to him; in fact, I wonder if he is even still alive. He certainly got what he was agitating for, and no doubt he was jumping up and down with glee when the Old Greeks turned up. I don't suppose he's so gleeful now, though, now that the Old Greeks have buggered off and left us all neck-deep in the proverbial excrement, with vengeful Turks beating down our doors.

You catch me at an awkward moment, my friends, and you may find my thoughts a little disconnected, but if you find me a little incoherent, if you detect that my discourse has come adrift, you will surely find me blameless, for I am at this very moment sinking slowly through the oily waters down to the harbour floor of this very lovely city that was Smyrna. I am, so to speak, neck-deep in the proverbial excrement only in a most metaphorical sense, as I am in reality considerably over my head in brine.

When you are not a strong swimmer, my friends, you are even less of a strong swimmer when fully dressed. This is a law of nature that no one can deny. I have been proving it empirically for the last hour or so. Sooner or later one has to give up the struggle, and the weight of one's sodden garments, combined with the extreme exhaustion brought about by panic and physical exertion, causes one to make peace with death at last, and then begins the long, slow descent to the murky realm of crabs and flatfish, seaweed, abandoned anchors encrusted with mussels and limpets, and inexplicable offcuts of thick rope and rusty hawser.

I can't convey to you the relief, the sheer pleasure, of abandoning the impossible struggle, the moment when one realises that it is less horrifying to die than to continue to struggle for life. It is nice, so very nice, to breathe the cold water deeply in and let it fill the lungs. One feels comfortable and clean, and a curious wavering solidity establishes itself in the head. I have just seen a large fish, and for the first time in my life have felt a pang of envy for the fishy lot.

Not far off I can see someone else sinking to the bottom, but her skirts have floated up around her face, and I wonder if she is concerned about dying in a state of immodesty, with her white camiknickers exposed for every drowning man to see. I would say that she has excellent legs, but I don't recognise them, so they probably don't belong to any of my little favourites.

All the canals of my nose have filled up, but my ears are hurting, and above me I can see the hull of a boat, and I have already become accustomed to the taste of salt. There are knocking noises reverberating through the water, and the sound of engines. They must be from the Allied warships that are watching with principled neutrality and cautious apathy as we struggle and drown. At first the water was stinging the burns on my face and hands, but now they are quite cool, I am pleased to say, and I can hardly feel the wound where the Turkish soldier shot me as I tried to swim away from the jetty.

I was very bitter about this death until I started to die it properly. I had envisaged a more ideal death, such as being shot at the age of ninety by a jealous lover of twenty-one whilst in the arms of her nineteen-year-old rival. Better still, and thoroughly ideal indeed, would have been never to die at all. I loved my life. Who could have had a more wonderful time? And the only price to pay for it was the occasional trip to the clapquack, and the occasional worry about rates of interest and whether or not the raisin harvest was any good. I had such a wonderful life that I was even inspired by my serene mood to commit unwise acts of philanthropy, such as erecting the little pump house at Eskibahçe, and not collecting debts from my friends.

What bothers me is that I am dying (albeit quite pleasantly) because of the most gigantic fuck-up, brought about by domnoddies, nincompoops and ninnyhammers of the first order who happened to find themselves in charge of fucking everything up. Excuse the strong expression of my feelings. I would not normally use strong language in the presence of ladies, but as a drowning man who has lost everything because of the antics of addlepates, I feel entitled to express myself picturesquely. (I have just been cursorily examined in the face by a harbour mullet, and it has swum away, presumably unoffended.)

Let's get one thing clear; I am not and never have been a dumbbunny. If I were a dumbbunny, I would not have made my substantial fortune, would not have paid almost no taxes, and I would not have made good connections at every possible level of society. Nothing, my friends, is as innocent as the pursuit of cash, the avaricious but honest exchange of goods and labour. I am a capitalist, and no good capitalist can afford to be a dunderpate. I have made money out of every commodity, and even out of thin air, and I have spent it liberally on both necessities and frivolities. I have generated so much employment that when I get to Heaven God should give me a medal and my own private whorehouse. Without me many a fig grower would be poorer, and many a little tart less well dressed.

I will tell you who the rattlebrains are, beginning at the top. Actually, there is not a top, because there are so many contestants for the lackwit championships that all come in equal first. Before nominations begin, let me make it quite clear that I am not an Old Greek. I don't come from Athens or any other poky little hole like that, where they don't even speak Greek properly. I am a rayah Greek, a twenty-four-carat Asia Minor Greek, and my family have thrived here in Smyrna for generations, and I will hobnob with any old Turk or Jew or Armenian or Levantine as long as they are inclined to strike a mutually beneficial deal. I make no distinctions of race and religion as long as there's some lovable cash in it or a good night out at Rosa's, which I fear has now been burned to the ground in this very conflagration which, from Bella-Vista Street to the Custom House, from the Custom House to Basma-Khane, and northwards to Haji-Pasha and Massurdi, is reducing the prettiest little playground in the Levant to a heap of ash composed in equal parts of bones and timber.

Here are some of the lackbrains in random order: the Greek people for electing to office a romantic, His Romantic Adventureness, Prime Minister Eleftherios Venizelos, who honestly thought he could annex the nicest half of Turkey and tack it on to Old Greece, even though no one had given him permission, even though most people here are Turks, and no one with any sense pisses off the Turks, because the one thing the Turks are very good at is overreacting when pissed off. Clodpoll number two, the Greek people again for being just as romantic as the aforementioned romantic, for thinking that just because the civilisation here used to be approximately Greek in the distant past and is now partially Greek, it should be forced into political union with Old Greece. Timbernonce number three, the aforementioned elected romantic, Eleftherios Venizelos, Prime Minister of Greece, prodigiously overendowed with Big Ideas.

Talking of which, what about the positive plague of firebrand priests we've been inundated with? All these men of God who want us to go out and kill Turks in the name of Holy this and Holy that? What about all this talk of rebuilding Byzantium? What on earth for? And some of them even talking with all seriousness about the imminent return of the Marble Emperor! What are we supposed to make of it when Archbishop Chrysostomos himself puts on his mitre and blesses our troops when they land at the quay, and strikes at Turkish gendarmes with his pastoral staff, and encourages his entourage to spit on them? I tell you what it looked like to everybody, without a shadow of a doubt. It looked not like an Allied occupation but another stupid Crusade, several hundred years too late. I admit I am sorry about what happened to Chrysostomos when the Turks took the town back. I don't think he deserved to be torn up by a mob, any more than I deserve to drown, but he was still a troublemaker and a Holy Fool, and I am only sorry that becoming a martyr will make people forget what a troublemaker he was.

And look what the Old Greeks did to the chief of police when they took over! He waited for them in his office so that he could hand over his authority, and they beat him and cut off his ears and gouged out his eyes, and everyone thought it a very fine thing and was pleased when he died that night in hospital, and you can bet that the same people who are horrified about the dismemberment of the archbishop were symmetrically gratified by the ditto of the police chief.

Rabbitbrains number four, all the Allied presidents and prime ministers for thinking it would be a good idea to let the Old Greeks occupy any bit of Turkey, because there's nothing like an Old Greek for harbouring grudges and grievances. How they nurse them and caress them and murmur endearments to them! An Old Greek nurtures historical hatreds like a botanist does a rare and exotic orchid. When an Old Greek turns senile he forgets everything except a grudge. If they were plants, these antique resentments would overwhelm the entire Levant and turn it into a jungle! And ninety-nine per cent of their most cherished and beloved grudges happen to be against the Turks. Did the British and the French and the Italians honestly think that Greek soldiers were going to be nice to the Turks after the landing?

Biggest fuckwit of all, now I come to think of it, must be that British Prime Minister, the Right Honourable Jobbernowl David Lloyd George, for encouraging the Old Greeks and the plausible Venizelos. I wrote to Lloyd George myself. I didn't address him as 'Dear Fuckwit', though I should have done. I said 'Honoured Sir'. I told him that this region can't be self-supporting because even though it might be pretty it doesn't have good land. I told him that all the trade comes from the hinterland, and this Greek occupation has cut us off from it. On top of that you had Greek soldiers and chettas and Bashi-Bazouks causing mayhem in all the rural areas, and on top of that we had Armenian bands and Circassian bands, and Turkish bands, and the net result was that the farmers couldn't work their land. I said in my letter that this city had been ruined and impoverished, there was no trade any more, I said that the rue Franque was virtually closed down, and that I personally was going to move my money to Alexandria. I didn't get a reply. I wrote the letter in French. I wonder what language the dead speak.

I nearly forgot King Constantine, coming here and landing at the very spot where the Crusaders landed, instead of landing at the port like a sensible and responsible monarch. And I nearly forgot General Hazianestis, Supreme Commander, rumoured to be mad, and sincerely convinced on one day that his legs were made of sugar, and on another that they were made of glass. This was his reason for not rising when one entered the room, in case they broke. I was once strolling with him along a corridor after a good dinner, and was just thinking about going to Rosa's, when I was startled by the General, who had just caught sight of himself in a mirror. He sprang to attention and saluted himself, his hand quivering with disciplined admiration. When he had finished, he said to me, as if it were perfectly obvious, 'One should always salute the commander-in-chief.' I heard that once he confined himself to barracks for walking on the grass when it was against regulations. Madman or noodle? Who knows? Whoever appointed him must have been both.

Please note that I don't place our dear High Commissioner, Mr Stergiadis, very high in my pantheon of nincompoops. The stupidest thing he did was to take on the job in the first place. He should have stayed in Epirus.

I'll tell you what I liked about Stergiadis; he was bad-tempered and he cultivated the noble art of alienating everybody quite impartially. When the notables invited him to a party, he didn't go, and neither did he have any parties and invite the notables. That's what annoyed them more than anything else. In fact, he just went home like everybody else after a day's work. It didn't bother me much, because I'd rather have gone to Rosa's than gossip with bigwigs.

He didn't take bribes either, and that was deeply annoying. That was the one way he annoyed me, in fact. 'How am I supposed to get things done, then?' I asked him, and I can tell you I was genuinely perplexed, and he looked at me as if I were mad and said, 'Mr Theodorou, you will have to go through the proper channels.'

I said, 'Proper channels? What proper channels? Round here there have never been any proper channels. I wouldn't know a proper channel if it came up and spoke to me in the street. I wouldn't know a proper channel if it introduced itself to me and handed over a calling card!'

He just shrugged and said, 'I sincerely hope that you and the proper channels become better acquainted during my period as High Commissioner.'

The other thing that annoyed everyone was that he was so scrupulously fair to the Turks that all the Greeks thought that he was anti-Greek. They thought it outrageous that he set the police on them when they got caught out, innocently and magnanimously inflicting atrocities on Turks. They thought it displayed a lamentable lack of Hellenic ideals, because what they really wanted was to clear the Turks out altogether. To be fair, in 1914 the Turks tried to clear all of us out as well, and God knows how many thousands of rayah Greeks got frogmarched to the interior and never came back. It was probably half a million. So don't misunderstand me, it isn't that I think the Old Greeks are worse than the Turks, what irritates me is that they think they're so much better when really they're exactly the same. God made them Cain and Abel, and whichever one happens to have the upper hand takes his turn as Cain. Whoever is unfortunate enough to be playing the role of Abel seizes the opportunity to bemoan the barbarism of the other. If I ever get to meet God In Person I shall suggest quite forcefully that He impartially abolish their religions, and then they will be friends for ever.

I went to see Stergiadis about something once, to complain about the murder of one of my Turkish customers who happened to owe me a lot of money, and by that time we were almost friends, and he confided something to me. He said that the Allies were getting very twitchy, and thinking that they had made a terrible mistake. There was a British general called Milne who had laid out the borders that would limit the occupation, but of course it was ignored. And then the British started getting inundated with reports from all quarters, about the antics of the Greek chettas and the Old Greek troops, and they started to put pressure on Prime Minister Venizelos, and he put pressure on Stergiadis, who tried to put pressure on the military, and didn't get anywhere at all. The fact is that the military were out of control and more often than not the high command didn't even know what the soldiers were up to. It was driving Stergiadis crazy. 'Mr Theodorou,' he said to me very gloomily, 'the sad thing is that I have to listen to so many people talking about our civilising mission.' He didn't say any more, he just left it at that.

As for me, I knew it was going to be a fiasco from the first day. Like everyone else I came down to the harbour when the evzones landed, and for a while I even felt like cheering and waving a Greek flag. It was certainly an exciting occasion, for a few minutes. Then some idiot fired a shot, and the soldiers opened fire on the Turkish barracks, and it went downhill from there. Excitement is only a good thing within certain limits, I would say, and that was a little too exciting. I prefer the more innocent excitements of the bawdy house. I think they killed three hundred Turks on the first day, and what's worse, the rayah rabble started looting the Turkish shops and stamping on fezzes and tearing off veils and committing the usual unimaginative horrors and bestialities. Thank God that Stergiadis turned up and re-established order. Even so, the soldiers and the rayah rabble continued to engage themselves in their exhilarating spree of self-congratulation, with their stupid flag-waving processions, and their ubiquitous portraits of Venizelos, and their thoughtless patriotic songs. There was one in particular that was going through my mind just now when I began drowning, and it was annoying me beyond measure, because when you are dying the last thing you want is a stupid song going round and round in your mind like the gibbering of a lunatic. Actually, I wish I had never mentioned it. The damn thing's coming back.

> Now that the fustanella
> Has come to Smyrna
> The fez will disappear
> The blood of the Turks will flow
> Now we've taken Smyrna
> Let's fly to Haghia Sophia.
> The mosques will be razed to the ground
> And the cross will be erected.

You know what annoyed me most about this song? It was the line about the fez disappearing. I watched a jaunty company of evzones marching up the rue Franque, and they were singing their hearts out, and it was this very song they were singing, and I thought to myself, 'And what exactly are those evzones wearing on their heads? Ladies and gentlemen, the headgear of an evzone is unmistakably a fez.' Of course the result of all this jubilant and thoroughly public crusading imperialism was that every self-respecting Turk hid his money, got his gun out of the cupboard and disappeared. The wind got sown, and here we all are, grimly reaping the whirlwind.

When Stergiadis turned up, that was all very well, and it was good to have Smyrna at peace again. But I am a merchant; I had to travel a great deal throughout the vilayet of Aidin and the sanjak of Smyrna. Things got desperate for me almost immediately. We had bandits coming over from Mytilene, whole villages wiped out in reprisal for the murder of one gendarme, a massacre at Menemem, where the rayahs painted white crosses on their doors so that the troops would know which house-holds to exterminate, officials going round forcing Turks to sign documents stating their delight about being occupied, soldiers taking away hunting rifles that were held under legitimate licence, the whole population of Karatepe getting locked into the mosque and burned to ash, soldiers parading about with fezzes and kalpaks on their bayonets, stealing everything, including the dirty handkerchiefs of Turks, gathering menfolk into mosques on the pretext of delivering a proclamation, whilst their valiant comrades raided their homes and molested the women, setting fire to houses to burn out snipers, imposing frequent roll-calls that made agriculture impossible, setting fire to the Turkish quarter at Aidin and putting machine guns in the minarets so that they could get anyone who preferred not to burn, the 8th Cretan Regiment embellishing daily its repu-tation for hooliganism, a tidy massacre at Ahmetli, rayah civil-ians being armed with weapons taken from Turkish barracks, Turks being charged fifteen piastres for the privilege of being compelled to buy rosettes and shout 'Zito Venizelos!', looting the office of the Italian Major Carrossi, who happened to be the Allied inspector of the gendarmerie, the usual impromptu Caesarean operations upon pregnant women, the usual ampu-tation of body parts, the breaking of teeth, the ransoming of

horses, the use of villagers as draught animals, the usual violation and defenestration of girls, the entertaining of idle troops
by letting them take potshots at muezzins calling the azan from
the balconies of minarets, the beating up of Turks who failed
to go into mourning on the solemn occasion of King Alexander's
death from a monkey bite, the shooting of tradesmen who
insisted upon piastres instead of drachmas, the knocking down
of a man and the putting of a foot in his crotch in order to
expedite the removal of his boots, the burning of every town
and village on the army's precipitate and humiliating retreat . . .
Oh, indeed, an infinity of errors great and small, constituting
the bitter reality of the glittering redemption of Constantinople
and the Asia Minor Greeks from the cruel and barbarous infidel
Turk.

And then the triumphant and vengeful troops of Mustafa
Kemal turn up, hordes of chettas mixed up with smart regulars,
and they crucify priests or garrotte them with knotted cord, and
they violate and defenestrate even the sweetest virgins, and they
pour petrol on to those trying to flee in boats, and they seal off
the Armenian quarter in the interests of their own entertainment, and then the city goes up in flames, and the identical catalogue of atrocity happens all over again, but now it's Turkey for
the Turks, and it's let's redeem Asia Minor from the cruel and
barbarous infidel Greek. Well, what can I do, except doff my hat,
make my salaams, and say, 'Gentlemen, fuck you all!'? I am at the
bottom of the harbour, my house and warehouses and Rosa's
whorehouse have all burned down, my money is in Alexandria,
and there is a wall of flame two miles long and a throng of
desperate humanity on the waterfront, waiting for the Allies to
bring their ships in and rescue them, which they gallantly show
no sign of doing.

I will tell you the one cruelty that offended me the most,
since time is short, even though time seems to stretch to infinity
when one is drowning, and I am indeed scarcely aware of my
body now that I am bumping gently up and down on the
seabed.

I had a client in Yeniçiftlik. His name was Kara Osman Zade
Halid Pasha. He was a very important man, a man with dignity,

and, if this means anything to you at all, the very best kind of Turk. It was a long journey, but I had to go out to see him on account of a shipment of figs. I found him dead at his house, with thirty-seven bayonet wounds, and without his nose, lips, eyes and ears. These items were removed from his head, which was in turn removed from his body. I had known Kara Osman for a very long time, but even I had trouble recognising him. I was only sure it was him when I saw that he was wearing his favourite silk shirt.

I looked down on his remains for some time, and I couldn't help the tears coming to my eyes, even though I did manage to conquer the urge to be sick. I did in fact owe him some money, but despite this I felt no relief about his death whatsoever. I was stunned by it, and I didn't understand it. I went to an officer nearby, and I could hardly speak, but I said to him, 'You've killed Kara Osman Pasha.'

This officer had a cutesy military moustache to which I took an instant and unconquerable dislike. He looked at me and raised an eyebrow, and in response to my observation replied coolly, 'So?'

I felt rage coming over me, and I couldn't restrain myself. I said, 'You're a cunt.' And then I turned and walked away, back to my horse, and I didn't see his reaction at all. I was expecting to get a bullet in my back, but nothing happened, and now, when I think of it, I realise it was the bravest thing I ever did.

I wish I'd had the sense to scamper off to Eskibahçe. I could have had a little holiday in the Italian sector. I could have built a neoclassical archway to go with the pump house. I could have repaved the meydan. I could have paid for a clapquack to look after the girls in the cathouse. But it's all dreaming now. My sight is fading, but it's dark anyway. I didn't know there were crayfish here in the harbour. I prefer the Atlantic lobster, really. I have become unaware of my body. I am already too dead to be worried about dying.

Georgio P. Theodorou, merchant and philanthropist, wishes you all a watery farewell. I would give you a wave but I don't know where my hand is, and more than likely you're not even there, whoever you are or aren't. Farewell Smyrna, farewell Rosa's, farewell my friends, farewell Lloyd George and Venizelos and all the other fuckwits, farewell my worldly goods, farewell even to myself. I just wish I didn't have to die with that stupid song about the fez going round and round in my head.

86

Mustafa Kemal (22)

It takes only a month for Mustafa Kemal to outwit and outface the British. He knows that the French and the Italians are happy to give him what he wants, which is the withdrawal of foreign troops from Thrace and Istanbul, and he himself is happy to guarantee passage for all ships bound through the Dardanelles to the Black Sea. His troops are now marching on the Dardanelles and on Istanbul. In Smyrna, which soon will become known as İzmir, Mustafa Kemal meets the woman he will ultimately marry, but unfortunately for both of them, her character will turn out to be just as strong as his.

Lloyd George announces in Cabinet that he will stand up to Mustafa Kemal, and Winston Churchill, ever warlike, wants to send an expeditionary force. New Zealand is the only Ally that feels like helping, however. Mustafa Kemal succeeds in convincing the French High Commissioner that he will be unable to restrain the victorious march of his troops on Istanbul, afterwards confessing to a journalist that he has no idea where his troops actually are. The French and Italians withdraw ships sent to help the British, and Lord Curzon goes poste-haste to Paris, where he has a bitter row with Poincaré that leaves him weeping. Turkish cavalry forces the British behind their defences at Çanakkale, but no shots are fired. It is during this time that Turkish officers come and borrow barbed wire from the British, on the gentlemanly understanding that they will return it when the crisis is over.

The French agree a plan with Kemal that gives him everything he wants, but the British are unaware of it. They decide to present him with an ultimatum, but General Harrington decides that it is better not to deliver it. He knows that he cannot defeat Mustafa Kemal when he has only a few thousand men. Poincaré is most relieved, and Lloyd George is furious, but in the end everything is smoothed over when armistice discussions are put in place. Ismet Pasha is a leading negotiator, and, since he is partly deaf, he simply pretends not to hear anything uncongenial or awkward.

In Greece, the fickle people turn against King Constantine, who they had welcomed back with such excess of joy only a short time before. They suddenly remember how much they used to hate him, and now they blame him for losing the war started by his greatest enemy, Eleftherios Venizelos. Constantine abdicates in favour of his eldest son, and will die in exile in Sicily within four months, a broken and heartbroken man. He has learned the bitter lesson of all Greek royalty, which is that it is better to mourn in exile than to reign at home, because the Greek people will only ever treat a king as if he is a president.

General Hazianestis and five ministers are put on trial and condemned to be shot. Rather than be degraded by anyone else, General Hazianestis strips his own insignia from his uniform before boldly stepping out to face the firing squad. His legs are firm beneath him, and do not, after all, turn out to have been made of glass or sugar. His execution and those of his comrades provoke outrage in the rest of the world, because it is obvious that they have been made scapegoats. Venizelos reappears, inexplicably disculpated, and the new military junta in Greece announces its intention to retain Thrace. Only Lloyd George has any patience with this vain ambition.

Kemal continues to threaten the Allies with war, and finally he gets his way. Eastern Thrace is to be Turkish after all. Its large Greek population leaves amid the usual heart-rending and pathetic scenes, the usual deaths on the roadsides, and it will be many years before it is replaced by Turkish refugees from Bulgaria and Greece, who will also have endured long and desperate treks from their homelands.

History begins again. The disastrous Lloyd George falls from power, and Winston Churchill loses office. Mustafa Kemal commences the construction of an entirely new country. He abolishes the sultanate, and then the caliphate. He sets up a secular constitution. He changes the alphabet from Arabic to Roman, thereby inadvertently ensuring that almost no future historians will really be able to understand the disordered archives left over from Ottoman times. He establishes equal rights for women, and outlaws both the veil and the fez. He sets up entire industries. He puts in motion events that are planned to lead to a Western-style liberal democracy just as soon as he dies, in which event he considers that he will automatically lose interest in holding on to personal power.

Mustafa Kemal also signs up to the Treaty of Lausanne, one of whose provisions is that almost all Turkish Christians, regardless of which language they speak, will be removed to Greece. Another provision is that almost all Greek Muslims, whether of Greek or Turkish origin, and regardless of which language they speak, will be removed from Greece and sent to Turkey. The criteria are explicitly religious rather than ethnic, and in the interests of preventing future strife it looks like a good idea, until one takes into account the innocent people concerned.

One day in Turkey they will call it 'The Demographic Catastrophe', because it is the Christians who know how to get everything done. Turks are soldiers and peasants and landowners, but Christians are merchants and craftsmen. Their loss will delay economic recovery for decades.

In Greece they call it 'The Asia Minor Catastrophe'. Those who leave will for ever feel that they have been arbitrarily thrown out of paradise. One and a half million of them arrive in Greece, causing the utmost difficulty for a government trying to accommodate and incorporate them. They bring with them their education, their sophistication, their talents, their nostalgia, and a music that will turn out to be rembetika. They also bring with them their absolute destitution and sense of injustice, and this will contribute perhaps more than anything else to the rise of communism in Greece, which will in turn lead to the Greek civil war.

In Turkey, committees are sent out to all the places where there are Christian communities. Their job is to assess the value of property so that it can be sent ahead, or its value reimbursed to the refugees on arrival. There is no transport provided, however, simply because Turkey has nothing left after the decade of war, and the goods will not arrive. For many of the refugees it turns out to be yet another death march.

In Eskibahçe they don't take the arrival of the committee very seriously. The Turkish and Greek Christians there, who have recently had a quiet time on account of the Italian occupation, feel little of the bitterness left over from the war with Greece. They still think that they are Ottomans, and that Mustafa Kemal is a good servant of the Sultan. Many of them still wear turbans, which were banned absolutely years ago.

The survivors of the conflict begin to trickle home. The celebrations that now seem to be occurring almost every day expose an inevitable undercurrent of terrible sadness. There are soldiers who return to find that their mother or father died years ago, or that they have lost their brothers. They find the fields overgrown, the animals gone and the houses dilapidated. Families wait in desperate anticipation as the lapse of time makes it increasingly clear that their sons are lost for ever. The town fills up with cripples. When Karatavuk returns, handsome, fully grown, upright, full of confidence and covered in medals, the joy in Iskander's house is unbounded. Nermin cannot stop weeping with relief, and Iskander, bursting with pride, tells his son that he too has had a good war, chasing the brigands with Rustem Bey. They take Abdul Chrysostomos's rifle and go hunting. Karatavuk and his brother both get a deer, and Iskander misses one. Karatavuk assures him that the ammunition must have been faulty, and deliberately misses the next target.

When Ibrahim comes back, he is abject and trembling. His hands shake so much that he cannot drink from a glass. He seems to be terrified of his mother and his sisters, cowers in a corner, and hides his eyes behind his forearm. Philothei can hardly resist the joyous impulse to run round to see him, but Ali the Broken-Nosed soon appears at Charitos's door and says that it is obvious that the wedding will have to be delayed. He offers to release the family from their agreement, but Philothei vehemently refuses when the idea is suggested to her by her mother. She works furiously at her trousseau. Ali says that Ibrahim is exhausted and very sick, but soon everyone is spreading the gossip that he has gone half mad. When Drosoula mentions this to her friend, Philothei becomes so infuriated that Drosoula never dares to bring it up again. Philothei finds that one kind of misery has simply been replaced by another. She remembers every time that she and Ibrahim have crossed each other's paths. She reminisces about them constantly. They are little stories, without trajectory or consequence, and soon Drosoula and Leyla Hanım resort to pretending that they are listening. Her nostalgia eats at her like a cancer. All her stories seem to begin with 'One day when I was out gathering wild greens . . .' She catches no glimpses of her betrothed even though he is only a few doors away.

The news has come through that Smyrna has been largely destroyed by fire and that all the Armenians and Greeks have gone. For months afterwards Iskander the Potter glumly surveys his shelves, packed out with five hundred children's birdwhistles. He hopes that Georgio P. Theodorou has survived, and that one day he will come and get the whistles. Otherwise he has no idea what he is going to do with them.

87

I am Philothei (14)

What can I do, but wait and wait and wait? I have waited so long, I've waited since I was a little child, and now I wish I'd married when I was twelve, because some girls do, but it was Ibrahim who was too young. Thirteen is too young for a boy. At that age boys are disinclined to seriousness.

I have whiled away the years tending to Leyla Hanım, who mostly seems just to want a little company, and who doesn't? And the coins I have been paid for this have been a benefit to my family. But all the time I've had this longing, for as long as I can remember. It's a longing that makes my throat ache, and my heart, and I have a kind of shivering whenever I think of him, and things begin to happen that affect me in my legs and stomach, and it's a kind of hunger and restlessness, and I keep picturing him in my mind, and it is as if I really see him, but it is a curious kind of seeing, because it is seeing in a manner of not seeing, and I see my beloved like that. I look up at the hillside and the hillside ought to have Ibrahim on it, and I look at the meydan and it ought to have Ibrahim in it, and when I see a goat, or hear one, I think of my beloved, because he is a goatherd, and sometimes I see Kopek, Ibrahim's mastiff, who is quite an old dog now. And when I used to see Kopek, I would wonder who would die first, me or Kopek, both of us dying from the yearning of waiting for Ibrahim.

They say that I am beautiful, and once they made me wear a veil because I was too disturbing to the men, and they say that I was beautiful even on the day I was born, and Abdulhamid Hodja came to see me, and he was a saint and he blessed me even though I was girl. And it was Leyla Hanım who taught me to be even more beautiful, how to adorn myself, how to employ aromas and balms, how to sit in front of the mirror and compose myself until I was perfected.

I have found that perfection is not enough. I would give up this perfection for the pains of childbed and the weariness of working in his father's house, and the humiliation of being the least among the women in that house, and the pity of seeing my perfection washed out of me by the duties of a wife.

I have waited seven years since my beloved left for the wars, and these have been seven years in the house of Rustem Bey, and I have been observing my perfection dripping away drop by drop because of the pain of longing, and I have been afraid that my beloved would lose his love for me if he saw me after his return.

And now he has returned. He has fought in a place called Mesopotamia, a desert place of scorpions and stones, and he has been in Syria, and he has been in the armies of Mustafa Kemal in the fight against the Old Greeks, and this has concerned me, because perhaps he wouldn't want me because my father is a Christian, and now there is bitterness against Christians because of the Old Greeks.

Now my heart is hurting and heaving in my chest, because he has returned and I have hardly seen him, not even in the company of his mother. And we have been betrothed by means of a gold coin, and he is very thin and has lost some teeth, and his voice is ragged, and his speech confused, and his laugh is high-pitched and peculiar, and his hands shake, and they say that he smokes continuously, even in front of his elders, so that his moustache has turned orange in the middle.

And Ibrahim's father came to see mine, and he said that my beloved was unsettled, and that he was not right in the head after coming back from the war, and my father agreed with Ali that the wedding should wait a little while until Ibrahim was back in balance, and when my father told me this it was like the stinging of lemons, and I wept because I had already waited so long, and perhaps I would have to wait another seven years or seven times seven, and I ran to the konak of Rustem Bey. In that house I wept with Leyla Hanım, who was like honey with me, and we went to the hillside and spied on my beloved, and the wind was booming over the sky, and we heard him playing the kaval, which is the sweetest sound in the world, sweeter than robins and linnets, and we saw him seated on a rock, and he put down his kaval and was caressing Kopek's ears, and then he began to sob and rub his face with his hands, and Leyla and I crept away because it is unseemly to spy on a man who is weeping.

Leyla Hanım took me back and sat me in front of the mirror and made braids in my hair and then undid them and redid them in different styles, and made me laugh a little by making me look unwonted, and she stroked my neck tenderly and kissed me on the cheek, and she said that since Drosoula had got married to Gerasimos, I had been much more than a handmaid and maid-servant, and she hugged me and I was comforted.

And I told her about the ache in my throat and the yearnings in my stomach, and the restlessness and shivering, and the deep hunger, and the never-ending hoping, and the seeing everything with him in it even when he was absent, and Leyla told me, 'I know a word for this,' and I said, 'Tell me the word,' and she said, 'The word is *agapi*,' and I said, 'What does it mean?' and she laughed and said, 'Silly girl, it means all those things you have just told me about,' and I said, 'What language is it?' and she said, 'Promise not to tell anyone?' and I said, 'Promise,' and she said, 'It's Greek,' and then she said, 'And do you want to know what to say to your beloved when you want to tell him about the feel-ings, when you are in his bed or you are lying privately in a field, and he covers you?' and I blushed and said, 'Tell me, Leyla Hanım,' and she said, 'You call him "*agapi mou*",' and I repeated, "*Agapi mou, agapi mou*", until it was memorised, and then Leyla Hanım said, 'When you want to tell him about your heart, when the feelings overwhelm you and they have to come out, you say "*S'agapo*",' and I repeated, '*S'agapo, s'agapo, s'agapo.*'

Leyla said, 'Now say, "*S'agapo, agapi mou*".' And I repeated, '*S'agapo, agapi mou, s'agapo, agapi mou*', and she stroked my face and said, 'This is the language of your forefathers that the Christians in this place have gradually forgotten,' and I said, 'Are there no words in my own tongue?' and she said, 'Silly girl, of course there are, but Greek is the best language for love.'

And every night before I slept I thought of Ibrahim, so close and yet so seldom seen, and made a picture of him in my mind, and I said to him, '*S'agapo, s'agapo, s'agapo*,' and when I dreamed of my beloved and I was running to him amid the tombs, I called him '*Agapi mou*', and eventually I realised that what Leyla Hanım had told me was true, that these words were the most perfect of any language in the world, and of all the words in the languages of the world, they were the most beautiful, and they were also the words that most meant what I was meaning to say.

88

Exodus

In the turbulence of his sleep Father Kristoforos dreamed once again of the funeral of God. The dream recurred in a thousand infinitesimally different variations, and for some time he had found it a potent source of psychological and spiritual strain. Lydia the Barren fretted about the dark rings under her husband's eyes, and the pallor of his face, but she had found no potions to yield him better sleep. In the version of this particular night, Father Kristoforos had dreamed that he had been the priest officiating at God's funeral, and the Angel Azrael, his maliciously aristocratic face gleeful with *Tödeslust*, had been the gravedigger. The latter had greatly shocked him by his irreverent comments about the state of the corpse, and Kristoforos had been awakened by his own shouts of protest, just as the gendarmerie arrived at dawn.

They were commanded by the same Sergeant Osman as had arrived years earlier to collect recruits, and with whom Karatavuk had left to join the army in the place of his father. The sergeant had aged greatly, partly because of the toll taken on his health by old wounds, and partly because of the parlous conditions of his life over many years. His limp had become more pronounced, and sometimes he experienced difficulty in breathing, a problem that he sought to alleviate by smoking continuously, a habit that had dyed most of his thick moustachio in various shades of brown and yellow ochre. He still considered himself a proper soldier, and his pride had caused his carriage to remain erect and his speech simple and direct. Upon arrival, after several days' march from Telmessos, he went immediately for a shave, and then, perfumed and refreshed with lemon cologne, set up office in the meydan under the same plane tree under which he had directed operations years before. Thence he dispatched his gendarmes to impart his orders to the populace.

At first no one believed what the gendarmes were telling them, but it soon became apparent that this was no prank. Sergeant Osman's orders were to collect the entire Christian population of the town and march it to Telmessos, whence it would be transferred by ships to Greece. Sergeant Osman had been given no transport, no provisions and no money with which to accomplish this feat. It was not long before he was besieged by groups of Christians who were at the very edge of hysteria.

'What about my house?'

'Lock it up.'

'What about my animals?'

'Ask your neighbours to care for them. Sell them.'

'What about my mother? She's sick. What will become of her?'

'No one can be left behind.'

'What about my son? He's away for three days. What will become of him when he returns?'

'He will be sent after us.'

'What about my samovar? It is very valuable.'

'Don't bring anything you can't carry all the way to the sea. If you have any sense bring food and clothing.'

'Tomorrow I am supposed to be meeting someone to talk about some land.'

'It's cancelled.'

'What about my things? I haven't got a cart to carry them in.'

Sergeant Osman would raise his hands to appeal for calm, repeating, 'Listen, all of you, in your new home you will get compensation to the exact value of everything you have lost. There will be an issue of certificates.'

'When? Where?'

'I don't know exactly. I expect it will get sorted out at Telmessos.'

'Where is Greece?'

'Over the sea. It's not far. Don't worry, you will be looked after by the Greeks and the Franks. They will find you new homes, as good as your old ones.'

'Are the Greeks Ottomans like us?'

'No, from now on you are Greeks, not Ottomans. And we are not Ottomans any more either, we are Turks.' The sergeant held out his hands and shrugged. 'And tomorrow, who knows? We might be something else, and you might be Negros, and rabbits will become cats.'

In their houses the Christians attempted to deal with the bewildering and impossible task of working out what to take. There were some families who regularly took animals up to the yaylas in the summer months, and were accustomed to trekking away into the distance with all they could carry, but even so they had never had to do so under such conditions of haste and uncertainty. Most people had been plunged quite suddenly into extreme states of emotion, and were completely confused. Some were shocked and silent, some hysterical and weeping, whilst others talked wildly of disobedience and defiance, of hiding until the gendarmes had gone, even as they obediently sorted through their possessions.

Some loaded themselves up only with food and water, and others deemed it better to take valuables that they could sell to raise cash, such as copper pots and dowry jewellery. Some sold their effects to their neighbours at knock-down rates, thinking that cash would be of more use than chattels. Some sorted out objects of sentimental value, and some looked, with greater or lesser irrationality, for things that may or may not turn out to be useful, such as small coils of rope, or the head of a hoe. It was one of those exceedingly rare occasions when blessed indeed are the poor, for by far the greater proportion of the people lived in such straitened circumstances that there were relatively few choices to make. These humble souls gathered what little they had into bundles, and foregathered in the meydan. Humbler even than them were the dozen beggars of Christian origin, who were alone in experiencing optimism in the place of despair. Some were mad, some retarded and some fugitive, but for all of them the hope of a new and better life in a new land was suddenly held out. They would follow the column of refugees, imploring alms from those who had nothing to give. Among their number was not to be found the Dog. He remained amid the tombs, removed from all considerations of race and religion by virtue of his speechlessness, his mutilation and his anchoritic life. Neither did any of the Christian prostitutes arrive from the brothel, being similarly removed from all considerations of race and religion by virtue of their profession.

Sergeant Osman's troubles truly began when the time came to marshal the people and get them moving. In the first place there was the problem of the teacher.

Daskalos Leonidas appeared in the meydan just when it seemed that at last the Christians were ready to depart. He was skinnier and more dishevelled than ever, the lenses of his spectacles were smeared, and his Frankish clothes were ragged and greasy. Because no one had seen fit to inform him, and he had no friends or relatives in the town who might have done so, he had not found out until relatively late what was about to happen.

Whereas to most of the Christians the disaster was a personal one, to Leonidas it was also a political and ideological one. He saw his dreams evaporating. Fired up with the courage of the outraged, he found enough audacity within himself to scramble clumsily up on to the very table under the plane tree where the town's gendarmes customarily played their infinitely repeated games of backgammon.

Sweating and trembling, he began to wave his arms and shout, in order to attract the attention of the milling crowd. 'Friends! Friends! Listen! Listen to me! You have to listen!'

'Get down and shut up, idiot,' demanded Sergeant Osman, looking up at him. He was ignored.

'Listen! Listen!'

There was something desperate and commanding in that thin dry voice, something that made even Sergeant Osman want to hear what he had to say, and so he stayed the hand of a comrade who was about to thump Leonidas in the back of the knee with the butt of his rifle. 'Go on,' said Osman. 'Say what you have to say, and hurry up about it. I give you a few words, that's all.'

No one suspected what Leonidas was about to say, and it came to them almost as a shock. They fell silent, their faces trained up towards him, and he made an eloquent gesture with both hands. 'Since ancient times,' he said, as if beginning a lesson, 'we have lived here. This is our home. In their greatest days our ancestors built the magnificent things that you see fallen about you in ruins. We had the greatest civilisation in the history of the world. They tell you that you are being taken to Greece, but this was Greece. This must be Greece again. It is Greece. We are Greeks and this is our home in Greece. We cannot leave. In this place it is the Turks who are foreigners. They arrived long after we did. You must all go back to your houses. We must all refuse to go. This is our home. This is Greece. This is the land of the Patriarch. We must refuse to go. You must stay here for the love of Greece and the love of God.' He let his hands fall to his sides, and then raised them again, holding them out beseechingly, palms upward.

The people looked up at him, unresponding. It was true that this was home, but how could they refuse to go when there were men here with guns and authority? How could they become defiant when they were probably under the orders of the Sultan Padishah himself, refuge of the world, and under the orders of Ghazi Mustafa Kemal Pasha, terror of the Franks? How were little people, most of them illiterate, bred to docility and hier- archy, suddenly supposed to become lions? The metamorphosis can be made under the leadership of a demagogue, but Leonidas up on his table did not amount to such; he seemed ludicrous, and a little mad.

Sergeant Osman looked up at him wearily, and tugged at the cuff of his trousers, saying, 'Come down now, or I will have to shoot you. It will give me no pleasure, unfortunately, but we are running out of time.'

Daskalos Leonidas looked at the upturned faces of those below. It seemed to him that they were regarding him with a curiously mild interest, as if he were a strange but harmless animal that had wandered away from a menagerie.

'Come down,' said Sergeant Osman, but instead of coming down Leonidas remained on the table, hung his head, closed his eyes and began to sob. His shoulders shook, and tears began to slide down his cheeks, gather on the point of his chin and splash on to his boots. The people watched, and Leonidas wept.

He was weeping for the loss of everything that he had believed in and for which he had fought. All his adult life he had dreamed and worked for the idea of Greater Greece, of the days to come when Greece would again encompass all the historic territories, of the days when Greeks would rule over themselves and cease to be anyone else's subjects. It had seemed for so long that history was on his side, as Greece grew bigger and bigger. Crete, the

Ionian Islands, Salonika had all become Greek. He had passed so many nights, engaged in a protracted epistolary conspiracy, writing about the inevitability of it all by the light of a stinking wick, and now it was impossible to imagine that suddenly history had changed sides, and created a country called Turkey in a Greek place. Leonidas was a nationalist in the days before the erosions and landslips of time exposed the miserable stupidity of nationalism. If he had lived three generations later, an intellectual like Leonidas would have thought of nationalism and religion as the unholy spouses from whose fetid conjugal bed nothing but evil can crawl forth, but these were innocent days, when orthodoxy was the sole and obvious truth, and nationalism was still romantic, reputable and glorious. Dry and cantankerous as he may have been, Leonidas was the highest romantic, and his tears were those of a romantic who has seen all his aspirations crushed. Leonidas, disowned by his family, all of whom had in any case irretrievably disappeared during the burning of Smyrna, friendless in this backward place, betrayed by history, now had not even his wonderful ideas for which to live. On the long march to Telmessos, he would speak only once, when the moment came for him to translate some Greek, the language he had for so many years tried in vain to teach to the children of the town, and which soon they would all have to learn, whether they wanted it or not.

When Leonidas finally descended dejectedly from the table, he turned and said bitterly to the sergeant, 'You will never be forgiven for this.'

The gendarme looked back at him, and replied simply, 'I have nothing to be forgiven for. I've got nothing against you. I don't care about you at all, in fact. I don't care if you live here or in Greece or on the moon or up a tree like an ape, or up the backside of a camel, and as a matter of fact one of my grandmothers was a Christian from Serbia, so I don't even care if you're an infidel. If you want to blame somebody, blame the Greeks for invading us and laying half the country to waste. This,' he said, indicating the proceedings all about them with a wave of the hand, 'is thanks to orders from above, and I just have to assume that those above us know what they're doing. If you give me any trouble in carrying out my instructions, you will find that I lose patience very suddenly, and no doubt one of my men will be glad to give you some indications of my displeasure. I hope this is all very clear to you.'

Daskalos Leonidas stood for a minute, scrutinising Osman's face. It was not the face of an enemy, and this perplexed him. The brown eyes were those of a grandfather. Leonidas turned and went back into the crowd, where he stood, his ears burning with shame, embarrassed and enraged both by these sheeplike people and by what was being done to them, repeating to himself the formulae which seemed to him to be so just, but to which no one wished to pay attention.

It seemed to Sergeant Osman that at last he could get everyone moving. To him, too, they were like sheep, but more skittish. Perhaps they were less skittish than goats. Everything was in place. As far as he knew, he had all the Christians gathered together in reasonably good order.

Surveying them, however, his heart sank. There were many very old people, some bent double from their lives' labours. There were pregnant women, and tiny children too small to walk long distances, but too heavy to carry. There were even beggars, mad people and idiots. He shook his head and rubbed his eyes with his hands. It was odd how when one thought of a generic human being, one had the mental image of a man perhaps between twenty and thirty, but here was visible proof that such generic ideas were impertinent to reality. He could tell in advance that without transport the whole operation was going to be a fiasco. Inevitably there would be deaths on the road, and delays brought about by those deaths.

The rest of the population had gathered to observe the departure, but were not apparently about to do anything untoward. They seemed curious, and oddly subdued, as if they were about to witness a passing procession of animals rather than the deportation of their friends and neighbours.

The first untoward event came not from the onlookers, but was sparked by Polyxeni, who had already been semi-hysterical for some time because her daughter Philothei was nowhere to be found. Now she suddenly remembered Mariora. 'Mother! Mother!' she cried, and abruptly she dropped the bundle she was carrying, left the side of her husband Charitos, and ran off in the direction of the little church at the bottom corner of the town.

There was the briefest moment of puzzlement as people thought, 'But Mariora is dead,' and then there was an equal moment of collective revelation as everybody realised what Polyxeni was doing. Once it had become clear, it seemed inconceivable not to follow her example. Likewise dropping their bundles, the people ran off, exclaiming and crying out to each other, ignoring the cries and warning shots of the gendarmes.

'Son of a whore!' muttered Sergeant Osman, his pistol in his hand, looking around at the mêlée, utterly confounded by this extraordinary turn of events.

Some people ran to the cemetery and flung themselves head-long upon the newer graves, speaking into the earth, 'I'll come back for you, I promise. I promise I'll come back.' Those who believed that their loved ones might have sufficiently rotted began hurried exhumations without the assistance of the priest, and without the customary washing with wine. Many were horrified to find that a particular body would need much longer in the earth. There are few things more unforgettably appalling on this earth than to see and smell the corpse of a loved one who is half decomposed.

Others more fortunate crowded into the ossuaries of the two churches, gathering up the linen-bound bundles. Polyxeni was lucky in getting there first. Her mother's bones were near the top, and the linen had not yet rotted. Against the tide of the crowd, triumphantly bearing her mother's remains, she found her way safely back to the meydan.

There were scenes that would have been amusing had they not been macabre. People altercated over questions of identity, particularly with respect to the older bones that had long turned brown. There were tugging contests whose inevitable consequence was that many bones were spilled, falling to the stones with a hollow clattering, becoming mixed up on the ground. The linen wrappings of the long dead crumbled apart, scattering their contents. Brothers argued over who had the most right, or the greatest duty, to particular relatives. There was much running

533

hither and thither to find sacks and bolts of cloth in which to carry the precious cargo.

It was a full hour before the Christians were once more gathered in the meydan, and ready to depart, now bearing bundles of bones in addition to their essentials. Sergeant Osman regarded them balefully. As far as he was concerned, it was sacrilege to disturb the remains of the dead, and he found himself feeling outraged and repelled. After some minutes of discussion with his corporal, he decided that it would now be impossible to travel any significant distance before the intervention of darkness, and he climbed up on the table to address the Christians.

'Return to your houses. We depart an hour after dawn. Listen for the azan, and make sure you are out of your houses promptly. Anyone causing delays will be dealt with very severely. Get well rested, and prepare yourselves for a long hard day. That is all.'

He jumped down, landed awkwardly because of his bad leg, and straightened up. He and his men would spend the night in the town's khan, and awaiting them they anticipated yet another unappetising dinner of bulghur wheat, bread, cheese and raw onions. They were more than delighted when a servant of Rustem Bey's appeared, bearing platters of kadin budu and chicken with saffron. Rustem Bey's sense of *noblesse oblige* had made it a matter of principle for him always to bestow hospitality upon new arrivals in the khan, and his servants were instructed so to do, even, as in this case, in their master's absence. That evening the gendarmes went to sleep replete, their bellies pleasantly rounded, and their mouths tingling with the softly bitter taste of cooled tobacco smoke, inhaled from the waterpipe that had also arrived from the aga's house in the wake of a tray of rosewater lokum. 'I tell you what, lads,' commented Sergeant Osman as he rolled out his pallet, 'I wouldn't mind staying here and forgetting about this whore's cunt of a job altogether.'

'Well,' said the corporal, 'there'll be plenty of empty houses if you ever feel like coming back.'

'I might just do that,' said Osman. 'I'm getting too old for all this.'

In the first light of dawn, as the sun ascended from behind the mountains and spread its rosy fingers across the horizon, the entire population of the town reassembled in the meydan, the Muslims remaining at its periphery under the lime trees, and the Christians milling about at the centre. There was a better sense of order than there had been on the eve, and Osman felt vindicated in having made the decision to postpone their departure. He was enjoying the first chill, and the first cigarette, of the morning, and was feeling more confident about the task that lay ahead of him. He had no delusions about the difficult decisions that awaited him, or the occasional brutalities that might have to be committed for the good of all, in order to keep the column moving. That morning, as he had touched his head seven times to the prayer mat, he had explicitly asked God to forgive him in advance, and to be merciful, and now he felt himself fortified.

Osman saw that the Christians must have spent much of the night in preparation. Those who owned goats had improvised little pack saddles for them, which were laden with provisions tied up in bundles of clothing. Chickens had been tied by the feet to these saddles, and they flapped and squawked as they repeatedly lost their balance. The few that possessed mules or donkeys had piled them with preposterous loads that would almost certainly topple off before long. The most curious thing of all was that everybody had, by some process of apparently telepathic unanimity, decked themselves out in their very best clothes, as if they were going to a wedding or celebrating a saint's day.

Just as Osman was thinking that it was time to go, Father Kristoforos appeared from the direction of the Church of St Nicholas. Behind him came Lydia, his wife, bearing a large bundle of bones upon her back, which was held in place by means of a band of cloth circumposed about her forehead.

Attired in his priestly robes, Father Kristoforos, his eyes half closed either in grief or in meditation, was singing the theotokian from the prayers for the departed. The people fell silent as his rich baritone sent the ecclesiastical Greek echoing from the walls of the town. 'O pure and spotless Virgin,' he sang, 'who ineffably bore God, intercede for the salvation of the souls of thy servants.' Suspended about his neck on a chain, and held out before him, his hands gripping the thick, elaborately engraved silver frame still draped with tamas of the faithful, Kristoforos bore the icon of the Virgin Panagia Glykophilousa.

The Christians fell to their knees and crossed themselves. How could they have forgotten about their icon? The Muslims, too, could not help but let out a low moan of despair. Was there any one of them who had not at some time asked a Christian acquaintance to solicit some favour on their behalf from Mary Mother of Jesus? Wasn't it true that the icon had for centuries watched over the town for all who had lived in it, and mitigated its bad luck, regardless of faith? Those who were destined to remain in that town suddenly had the appalling feeling that they were being left helpless.

Father Kristoforos processed through the kneeling people, and stopped before Sergeant Osman. 'Sergeant efendi,' he said solemnly, 'you will not drive my flock. I will lead it.'

There was one of those moments that sometimes pass between two people, when they look into each other's eyes and come instantly to a kind of understanding which is akin to the recognition of oneself in another. Osman looked at Kristoforos, with his haunted and unhappy face, and his tatty black robes, and realised that in the priest's position he would have demanded exactly the same thing. He found it admirable that the priest had found the courage to address him so directly, when there was such a disparity of power between them. Normally a gendarme would have had no reason to take notice of any demand or request from the likes of Father Kristoforos. Kristoforos, for his part, thought that he detected a certain humanity, a lack of self-consequence, in the gendarme that made it easier to approach him so directly. The two men regarded each other for a while, the one downcast but proud, and the other weary but humorous. 'As you wish,' said Osman, eventually, 'just as long as we arrive in Telmessos. If you want to play the shepherd, my men and I will be happy to play at being the dogs, as long as it is understood that in this case it is the dogs who are in charge.'

'We will arrive in Telmessos,' assured the priest. He turned about and raised his voice. 'Be comforted,' he called, 'and follow me. We are all in the hands of God.' With great dignity and at a measured pace, he set off in the direction of the entrance to the town, holding out the icon before him, reciting the kontakion to the Mother of God: '. . . Do not despise the voices of we sinners as we pray. In your love, haste to help us who cry to you in faith. Hurry to intercede, make speed to entreat, O Mother of God, for you ever protect those that honour you.'

The crowd began to drift in his wake, with the bemused gendarmerie bringing up the rear, but no one had gone much more than fifty paces before the first small drama had occurred. Polyxeni, already deeply distressed by the inexplicable disappearance of her daughter, Philothei, when there was so much to carry, was incapable of walking any further, because of the burden that she had taken upon herself. She and Charitos had argued about it for much of the night, but there had been no possibility that she would ever agree to leave behind her ancient great-grandfather, Socrates, or, God forbid, do away with him as a matter of mercy.

Socrates had gone past the age when it was possible to age any further. For years he had remained the same, propped in a corner of the house, repeating the same senescent inanities, and mulling aloud over the same memories. He was tiny and wizened, his birdlike bones shining through the yellow and mottled skin of his face and limbs, his few wisps of hair concealed under the same rotting turban that he had been wearing for decades, and from which he had always refused to be parted. Finally Charitos had agreed that he would carry the heavy bundle of essentials, and the bones of Mariora too, but Polyxeni would have to carry the venerable Socrates on her own back.

Socrates was delighted to be out in the light, surrounded by so many people. 'I'm ninety-four, you know,' he said, in his small, cracked voice.

'You're much older than that, Socrates Efendi,' said somebody, but the old man's mind was away on its own. 'I've got twelve children,' he said.

Polyxeni was not a big woman, and she was by no means young herself, but even so, it had seemed to her that it ought to be possible to carry her great-grandfather on her back all the way to Telmessos. He was as light as a straw, after all.

However, with his arms tightly around her neck, so that she

felt she would choke, and the weight of his body bearing down on her arms, she stumbled almost immediately over a stone down by the new wash-house at the entrance to the town, and she and her great-grandfather fell together to the ground. Despair gripped Polyxeni suddenly, and she sat up in the dust and began to wail, her hands over her face. She rocked and howled, and everything came to a halt around her.

Sergeant Osman hurried over, saying, 'Get up, woman, get up. Keep moving.'

'Oh God, oh God,' cried Polyxeni. She had fallen face down on the stones, unable to protect herself because of the greater need to protect the old man. Her nose bled, and her cheeks were cut. One knee of her shalwar was slashed, and underneath she could feel a wound beginning to bleed. 'Come on, get up,' repeated Osman, and old man Socrates lay on his side, parroting, 'I've got one hundred and twenty great-grandchildren.'

Polyxeni was immovable. She knew that it would be utterly impossible to carry the old man, and the desperation and grief of it overwhelmed her completely. Osman prodded her with his boot, and was beginning to think that he might have to beat her. 'They're all shit,' said Socrates, triumphantly.

'Oh God, oh God,' moaned Polyxeni.

'Will no one carry the old man?' asked Sergeant Osman of the people who had gathered around. It was impossible. Everyone was fully laden. No one spoke, but each of them felt a pang of guilt.

It was at this point that Ali the Snowbringer intervened. He had been planning to go and fetch ice after the Christians had gone, and was stationed at the entrance to the town, preparatory to his own departure. He had found himself feeling increasingly upset as he began to realise the full import of what was happening, and now he was quite suddenly moved to action. He came forward with his donkey, bent down, and placed the rope of its halter into Polyxeni's hand. She felt the strange sensation of the rope's roughness between her fingers, and looked up through her tears, to see Ali the Snowbringer leaning over her.

Initially she was puzzled. Ali the Snowbringer was not someone with whom she had ever shared any discourse. For many years he had lived in the meydan, in the hollow of a gigantic tree, with his wife, children and donkey. He was among the world's poorest and lowliest of beings, an emaciated old man now, his teeth broken yellow stumps, his face creased and baked dark brown by his lifetime's treks into the mountains. His clothes were barely better than rags, and more often than not he went barefoot.

He indicated his donkey with a wave of his hand, and said humbly, 'In the name of God.'

Polyxeni took some moments to understand what he meant. 'In the name of God,' he repeated, gesturing again towards the donkey.

'You are giving me your donkey?' asked Polyxeni incredulously.

'Not giving, Polyxeni Efendim, lending. When you arrive at Telmessos, inshallah, let her go, and she will find her own way back, inshallah. She is a good donkey, and she has been lost before, and found her own way back.'

'Get up, woman,' said Sergeant Osman, 'you will never receive such an offer again. I for one am glad that I lived to see it.'

Polyxeni did not get up. On her knees before the Snowbringer, she took his right hand in her own, kissed it repeatedly and pressed it to her forehead, all the while sobbing with gratitude. She looked up at him at last and said, 'Snowbringer, for this one good deed you will rest for ever in paradise.'

Ali the Snowbringer had never previously had his hand kissed by any other than his own children and grandchildren, and the unexpected respect nonplussed him. He was moved by it, and his lips began to tremble. It seemed to him that his life had been worth living, now that this point had been reached. 'Apart from Rustem Bey I have no customers any more,' he said, *sotto voce*, as if to excuse his self-sacrifice.

Charitos, who had dropped his own bundle in order to attend to his wife, began to help her to her feet, now that she had recovered her hope, and with it her strength. Then the two men lifted Socrates on to the donkey, and some of the load with which Charitos had been laden. Into the ice bags Polyxeni put the bones of Mariora.

Polyxeni kissed Ali's hand again, and then Charitos kissed it, saying, 'Blessings be upon you.'

'And upon you be peace,' said Ali.

'I have sixty grandchildren,' interjected the bemused old man astride the donkey.

This scene had produced a great effect upon everyone present; it had brought home the true significance of what was occurring, and caused a welling-up of emotion in the witnesses. A woman's voice rose up clearly and desperately into the morning air, echoing from the stone walls of the buildings: 'Don't go! Don't go! Don't go!'

It was Ayse, widow of Abdulhamid Hodja, who had lost all her sons in the war, and now understood that she was losing many of those who had kept her going in the subsequent years of want and despair. She had made her farewells with Polyxeni only an hour before, and they had already wept together, but now she was confronted by the reality of this final departure. She would never see her life's best and most long-standing friend again. Never again would she enter Polyxeni's house through the haremlık door, and throw herself down on the divan, sighing and giggling in their gentle conspiracy of intimacy and affection. 'Don't go!' she cried. 'Don't go!'

Ayse's wailing was infectious, and others among the onlookers began to moan as the Christians passed them by. Before long the men were choking back tears, and the women were giving free rein to them. Soon it was like the howling and ululation of those who become carried away by grief at a burial, multiplied beyond understanding by the sheer number of people. Up in the ancient tombs above the town, the Dog cocked his ears to listen, and down among the refugees, Sergeant Osman felt that he had never heard anything quite so disturbing in all his life, not even when men are dying between the lines after a battle.

So it was that, long after they had entered the serene and scented pine forest below the town, the fearful Christians began their odyssey into hardship and loss with the heart-rending lamentations of those who remained still echoing in their ears. In the trees they passed the Muslim dead, melding silently and obliviously into the earth in their tilting whitewashed graves. The people gazed at everything they saw with that special intensity brought about by the knowledge that only in precious memory would they ever behold the face of their homeland again.

Ahead of them, leading them away, almost unable to see through his tears, bearing the icon before him, pausing in his orations to kiss its silver frame, Father Kristoforos continued to intone every prayer for mercy that he could remember. 'Chief Captains of the heavenly armies, we the unworthy implore you to protect us by your supplications, with the shelter of the wings of your immaterial glory, as you guard us who fall down and insistently cry out; deliver us from dangers . . .' he sang, acutely pained by the irrepressible suspicion that his prayers were winging up to an empty sky.

89

I am Philothei (15)

When the committee came to value our property none of us was very concerned. We didn't think we would be deported anyway, because we didn't speak Greek. Only Leonidas Efendi knew Greek, and Father Kristoforos.

And we said, 'We aren't Greek, we are Ottomans,' and the committee said, 'There's no such thing as Ottoman any more. If you're a Muslim you're a Turk. If you're Christian and you're not Armenian, and you're from round here, you're Greek.'

We said, 'We ought to know who we are,' and they just ignored us and carried on valuing our property.

So when the gendarmes arrived with an official firman, and we were given almost no time to get ready for leaving, it was a terrible shock to all of us, and no one knew what to do, and what to take with them, and I can't describe the panic.

Most people were looking for neighbours to sell their property to, but because everyone was trying to sell, no one could get a good price. My father Charitos was walking about like everyone else, laden down with pots and carpets, trying to sell them. My brother Mehmetçik was an outlaw because he'd deserted the labour battalion, and there was no way to get a message to him. My mother Polyxeni was weeping and clutching at her head with both hands even as we tried to sort out our possessions and gather provisions. In the end she decided to leave her trunk with Ayse, widow of Abdulhamid Hodja, in the hope that one day she could come and get it. I helped her carry it to Ayse's house, and Ayse Hanım was very upset and we had to reassure her.

The worst thing for me was that I was torn in half because I was betrothed to Ibrahim, and he was far away in the rocks with the goats and Kopek, his dog. I was a Christian, but if I married him I would be a Muslim. I didn't know what to do. I loved him but I knew he was still not in his right mind, but I also knew that he very nearly was. I loved my father and mother and wanted to leave with them to our new home, but I also wanted to stay and be married to my beloved if he got better.

I was revolving these problems in my mind until I couldn't bear it any longer, and I thought I was going to go mad with the distress, and when my mother wasn't looking I ran away up the street, past the grand houses that used to belong to the Armenians, and then I ran through the thorns and the tombs, and I came across the Dog and I said to him, 'Please, Dog Efendi, where has Ibrahim taken the goats?' and he pointed over the hill towards the sea, and he wagged his finger at me as if to say 'Don't go', but I went anyway.

90

Leyla Hanım's Letter
to Rustem Bey

When Drosoula had run to Rustem Bey's house to make her hurried farewells to the mistress that she and Philothei had served for so long, she can have had no idea that Leyla would react as she did. Instead of the shock and dismay that everybody else had expressed at the arrival of Sergeant Osman and his gendarmes, Leyla Hanım had evidenced excitement and agitation.

'Are they really taking you all to Greece?' she had kept asking. 'Where in Greece? How are they transporting you? How long is it going to take?' and Drosoula had been obliged to shrug and repeat, 'Nobody knows, nobody knows. We have to gather in the meydan with all the things we can carry. That's all we've been told.'

'Greece,' Leyla had said, wonderingly, 'they're taking you to Greece.' There had been a light in her eyes that was like the prospect of intoxication.

Drosoula had had no time to linger and deal with Leyla's strange wonderment. She had returned to her mother, who was trying to deal with the paterfamilias, who was already drunk and incapable on account of the raki that he consumed each morning in order to suppress his perpetual toothache. In addition, Drosoula had had to await her own husband's decision about what they should do. Gerasimos had a plan that seemed both mad and the only possible course of action. Accordingly, Drosoula had embraced Leyla Hanım, each promising the other that they would meet again if God willed, and then Drosoula had hurried away through the gathering chaos of that improvised departure.

Shaking with excitement, but horrified by the foolish actions that she knew she was about to commit, and the perilous mis-adventures that she was about to bring upon her own head, Leyla had sat for a moment in the haremlık, and attempted to think sensibly.

Rustem Bey was away for a few days, hunting in the foothills, and now it wrenched her heart to think about what she was about to do. She called for paper and a pen, and sat at a table to inscribe, with painstaking care. Tears running down her cheeks, she wrote:

My Lion,

I write this in a terrible hurry, because I have so much to do in a very short time. I think that very probably you will not ever be able to read this, but I would feel very bad if I were to leave you with nothing. I still don't know if you can read. I never found out. Anyway, I have to write in Greek, with the Greek letters, because that is all I know how to write. I don't have time to work out Turkish in Greek letters, and I don't know the Turkish letters at all. It occurs to me that I am, after all, writing this letter to myself.

My lion, you should know that, after you bought me from Kardelen, I loved you first out of fear and out of necessity. Then I grew to love you completely with all my body and my heart. Those were our years in paradise. Then our love eventually became like the love of brother and sister, and those were our years of contentment and peace. Because of this, because of what our love has become, it is now possible for me to leave this place, and to continue to love you without too much grief. I will miss you, and there will be a hole in my heart for ever in the shape of Rustem Bey, and I will remember you every time I play the oud, or eat garlic, or do all sorts of things that we used to do together. I will miss you, but my sorrow will not be unbearable, because our love is now of brother and sister, and not of lovers. I hope that there will always be a hole in your heart that is in the shape of your Ioanna.

My lion, I am not Leyla. I have deceived you for a long time. I am not Circassian either, and I know that you prized me more greatly because you thought that I was. I must tell you that I am not after all a Muslim either, and my name is Ioanna, and I am a Greek. I am from a little place called Ithaca, and ever since I left it I have been longing with all my heart to return. I have always had a hole in my heart which is the same shape as Ithaca. Now that there is passage organised to Greece, this is my chance to go home to Ithaca. I think now that I will never have children, and this is a reason for me to seek what relatives are left, so that one day my bones will rest in the right place.

My lion, when I was a little girl I came from a good family. As you see, I can write, which is the proof. I was abducted by bad men who found me hiding in the olive grove behind my parents' house, after they had beached their boat, and come ashore, and beaten my mother and father, and taken their goods and their animals, and destroyed their house out of wantonness. They treated me badly and I was very much abused, and I was traded first in Sicily, and then in Cyprus, and then to Kardelen in Istanbul. I suppose that you did not realise what Kardelen really was, as you are not wise to the world even though you are the aga hereabouts. You have never been corrupted in a city. Kardelen was a man who was also a woman, he was one of God's victims, but he was the first to treat me well, and he made me what I am. He arranged for me to learn the oud, which has been the great pleasure of my life, and he taught me how to be a good hetaera and how to appreciate luxury. He gave me a lot of the money that you bought me with, and you didn't know it.

My lion, you have been fooled all these years, and in more ways than I would like to confess. I am ashamed of my deceptions, but I have made up for them by means of the very many pleasures that we have enjoyed together.

My lion, I am longing to hear Greeks call me by my real name, to speak my own language, and to hear the sweet melody of it in my ears. I was disappointed when I arrived here and found that the Greeks did not speak Greek. Now they will have to learn it.

My lion, if I had stayed here, I would have died with the name 'Ithaca' on my lips. Now, however, in Ithaca when I die the name on my lips shall be yours. I shall say 'Rustem, my lion', and then I shall die. When you die, let the name on your lips be mine, and the face in the eyes of your mind be mine also.

My lion, please do not come after me. I am going to find Ithaca, which has occupied my dreams for so many years, and which has been fastened to my heart like an invisible rope, and is now drawing me back, even against my will. May you also find your Ithaca, if you have one. If you do not have one, you should raise one up before you.

I am leaving you with Pamuk, who is too old and idle to travel, and too used to blissfulness, and has come to love you more than she ever loved me. You must be good to her because she never tried to eat any of your pet partridges, despite your fears. Remember to feed her with cheese, and pieces of liver, and to comb her so that the fur does not mat, now that her teeth have all fallen out and she cannot remove the matting herself. When she dies, cause her to be buried decently under the orange tree in the courtyard, in the place that she likes, and do not cast her out to be eaten by dogs or birds. I am taking only necessities and my oud, and the string of gold coins to go around my forehead, which was the first present you ever gave me, and which is the thing in the world that I prize the most, and I am taking other gifts you made to me, so that I can remember you, and not so that I can use the wealth.

My lion, farewell with a full heart, and with love and gratitude for ever, and until we meet again in Heaven, this is your Ioanna who was Leyla, and who loves you under all names she has ever had, and regardless of names.

She waited until the very early dawn of the day after the Christians' departure, and then, having picked up Pamuk and, for a long moment, pressed her face into the fur of her neck for the last time, she slipped out before the servants were awake. With her oud and a small cloth bag over her shoulder, dressed in the least immodest of her mistresslike clothes, and with her thickest-soled slippers upon her feet, she set off in the wake of the refugees, secure in the knowledge that she could catch them up, but terrified in case she should fail to do so.

When Rustem Bey finally returned from his hunting with a deer slung over the saddle of his horse, he was astounded to find the town half empty, and many of his servants gone. Those that remained were almost too terrified to explain what had become of Leyla Hanım. In the haremlık he found the letter. He sat down heavily on the divan, and stared at it as if he could make it speak by sufficiently tenacious scrutiny. Angrily he went out into the town to find somebody who could read it, but in any case there would only have been Daskalos Leonidas, and he had left. For some reason he did not set off in pursuit of the Christians, as if he knew in his core that Leyla had forbidden it.

Rustem Bey kept the letter carefully, folded into the family Koran, and never had it translated. Its perpetual obscurity raised its status in his eyes until it became as sacred as the book within which it resided. Rustem Bey was a restrained and dignified gentleman, and it was a long time before he realised what the strange circular washings of the ink on the letter must have been.

Leyla Hanım caught up with the Christians on the evening of the second day. She was filthy, hungry and exhausted, but in good spirits, and when she entered the encampment she made a special point of walking confidently and holding her head high. She had anticipated a hostile reception, and was not surprised when she received one. After their initial surprise, the Christians, and especially the women, soon began to mutter against her. 'What's she doing here? We don't want Rustem Bey's Circassian whore. Why should we walk with a slut like that?'

Having received the representations of the respectable, Father Kristoforos approached her as she sat on the ground near the fire, removing the shoes from her blistered and aching feet. 'Leyla Hanım, why are you here?' he demanded. 'You have no place among us. What makes you think you can come to Greece? None of us here wants you with us.'

Leyla Hanım did not even look up at him. 'Eimai pio Ellinida apo olous sas,' she said tartly. 'Genithika stin Ithaki kai esis den isaste para mia ageli apo bastardi Tourki.'

Father Kristoforos's Greek extended only to the snippets of

548

the old ecclesiastical variety that he had learned by rote for the purposes of his ministry, and he was taken aback by this unexpected reply that he barely understood. He had spoken to her in his native Turkish, and now asked of those at the fire, 'What did she say? What's she saying?'

Sitting near the flames, Daskalos Leonidas had been momentarily awakened from his mute dejection by hearing his own tongue spoken, and he stirred and looked up wearily at Father Kristoforos. 'I'll translate for you,' he said. 'Leyla Hanım said, "I am more Greek than any of you. I was born in Ithaca, and you are nothing but a pack of mongrel Turks."'

'She said that?' asked Father Kristoforos incredulously. 'Christ have mercy!'

'From now on,' said Leyla Hanım, reverting to Turkish, 'my name is Ioanna, and you will speak to me with respect.'

91

Exiled in Cephalonia, Drosoula Remembers the Death of Philothei

It hardly seems credible to me now, the way we were just gathered up and taken away. I am sure it couldn't happen nowadays. Look at all the trouble it caused. Nowadays no one would say, 'I think we'll remove all these people from their homes and send them to another country.' In those days we didn't question so much. If the gendarmes turned up and told you to leave, you just left. We were simple people then. We were docile and we had the habit of obedience to authority, so you see, we weren't like Greeks at all. Some of the Turks used to refer to us as the Raya, which means Cattle.

My husband wasn't so simple though. He didn't have the cattle mentality. It just so happened that he wasn't out fishing when the gendarmes arrived. If he had been, then God knows I might have had to set out without him, because there wouldn't have been any choice, and who knows where Mandras and I might have ended up? It shows that fate depends upon the smallest things.

You know about my son of course. We called him Mandras because I had a dream in which my dead grandfather told me his name was to be Mandras. Everybody said, 'Mandras? What kind of name is Mandras? Whoever heard of this name?' and I said, 'I heard of it, it's what my grandfather told me when I was eight months gone.' They said, 'But he should be called after his father, or his grandfather, or somebody. At least his name should be the name of a saint. And everyone knows that pregnant women have strange desires.' There were lots of arguments, but I was very obstinate, and finally one day my husband took me aside and said, 'Look, I am sick of all this dispute. Why don't we baptise him by one name and just call him by another? Everyone has a nickname after all.'

I resisted for a while, but in the end the common sense of my husband won me over, and so he was really baptised as Menas, after the saint. Naturally I called him Mandras all the time, and that's what he became as far as most people were concerned. Mandras died a long time ago, at the end of the war with the Germans. It was his own fault. He came to a bad end. If a mother doesn't have one sorrow, then she invariably has another. You know, they say a walnut tree brings death when first it fruits. Mandras was my first and only fruit, and I was like that walnut tree. He had a fiancée for a while, and with time this Pelagia has become like a daughter to me, thanks be to God. She made me like the almond tree, that blossoms in midwinter. We set up this taverna, and so that's how we live.

Anyway, Mandras was only a tiny boy at the time, and he was a very pretty boy, he didn't take after me at all, but after his father, which was lucky for him. He began to look more ugly, like me, after he came back from the war.

When the gendarmes arrived and told us we had only a few hours in which to prepare to leave, we were at first dumb-founded, and then there was a kind of panic. The first thing I did was run to Leyla Hanım, because I was her maidservant. She had a strange reaction, she seemed very excited, but I was too hurried to consider it. She gave me money for the journey. Then I rushed to my parents' house, where my mother was trying to organise herself. My father was already drunk, and my mother was shaking him and slapping his face, and saying, 'You good for nothing son of a horse, I am going to leave you behind, you sow's backside.'

Well, my husband Gerasimos arrived at that point and said to me, absolutely straight, 'Come on, we're leaving. Come back to the house and get ready, and get some food in a basket, and as many water bottles as we can carry, and some warm clothes, and then we're going.'

'What?' I said. 'What do you mean? I know we're leaving.'

He looked at me, and he was very cool. He said, 'We're leaving in the boat.'

I was aghast, and so was my mother. I said, 'The boat? I've never been in the boat. What about my mother and father?'

'You have other sisters. They can go with your mother and father. You and the boy are coming with me in the boat.'

My mother and my husband were looking straight at each other with a kind of honesty that was very hard, like metal. My mother turned to me and said, 'You should do as your husband says. We'll be all right. We'll manage.'

'But, Ana,' I said, and my mother placed a finger on my lips. 'Go with your husband,' she said. 'Your place is with him. We will meet again if God wills.'

'We are going to Cephalonia,' said my husband. 'Can you remember that?'

'Cephalonia?' said my mother.

'Repeat it,' commanded my husband. 'Repeat it until you remember it.'

My mother stood there, saying, 'Cephalonia, Cephalonia, Cephalonia.'

'Have you remembered it?' demanded my husband.

'Cephalonia,' repeated my mother, with her eyes full of tears, and her voice choking.

'When you get to Greece, find your way to Cephalonia, ask for the family of Drapanitikos. If God wills, you will find us.'

'Drapanitikos, Drapanitikos,' repeated my mother, 'Drapanitikos.'

My husband kissed her hand and touched it to his forehead and then to his heart, and then he embraced her. He embraced my sisters, and then took my father's hand and kissed it, even though he was in a stupor and not far from being sick, because he'd been drinking to kill the toothache as usual, and Levon the Armenian had never after all paid to have the bad teeth pulled, because all the Armenians were taken away before the return of the drawtooth.

I kissed my mother and my sisters, and to tell the truth I was too stunned to weep. I hurried after my husband, who had already left, and I said, 'Why Cephalonia?' and he said, 'Because it's the only place in Greece I've ever heard of. My grandfather, who was shipwrecked and was washed ashore here, was from Cephalonia, and his name was Gerasimos Drapanitikos, and I was named after him. He met my grandmother and never went home. He said that Cephalonians are wanderers who are hardly ever buried in their native land, so he considered it natural that he should die here.'

'Why aren't you called Drapanitikos?'

'Because I am not. It's a second name, and no one has one round here anyway.'

This conversation took place whilst we were almost running up the hill back to the house, and so it was not very complicated, on account of our breathlessness.

'Where is Cephalonia?'

'In the west. Somewhere. We'll ask after it, and when we get there we will find the family of Drapanitikos. Then we won't be nobodies in a land of strangers.'

'What about my mother and my sisters?'

'The boat isn't big enough. We'd sink, and that would be the end of all of us.'

'Why have we got to go in the boat? Why can't we go with the others? We can go to Cephalonia later.'

He stopped and looked at me very candidly, and he said, 'For one thing, the boat is the only thing I've got. With that boat I can earn us a living wherever there's a sea. For another thing, I don't trust the gendarmes. Remember what happened to Levon and the other Armenians? They didn't get a day out of here before they were dead. That's what everyone said.'

'Those were Kurds that took them away. They were tribesmen. They were wild men from the east. They weren't even proper soldiers. Everyone knows that the Kurds hate the Armenians. These are gendarmes, and they don't hate us.'

'All the same,' said my husband. 'Do you see horses and carts, do you see any provisions made for us? Any shelters loaded on mules and donkeys? If you ask me, we'll be lucky to arrive anywhere without half of us dying.'

'But my mother . . .' I said, 'and my sisters.'

He looked at me and replied, 'I give you the choice. I don't order you. You are my wife, but I don't order you. I could order you, but I don't. If you want you can go with your mother, and meet me in Cephalonia, when you find the family of Drapanitikos.'

It was then that I made the most difficult decision of my life.

I didn't choose between one duty and another duty. I chose between one kind of love and another, and I never saw any of my family again, and I never found out what happened to them.

It was when we were on the beach preparing the boat and putting food and water into it, that the most terrible thing happened. It overshadowed the whole voyage and has been with me all my life. I often dream about it, and I can't get the images out of my mind even if I get up and take a big swig of raki in the middle of the night. I think it was worse than saying goodbye to my family, because I didn't know then that I would never see them again.

I expect that I told you about my childhood friend, Philothei. She was betrothed to a goatherd called Ibrahim, who was also a childhood friend. Philothei was pretty enough to marry the Sultan, but she was happy to marry Ibrahim because they had always loved each other, it had been arranged since childhood, and anyway, a goatherd earns a good living because he takes payment for looking after other people's goats. There were some people who hardly saw a coin from one year to the next. With him she would have been rich by comparison. The only disadvantage was that she would have had to change her religion, but in that place back then, it never amounted to much for a Christian woman to change to a Muslim if she married one. The beliefs were all mixed up anyway, and sometimes Muslims came to Christian services and stood at the back with their arms folded. I don't know why they always folded their arms. Anyway, Philothei would have carried on going to visit the icon whether she'd turned Muslim or not. It wasn't like now, when everyone has to be one thing or another.

When the gendarmes came to take away the Christians, I suppose that Philothei ran off to find Ibrahim, because they weren't married yet and she would have had to leave without marrying him. I don't know what they could have said to each other. You can only guess. The trouble was that Ibrahim wasn't normal after he came back from the wars, and the families were waiting for him to get normal again. If he hadn't been mad maybe he wouldn't have pushed Philothei off the cliff.

I saw them up there on high. They were running back and

forth in a very curious manner, and they were shouting and gesticulating at each other, but I couldn't make out the words, and I saw them do things like put their hands to their heads and over their eyes, and grab at each other's sleeves. You can only imagine the turmoil they were in, especially with him not being normal yet. It looked to me almost as if they were fighting, and Ibrahim's huge mastiff dog was jumping up and down at them and barking, and making everything worse. Then I saw Ibrahim lunge forward and Philothei sort of spun round and fell.

Philothei hit an outcrop of rock a few yards down the cliff, and bounced as if she were made of wood. Then she fell straight down and smashed into the slope of scree at the bottom of the cliff, and bounced off that, and ended up a few paces away on the shingle.

Gerasimos and I were paralysed for a moment, and just looked at each other dumbly. Then I ran over to Philothei and turned her over. I felt like a machine because all the feelings hadn't arrived yet.

I find it hard to tell you about the state she was in. When I think about Philothei I realise that there isn't much to describe. I mean, she wasn't intelligent or funny or particularly interesting. She didn't have any knowledge or education. She didn't really have any high spirits. She only had two ambitions. One was to be beautiful, and the other was to marry Ibrahim. No doubt she would have lost the beauty after a few children, and she wouldn't have minded by then, because motherhood makes you too busy for vanities. In lots of ways Philothei was nobody at all and she only lived in a very little world, and she was destined to be ordinary. I expect that if she had lived to old age, you could have written her biography in half a page, and I expect that if she had never been born, it would have made no difference to the world at all.

But the fact is that everyone who knew her loved her. She was very gentle and sweet-natured, and she had no complications and no malice, and on top of that she was exceedingly pretty, and she loved pretty things. You could tell from her face and her expressions that she was sweet of soul.

So when I saw her at the bottom of the cliff, I could hardly bear the horror, because the stones had scraped deep cuts into her beauty. The cuts were more like tears than cuts. They were V-shaped, and full of little pieces of stone. Her clothes had been torn open. Her face was scraped to the bone in places, and the tip of her nose had gone. I tried to wipe the blood from her eyes, but they kept filling up again. I was saying, 'Philothei, Philothei, Philothei,' and I could feel my voice filling up with sobs and anger.

She heard me, because she said 'Drosoulakimou' very softly, and she smiled a little bit as if she was remembering me, and when I cradled her head the blood came out of her mouth and ran down the sides of her chin. I remembered that Leyla Hanım had called me that, and Philothei had learned it from her.

After a moment Gerasimos put his hand on my shoulder and said, 'She's dead,' and I realised that he was right.

It was then that I saw that Ibrahim and his dog were at the top of the cliff, two little specks looking down at us, and my soul filled up. I felt as if I were possessed.

In this rage of possession I shouted curses at Ibrahim, and now they come back to haunt me, and I wake up hearing them come out of my own mouth. I said, 'May you never have a son to lay you in your grave, may you never have a daughter to mourn for you, may your eyes well up with blood, may your ears be full of howling, may your bowels fill with stones . . .'

I don't know where these curses came from, because I had never heard the like of them from anyone before. When I hear them in my memory, those Turkish words that don't sound right in this place, with my own voice ringing them out from somewhere deep inside my chest, I put my hands over my ears, but nothing blocks them out, and I can't forget them. I was full of the white rage, and this rage has never entirely left. Sometimes it has made me strong, but I would have had a better life without it.

The only other time I have felt that rage was when I found my son Mandras on the point of violating a woman, and I told him that he was not my son. I said, 'I disown you, I do not know you, you will not come back, never in my life do I want to see you, I have forgotten you, my curse goes with you. May you never know peace, may your heart burst in your chest, may you die alone.' I said to him, 'Get out before I kill you.'

That was a strong curse, but it was nothing compared to the one with which I cursed Ibrahim, even though Ibrahim was a friend of my childhood and was well loved. I have often wondered whether these curses that welled up from inside me are a sign that I am an evil woman. I sometimes wonder if, because of me, Ibrahim walked accursed for all the days of life. When I had finished cursing he just stood there unmoving, and he was still standing there when we were out at sea.

Of course I didn't forget my son Mandras. I loved him as a mother has to love a son, and you don't forget your son even if you announce that you have done so in a curse. To lose a child is the hardest thing that a human has to bear. Mandras died in the sea, just like my husband Gerasimos, and now I am here in Cephalonia with no family at all. I was orphaned by my own decision in Turkey when I was faced by an impossible choice, then I was widowed by my husband, and then I was orphaned by my own child.

Even so, I am not complaining. Don't misunderstand me. I have had some happiness, and I am grateful for a lot of things. Home isn't only the place you come from, after all.

Now I will tell you how we got from Turkey to Cephalonia.

92

I am Ayse

On the morning after the Christians departed there were very many of us who were left bewildered, and we were very sorry, and we began to be frightened about what would happen to them. They had so many things to carry and such a long way to walk, and as well as that, we knew that when Levon the Armenian and the other Armenians were taken away, they were killed only a day's journey away, because Stamos the Birdman found them when he was going to Telmessos with a cage of finches, and out of modesty he went into the woods to do his business. He said that he found skeletons with holes and cuts in their heads, and there was clothing, and he recognised the head-scarf of the wife of Levon the Armenian, and he said that when he looked at her bones he saw that her feet had been nailed to donkey shoes, and I know I'm no one to have an opinion, but when I heard of that I thought it was a good thing that Rustem Bey had brought back the daughters of Levon the Armenian even though at the time I didn't care if every Armenian in the world got killed, because we hated them so much, but now when I think about it, it wasn't our Armenians in this town who ever did anyone any harm, but the ones who attacked our army when we were fighting the Russians, and Levon was a good man and his wife was a good woman and his daughters were sweet-natured girls.

So some people decided to follow the Christians and help them on their journey by carrying things, and some of the men took their guns and swords because they wanted to make sure that the escort was behaving, and they followed on after the Christians and caught them up quite soon. Some of the women went, but I couldn't go because, since Abdulhamid Hodja my husband died, I had no man who was a relative to protect me, and for the same reason my daughters didn't go either, but we wanted to go very much and it caused me great pain that I might never see Polyxeni again, and so I gave an embroidered scarf and a coin to Nermin the wife of Iskander the Potter so that she could give them to Polyxeni as another farewell gift, and I sent pitta bread stuffed with cheese and honey, and I asked Nermin to ask Polyxeni to come back whenever she could, and to tell Polyxeni that I would always keep the trunk she left in my care that has all the things from her dowry in it, and I will keep it until I die and after I die I will give it into the care of my eldest daughter, and like that it will be safe for all time. I am proud to say that even though the trunk is not locked I have never lifted the lid once, and neither will I ever lift the lid and that way my hands and my conscience will be clean and I will have no temptation even though I am poor. I wish I had had more money to buy things from her before she left.

It turned out that the Christians were not being badly treated, because the escort were gendarmes and not tribesmen, but they were still weary and desperate, and so it was that our people helped them to carry their things. They were astonished to find that Leyla Hanım was with the Christians, and she had nothing except a bundle and her oud, and I think to this day that Rustem Bey does not know why she went. They also found that Polyxeni was weeping and crying out because her daughter Philothei had vanished and had not come with them.

At Telmessos some Christians kissed the earth, and some Christians took a leaf or a flower or even an insect or a feather or a handful of the earth because they wanted something from their native land, and when the time came for the ship to leave the quay, there was much hugging and weeping, and promises were made, and the little boys who could swim swam out after the ship for a little way, and the women who had mirrors took them out of their sashes and they held them up to the sun so that the little flashes could sparkle on the ship until it was out of sight, and that way the sunlight of their native land followed the exiles even when they left it. And there were people who were saying, 'A curse on all those who are responsible for this, we curse them and we curse them and we curse them,' but I never did find out who was responsible except that it was probably the Franks.

And it was said that the ship took our people to Crete, which is a land in the west, and it was from that land that some Muslims came to replace them, but not as many as the number we lost. And these Cretan Muslims are rather like the Christians that we lost, so that we wonder why it was necessary to exchange them, because these Cretans dance and sing as our Christians used to do, except that they have a new dance called pentozali which it lifts the heart to watch. A few of these Cretans speak only Greek. At least all of our Christians knew how to speak Turk. Not that I am anyone to have an opinion of course, and one good thing is that my daughter Hasseki has found a good-looking husband among them who is a good Muslim and knows how to make locks and hammers and ploughs and all sorts of useful things made of metal.

And when our people came home from seeing the Christians leave, two very strange things happened. One was that the bell of the church fell off the bell tower of St Nicholas, and broke into two pieces on the paving stones, and the other thing is that for days afterwards all you heard at night was the crying of the cats. They drowned out the bulbuls and nightingales, crying and crying, lamenting and complaining, complaining and lamenting. They were on the roofs and in the alleyways, they were on the walls and in the almond trees, in the courtyard of the mosque and in the cemetery of the Christians, and they were wandering about, distressed, crying that low moaning cry and some of them wailing, and it was a terrible sound and it was frightening, and I lay on my pallet listening to them, and I couldn't sleep, and I understood why they were crying in the great sudden loneliness and strangeness of the town, and that is what I remember more than anything else, the crying of the cats.

93

I am Ibrahim

They like to call me Ibrahim the Mad, even to my face, because they think I am beyond understanding, but there is a little part of me that never went mad, and this little part is like a tiny man who lives in the corner of my head, and he watches the rest of me being mad, and thinks about it and makes comments about it, and sometimes when I am very mad he becomes frightened and hides in my head or somewhere else in my body, and doesn't come out until the danger has passed. This tiny man knows that I am not completely mad, and it is he who is able to watch over the goats and return them to their owners at the right season, and it is this tiny man who cares for my dog Kopek, and he knows how to play the kaval out among the tombs and he uses the music to calm the rest of me down so that the mad part of me sometimes gets a rest. He is very good on the kaval, and the naked man they call the Dog who lives out among the tombs and near the tekke of the saint likes to hear him play it and sometimes he comes out and sits with me when I play, and he doesn't say anything because he can't speak, and anyway his mouth and tongue were destroyed by a red-hot iron. The Dog writes things in the dust with the end of a stick, and then he rubs it all out again, and he points at the dust where the writing was, and laughs. The Dog is the only friend I have now, because I am mad, and even Karatavuk who was my friend from childhood doesn't talk to me any more because when he speaks to me it is the mad part of me that answers, and not the little tiny man who is not mad and hides in a corner of my head, watching.

When there were Christians here they used to tie the mad up in their church for forty days, and that would cure them, and after they left my family tied me up in there for forty days to see if it still worked, but there was no success.

561

I am the little tiny man. I am the one who contemplates the gibberish and confusion, but I am taking this moment of clarity to report that when I was a little boy it was Iskander the Potter who told me that to fall in love was the worst misfortune that could ever come upon a man. He was a great maker of sayings, and I still don't sit in the shade of the red pines because he once made a proverb which was 'He who sits in the shade of the red pines gets shat upon by doves'. Iskander told me about the misfortune of falling in love because even when I was a little boy he could see that I was in love with Philothei, and she was a Christian and I was not, and probably we would not be able to marry, and he said that the man who is in love should never marry the one he loves, he should instead learn to love the one he marries. I never understood what he was talking about, but now I know that the churning and churning and aching and aching was what he meant, because it makes all life impossible. But even so, I was going to marry her and there was no problem because our families were agreed and we were betrothed by means of a gold coin, and she also loved me with the same aching and churning, and then the terrible accident happened and there was no more Philothei and no more marriage, and then Drosoula laid her curse upon me, and that was when the madness came down and there was only me in the corner who didn't go mad.

And now I have times when the pictures come before my eyes and I see them before me among the stones and in the shadows of the tombs, and these pictures are not just of Philothei, but of all the things that happened in the long years of war. They are things from the campaign against the Greeks.

Sometimes I look back with wonder and think it strange that after the war with the Franks was lost, I should have begged and stolen my way for hundreds of miles from Aleppo to join Mustafa Kemal in Ankara. I could have come home and married, but there was something in me that would not accept defeat, and so when I heard that the Greeks had invaded at Smyrna, and I heard that Mustafa Kemal was gathering an army against them, that was when I set off, and I passed not far from this town, and I didn't come back to it even though it would have been easy and no one would have thought badly of me, and I could easily have joined a band of chettas and fought against the Greeks like that, but I was a proper soldier and I didn't want to be a bandit. By the time I got to Ankara I was in no condition to fight anyway, and maybe part of me was already mad, but not a very big part, and this would have been because of all the fighting and suffering I had already done, but it wasn't long before I was well, and I was at every battle that we fought for the three years. In Cilicia our soldiers were driving out the French and their Armenian legionaries, and in Armenia General Karabekir defeated the Armenians altogether, but I was not there. I was facing the Greeks, and I was at both the battles of the Inönü. I remember how we beat the Greeks and still had to retreat, and how bitter that was, and then I remember how finally we broke the Greek army at Sakarya, and they had no second line to fall back on, and finally we chased them across the countryside until all the soldiers got into ships and left, and we entered Smyrna and then immediately went north to confront the British.

There is something I have always wanted to say, because I have a certain guilt, and this guilt is as bad and gives me almost the same churning and aching as being in love, and the same aching and churning that I have because of the accident to Philothei, but I have an excuse.

The excuse is that when we were advancing towards the sea and driving the Greek army before us, we found that they were destroying everything and leaving behind them nothing but a smoking desert, and from the survivors who had not managed to flee to the Italian sector we heard terrible stories about what the Greeks did to our people. There was town after town, village after village, laid waste and devastated, everything looted and stolen, the farmland destroyed. I saw so many sights.

There would be children crucified on doors, gravestones smeared with shit, mosques that had been made into latrines, mosques full of the corpses of people who had been pushed in and had a grenade thrown among them, people burned in their houses, men who had been hung up by their feet and had piles of straw ignited beneath them, little boys buggered and bayoneted, women who had been stripped naked and tied to the ground and had fires lighted on their chests.

I learned that there is no end to the number of things that can be forced up inside a woman. You can kill them by running in a red-hot iron. You can impale them upright on pointed rods that are set into the ground. We found one whose arm was cut off and put inside so that it looked as if a hand was waving at you from between her legs, and she had a breast cut off and put into her mouth. Then there was a woman who was dead in her house, and her husband had managed to hide, and he said that she had been told that she would be spared if she were baptised as a Christian, and so in her fear she agreed to undergo it, and when the ceremony was over they took her from the church to her house and raped her and flayed the skin from her face and killed her.

I don't know how much of this was done by the Greek soldiers, and how much by the Greek chettas, and how much by the Christians of the villages who fled in the wake of the army, but I do know that by the time we reached Smyrna there was nothing that we wouldn't have done for the sheer sweetness of revenge, because there was no limit to our rage.

All of that is my excuse. We had orders from Mustafa Kemal himself that we had to behave well, on pain of death, and in the big public places we did behave, but no one could stop us going about the little alleyways, and sealing them off with sentries, and going into the houses in the Greek quarter and the Armenian quarter, and it wasn't possible for our officers to be with all of us at once. There was a corporal who was mainly interested in rape and he took four of us from house to house and he would knock on the door, and when it was answered he would smile politely and say, 'We mean no harm, we only want to fuck the women,' and then we would have to kill the men who attempted to resist, and I would have to help strip the women and hold them down, and I would have to pretend to rape them when my turn came. I was no good at it, I couldn't manage it, but I had to pretend, and I would kneel down and lean forward before exposing myself, so that no one would see that I was having to pretend, and I don't even know if it made any difference to the women that I was pretending, because they cried and wailed just the same, whoever was on top of them. Once I said to the corporal,

'I can't fuck this woman, she's bleeding,' and he said, 'That makes it slip in and out more nicely.' Once there was an old Greek man that I had bayoneted, and the bayonet was still in his guts and he was holding on to the muzzle of the rifle to prevent me from moving the bayonet, and we looked at each other and because he had a broken nose he reminded me of my father, and he said, 'Filthy Turk, you are nothing but an animal.'

I was cold and said, 'We are doing nothing to you that you have not been doing to us,' and he said, 'And we have done nothing to you that you have not been doing to us.'

Then I pulled out the bayonet suddenly, and he staggered forward a couple of paces and fell to his knees, clutching his stomach, and it looked as if he were about to pray, and before he fell on to his face he looked up at me and said, 'As for me, I never harmed anyone in my life.'

It was when we were marching north to face the British, just after the city burned, that the shame suddenly descended on me. My face filled up with blood and my ears started to burn, and the misery came into my heart like a heated knife, and this is why I didn't marry Philothei the moment I came home after the war, and delayed it, and it was because she was a woman, and after my experience I couldn't perceive her in the same way as when I was pure.

I am Ibrahim the Mad, who used to be called Ibrahim the Goatherd, and I have an excuse, and there is a little tiny man who is not mad, who hides in one corner of my head.

94

Drosoula Remembers the Voyage into Exile

Gerasimos and I were lucky in one way. There was an El Saleeb wind that did not happen very often. It used to blow for maybe two or three days in the late summer, and on this occasion it wasn't too violent. We arrived in the port of Rhodes much quicker than I expected.

I had wanted to bury the body of my friend there, the one I told you about. I don't know now why we didn't bury her on the beach where she fell. Maybe we were anxious to get away before we were discovered. Maybe I was too upset to part with her straight away. I said to Gerasimos, 'Help me get her into the boat,' and that's what we did, without even arguing about it. It was only after a few hours that we started thinking about what to do with her.

I didn't want to drop the body into the sea because it might float about and be eaten by fishes, but Gerasimos said that if we arrived in port with a dead body in the boat, we would surely get arrested on suspicion of murder. That is why we had to decide to put the body into the sea after all. I took the crucifix from around my neck and placed it round hers, and we crossed ourselves and tried to think of prayers, and then we tipped her gently over the side. She floated for a while, but then the weight of the water in her clothes made the body sink, thank God. Her beautiful black hair floated behind her in the water as she sank, and I thought, 'What use is being beautiful now?' and an emptiness came over me that has never been filled. Saying farewell to Philothei and watching her slowly sinking out of sight in the blue water was like saying goodbye to Anatolia and to the life that I would have had there, and these farewells always leave you empty. I wonder where Philothei washed up. My clothes had her bloodstains on them until I was able to obtain new ones.

I was very sick, both with grief and because of the sea, but my little boy Mandras wasn't too bad. Sometimes I got very cold even though the weather wasn't too severe. I was sunburned as well. I hated having to go over the side, if you know what I mean, even when Gerasimos was averting his gaze. The worst thing was when we were caught out at sea at night. Believe me, I know what terror is, and I know what it is to be caught up by the whims of God.

I learned things about my husband. He had never sailed across open water before. A sensible fisherman stays close to the rocks around the coast, where all the fish are. A sensible fisherman always keeps land in sight. What I learned about my husband was that he had fantastic courage and fantastic wisdom. His courage was not the foolish kind of a young and silly man. It was the courage of a man who looks danger in the face, and forces himself not to flinch. He had the calmness of a condemned man who is reconciled. My love for him increased because of those voyages, and it was a love that I wouldn't have had otherwise. I am pleased that I experienced that kind of love. My husband sailed success-fully even though he was ignorant. He never sailed if there was the slightest sign of a storm and heavy seas, because he had all our lives to consider. He made a prayer to the Panagia, prom-ising that if we arrived safely in Cephalonia, he would silverplate an icon in her honour, and this is what he eventually did, once he had earned enough money to do it. At some point the Virgin stopped watching over him, though, because a few years after we arrived he was drowned in a sudden squall between here and Zante. After that I lost my respect for the Panagia, God help me. In my opinion Gerasimos should have learned to swim, but all the sailors and fishermen say that you shouldn't, because it's better to drown quickly than to struggle for hours in a state of desper-ation. In my opinion he should have learned to swim, and then he could have swum ashore, like that English sailor from the submarine that sank during the war.

I remember everything about those travels, which lasted for many months. I discovered that there are two kinds of people: those who are thoughtless, and those who have hearts. The thoughtless ones call you a filthy Turk, and spit at you, and tell you to go to the devil, and say 'Piss off back to Turkey', and the heartful ones give you coins and bread, and offer you work, and make a fuss of your little boy, and offer you clothes they have finished with, because they pity your rags.

We stayed in Rhodes for about a week, because there were people there who spoke Turkish, and could tell us what to do next. In those days the Italians were in charge, just as they had been for a while back home, and just as they were here in the first years of the war. I feel familiar with Italians. God knows, they don't ever manage to stay long, but they aren't too bad, unlike some I could mention. Anyway, we harboured at a little place called Mandraki, which had two nice little statues of a fawn and a deer on top of a column at each side of the harbour. I loved those statues. I had never seen a complete statue before, because at home all ours were very old, and they were all broken and lying about. We had to sleep in the boat under the sailcloth, because some people were unkind to those who slept in doorways. I got used to it. I felt an affinity to the port of Mandraki because it was like 'little Mandras' and when my son was a small boy I often called him Mandraki from that time on.

Then we sailed to Halki, which was not too far. I liked it, but there was almost nothing there. There was only one village, called Nimborio. It also had Italians, who weren't too bad. That's all I remember about it. The houses were pretty.

After that, we sailed to Tilos, where there were one or two Italians, but everyone else was a peasant. In Livadia we made repairs to the boat with the help of a fisherman who could understand us. We walked all the way to the Monastery of Pantaleimon so that we could make homage to the saint, and ask for help on the next part of our voyage. We did this on every island, but sometimes the monks were hostile and called us filthy Turks. You should expect better of monks, in my opinion.

We went to Astypalaia next. It was a long voyage, and we were nearly overturned in the bow-wave of a great warship that came too close without caring about us, or perhaps without seeing us at all. The nice thing about Astypalaia was seeing the town all gleaming white on the hill, and the windmills all whirling away. We went and prayed in the Monastery of Our Lady Fevariotissa.

We stayed there all winter, because the weather became too rough, and Gerasimos pulled the boat up on to the beach and caught fish with a handline. A widow took pity on us, and we slept under her table instead of out in the boat. My husband carved her an eagle out of driftwood, and gave it to her when we left, as a sign of our gratitude. There were Italians there as well.

In the spring we meant to go to Amorgos, the place that someone wrote that famous poem about, but something went wrong with the wind or the currents or something, and we went to Anafi instead. It was a mistake, but it didn't matter very much. We were lucky it happened to be in the way, as a matter of fact, or God knows where we would have ended up. We prayed in the Monastery of Our Lady Kalamiotissa. We were surprised because there weren't any Italians. After that we went to Santorini, which wasn't far at all. I was becoming a very excellent sailor, and Mandras was healthier than I expected.

In the middle of the harbour at Santorini was a volcano, and we thought it was mad to stay there. We thought that this was the reason that there were no Italians there, but the Greeks were mad enough, that's for sure. We prayed to St Irene, and left as soon as the wind blew well. We unintentionally went straight past Thirasia and landed in Sikinos, which turned out to have a harbour in a very sensible place where the meltem wind couldn't batter it. We prayed to the Panagia Zoodochos Pigi, and when it was fine we went on to Folegandros. I think it was Folegandros. It was all so clear once, but now my memory plays tricks. I am sure it was Folegandros. That was where I was ill for a while, and Gerasimos helped someone build a house, and Mandras was scratched by a cat.

After that it was Milos, and after that we had the worst voyage of all, because we wanted to go to Malea, but we went off course, and we were lucky to arrive in Kythera, which was a place I liked so much that I wanted to stay. They say that Aphrodite was born there, whatever the Cypriots think. Anyway, Gerasimos liked Kythera too, but he was determined to go to Cephalonia because of the family. In Kythera there was a little port with a great castle at the top of the hill, and we were impressed because St John had begun to write a book up in a hole in the cliff, so it was a very holy place. There was an icon of the Black Virgin, and we went to see it. It was a very long walk indeed, but the place was beautiful. The monastery nestled in a valley of oleander.

After that it was just a question of sailing along the coast and stopping wherever we could, to ask the way, and to take water and food on to the boat. Gerasimos always worked when we needed money, and so did I. By this time even little Mandras was beginning to pick up words of Greek, and I knew the words for most of the essential things. The last place we stopped was Zante, which was as pretty as Kythera, and I could have stayed there too, if only Gerasimos had agreed. It was on Zante that the people sang cantadas, which were the most beautiful songs I have ever heard, and the old men would sing them at the table after eating, and they would play accordions and guitars and mandolins. I was in Zante when I first heard cantadas, and I realised properly that there was after all something beautiful and joyful about the human soul. When Antonio arrived here with his mandolin during the war, it couldn't help but remind me of happy days in Zante. We went to see the relic of St Dionysus, and promised to call our next son Dionysus if we got to Cephalonia. The people on Zante told us to watch out for Cephalonians. They said, 'They think they're eggheads, but actually they're mad.'

Well, we did arrive, as you can see, and the first thing we did was tie up the boat in Argostoli harbour, and go straight to the monastery and pay our respects to St Gerasimos, who watches over the mad, and must surely have been watching over us. That was another long walk, and in those days the roads were even worse than they are now. We had to go over English Bridge and then find our way through the hills. My husband was very moved to see the body of the saint for whom he and his grandfather were named, and the nuns let him kiss the saint's embroidered slipper. He said to me, 'We are home at last,' and when we went outside we embraced, even though it was in public and there were some nuns.

We were very thin, and weary, and we had been travelling for almost a year, on and off. It was the only time in my life that I was thin, and it wasn't long before I was fat again. When I think about it, it is a miracle that we even got as far as Rhodes. In

Argostoli harbour the boat practically had to be reconstructed. Of course, the irony is that the Drapanitikos family thought we were just dirty Turks. They knew that someone called Gerasimos had been a sailor and had disappeared, but apparently he had been a black sheep anyway. They'd never heard of us, and didn't want to have anything to do with us. We took the name 'Drapanitikos' anyway, and maybe one day the rest of the family will think me respectable enough to acknowledge, not that there's any sign of it after all these years. Then Gerasimos drowned in the sea between here and Zante, before we could even have a son and call him Dionysus. After all that sailing and praying! After plating that icon at such expense! Just think of it! Still, before he died, Gerasimos got the nickname 'Odysseus' from the other fishermen, and he was very proud of that. He was more of a sailor than all of them put together. He was greatly admired for sailing such a little fishing boat all the way from Turkey. I think that's why we were so easily accepted, even though we spoke Turkish to each other, and Gerasimos liked to wear a turban when he was out at sea, instead of a hat.

Did I ever tell that after all this time I sometimes still dream in Turkish?

95

The Wounding of Karatavuk

It was not until the following spring that Mehmetçik reappeared in the area. Late at night he scratched at the door of the family house, and whined like a dog. This had been for very many years the agreed signal, so that the family would know that it was him. If there was anyone inappropriate in the house, all his father had to do was open the shutter and call out, 'Get lost, stupid dog, go home!'

On this occasion the door was opened by a wall-eyed middle-aged man with an enormous moustache, wearing curious night attire and bearing an olive-oil lamp in one hand, who had plainly been expecting his visitor to be a dog, and had been preparing to give it an indignant but cursory kick.

By the light of the dim little lamp, he and Mehmetçik looked at one another in surprise and perplexity. 'Who are you?' asked Mehmetçik, unable to think of anything else to say.

The man said something quite incomprehensible, and held up both hands, as if surrendering. He was beginning to tremble. It looked most odd because he still held the lamp in one uplifted hand. In a moment a thin woman who must have been his wife appeared at his side. She gasped at the sight of him, put her hands to her mouth in fear and ran back into the house.

Mehmetçik's puzzlement as to their behaviour vanished suddenly, as he realised that what they were seeing was, to all intents and purposes, a bandit. Over his shoulders he was wearing two bandoliers full of cartridges. In his sash was a pistol and a yataghan. On his head was a filthy old turban. His boots were holed at the toe and scuffed, and his shalwar were much misshapen by heavy rips that had been clumsily repaired by someone who plainly did not know how to sew. His sunburned and weather-beaten face was obscured by a week's stubble, and not a little of the filth of travel. In his left hand he carried a carbine.

Confused, Mehmetçik asked, 'Where is my father?'

The man said something else that was incomprehensible, and began, with his free hand, to fumble in his sash. For a moment Mehmetçik thought that he might be searching for a weapon, but after a few moments he produced a small drawstring leather purse that he held out to Mehmetçik, his hand shaking. 'He goes to bed wearing a sash with his purse in it,' thought Mehmetçik, wonderingly.

'I have not come here to steal,' he said. 'I don't want your purse. Where is my family?' The frightened man held the purse out to him with an imploring look, as if begging him to take it and be gone. Mehmetçik shook his head, and left. As he ascended through the town to the ancient tombs above and behind it, guided by his memory and what little light there was from the stars, he was assailed by deeply troubling thoughts. 'Surely I can't be mistaken about the house? Have they gone, and not told me? Where can they be?' Concerned not to disturb the Dog, should he still be living, Mehmetçik settled in an empty house-tomb far enough away from the one habitually frequented by the former. He lay down on a low stone shelf intended anciently for a rich man's corpse, and resigned himself to a long and cold night. He had experienced many such nights during his years as an outlaw, and had even learned to sleep in the open in storms of rain. He would wake up aching all over, but nonetheless he slept. He listened to the scuffling of small nocturnal animals, and then a bulbul began to sing. As he listened to the liquid notes cascading into the night, he remembered how, in the old days, people used to be driven mad with insomnia by the night's massed choristers. On account of the birdsong, he suddenly had a good idea about what to do on the morrow, and at that point exhaustion overtook him. He had been trudging all day on vertiginous goat paths through the mountains, and now he fell into a turbulent sleep.

He awoke shortly after dawn, and flexed and stretched his muscles in order to free them up. He experienced a moment of doubt as to why he was inside a tomb, but then remembered the events of the night before, and sat up quickly. Hardened by frequent necessity, he did not think of breakfast. These days food came in his direction whenever a capricious fate looked upon him kindly, and not otherwise.

Cautiously he put his head out of the door of the house-tomb, and looked about. He regretted, not for the first time, the vanity that caused him always to wear a red shirt. He had always done so, ever since he and his friend Karatavuk had whimsically adopted the identity of birds in their childhood. It had been something intrinsically innocent. Now that he had been an outlaw and a brigand for years, however, the red shirt had become a trademark that he could not abandon. To do so would have been somehow to diminish his status, to allow his own legend to tarnish. It had become very simply a question of manly pride. It was amazing to him that, after all these years of being a conspicuous target in any shoot-out that might occur, he had still only ever been wounded but slightly, and sometimes he cursed inwardly that the position he held among his men prevented him from wearing sober colours, like any other sensible renegade in everyday need of camouflage.

Ducking down, he hurriedly made his way higher up the slope, picking his way through the maquis, with the intention of surveying the town. After the surprise of the previous night, it was almost as if he wished to reassure himself that the town was really his. From behind a large white boulder he tried to discern what was going on below, and he saw that there was very little activity, considering that it was past dawn, and people ought to be about the business of the early day. He decided to go higher, near the tiny white chapel that had been built centuries before as some forgotten person's private act of piety.

When he arrived there he saw that the door had been burst open. He went inside, and saw to his dismay that the frescoes of the apostles had been defaced. They had all had their eyes carefully scratched out, and this gave them the disquieting appearance of the newly blinded. Feeling outraged and dismal on account of the sacrilege, he went back outside, and heard the bleating of Ibrahim's flock of goats, over by the hole in the hillside where since antique times the townspeople had quarried lime for the construction of their houses. He listened carefully, and just made out the sound of Ibrahim's kaval. It was a thin, curiously wavering and disconnected melody. Calculating that a childhood friend like Ibrahim could surely be trusted, he made his way to the hollow by the limepit.

When he crested the brow of the hollow, Ibrahim's great dog was the first to see him. Kopek was a giant among dogs, of that breed which in Anatolia has been used for centuries to fight off the wolves, feral dogs and lynxes that harass the flocks of sheep and goats. Some herders take particular delight in the terror that these dogs evoke in the human strangers that they confront, and certainly Mehmetçik could remember Ibrahim's relish when recounting tales of Kopek's feats of intimidation. The dog was possessed of a formidable memory, and knew exactly which goat to return to each owner when the flock was brought down into the town in the evenings. He also knew the smell of everyone in the community, and therefore knew who to threaten and who to leave unmolested. Whether he knew this because living there caused everyone to share something common in their scent, or because he knew the smell of each person individually, is a question that cannot be answered, although everyone assumed that it must be the latter.

Mehmetçik felt a prickle of fear in his throat. He had had some memorably terrifying encounters with these dogs during his years of brigandage, and considered them to be more truly dangerous than most of the human flotsam with whom he had had to deal. Once or twice he had been forced to shoot particularly aggressive ones, and this had always weighed very heavily upon his conscience, because it was common knowledge that, whereas one sheep or a goat was not too unbearable a loss, a good dog was a herder's most precious possession, combining the roles of stalwart protector, loyal friend and body-warmer on freezing nights.

Kopek hunkered down into the stalking position, and Mehmetçik's heart sank. He saw Ibrahim sitting on a rock amid the black goats, playing his kaval, but apparently paying no attention to the dog. Then Kopek rose suddenly to his feet, and began the ritualised routine of the hunt. His hackles standing in a bristling ridge, raising his forefeet delicately high, pausing at every step, he advanced on Mehmetçik, a deep growling rumbling in his chest. Mehmetçik knew that this was a preface to his being violently rushed, and most probably pinned to the ground with the animal's feet on his chest, and its teeth in his throat. He struggled to remember the dog's name, and did so only just in time.

'Kopek, Kopek,' he called. 'Kopek! Good dog. Kopek, it's me, it's me!'

The dog stopped dead just as his charge commenced, and raised his ears as if thinking, 'I wonder who this person is, who seems to know me?' He sniffed the air to catch Mehmetçik's scent, his black jowls quivering.

Courageously, Mehmetçik came forward slowly, extending his hand to the dog so that it could be sniffed. Kopek did so, and considered the matter. The hand did seem a little familiar. 'Good dog,' said Mehmetçik, in as confident and friendly a voice as he could manage under the circumstances, and Kopek recognised something in the voice as well. He licked the proffered hand, and decided that its owner was acceptable. He allowed Mehmetçik to pat him on the head and ruffle his chest, and then he rolled over on the ground and submitted.

Profoundly relieved, Mehmetçik ruffled the animal's ears and chest, and then approached his old friend, with Kopek following happily at his heels. 'You could have called him off,' said Mehmetçik.

Ibrahim did not reply. He sat on his rock and continued to play the same thin and meandering melody.

'Ibrahim,' said Mehmetçik, putting a hand on his shoulder, but Ibrahim merely played on. Puzzled, Mehmetçik stood back a little and looked down. He bent to look into Ibrahim's face, and was shocked by what he saw. Ibrahim was not just eight years older, he was also quite clearly in a reduced state. His face was drawn, pale and thin, saliva trickled from the corners of his mouth as he played, his lips trembled, which perhaps accounted for the attenuation of the flute's sound, and his eyes darted about without settling upon anything. He would not, or could not, look Mehmetçik in the eyes, and quite clearly did not recognise him.

'Ibrahim, Ibrahim, old friend,' said Mehmetçik sadly, feeling utterly helpless. Seeing his old playmate in this condition made him feel unnaturally strong and healthy. He could make no connection between this haggard ruin and the bright and funny youngster who had once kept everyone entertained with his bleat of a goat that is surprised, a goat that is looking for its kid, a goat that is protesting, a goat that is hungry, a goat that is in rut, a goat that has nothing to say.

'It was me,' said Ibrahim abruptly, removing the kaval from his lips.

'Ibrahim?' said Mehmetçik.

'It was me. I did it.'

'What did you do? Ibrahim, what are you saying?'

'I killed the little bird.'

'The little bird?'

'It was me.'

'What's this little bird?'

'It tried to fly,' said Ibrahim.

'They do fly,' said Mehmetçik.

'It was my fault,' said Ibrahim, and he resumed playing the kaval. As he did so, he began to weep silently in a most unnatural fashion, without sobbing or catching his breath. Large silent tears followed each other down his cheeks and disappeared into the corners of his mouth, as if he were drinking them as he played.

'Come,' said Mehmetçik, 'a man doesn't weep like this. You must stop, Ibrahim. Ibrahim, you must stop.'

The dog Kopek settled next to his master, and looked up at Mehmetçik, as if to say: 'Oh well, what's to be done?' Mehmetçik stooped to place his hand on the dog's head, as if in benediction, and then stood upright. He looked down at the abject Ibrahim for a few moments, and then turned on his heel and walked away. There was nothing to be done. The fact was that in this life things change and pass away, and, whatever the reason, the days of Ibrahim's radiance had clearly gone for ever.

It was not long afterwards that, down in the town, Karatavuk heard something that made him stop his work, stand perfectly still, and listen. He heard it quite distinctly. It was the sound of a robin, singing very loudly and clearly. It was a little too loud and clear, and it was not exactly like a robin. It was more like somebody executing a near perfect imitation. His heart seemed to leap in his chest, and he stepped out of the tank, hastily wiped his feet on a piece of rag, and ran indoors. He rummaged about among his few possessions and found what he was looking for. He took the small terracotta whistle to the water jug on the table, and carefully filled it with water. He blew into it to make it warble, and, emptying a little out, he tried it again.

He ran outdoors, and listened for the robin, but heard nothing. He put the small clay bird to his lips and blew a few notes. The song of a blackbird, very loud and clear, floated out over the town. He stopped to listen. Out among the tombs, the song of the robin briefly resumed, and stopped. He played a few more notes of blackbird. The robin in the tombs answered, mimicking the same intervals. Elated, his heart thumping with excitement, Karatavuk ran up through the narrow streets, tripping over dogs and recumbent mules, accidentally elbowing people in his passage, and then he emerged into the dense maquis of the hillside, and paused to blow into his whistle. Further up, the robin replied.

In this manner the two friends found each other behind the boulder whence Mehmetçik had previously surveyed the town. They embraced, kissing each other on the cheeks, and giving each other great thumps between the shoulder blades. 'Oh, my friend, my friend,' exclaimed Karatavuk, wiping his eyes with his sleeve, 'I never thought I would see you again.'

'It's been eight years,' said Mehmetçik.

'Eight years,' repeated Karatavuk.

'Look at the state of you,' chuckled Mehmetçik. 'What on earth have you been doing?'

Karatavuk looked down at his own legs as if he did not know how they had been occupied. They were caked and dripping with a grey earthy slime. 'I have to tread the clay in the tank these days,' he said. 'It's down to me to find the little stones with my feet, and get them out. I've developed very deft toes since you saw me last.'

'I thought you had an old man to do that.'

'We did, but he died.'

'Oh, I am sorry.'

'It was a good thing in the end. He became very ill.' Karatavuk paused. 'So, everything's changed for you, according to all I hear.

You've gone from being a little robin to being the great big famous Red Wolf.'

'Another outlaw,' Mehmetçik shrugged, a little abashed.

'A very famous one.'

'Half the stories aren't true. A lot of those things were done by other people. Everyone blames me and my men for everything. We don't commit half the cruelties that people say we do. We're not the only bandits in the mountains. By the way, do you remember Sadettin, the son of Yusuf the Tall?'

'The one who left after his father made him shoot his sister? Yes, we all remember him.'

'When I joined the outlaws, he was the leader. They captured me when I was trying to make my way home, and then I realised that I ought to ask them if I could stay, because no other life was possible as long as the authorities were looking for me. I looked at all those men, and they were all kinds. There were Christians and Jews and Muslims, and Armenians, and two Arabs, and even a black man from Ethiopia. Sadettin remembered me, and he asked me about the town and about his mother, and they accepted me, all because of Sadettin. Otherwise I think they might have killed me.'

'What became of Sadettin?'

'He was very reckless and brave. Some of us considered that he took great risks on purpose, because he wanted to get finished with life. He was never reconciled to having killed his sister and lost his family, and he used to talk about it when he was drunk. The raki made him stupid, and one day he was killed by a gendarme. He was going to shoot the gendarme, and confronted him in broad daylight in the meydan of a town near the place we were hiding. He had a pistol with a safety catch, and he forgot to release it, so by the time he realised why the gun wouldn't fire, he was dead, with the gendarme standing over him. We had two more leaders after that, and now it's me.'

'The famous Red Wolf! I can't believe it's you! But tell me, how did it happen? I mean, what happened that made you run away to be a brigand?'

'It was the labour battalion,' said Mehmetçik. 'Didn't you hear?'

'No, I didn't. How should I know what happened? I just heard you were a deserter. I was ashamed for you when I heard.'

'A deserter? That's not how I would put it.' Mehmetçik thought about what he was going to say, and then began: 'After they wouldn't take me into the army when I volunteered – you remember, we went along together, and they wouldn't take me because it was a jihad, and I was a Christian – well, you remember how disappointed I was. I wanted to serve the Sultan and the empire very badly, but I wasn't allowed. I took it as an insult, and I am still often offended when I think about it. It was a great slight to my honour.

'Not long afterwards the recruiting people returned, and they enlisted all the Christian boys into the labour battalions. They said we could serve the Sultan and defend the empire against the Franks by doing essential work, you know, building bridges and roads, making railway tunnels, constructing docks, all those kinds of things. They were going to feed us and pay us, and they made it seem an honourable way to serve.'

'And it wasn't?'

Mehmetçik shook his head. 'It certainly wasn't. They treated us not like men, but like slaves. We worked from dawn to dusk, without food or water, more often than not. If we were sick, or fainted, or rested they beat us and kicked us, or even whipped us. We became skeletons draped in rags. We were covered in sores and blisters, and the fleas and lice tormented us. We slept in a sort of tunnel made of scraps of wood and cloth, all crammed together without a pallet and with nothing to cover ourselves, and all the time we were shitting ourselves with diarrhoea, and some people were even shitting blood, but we still had to work.'

'It sounds a bit like being in the army,' observed Karatavuk.

'At least a soldier is a man and not a slave. I could have taken it if I hadn't been a slave.'

'Anyway, for us it was holy war,' said Karatavuk. 'The thought of that kept us going.'

'There was nothing holy about being in a labour battalion,' said Mehmetçik. 'It was when the men started to get typhus that I ran away. That wasn't how I wanted to die. I knew I would die if I stayed, and that isn't how a man should die, not a man who wanted to be a soldier, and face the enemies of the empire.'

'Most of my comrades didn't die of bullets,' said Karatavuk, 'but I suppose we weren't slaves.'

'Well, I've gone from being a slave to being a bandit,' said Mehmetçik bitterly. 'At least I've gone from a greater shame to a lesser one.'

'Some people admire you,' said Karatavuk. 'I suppose you know that there is a big reward for information leading to your death or capture?'

'I know that. It was after that business with the governor's administrator.'

'You don't think it was a big mistake to rob and strip one of the governor's men, and make him walk away naked? And tell him that Red Wolf wishes him a safe journey? It made everyone laugh who heard of it, but you didn't think that was a stupid thing to do?'

'Yes, it was stupid,' agreed Mehmetçik, 'but the man was an arrogant piece of shit, and he asked for it. He annoyed us all by repeating how important he was, and telling us of the things that would happen to us.'

'Take my advice,' said Karatavuk, 'get rid of your red shirt that makes you such an easy target, and go and find your family, and till the soil like everyone else, and live in peace.'

'I noticed that you don't wear a black shirt any more.'

'I would if I had one,' laughed Karatavuk. 'All I have now is the nickname. If I ever have any money, perhaps one day it will be a vanity I can afford, and my wife can cut me a new one from black cloth.'

Mehmetçik held up the small clay birdwhistle. 'And you still have one of these. I've had mine all these years, and I have never broken it. It's a miracle when you think of all it's been through. Does Iskander Efendi still make them? You know, I have always wondered why he made mine with a turban on its head. Whoever heard of a robin wearing a turban?'

'It was just my father's fancy. There isn't a reason. He still makes them like that, and now I know how to make them myself. I have taken up my destiny after being so much interrupted, and now I am a potter like my father, just as it was always set out for me. All my brothers but one were killed in Mesopotamia, and now we two are the only ones left to carry it all on. Now I have a wife, so I have some hope that all will be well.'

'I have gone a long way off course,' reflected Mehmetçik sadly, carefully replacing the whistle in his sash. 'I am very like Sadettin.' He paused, and then looked up. 'I have to ask you . . . actually, this is the reason I had to speak to you . . . who are those people in my father's house? Where have my family gone?'

Karatavuk looked at him with astonishment. 'You don't know?'

'I have no idea. In the last years I've been everywhere from Kemer to Konya. I haven't been able to return.'

'You must surely know that all the Christians have been deported?'

Mehmetçik blanched. 'All of them?'

'As far as I know, all of them. They've all gone from round here. It was some months ago. The gendarmerie from Telmessos came, and took them all away. My father has the keys to many people's houses.'

'How long have they been taken for?'

'For ever, it seems.'

'Holy Panagia, have mercy,' exclaimed Mehmetçik, utterly appalled. 'Obviously I knew that all the Greeks had been taken away. I saw the columns. But I didn't think my own family was included, I didn't know we counted. Where have they gone?'

'Well, the people who came here to replace them were from Crete, wherever that is. They were a sorry bunch when they arrived, and they were many fewer than the number of people who left. That's why the town seems so empty. There's a big shortage of customers for us, and naturally the Cretans have nothing at all to buy anything with.'

'Crete,' said Mehmetçik, wonderingly. 'Where is it, though?'

'I heard that it's in Greece, which they say is not far across the sea in the west. If I were you I would go to Crete and try to find them. You should give up this outlaw business. You'll come to a bad end, all for nothing, with no children or brothers to follow you to your grave.'

'We don't know how to speak Greek,' said Mehmetçik. 'What will they do in Greece?'

'Well, these Cretans are Muslims, but they mostly don't speak Turkish. They mostly speak Greek, and life is very hard for them here. There are many people who spit at them and call them filthy Greeks, because of the bad feeling after the war. The ones in your house are Cretans. But you shouldn't worry about your family. It was agreed by the great Frankish pashas and Mustafa Kemal that when they arrived they would receive compensation to the same value as everything they lost when they left.'

'That would be a good thing. I hope it has happened. They were not born to be beggars. But how will I find Crete?'

'Go to Kaş. I have heard that just opposite the town is a very small island called Megiste, which is full of Greeks, except that the Italians took it over a couple of years ago. You should get to the island. Perhaps a fisherman will take you. The Greeks on the island will probably know where Crete is and how to get to it. I think that's the best thing to do. A lot of people who got left behind have done the same thing, which is how I know about it. Apparently the Greeks on Megiste and the people of Kaş smuggle between each other at night.'

'The Cretans in my house. Are they good people? I would hate to think of my house full of bad ones.'

'The Cretans are mostly good. They have strange dress and customs, and they eat snails, but they do a dance called pentozali which is very good to watch. It makes us like them. Some of our young men are starting to do it. It's good that they have some high spirits, because it reminds us of all the saints' days that the Christians used to have.'

During the process of this long conversation, things were happening down in the town. The Cretan householder who had been disturbed by Mehmetçik's appearance late the night before had hardly been able to sleep for fear and worry, and in the morning he naturally told his friends. One of these was a Turkish speaker, and he in turn went and told the two gendarmes who were to be found, as always, playing backgammon in the meydan on fine days, or in the coffeehouse on inclement ones.

What mobilised the gendarmes and the townspeople was the

prospect of a large reward, because it was very obvious from the description of the man with the red shirt and the bandoliers that he was none other than the notorious Red Wolf, bandit and outlaw. Since Mehmetçik's family had kept absolutely quiet about his new identity, there was no one remaining in that town who had the smallest idea that Mehmetçik and Red Wolf were one and the same. Otherwise the reaction of the townspeople might have been a little different. As the rumour spread that Red Wolf had been seen in the vicinity, men got out their muskets, rifles and fowling-pieces, and began to gather in the meydan, where they were mustered into some kind of order by the two gendarmes, neither of whom would normally have been tempted from their backgammon by anything less than the prospect of a large bounty. Among the men who retrieved their weapons, hastily serviced them and rummaged for ammunition, was Iskander the Potter, who had cherished his rifle and his pistol for very many years, ever since the extraordinary Abdul Chrysostomos of Smyrna had finally produced weapons that conformed to the potter's require-ments. It was true that these beautiful guns had made Iskander feel more of a man, and he took great pleasure in hefting their weight in his hands, and aiming them at nothing in particular with one eye asquint. With the rifle Iskander had shot one or two deer, and a goose. In truth he was a little short-sighted, which unsuited him to great feats of marksmanship. Now, with the loaded pistol in his sash, and the rifle over his shoulder, he milled about with the other men in the meydan, awaiting the most exacting and exciting hunt of them all, whilst the women fussed and fretted about them, begging them to be careful. The men's thoughts were busy whirling in their heads, however, as they privately rehearsed possible arguments about how the bounty should be shared in the event of success. Very soon they would fan out and spread up the mountainside, where, amid the rocks and ancient tombs, were to be found the most obvious hiding places for a fugitive. None of them honestly believed that they would find the Red Wolf, but in any case the true point was to have an interesting and exciting day out.

Oblivious to these events, the two old friends relaxed in each other's company, and continued their conversation. 'I saw Ibrahim, this morning,' said Mehmetçik. 'He looks terrible, and he wouldn't even talk to me.'

'He's gone mad,' said Karatavuk. 'No one really knows why. It happened almost as soon as the Christians left.'

'He kept saying, "I killed the little bird."'

'I know. That's what he says all the time, "It was my fault. I killed the little bird."'

'Wasn't "the little bird" his name for Philothei? He didn't kill her, did he?'

'Not as far as I know, but I don't know what happened to her. I suppose she left with the others.' Karatavuk paused. 'You know the oddest thing?'

'What?'

'Leyla Hanım, you know, Rustem Bey's whore. She left with the Christians.'

'Really? Why would she do that?'

'It's a complete mystery to everyone. She must have been madder than Ibrahim.'

Appropriately to the talk of madness, the two friends were quite suddenly interrupted by the Dog, who sprang out before them, clearly in a highly agitated state, giving them both a very considerable surprise, and causing them to exclaim 'Ey!' and leap to their feet.

The Dog was now an old man. His eremitic and arduous life among the tombs, all but naked, and subsisting on the charity of the desperately poor, had greatly reduced him. He was skeletally thin, his meagre hair fell in long white wisps upon his shoulders and face, and his black eyes had shrunk back into his wizened and sunburned face. It is true that people had long become reconciled to his grotesque and horrifying smile, and people pitied him that he must once have had his lips pinned back, and been made to bite down on the red-hot iron rod that had been forced into his mouth. The state of his gums, tongue and teeth had long ceased to shock, but he still carried with him a daemonic air that continued to frighten people, and it was common for mothers to threaten their mischievous children with him, as if he were a bogeyman. This did not, however, prevent the same people from believing that he must be some kind of saint, since the popular imagination inexplicably but routinely associates sainthood with physical deprivation, suffering and the many varieties of masochism.

Now he appeared, almost dancing with excitement, before the two men, grunting incoherently, and gesticulating, with a strange curving motion of his arm, as if pointing over the boulder behind which Mehmetçik and Karatavuk were concealed. It took a moment for the two to gather their wits, and another for them to realise that they were being told to look over the boulder. When they did so, they both swore.

'Orospu çocuğu!' exclaimed Mehmetçik. 'They're coming after me!' Down below could plainly be seen the men of the town, spread out across the hillside, picking their way through the maquis, some armed with swords and knives, some with cudgels, and a great many with rifles and pistols. He turned pale, and ducked down behind the boulder. 'Shit!' he said. 'Shit, shit, shit.' He turned to the Dog, and grasped his hand, bringing it to his mouth and kissing it on the back. He pressed it to his forehead and then to his heart. 'Thank you, my friend, thank you,' said Mehmetçik. Astonished and amazed by this gesture of gratitude and respect, the Dog stood motionless for a moment, examining the back of the hand that had been thus treated. Then he ran off, oblivious to the thorns and stones that cut into him, uttering strange and piercing cries of joy.

'Give me your shirt,' demanded Karatavuk.

'What?'

'Your shirt, idiot, give me your shirt.'

'Why? Look, I've got to run.'

'Give me your shirt. Swap shirts and I'll lead them astray. When you see them coming after me, go in the opposite direction. For God's sake get to Kaş, and take yourself to Crete. Come on, your shirt.'

'What if they shoot you? I can't let you die for me.'

'Everyone dies,' declared Karatavuk curtly. 'For your mother's sake give me your shirt. Come on, come on!' He made an impatient beckoning motion with his fingers, adding, 'I got through eight years of war and nobody managed to shoot me.'

Mehmetçik hesitated a moment, and then gave in. His friend

commanded so imperiously and emphatically that he was ceded no choice. With both hands he seized the waistline of his shirt and hauled it upwards. There was a small crash at his feet, and he stood holding his red shirt, looking down at the fragments of the small terracotta birdwhistle that he had inadvertently jerked out of its place in his sash. 'Shit,' he said.

'Never mind, take this,' said Karatavuk, handing him his sober and tattered working shirt.

They stood looking at each for a moment, caught between the reluctance to part and the necessity of flight. 'Go to Megiste, get yourself to Crete,' said Karatavuk, and he stepped forward, embraced Mehmetçik and kissed him on both cheeks.

'Until paradise, if not before,' said Mehmetçik, smiling sadly.

'Stay here until you are sure they are following me, and then run,' said Karatavuk. Before he went, he took his own birdwhistle out of his sash, and gave it to Mehmetçik, saying, 'I know it sings like a blackbird, but take it anyway, and remember me. I'll make myself another one.' He turned abruptly and began to scramble away up the rocky path.

Mehmetçik watched him go, and noticed how he took pains to make himself conspicuous. Sure enough, a shout went up down below, and the line of hunters began to wheel about in pursuit of Karatavuk. Shots crackled and snapped, and bullets began to ricochet off the rocks. 'Son of a whore,' muttered Mehmetçik to himself, ashamed of leaving his friend to take the bullets. He hesitated, torn between the alternatives, and then made off as fast as he could up a goat track which intersected with another that would lead him away. 'Son of a whore, son of a whore,' he repeated to himself, as if it were an incantation against adversity.

Karatavuk laid low behind the tomb of the saint, his heart thudding. He had decided on a gamble, and now he was committed to it. He put his hand under the tomb and felt for the hole at the bottom where the olive oil trickled out, having passed over the bones of the saint. There were some drips still clinging to the stone. He touched oil to his lips and his forehead, and placed some on his tongue. He asked help from the saint and from Mary, the mother of Jesus the Nazarene, and hugged his knees to his chest. He rocked back and forth, attempting to conquer his fear by a stupendous effort of will, and, when at last he reckoned from the voices that his pursuers were only a few paces away, he stood up, raised his arms high in the air, and turned to face them. Thinking for the first time that he was going to have some explaining to do, in his embarrassment, he smiled sheepishly.

Iskander would never understand why he did it. It is true that he was short-sighted, and therefore did not recognise his son, but it is also true that he could see well enough to know that the fugitive had raised his arms in surrender. There was something about being keyed up with excitement, about being ready to shoot at a real man for the first time in the many years since his military service, about the chance to gain some notoriety and kudos as the one who had brought down the Red Wolf, about the chance to use in earnest the beautiful gun that had been made specially for him by Abdul Chrysostomos of Smyrna.

Iskander raised the rifle to his shoulder, aimed it at the slightly blurred figure standing not twenty paces in front of him, and pulled the trigger. As soon as he felt the bruise of the recoil against his shoulder, as soon as he heard the snap of the shot, as soon as he saw the cloud of cordite blossom from the barrel, he knew that he had dishonoured himself and made an irretrievable mistake.

In this way Iskander joined the ranks of the very many in those days who did wanton things for which they were never able subsequently to forgive themselves.

It was for this reason that Karatavuk entirely lost the use of one arm, and at the same time his destiny as a potter.

When the time came, however, for Mustafa Kemal to abolish the writing of Turkish in Arabic letters, Karatavuk swiftly learned the new Roman letters and, albeit endowed with an imaginative sense of orthography, became the town's letter-writer. When it became clear that no one was coming back, he moved his growing family into the former house of Daskalos Leonidas, wrote at the same desk by means of the same stinking wick of the same oil lamp, used up Leonidas's stock of writing paper, and kept a singing finch in the same wire cage outside the front door. Sometimes he even wondered if he were growing into the same irritable and cantankerous character.

Karatavuk prospered modestly, even though there were some people who adamantly refused to use his services because he was obliged to write with the left hand. By the time that the inevitable blindness overtook him in old age, there was very much less need of his services in any case, and he had become a legend in his own right. He was a hero of the great victory at Çanakkale, he had lost the use of his right arm in a most romantic and honourable way, he had been the friend of the Red Wolf, and he was a scholar who had read many books, and intervened to help many illiterate people in their troubles. He was therefore able to enjoy the pleasure of whiling away the darkness of his declining years in the meydan, seated upright on a stone bench under the plane trees, with his left hand propped on a walking stick, a cloth cap set squarely on his head, receiving the respectful and affectionate greetings of passers-by, and telling stories about the old days to children who clung to his legs, or sat themselves before him in a semicircle in the dust.

EPILOGUE

I

What the New Imam Did

The new imam was one of those hardliners stereotyped by the religious colleges in Konya, and it was not long after the departure of the Christians that he was righteously inspired to fire up a few followers to perform the following sacred duties:

Firstly, they broke down the locked doors of the abandoned houses. They did this because they felt it unnecessary to find the neighbours with the keys, and because God rewards the superfluously zealous. Inside the houses they located the stores of wine jars, carried them out into the streets, and emptied them into the alleyways. Then they smashed the jars because of their having been contaminated by wine, and then they went to the vineyards and tore out and burned the vines, even those whose grapes were cultivated solely for the manufacture of raisins.

Secondly, they entered the Church of St Nicholas, the little church at the bottom of the town with the owl on the crossbeam, and the little white chapel at the top of the hill behind the town and above the ancient tombs. In these churches they assiduously scraped out the eyes of all the figures depicted in fresco, and broke any religious ornaments that were left.

Thirdly, they took the few Christian bones that remained in the ossuary behind the little church with the owl, and threw them over the cliff.

Fourthly, they defaced all figurative work on the tombs left by the Lycians from ancient times.

Fifthly, with very long poles, they rounded up a small group of pigs that had perforce been abandoned by their old owner. These pigs they drove to the top of the cliff above the little chapel, and, in front of Ibrahim, who was up there with his goats and was still in a state of horror over what had befallen Philothei, they herded them squealing and shrieking over the same cliff where they had disposed of the bones of the Christians.

Out of all these actions the only one that met with the overt approval of the general population was this last, as the taboo against pig flesh is inexplicably the deepest ingrained in the average Muslim. There were many, however, who would never forget that mouth-watering aroma of roasting pork that used to drift across the town, arousing simultaneous feelings of longing and revulsion. The other sacred acts, most especially the disposal of the wine, were greeted with various degrees of disquiet or horror, but the people were cowed by the mad light of moral certainty in the eyes of those who acted on God's commands as laid down in holy books that no one was able to read. For that town these events began the interminably tedious years of respectability, observance and decorum that made everyone think that they had lived twice as long as they really had, so that even the Cretan exiles forgot how to sing their sustas and dance the pentozali. Only the substantial number of Alevis, feeling like a minority for the first time in their history, now that they were the only minority left, stubbornly continued in their old habits and escaped the deadening longueurs of a disenjoyed life.

In Greece the abandoned mosques were almost all demolished, and the graveyards of Muslims desecrated. No doubt these deeds were performed with a choleric and righteous zeal essentially identical to that of the holy vandals of Eskibahçe.

2

I am Karatavuk

About one year after the Christians were taken away and the Muslim Cretans brought to take their place, I was looking for a small knife that I needed to cut some cord, but I couldn't find it anywhere. Then I remembered that when I was in the army I used to have one in my knapsack, and it occurred to me that it might still be in there.

I found my knapsack and put my hand in it, and rummaged about, but didn't find anything, and so I turned it upside down just in case anything would fall out. What fell out on to the floor wasn't a knife but a little leather purse, all old and dry.

I picked it up and looked inside, and I beheld the little handful of soil that my friend Mehmetçik had given me to take away to war, when we were about fourteen years old. I remembered him saying that when I came back from the war I should replace it in the same spot from where it had been taken, and I remembered saying to him that the soil of this place has a special and particular aroma.

I put the purse to my nose and smelled it, but now it smelled of the leather of the purse. I went to the house of Abdulhamid Hodja where his widow Ayse still lived, and I found the place by the wall where the soil had come from. I had a moment of hesitation because it occurred to me that I might have to go to war again, but then I tipped it back on to the ground in order to honour Mehmetçik's suggestion. I looked at the little heap of soil for a moment, and then I rubbed it back into the earth with my feet, until it was properly mixed in again. Then I knelt down and smelled the earth – and no doubt anyone who saw me might have thought I was making a salat – and it smelled once more like the proper soil of this place.

I had some sad thoughts about my friend Mehmetçik, and I thought it was almost certain that he had not been able to take any of the soil of this place with him. I wished I knew where he was so that I could send it to him.

Later on I was talking to the father of the family that had moved into Mehmetçik's house, and he was one of the few Cretans who could speak Turkish. I told him about this business of the soil, and his face lit up, and he went into his house and came back out with a little purse, and he loosened the draw-string and showed me inside, and he said, 'Soil of Crete.'

I said to him, 'Sooner or later it starts to smell of leather,' and he just shrugged and said, 'Everything changes.'

Soon after, he told me that he had put the soil into a pot where he was growing basil with seed that he had brought from home, so that the soil could make a true Cretan plant. It came up very strongly, and from that plant he took the seeds, and he took the seeds from the new plants that he grew, and he gave seeds away to other people, and in this way all of us here now have Cretan basil on our window sills, to flavour our food and keep away the flies.

I never did find the knife.

3

Pamuk

One day in early summer, Rustem Bey was sitting out in his courtyard, smoking, when one of his servants came hurrying out, calling 'Master, master!' Rustem Bey turned and the servant said, 'The cat Pamuk is very sick.'

It was true. The cat was lying on its side in the haremlık, its paws twitching, with saliva coming from its mouth, and a look of blank terror in its eyes. Its breathing was hoarse and irregular. Rustem Bey knelt down and said, 'Oh, poor little Pamuk.' He put his hand on the cat's head and felt the velvet of the ears and the bones of the skull underneath. 'She is very old,' he said. 'She is just bones and fluff.'

'She had great spirit,' said the servant, adding, 'What will you do, master?'

'I think we should kill her,' said Rustem Bey. 'I think this is her last suffering, and we should put an end to it.'

The servant was disconcerted. He was fond of the cat and was fearful that Rustem Bey would tell him to do the deed. 'Master,' he said, 'please don't ask me. Please ask one of the others.'

'I wouldn't let anyone else do it,' said Rustem Bey.

The servant was very considerably relieved. 'How should we do it?'

'We could drown her, break her neck, cut off her head, strangle her, or shoot her,' replied Rustem Bey, but in a gentle tone of voice that belied the honest brutality of the words.

'It would be a shame to get blood on the beautiful white fur,' said the servant.

'I'm going to take her outside,' said Rustem Bey. 'Bring me a thick cloth of some sort.'

Out in the courtyard he wrapped the cat in the cloth so that she was well bound up. He sat in a chair with it against his chest,

597

and the top of her head beneath his chin. He could smell her sweet dusty aroma.

Rocking back and forth in his unhappiness, with his eyes closed, he held the ancient cat across his chest, and hugged her. His right forearm was across her upper flank, and he was hugging just a little too tightly. He hoped that the animal was too sick to know what was going on, and under his breath he muttered, 'Bismillah allah akbar, bismillah allah akbar, bismillah allah akbar,' the words helping him focus his mind elsewhere than upon this present sorrow.

He knew that Pamuk had stopped breathing when her head fell, and the small pink tongue emerged and lolled to one side. He continued to hug the cat tightly, and sat for a very long time.

Finally he mastered himself and went back indoors with Pamuk still wrapped in the cloth. 'She's dead,' he said to the servant, who had been hovering at a discreet distance, just inside the door of the house.

'What shall we do?' the latter asked. 'Do you want me to take her and leave her up in the rocks?'

'No. Fetch me a spade. It was always agreed that Pamuk would be buried here in the courtyard in the place where she liked to lie, under the orange tree. She had many happy hours of idleness.'

'Don't you want me to do it, master? With your permission, it would please me very much to do it.'

'No. I will bury her myself.'

Afterwards, Rustem Bey looked down at the small heap of earth, and remembered when he had first encountered the young Pamuk, staring and hissing angrily from a large wicker birdcage on top of Leyla's heap of luggage back in Galata all those years ago. The cat had one blue eye and one yellow eye, and its coat was entirely white. He had said, 'What's this?' and Leyla had said, 'It's a cat.' At that time he had not liked cats, and had replied stiffly, 'I reckoned on no cat.'

'There was a lot I hadn't reckoned on,' thought Rustem Bey, reflecting on the irony that the bond with the cat had outlasted that with its mistress, except that there was a somewhat mystical sense in which no profound bond ever comes to an end.

Because he did not wish any of his servants to see him upset,

Rustem Bey went and found the letter from Leyla Hanım that he had never read, and put it in the pocket of his jacket. He went through the town, up past the fine houses where the Armenians had once lived. He paused at the place where he had begun to build a mosque in fulfilment of his promise. It was now over-grown with weeds and thorns, and an almond tree was growing up from the middle of it. It might as well have been another ruin left by the ancient Greeks. He realised that he ought to feel ashamed of never having completed it, that he should do so now that there were men to build it, and that it was a disgrace in the eyes of the townspeople, but the thought of doing so merely filled him with an immense weariness of spirit. He shrugged and said to himself, 'After all, God has no shortage of mosques.'

He left, and picked his way through the thorns of the maquis on the hillside. He passed the Lycian tombs where the Dog lived, and the tomb of the saint. He saw Ibrahim the Mad and his dog Kopek, and their flock of goats. He stopped a minute to listen to Ibrahim's strangely beautiful but disconnected playing on the kaval. Finally he took a goat path up to where the land ends.

It was when he was up there, turning Leyla's letter over in his hands as its corners fluttered in the sea breeze, that it finally occurred to him that the round, irregular stains on the paper must have been tears.

Rustem Bey sat on a rock at the clifftop until it grew dark, looking out across the sea, feeling as if he had lived too long.

4

The Epilogue of
Iskander the Potter

You may recall my observation that the people who remained in this place have often asked themselves why it was that Ibrahim went mad. I said that I was the only one who knows, and that I have always been committed to silence, because he begged me to respect his grief, or, as he also put it, to take pity upon his guilt. Now that he is mad, and the sun has long since dried the rain that washed away the blood upon the rocks, and there is almost no one left who remembers her, I have indeed decided that no one would be betrayed if finally the truth of it were known. It is the story of a curse, and I have an inkling of how Ibrahim feels, because once I shot my own son, and have cursed myself every day of my life. At least Karatavuk lives, however, and at least he has forgiven me, and has a wife who has borne him sons to plough his field and daughters to hoe it. It is worse by far for Ibrahim.

The fact is that Philothei, sweet-natured, Christian, vain and beautiful, was killed by Ibrahim, and it was this that drove him mad. I am no great pasha who understands the great world, I have no education apart from the recitation of the first sura of the Holy Book, and I will probably never know all the causes of things, but to me it seems that Ibrahim was not truly to blame, even though he believed himself to be so.

I say this not because her death was an accident, but because there would have been no accident if it were not for the great world. It was the great world that went to war with us and attempted to divide us up, and then it was the Greeks who invaded us after the war with the great world, when we were weak and they thought it would be easy to beat us. We won that war, and the Greeks lost it, but it was because of that war that the pashas of the great world decided to take away the Muslims from the Greek land, and deliver them to us, and to take away the Christians from this land and deliver them to the Greeks, and it was because of this decision that Philothei ran to find Ibrahim, and suffered the accident that killed her.

When the gendarmes arrived unexpectedly, and ordered our Christians to get ready to leave within a few hours, there was terrible confusion. The Christian women were wailing, and there was a panic because none of them knew what to take. We had all heard the stories about the departure of the Armenians eight years before, when they took along their finest jewellery, hoping to sell it when they arrived at their destination, but they lost all this jewellery because the soldiers who escorted them stole it from them almost immediately. For this reason our Christians were wondering whether to take practical things or precious things, and did not know how long the journey would be, and whether or not they would be fed, and they were going to their Muslim neighbours, saying, 'Please, efendi, look after my things until I get back, and take this key to my house, and lock it when we have gone, and look after it until we come back.' I myself have three keys of my old neighbours, and I hang them near the door on a nail, where they get more rusty by the year. I also keep an eye on the land of those neighbours, and keep it in good condition by working on it and growing food on it, and I have their goats, which have bred many times with mine, so that now I would be hard put to work out which kid belongs to which neighbour. This is some recompense for me, since I lost most of my trade when the Christians left, and I was made extremely poor.

Because of the panic and the hurrying, and the making of last-minute arrangements, Charitos and Polyxeni did not notice that one of their daughters had disappeared until it was too late, and neither did Drosoula notice, who was her best friend, because Drosoula and her mother were trying to get some sense out of her own father, who was always drunk, and Drosoula was planning to run away with her husband.

This is what happened, and this is what Ibrahim told me when he rushed down the hillside and into the town, pushing aside the poor people who were preparing to depart. I have often wondered why he chose to come to me, and perhaps it was only because my workshop was near the edge of the town, or because my son Karatavuk was a particular friend of his.

What happened is that the lovely Philothei, fearing that she might never see Ibrahim again, left her father's house, and went up the hillside through the ancient tombs where the Dog lived, in order to look for her fiancé. He was still her fiancé because they had never married, and they had never married because Ibrahim had been forced to leave and join the army, and since then he had been fighting for about eight years, first against the Franks, and then against the Greeks. He and Philothei had not had the good fortune to marry before he left, but they were due now to be married at some future time.

Ordinarily a woman would be disappointed to put off her wedding, but it would not destroy her. In this case, however, Philothei was distraught beyond all measure because she and Ibrahim had had the misfortune to have become besotted with each other, and had been thus besotted since they were little children.

To be in love is generally the worst thing that can happen to a man or to a woman, and when it happens we all look at it and shake our heads, and thank God that it has never happened to us, and pray that it may never happen to our children. It makes people foolish and obsessed, and they disobey their parents in matters of marriage. They do not concentrate, they dream even when awake, they weaken physically, they lose the capacity both for sleep and work, and they become foul-tempered when their reveries are disturbed. It is a sickness that is probably the result of bewitchment or the evil eye, and is something to be shuddered at because it takes away all reason. The drinking of this besotment causes drunkenness that is worse than the stupidity of raki or the vacancy of opium, because it lasts much longer and has no known cure apart from time, or possibly marriage.

In the case of Philothei and Ibrahim, however, the besotment had been with them since the days when they had played together with Karatavuk and Mehmetçik and all the others of their friends. People used to laugh at the way that Ibrahim followed Philothei faithfully like a dog, and they would note that he was the only boy with whom she was not flighty or coquettish or spiteful or shy. It was as if they both knew that kismet had picked them out for one another. To put it another way, it seemed obvious to all that they had been born married.

Fortunately, Charitos and Polyxeni had all their lives been friends with Ali the Broken-Nosed and his wife, and not merely friends, because they were all related in one way or another by marriage. With us it was the custom that although a man could not exchange his faith, the woman should take her husband's religion upon her marriage. It was understood that most often the woman kept her faith in private as long as this never became known. In any case, we all had the custom of offering tamas to the mother of Jesus because this was effective in the event of sickness or ill luck, and, after all, the faith of a woman is not of great concern to God, and therefore it was not a great concern to us. For all these reasons it had been agreed for many years that Philothei and Ibrahim would be married, and so Charitos never placed an empty bottle on the roof of his house even when Ibrahim was away at war and no one knew whether he was alive or dead.

Now, with the whole town in an uproar, and everybody in tumult, Philothei ran away to find Ibrahim, who was minding the townspeople's goats on the hillside. He would spend every day up there, and he would have beside him his great mastiff, Kopek, and he would sit there playing softly on the kaval, as he still does, because a goatherd has little to do for much of the time, and so it behoves him to play the kaval. The sound still drifts over the town, especially when the wind comes from the direction of the sea, but the tunes no longer make sense now that he is mad.

As you know, we have a river that runs across the bottom of the town and curves away below the meydan. It goes round the hill and enters the sea. The hill behind us is very high, and this is where the Dog lived, and you could find the tomb of the saint and the ancient tombs. This is also where Ibrahim and his dog minded the goats that lived off the maquis. The hill goes up and up until it reaches the very small chapel that was used only once or twice a year, and of which no one knew the origin, and then it starts to curve down again, but it is interrupted by a very steep cliff that plummets straight down to the beach. It is a bad place to walk in the dark, because it is easy to walk over the edge; the edge is very liable to crumble away beneath one's feet, and there are very many demented ghosts of those who have thrown themselves over on purpose and have become accursed by God. Ibrahim and Kopek always returned with the goats before dark because of these spirits. In other places a goatherd will often spend many nights out in the hills with only the wolves to worry him.

When Philothei found Ibrahim, she was exhausted and she was crying violently. He was right at the clifftop because he was looking down at the beach, where he could see Gerasimos and Drosoula, with their little son Mandras, apparently preparing to put to sea in his little fishing boat. Ibrahim knew nothing of the arrival of the gendarmes to take away the Christians, and he was puzzled by what he saw, and he was waving to them and shouting, but the cliff was very high, and there was wind, and they couldn't explain anything to him for lack of being heard. Ibrahim was wondering why Gerasimos should be going fishing with a woman and a child, which was not normal, and was not good luck.

So Philothei found Ibrahim, and she was, as I said, exhausted and tearful. She had been badly cut because in her haste she had fallen frequently among the rocks and thorns, and her hands and face were bleeding. Her clothing was torn. She tried to explain to him what was happening, and at first he could not understand, because it was not a usual thing for the gendarmes to arrive and take away people with no explanation, and it had not happened since the Armenians were removed about eight years before. The reason he was uncomprehending was that it was completely unexpected, and made no sense to anyone. I myself never understood the purpose of it.

Philothei grew wild and he could not restrain her, and the reason for this was that she was divided into two pieces. Should she go with her family, or should she stay with her betrothed? She could not decide between the two. She was like Nasreddin Hodja when he was given two identical plates of kız memesi kadayıf, and was in danger of starving to death because he could not decide which to eat first, or like Nasreddin Hodja's donkey, who was in danger of starving to death between two equal bales

604

of hay, except that these examples are frivolous. Perhaps it was more like the man who is forcibly given the choice of sacrificing one of two equally beloved twins. For Philothei the situation was desperate because her heart was torn in matching parts, and whilst Ibrahim was on his knees pleading with her to stay, she was turning away to go, and then turning back to Ibrahim. This she did over and over again until a kind of madness overcame them both and neither of them knew what they were saying or doing. Ibrahim was waving his arms and shouting, and she was rushing back and forth uttering little cries that he said were cutting into his belly like a sword. To make it worse, their behaviour bewildered the dog Kopek, who began to bark and throw himself upon them.

It was at one moment when Ibrahim was on his knees with his hands at his temples that he noticed that Philothei was getting too close to the edge of the cliff. She was weeping and gesticulating too much to notice where she was. Overtaken by a sudden panic, he leapt to his feet and tried to grab at her clothing, but in doing so he stumbled, and instead of grasping her to pull her back, he fell against her with his outstretched hand, and she fell backwards over the edge. As she went over, she looked at him with her beautiful eyes so wide with terror and disbelief that the memory of them is one of the reasons that he has never slept a peaceful night again.

Prone at the edge of the cliff he watched her hurtling down the precipice. He says that it seemed to happen very slowly, and that her body bounced on the outcrops of rocks as if it was not a body but something made of wood. He says that it seemed to take an eternity before she bounced off the last rocks and came to rest on the beach not far from where Drosoula and Gerasimos were preparing the little boat. He says that the two of them ran over to the body, and that when Drosoula saw who it was, that it was her best friend whom she had loved since youth, she threw herself on the body, but then gathered it in her arms and cradled it, stroking the head, and rocking back and forth. Then Gerasimos touched her shoulder and said something, and Gerasimos picked up the body and began to carry it to the boat.

Drosoula looked up at the top of the cliff, and saw Ibrahim

looking down. Ibrahim says that he was helpless. There was no way down to the beach, and he was too horrified to move. He says that he had at that moment no feelings inside because the feelings were too great to feel without breaking him into fragments like a fallen pot, and causing him to die. He says that Drosoula seemed tiny so far away down on that beach. He says that then Drosoula raised her arms and cursed him. He says that despite the distance, he heard every word of the curse, and will never forget one word of it. He says that the curse is too terrible to repeat aloud, and he has never told me exactly what it was. He says that it was a very long curse, and that it made the sweat pour down his back as cold as snow. He says that it took the spirit out of his body and twisted it like wire, and that it took his body and removed the goodness and the flame. However, Ibrahim says that Drosoula's curse was not as terrible as the curse which at the same time he was making against himself, and which he has never ceased to make more telling in the years that pass.

I will never forget the day when the Christians left, and Ibrahim ran to find me. He was bleeding from many cuts because he had fallen a great deal among the rocks and tombs as he came back to the town. His eyes were blinded by tears, and he had been running, and the madness was already beginning to come upon him. His voice was strange and agonised, and when he could speak, the first words he said were 'I've killed the little bird'.

It was for these reasons and causes that Ibrahim went mad, and for these that the lovely Philothei was killed. Ibrahim, as I have said, blamed himself, and now he is too insane ever to be persuaded otherwise, but in my opinion, as I have also said, everything that happened was made to do so by the great world.

5

Mehmet the Tinsman and the New Copper Dish

All these events having transpired, and the Christians having been deported, the people that remained in that place soon got into the new habit of referring to their former neighbours as Greeks. Certainly, it was to Greece that they had been deported, and they had become Greeks whether they had wanted it or not, even if their new compatriots often deprecated them as Turks. The word 'Ottoman' would fall into disuse and disrepute until such time as the inevitable revisions of later days, when the world would realise that the Ottoman Empire had been cosmopolitan and tolerant.

The population of Anatolia was in mourning. Ten years of war, in the Balkans, then against the Franks, then in the War of Independence against the Greeks, had left tens of thousands of widows and orphans, tens of thousands of parents without inheritors, tens of thousands of brotherless sisters. It was a people bereaved and worn out beyond endurance, and it would climb out of the pit of misery only because it would have the miraculous good luck to fall under the quirky but brilliant leadership of Mustafa Kemal, who had recently decreed that from now on everyone must have a surname, and that his own was Atatürk.

It was bereaved also of those who had not died. Eskibahçe was dying on its feet because not enough Greek Turks had arrived to fill the empty houses of the Turkish Greeks, and in any case they had brought virtually no wealth with them. Some of the abandoned houses were looted, especially those whose owners were reputed to have secreted treasure, but those whose owners had left keys and a trust of guardianship with their Muslim neighbours simply rotted slowly away against the return of their owners, until the timbers sagged, the roofs collapsed, the cisterns clogged, and the door jambs and window frames fell away from the walls.

The wrought-iron gates of the two Christian ossuaries rusted and the few ribs and teeth that were left became the playthings of ghoulish little children.

Down at the entrance to the polis, the great pump house built in 1919 as an act of philanthropy by the garrulous merchant of Smyrna, Georgio P. Theodorou, broke down and fell into disuse, because there was no one left who knew how to repair it. Travellers emerging from the pines were no longer met by the joyful sound of cool running water, and their thirst was unslaked, their hands and faces unrefreshed.

Indeed, almost no one remained who knew how to get anything done. There had been such a clear division of labour between the former inhabitants that when the Christians left, the Muslims were reduced temporarily to helplessness. There was no pharmacist now, no doctor, no banker, no blacksmith, no shoemaker, no saddle-maker, no ironmonger, no paint-maker, no jeweller, no stonemason, no tiler, no merchant, no spicer. The race that had preoccupied itself solely with ruling, tilling and soldiering now found itself baulked and perplexed, without any obvious means of support.

There were only two artisans left, Iskander the Potter, much diminished by the terrible wound that he had inflicted upon his favourite son, and Mehmet the Tinsman.

Mehmet was descended from Armenians who had arrived in the time of the Seljuks, and converted to Islam, and the family had provided the town with an unbroken line of coppersmiths for many generations. Although Mehmet did not know it, his skills and designs had filtered out of India three thousand years before, but he was still conversant with the esoteric meanings of the goats, griffons, winged lions, fish and hexagrams with which he adorned his dishes, his cooking pots and his spring-lidded powder horns. Indeed, Mehmet was one of the few of his family who still made these representations and knew their semiotic, for the more devout had ceased to do so entirely, decorating their work only with complicated geometrical designs.

Mehmet the Tinsman loved his work, and there was nothing else that he was willing or qualified to do, but the fact was that a good half of his clientele had disappeared overnight. His mainstay had always been the retinning of copper and brass pots, and he found that, instead of waiting happily in his workshop for customers to arrive, he was obliged to travel from place to place in order to improvise any kind of living at all. With one exception, all the rich people had gone and now there was no one to buy his new copperware. 'Perhaps,' he often thought, 'it is just as well, because I no longer know where to get my acids, my nisadir powder, my sheets of raw copper, and I no longer know where to get my tin. God help me when my stock runs out.' His copper used to arrive from Smyrna in huge, blackened, fifty-kilogram sheets, and his tin used to come from a far-off, exotic, barbarian, Frankish place of which it was impossible to conceive, and which was named 'Cornwall'. Mehmet had never had much desire to travel, but his Cornish tin had a special crackling sound to it, and he imagined the shining rods being rolled in the great hairy hands of Cornish djinns that lived and laboured underground in the stannaries, and possibly had one eye, or perhaps three. It was his ambition, one day, to travel to Cornwall and see the tin djinns for himself.

Nowadays, his enforced travel was confined to the surrounding towns and villages, whose populations had likewise halved, and whose craftsmen had similarly disappeared. He had acquired a donkey, and was therefore able to take advantage of the fact that he was the only tinsman left in the area. If it were not for him, all the pots would wear down to the copper, and people would be poisoned by their own cooking. Recently, indeed, people had begun to walk for miles to bring him their pots, because somebody in the family had already fallen ill. Sometimes Mehmet thanked God that tinning lasts only for eight months, because otherwise he would have had no prospect of a long life.

One day Rustem Bey walked into Mehmet the Tinsman's workshop, and, unbeknownst, watched the latter diligently tinning a skillet. He was at his bench, surrounded by the clutter of his extraordinary collection of strangely shaped hammers, anvils, dollies and punches, sprinkling the white nisadir powder over the copper, and repeatedly wiping it over with a cotton wad that he was dipping in a pot of molten tin that bubbled on the brazier beside him. Rustem Bey marvelled that the tinsmith did not burn his fingers. When Mehmet had finished, he sensed that someone was watching him and looked up. He stood and took the aga's hand in respect, touching it to his heart, his lips and his forehead. Rustem was the only wealthy man left in the whole district, and it was widely known that he was charitably using his wealth in order to create work for those less fortunate.

'Fortunate' is a relative term, and certainly Rustem Bey did not feel fortunate. The interesting people with whom he used to socialise and converse, including the Italian officer, had all gone. The abscondence of Leyla Hanım had left a hole in his heart and in his life, even though, out of opportunism and loneliness of the spirit, he had finally taken all three of Levon the Armenian's daughters as his mistresses, keeping them in houses at opposite extremes of his estates. He had not grown cynical about love itself, but he had resigned himself personally to the idea that he would never have it, that it was not something intended for him. He had long since buried his rejected wife Tamara among the white graves in the pine woods.

He often remembered how it had felt like a blow to the stomach when a messenger had arrived from the brothel, to tell him that Tamara Hanım had died, and asking him whether he had any instructions as to what to do with the body, because otherwise they would leave it under stones among the ancient tombs where the Dog lived. They said that she had died of the plague that comes back with the haj, but he knew in his heart that really she had died of attrition. He had been convinced of this when he had collected her body and seen what appalling ravages had befallen her once comely face. He provided her with a respectable shroud, and made her a decent and honourable grave. He attended the burial, which was carried out by the new imam and his servants, and felt a lurch of dread and sorrow when the body was lowered into the ground. He had the tomb painted white, with the exception of the headstone, which was made in the shape of a tulip, and which was picked out in green and painted red. When he walked away from the place after the interment, he felt again that weariness of someone who knows that they have lived too long, and which can come upon a person at any age.

Like many others who remained, living amid so much absence, Rustem Bey felt like a ghost in a land of ghosts. Nowadays he had to imagine what had once been a daily reality; the clanging of the bell at angelus, the raucous and drunken Christian holy days that seemed to happen every week, the sheer exuberance and variety of the community's former self. For his own part, he had grown resigned, and wiser. He had been defeated and subdued by life, but he had remained dignified and had never lost his sense of having a role in the scheme of things. He still had no children, despite having the three mistresses, and despite having had a wife and Leyla Hanım. This caused him much grief and self-doubt.

Physically he was greatly changed. He had lost the muscularity of his prime, but without losing much of his strength, and he looked visibly smaller. His cheeks had sunken in because he had begun to lose some of his teeth, and his hair and moustache had long since begun their journey from black to snowy white. Because he was a modern man he had ceased to wear breeches and a sash at all, and wore Frankish clothes as a matter of course. Nowadays he seldom wore his silver-handled pistols and dagger, and ever since Mustafa Kemal had forbidden the wearing of the fez because it was ridiculed by the rest of the world, he had taken to wearing a trilby. He had put his fez away in a box, and in secret every now and then he retrieved it and turned it over in his hands, because without it he felt somewhat unlike his authentic self.

When he had been greeted in Mehmet the Tinsman's workshop, he said, 'Mehmet Efendi, I have come to ask you to make something for me, for which I am prepared to pay you an honest price.'

'An honest price is all I ever demand,' replied Mehmet, flattered that Rustem Bey had addressed him as 'efendi' when he was not an educated man at all.

'I had a dream,' said Rustem Bey. 'I dreamed of a great copper plate, a big ekmek saç, you know, a big bread-baking plate, and it had a particular pattern, and when I awoke I felt that I would like this plate made. I remembered the designs.'

'I will do it if I can,' said Mehmet, and when Rustem Bey had explained his intentions, he exclaimed, 'Why, those are old ones!

My father used to like to do them, and my grandfather too, but not with all of those beasts on one plate. You would have each on separate plates.'

'Perhaps I have seen them before somewhere,' said Rustem Bey. 'Quite often a thing goes into your mind without you realising it, and then you can't remember why it is there. In any case, it's the one I dreamed, and I would like it made, all on one big plate, if you have the time, and since it's a big plate, you should be able to fit in all the beasts.'

'I could do it now,' said Mehmet with enthusiasm.

'How long will it take?'

'Who knows? That depends upon how well it goes. God's in charge.'

'I will stay and see you begin,' said Rustem Bey. 'I am not as busy as I was.'

Mehmet went to his stack of crude, oxidic copper sheets and scratched a large circle in the one on top, using a wooden pattern and a long pointed scriber. He cut the shape out with a heavy, blackened pair of shears that must have been in the family for generations, and brought it over to his table. He threw charcoal dust and some oil on to the very big brazier that stood, permanently aglow, in one corner of the workshop, and fanned it up to temperature, putting on more coals as the temperature rose. When he was satisfied, he laid the copper roundel across the griddle, and stood back as it heated up. Rustem Bey observed him, envying him his skill and his sense of belonging in the world. It was true that Mehmet was filthy and stinking, it was true that his complexion was reddened, coarsened and ruined, that his hands and forearms were covered with the healed scabs of a lifetime's minor burns, that his clothes and even his turban were everywhere full of charred holes, that his fingernails were broken and his fingers engrained with grime, but it was also true that Mehmet was fulfilled and that he knew happiness by personal acquaintance. Happiness and contentment were indeed his wife and mistress, and they slept with him in the same bed.

The copper slowly ascended to red heat, and Rustem Bey stood further and further back. Mehmet removed the glowing sheet with two pairs of tongs, and laid it across four flattened stones to cool off. 'Does it take much longer?' asked Rustem Bey.

'Well, efendi, you have to beat it, which is very noisy indeed, and then it is so hard that you have to heat it up again to red heat, and you can either quench it or let it cool on its own, and then you can begin to make the designs.'

'So it all takes a very long time?' interrupted Rustem Bey. 'I think I may not have time to stay and see all of this.'

'Indeed,' replied Mehmet. 'It takes a long time, but a long time to us is a short time to God, and a long way for us is a short way for a bird, if it has wings.'

'You are speaking in proverbs, just like Iskander the Potter,' said Rustem Bey, laughing lightly. 'But in any case, God's time is not a time that I would want to wait, and the heat in here is becoming intolerable. When shall I come back?'

'The engraving will take time if you wish it to be good.'

'I wish it to be good,' confirmed Rustem Bey.

'Then come back in three days, just before the evening azan.'

Rustem Bey duly arrived three days later, just before the call to prayer, and found Mehmet the Tinsman, amid much huffing and puffing, vigorously shaking a large black goatskin bag. His initial impression was that Mehmet must have gone mad. The latter stopped for a moment, and explained breathlessly, 'Water and river sand. Giving it a polish in the old way. Can't use acid. Nearly run out.'

Mehmet sat down for a while to recover his breath, and rolled a fat cigarette as consolation and reward for his efforts. The heavy perfume of Latakia tobacco superimposed itself upon that of hot metal and coals. When he had recovered, he removed the huge platter from the goatskin, and took it over to a pail of water, where he carefully washed it down. For a moment he held it up and admired it, pristine, virgin, untarnished, brilliantly shining. He turned and presented it to Rustem Bey, saying, 'From my hands to yours, Aga Efendi, may it go with good fortune.'

Rustem Bey took it reverentially and felt an unfamiliar pang of aesthetic pleasure. It had come out even better than he had dreamed of it. Around the rim, in Arabic text that he could not read, there was a line from the Koran. In the centre, set amid

613

swirling acanthus leaves, were five beasts. One was an eagle with two heads growing out of the one body, each head looking in opposite directions. Two of the beasts were identical geese, breast to breast and paddle to paddle, but with their heads flung directly back over their bodies so that they saw both the world and themselves upside down, but could not see each other, and two of the beasts were the prettiest and most elegant antelopes imaginable, identical, both winged, tails flicked high, both hoof to hoof and chest to chest. They might have been sisters, twins of the same dam, but they too were looking not at each other, but in diametrically opposite directions, backwards over their shoulders.

6

The Epilogue of Karatavuk the Letter-Writer

I have just reminded myself of someone I should not have forgotten, since now I live in what was his house. I was sitting here whilst my family slept, with the paper before me and a pen in my left hand, wondering how to start. I was looking at the glow of the oil lamp, when I suddenly remembered Daskalos Leonidas, who was the teacher to the Christian children in the years just before they had to leave. He was not well liked by anyone, but I have reason to think that there was some warmth in his heart, because he was kind to my parents during the war when they asked him to read a letter, and to write in reply. Also, he knew that it was me who exchanged sparrows for the song-birds in his cage, but he never pursued me for it. The reason I am reminded of him is that he used to write all night. There was always a light coming through his shutters. No one knew what he was writing, and I cannot myself read the papers he left behind, but it was said that he was a conspirator and was working out plots to make all these parts Greek. Perhaps he is dead by now, but wherever he is, he must know that all the plans like his ended up with these parts becoming completely Turkish, and that this happened after we had all had to wade in lakes of blood. My father Iskander would have thought of a proverb to illustrate the futility of great plans and big ideas, but I am reminded of a story about Death, who sent a message to someone to say 'I will see you tomorrow night in Telmessos', and so the man ran away to Smyrna, thinking that he had made a fortunate escape, and then he was walking along in the Armenian quarter, and he met Death coming the other way, and Death said to him, 'How fortunate! I had been planning to meet you in Telmessos, but something came up, and I had to come here instead.' This is to say, that in seeking our good ends we often bring about our own misfortune.

615

When I think about it, I realise that without Daskalos Leonidas, I would not be sitting here writing whilst my family sleeps, because it was he who taught my friend Mehmetçik to read and write, and it was Mehmetçik who taught me. In our day the Muslim boys learned to recite only the first lines of the Koran, in Arabic, and that was all our education, which was why we were always helpless when the Christians wanted to outwit us. I pestered Mehmetçik until he gave in, and every day in the rocks above the town, where the Dog lived, he would teach me as Daskalos Leonidas had taught him, which is to say that he put on an irritated tone of voice and hit me frequently with a stick, and I would scratch out words in the dirt with a stick. I still smile when I remember the antics of our childhood, all that running about in the rocks and blowing on birdwhistles and finding interesting things to piss on. I wonder if he still is wearing red things, should he have managed to escape. I still have birdwhistles that my father made, and I wonder if Mehmetçik still has the one that I gave him when I last saw him, just before my own father maimed me.

Well, after that I had to change my course in life, since a one-armed potter is an impossibility. It is also because of that meeting that I am writing this with my left hand, which, according to my wife, is the hand of Satan. She says, 'Nothing good comes out of what is done by the left hand,' but this is not true, because now I write with my left hand, and this is how I live.

I agree that nothing will come of this particular writing, neither good nor bad, but not for the reasons proposed by my wife, who thinks like a woman, and is preoccupied with female things. Mehmetçik taught me to write in Greek characters, teaching me all the sounds that the letters signify, and so I used to write my own Turkish language in Greek letters. There used to be many others who did this, but I don't know if there are any left. I have heard that it is still done on the island of Rhodes. After the wars were all finished, Ghazi Mustafa Kemal Atatürk Pasha made everyone learn to write in the Roman letters used by the Franks, and so now no one can read what was written in the old Ottoman script, and no one can read what was written in Greek script either, except for a few people like me, and then only if the language is Turkish and not Greek. Mustafa Kemal also made us take second names, and so obviously I took the surname Karatavuk, so now I am Abdul Karatavuk Efendi, and I am 'Efendi' because I can write, and this has brought me great honour, which is a consolation.

This new way of writing, with Frankish letters, is a good one. I can write knowing that I will be understood. Not all writing, however, is done so that other people may understand. If I write in Greek letters, as I used to, then it amounts to a very good code that only I can read, and the only other people who will ever understand it will be those who will take the trouble to work it all out with great sweat and labour. The reason to write like that would be if I had things to say that I did not wish to become common knowledge. As it is, I wish only the fine things I have done to be remembered, and these are things that I can tell to my sons by word of mouth, and to my friends in the coffeehouses, and I would write them in the new Roman letters so that I will be remembered for them.

I have heard that there is a type of Christian who goes to their priest and tells him all the bad things that they have done, and then the priest forgives them on God's behalf, because it is said that Jesus Son of Mary gave his disciples the power to forgive sins. I don't know anything about this, but I do know that if there is someone to whom you can tell the bad things, then it takes the burden from your shoulders, if only for a little time. I have only paper to tell these things to, and paper has no power of forgiveness.

Fortunately, I have had long years of practice in writing with my left hand, which used to be awkward and clumsy, but now it is so easy that I would only cease if the price of lamp-oil became too great. I have become the town's letter-writer, and so I always have work, and I sometimes write to make myself feel better about the things that I experienced, because it is better to confide to a piece of paper than not to confide at all and to feel the dishonourable things eating at your guts like a rat in the night. I have dishonourable things to remember from the years when I was at war.

Here are the things that I would like to tell Mehmetçik if I knew where he was. I am sorry that you were not allowed to fight for the empire like an honourable soldier, and although it was a jihad I think that those who wanted to fight for the Sultan should have been trusted. There were Arabs at Çanakkale who were Muslims but did not fight, and were traitors to the empire, and ran away. Also the Franks had Muslim soldiers from India who fought very fiercely for them, and did not believe it was a jihad. Therefore this proves that to exclude Christians from the army was beside the point.

I am sorry that you were taken away and used like a slave in the labour battalions, because they should have used convicts, and not men who wanted to be soldiers. I am sorry that in this way you were made to lose your allegiance, and become an outlaw. I am also sorry that all the Christians have gone, because many of us were comforted by the presence of the icon of Mary Mother of Jesus, and because the Christians were merrier than us. It is fortunate that the new Muslims from Crete brought some of their high spirits with them, but unfortunately we have too many sanctimonious old men here who are always telling us that to enjoy ourselves is a sin, and so we spend too much of our lives sitting grimly and waiting for death, because it is only after death that we will be allowed to have a good time.

I have written many of the things that I would have told Mehmetçik after the wars were over, and many of the things that I would have told him if not for the intervention of fate and my father wounding me. I wrote them whilst imagining that I was with Mehmetçik in the rocks, before my father interrupted us with his rifle. The papers will be found after my death no doubt, and then who knows what will happen to them? I originally began it like this:

My dear and well-loved friend who has long gone from me, when you came back after all the wars, I had been sure that I would never see you again. Your family had left for wherever they were sent, and your house was occupied by those who came from Crete. These people slowly became like us, and now they are Turks. They have learned Turkish, especially the children, but sometimes they still use the Greek language, and they gather snails and make them into dishes with tomatoes and onions and rice, and they have beautiful songs and a kind of dance which is very popular with us at feasts when we ask them to dance for us. My dear Mehmetçik, you would not be bitter if you saw them in your old house, because they are good people and your house is as happy as it was before, and no doubt the old Cretan people in it long for their old home as much as you must long for yours. I know what it is to long for home, because I was at war for eight years and lost my youth and much of my decency when I should have been at home making pots and making sons, and when I came home everything was changed. Who knows? One day it all might change back again, and your people will be back with us, and our people with yours. In the meantime, I remember you with a smile, and hope that you also remember us.

I smile about the time when I last saw you, when you told me that Sadettin had become the Black Wolf, and you were the Red Wolf. I couldn't at first believe it when I heard such a familiar sound of robins coming from beyond the town, up the hill where the Dog lived among the tombs. I thought, 'That music sounds just like Mehmetçik's bird-whistle,' and I began to think of the days of our childhood when we were friends. And then I thought, 'That music is going on a long time, and is not completely like a bird.' I often listened to birds when I was at war, because when the battle goes quiet, and you are perhaps behind the lines in the reserve area, perhaps in a patch of woodland, you often hear the songs of the birds loudly and clearly, because they are saying to each other, 'When these people have gone, this land will be ours again,' and I remember when the long battle against the Franks was over, and we moved into their trenches, and the guns were silent at last, all you could hear was the song of birds, and at night we heard the nightin-gales and bulbuls, just as we do here in this town.

Of course I suddenly knew it was you out there in the rocks, and it made me very joyful.

When I saw you again, I didn't know what to say at first. How much you had changed! Your skin was dark from the sun, and you had a great beard, and your body had filled out, and you were dressed like the outlaw you were, with a cutlass and pistols in your sash, and a bandolier full of bullets across your chest, and a rifle in your hand, and round your brow you had wrapped a red cloth so that it was like a turban, and you stepped out from behind the tomb and embraced me.

I had heard so much about this Red Wolf, who was an outlaw and a brigand, a plague to the gendarmes, but it had never occurred to me that it was you. I said, 'I thought you must have left with your family and the other Christians,' and you said, 'How could I? I wasn't here. I was already hiding.'

It was then that we sat by a tomb and I began to tell you all that had happened to me, because our bargain was that I would speak first, and then you would speak, and so we would swap histories.

Of course it didn't work out, because we were interrupted, and now finally I have decided that I will not write my story as a long letter to you. I have no idea where you are or even if you are alive, and it pains me to write to you when you might indeed be a ghost. What I will do instead is to imagine that I have readers that I do not know, and so I will begin my story again, with the words 'I will not relate what happened during my training'. This will be left for my children to read, and anybody else who may have an interest.

This is the last time I will speak to you, by means of this writing that you will never read. There was a custom you may remember, of sending birds to take messages to the dead, and how I wish that I had a bird who could take my thoughts to you. If you know me at all, you will know that I have missed you all of my life, and I still miss you now that I am an old man and my eyes are beginning to fail, as a scribe's eyes always do. I have a wife and children and grandchildren, and I have seen my country grow into a great one with a new purpose. It is not frightened by anyone. I have mainly lived a good and honourable life and I have forgiven myself for the things of which I was ashamed. This place is still very beautiful, and the bulbuls and nightingales still keep us awake at night. The gendarmes still play backgammon in the meydan. It is easy to be contented here. All the same, I miss you, my old friend, and in the hope that there is a life after this, I will enter death anticipating that we will become boys again in the old paradise, filling our birdwhistles with water, running about and flapping our arms, and calling to each other among the tombs, and that there we will find the people of our childhood who have all slipped beneath the earth: Rustem Bey, Leyla Hanım, Ali the Snowbringer, the Dog, the Blasphemer, Ali the Broken-Nosed, Stamos the Birdman, Mohammed the Leech Gatherer, Charitos and Polyxeni, Ayse and Abdulhamid Hodja, Lydia the Barren and Father Kristoforos, my own father Iskander and my mother Nermin; and there we might find again the companions of our childhood: Philothei the Beautiful, Drosoula the Ugly, Sadettin who had to kill his sister and then ran away to become Black Wolf, and Ibrahim the Mad. There perhaps will also be Fikret from Pera, and my comrades from the wars, and there we will find again our old enchantment.

For me the stars are growing dim, and everything has almost gone, and I wonder if you have come to the same conclusions as I have. It is often useless to plan for things, even when you know exactly what you are doing. The present is confounded by the future, the future is confounded by the future beyond it, and the memories bubble up in disorder, and the heart is unpredictable.

You and I once fancied ourselves as birds, and we were very happy even when we flapped our wings and fell down and bruised ourselves, but the truth is that we were birds without wings. You were a robin and I was a blackbird, and there were some who were eagles, or vultures, or pretty goldfinches, but none of us had wings.

For birds with wings nothing changes; they fly where they will and they know nothing about borders and their quarrels are very small.

But we are always confined to earth, no matter how much we climb to the high places and flap our arms. Because we cannot fly, we are condemned to do things that do not agree with us. Because we have no wings we are pushed into struggles and abominations that we did not seek, and then, after all that, the years go by, the mountains are levelled, the valleys rise, the rivers are blocked by sand and the cliffs fall into the sea.

POSTSCRIPT

Fethiye in the Twenty-first Century

O ne story is that in 1913 Fethi Bey, an intrepid Ottoman aviator endowed with a Blériot monoplane and memorable moustaches, crashed into the bay of Telmessos and was untimely killed. In 1923 the town of Telmessos changed its name in his honour, and became Fethiye.

On the other hand it might be that in 1913 Fethi Bey, an intrepid Ottoman aviator endowed with a Blériot monoplane and memorable moustaches, undertook to fly from Istanbul to Cairo and was killed when his plane crashed in Palestine. Louis Blériot, world-famous not only for flying the English Channel and winning the thousand-pound prize offered by the *Daily Mail* but also for his own unsurpassable record of spectacular and marvellous crashes, most charmingly and honestly acknowledged that the wires above the wings of his aeroplanes were insufficient to withstand the download caused by turbulence. The French army grounded its Blériot monoplanes, and in 1923 the town of Telmessos changed its name to Fethiye in honour of the first Ottoman pilot to have been killed by a design fault.

Another version is that in 1923 the town of Telmessos changed its name to Fethiye in honour of a pilot named Fethi Bey, who had been killed in action during the Turkish War of Independence.

Since 'Fethiye' means 'conquest', however, the town might equally have been renamed to celebrate Atatürk's expulsion of foreigners and the establishment of the modern Turkish state. The identity and manner of death of Fethi Bey, aerial, intrepid and unfortunate, are concealed for ever behind the tangled contradictions of multiple and congenial myth, and he lives on solely in the name of a pleasant and modest town that may not indeed be named after him, having existed, it seems, solely for the purpose of demonstrating the impossibility of history.

Every Tuesday there is a market in Fethiye that bestraddles the sides of a shallow and limpid canal that carries the water of the mountains into the sea. It is a market that seems to go on for ever, to be crowded by every nationality, and to sell the strangest possible combination of touristic handicrafts and daily necessities.

There are agriculture and carpentry stalls, laden with nails, adzes and sickles, stalls with generous and redolent bags of spice and saffron, stalls with brass teasets, coffee grinders, kebab skewers, and mortars and pestles, stalls with wondrous aubergines and turgid watermelons, stalls with tapes that alternately blast out the equally lamentable pop songs of both Turkey and America, stalls selling priceless carpets inveigled for a song from the naive peasants of Anatolia, stalls selling hand-sewn silks, waistcoats, hats and socks, and stalls selling seductively beautiful musical instruments, geometrically inlaid, which Turks can play by instinct, but which Westerners find impossible, even in theory.

Many of the traders have formerly lived in London; 'Cheaper than Tesco,' they cry, 'cheaper than Asda, better than Harrods. Buy one and get one for nothing. Pay me next year. Who cares about the money? Look, look. English? Deutsch? Please, please, very nice, very cheap. Lovely jubbly.' They trade con brio, bursting with joy and panache, and each of them has a samovar on a portable gas ring in order to fill themselves and their customers with hospitable and inexhaustible draughts of sweetened apple tea.

There are old ladies crouching in the dust next to cotton cloths upon which is arranged complex and exquisite silver jewellery set with rich semi-precious stones. Young men wander among the throng insisting upon the purchase of genuine Lacoste socks and genuine Cartier watches and genuine Reebok trainers and genuine Chanel perfume. Middle-aged women intent upon the weekly stocking of provisions curse the tourists and mutter to each other irritably as they haul their baskets through the cosmopolitan muddle. A boy is determined to sell his authentic French designer fragrances: 'Ten pound for one,' he exclaims, and then, 'Eight pound for one. OK, five pound for one. OK, one pound for one. OK, OK, ten for one pound.'

Noisy women from Manchester and Newcastle howl and cackle like hens as a spouse tries on a fez. Roasted and rubicund middle-aged blond couples from Amsterdam and The Hague blink in confusion as a dark small boy attempts to sell them a self-illuminating yo-yo or a small carving with an astounding phallus. Policemen on duty, stupefied by boredom, smoke surreptitiously, their aromatic cigarettes smouldering in cupped hands behind their backs.

There is a tall and heartbreakingly lovely German girl. She is golden-haired and freshly minted, moving with catlike confidence and grace through the crowds between the stalls. She wears the skimpiest of tops, and her interminable legs disappear into the shortest of shorts, which have been slashed deliberately across the buttocks in order to expose firm alabaster flesh of inestimable delight. She astounds the local men, who gaze after her with popping eyes, their mouths agape with censorious longing and disgusted desire.

There is only one woman completely enrobed in black, in the Iranian style. There is another who is also clothed in black, except that she wears an ordinary black headscarf and skirt, and a black T-shirt. She is trying to be both East and West, and she is indeed fortunate that she is innocent of the English tongue, for her T-shirt bears the immodest and un-Islamic message 'Red Hot And Ready To Go'.

All this is quite normal and unremarkable for the town of Fethiye, whose old name was Telmessos, meaning 'City of Light', or 'Megri', meaning 'The Faraway Land'. The truly anomalous and remarkable thing about Fethiye, its market and the region of Lycia, is that there are no Greeks.

Sofia
Black Sea
Edirne
(Adrianopolis)
Istanbul
(Constantinopl
Salonika
(Thessaloníki)
Marmara Sea
Gallipoli
Çanakkale
Aegean Sea
Athens
Crete